FAREWELL, MY BEAUTIFUL HOMELAND

The secrets of the state are darker than those of the earth...

FAREWELL, MY BEAUTIFUL HOMELAND

AHMET ÜMIT

TRANSLATED BY RAKESH JOBANPUTRA

ANTHEM PRESS

Anthem Press
An imprint of Wimbledon Publishing Company
www.anthempress.com

This edition first published in UK and USA 2020
by ANTHEM PRESS
75–76 Blackfriars Road, London SE1 8HA, UK
or PO Box 9779, London SW19 7ZG, UK
and
244 Madison Ave #116, New York, NY 10016, USA
Original title: Elveda Güzel Vatanım

British Library Cataloguing-in-Publication Data
A catalogue record for this book is available from the British Library.

ISBN-13: 978-1-78527-103-8 (Pbk)
ISBN-10: 1-78527-103-2 (Pbk)

This title is also available as an e-book.

Dedicated to the peace protestors that were slaughtered in Ankara on Saturday 10th of October 2015...

A plan to assassinate me upon my arrival in Izmir on the 16th of June has been unearthed. The primary culprits were caught in the act and have been detained. The detainees have all confessed to their involvement in the plot. Sarı Efe, for whom an arrest warrant has been issued, is amongst the conspirators. There is no doubt that Sarı Efe has friends and organisations backing him in Istanbul, where he is based. In the event of the plot succeeding, meetings are expected to be held this evening and tomorrow by the organisation in question to discuss the necessary measures to be taken in regards to the politics to be pursued in the wake of the assassination.

If Sarı Efe has been detained, the initial intelligence obtained from his interrogation must be used to help us find the organisation in question and discover the location of the planned meeting; if, on the other hand, he is still at large, our priority is to obtain the aforementioned information once has he has been detained.
–Excerpts from a coded message sent by
the President of the Republic Gazi Mustafa Kemal
to Ekrem Bey, the Chief of Istanbul Police

Mister President, Your Excellency, let me now speak directly on this matter of the 'clandestine organisation', the clandestine organisation whose existence you have assumed since the day the Committee for Union and Progress' agenda was drawn up. I absolutely and categorically have no information regarding the assassination as ordered by that organisation. Proof must be provided for the actions a man has taken. How am I to prove I have not done something? I have never, in my life, engaged in violence against anybody, even against my worst enemies or those that have violated my rights, my dignity or my honour. Nor have I ever espoused the use of violence. I am a man that has always maintained his impartiality. You will not find violence or the championing of violence in any of my actions, writings or speeches.
–From former Minister of Finance Cavit Bey's defence
during the trial pertaining to the Izmir assassination
in the Independence Court

Contents

viii

Death Begins with the
Loss of Our Cities…

Good Morning, Ester (Morning, Day 1)

The sun finally rose. The dim grey that had been trying to steal through my window gave way to the clearest, deepest blue. I opened the balcony door, stepped outside and felt a damp breeze caress my face. I breathed in the clammy morning air, hoping that it would dispel some of the heaviness in my head. There was something about the chill that I liked, however, something invigorating. The city had awoken. Shouts and cries rose up from the street below; jokes and wisecracks, the rattling of yoghurt vendors' carts, the rumble of carriages trundling past… the familiar rush of the streets of Pera. Down below, the glowing white waters of the Golden Horn stretched away like a lake of milk, flecked by the ashen stains of a few boats bobbing on the waters. I cast my mind back to the tranquil waters of Salonika. That endless blue stretching from the bay out towards the open sea…

If I remember correctly, the balcony of my house in Salonika was wider than this one… How my heart aches when I say the word *remember*. Is it possible for someone to forget the city of his birth? The house in which he was raised? Of course not. One cannot forget but time, slowly, inexorably, begins to erase the memories, one by one. *Death begins with the loss of one's city.* I can't remember who said those words, but how unfortunate that he was right. There is one crucial omission, however: death begins with the loss of one's city and is completed with the loss of the homeland. That is the feeling that now haunts me. My city I have long since lost. Now it is time to lose my homeland. Perhaps I have already lost it and I am just oblivious of the fact.

Indeed, what is a country? A handful of earth, wide seas and deep lakes? Is it rugged mountains, fertile plains, lush forests, crowded cities and scattered villages? No, a homeland is more than just that. It is not just a handful of earth or river plains or rows of trees… The homeland is our mother's love for us, it is the specks of white in our father's beard, it is our first love, the birth of our children, our grandparents' graves… Those without a homeland are also without life. At one point, my heart and mind were full of ideas like these. And now? Now, I am not sure.

Just as that vast land is now disintegrating and facing annihilation, so too are my thoughts, goals and ideals. Indeed, my entire life now seems to be evaporating in front of my very eyes. No, don't worry, my body is fine, but my mind and my soul are in torment. Such is the pain that I sometimes ask myself why I am prolonging the torture. There are times I wish to end this macabre escapade with my own hands. But then I desist. Not because I fear death, or because I love life, but simply out of some strange curiosity. I may not need to do it in the end because the new masters of the land may soon decide to end the beating of this heart that still clings stubbornly onto life in my otherwise weary, jaded body. The possibility is very real… It happened to my friends, and I imagine the same fate may also lay in wait for me. My life shall come to an end either with a bullet to the head in some dark, grimy corner of a dingy room or at the end of a rope in the wake of a verdict and sentence passed by a hastily assembled court. I feel it; every day, every hour, every second. The circle is closing in on me. That is why I am writing this to you. I know I do not have the right to do so, but believe me, I have no choice.

They are after me, Ester. They are hunting me down. They do not spare any of the old members of the party. None of them have been spared. The assassination attempt in Izmir on the president was a pretext, a smokescreen. The reckoning has finally begun. The gallows set up in Izmir were not enough;

they also hanged our men in Ankara. Guilty or innocent, they don't care. Take Kara Kemal, for instance. He had nothing to do with the assassination plot, but they got rid of him anyway. They say he killed himself, and in a henhouse too. Who could actually fall for such nonsense? What do they take us for? Not only are they telling us he committed suicide, but that he did it in a chicken coop too. What they're doing is blackening his name. Humiliating him completely. They're getting rid of them all, of everybody, one by one, and I am next. I can feel it. A power that can have so many committee members imprisoned and so many more exiled would never deign to leave me alive. That is why I left the house in Beşiktaş and came here, to the Pera Palace Hotel. Because when my landlady Madam Melina died, I had nobody left in the world, nobody to care for me, and I want witnesses if I am arrested, I want somebody to see it if I am killed, someone to notice. I am ready to die, but not in disgrace. I don't want what happened to Kara Kemal to happen to me. And no, this is not paranoia. Of this, I am absolutely certain, even though I do not pose any threat to them. Not that it matters anymore. What matters is that we have been defeated, that our castle has been overrun, and it is clear that there will be no turning back from the decisions that have been made.

They are coming after me, Ester. And no, I am not trying to make you feel sorry for me. I am not begging for pity. This is just something I need to do. I need to write to you. Please forgive me. Please do not be upset. I know that you are upset, that you may not believe me. You may think I still harbour political aims and objectives, but I swear upon my honour that I do not. Do not take this as an outpouring of grief or as a form of confession; rather, it is a form of self-appraisal, a way of coming to terms with the self. You may ask why, after all these years, I am involving you in an appraisal of my life. Well, the fact is you never left my thoughts; without you, there is no such thing as me.

So yes, that is the truth, whether you believe it or not. Even when you left me that day on the narrow streets of Salonika, I was still madly in love with you, perhaps even more so than at any other time. You may say that you did not leave me and that I was the one that left you. And you may say that I did not honour the decision we made and that I abandoned you. And yes, you would be right. That is what happened. I was the one that ended our affair, not you. And why? I could say it was for the motherland, for the nation and for the sacred cause, but that would not be enough. The truth is far more complicated…. And that is why, in a way, I am writing: to search for the answers to that question. Because even I do not know exactly why I left you. If I could go back to the beginning, if I could remember with certainty everything we have been through together, if I could start living again, then I may find the answer to the question of why I ran away.

I know you may never open these envelopes, that you may never read a single line of these letters. It matters not. Even if you never open these envelopes, I shall imagine you have read these letters and will tell myself that my last days have been happy ones. Yes, I shall close my eyes, my mind and my heart to reality and tell myself that my soul's wishes have been fulfilled. You may call what I have done selfishness or even cruelty. You may see it as reprehensible… I accept all the vilification that comes my way. Such conduct does not befit me. You are right, the Şehsuvar Sami you knew would have never stooped to such lows, would have never been embroiled in such sleazy affairs. But I need to tell somebody what I have been through. And unfortunately, in a world gone mad, in a country that has long since ceased to be a homeland, I have nobody else with whom to share my secrets but you.

Are You Going to Be a Killer?

Hello Ester (Afternoon, Day 1)

Your voice echoed through the room this afternoon. *Are you going to be a killer?* It wasn't a dream. I swear it wasn't a dream. Your voice was so close to me and so clear, it was as though you were standing next to me. You were shouting at me, your voice full of fury and anxiety.

'Tell me, Şehsuvar, are you going to be a killer?'

Your voice was so real I could almost feel your sweet breath on me. I momentarily succumbed to a futile hope and scanned the room, this hotel room in which I am probably spending the last days of my life. Of course, you were not there, but such is the power of hope I still got up and looked for you in the bathroom. I even opened the door and looked up and down the hallway. You were not there, nor could you have been. Those words I heard you had uttered a long time ago, before our bodies were this jaded, before our souls were this battered, at a time when our hearts were still full of hope...

It was the end of summer. We were in that garden crowned by purple grapes hanging down from the vines, by the stone pond whose fish had long since died. Your face seemed paler amongst the yellowing leaves. Your gaze bored furiously into mine. Actually, I had already guessed that I would not be going to Paris with you. News had already probably reached you of my joining the movement. Even if you hadn't heard about it, you sensed it.

The moment I told you I was joining the Committee of Union and Progress, you could not hold back your anger and erupted.

'So are you going to be a killer?'

It was the first time I had seen you so livid, and so desperate and helpless too. I tried to console you but you would not listen. And you were right not to, because I had lied. The truth is I had long since been a member of the Committee.

Yes, I feel ashamed now telling you like this; that was something else I had withheld from you. It was a year earlier, in the summer of 1907, when you were in Paris writing me those letters peppered with lines by Baudelaire.

'*The sunset's rays enfold / In hyacinth and gold / Field and canal / Life sleeps and all / Lies bathed in warmth and evening light…*'

Ah, the way you spoke about the capital of love, liberty and poetry, the delight and the elation your words carried…

'We have to get away,' you wrote. 'We should live here. In a little place of our own, a rooftop flat in an apartment overlooking the Jardin du Luxembourg. You should start your first novel here, when the leaves on the trees fade with a sweet anguish…'

You wandered around the Pantheon, that grand shrine to civilization, the entrance over which are inscribed the words *Aux Grands Hommes, La Patrie Reconnaisante*. 'To great men, the grateful homeland.' Inside, you circled in reverential silence the statues of Voltaire, Victor Hugo and Jean-Jacques Rousseau.

'This is it. The palace of free thought. I am here, in the temple of humanity liberated from the squabbles and differences caused by language, race and religion. This is where we belong. Vive liberté, égalité, fraternité! Vive *hürriyet, müsavat uhuvvet!*'

I too had once wandered those streets, and I too had once gazed, partly in bewilderment but always in awe, at those statues of those great men. I knew all too well how you felt, so much so that I even knew the feelings you did not write about in your letters. Because while you were writing those beautiful and impassioned letters, I was busy joining a movement that aimed to bring those principles and slogans in your letters to life in our country.

'Long live liberty, long live equality, long live fraternity…'

While you walked amongst the tombs of those great men, I had already chosen their ideals as my own guide. A guide that would change the entire course of my life, a guide that would shock my loved ones, a guide that would possibly even lead to my death. Don't get me wrong; I do not hold you responsible for my joining the movement. Seeing as it was your Uncle Leon that took me to the oath-taking ceremony, it would be unfair to say I joined because of you…

That's right. Uncle Leon. I'm sure you'll be stunned to know but that is the truth. He was the one that recommended me to the committee. I kept it a secret for years, but now I no longer have any secrets to hide. There are now no secrets, committees or comrades that need protection, in contrast to that summer evening in 1907, when Uncle Leon took me to the Committee's headquarters in the strictest confidence.

Please do not be angry with Uncle Leon. He is an incurable romantic. What's more, like most of the people in the Committee, it was not an empire on the verge of collapse that he wished to rescue; rather, he was a romantic rebel, intoxicated by the rallying cries of the French Revolution. Actually, I was also the same. We all were. But he was different from the rest of us; maybe he was still dreaming of a socialist order. You remember Avram the Bulgarian, the trade unionist? He and Uncle Leon were the best of friends. As thick as thieves, as they say. Anyway, Avram once gave me a copy of *The Communist Manifesto*.

'Here, you need to take a look at the rebellion from this perspective.'

I read it, but I can't say it truly appealed to me. Anyway… Uncle Leon did not recommend me to the Committee in order to separate you and I, not that he was overly ecstatic at our relationship in the first place. In introducing me to the movement, he had just one aim and that was for me to take my place in the cause, the cause for freedom. I never blamed him either, or held it against him. We had no blood tie, but he was a central figure in my life. He helped me see the world in a whole new way, with different eyes. And I suppose while I am it, I should also make another confession – he was the one that dispelled my prejudice against the Jews, years before you were a part of my life. Who knows, perhaps he was the one that prepared the ground and cleared the way for us. Purely by accident, of course…

On one of those nights when your mind was swimming with visions of our future life together in Paris, Uncle Leon took me to the ceremony where I would pledge my allegiance to the cause. I had been blindfolded in the car so I would not know where we were going, but I could tell from the sounds and the scents and from the salty tang on the breeze that we were on one of those narrow streets leading down to the harbour. Had I concentrated a little harder, I may even have been able to identify the road we were on but I didn't. I chose instead to block out my thoughts so I would not know and would not notice. We eventually arrived at a house on the ground floor of a low building. Actually, it may not have been a house at all, as it could have very well have been the offices of a law firm or a government agency. Like I said, had I tried a little harder, I could have perhaps identified the place and the location but I chose not to. When we knocked on the door, a high-pitched male voice called out from inside.

'Who is it?'

'Hilal', said Uncle Leon, using the code word.

That was all. I heard a metal click and the door opened in seamless silence. Not the slightest creak or groan.

Once we were inside, I was struck by the acrid smell of stale tobacco but even that somehow smelled agreeable.

'This is as far as I go,' Uncle Leon said. 'You're in his arms now. God be with you.'

I tried to mutter something but I was so overcome with nerves, even I did not know what I was trying to say.

'This way', the heavy smoker said. He took me by the arm and gently shepherded me in. 'We'll take a turn to the left a little further on, so watch your step,' he said. Ten or fifteen paces later, he said, 'Another turn to the left now.' We carried on walking. 'We're turning right now. Good, now stop.' We stopped. I heard him open another door. 'Yes, we're going in now.'

We walked in. The place reeked of mildew. I don't know why, but I felt we had entered a wine cellar. The darkness of the blindfolds seemed to have been momentarily lifted, but I still could not see anything. As far as I could make out I was standing under a bright light. The man with the cigarette breath had gone. That is when I heard the other voice.

'Why do you wish to join our movement?'

It was a deep, confident voice, but there was no feeling in it, neither friendship nor enmity. It was cold and emotionless, like a military command.

'For... For... For the motherland', I stammered. 'To defend the motherland. For liberty, for fraternity...'

Just as I was beginning to get a hold of myself, that cold, deep voice growled. 'You know that this movement requires sacrifices, don't you? That it may require you to kill or be killed?'

I swallowed nervously a few times before the words came out of my mouth of their own accord.

'I know... For this sacred cause, for the motherland, I am prepared to kill and to die. My life has no other purpose.'

There was a short silence, after which I heard footsteps growing progressively louder, followed again by the stench of tobacco. Somebody removed my blindfolds. The light in the room was dazzling. Three men in black capes and black hoods were sitting on three chairs in front of me, with a single table positioned between us. It would be impossible for me to describe those three men but I'm sure the cloaks made them look larger than they actually were.

'You need to take the oath', the man in the middle said. His was the voice I had been hearing. A hand came out from under the cloak and pointed at the table. 'Swear on the *Qur'an*, the gun and the flag!'

I placed my right hand on the gun and my left on the *Qur'an*. 'I hereby swear to fight with every last drop of my blood for the motherland, for liberty, equality and fraternity, and for justice.'

'Welcome to the brotherhood', he said. 'May your membership of the Committee of Union and Progress be auspicious. 1117. Yes, that is your number. Do not forget this number. Ever. Remember it in such a way that it will never be deleted from your memory. I hope you always remain loyal to your oath and that you defend the honour and dignity of your love for the motherland with every drop of blood you have. May Allah be with you.'

That is how my adventure with the movement began. Actually, despite the solemnity of the ceremony, I didn't think I was that important to them and that such grandiose rituals were the norm when initiating new members. But I was wrong. Just two weeks later, my assignments began. No, it was nothing dangerous. I was a courier, a simple courier, and I travelled countless times from Salonika to Bitola, from Bitola to Skopje, and from Skopje to Ohrid.

'You have an innocent face', my contact within the movement used to say. 'Nobody will suspect you. As it is, they're too busy looking for soldiers. But your innocent looks and your youth work in our favour.'

But after a while I began to grow bored. Was this going to be my sole contribution to the cause – working as a lowly courier for the duration of the struggle? I did not voice my frustrations, however, and a good thing too. Good things, as they say, come to those that wait… And the 'good thing' here, the incident that would make me smile, would also turn me into a killer, long before you asked me that fateful question that day.

You do not know whom it is I am talking about but be patient, all will be revealed. As for this morning, that question from the past that kept on pestering me, the question of whether I was going to be a killer or not, felt like a sign of sorts but the fact is, it had come too late. I had become a killer long before you asked me that question!

An Idea Whose Time Has Come

Dear Ester (Late Afternoon, Day 1)

'The important thing', my late father used to say, 'is to conquer your fear. If you do not, that vile emotion will bring you to your knees'. The incident that made me remember my father saying that occurred this afternoon. I had sat down at the desk to continue writing to you when I heard some noises just outside my door. I leapt up and listened. Something was happening in the hall… Screams and shouts and a general hullabaloo. At first, I thought it was the police, that the time had come for them to slap the handcuffs on me and drag me away. And how quickly they had come too! But why was I surprised? I was already expecting them and now here they were. Finally. They had arrived. I steeled myself and opened the door, expecting to see a mass of stern, hardened police faces but what I saw instead was a hotel maid staring at me in wide-eyed fright.

'A fire!' she shouted. 'A fire has broken out, sir! Please, let's go downstairs!'

I suddenly began laughing. The poor woman did not know what was going on as she watched me double over with laughter. I eventually managed to pull myself together and we made our way down to the lobby. It was pandemonium downstairs, with ladies screaming and fainting everywhere… Thankfully, it was not a serious fire. The flames had not spread and once the fire had been put out, we were able to return to our rooms.

I did not return to my writing immediately. Hanging a few hand widths above the cupboard on the wall by my bed is a photograph in a silver frame. I have seen it many times but now, as I write to you, its significance dawns on me. It is a photograph of the Rue des Petit Champs, the street on which the Pera Palace can be found, taken on the 24th of July 1908. The little square is teeming with people and at the foot of the photo, in French, is the following: *A march by military cadets on the 24 July 1908 celebrating the declaration of the new constitution.* Exactly eighteen years ago today…

It is no coincidence, if you ask me, that I am staying in a room with this photograph. The young manager of the Pera Palace, Reşit Bey, is the son of Yusuf of Salonika, who was killed in Tripoli. I have known Reşit Bey since he was a child. Indeed, I remember spending one summer teaching him French. Like me, he is a graduate of the French high school, the Galatasaray Lycée. I suppose I am kind of a big brother to him, which is why, I believe, he is extra attentive to my needs and treats me with such affection, as though I am a guest in his own house, even though he is fully aware of the danger I am in and the risks he is taking in hosting me. Indeed, when I am plunged into a morass of self-doubt, the look of admiration and esteem I often see in his chestnut eyes is a source of rare and indescribable consolation for me. What I am trying to say, my dearest Ester, is that Reşit Bey may have given me this room – with this particular photograph hanging on the wall – on purpose, a token and a memento of our struggle for liberty, as it were. I don't know. Perhaps I am labouring under a delusion. Perhaps I am in this room purely by pleasant coincidence, but I must admit, the possibility that it may not be a coincidence does warm my heart.

The 24th of July 1908… Actually, it was on the 23rd of July 1908, the day before, that the photograph was taken. A revolution that would determine the fate of the entire Ottoman homeland from the Persian Gulf to the Adriatic was taking place. Although there are attempts now to dismiss its importance, the events of that summer represented a transformation that would send shockwaves not just through our country but throughout the whole world. A constitution that had been suspended for years on the orders of the Sultan had now been enforced by the will of the people, and it was a constitution that promised even more freedom than before. The sound of liberty was first heard in Bitola, and it then began to spread across the three continents. That sound was so powerful, so righteous and so compelling that the despot on the throne, the sultan, who, given the chance, would not take a single step forwards or back, had no choice other than to acquiesce to the people's demands.

Yes, that was the day we saw our dreams come true. The 23rd of July 1908... Salonika... Do you remember the day? There was such a sweet, wonderful breeze in the air that morning, a breeze that soothed not just our faces but the fires raging in our hearts and minds too. The sea was the deepest azure, and it felt as though heroes from ancient times, heroes from millennia past, would appear on the horizon in their longboats and join us...

It was early when we met, very early. We were in a little park on the coast, on a usually empty patch of green that was now a sea of people. Five people had somehow contrived to perch on the bench we usually sat on. The whole city it seemed had poured on to the streets, some walking and talking together, others deep in conversation and debate. Even the declaration itself howled against the centuries-old wall of silence with the same demand: 'Let the Constitution of 1876 be restored!' 'Long live the constitutional monarchy!' And then there was an explosion of banners and placards of every colour under the sun, all featuring the same slogan: 'Vive liberty, equality and fraternity! Vive justice!'

We were like children, enchanted, overcome by delight, squirming and grinning with joy. I recited those lines by the poet Namık Kemal to you: *Ah liberty, how beguiling is your countenance / We have escaped captivity and are now captives of your love...* The faces around us seemed to glow with vigour and zeal, with a beauty that had never been seen before ... Something completely new was stirring in the city, something that could be sensed by even the most unlettered and ignorant.

The seamen, the porters, the farmhands, even the city's 'ladies of the night'... And the same applied to the affluent too, to the owners of the tobacco factories, the merchants, the bankers, the masons... Turks, Greeks, Bulgarians, Albanians, Serbs, Jews... That day, all the nations of the empire, all its peoples, faiths and religions gathered under the Ottoman banner. Muslim, Christian, Jew and all the others; we were all on the streets, standing side by side, shoulder to shoulder, for a new society, our petty differences now cast aside.

But you know all this. What you do not know was that in that seething mass of people, nobody could have been happier than me. Not only because I was seeing my most hallowed ideals come true but because you were there with me too. You may smirk upon reading this; your lips may curl up into a wry, unbelieving smile as you read what you think are nothing but preposterous lies but that is the truth. Your frail body standing by my side, your tiny hand throbbing like a second heart in my hand... If only we could have stayed like that forever. If only you had been by my side when we fought for our freedom... But alas, it was not to be. That is not how it played out. I may not have thought so at the time, but now I realise that one can only fail against fate. Even if you possess a will strong enough to alter the course of your homeland's history, you can rarely, if ever, find the strength to change the course of your own life. This is not an attempt at an excuse but if the people hunting me down were to give me the chance, and if I had enough life left on this earth to tell you what is in my heart and mind, then you would know what I mean...

But let us return to that glorious day. We joined the crowds and made our way along the coast to Olympus Square, the two of us hand in hand the whole day. You did not let go of my hand, not even once. Nobody actually saw us holding hands that day anyway, not that we would have cared. A Muslim man holding hands with a Jewish girl, yes, but who would have cared about such a supposed impropriety when a revolution was taking place? It was not just us, two foolish lovers, demanding our rights but the whole of Salonika; its sea and its sky, its trees and its streets, its buildings and its people, as one body, one voice and one will. If there is anything, any act, that deserves to be tolerated during a revolution, then it must certainly be love.

When we arrived at the café in Olympus Square, it was already packed to the rafters. But amidst the tumult and confusion, the people's eyes there were shimmering with hope, their hearts were aflame with joy and their hands had curled up into fists brimming with belief.

'We simply want what is needed!' the speaker was saying. 'We want what the countries that have chosen freedom already have. There is no other way for the prosperity of the nation!'

We then spilled out once more onto the streets, invigorated not by the breeze coming in from the sea but by our dreams of revolution. And you? You looked so beautiful that day that I could not help myself and I kissed you on your lips there and then on that bustling street corner. I remember the way you blushed and gently pushed me away with a whispered warning.

'Don't. This is not Paris. We may be in the middle of a revolution but this is still Salonika.'

We then began running along the coast, carefree like children. Nobody cared, nobody looked, nobody scowled in condemnation or contempt. Those were amazing, extraordinary days of amazing and extraordinary emotions. Although not abolished altogether, traditions that had been dominant for thousands of years were forgotten, if only for those few heady days.

Finally, that night, the city tasted freedom. The multicoloured banners of the revolution carried the same fervour over to the next day. The highpoint of the revolution was undoubtedly the speech given by the Inspector General, Hüseyin Hilmi Paşa, from the grounds of the city hall, where he read the telegram that was the proof that the despot residing in Yıldız Palace had yielded. We pushed our way through the vast crowds to get closer to Hilmi Paşa, a man who had managed to maintain cordial relations with both Sultan Abdülhamit and our movement but who now looked nervous and astonished. His greying moustache was quivering and his voice was wavering. He may have been reading the telegram giving the news that the new constitution was to be implemented but his eyes and his body language gave away his unease. What if the new constitution was also to be suspended, as had happened thirty years earlier? What if the sultan, using the existence of bandits in the mountains or the loss of imperial territories as a pretext, were to return the country to absolute monarchy? And what if he were to bring the officers implicated in this rebellion to trial? But his fears were in vain. The tide could not be reversed, and it was not just our country either that was waking up to a new era: the desire for freedom had erupted amongst the masses in Russia three years earlier and in Iran a year after that, and the people of the neighbouring countries were now also rising up. The domestic and overseas circumstances were ripe, and the constitutional era was beginning. As Victor Hugo said, there is nothing more powerful than an idea whose time has come.

But of course, for the idea to succeed, a price had to be paid, courage had to be shown and lives had to be taken and given. Like birth itself, the revolution, midwife at the birth of a new era, could not be bloodless – this is the ancient law of history. And for the laws of history to manifest themselves, heroes are always needed. I shan't name them here as you already know who they were – those giants of men from the *İttihad-ı Osmanlı Cemiyeti*, the Committee for Ottoman Union, that had been struggling fearlessly for freedom since its inception in 1899, its members risking exile, torture and death for the cause. Back then, it had still been too early; the iron was not ready and history could not hand us our victory as the conditions were still not right. Not until 1906 that is, and the awakening in Macedonia, and then two years later in 1908, when Captain Ahmed Niyazi twirled his moustache and took to the mountains with his troops, after which he would inspire similar actions by Eyüp Sabri of Ohrid, Captain Enver and the other patriotic sons of the soil.

The despot, of course, responded immediately to these moves. In order to preserve for eternity the dark and bloody regime over which he ruled from his abode in Yıldız Palace, Abdülhamit send the most brutal of his generals out to pursue the mutineers. Yes, I am referring here to the Albanian Şemsi Paşa, the sultan's ruthless executioner. He was a man whose very name made even ethnic Albanians tremble with fear but on the 7th of July 1908, sixteen days before we poured out on to the streets with such revolutionary fervour, he was killed. Yes, this time it was not the sultan's man but the patriots that won the day. The tyrant that had been despatched to strangle the life out of the rebellion had instead had his own life snatched away from him.

And before you ask, no, I was not the one that pulled the trigger that day, although I did have a part in the operation. And I say that not to alleviate any guilt I may have because I would have pulled the trigger without a second's hesitation had I been ordered to do so. I would have done it out of a sense of duty to my homeland, whose desperate circumstances demanded my allegiance. Şemsi Paşa wished to extinguish the flames of freedom that were spreading throughout the land and so we in turn extinguished the flame that was his life.

Your Decision

Good Evening, Ester (Evening, Day 1)

I sent my letters to you from the hotel's post office this evening, just before dusk. The main post office on the *Cadde-i Kebir*, the city's most central and most glamorous street, is not safe. The second I leave the hotel, they are on my trail, following me, sometimes undercover, sometimes quite openly. Almost as though they expect me to be afraid, to panic and so try to escape. But I shall not give them that pleasure. No, I shall not let the official archives write 'Şehsuvar Sami panicked and ran'. But at the same time I do not want them to stop my letters reaching you, so I have been using the postal services in the hotel to send them.

If I could just write it all down in one go, in a single sitting. Just let it all out... Not because I am impatient but because I am worried. What I have sent you is just a small part of what I want to tell you. A prelude perhaps, maybe just the first pages of a novel... An outpouring of the last twenty years, the story of a world turned upside down, of an empire in upheaval, of lives turned inside out, of our lives... The story of an accursed war that drenched the world in blood, of shattered hopes and dreams, of torn ideals and of a love that never died. Do not be so quick to frown. I know I have no right to speak about love after everything we have been through. But please, I implore you, even if you do not believe what I write, at least wait until the last lines before you pass judgement. Please, at least grant me that one indulgence.

Instead of the stairs, I took the lift down to the postal bureau to post my letters to you. You know how machines and machinery have always fascinated me. There were three other people in the lift with me. Three French ladies. I won't lie, they looked so sophisticated and they exuded a heavenly aroma. The scene reminded me of that day we went to dinner with Ahmed Rıza Bey on the Rue des Ecoles in Paris. Although the restaurant was full of stunning women and elegantly dressed men, you were still the most beautiful woman there, even though we were barely out of our teens. However, I must admit I didn't really spend much time observing you or anybody else there because I was so completely focused on Ahmed Rıza and what he was saying about our country, about the world and about religion. He was so courageous in his words and the way he thought was always so logical, with everything he said coolly and rationally substantiated. Back then, I used to think that life could be explained purely by reason and by logic and science, and I used to believe that the force of human will could change not just society but history itself and the world, but Ahmed Rıza's words, one by one, undid the knots in my mind, banishing my doubts and answering my questions. For me, he was not just the ideological father of the Committee for Union and Progress but also a supremely wise man and an honourable and decent Ottoman intellectual. You saw for yourself the deference with which even the French greeted him.

Back then, Ahmed Rıza was my only hero. I often wish it could have stayed like that and that I had followed in his path. Had I done so, then your wishes would have come true and instead of being cooped up here in this hotel room like a caged animal waiting to be hunted down and captured or killed, I would have gained fame as a writer for my novels. Who knows, perhaps my novels could have become some type of invisible armour shielding me from danger…

But would they have? Did novels, after all, work for Halide Edip Adıvar? Did they form a protective suit of armour around her? Because heaven knows what has befallen that poor woman now as she desperately tries to eke out a living in some godforsaken land overseas. Such are the times we live in now that we can forget our tomorrows; we cannot even be certain about today. But I have no regrets. All I have is my fury, and a profound disillusionment. It is as though my entire life has been snatched from my very hands. And I know what you'll say in response to that. You'll say, 'Don't complain. It was your decision'. And you'll be right. I chose this path. In spite of you, and in spite of the chance of living another life, which I also wanted. But that is a topic to which we shall return, eventually. Let me continue with my story. Let me go back to the scorching hot month of July 1908, to the days just before the inauguration of the Second Constitutional Era, and to my first assassination. Let me tell you about the way we murdered Şemsi Pasha in the middle of Bitola in front of what seemed to be the population of the entire city.

I don't know if you remember the 3rd of July 1908. It was the day Captain Ahmed Niyazi of Resen took to the mountains... The day a chain of critical events was set in motion... Whether Abdülhamit, who had received news of the officers' rebellion, grasped the gravity of the situation or not is unclear but, with his usual obsessive fear, he was quick to react and his countermeasure was cunning in the extreme, sending into action Şemsi Pasha, also known as Şemso, the bane of the rebel gangs in Macedonia and a man who had won the praise and acclaim of nearly all Albanians.

'A band of ignorant upstarts including members of the military has taken to the mountains and dared to defy the authority of the Ottoman state. Deal with these traitors to the motherland and the nation. Let the treatment meted out to them serve as an example to others that would dare follow their lead. Do whatever it takes to crush their cause. Use any means and as many men as necessary.'

At the time, Şemso was in Mitrovica. Upon receiving the padishah's telegraph, he threw himself into his preparations. Not that the seasoned old warrior was bristling with excitement at the prospect at hunting down his quarry; over the years he had crushed numerous rebellions, and this latest band of insurgents was just another mob that he would deal with swiftly and summarily. Or so he must have thought, because this time, for the first time, he was wrong. This was not a gang of thugs and madmen disturbing the peace and looting the wealth of the people but a well-drilled band of patriots with history on their side fighting to carry out the will of the people and make it the supreme force in the land.

As Şemso's preparations continued in earnest, a second telegraph from the palace arrived reiterating the commands of the first and bearing the personal greetings and blessings of the sultan himself.

Heartened by this rare royal tribute, the old wolf quickly assembled his force, consisting of two full battalions and an additional troop of around thirty Albanian guards, and they set off on a train that had been reserved specifically for their use. But even before the train had set off, we were privy to these developments and we knew amongst ourselves that Şemsi Paşa and his men had to be stopped and at any cost, and immediately too, at the first station at which the train stopped. That meant Salonika, and if he was not stopped at Salonika, then it would have to be in Bitola, and if not in Bitola, then in Resen. And what if he was not stopped in Resen? There was no what if there. Whatever the cost, however arduous the mission, Şemsi Paşa had to be stopped, otherwise the people's uprising was in danger.

How did I know all this? Because I was the person carrying the message from the Committee of Union and Progress in Salonika to our people in Bitola telling them to get ready to eliminate Şemsi Paşa if he was not taken out in Salonika. We usually used coded telegraphs to communicate, but for something as crucial as a planned attack on Şemsi Paşa, the organisation used its most trusted and reliable members as couriers. I had carried countless communiqués since joining the movement but none had been as critical as this one. None could have changed my life the way this one would.

I doubt you'll remember now but the previous day, I had told you I would be visiting my uncle Mehmet Ali Bey in

Bitola to discuss the details of my grandfather's inheritance. It was a lie of course, and it was not an innocent or insignificant one either. It was deliberate and duplicitous and I did it not just to conceal our murderous plan but to protect both you and our party. On the morning of the 5th of July, when Şemsi Paşa was boarding the train at Mitrovica, I was leaving Salonika with a message for our people in Bitola telling them to deal with the incredibly brutal and dangerous man that was on a train heading their way.

You may ask me why we were so ruthless. Why we chose to kill him rather than sit down with him and try to negotiate, to try to persuade him of the righteousness of our cause.

Indeed, there were some amongst us that wanted to try just that, who argued that Şemsi Paşa, ultimately, was also an officer of the Ottoman armed forces and that he would therefore understand that the nation was heading for calamity and that he could be won over to the cause. They did in fact manage to speak to him on one occasion. One of the men that sat down with him to speak to him was his future son-in-law, Rıfat Bey, the Chief of the Bitola Gendarmerie Brigade, who openly told him that his troops would not obey him. Şemsi Paşa, however, was not the type to surrender so easily. Not only was he fiercely loyal to the sultan, he had a toxic loathing of insurgents and of the very notion of constitutional monarchy. He therefore left our revolutionary officers no other option – he had to be eliminated.

Şemsi Paşa's train arrived in Salonika on the 6th of July. The movement did not wait and nor indeed could it wait. It wanted the murderous tyrant dealt with there and then, on that very day, which is why our men had slipped into the station the previous night and taken up their positions in readiness. But things did not go according to the plan. The authorities in Salonika had taken massive precautions against a possible assassination attempt on the pasha and Şemsi Paşa's Albanian bodyguards were as vigilant and as thorough as ever. None of our movement's men – amongst whom were trusted and reputable fighters like Yakup Cemil, men known to always successfully complete their mission – were able to even get close to the target. The only way to finish off the job was to kill him as he made his way to the Marshall's offices, which is where Şemso would be going to speak to Ibrahim Paşa and be briefed on the latest developments. Unfortunately, however, this plan did not work either. The movement was frightened that the man who pulled the trigger in such an audacious plan, in the middle of the city and in broad daylight, could be captured and if he were to talk, then… Moreover, if Şemsi Paşa were to survive… Abdülhamit's spies would round up everybody and our movement would be crushed.

And so the sultan's man was able to stroll in undisturbed leisure to the Marshall's offices. Ibrahim Paşa greeted this honoured guest with all the requisite pomp and ceremony but somehow I don't think Şemso would have stopped to enjoy the cup of sweetened coffee that had been handed to him upon arrival as Ibrahim Paşa had no doubt informed him of the gravity of the situation and the importance of him being there. This latest uprising was not like the other rebellions that had been quashed in the region. This time, the insurgency had the support of the army and from people from all walks of life across the whole country. He also informed him of an incident that had taken place a few days earlier, when shots were fired at two government officers, Hacı Hakkı Bey and Şuayıp Efendi, as they were exiting the gardens of the White Castle in Salonika. Hacı Hakkı Bey managed to survive the assassination attempt, but Şuayıp Efendi had not been so lucky.

Perhaps it was at that moment that Şemso Paşa, usually as cold-hearted as a snake, began to feel the first traces of concern. Perhaps that is when the seriousness and the intricacy of his task began to dawn on him. But of course, that would not have deterred him. He had been commissioned by Yıldız Palace and with the personal greetings and approval of the sultan himself. Admittedly, he was nearing sixty years of age and the lustre in his eyes may have faded somewhat, but that cold, dark heart of his beat as ominously and as viciously as ever. He may have been worried for a moment but only for a moment, a single, fleeting moment, after which he most probably made a personal vow to crush this insolent uprising as mercilessly as he had crushed the others. Not wanting to waste a moment, he returned to the station so he could set off and engage with the rebels.

The atmosphere at the station was tense. Our men were in position, their fingers on the trigger ready to fire the moment Şemso appeared. He had already managed to wriggle out of our grasp once but this enemy of constitutionalism would not get away again. However, once again we were foiled. The committee, surprisingly, decided not to kill the pasha in Salonika, the reason being that opening fire on him in or around the station would almost inevitably cause his entourage to return fire, which could lead to the deaths of bystanders, and if any foreigners were killed in the exchange, this would provide the foreign powers, Great Britain and Russia in particular, with a reason to intervene in Macedonia. Only a few weeks earlier, the King of England, Edward VII and the Russian Czar, Nicholas, had met at a summit at Reval, where they had discussed the fate of our homeland, which is why the movement decided not to shoot Şemso at Bitola. The decision was to have a profound effect not just on Şemso but on me too. If the Albanian had been shot that day, I may not have joined the movement's armed wing and would have probably remained a simple and rather anonymous courier. Perhaps the dreams you and I had shared would have come true and we would have fled to Paris to start our new life, away from Jews and from Turks and who knows, perhaps even away from history itself. But it was not to be. Coincidence and the random workings of the world, it would seem, affect not just the individual choices we make but the course of entire human lives too.

Wait. Hold on.

Someone is knocking at the door. It must be the cleaner. I'm sorry, I have to stop writing. But I promise, I won't be away for long.

Dogs Smelling Blood on a Hunt

Good Night, Ester (Night, Day 1)

I say good night, but who knows when these letters will reach you and at which hour on which day you'll be able to read them… It doesn't really matter, so long as you read them. That would be more than enough for me. But I would still like you to know the state of mind I have been in whilst writing to you. This evening I was going to write about the assassination of Şemso and how the incident changed my life but I had to leave the room before I could finish because there was a knock on the door. It was the porter, bringing a message from Reşit, the hotel manager, reminding me of our dinner appointment this evening in the hotel restaurant. He wants me to open up to him and share my woes and, gentleman that he is, thinks that by spending some time with him I may feel something akin to relief. But if I were to really spill the beans to him and let him know of my worries, he would be at great risk and I cannot allow this to happen out of the respect I have for his dear departed father Yusuf Bey and out of the gratitude I have for the kindness and care Reşit himself has shown me.

The worst thing about all this is being unable to explain my seeming evasiveness. Perhaps he would not be so curious – and would be less concerned – were I to provide some kind of explanation regarding my circumstances but I cannot. And it was the same this evening during our meal when he peppered me with questions, although he never veered into any discourtesy or vulgar nosiness at any time. As for me, I dutifully and respectfully answered his questions with a verbal dexterity that would make the most seasoned diplomat beam with pride. When I found myself at an impasse, I would turn the conversation to the food, and credit must be given to the hotel cook here for he had prepared a truly exquisite feast for us: cream of chicken soup, buttered fillet of bream, assorted puff pastries, sautéed chicken with vegetables... And as for the dessert revealed at the end: wafer-thin strips of pastry encrusted with hazelnut pieces and topped with the most delightful sauce... It reminded me of the *samsa* desserts we used to have at your place... Grandma Paloma used to make them so well!

'This is the most delicious sweet of the many the Sephardic Jews brought over from Spain,' she would say, and let out a wonderful hearty chuckle. 'And the most sumptuous *samsa* desserts of all are made in this house, I'll have you know.'

Actually, I have been thinking of Salonika a lot recently. The green shutters, the lime white houses, the cobblestoned pavements along which you and I used to stroll... The memories haunt me. They torment me so much that the present is no longer of any interest to me. I have yet to reach forty and yet I am like an old man, stuck in the past, living on his memories. Sometimes I am struck by such vivid recollections that I am taken aback. Perhaps it is because I have nothing else to do, no work to take up my time, no meaningful goal or purpose in life for which to strive. Maybe it is because I am walking towards death, step by grisly step. Of course, I often remember the conversations we used to have, and every day I realise how right you always were.

'Don't do it, Şehsuvar', you used to say. 'You are not cut out for politics.' You know me better than I know myself. You were right. Armed resistance, heroism, valour; none of these are for me. Don't misunderstand, these are not words written in regret; they are simply the summation of the last twenty years. And please do not misconstrue this as a disparagement of what I have done, either. I have always remained truthful to my ideas and my principles and have betrayed neither, nor have I betrayed my friends, the party or the cause. There were times when I was afraid, yes, times when I was scared out of my mind, but I learned to control those feelings. My cause was a form of self-realisation, a turning inwards into the self. When a man is without hope, like a boat that has been plucked from a raging torrent and has been abandoned instead in a dead sea where all it can do is wait to slowly and inexorably sink into its murky depths, he has a macabre opportunity to step back and evaluate his life. I do not deny that the turmoil in the world of the last twenty years – the assassinations, the coups, the wars – may have left my spirits battered but their impact cannot have been that intense or distressing as when I look back, all I can picture, in all their radiance and vivacity, are you and Salonika.

I'm sorry, again I digress. Perhaps literature is not my true calling after all… Where was I? Ah yes, Reşit. He was so keen to know about my problems. At dinner, while I pondered his motives, trying to figure out whether he was asking merely out of courtesy and curiosity or out of a genuine desire to help, I noticed something in his expression, a look that was so odd and so sly, insidious even, that I could not help but feel a shiver of fright run down my spine.

Was he blaming me for his father's death? Holding me responsible because I had not protected him in Tripoli? Because I had abandoned his father there and returned safely to the capital? No, Reşit was too clever and too rational to be swayed by such outlandish speculations. And it was not anger I saw in his eyes but something more temperate and measured, as though he was harbouring some surreptitious agenda of his own. Or was he also…? I began pondering… Was the meal we were having, that exquisite feast, part of the some wider plot that would see me delivered into the hands of the executioner in the middle of the night?

No, I was doing the man a gross injustice, and I immediately banished those thoughts from my mind. There was little to be gained from such paranoia. Reşit's only intention was to help a friend of his father, a man his father had attended school with and who had acted as a big brother towards him. But I still could not tell him about what had happened to me, or about the questions and issues that plagued my mind. Even if I had, he would not have understood. He would not have understood even though he lost his own father in the same bloody conflict.

There was and is just one person on the face of the earth that can understand me – you. Because you are the one I have caused to suffer the most, the one I have disappointed more than any other, the one whose happiness I have snatched away and whose spirit I have broken. Yes, along with my own, I have also ruined your life. You may say that it is all in the past now and that it no longer matters but it does matter. It matters a great deal. Even if you do not read these letters, and even if you do not want to know, I need to tell you. That much I owe you. I have to tell you why I made that choice, why I made that awful decision, if, indeed, I can... I should at least try. Please don't stop reading, please try to understand. Even if I don't deserve it, please at least grant me this one privilege.

So Şemsi Paşa left Salonika alive and well. As the train that carried the men that had come to crush our dreams pulled into the station, our men in Bitola were in a state of high alert. If Şemso could not be shot in a city like Salonika, where the movement's presence was at its strongest, how could he be killed in Bitola? Time was not on our side either. Just as our men in Bitola, in an act of desperation, were on the verge of hiring a professional assassin, a young volunteer by the name of Atıf spoke up, emerging as a modern-day Alexander offering to untangle our own Gordian knot.

'I'll do it'.

It was not the first time he had volunteered either. Two days earlier, he had made the same offer, and with the same steely determination.

'If Şemsi Paşa is not dealt with in Salonika, I'll shoot him in Bitola.'

The first time round nobody had paid the youngster any attention but now they were all ears and slowly began to realise he was serious. Yes, I was there, with Mehmet Ali Bey. Süleyman Askeri Bey was also there with us. Actually, had I possessed the courage, I would have spoken up before Atıf and offered to shoot Şemsi Paşa; the atmosphere there was so tense and so downbeat, somebody needed to speak up and say, with the necessary resolve and authority, that they would successfully do what had to be done. But nobody would have listened to someone as young and as inexperienced as me. Moreover, I was not a member of the *fedaeen*, our paramilitary wing, so it would never have occurred to any of them that I knew how to use a gun. Only Uncle Mehmet Ali knew that my father, ever one with an interest in such matters, had raised his one and only son to be proficient in the use of weapons.

We need to be able to defend ourselves, son. We are living in such dangerous times, I'm afraid you may have to fight, even if you are not a soldier.

After my father's death in that hellish city to which he had been exiled, I became even more interested in firearms. Well, until I met you, that is. I won't lie – after I met you, I stayed away from guns and I may never have laid hands on one again had events not placed me bang in the middle of the plot to assassinate the Semsi Paşa.

His train arrived in Bitola on the 7th of July. A piercing blow of the horn alerted the whole town to his ill-starred arrival. Although young Atıf had said he would kill him, neither he nor anybody else in our movement had undertaken any preparations for such an operation. You may ask how an organisation such as the Committee for Union and Progress could be so inept but I'm afraid it is the truth. All we had were brave, resolute and determined men, men like our young Atıf. His deep, serene eyes revealed a man ready to make any and all sacrifices for his cause, including death. As I watched the meeting proceed, wondering how the mission would be completed, my uncle Mehmet Ali Bey discreetly led me to one side, to a quiet corner of the room.

'You can see for yourself how grave the situation is, Şehsuvar,' he said, looking straight into my eyes. 'Atıf is sacrificing himself. His valour must not be spent in vain. This mission has to succeed, otherwise our friends in the mountains are doomed, and we will all be killed. The revolution will be finished before it has even started. Atıf has to pull that trigger and his bullet has to find its target. But if it doesn't… If that bullet does not go where it is supposed to…' He put his right hand on my shoulder. 'I know it is not your charge and that you haven't received the necessary training but we have been caught unprepared. I'm too visible to do the job. Rumours that I am one of the leaders of the movement have spread and are now too loud to be ignored. I cannot risk trying to protect Atıf. If I do and I am seen, it may damage the cause. The organisation may have taken some precautionary measures but I cannot be sure. Şemso should have been dealt with in Salonika. We should have finished him off there and it now may be too late. What I'm trying to say is that nobody here knows you. If you stand behind Atıf… Well, Atıf will probably get him but if he doesn't… I do not have the authority to ask this of you but if Atıf does not succeed…'

The trust he had in me was so moving I did not even let him complete his sentence.

'I'll finish off what he starts', I said in one breath. 'Just give me a gun'.

There was a glimmer in his eyes. He pulled me in and embraced me.

'Were he alive to see this, your father would have been so proud.'

'This will also be revenge for my father. When the cause succeeds and the new constitution is implemented, his soul will finally be able to rest in peace.'

'Absolutely', he said, letting me go. 'The souls of all the martyrs murdered by the despot shall rest in peace.'

He reached behind his shirt, pulled out a Nagant service revolver and handed it to me.

'It has never let me down. *Inshallah*, it will not let you down either.'

From that moment on, I was like Atıf's shadow. It was impossible for him not to notice but he did not turn around to look at me or to greet me. He did not even smile in acknowledgement.

Perhaps he thought I had been assigned to the mission by the movement and was pretending not to notice so as to not alert any of the spies thronging the area. Perhaps my uncle had whispered to him that I had been assigned as his bodyguard.

At this point, Şemsi Paşa had left the station by car and had gone to the telegraph office, probably to send a report to the palace. Like me, Atıf Bey must have also seen this as a golden opportunity to strike as he also headed for the telegraph office, which was located across the Dragor, the river that flows through the centre of Bitola. Atıf was the epitome of calm, taking light and easy steps along the street in front of the telegraph office, as though he had gone out for a leisurely stroll rather than on a deadly and possibly fatal mission to kill. At one point, he even entered a restaurant and had a bite to eat. He stopped to chat to friends from the military that recognised him and he greeted passers-by but not once did he take his eyes away from that telegraph office.

It was a hot, humid and sticky day and the street in front of the telegraph office was heaving. Everybody had come out to catch a glimpse of the famous pasha that had once hung the heads of captured bandits from ropes in town squares like beads on a rosary. The same question was on everybody's mind in the city and in the square: would Şemso succeed this time too? Would he crush the rebellion and restore the honour of the empire? Doubt and tension filled the air, made only worse by the muggy weather. At one point, a cool wind blew down from the mountains and seemed to stop for a moment before it showered the people gathered in the square with all the dust and grime it had gathered from its journey over the plains and the mountains. A ripple passed through the throng but nobody budged.

'An earthquake is on its way', said one old man, wiping away the dust that had coated his face. 'These are all signs, I tell you! Portents! Omens of an imminent earthquake. Dear me, this heat! May Allah save us.'

A few people turned and scowled at the old man.

'What? What are you looking at?' he scowled back. 'Have you ever seen such filthy air?' He looked up at the grey, ashen sky. 'Look. It's the middle of the summer and the sun has disappeared.'

'It means it's going to rain, Uncle Şaban, that's all', one scrawny youngster piped up. 'The same thing happened last summer, remember? The whole town was almost flooded.'

Uncle Şaban was about to reply when the crowd began to quiver and sway like the poplars lining the river.

'He's coming, he's coming… Şemsi Paşa is on his way…'

I turned to look at the table at which Atıf was drinking coffee but he wasn't there. He had disappeared. Anxiety began to creep in. Where had he gone? Had he given in to nerves and scurried off in fear? Because if he had, it meant I had to step up and do the job. My right hand moved of its own accord down to my holster to touch the revolver there. There it was, nestled tightly in my belt, a trusty old friend. I looked up and saw Atıf. He hadn't fled. Nothing of the sort. He was striding purposefully towards the telegraph office, graciously asking the people in front of him in a whisper to let him through. Every step took him closer to his target, to the man he would shoot dead.

Şemso was still nowhere to be seen but his men were still there, as vigilant as ever. His Lândon carriage was ready in front of the telegraph office and his Albanian guards were walking to their horses. They looked confident and relaxed, so much so they didn't seem to have taken any exceptional precautions. Seeing as nothing had happened to them in Salonika, the city in which the CUP had its strongest presence, the guards and perhaps Şemso too, were probably confident that they would not face any assassination attempt in a city like Bitola. It was not for nothing that my father used to say that *man is at his most vulnerable when he feels strongest* and that is the fatal mistake that Şemsi Paşa would make and which would lead him to his death. Of course, Atıf was way beyond such rational explanations. He was walking steadily and resolutely, almost like the bullet that would burst out of his own gun when he pulled the trigger, towards the telegraph office where he would commit his first and probably his last murder. He knew too well that he would almost certainly be killed during the operation.

I also began walking not to lose sight of Atıf, but I was also worried that my lack of experience may cause me to slip up and make a mistake that could draw attention to our presence there and jeopardise the operation. I mingled with the huge crowd, whilst also making sure I kept Atıf in my sights. Blending into that sea of turbans, fezzes and hats whilst also keeping an eye on Atıf was no mean feat but I stuck to it and eventually, after much pushing and shoving, I managed to get to the entrance of the telegraph office.

Atıf had stopped and was standing behind a line of people. I took up position just behind him. The large crowd that had gathered there was waiting impatiently, staring intently at the entrance to the premises, but none of the people in that group were as focused as Atıf or I. At one point, he turned his head ever so slightly to one side. We came face to face and I smiled as a way of reassuring him but there was not even a hint of a response in his countenance. For all I know, he may not have even noticed me. He discreetly turned back around and kept his eyes fixed on the wooden front door of the offices. Again my right hand went down to my gun of its own accord, as Atıf's hand must have too. But despite the commotion at the entrance, Şemso was nowhere to be seen. My throat was parched and the hot, dry weather was only exacerbating my tension. I felt I was the one that was to pull the trigger, not Atıf. Actually, it was not that far from the truth. As Mehmet Ali had said, if Atıf did not or could not do it, it was up to me to finish the job. Remembering my charge, I suddenly realised my position – if and when I had to shoot, I needed to be better placed and so I pushed aside a tiny man in front of me wearing a red fez at least two sizes too big for him and moved up until I was in the same row parallel to Atıf. Now there only a few people between us and only one row of people in front of me, with Şemso's carriage just a few metres ahead and it would have remained there had one of the horses pulling his carriage not decided to empty its bladder all over the cobblestoned pavement, forcing me and those around me to take a few steps back to avoid the mess.

Although I had not been there all that long, the seconds seemed to drag on. It felt as though I had been standing there for hours waiting for Şemso, and I'm sure Atıf was feeling the same. What was Atıf thinking at that moment? Was he perhaps wondering why Şemso wouldn't just turn up so the torment could at least end? Or was he really as serene as he looked? After all, why would a man who has decided to stare death in the face have anything to fear from Azrail?

'Looks like he's not coming out', a man in a turban standing to my right remarked. He reeked of sweat. 'We're wasting our time here'.

'Really? We're wasting our time, are we? He's not going to come out, eh? And why exactly would he not come out?' The response came from a man in a black hat standing in front of me. 'What's he going to do in there? You think he's going to spend the whole night in a telegraph bureau? A pasha of the realm, no less, spending the night in a dingy telegraph bureau?'

The man in the turban did not reply. He simply glowered at his critic. The crowd began to surge excitedly again.

'He's coming out, he's coming out! There he is!'

And they were right. The wooden door of the offices had opened and two soldiers had walked out. As the carriage drivers quickly stood to attention and prepared for departure, I turned to have a look at Arıf. I sensed a slight, almost imperceptible, quiver of movement in his right shoulder, a sign that he was reaching for his gun. It had begun… I swallowed hard and grasped the butt of my revolver. Masses of people, uniformed and civilian, were streaming out through the front door. And then, finally, he appeared. Şemsi Paşa emerged, leaning on his walking stick, exiting the building with slow but deliberate and assured steps.

I must confess, I was disappointed. Was this doddering old man barely able to walk really the monster about whom I had heard so many grisly stories? Again, I couldn't help but wonder if Atıf was thinking the same. I shot him a glance but he was not letting anything distract him. His mind was focused on the job and his eyes firmly fixed on his target. I did the same, but that also meant I could not watch Atıf. Cursing my own ineptitude, I turned to watch Atıf again. I saw him slowly take out his gun, a Nagant just like mine. He was holding it steadily, using the man standing in front of him as cover. Until that moment, nobody had seen him. I also took out my own gun but I did not lift it to aim. Atıf, however, was already aiming his gun at Şemsi Paşa over the shoulder of the anonymous man in front of him.

I remember being amazed at his composure. Forget shooting someone, just witnessing the events unfolding there was frightening enough for me, but the courage shown by our young lieutenant was enough to put the brakes on the fright that had threatened to overwhelm me. The fear I had been feeling up to that point had been enough to make me turn tail and run from that crowd, leaving Şemsi Paşa and his coterie of ruthless guards far behind me.

As I stood there taking deep breaths to try and pull myself together, Atıf's gun suddenly went off. The sound was met with a deep silence at first. I turned to look at the pasha. Rather than fear or pain, there was a look of astonishment on his face, a look that seemed to express amazement that somebody would have the audacity to even attempt such a heinous act. I realised then that he had not been killed, and that the bullet had merely grazed his head and then whizzed past. The deep silence then turned into pandemonium, and as shrieks and shouts filled the air, Atıf's gun went off again. I saw Şemsi Paşa stagger on his feet and a frail cry emerged from his cracked lips. His eyes, still wide open in astonishment, turned in the direction from which the shot came but he crumpled to the ground before noticing anything. Atıf pulled the trigger once again, wanting to leave nothing to chance, but the shot was in vain. The people that had seen the pasha fall to the ground had spotted the assassin and were now pushing and shoving as they desperately tried to get away as quickly as possible. Some escaped into the side streets, others rushed into the coffeehouses and restaurants thronging the area, while other, less fortunate, souls found themselves in the Dragor River as a result of that chaotic stampede.

As for me, I could feel the wretched fear that had been sapping my soul disappear completely. Now, instead, an elation bordering on – and stemming from – pride lifted my spirits. We had done it. We had eliminated the man that had come to crush the revolution. It is only now, today, that I grasp the magnitude of what we achieved that day.

Atıf had done his duty; now it was my turn. I had to defend him, at all costs, and stop him from falling into the hands of those vicious Albanians. I ran after our young brave, who was bumping and crashing into the people around him as he also tried to make good his escape. He was heading for the section of the street that led to the local government offices, knowing it would be quieter there, but there was one glaring drawback to taking that route – precisely because it was so quiet, he would stick out like a sore thumb. He was running as fast as he could but he had forgotten to remove his sword and it was now impeding his movements. Twice, in fact, he tripped over his sword and stumbled but, thankfully, he did not fall. I took out my gun and released a few successive shots into the air. The guards turned and stared at me in shock, their weapons at the ready. One of them raised his gun and pointed it at me, but when one of his comrades, a bearded comrade standing next to him, said, 'What do you think you're doing? The real killer is getting away,' he focused his attentions back on Atıf. Those few shots I fired into the air hadn't done much good. The Albanian guards had overcome their shock, and were now chasing after the assassin, their Mausers cocked and ready.

Because I was not as quick to react as Atıf, I found myself behind the others. I started running and would soon be in the Mausers' firing range. Luckily for me, the Albanian troops were standing still so they could take better aim and that meant they made easier targets for me. Seeing Atıf rush towards the ends of the street gave me some hope. All he needed to do was hold on and turn the corner and then he would be safe. At one point, he also stopped and he turned and fired two more shots, surprising the Albanians, but their surprise only lasted a moment. They resumed their shooting, whilst our nimble young Atıf continued his escape. He was about to reach the corner, when he stopped and bent down to look at his right leg. *Damn*, I remember thinking. *He's been shot. Any second now and he's going to fall. The prey is going to be devoured by the hunters.* I turned my gun on the Albanians and was about to start firing when Atıf began running again. True, he was not running as comfortably as a few seconds ago and his right leg was not landing properly on the ground but he was still able to move. He took five steps, then ten steps, twenty more… And then, finally, he turned the corner and vanished…

But of course the Albanians would not give up the chase. Like dogs that had sniffed blood on a hunt, they rushed after him. Nor could I just stand there and watch and so I fell in after them. By then, the area was so crowded, it was difficult to work out who was whom. There were even some civilians amongst us. Some local members of an organisation that was trying to stop the Albanians were now part of a huge affray.

When I reached the end of the street, I looked around. Atıf, thankfully, was nowhere to be seen. The panting Albanians were looking around too, asking one another where he could be.

I knew they would come after me once they realised they had lost their assassin so I quickly escaped into the nearest side street. I learnt of Atıf's fate later – knowing escape was impossible, he played smart and hid in a shoe shop on that street and didn't come out until things had calmed down, after which he went to Mahmud Bey's house, where he would be safe for at least a few more hours. Later on, he would be escorted to Resen by Süleyman Askeri Bey and then taken on to a safe house in Ohrid. Years later, when we were to meet again in Istanbul, this is what he would have to say to me:

'The worst part of that entire operation was not the torture of waiting for Şemsi Paşa or the hail of bullets from those Albanians' rifles but the horrible black burka I had to wear on the journey from Bitola to Resen.'

The Meaning of This Empire for Us

Good Morning, Ester (Morning, Day 2)

I missed out on breakfast in the hotel this morning. When I woke up, it was nearly midday. I had become so engrossed in my writing last night that when I finally lay down on the bed and closed my eyes, it was nearly dawn. Not that I am complaining. On the contrary, it gives me a certain sense of pride, as for a few blissful moments I felt like one of those great literary masters falling asleep at his desk in the midst of writing a masterpiece. But joking aside, you have no idea how happy it makes me to write to you, to reach out to you via these letters, to think about you and relive the things we experienced together over and over again in my mind. You dominate my days and my nights and my thoughts and feelings. You were even in my dreams last night. We were strolling along the narrow streets of Salonika. Some old men were sitting by a table in one of the pavement cafés playing dominoes. One was swearing in Greek, another was singing a song in Spanish, while another was haggling with a nearby trader in Turkish.

'We would never see this in Paris', I said to you. 'This is an empire. A garden of intermingling languages, faiths and ethnicities.' You smiled alluringly and replied, 'Yes, but this empire also means our relationship can never be realised, Şehsuvar.' You were, somehow, discreetly nuzzling up to me whilst at the same time edging away from me without even letting us touch. 'In Salonika, this is the closest you'll ever get to me.' You shook your head. 'But in Paris... Don't you see, you dolt? The only place we can be free as lovers is Paris! This is a dying empire but Paris is a whole new world. A world of new hopes and new beginnings…'

Then we were sitting side by side. I think it was the Odeon Music Hall. We were waiting for the operetta *The Count of Luxembourg* to begin. Your heavenly scent, the locks of your red hair tumbling down over your tiny ears, that smile of yours which makes your black eyes turn indigo… I woke up when the orchestra began playing. Well, I thought it was the orchestra but in actual fact, it was the chambermaid knocking on the door.

'Not today!' I shouted. 'Why do you keep bothering me?'

The poor woman did not even know why I was so furious. How could I tell her she had interrupted a dream and destroyed a delicate marvel? That she had snatched away from me the recollection of one of the happiest moments of my life?

When I woke up, I could not get straight out of bed. You were still there with me, everywhere, in my mind, body and soul. What was it I had just seen – was it a dream, or a memory I have been unable to forget? It was so real, like the wind driving away the clouds from the top of Mount Olympus to reveal the snowy peak in all its unadorned glory. So real and so vivid… But dream or memory, it had been ruined, and the only thing that could save me from my disappointment was to go back to my desk and carry on writing.

I got up in a feverish haste and washed my face but did not bother shaving. I did not even go downstairs to eat. I was not going to be distracted from my writing by the meaningless humdrum of daily life and so I asked for lunch to be delivered to my room. After having a few measly bites to eat, I went back to my desk…

I was not the one that pulled the trigger at Şemsi Paşa's assassination, nor indeed did I help Atıf in any significant way, but my role in the incident was roundly commended. The members of the movement that had been there watching duly noted how I had stayed in position until Atıf disappeared, and they also noted my armed response, the shots I had fired and the way I had dived into the crowd and stood up to the Albanians. Eventually, on Uncle Mehmet Ali's recommendation, I was promoted to the *fedaeen*, the armed wing of the movement. I cannot tell you how delighted I was when I was given the news. Of course, I am no longer part of that section of the movement, and yes, it may even have been better for me had I not been part of the squad assigned to assassinate the pasha. Indeed, there is no 'may' about it: it would definitely have been better for me. But even if I had not been involved in the plot, would I have still been able to defend myself from the effects of the rebellion that was threatening to turn the country upside down? Faced by the whirlwinds of history, man is like a shell adrift on the ocean. No matter how hard we resist, or how conscientious we may be in our thoughts and our actions, our fate is at the mercy of the waves. You can be certain that had I not been there at Şemsi Paşa's assassination, I would have been on the front lines in another fight.

You may deny the validity of what I am saying this and give yourself as an example, saying you have not taken my path. But your father was not sent into exile to the wastelands of Fezzan without even being granted a last chance to say goodbye to his wife and his son. Your father did not die in exile at a senselessly young age. And no, this is not hubris on my part, nor is it a grievance. I have not forgotten how you also lost your mother at a young age. All I am trying to say is that one cannot live in these lands and remain silent or undisturbed by the events that surround and shape us.

In response, you may well say that some have remained silent and then ask why I have not and you would be right to do so. Yes, there were those abject individuals that chose to ignore what was happening around them, those that bowed their heads in subservience, who crawled on their hands and knees and who degraded themselves to preserve their favour with the palace and thus continue with their wretched lives. I myself would have rather died than live such a life, and I know you think the same. I know — I am certain — that your soul, ever proud and ever free, felt and feels the same as mine. I've always maintained that it was not the ardour of our young bodies that brought us together but the defiance in our souls and the desire in our hearts to discover the new. You wanted us to choose the literary life. Yes, literature is the eternal revolt. Like politics, it is not restricted to just one era, to one period, to today. And yes, maybe you were right, maybe literature could have been our liberator, but the revolution caught me unawares. That chain of events, the great pains we suffered and those grand hopes overwhelmed my young and naïve dreams. Please, I beseech you, do not think of these as justifications or excuses. I am fully aware of my faults and my culpability. If you like, I can also make that confession. So yes, the fault is mine. At any time I could have stopped it. Yes, you're right, I could have made our relationship mean something more than it already did. But I didn't. You're right, I was mesmerised by the charm and the appeal of rebellion. Revolution, in this case, transcended and overcame the allure of love.

If only I had told you all this at the time. I could have told you that I had changed my mind, that our personal lives no longer mattered, and that our insignificant little affair meant nothing compared to the salvation of the empire. But I didn't. I couldn't. But I do not want to be unfair to myself either: such a confession was against the nature of the struggle I had joined. I was a member of an organisation that was fighting against a tyranny that had lorded over us for thirty long years. I was part of a movement that faced constant danger, one whose followers had been thrown in prison, exiled and even killed. I say followers but we were more than that; like the others, I had dedicated my youth, my pride and my honour to the movement. That is why I could not share the details of our struggle with anyone on the outside, not even with the person I cared for most in the world – you. Had I told you about our activities, I could have placed my comrades in danger.

So yes, that is partially the reason for my silence. I had, in a way, been expecting you to understand as we had finally begun to look at the world in the same way, to look for liberation in the same ideas, to adopt the same lifestyle. Isn't that why we loved each other in the first place? The first time we met, that day I was with Uncle Leon; the day we first set eyes on each other on that dark winter afternoon... The way you lifted your head, like a rising, sparkling sun, the way you spoke of that French female writer who used the *nom de plume* George Sand... The way you spoke, as though you were rebelling against life, against time, against people, even against me... And my gradual discovery of your beauty while listening to you speak... Or should I say, your intoxicating beauty's gradual capture of my heart...

Yes, I know perfectly well why I love you, and why I have not forgotten you either... I could write page after page telling you why, while at the same time I could also sum it up in a single line. But I should also admit that I still do not know why you loved me. You never told me why and I never asked you. And yes, before you say it, you are right: I did not ask because of my stupid pride. How can a man ask his woman why she loves him? At the end of the day, we are still Ottomans and I am still a man of the East. The East still flows through my veins. Although I do remember what you said to me on one occasion. 'You're different', you said. 'You're not like the others.'

I wonder, is that why you loved me? Because I was different? If so, what was that difference? My wanting to be a writer? Because of those few clumsy amateurish stories I once dashed off? Maybe you loved me because I was brave enough to love a Jewish girl, as that meant inviting the wrath and the disdain of every member of my family, my mother Mukaddes most of all, as well the ire of my friends in the movement. Yes, even them. My comrades. No matter how progressive the ideas they were defending may have been, when it came to women, they were no different to our ancient ancestors. I remember what Ahmed Rıza once said to me when we were sitting in one of the cafés in front of the Sorbonne in Paris. As the waitress who had brought us our coffees walked away, he said:

'There are two things in Paris that confound the Ottoman elites. The first is seeing women so free and so much a part of life that they can work as waitresses.' He then pointed to a statue of Auguste Comte that was standing a few yards away. 'And the second is monuments such as this. Both are quite alien to us. Progress, my dear friend, is a matter of time. And we are going to need a very long time indeed before equality and beauty become integral parts of our society.'

Even an intellectual as ahead of his time as Ahmed Rıza knew. My falling madly in love with a Jewish girl and my willingness to live my life with her required immense courage precisely because of the attitudes prevalent in our society. Yes, I can say with the utmost confidence that I really was ready to risk everything. Of course, you can also say the same, indeed more, as the risks you were taking were even greater. Your people and your community were just as conservative as mine, if not more. And also, being a woman… But you didn't care what anybody said, not in Salonika, not in the whole world. When I looked at you, it was like looking at somebody that had come from the future. In your eyes, nothing in the world mattered except our love.

'Love is the most wonderful selfishness in life…'

Yes it is, and it is also one of the most destructive and most merciless of feelings. The intensity of your passion and your strength made me happy but they also frightened me. I often used to sit and wonder, what if you were to one day stop loving me? I knew for sure that were that day to come and you left me, you wouldn't even turn around to look back, not even once. Perhaps it was that fear that kept my feelings for you alive – the fear that I could lose you at any moment.

I remember once telling you that our love was impossible. It was one of those wonderful moments when we were alone in your Uncle Leon's office. 'How is this all going to end, I wonder?' I wondered out loud.

'All loves are impossible, Şehsuvar', you replied. 'If there is no impossibility, the love fades away. And most important of all, my handsome fool, love is not commerce. It is not a business deal that concerns itself with ends. It looks only at today. Not even today but at the moment. It exists while the fire burns. And when the fire burns out and the passion dies….'

And that is what I had always feared – the passion dying out. Of you leaving me for another man. There were, after all, so many young men swarming around you vying for your attention. Yet just look at the quirk of fate – it was not you that left me but I that left you. Not that I actually left or went anywhere. My body and my mind may have left but my soul was always with you. It always has been and always will be. To paraphrase what you once said, *It is the impossible that keeps love alive… The impossible never lets love die.*

When I joined the movement, I never thought I would leave you but I was clearly deceiving myself. It is an old childhood habit of mine, one that has never gone away. I was going to be one of the heroes that would bring freedom, fraternity, equality and justice to the country and you would love me more as a result. I would become a hero in your eyes and after our victory, we would go on to live better, happier and fuller lives. After all, how long can a revolt last? How long can a despot defy the rebels and cling to his power? Abdülhamit would eventually have been deposed, a constitutional monarchy would have been declared and the paradise on earth for which we yearned would have been established. And then, once we had won, we would move to Paris, as the eminent and upstanding artists of an honourable and honoured country.

I was young back then and so naïve and wildly optimistic that I actually believed everything would out turn the way we wanted when we all know that ultimately, it did not. We hit the wall. And why? Because history has no conscience. History does not take people into consideration. Not people, or loves or lives. We may try to control history and direct her but she moves according to her own whims. Countries may be torn apart, whole nations may be wiped out, cities pillaged and plundered and people slaughtered but history does not care!

Actually, I did not want to write about this. Who am I, after all, to expound upon the relationship between the individual and history? But once you begin to question yourself, you don't know how to stop. Forgive me if I have digressed, I should return to our subject… The assassination of Şemsi Paşa.

The news of his death hit the palace like an earthquake. For the first time, the sultan began to grasp the depth, the urgency and the immediacy of this new threat. As you well know, Abdülhamit had been living in fear ever since the death of his uncle Abdülaziz. Events that began with the overthrow of his uncle may have led to Abdülhamit being crowned sultan but that did not mean he was able to shake off his paranoia. Even after having so expertly and so deviously engineered the arrest, imprisonment and execution of a statesman of the stature of Mithat Paşa, whom he suspected of murdering his uncle Abdülaziz, he was still not able to free himself of those gnawing fears. Years of complex power struggles, the ruthless elimination of the princes and other rival claimants to the throne and the fear engendered by numerous cunning plots and mutinies had taken their toll on his tall, thin frame and that hapless fear, which he wore almost like an invisible cloak, followed him to the grave, as though it had now seeped into his soul and become an unshakeable part of his character. But now the situation was different. Now, it was not an imaginary fear but a very real threat. A pasha, no less, had been gunned down in broad daylight in one of the empire's most important provinces, while at the same, soldiers continued to abandon their posts and swarm to the hills to join the rebels. The omens were not good. Nevertheless, it was not until he was told that Tatar Osman Paşa had been kidnapped and taken to the mountains that he grasped the true significance of the rebellion.

Do you remember those days? The morning after my return from Bitola, I stopped by your house to see you. As always, Grandma Paloma was sitting on her divan in the corner of the veranda singing one of those *romanza* folk ballads. I assumed she was just relaxing and enjoying the morning sunshine, but then I noticed the tray of green beans in front of her and realised she was actually busy preparing them for the evening meal. She was so immersed in what she was doing, although whether it was the beans or the sad story behind the song she was singing that had captivated her, I could not tell. I must have been blocking out the sun as she suddenly stopped mid-song. She lifted her head and squinted up to see who it was. She smiled when she recognised me.

'Şehsuvar, is that you, my little lamb?'

'It is, Grandma Paloma', I said, laying a hand gently on her shoulder. 'How are you? I hope all is well.'

'Thank you, dear lad. Here, come and have a seat.'

I didn't really want to take up her time and asked if you were in. Her old tired eyes seemed to cloud over with worry at the mention of your name.

'Ester is here, but you just forget about her for a moment.' She pointed to the divan. 'Here, come and sit next to me.'

It would have been rude not to so I sat down beside her.

'You're an educated lad, Şehsuvar. Tell me, is it true that they have shot a pasha in Bitola? You should see our Leon. He is so happy. Over the moon, I tell you. You'd think he'd been made the sultan. He says the soldiers have taken to the hills and that the palace is being bombarded with telegrams demanding the opening of a parliament. He says a revolution is underway. I keep asking them but neither Leon nor Ester bother to tell me what is going on. You're a good lad. Tell me, what is this revolution they're on about?'

'The despotism shall soon be smashed, Grandma Paloma,' I said happily. 'We shall finally be free. Free from the rule of the tyrant. The nation is rising up, Grandma Paloma. The constitution of 1876 will be re-instated.'

But the more I told her, the more her adorably sweet face seemed to darken, in contrast to my delight.

'So it's true'. She sniffed and went back to snipping the ends off the green beans. 'I would say let's hope for the best but no good shall come of this, I tell you. No good at all.'

'Why do you say that, Grandma Paloma? We shall have freedom and equality. We shall all be brothers once again. People of all faiths and religions united as brothers and sisters.'

She turned and stared straight at me.

'We shall have nothing of the sort. It will only get worse. This country will be destroyed. God help us all. They won't even let us into this city.'

It was not so much her words that moved me but the worry in her eyes. I could not help but ask.

'Who? Who won't let us in?'

'The Christians', she said nervously, almost afraid of being overheard. 'As though you didn't know. The Christians, of course. The Greeks, the Bulgars, the Vlachs, perhaps the Serbs too. Whoever has the strength and the will.' She shook her head in despair. 'The Ottomans will be overthrown, my boy, and it will be calamitous for all of us. Once again, we shall have to abandon our grandfathers' and our forefathers' graves and take to the roads. You Turks shall have Asia Minor, but what about us Jews? Who knows where we will end up. I cannot leave though.' A muffled cry of pain escaped her lips, as though she had only just grasped the enormity of the situation, before she sighed, 'Ah, such a calamity!' and raised her arms to the sky. 'Dear God, please, I implore you, take me away as soon as possible. Please, I beg you, do not let me witness the disintegration of this beautiful country. Please, do not let me die in another city.'

That is when you appeared. You were wearing a long scarlet dress that made you look even slimmer and an olive-green scarf under which your hair fluttered and sparkled in the brilliant July sun. You had that familiar carefree, daring smile on your lips and as soon as I saw it, I forgot about Grandma Paloma's woes. Not that it had really affected me but she was right to be worried as everything she had prophesised was soon to come true. She had foreseen the imminent calamity before any of us but we were so engrossed in ourselves and in our own personal struggles that we had failed to see what lay in store for us.

The only consolation for Grandma Paloma was that she was buried in her beloved Salonika and that she died before the nightmare she had foreseen became a terrible reality, breathing her last before the empire began to disintegrate and the war brought fire and destruction in its wake.

That July day when you approached us, you did not know that Grandma Paloma and I had been talking about but you did joke with me about what I had been doing during my absence.

'You went away to Bitola and while you're there no less than an Ottoman pasha gets killed,' you joked. 'If I didn't know better Şehsuvar, I would start to think there was something sinister about you…'

For a moment I was afraid you had found me out and I turned to look at you in surprise. Luckily, you didn't notice the look in my eye.

'I'm sorry, did I say something out of line?' you said before taking me by the arm and dragging me down to the end of the garden. That is when I had a sudden urge to tell you everything that had happened. I wanted to be free of the suffocating weight that grand lies always bring but I then remembered the oath I had taken with the movement and resisted the urge to reveal all. Things were now moving so fast, I was beginning to believe, in contrast to Grandma Paloma, that the revolution would create an even better life than the one that had been promised to us, and that it was not far off either. And ultimately, that is what happened. Sultan Abdülhamit, for one, lost control over the situation. The day after Şemsi Paşa was killed, the Albanians in Ferizaj, upon hearing that their lands would be ceded to foreign powers, took to the streets. The man sent to crush the protests was Galip Bey, the Captain of the Gendarmerie, and he was a loyal member of the Committee for Union and Progress and a close friend of our very own Mehmet Ali, so when he reached the troubled region, instead of obeying the wishes of the sultan and the government, he turned to the thirty-odd thousand protestors gathered there and roused them to revolt against Yıldız Palace, saying, 'If the constitution is implemented, no one shall take an inch of your lands.' It did not take long for his words to take effect. Twelve days later a telegraph carrying one hundred and eighty signatures representing thirty thousand Albanians living in Skopje, Tetovo, Gostivar, Mitrovica, Pristina and Novi Pazar was sent to the sultan demanding the implementation of the constitution and stating that if the demand was not met, the people would take up arms and march to the capital. Although this unexpected demand by the Albanians, who were usually the most loyal subjects of empire, was a severe setback for the sultan, the blow that would eventually oust him was undoubtedly the kidnapping of Tatar Osman Paşa.

After the assassination of Şemsi Paşa, Tatar Osman Paşa, the Commander of the Skopje Regional Unit Forces, was summoned to the palace by Abdülhamit and all control over the region was immediately handed over to him by a monarch livid that the Ottoman state had been disgraced in such a manner. The honour and the dignity of the state could not be sullied so outrageously. Where Şemso had failed, Osman Paşa was to succeed. However, it was too late. We had already learnt of his appointment and the movement immediately convened a general assembly to assess all aspects of this new threat. This time, the movement did not decide on assassination. Rather than eliminate the pasha, he was to be captured and brought to the mountains, and the mission was to be headed by Niyazi Bey and his company, who were already ensconced in the hills. A written communiqué later explained why the pasha was not to be killed.

As you've probably guessed, I was the one entrusted to take the communiqué to Niyazi Bey of Resen, also known as Resneli Niyazi. The reason for my setting off again for Bitola fourteen days after returning was not actually to deal with some family inheritance issues, which is the excuse I had come up with at the time, but to deliver that letter to the rebels in the hills.

And yes, I can almost feel your anger and see your astonishment at the fact that I did not even blush when I lied to you and that I did not feel even the slightest discomfort at uttering such blatant lies. But you're wrong. I was not happy at having lied to you. I was deeply uncomfortable about it. Indeed, uncomfortable is not the world. Shame is what I felt. So much shame that I wanted to sink into the bowels of the earth and disappear. But I had no choice.

Hold on. Something is happening in the hall... I think somebody is standing by my door outside. He has put a key into the keyhole. My God, somebody is actually trying to enter my room! Is it the maid? I'm sorry, I'm going to have stop writing...

Confronting Death

Good Evening, Ester (Evening, Day 2)

Now I understand. A writer's wish to be left alone in a hotel room so that he can work on his masterpiece without disruption is an impossible wish. Every day, indeed, almost every hour, I am disturbed by some new incident. This time it was caused by a gentleman at my door claiming to have forgotten his room number. I heard the jangling of keys in my keyhole and so I got up and opened the door. Standing there was a rather stout gentleman trying to open the door to my room. When I asked him why, he said he had made a mistake and that he had got the floors mixed up. I glanced down at the number on the key in his hand. It was room 310, whilst mine is 410, which meant his room was the one directly beneath mine.

'My apologies', he said sheepishly. 'I must have had a little too much of that Italian wine this afternoon.'

Of course, I did not fall for it. He was with them. With the police, who are keeping an eye on me while I am cooped up in here. You see, I did not leave the hotel today and so they must have been wondering whether I was still in my room or not. Let them. I couldn't care less. I played along with the man, however, and accepted his apology. Indeed, to appear even more convincing, I said, 'Perhaps a nice, strong cup of Turkish coffee after so much wine would have helped you remember where your room is.' He apologised once again and walked away but by then, my sense of comfort as well as my desire to write had vanished. I stepped out onto the balcony and into a spectacular evening. The sun setting slowly over the banks of the Golden Horn glittered in the windows around the city, bathing the whole of Istanbul in a honey-coloured light.

The street was its usual flurry of activity. For some, the day was ending, while for others, life was only just beginning. I felt a huge urge to go out, to see people heading back to their homes, to bump into the pleasure-seekers streaming on to Independence Street. I thought it might cheer me up and reignite my urge to write so I rushed back into my room, gathered up my pen and my notes and sheets and hid them away in their secret hiding place under the ornamental tiled stove. After that, I shaved, washed and got dressed.

When I went downstairs, I noticed a group of foreigners – men and women – mingling in the lobby. I was surprised to see them at first but then realised they were passengers from the Orient Express. The Express had arrived late in town and its customers were now eagerly waiting to be registered at the hotel so they could retire to the comfort of their rooms and unwind. They were all Europeans, and all rich to boot, most of them having probably made their fortunes during the Great War, although why I found myself standing there and casting judgement upon these people I did not even know and whose personal lives I knew nothing about was a mystery to me. For all I knew, they may have had nothing to do with the war. But the war had had such a shattering impact on our lives that I could not help but cast aspersions on these people who were, just a few short years ago, part of the enemy camp.

Well, whatever they were, you know I have never been one to stomach large crowds but on this one occasion I was actually pleased to see them as their presence there would help me slip past any snoops that may have been lurking in the hotel. I didn't notice any suspicious looking characters, not even the guy that had been trying to get into my room earlier but I knew they were there, if not in the hotel then outside on the street. The second I saw the man in the creased suit and trilby standing by the tobacconist's shop on the corner of the street, I knew he was a member of the same squad that has been following me like a shadow in Beşiktaş. Whether I am strolling along the coast or getting on the tram, they are there behind me. The strange thing is, when I noticed him, I felt a surge of excitement. My slumped shoulders straightened up, I felt an unexpected vigour return to my knees and my mind seemed to suddenly awaken from its long, protracted lethargy.

'Confronting death is better than thinking about dying', the late Major Basri used to say. 'Therefore, do not ponder potential dangers for too long. I am not telling you not to be vigilant or not to take necessary measures but there is no need to dwell on potentially dangerous outcomes for too long. The moment you encounter the enemy; indeed, the moment the first gun is fired, you will feel much better.'

I did not think any guns would be fired this evening here in the middle of Pera but I now knew I had a much better idea of what Basri Bey meant.

One by one, the lights from the shops lining Istiklal Street were blinking into life. The crowds had yet to appear but the shopkeepers had long since completed their preparations for the customers that would soon arrive. I walked along the pavement lit up by the lights and colours from the store windows up to the Tepebaşı Theatre. Naturally, my tracker in the grey hat had also started moving. But he was not the only one: when I reached the theatre, another man, wearing a black leather jacket and brown flat cap, joined the party. There had to be another one, as these squads usually consisted of three members. I knew that from the days of the *Teşkilât-ı Mahsusa*, the Ottoman Special Organisation, as we had employed similar tactics when stalking people. They were usually foreign spies or other suspicious persons, but the list also included anybody the movement deemed dangerous.

You may wonder how young idealists fuelled by a love of freedom and with a wish to usher in a constitutional monarchy could become embroiled in such underhand strategies but don't worry, all will be revealed.

When I reached the Tepebaşı Theatre, I stopped and pretended to examine the posters for that evening's bill, which featured Dumas' *La Dame aux Camellias*. What I was actually doing was watching the man in the brown flat cap on the other side of the road through the window that housed the poster advertising the show. He was standing in the doorway of the Italian House, ostensibly lighting a cigarette. But he made a crucial mistake: he looked over at the Bristol Hotel and made a gesture. It was a quick and almost imperceptible gesture but I saw it.

I calmly turned around. There he was: the third man, a short, squat fellow. Feeling especially roguish, I began walking towards the Bristol Hotel and to his side of the street. When he saw me walking towards him, he was confused and looked away but I carried on walking towards him. He began to panic, not knowing what to do. It was too late for him to turn around but he could not just stand there either as that would have looked odd so, with no other option, he began walking towards me. Because I was keeping my gaze fixed on the building behind his left ear, using it as a focal point, he did not know if I was looking at him or at something else, which was making him increasingly irate. If his superiors were to find out I had noticed him, he would receive a stern reprimand, and perhaps even be removed from duty. We were closing in on each other, step by step. He could not bear the tension anymore and, with just a few paces left between us, he finally looked at my face to work out my intentions, but I did not slow down or alter the direction of my gaze. He quickly looked away again. He took a step forward and I responded in kind, until we were face to face. I slid a little over to the right and quickly walked past him. He let out a deep breath. Such was the relief he felt, I could feel his breath in the air even after I was a few steps past him. I had to stop myself from laughing out aloud as I carried on walking along the now thronging pavement towards the Grand Hotel de Londres.

My trackers had probably overcome their confusion and were back on my trail but the short, squat man would be more careful from now on. I stopped when I reached the entrance to the Hacopulo Arcade and looked back at the direction from which I had come. Yep, they had smartened up: I could not see them now. With an inexplicable lightness of spirit, I entered the arcade. I have always liked that particular place, and I know you used to as well. Remember when you came to Istanbul the year I graduated from the Lycée de Galatasaray? It was supposedly to visit your Aunt Lillia, although we both knew it was to see me. It was the finest graduation present I could have wished for. And do you also remember the day we came to this passage together, and I showed you where Namık Kemal's newspaper *İbret* was published? It was printed on the premises under the house in which Ahmed Mithat Efendi used to live. In fact, he was the owner of the press on which the paper was printed. We talked about those two writers and their years in exile…. Then we bought you a navy blue hat. The Armenian tailor swore that they were all the rage in Paris. It was the beginning of summer and the flowers in the arcade were in full bloom. Wonderful days they were… Sweet, sweet days…

As I strolled around in the shimmering evening light, the trackers dutifully following me, once more I realised how much I missed you. My nose tingled and my eyes misted over. I swallowed back the tears, of course, as there was no way I would let the reports filed by my trackers say that I had suddenly started blubbing right there in the middle of the street. While passing through Hacopulo Arcade, I thought about going to that Iranian restaurant we used to frequent together. I had always liked their saffron rice although truth be told, I cannot remember any of their other foods. In the end, I decided not to go in. There is little point in awakening old memories and I did not want or need any more sentimentality and so I made my way through the maze of tailors, restaurants and coffee houses in the arcade until I arrived at the *Cadde-i Kebir*.

The street was thronging with so many people that my trackers must have been worried they would lose me in the crowds. I kept on walking, calmly and leisurely, along the street, as though I had come out for a nice relaxing evening stroll. The occupation of the city had ended only three years ago but the street had already regained much of its former glory. Beautifully dressed women and smart-looking gentlemen were passing me by on the street, while all manner of expensive goods were on display in the shop windows. For the poor, war and scarcity are disasters, but the rich always find a way to survive and to prosper, whatever the circumstances. As I walked along, I ignored the expensive fabrics, jewels and clothes on display in the gleaming shop windows and watched the people instead, many of them out enjoying the autumn evening. Eventually I reached the Galatasaray Lycée, formerly known as the *Mekteb-i Sultan*, the Imperial High School. Gazing at the grounds of the school that had been home to me for years, it was not my friends in general or one particular friend or classmate but the school's celebrated – indeed, legendary – headmaster, Tevfik Fikret that I suddenly thought of, that great poet who had stood in front of the school gates on the 31st of March to stare down an angry mob of conservatives that were against the very idea of a constitutional monarchy and say to them, 'You shall enter the grounds of this school only over my dead body.' He was a decent man, a man of honour that felt all the pain and the turmoil of the world and of his country. Over the following years, the movement even managed to make him an enemy too. I felt a twinge of sadness and hurriedly looked away, as though doing so would somehow help me forget the past.

I left the teeming crowds on the street behind, entered the Cité de Péra and walked past the patisserie, the tailor's and the bakery until I arrived at Yorgo's Tavern, where I finally let out a deep breath and let myself relax. As soon as I entered, I heard Hristo's cheery voice ringing out.

'Well, if it isn't Mister Şehsuvar himself! You're a sight for sore eyes, aren't you?'

I had no wish to drink as I needed to keep my wits about me and so when I sat at my usual place at the table by the window, I only ordered a few light mezzes but Hristo insisted I have a drink.

'One small glass won't hurt you, Şehsuvar Bey', he insisted. I couldn't refuse. The waters have been rich with bonito this season and so I helped myself to a dish of that lovely blue-scaled fish and a salad piled high with rocket leaves. The snoop in the leather jacket went past my window once but I didn't let it bother me. I was no longer afraid of them, nor was I angered by their presence. There was no reason for me to take them seriously. They were just some guys trying to do their job, nothing more.

Coming back to the hotel, I felt much better, even though my worries and woes are still as bad as ever. I felt free, as though I had been liberated from this world, this country, this city and the threats and dangers that await me, and it was with this elated state of mind that I sat at my desk and began writing about those better days, those days of rebellion and revolution, days that were so much happier and full of hope than today.

From his abode in Yıldız Palace, the padishah had appointed Tatar Osman Paşa to crush the rebellion and to finish off the job Şemsi Paşa had been unable to do, no matter the cost. Of course, the palace and the government were on high alert, with much greater caution and vigilance now being demanded. After all, what would become of the Sublime Porte if another of its pashas were to be slain? Appropriate measures had been taken but one had to remember that this was an underground movement the throne had to combat. Moreover, even if Tatar Osman Paşa was clean, the fact that one of the officers closest to him was a member of the Committee for Union and Progress was almost too horrible to consider. Poor Osman Paşa was all too aware of this but there was little he could do. The orders had come from above, from the highest authority in the land, and those orders had to be carried out, even if it ultimately meant death. Nevertheless, the pasha, wily and long in tooth, decided to adopt a different approach. When he arrived in Bitola, instead of dispatching his troops to the hills or rounding up suspects in the city, he set up a committee of his own in an attempt to identify the movement's members. But it was too late. No matter what he did, he would not have been able to suppress the insurgency. The committee could not put out the fires of rebellion that had broken out in the mountains of Macedonia.

The patriots had won a moral victory with the shooting of Şemso. More importantly, the people now knew that the sultan's pashas were mere mortals. Their fear of the palace had, it seemed, diminished. I say 'seemed', because absolute victory had yet to be achieved. A hard, firm retaliation by the palace could have radically altered the situation in an instant and people that had never experienced any serious upheaval or rebellion and who had bowed their heads in blind, terrified submission to kings, emperors and sultans for thousands of years would have been all too delighted to declare us traitors the moment they felt the crushing might of the state upon them and would have happily accompanied their shrieking condemnations of us and our actions with lusty shouts of 'Long live the sultan!' Moreover, the assassination in quick succession of two pashas could have easily generated a negative reaction, which the palace could have then feasibly used to turn the masses against us by duping them into believing the rebels were collaborating with outside forces, thus making us traitors in their eyes. The movement did not want to play into the hands of Abdülhamit and give him such an advantage, which is why the decision was made not to have Tatar Osman Paşa killed but to have him brought to the mountains and held there.

This is why it was vital that the message sent by the Central Committee of the Committee for Union and Progress to Niyazi of Resen reached him on time. Of course, at the time, I had no idea of the contents of the coded message I was carrying. It was only later, after the implementation of the constitution had been declared, that I discovered what was actually written in the message that I had carried under my shirt that day, a message I held less as a letter and more as a sacred covenant carried over my heart.

First, I took the train back to Bitola, the return of the voyage I had taken ten days earlier. Mehmet Ali was there at the station to receive me and he embraced me warmly when he saw me. Even within the relatively short period of time in which we had not seen each other, major events had taken place around the country. The people were beginning to rise up and we were both jubilant at our role in the resistance and the enormity of what we were doing. Nevertheless, we did not sit on our laurels and bask in the glow of our achievements. We had precious little time; every hour and every minute were crucial. While waiting for the carriage provided by our guys in Bitola to arrive, I stopped off at the restaurant Atıf had been in ten days earlier while he was waiting for Şemso to appear and ate my fill there. Mehmet Ali did not leave my side for a moment. As you have probably guessed, he had come to the station to welcome me not as a relative but as a member of the movement, but I am sure that he would have jumped straight in to defend me as an uncle had I been in any danger. In terms of protection, I could not have wished for more.

Luckily for us, nothing dangerous happened. Two hours after disembarking from the train, I was in a carriage pulled by two black horses heading for Resen. Sitting next to me was Ulviye Hanım, who, for the purposes of my journey, was my maternal aunt, and her ten-year old son Hasan. The committee did not want to leave anything to chance as they knew that throughout his thirty-two years in power, covert surveillance had proved to be one of Abdülhamit's strongest points, although I should also add that there were signs that he was beginning to slip up in that area. The sheer volume of reports coming in was so dense that it was difficult to distinguish the genuinely important ones from those that were simply attempts to gain recognition and thus possible promotion by eager intelligence officers. Nevertheless, surveillance and intelligence gathering remained crucial operations for the sultan and he had not lost faith in his agents, even when his men had not been able to stop an assassination attempt in 1905 by a Belgian anarchist called Edward Jorris. On that occasion, Abdülhamit survived only by the purest of good fortune that came in the shape of a sudden and unexpected delay that caused the bomb to miss its intended target. Despite that slip, Abdülhamit continued to place his trust in his agents. He had little choice. How else was he supposed to handle the multitude of rebellions that were breaking out all over the empire, despite the scores of brutal suppressions that he had ordered?

We got out of the carriage at Şaşı Fehim Ağa's farm on the borders of Resen. Yes, Fehim was nicknamed Şaşı, 'the Cross-Eyed', but in reality it was only a slight squint. Otherwise he was a tall, lean and extremely handsome man who walked completely upright and with his head held high, even though he was in his seventies. Moreover, despite his advancing years, his mind and his memory worked like clockwork, better even than mine. He welcomed us as though we were his own sons, having food prepared and brought out to us on a makeshift table under a huge sycamore tree. While we ate our fill, he told us Niyazi Bey was already marching towards Lavci and that he would soon arrive, if not that night then the following morning. Once Ulviye Hanım and her son Hasan had departed, he looked at me worriedly.

'You look terrible, cousin', he said. 'Exhausted, if I may. Why don't you stay the night here? You can set off again tomorrow.'

Yes, I was tired and had not rested but stopping was out of the question. Even if it meant risking death, I needed to find Niyazi of Resen as soon as possible.

'Many thanks, Fehim Ağa', I replied resolutely. 'But the mission cannot be delayed.'

He did not insist. Instead, he gave us a black steed and assigned two armed men to accompany us on our way. The mountains were dangerous, teeming not just with our men but with bandits and robbers. We set off at dusk. It was a warm summer night but there was a cool breeze in the air, one that ruffled our horses' manes. We travelled undisturbed for a good three hours without any sign of robbers, bandits or soldiers. Eventually, while we crossing a valley in which the trees had begun to thin out, a stern voice called out in the darkness.

'Halt! Stop right there! Where are you headed?'

Fehim Ağa's two men stepped out in front of me.

'We're coming from Resen', said the one on the bay horse. 'We're going to Lavci'.

'And whom do you plan on seeing there?' the voice in the trees growled.

'My brother', our escort replied. 'We're going to see my brother Sakar in Lavci.'

That was the code we had been given and it worked. The gate was unlocked and around a dozen men emerged from the trees. They had revealed themselves but they still did not let down their guard. Their fingers remained on their triggers. But then they came a little closer and burst out into laughter.

'Well, well, well! Bald Hamdi, is it really you, you rascal?'

The man on the bay horse erupted into laughter.

'Why, if it isn't Nuri of Tikveš! I should have recognized the voice. I don't know anybody else who sounds like a braying donkey whenever he tries to speak!'

Hamdi deftly leapt down from his horse and embraced Nuri. Nuri told him that gangs of Bulgarian bandits had been seen roaming the hills and that they had taken to the road in fear of a surprise raid. However, there was some good news in that Resneli Niyazi was about to reach Lavci. So, once the men had quenched their thirst from the stream by which we were camped, we set off. As the night set in, the air cooled, and dew began to form around us. I was shivering inside but I didn't let it show, not wanting the others to think this rookie youngster was shaking like a leaf out of fear. When we reached Lavci, all was calm. Clearly, Niyazi Bey and his men had yet to arrive.

'Let's stay outside', Hamdi said, leading his horse off the path. 'We can wait here in this little nook. When morning comes, we'll show ourselves.'

We took our blankets down off the horses, spread them out on the ground and lay down to rest. I was so tired, I fell asleep at once, only to be woken up by a rifle poking me roughly in the back. When I opened my eyes, I saw none other than Niyazi Bey of Resen in all his pomp, a pair of binoculars around his neck and a rifle in his hands.

'So this is how you perform your duties, is it, eh, youngster?'

I hurriedly pulled myself together and jumped to my feet.

'Sorry, sir, I was just, ahem…' As I stood there stuttering and stammering, the rest of the company burst out laughing. You have no idea how embarrassed I was at that moment. The look in Niyazi Bey's fearless eyes changed to one of impish mischief.

'I'm just teasing you, lad', he said, a warm smile revealing a row of teeth under his smart handlebar moustache. 'The others told me you've been on the road for hours. You must be exhausted. And so we are, I should add.'

I looked around. Bald Hamdi and the other men were all chuckling away but I did not have the luxury of taking offence. From under my shirt I took out the letter given to me by the Central Committee and handed it over to the man who was at the epicentre of the rebellion. He took it, unfolded it, and then, when he realised it was written in code, said, 'Come with me'. We walked over to a walnut tree a little further up ahead, where he handed the letter to one of his men and said, 'Here, Bahri, decipher this message, if you please.'

Bahri opened up a portable desk the troop carried with them and took out some books and notebooks while Niyazi Bey and I silently watched on. Bahri eventually stood up and pointed to a sheet on the desk.

'The letter is ready, sir.'

'Thank you Bahri', he said. He sat down at the desk and began silently reading the communiqué.

While he read, I peered at this legendary fighter's hat. It completely covered his head and nearly touched his eyebrows. I also looked at the inscription above the peak, which read *Defender of the Motherland*. When Niyazi, oblivious to the fact I was staring intently at him, had finished reading, he muttered, 'So it's true'. He then turned and looked at me. 'May God be on our side, son. The mission has been set. It shall be accomplished.'

That morning we ate our fill from the foodstuffs that had arrived from Resen and the villages in and around Lavci. For days, it felt strange being amongst these people that had taken to the mountains. Niyazi's men were nothing like the revolutionaries in Victor Hugo's novels. Not that I was disappointed, mind. On the contrary, these tall, bearded, scruffy-haired soldiers in dirty uniforms standing up to a despotic sultan were, in my eyes, grittier and somehow more real than the French revolutionaries I had read of in novels. They also had a certain naivety to them and I would have given anything for them to invite me to join them but alas, I had to return to Salonika to inform the executive that the communiqué had been delivered.

With my two armed guards, I went back, first to Resen, then to Bitola, and from there I boarded the first train back to Salonika and to you. While I was making my way home, Niyazi Bey was carrying out his orders to the letter. On the night of the 22nd of July, he and his men swooped down into Bitola, burst into Tatar Osman Paşa's quarters and took him to the mountains. The next day in Manstır, to the sound of cannons fired in jubilation, the new constitution was declared, after which the provinces of the empire, one by one, like dominos, recognised the legitimacy of the constitution. And while all this transpired, little Abdülhamit sat utterly alone and forsaken in his palace in Yıldız, unable to do nothing as the storms of history raged and howled around him.

The Ancient Wound

Good Morning, Ester (Morning, Day 3)

The strange thing is I woke up quite early today, even though it was nearly midnight when I finally went to sleep last night. What's more, I had weird dreams the whole night. In one, I was on a boat with Resneli Niyazi going to France. We were supposed to be going there to shoot an English general but it turned out the person we were really going to shoot was our own Enver Paşa and it was not actually Niyazi Bey I was with but our movement's own intrepid marksman, Yakup Cemil, somebody with whom I have never really got on, to tell the truth. But that was the dream, anyway, and that is when I woke up. Not in a film of cold sweat but with an inexplicable sense of delight, despite the bizarreness of my nocturnal visions. I used to feel the same joy during my high school years when getting on the train at Sirkeci that would take me to Salonika and straight to you. It was surprising, as it had been some time since I had felt such happiness. After relentless despondency, one begins to fear hope, but life, even if one does not lift a finger, has a way of filling a man's heart with joy.

I took a bath first, then got dressed and went downstairs to breakfast. Even bumping into the swarm of tourists that had arrived on the Orient Express yesterday could not dampen my spirits. With his usual swiftness and foresight, Ihsan, the hotel restaurant's head waiter, had the corner table set aside for me, granting me some reprieve from that group of noisy tourists. I may have put on some weight of late but this morning I was ravenous and I feasted on a sumptuous breakfast of eggs, honey and milk. As I was chewing on the last bite, the fat man that was fumbling around outside my door yesterday evening entered the dining area. He was looking for an empty table, and when he saw me, he was startled but quickly pulled himself together and bowed his head lightly in acknowledgement. I accepted his greeting and even smiled in response, but when Ihsan approached my table, I had to ask.

'Tell me, Ihsan Bey, would you by any chance happen to know that rather portly gentleman sitting on the table to the left of that door over there?'

He very subtly glanced at the door and table in question.

'That's Nurullah Bey. He's a grain merchant from Sakarya. He's one of our regular guests.' He looked the gentleman up and down out of the corner of his eye. 'Not that it has anything to do with me but they say he made his fortune during the war. One of those guys that made a killing trading in the state wagons. They say he made his fortune thanks to the support of the Committee of Union and Progress. He's a courteous fellow, and generous too. However, he does have a weakness for booze. They say it was love that drove him to drink. That he fell madly in love with a Russian girl called Galina who works at the Maksim jazz club. A real stunner she is too, apparently. A right *harasho*, as they say in Russian. He proposed to her but she told him she would not leave her husband. If you ask me, she was just playing hard to get and leading the poor man on, hoping to squeeze him dry. Anyway, when his advances were spurned, Nurullah Bey hit the bottle. He spends around six months a year here in Pera. If you ask me, Şehsuvar Bey, I'd say it's divine justice. The whole country is starving and yet you somehow manage to make a fortune trading in scarce commodities like sugar and flour, only to go and lose it all because of some Russian tart. Well, you know what they say – what goes around, comes around.'

I listened to Ihsan in amazement. Amazed not at the man's story but at my own paranoia. How certain I had been that this fat, wealthy merchant, who puffed and wheezed with every step he took, was a government agent watching over me and my every move! But that is what they do. That is their style. They slowly but surely drive a man insane. The fault is mine. I should be keeping my cool, staying calm and not letting the fear take over. Who knows, maybe I'm making too much of it. Maybe there is nobody spying on me at all. Why should they spy on me anyway? I am all washed up, after all. I may not be that old but I have given everything I have to give and now I am spent. And more to the point, I am no longer a threat, no longer a dissident or critic of the regime. And why should I be a critic? The country is now a republic and has a system of government for which we had fought. There is no reason for me to dissent and yet, for some reason, these people cannot be convinced that I am not working against them and the new regime. Why are they following me, and so openly and brazenly too? What do they want?

Maybe they are just trying to figure me out, trying to work out my true aims and intentions. Yes, that is it. Perhaps they just have a few simple questions that need answering, a few simple doubts that need dispelling, rather than any true ill will. If I could just dispel those doubts and explain my intentions to them, I will have no reason to fear them.

As I sat at the table and listened to Ihsan and pondered these issues, the future struck me, as clear and as bright as the light striking the window. I rose from my table with a newfound hope. Not wanting to dampen my high spirits by watching the grain merchant Nurullah Bey noisily scoffing down his food, I decided to take my coffee in my room, a minor indulgence I would not be denied by the hotel manager seeing as we were such good friends. I also asked for the newspapers to be delivered to my room with my coffee.

The papers arrived before the coffee. I picked up the day's edition of *Cumhuriyet*, a paper that began its print life in the *Pembe Konak*, a mansion that served two years ago as the headquarters of the Committee for Union and Progress. As one can infer from the name, the newspaper was and is a vociferous defender of the new regime. The front page today featured the entirety of a speech given by the President of the Republic, Mustafa Kemal, while the rest of the news dealt with the aftershocks of the war, stressing 'the urgent and pressing need for an economic and social transformation in the country'.

I also flicked through *İkdam*. It was much of the same: the same news and a few columns here and there. *Vakit* was not that different either, featuring an exultant article on the front page proudly revealing the English hand in the Kurdish uprising that was crushed last year. The article also criticised the Progressive Republican Party, and highlighted the role former members of the Committee for Union and Progress had played in the Kurdish rebellion. Mostly lies, it should be said. I actually know the writer of the piece too: he is one Ibrahim Naşit, also known as Ibrahim the Toff. The various branches of his family tree go all the way up to the palace itself but he is an ignoble and contemptible lowlife if ever I saw one. During the occupation of Istanbul, we asked him to hide one of our comrades but he point blank refused. Nowadays he presents himself as an avid supporter of the new republican government but when we were in power, which was, admittedly, for a very brief period, he was behind us all the way. And yet, during the Armistice, he gave his support to Damat Ferid Pasha's conservative reactionaries. In other words, as you can see, he is a grotesque excuse of a man who throws his weight behind whoever he thinks is winning and in hurling these vile accusations in the newspaper, he probably thought he could erase the ignominy of his decisions during the Armistice. By the time I reached the middle of his rancid attempt at journalism, I was bored and wanted to throw the paper away but something told me to keep on reading to the bitter end, and it was good that I did because as I read, line after line, I realised the article could not have been written by Ibrahim Naşit, rogue that he is. It had obviously been penned by an official for a government that wished to purge all unwanted elements in both state and society. The article finished with these lines: *As evinced by the rebellion led by Sheikh Sait and the attempted assassination of the President in Izmir, it is imperative that we show no leniency or indulgence towards the treacherous elements that continue to reside amongst us. The Republic has reached a crossroads and the successful completion of our revolution will be impossible without a thorough purging of those rotten and decayed relics of the past that persist in their incitements.*

What he was saying was not new but the subtext was that the operation to wipe out those deemed threats would not be complete until every last member of the CUP had been reeled in and brought to account, which clearly meant they would not leave me in peace. At least I now knew. The fact that I am innocent and that I present no danger to them or to anybody else is irrelevant. What matters is my tainted past, and it is something for which I have to atone. Like Kara Kemal, Cavit Bey and countless others that have been killed on the pretext of involvement in the attempted assassination of Mustafa Kemal in Izmir, I will also be eliminated. Indeed, the fact that I am still alive is a miracle in itself. The buoyancy I felt at the breakfast table was suddenly extinguished and was replaced by fear and dread. Most worrying of all was a sudden fear that I would not be able to complete my memoirs, my account of the past, and that is why I sat down at my desk once I had finished my coffee, picked up my pen and went back in time, this time back to those wonderful, heady summer days of eighteen years ago when our spirits were buoyed by an incomparable joy and hope.

The declaration of the constitution had, indeed, been a source of jubilation for us all. Absolutely everybody – yes, everybody – seemed drunk on happiness. Things we could never have even envisaged, developments we could have barely dared to imagine, were beginning to transpire. The Greeks, the Bulgarians, the Vlachs and the Albanians – all of them sworn enemies – came down from the hills to lay down their arms, surrender and swear their allegiance to the constitution.

'This is what it is all about', I remember Uncle Leon saying euphorically at the time, clenching his fists in pride. 'This is what our revolution was all about. A little late, yes, but we've done it! Freedom has finally arrived in the Ottoman lands!'

I agreed with him completely and shared in his euphoria but you were not the same. You had your reservations and the elation you felt on that first day began to inexorably fade away. The speeches and the demonstrations were not having the effect they used to. Obviously, you were not as pessimistic as Grandma Paloma, who thought the revolution was going to bring a catastrophe upon us all, but for some reason you were not as moved or as excited as the rest of us. There was something in you that was distant; distant, cold, reserved and more cautious. A few days later, when a meeting of the party's ladies was being held in one of the local clubs, I came to your house and suggested going but you refused.

'Let's stay here', you said. 'Read me some poems by Poe'.

You looked so sad and so despondent, I could not refuse and began reading Poe's poem *The Raven*. As I read, you closed your eyes, as though you wanted to feel every line and every word deep in your soul. When I finished, you reached out and touched my hand.

'When we learn to mock our pain the way Poe does, perhaps then we may have taken one step closer to being human.'

I didn't know what you meant, and, to be honest, I was a little upset. What pain could you be talking about when the people of the country had united as one to win their liberty and create a new country? What was this pain of which you spoke when the country was drunk on rebellion? And as for being human, that was precisely the time to be human. The country had been freed from servitude and the Ottoman nation had become one, a unified nation, with linguistic, religious and ethnic differences cast aside. What higher ideal could one wish for? And at the time I told you so as well, perhaps a little too sternly even, but as always, you were ready with your answer.

'Those are all empty slogans, you dolt. I'm talking about us. About ourselves. About the individual.' You saw me frown in puzzlement and went on. 'How many of these people here on the streets feel the pain and the anguish of simply being human the way Poe did? This mighty uprising of theirs is not in any way as meaningful as one mortal person's struggle to survive. Yes, we are socialised peoples and yes, we have come far enough to demand liberty, fraternity and equality, but our actions are still a long, long way away from having the depth and complexity of being an individual. And no, I am not disparaging these grand ideals. I'm not talking about politics, or democracy or rebellion here. I am talking about the essence and the meaning of existence. Why are we alive? Do we have a purpose? That is the issue and the question of existence. It is the ancient wound in our souls…'

Not only did I not agree, I was actually angry with you. Was this the time to indulge in our own personal issues and despondencies, when nations that had been under the heel of despotism for years were breaking free of their chains and rising up against the tyrannies that sought to crush them?

'You feel like that because you are not directly involved in the uprising', I said disdainfully. 'If, like the rebels in the mountains, you were to…'

You threw the words right back in my face.

'What on earth are you talking about? If I wish, I can join them any time. Uncle Leon can give them my name and make me a member of the party's women's wing in an instant. Indeed, you can take my hand right now and take me yourself to the meeting, the one that is about to start. They may not be remembered at other times but at the moment, those women are quite the ticket. 'The freedom-loving women of the East suddenly rising up and fighting for their rights…' It makes for quite the headline, doesn't it? I can join at any time, I tell you. I know I write well and I am also articulate. It wouldn't take long for me to be noticed. Within a week, they'll proclaim me their champion and hero. And what a triumph for the constitutional movement it would be too, having a young woman as one of its heroes. If the French have Joan of Arc, then we…'

You must have been worried I was misunderstanding as you suddenly stopped. All you did was shake your head, and then look up at me with your big, black eyes.

'Yes, this uprising, this fight for freedom, is commendable, and yes, it is necessary, and yes, of course, it is a part of life. But we also exist as individuals. Yes, we may form something known as a community with other people but we are still distinct from them. You, for instance, want to be a writer. That is your difference, the thing that sets you apart from the others. You do not feel like them, or see the world like them. You do not think like them or see and assess the world the way they do. Yours has to be a new and completely different point of view. And that is because a writer is just not a chronicler; he does not interest or confine himself simply to what has transpired in history. He writes instead of the impact of what has transpired in history on the characters he has created. And we, the readers, adopt the same state of mind as his characters and his heroes, and in doing so, we are given the opportunity to confront our own selves.'

You then reached out and took the book of poems from me.

'No, let's not go the women's meeting. All we've been doing for days anyway is listen to people. Let us return to poetry. Let us return to literature and to beauty.'

But I did not listen to you. I could not stay in that garden any longer, even though the air was growing heavy with the scent of the flowers in the summer sunshine and was enough to make anybody languid and drowsy. Even if it meant hurting you; indeed, precisely because it hurt you, I got up and left you there under the cherry tree with Poe's poems. I was so convinced of my own righteousness, I mumbled angrily to myself the entire journey, reassuring myself of the rectitude of my actions. But later, much later, after we had split up, during those moments when I was far from war and from politics, I would look back on what you had said to me on that hot summer day. Although there were moments when I could see what you meant, on the whole I disagreed. At a time when the world had turned into an inferno and during a period of history in which people – men and women, young and old, it mattered not – were being mown down, it struck me that pontificating on the torments of the individual was something of a frivolous indulgence. But over the ensuing years, and now, as I sit here in this hotel room alone with nothing but my own thoughts for company, your words that day have struck me as ever more relevant and I feel as though I am beginning to slowly understand. I say beginning, as some ambiguity and doubts remain and I am still not certain as to what is true and what is false. Such a stark contrast to the July of 1908, when the truth was in front of my own eyes! The truth then was as clear to me as your slim body, your coal black eyes and your red hair fluttering in the breeze like a revolutionary banner.

The reason why I woke up in such high spirits this morning was the recollection of those days. Perhaps not quite remembering them but somehow *feeling* them again. Yes, I woke up and felt something of the joy I felt during the upheavals of all those years ago. And yet now that zeal has vanished and the fervour has turned to dust. As Grandma Paloma so rightly said, the revolution did not bring us happiness; instead, it only brought us more pain and misery. But of course that was not how I felt during the stiflingly hot July of that year, especially when we were in Liberty Square listening to Enver Bey, the hero and the champion of the liberation himself… That speech was one of the most memorable moments of my life, and it was the first time I was seeing Enver Bey – or Major Enver, as he was then – so close up. He was certainly different to Resneli Niyazi. Yes, he was fearless like Niyazi, but he was also more handsome, and he had something else flickering in his eyes: a steely tenacity and a fiery passion, rather than simple determination. He seemed to possess an inextinguishable passion as well as a profound self-belief, a belief and faith in himself that was so unwavering that he would eventually begin to confuse his own dreams with reality and, more ominously, draw those around him into the fallacies of his own delusions. But that was also a sign that he, like all true leaders, had the ability to influence people. He was not a tall man but he stood absolutely upright, as though his head could almost touch the clouds. And that day, he spoke so eloquently and so magnificently that his audience was electrified.

'Citizens!' he roared. 'Brothers! The tyranny has come to an end. The era of rotten government is over. We are now no longer Greeks, Bulgarians, Serbs, Romanians, Jews or Muslims. Under the vast blue skies above us, we are all now equal. We are all proud Ottoman brothers. Europe must now accept that her domination over our empire has been broken.'

Yes, his sentiments were overly optimistic and his manner could at times be needlessly ornate but as I said before, the rebellion had overwhelmed and intoxicated us all, and Enver Bey was probably more drunk than any of us. Moreover, the rhetoric he employed seemed to fit the mood and at the time, it did not sound overblown. Our words were no longer just ineffectual noises floating aimlessly in the air. In a country that had groaned under Abdülhamit's tyranny, the doors of the dungeons were one by one being flung open and the sons of the Ottoman dynasty, for so long captives in their own lands, were now, one by one, reaching out to claim their rights. Those governors that insisted on defending the sultan and his interests were being ousted by the people in their own districts, the sultan's spies and informers were being targeted and captured and in the capital, a crowd of fifty thousand was marching on the *Bab-ı Âli*, the seat of government. The entire Ottoman homeland, from Bursa to Beirut and from Serres to Harput, was celebrating the transformation. But behind the revelry and laughter, the reality was very different; despite the huge turmoil and the profound upheavals, a decisive victory had yet to be achieved. The constitution may have been declared but the despot that had tyrannised over the nation for thirty years was still there in Yıldız Palace and his spies and his troops were still actively defending his rule. There was talk of holding elections but our own movement, which had operated underground for so many years, had yet to attain legal status. As Uncle Leon said, we had started a revolution but we had not gained power.

He said that to me when we were on our way to a law office after listening to Enver Bey speak. At that moment in time, you were most probably sitting under the cherry tree, reading poems written by some melancholy poet or another. You were probably angry with me too, perhaps even hurt, but I doubt you cried. Even if the hatred inside you was tearing you apart, you were never one to display that particular weakness. Even when you were by yourself, your eyes would never glisten with tears. How is that even possible? Is it possible for a person to be that strong and that defiant? Or is it precisely because you were so powerless and so fragile that you chose to appear strong? Was that mocking, sardonic indifference of yours just another layer of armour?

It is something I have pondered numerous times. Perhaps it was losing your mother when you were still just a child and your father abandoning you and leaving for Paris to marry another woman that made you so stern and so severe, the result of a maturity that had been forced upon you at such a tender age. Not that you grew up without love, as Grandma Paloma and Uncle Leon showered you with so much love and affection that one could even say you were pampered as a child. That day, as we walked along the coast, Uncle Leon and I talked about you.

'Where's Ester?'

I told him you no longer had any involvement in such gatherings. But he was a wise man, a man of the world and when he saw the tautness of my expression and the catch in my voice, he understood.

'So you had a row?'

I told him about our little discussion. He listened and nodded his head thoughtfully.

'She is looking for a way out for both of you', he muttered. He suddenly stopped and looked me straight in the eye. 'You are going to have your work cut out. You do know that, don't you, Şehsuvar?'

I could not tell if he was angry with me for complicating his own life or if he was berating himself for allowing me into the movement.

'I know, sir', is all I managed to say. 'I know...'

We resumed our walk.

'Ester is unlike anybody else you'll ever meet. She is completely unique. I do not say this because I raised her or because I love her like my own daughter. She really is special.

She is way ahead of her time. And it has nothing to do with the fact that she received a fine education, or that she studied in Paris, or anything of that sort. This may strike you as odd but she has a certain talent. A gift from above, you could say, although some may say it is more a curse. She has an extraordinary sense of intuition. My mother had it too. It is something Jewish women have. Seriously. It is a gift I have seen in every Jewish woman I have known, a gift that has been nurtured over thousands of years, ever since Moses freed our people from bondage in Egypt, and it has grown and evolved over the years as we have been cast out from one land after another...'

We both fell silent and carried on walking, each of us reflecting on the matter in our own way. Eventually, he spoke up again.

'So yes, Ester is searching for a solution, a way for you and her to remain together. Of course, she is doing this for her own happiness because she loves you and she wants to be with you. She knows the more involved you become in political activities, the more the two of you will drift apart. That is why she wants to go to Paris. Perhaps she sensed all of this a long time ago, before any of this even began. She believes, naively, childishly even, that art can save you both. That you will become a writer and she a poet, and Paris, the city of art and of romance, will welcome you into her heart and embrace you as her own, and not as Jews or Muslims or whatever. Over there, what you will have is a completely different religion and faith, one that may be called the finesse of culture. When that happens, when the things that divide you are removed, you shall be united...

'That is Ester's dream. No, she has never openly told me this but I know. Like everybody else, like all of us, like the whole world, she feels trapped, as though she is at a dead end, and this is her solution. Whereas we — you and I, that is — have taken a very different path for our solution. However, we are now so far down our path and so deeply involved, it is too late for us to go back or to change direction.' He stopped again. 'Am I wrong? Now that the country is being convulsed by the uprising and our freedom is so tantalisingly close, can we really give it all up, turn around and say to the others, "Thanks guys, I'll be off now"?'

He had me cornered. All I could do was shrug.

'When Talat Bey sent you to me, he had lots of good things to say about you. But even if someone as important as him had not vouched for you, I would still have taken you on because the more I get to know you, the more I like you. You're real. Genuine. A true patriot, and an honest and trustworthy lad. You are not the type to turn your back on your country for the sake of your own happiness, are you? When the motherland itself is in flames, you would not turn your back on her just to fulfil your own heart's desire, would you? Would you break the vow you gave when you joined the movement? Would you give up the fight for liberty, equality, brotherhood and justice?'

I didn't know what to say. I was incensed but at the same time, I was ashamed and horrified. He was right. I had asked myself the same question countless times, and each time I had come to the same conclusion. But when asked like this, I saw it as an attempt to entrap me and to drive a wedge between you and I. I suddenly began to harbour serious doubts and in my heart, I felt a dark, swirling mistrust... *So all along he has been against our relationship*, I thought. As it is, his seeming approval of our relationship had always struck me as odd. And now, I thought, his warm and genial attitude towards us and towards me had been a lie all along. A ruse in which he had only pretended to approve. After all, no matter how progressive, open-minded and liberated he may be, which Jewish man would want his only niece, the apple of his eye whom he loved like a daughter, to marry a Muslim? It was a strange feeling for me. On the one hand, I was humiliated, while on the other, I felt a surge of raw, pounding fury. That wise and deeply compassionate man for whom I had had such esteem had, thanks to centuries-old religious enmities, turned, in my mind, into a demon. He was a Jew, at the end of the day, and the only reason he had joined our organisation was to help set up a government in Salonika that would serve the interests of his people. And there he was, having the nerve to talk to me about brotherhood, equality and justice. As I stood there, plagued by sinister and evil thoughts, I heard his voice come through the mist of suspicion.

'Don't be angry with me, Şehsuvar. I am not your enemy. On the contrary, I am your brother in the cause. Nor am I against you seeing Ester. Had I been against your relationship, I could have intervened long ago. If you were to tell me now that you are going away with Ester, it would not matter to me and I would do everything in my power to get you both to Paris. I would not judge you or condemn you, either. Remember, I was also young once. I too have experienced that sensation they call love. But we're talking about you here, not me. Only yesterday you were telling me that being a courier was too simple and that you wanted to be a part of the armed wing. Now, when the rebellion has kicked off and is spreading all around the country, are you really thinking of fleeing to Paris with Ester?'

He was right. I looked away.

'That, my dear Şehsuvar, my friend, my brother, is all I want to say. I am not telling you to leave Ester or to break it off with her. I just wanted to tell you what is on my beloved niece's mind so you know, so you can better understand her and what she wants. And nor shall I hide the fact that I am doing this for her and her happiness, and not for you.'

The rage that had gripped my heart had not abated but I now at least knew that Uncle Leon had been honest with me and had not had another agenda. He had not been hiding anything from me. Regardless of the veracity of what he was saying, he had been honest and sincere. I, however, was less virtuous. I was a liar and I carried on with my hypocritical charade, shamelessly hiding my own wicked and duplicitous thoughts.

'Sir, please, I humbly ask you, why would I be angry? I simply wished to explain the situation to you.'

Naturally, he did not fall for it but he did not want to embarrass me any further and so let the matter rest.

'Very well. But there is something you should know, and that is that the road ahead is not an easy one. The Ester I know is very obstinate. She always knows what is best and does not waver from what she believes to be right. I should also add that if Ester should, in the future, wish to go to Paris alone, I will not hesitate in supporting her. Obviously I do not want it to come to that but should that day come, please do not misconstrue my behaviour as a criticism or attack on your good self.'

It was at that moment I realised why honest people have no need for lies. It is because their beliefs and their actions are one. They have their own notion of what is right and nobody can make them think or behave otherwise. He may not have known it at the time but Uncle Leon was one of the finest teachers I ever had. It is such a shame that I never had the chance to tell him.

Although what he told me that day did clarify things to some extent, it had not managed to dispel the many doubts in my mind. Not just his words but my own internal explanations and justifications, the discussions I had held with you even when you were not with me, the frequent hauling up of the past and the subsequent disappearance into an endless abyss of reflection and analysis – none of them could provide the answers to the questions that were plaguing me.

I suppose that is why I reached the point of despair. That is why the relentless emotional upheaval, the mental ups and downs and the frequent bouts of anger followed by a sudden calm have never gone away. And I imagine that it is precisely because you are the only mystery I have never been able to solve and that I have never been able to forget our love. Like a sacred wound that will never heal, I have always held on to it as the most hallowed and revered part of my being.

Yes, you may mock me and you dismiss these ramblings of mine. You may even be infuriated by what I have written here and ask me why I left you. Why I did not come with you. I have so many answers and yet at the same time, none at all. In other words, even I cannot explain to myself why I did what I did. Sometimes I find a reason that appears valid, whilst at other times, all the reasons and justifications I have, no matter how logical they may seem, strike me as nothing short of absurd. Maybe you have better answers and better explanations than the ones I have.

Hold on… Hold on a minute… The phone is ringing. I could ignore it…

No, it is still ringing… So persistently…. No, I won't answer it, no matter who it might be…

But why do they insist? Why don't they hang up? Why this stubborn insistence? Perhaps I should answer it. It may be important.

I'm sorry Ester, I'm going to have to stop writing for a moment…

The Essence of the State

Hello Ester (Early Evening, Day 3)

After being interrupted by the telephone, I was able to return to my writing. I truly am in the strangest situation with the men that have been sent to snoop on me. What they want to do before hauling me in is break me and break my spirit. That way, they will be able to mould me the way they like and turn me into whatever they want. I now realise that in underestimating the new regime's network of spies and informers, I have made one elementary mistake: I forgot that the essence of the state is continuity. The men who are on my trail are part of a centuries-old Ottoman policing tradition, the ways of the *zaptiah*, and they have inherited all its traits too – its cruelty, its cunning, its savagery and its guile.

But let me not keep you in suspense too long. This afternoon when I answered the phone, I heard a familiar voice say, 'Mister Şehsuvar, a friend of yours is waiting for you in the Domed Lounge.' I recognised the voice immediately – it belonged to Ömer, the young lad at reception.

'You mean Mister Reşit?' I asked, thinking he was referring to the manager.

'Erm, no', he said uneasily. 'Another gentleman'.

'Who? Did he give you a name?'

'If you'll just hold on a second, I have written it down here somewhere. Ah yes, here it is. Captain... Captain Basri.'

The hairs on my neck stood on end. Captain Basri, just like Reşit's father Yusuf, had died fourteen years ago in Tripoli.

That's right, in my arms, in an almost paradisiacal oasis in the middle of the desert… Somebody was clearly playing a nasty game but the question was who? Who else could it be but the men following me. Even if I went down, there was a chance that there would be nobody there. I was tempted to just stay put in my room and pretend the phone had never rung… But then I had a better idea.

'Is he still there?' I asked. 'Because I have a favour to ask. Could you go and have a look for me and see if he is still there?'

I'm sure he found my request odd in the extreme but he did not object. After a short silence, he returned and said, 'He is still there, sir'. Then, as though he did not want the mystery man to hear, he whispered, 'He is drinking his coffee and waiting for you, sir.'

Seeing as I was expected and that I could only hide for so long, I decided to go down and meet the shady visitor.

At first, when I entered the Domed Lounge, I did not recognise the handsome-looking man with the unnervingly obsequious smile sitting on the maroon velvet chair. Of course, it was not Basri Bey. I took a few more steps and then recognised him. It was Mehmed Esad from Skopje, my first comrade-in-arms in the movement (apart from Basri Bey, of course). Why had he withheld his real name and used Basri Bey's instead? Why else but his usual recklessness. His idea of a prank. As he stood up, the ends of his upturned moustache broke out into a smile. I also put on a smile, masking my true feelings.

'Well, well, well, brother Şehsuvar', he said, embracing me. 'You haven't changed a bit!'

It was a lie. I have changed. The thrill of the chase has gone from my eyes, as has the old fire of youth that once burned in them. The lines on my face have deepened, my hairs are beginning to grey and even my posture has a slight stoop now. But I went along with it and churned out the same lie for him.

'You haven't changed a bit yourself.'

He was clean-shaven and sported a well-kept moustache, yet his greying curly hairs betrayed his age. Like me, Mehmed

Esad was not yet forty, but if one looked closely into the depths of his brown eyes, one could see the exhaustion of the years he was trying to hide. He smiled generously in an attempt to conceal that exhaustion.

'And why should I? We're the generation that rewrote history, after all. Do you really think that the pest they call time would be able to take us on?' He gave a little chuckle. 'What do you think – pretty poetic, eh? That's what comes from being friends with Şehsuvar Sami.' He suddenly turned serious. 'How's the writing going?'

I felt a jolt of anxiety How did he know I was writing? Or has he somehow managed to get hold of these letters I have been writing to you?

'You always used to say you would write a novel. You told me once when I was in hospital, remember? Well, have you gotten round to actually writing it?'

I relaxed. He only knew about my love of writing through a casual and offhand remark on my part years earlier.

'Write a novel – me? As if. Those were nothing but empty dreams. But enough of that. Let's sit. Tell me, how did you know I was staying here at the Pera Palace?'

'All in good time', he said, taking a seat. 'Tell me, do you have anybody left in Salonika? Family, that is?'

Once more a worm of suspicion popped up inside. In mentioning Salonika, was he perhaps alluding to you?

'Just my mother's grave and a few memories, Mehmed. No more.'

He smiled bitterly.

'The same story' It was the first time he sounded sincere. 'It's the same for us in Skopje. All we have left are the family graves. A once mighty empire, Şehsuvar... A once mighty empire has been brought to its knees.' He swallowed and looked around nervously but there was nobody around to arouse any suspicions. The spacious and beautifully furnished lounge we were in seemed completely calm. In one corner, an elderly French couple were sipping wine, three young ladies whose nationalities I couldn't quite work out were perched comfortably on a divan by the window chatting happily away and Ihsan Bey was waiting attentively as ever at the entrance. When he saw me looking at him, he came over to us.

'Can I get you anything, Şehsuvar Bey?'

I looked over at Mehmed, who showed me his empty coffee cup.

'I've had one already, thanks'.

'I won't have anything either, Ihsan, thanks. Maybe later.'

As he walked off, I turned and, appearing as nonchalant as I could, asked Mehmed, 'Why didn't you give your real name to the kid at reception? Why did you say you were Basri Bey?'

Instead of answering, he took out a packet of cigarettes, tore open the flap and shot me a doleful glance.

'For the sake of the past. So we remember. Nowadays, nobody wants to remember the old days.' He gave a vague smile. 'I hope you aren't upset or offended?'

I shrugged my shoulders.

'Why should I be offended? I just found it a little odd. It's not everyday you're told that the commanding officer under whom you fought and who died years ago is waiting for you in a hotel lounge. That's all.'

He seemed unperturbed by my remark and held out his cigarette box.

'Help yourself'.

There they were, rows of cigarettes produced by the Republic in its factory in the neighbourhood of Cibali, beckoning me to take one and light her up. Tobacco had become a dear friend to me during those endless nights in the trenches during the war and those endless days of crushing political setbacks when all seemed lost. But now, just like my days of wild adventure, they were a thing of the past.

'The doctor has advised me not to', I said, shaking my head. 'I had TB and have only just got over it. Got it while in Bekir Ağa's company in the army. I was lucky. They spotted it early on and I managed to pull through.'

He seemed worried. Like the rest of us, he had changed and the old devil-may-care attitude he once had had now gone.

'I'm sorry to hear that. You have to take good care of yourself. We need you.'

What or what did he mean by *we*? With a deadpan expression that gave nothing away, he took a cigarette out of his case. He put the case back in his pocket, lit his cigarette, took a deep drag and then, with a serious look in his eye, he went on, blowing silvery-grey smoke out into the emptiness of the lounge.

'Our old friends have sent me here. They're curious as to what your current ideas are.'

What the hell was he talking about? What nightmare was he trying to drag me into? I leaned back in my chair.

'What old friends? Because if you ask me, we don't really have any friends left. After the assassination attempt in Izmir, the CUP has made enemies of everyone.'

'Don't be so pessimistic', he said, the disappointment clear in his handsome features. 'Our movement may no longer be active but it is our ideas that rule the country. Think back to the days when we were up against Abdülhamit's spies. Those days are over. We beat them.' And then, lifting the hand that was holding his cigarette and, in a somewhat pompous manner, he began reciting the following lines by Tevfik Fikret:

Our hope is that even if we die, we shall live, absolutely,

The motherland is with you, far, far away from this dark dungeon!

'The dungeons have been overthrown, Şehsuvar. Wasn't constitutionalism the dream and the goal for all of us? Well, look around. That is what we have. Indeed, something even better. A republic has been proclaimed. Would you have ever dared to imagine it? The sultanate has been abolished, Şehsuvar. This is a revolution. A massive revolution.'

Despite the passion of his words, the uncertainty in his voice gave him away; even he did not believe what he was saying. He had been given a mission and was simply trying to carry it out. At first, I didn't think about raising any objections and thought I would just silently agree but I had been silent for so long, I could not hold my tongue.

'That revolution occurred in 1908, Mehmed. You know all too well that this parliament was not founded on the 23rd of April 1920 but on the 17th of December 1908. But of course nobody wants to remember that anymore. Everyone is acting as though this country's fight for freedom began in 1919. Everyone seems to have forgotten the thirty-year fight that was carried out against despotism and the men that fought and sacrificed their lives in that struggle; the men that were left to rot in prison or left to waste away in exile. That is where the roots of our War of Independence lie. That struggle represents the foundations of any victory we have now. Don't misunderstand; I am not blind to the mistakes that were made later on, or to the magnitude of what has been achieved today. The republic was a dream for all of us, and now it has been realised, with a huge collective effort. Don't get me wrong; the people that founded this republic have my utmost respect but at the same time I am not blind to the ancient law which states that it is the victors that write history. That has always been the case, and always will be. I know it and I accept it. I have no objections, believe me. And yes, I also believe the victors should be supported.' I looked him straight in the eye. 'I have just one request and that is that we are honest with each another. So, for the sake of the old days, please, tell me – who sent you, and what do they want from me?'

He did not answer straight away. Instead, he swallowed twice and took a long drag from his cigarette. It must have been too bitter for him as he stubbed it out before he was halfway through.

'National Security…' he stuttered. 'The government, in other words. But don't ask me for names…' He turned and glanced fearfully at the entrance to the lounge. 'This is not the *Teşkilat* we're talking about here but a completely new organisation, one built up from scratch. But I will say this – a verdict has yet to be reached about you. They are still trying to figure you out.'

So is that why they are following me? Are they trying to work out what I want by identifying the people I am speaking to? Perhaps I should have asked Mehmed Esad why I was being followed. No; instead of exposing myself, it was better to sit back and listen to what he had to say.

'I'll be frank with you', he went on. 'After all, I owe you a life debt. Don't think I've forgotten how you saved my life that day in Salonika.'

'It wasn't me. It was Basri Bey that saved your life. If he hadn't told me to, I would have left you there in your injured state.'

He didn't believe me and looked at me gratefully.

'You wouldn't have. You're not like that. I would have gone because I believe people should pay for the blunders they make. I was the one that rushed things that day. I made a mistake and as a result, I got shot and because of my mistake, you could have been caught too. You should have left me there and escaped but you didn't. So ultimately, you and Basri Bey, God bless his soul, saved my life… This is not the time to debate and evaluate the past, but the memory of that evening when you carried me on your back has always stayed with me and that is why I'm going to be honest with you. It's true, yes, they are curious about you and what you think about what happened in Izmir and the guys that were executed. And, more importantly, they are wondering whether you would be willing to work for the government or not?'

I was absolutely dumbfounded. All this time, I had been assuming they wanted to arrest me, interrogate and torture me if necessary for information, or just pick me up, stick a bullet in my head and do away with me, but instead they had sent an old friend and comrade of mine to talk to me. It was a highly unconventional approach… Noticing my silence, Mehmed asked again.

'What do you say, Şehsuvar? How does the offer sound to you? You carried out critically important missions in the past, so why not now? Of course, it would all be confidential. Nobody would know a thing, just like it was when we were in the *Teşkilat*. You'll work in secret, the way you used to.'

I could barely believe what I was hearing.

'Work? You mean the government of the Republic is offering me work? Is that what they told you?'

He backtracked immediately, knowing he'd blundered.

'Not in those words exactly but if you ask me, that is what they mean.' He noticed the disbelieving look in my eyes. 'Don't be like that, Şehsuvar', he said forlornly. 'We've been involved in this politics lark for decades, let's not be like this.'

Either he was mistaken or wanted to mislead me. When all the old CUP members were being hunted down and eliminated after the attempted assassination of Mustafa Kemal in Izmir, why would they want to bring someone like me, a loyal CUP man, on board? It didn't make sense. I needed to play the fool.

'They don't think I'm a risk?' I asked. 'They don't think I'm a danger to them?'

He shook his head firmly.

'Not at all'.

My lips formed a sardonic smile of their own accord.

'There is no need to smirk like that', he said. 'I said they don't think you're a danger. I didn't say they had reached a final verdict. They want to understand. They want to know what you think of the current regime and what you think about Gazi Mustafa Kemal.'

'And whether I had anything to do with the assassination attempt in Izmir', I added caustically.

He nodded in agreement.

'Well, there is that too. Actually, they know you never liked Ziya Hürşit and we know he has always wanted to kill Mustafa Kemal, and they're also aware of the bad blood between you and Sarı Edip Efe. But, as I'm sure you'll appreciate, the incident in Izmir was something extraordinary, from whichever angle you choose to look at it. And don't forget, many members of the secret service today are old CUP guys. There are forty of us in total, and all forty of us know what's going on.'

He could be right. It was true that pretty much the entire leadership of the fledgling republic consisted of old CUP members, and seeing as I was an old CUP hand myself, they would be unable to keep up the pretence or their distance from for too long. Assuming they did want to work with me, there was a part of me that liked and preferred easy options and it was inclined to accept the offer, but the same question arose once again – why had they sent Mehmed Esad to talk to me instead of using official lines of communication to contact me?

I looked at my old friend up and down. Despite his elegant attire and the air of confidence he had, there was also a strange caginess about him and his movements, as though he was concealing some ulterior purpose. What if everything he was saying was a lie? What if it was the party that had sent him? It was still a possibility, seeing as the authorities were hardly able to arrest and hang every ex-member of the movement. What if he was just sounding me out and testing the waters as he looked around for men to revive the movement? No, there was no reason at all for me to trust Mehmed Esad. I call him an old friend and what-have-you but ever since our first encounter, I had never really warmed to him. As for him asking about my writing, that was all just a ruse too as he had always mocked my wish to become a writer. On top of all this, I had not seen him for years and therefore had no up-to-date information about him. Of course, these doubts and misgivings I kept to myself. What I needed to be was honest; honest and transparent, as I had nothing to hide.

'Very well then, I'll tell you', I said, raising my voice a little. 'I have nothing to do with politics. I didn't even join Karabekir Paşa's Progressive Republican Party. I won't lie, Karabekir Paşa personally asked me to join. Not just that, he said I should be given a proper role in the party. But I rejected his offer, and unreservedly too. Doctor Adnan Bey intervened and tried to persuade me to join but I still refused. Nor was I swayed by the late Kara Kemal's attempts to bring me around. I want nothing to do with politics, even if it is legitimate and above board. And I knew I'd made the right decision when the party was shut down and that's because I'm of the same opinion as you – even if we're not in power ourselves, the ideas we fought for are now embedded in the government. It's of no concern to me that Mustafa Kemal is the head of state rather than Talat Paşa or Enver Paşa. I have no truck with the republic or the government. My only wish, my only desire, is to be left alone to live out the rest of my days in peace.'

He was listening intently but there must have been something on his mind as he kept stroking his moustache.

'Don't get me wrong', he said, finally pulling his hand away from his moustache. 'It's not that I don't believe you. You know how these things go. It's just that my questions need answers.'

'Go right ahead. Ask away'.

'Tell me, why did you leave the house at Beşiktaş? I looked for you there but couldn't find you.' He looked up and his gaze wandered around the Tea Lounge. 'Why are you staying in this hotel?'

I did my best to answer honestly.

'Because I'm afraid. Of being arrested, of being tortured and of being killed. If something happens to me, I want it to be seen and I want it to be known. And please, don't look at me like that. That is the truth. I really am scared. Innocent men were hanged alongside the guilty after that botched assassination attempt in Izmir. Poor Cavit Bey! He had nothing to do with it. If Ismet Paşa had not stated his concerns and had those officers not arrived at the courthouse, then Karabekir Paşa would have been strung up along with the others too. That's how they got rid off Kara Kemal. First a few accusations, then they say he committed suicide, and that in a chicken coop too! Lies, all lies. Lies and fabrications.

'So yes, seeing as we're being frank, I should also tell you that the President is still frightened of our organisation and thinks the CUP is planning a coup. Any ex-CUP members that do not give him their wholehearted support he sees as traitors. And yet the fact remains, the CUP is defunct. It no longer exists. There are no members out there, no activists willing to take up arms and overthrow the government. All we have left are a few ragtag squads like the one led by Sarı Edip Efe, and all they know is how to shoot. They have no grand ideas, no grand schemes. They're not the type that can operate or succeed on the big stage. That's why they got involved in that fiasco in Izmir in the first place.

'The simple truth of the matter is we lost and we have to accept it. History presented us with an opportunity and we blew it. We failed, and so we had to exit the stage. As for Talat, Cemal and Enver, the leaders of the movement – they're all dead. It's over. I simply don't know why the remaining partisans and sympathisers don't accept this and move on. I mean, for God's sake, there are people out there that still think I am a threat when believe me, I'm not. I swear on my life and on my honour that I am no longer involved and am no longer a threat. I have nothing to do with politics now, nor am I in touch in any way with what's left of the movement…'

As he listened quietly and intently, I leaned over towards him.

'I'm tired, Mehmed. Tired and fed up with it all. Like you, like all of us, like everyone else coming to terms with the collapse of a once mighty empire, I'm just tired. If I could sleep for a hundred years without moving a single muscle, I still wouldn't get over this exhaustion.'

He sighed deeply, reached for his case and took out a cigarette. He tapped one end on the table and then, before putting it between his lips, gazed at me with the gravity of a judge about to pass the death sentence on a defendant.

'I see', he said slowly, nodding his head. 'I understand. Really, I do. But the problem is trying to explain this to the others.'

An extended silence ensued. He tried a few times to revive the conversation but I was no longer in a convivial mood and was content to reply with short, brusque answers. He realised and chose not to press me, eventually rising to his feet to tell me he was leaving. Before he left, however, he did not forget to ask me if he could come and see me again.

'No need to ask', I said with a sarcastic grin. 'Yours truly is holed up in voluntary exile here in this splendid hotel. It's not like I'll be disappearing any time soon. And even if I were to try and disappear, your men wouldn't allow it.' Then, in a show of seeming amicability, I tapped him on the shoulder and said,

'Only joking. I'd be delighted to see an old friend like you again.'

After he'd left, I was left there in the lounge of the Pera Palace with a host of unanswered questions swarming about my mind. I must have looked terrible as even Ihsan felt a need to approach me and ask me if I was okay. I needed to get my head together, and quick. For a few short moments, I thought I could pretend Mehmed had not come at all and that our disturbing little conversation had not taken place; that I could make myself forget it all and just go back to my room, back to my desk and back to my writing, where I could escape the darkness of today and retreat to the heady and hopeful days of rebellion we lived through eighteen years ago. I almost did, too. I have come back to my room and my writing – these very words – but the questions continue to haunt me. What you have just read above is little more than those fears and anxieties spelled out in ink on paper.

I don't know how these words will affect you but I should confess that they are not aiding or comforting me at all. A darkness more foreboding than the approaching evening outside grows within me. Perhaps I should take a break. The beige walls, the light green curtains, the antique dresser, the landscape painting on the wall and the old photographs in this otherwise lovely room are beginning to get to me. They are beginning to smother me and squeeze the life out of me, just like that cold, merciless cell in the Bekirağa Bölüğü prison in which we were incarcerated by the English during the occupation. I can't breathe… I need air, fresh air… I need to get out and walk around. Sorry Ester, but I have to go.

Becoming the Hunted

Good Evening, Ester (Night, Day 3)

I hope I have not caused you any anxiety in writing to you like
this. I am much better now. Mehmed Esad's visit caught me
unawares, that is all. Or rather, the manner in which the State
Security apparatus decided to contact me caught me unaware.
Although I still do not know why they contacted me, at least
now I have regained some semblance of my old serenity. And
stepping outside for some fresh air was also a good idea; taking
a stroll through this ancient city's old, worldly streets, browsing
Pera's gleaming shops and stores and losing myself amongst
throngs of people out to enjoy themselves did me the world
of good. The more I walked, the more my woes seemed to
vanish. The damp breeze coming in from the sea blew away
the gloom that seemed to have stuck fast to the corridors of
my mind. Which writer was it that said it was when he was
walking that his stories came to him? Of course, my situation is
not fictional like his; indeed, my situation may still prove fatal.
But it is still possible that somebody may have conjured up
such a scenario whilst walking.

So yes, this time I went for a long walk. From Pera Palace all
the way to Pangaltı... Not a brisk walk but more of an amble,
where with each step I reflected upon my predicament, imag-
ining, speculating and envisaging what may lay in store for me.
And at the end of this two-hour stroll, I came to a decision as
a result of my ruminations, and the decision was that I should
wait. Just wait, without any action on my part. Just wait, today

and tomorrow. Because I am the prey. The target. What's more, I have already surrendered. I have handed myself over to my trackers, without resisting, without any attempt to flee. The men stalking me most probably sensed this decision and decided to leave me in peace as nobody followed me this evening. Not the three men from yesterday nor any others were on my tail, which made Mehmed Esad's tale all the more plausible. Once he'd made contact with me, he'd called his snoops off... End of story.

But I still do not have enough information to make a proper, informed decision, which is why I need to wait. Yes, that is what I need to do. Wait patiently and keep my hopes in check, because I no longer have the strength for more disappointments.

You'll say waiting must be a nightmare, and you're right. There is only way to cope with these dull, tense days that merge into one another, and luckily it is a pleasurable one, and that is to write. To write and think of you while the words come tumbling out onto the paper. To write about the past, with all its nuances, with all its cruelties, with all its hideousness and all its beauty... Not just to recall but to relive. That is the miracle writing to you has bequeathed me – to be able to see, to touch and to say all those things I had previously been unable to see, touch and say and to feel them as though I am experiencing them all over again.

As soon as I got back from my walk, I sat in front of the blank sheets of paper, took out my pen and began writing. I know you'll think I'm overdoing it but I really do feel like a diligent author, like a fortunate artist the muses have decided to bless. If it weren't for the call of nature, I would not even bother getting up from this desk. So yes, I'll admit there may have been a grain of truth when you said I had a writer in me. True, what I am writing is not fiction but reality, and not just reality but simply recounting my own personal experiences, but this momentous urge I have to take up my pen and write cannot be denied. Not that that by itself makes someone a writer, and especially not at this age.

I am all too aware that the train has already left the platform and that becoming an author, like our happiness, is now an impossibility. Had I gone with you to Paris in the autumn of 1908 instead of coming to Istanbul, maybe then our happiness may have been realised. But I didn't. Instead of taking me to the city of poetry and romance, events dragged me off to our old and jaded capital. But wait, we haven't got to that part yet. We are still in July. The whole country is talking about the forthcoming autumn elections and I am torn between you and our personal dreams and desires on the one hand and on the other, this astonishing revolt that is setting hearts and minds — my own included — ablaze.

'One day, you'll forget me', you once said. 'You'll be a great writer and women will flock to you like moths to a flame, clamouring over each other to get to you, to talk to you, to touch you and your dark skin. And they'll be so beautiful, these women, so stunning, that eventually you'll fall for one of their charms and disappear.'

It didn't happen. I won't deny that there were adventures with some women, and some of them very beautiful indeed, but none of them could hold a candle to you. It was not women that were your rivals but the revolution. The rebellion of July that year had captured my heart. The day I left you under the cherry tree alone with your book of poems by Poe was the day we began to drift apart. It was on that day that you first sensed the miserable future that awaited us. But still, you did not give up on me straight away, for which I am grateful. We soldiered on another two months and I now realise that those two months were the best days of my life. I won't lie: despite the rows, the fights and the pain, it was during those two months that I took those critical political steps that would determine the rest of my life and my fate, and that is what I want to write about now — all those things I was not able to talk about with you years ago.

So yes, my dream had finally come true and I had been accepted into the ranks of the *fedai*, the armed wing of the movement. It was a great honour, reserved for those members of the movement whose patriotism, courage and honour were beyond doubt. I suddenly began to see myself as a better man, as a man of consequence. I cannot write without telling you about the strange feelings I had back then. Once I had been made a *fedai*, at one point I began to feel like our young marksman, Lieutenant Atıf. It's silly, I know, but whenever I pictured myself, it was always the face of that brave young man who shot Şemsi Paşa that emerged in my mind, as though I was no longer Şehsuvar Sami but Lieutenant Atıf. Why it was Atıf and not my father, who sacrificed his life for the freedom of our nation in the sands of Fezzan, I do not know. My father was a sweet-natured man, a thinker who loved to read. He did not have an ounce of viciousness in him at all. In fact, he despised Robespierre and used to rail against him. 'What rot this guy spouted! Violence is not essential for a revolution to succeed!' My father was a great marksman too but he never used his gun. Well, not on any living creature at least. Although many of my friends used to say that my father would have been proud of me, I had my doubts. He had always been a man of theory, my father, someone that found ideas more compelling than action. He was also like you and would have wanted his son to be a writer instead of an assassin. 'The most crucial battle is the battle of ideas', he used to say. 'Violence is like a boomerang. It always finds a way back on to those that use it.' If he had not died, then perhaps the two of you would have come together to try and change the direction my life was taking. Alas, that was not to be as he was killed. Killed by Sultan Abdülhamit himself, who made sure of his death by sending him to that distant town in the deserts of North Africa, where my poor father all but roasted to death. Perhaps that is when my dream of becoming a writer also died; when the last few pieces of skin and bones that were all that was left of my father were finally placed in his coffin…

Pain, mourning and loss… These are what make up the critical junctures of our lives. Tales of pain and suffering.

But back to Salonika. The day after Enver Bey's speech, you turned up at the law firm's offices. I found your visit surprising as I thought you were too angry to want to see me or speak to me, but when you did turn up, you were so warm and affectionate. You were holding a book in one hand, a copy of Voltaire's masterpiece *Candide*. It was a gift for me, a gift that eradicated all the pessimism and despair of the previous night's conversation with Uncle Leon. 'You'll love it', you said. 'It's a splendid satire, and told in such a wonderful style.' Not that I could care less about the style. You had come to see me, you were smiling at me, you were taking time out for me and talking to me, and that was all that mattered. You opened the book and were about to read aloud a few lines but before you could start, I took you in my arms and looked deep into your eyes. We stayed like that for some time...

'Don't ever leave me, Şehsuvar', you said, with a note of surrender in your voice. 'Don't ever do that evil to me, or to yourself.'

I reached out and kissed you on the lips. Not because I did not have a response to what you said but because I wanted to take you into my heart and into my being. To completely eradicate the distance and the gulf between us, to free us off the prison of our individual bodies and our individual selves, to become one with you, to become a single person, a single entity... If at that moment I had been asked what the purpose of my life was, my answer, without hesitation, would have been, 'Ester. Ester's love... Give me a life with her and that will be enough. I'll ask for no more'.

You must have felt it too as you whispered in my ear.

'This is a chance. An opportunity. Love does not always smile like this upon just anyone. Let's not waste this opportunity.'

'We won't', I said, holding you tight. 'We never will'.

And no, I'm not lying to you or trying to pull the wool over your eyes; at the time, I really meant it. However, later that afternoon, when I met up with the other *fedai* at the Committee's headquarters, a completely different state of mind had taken over.

It was my third meeting with the *fedai* group. The first meeting had taken place on the fifth day after my return from Salonika and the attack on Şemsi Paşa. The only person present at that first meeting had been Basri Bey. Basri Bey… The finest and bravest man I had ever known, a man who, years later in Libya, would die in front of my very eyes.

That meeting had taken place in one of the gardens around Salonika's famous landmark, the White Tower. He was a stocky man of medium height, with chestnut-coloured eyes that shone with human warmth. He had a large nose but his bushy moustache helped conceal this slight flaw, giving him a noble, imposing bearing. I took to him immediately, this Basri Bey, whose rank in our movement was equivalent to that of captain. With the sea breeze blowing over us while we sipped on our cold beers in the summer heat, Basri Bey, my first commandant, made sure I knew what I was letting myself into.

'Being a member of the movement is one thing, but being a member of the *fedaeen*, of the armed wing, is another matter. That is the front line of the battle. The missions given there are far more important and far more dangerous. What I'm trying to tell you, Şehsuvar my brother, is this – you're still young and if you accept this position, you may have to kill. Worse yet, you may be killed.'

More important, very dangerous, die, be killed… I was so excited and so elated at being part of such a group that his words just went in one ear and came out through the other. If somebody had taken out a gun at that moment and fired every bullet into my body, I wouldn't have cared one jolt. It wasn't the beer that was making me drunk but sitting next to one of the movement's most important commandants that was so intoxicating. This wasn't an ordinary officer like Atıf talking to me now but a captain, a *kolağası*.

'I'm ready for anything, sir'.

He looked long and hard at me.

'You're answering without thinking. Youthful exuberance.'

'Not at all, sir. I know what I'm saying. I've made up my mind.'

He raised his right index finger to silence me.

'No. No objections. You're going to go home now and think this through. We shall meet here again tomorrow morning.

If you don't come, I won't be angry or upset. Don't worry. I won't think you're a coward, nor will I write anything of that nature in my report to the party. There are other areas in which you can help the movement, other ways in which you can contribute. I need to be sure you want this and that you want to join, and more importantly, *you* need to be sure. Understood? You have until tomorrow. Think it over until you're absolutely certain, and then see me. Then and only then. Because once you're in, there is no going back. Once you're in, we don't want you having second thoughts. We cannot let you put us in an awkward position.'

I was hurt and affronted. What was that supposed to mean? Didn't he have any faith in me? Didn't he think I was up to the task? Admittedly, I looked young for my age but what did that actually matter? I had dedicated my body and my soul to the cause. I was ready. I walked back home, distraught and despondent. My poor mother was beside herself with worry when she saw the state I was in and kept asking me what was wrong, but I just climbed into bed.

I didn't sleep a wink that night. I didn't have any doubts. I had made my decision and it was final. What did they think I was – some fly-by-night adventurer who was only in this for a quick thrill? Did they think I was only going to care about myself and my own life when the country was under the heel of a tyrant? That I was momentarily drunk and that in the middle of a mission I would sober up and tell them I was off and then scarper? I will never forget that night. Those long, dark, seemingly never-ending hours were horrendous and I was desperate for the morning to come. My greatest fear was being deemed unworthy by the party, just when I had my foot in the door. Of being deemed incompetent and lacking in courage for what was, for me, a sacred calling.

The hour of the meeting with Basri Bey finally arrived. I went to the beer garden with my heart in my mouth. What if he didn't turn up? What if he didn't even deem me worthy of his time? I was afraid I had been cast aside but my fears were in vain as he was there, at a table under a nettle tree sipping on his morning coffee. When he saw me approaching, he kept his eyes on me, watching and assessing me. Trying my best to conceal my nervousness, I sat on a stool facing him and waited for him to ask me my decision.

'What will you drink?'

'Coffee', I replied, almost automatically. 'No sugar'.

Don't laugh, Ester. I know I like my coffee sweet but I could hardly ask for a coffee with plenty of sugar in the company of such an important and serious man. It sounds childish now when looking back but that is how I felt. Had I been mature enough, and had I had the mind I have now, perhaps I would have asked for a coffee with sugar. Who knows? Perhaps I would have said, 'I'm sorry Commandant Basri, I don't think this is for me. I'm off to Paris with my girlfriend'. I don't know. Anyway, he ordered my coffee and then turned back around and focused his warm brown eyes back on me.

'So? What's it to be?'

There was no need for him to ask. He already knew the answer.

'My decision hasn't changed, sir. If you deem me worthy, I would be honoured to be a part of your team.'

His face lit up.

'Well, in that case, welcome aboard, brother Şehsuvar.'

In an instant, the torments of self-doubt and self-denunciation of the previous night seemed to disappear.

'From now on, you are one of us'. He then lowered his voice and asked, 'Do you have a gun?'

'I have the revolver my father left me. I'm pretty used to it, actually. It fits my hand quite well.'

'Fair enough. If it works, it works. Who are we to interfere? Otherwise we can sort that out too. There will be a training session this afternoon. Let's see how good a marksman you are, eh?'

I liked the fact that things were moving so quickly. That afternoon, we got on a carriage and crossed over the Salonika city boundary, eventually stopping in a rocky field somewhere beyond the seven hills that surrounded the city. We left the carriage and its driver behind and walked into a small valley. Although it was nearing late afternoon, it was still scorching hot so we took refuge in the shade of an old willow tree. Basri Bey pointed to a stone wall around thirty metres away.

'Is that a good distance?'

'Fine', I said, nodding my head. 'It could be a little further'.

He looked at me disbelievingly.

'Let's see what you're like from this distance first and then we'll see.'

Oblivious to the sizzling heat, he walked over, took three bottles of beer from behind the wall and lined them up on top. When he got back to the shade of the willow, he was caked in sweat. He took off his fez and wiped the beads away from his forehead, after which he said, 'Well then, let's see what you've got'.

Whether it was because of the heat or my nerves at being tested like this I do not know but my throat suddenly went dry and when I reached down to my waist to get my revolver, I noticed my hand was shaking. It was slight but it was still shaking. It wasn't a good omen but I then remembered what my father used to say to me.

When you shoot, the strength of your wrist or the keenness of your eye is irrelevant. The important thing is to always remain calm. The gun should feel like an extension of your arm. The rest will come naturally.

I took a deep breath and calmed myself. I raised the revolver until it was level with my shoulder and took aim at the bottle on the right. I aimed, steadied my arm, and then, without flinching, pulled the trigger. The crack of the firing gun was shortly followed by the sound of a bottle shattering. I pulled the trigger again, which led to another crashing sound, and then a third time, with the same result. The heat seemed to dissolve and I felt relief, as though a cool breeze was blowing over me.

'Excellent!' Basri Bey cried. 'Three out of three. Now, let's make the targets a little smaller...'

'I can do it', I offered as he began walking to the wall.

He shook his head sternly.

'Let me deal with that. Your job is to hit the target.'

This time, he placed three small tins on the wall.

'Well?' he said when he got back to the shade. 'What are you waiting for? Knock them over.'

I took my time. I remembered my father's words. *When you shoot, your greatest enemy is overconfidence. Never underestimate your target, no matter how big or small it is. It can be a stone or a bird, but never underestimate it. Don't ever be certain you'll hit it. A part of you should always be cautious. There should always be a hint of concern.*

I lifted the revolver and aimed as though it was the first time I was firing a gun. I pulled the trigger three times, and all three cans went up in the air. I saw the doubt in Basri Bey's eyes disappear.

'So it's true what they say. Emrullah Bey, bless his soul, taught you well.'

Although he said this, the test was still not over as he set up nearly a dozen more targets for me. Thankfully, except for two, I managed to hit them all. It was only then that he shook me warmly by the hand.

'If you're as brave as you are accurate with a gun, then the movement has gained a truly fine marksman.' There was a look of warmth and trust in his eyes as he looked at me and said what he had said earlier that morning. 'Welcome to our movement, Şehsuvar Sami.' This time, however, there was a greater depth and conviction to his voice and as we walked back to the carriage, he spoke to me more casually, as though we were old friends going back forty years. He started talking about my father, asking me how my mother had been coping since my father's death and what kinds of difficulties we had been facing. He spoke more like an older brother, taking a close interest in such personal matters. Of course, I did not mention you, and he didn't ask. He knew I worked in your Uncle Leon's office but he didn't know about us or about the special bond between us. He eventually told me he would call me in the near future. Of course, the small matter of my couriering that message for Niyazi of Resen would soon follow and I didn't see captain Basri Bey again until the day you gave me that copy of Voltaire's *Candide*.

That day, after seeing you, I went to the address I was given. It was a little office that had been rented out by the movement, which used fake documentation that said the premises were going to be used by a group of tobacco merchants. Basri Bey was not the only one there; standing next to him was a curly-haired young man with a coal black moustache and eyebrows. Yes, it was none other than Mehmed Esad, the man who turned up at my hotel earlier today. The moment he saw the book I was holding, he sneered.

'Turning us into some kind of high school now, are they?' he muttered caustically. 'We need men that can fight and they send us these kids.'

Mehmed Esad was a volunteer in our movement and because of his status as a soldier, he saw himself as my superior. I'd heard those arguments before. Many were of the opinion that the Committee of Ottoman Union movement, founded on the hundredth anniversary of the French Revolution in 1889, only began to gain any real power in 1906 when it started allowing actual serving soldiers to join, and I think Mehmed Esad was one of the simpletons that touted that particular line of reasoning. It was troubling, this display of arrogance from a fellow member of a movement I had pledged to defend and fight for to the death. Troubling enough to put a real dampener on my zeal. Luckily, Basri Bey stepped in to calm things down.

'Leave him alone, Mehmed', he said. He glanced down at the book. 'The boy's reading Voltaire, after all. What's wrong with that?'

Mehmed shrugged his shoulders dismissively.

'The time for reading is over, Commandant. The time has come to take up arms.'

Our commander looked at me affectionately, his expression telling me not to take Mehmed Esad too seriously.

'And that we shall', he said. 'But to succeed, we also need to think and know what we are doing and for that, we need to read.'

We both looked at him in astonishment.

'Take a seat, gentlemen', Basri Bey said, gesturing to the table. Mehmed Esad pulled out a stool and sat as far away from me as he could, as though I was carrying an infectious disease.

'We have intelligence regarding a possible assassination plot. Two of Şemsi Paşa's Albanian bodyguards are planning on taking out the movement's top brass. They swore on the *Quran* at Şemsi Paşa's grave to take revenge. Rumour has it that they are receiving their orders from the palace. This decision was taken two days after Şemsi Paşa was shot. Not just the decision but the plan, the programme, the itinerary and the day on which it is to be executed have all been prepared. The wheels are in motion. Out of some fanatical sense of devotion to Şemsi Paşa, these two cloth-headed fools who don't know the slightest thing about tact or diplomatic nuance are going to pull the trigger and the man in their sights is Talat Bey.'

Both of us – this arrogant young officer sitting across from me and myself – were stunned.

'I'm afraid so. They have set their sights high. Just as we stopped the attempt to crush the rebellion by getting rid of Şemsi Paşa, they are planning on weakening our rebellion by taking out our movement's brain and that, gentlemen, we cannot allow. It is our duty to send them into that cold ditch they think they have prepared for Talat Bey.'

Even while I was still trying to work out what was happening, Mehmed Esad already had a grasp of the situation.

'Who are these guys?'

Basri Bey took an envelope and a chart out of his bag.

'Yanık Halid and Kısır Ismail'. He took a photograph out of the envelope. 'This is them'.

The lieutenant grabbed the photo and stared intently at it, scanning it carefully, but the look of earnest concentration in his eyes soon vanished and he handed the photograph back.

'Don't know them. Never seen these upstarts before in my life.'

It was my turn to reach for the photo and Mehmed Esad was quick to butt in.

'And what makes you think you'll know them, eh, book-worm?' he said derisively. 'Don't tire yourself out for no reason. You won't recognise them either.'

I chose to ignore him as I realised that the tension and mistrust between us were now there to stay and focused on the photo. There were three people in the picture and when I looked closely, I could see from the clothes the person in the middle was wearing that he was a Bulgarian guerrilla. I could also tell he was dead by the bloody black scar a few centimetres above his right eye. He must have been a dangerous man; otherwise Şemsi Paşa's two men would not have gone to the trouble of hunting him down and having a photograph taken of themselves alongside his corpse. But what I found even more disturbing was that the two men did not strike me as strangers. The shorter one, in particular, the one with burn marks scarring half his face, seemed quite familiar …

'Where have I seen these guys before?' I muttered. 'I've seen them somewhere before. I know I have.'

Basri Bey was watching me carefully at me but the other one, the cocky one, couldn't take me seriously.

'In your dreams perhaps, sunshine. These are nasty guys. Not the sort you'll find prancing around at your nice little school.'

He was becoming more and more annoying but I stayed calm and focused on the picture.

'In Bitola…' I suddenly remembered and turned to Basri Bey. 'I saw them in Bitola. When Şemsi Paşa was shot.'

He listening intently but again, Mehmed Esad was intent on mocking me.

'Next you'll be telling us you were there with Atıf that day.'

I shouldn't have said it but I couldn't help it, a result of foolish naiveté and mounting frustration.

'I was, actually. I was there as back-up to Atıf. If he hadn't shot Şemsi Paşa, I would have done it.'

He gave a theatrical laugh.

'Don't even try that with me! You and Atıf? Who the hell are you to back up Atıf?' He turned to Basri Bey and, with a grave expression, said, 'This is a critical mission, sir, and I don't think we have space for deluded dreamers like this one. What say you, sir?'

The commandant's face turned to stone and he leaned forward in his stool to address Mehmed Esad.

'Maybe you're the one we shouldn't be taking along. You've been making fun of him ever since he got here and yet you don't even know him. What do you know about him or his past?'

Mehmed Esad was stunned.

'But… But, sir', he stammered.

'No sirs, nothing. The party has selected us for a mission and we're here because we have the necessary skills and qualities. The movement knows all three of us well enough. So that's me, you and Şehsuvar here. We're here for a reason and they chose the three of us for a reason. If you like, you can write a formal request to general headquarters and ask to be transferred to another mission.'

The young lieutenant's face fell.

'Of course not, sir. How could you even…'

But Basri Bey was not in the mood to listen.

'Trust is the most important thing we have. It is what binds us together. When push comes to shove, I should be ready to sacrifice my life for you, you should be ready to take a bullet for Şehsuvar and Şehsuvar should be ready to take one for me. Are you trying to tell me that you do not have absolute trust in your own comrades?'

'Nothing of the sort, sir', Mehmed replied abjectly. 'I was just joking around'.

'There's no such thing as joking around in matters like this, and especially not between us. I don't want to hear any more of this nonsense. Are we clear?'

'Absolutely, sir', he replied. He tried to put on a brave smile but he only ended up looking even more wretched. 'As you command'.

The matter was seemingly closed but now I was rattled. I knew this arrogant guy would start a fight with me once we were alone and once that argument kicked off, anything could happen. All I could do was smile and go along with it. Sometimes matters sort themselves out without any effort or interference on our part.

That day we studied the plans of the house in which the Albanians we were going to assassinate were staying. Basri Bey gave us all the details – the house, the streets, where, when and at what time the Albanians came and went, everything. And as if that were not enough, he had drills and trials planned for that day too so we would be ready for the real thing the next day and the successful completion of our mission. For a second time, I would be on the hunt. I would lift my gun, look my victim in the eye, aim and pull the trigger. Remember that time you asked me if I was going to be a killer? Well, now the answer was clear. This time I was.

Like Two Wistful Flowers

Hello Ester (Dawn, Day 4)

Once again, that terrible dream woke me up in the middle of the night... I haven't had that dream – that nightmare – for some time but now it has once more become an obstacle to any improvements or changes that may occur in my inner world. I got up, switched on the light and drank some water. It was dark outside and for some reason I refrained from opening the window. Instead, I wandered around the room a little before sitting down on the edge of the bed. I stared at my pillow for some time but all it did was stare back at me... Sleep was truly evading me. Lying down and closing my eyes was not going to do me any good so I went into the bathroom and washed my face, after which I sat down at my desk and decided to carry on with my writing.

I first had this nightmare the night after the uprising of the 31st March. Or rather, the night of that Saturday after the crushing of the attempted uprising and the defeat of the plotters. I shall write to you about those days in more detail but now I want to tell you about this awful reoccurring dream of mine. I'm in Salonika. It is an autumn night and I'm at the party's swearing-in ceremony, the same as the one I had participated in for real years earlier. Uncle Leon brings me to the front of a building, although I can't really tell as my eyes are covered. The password is given and a door opens. Uncle Leon leaves me there by the door and disappears. Just as in the actual event, a man whose breath reeks of tobacco takes me by the arm. Only this time it feels different. This time I'm scared, whereas years earlier I had been more excited than afraid. As we make our way down the hall, I hear faint sounds and the low hum of whispers tangled in the wind. I feel as though I am passing through a crowd of people who are pointing at me and talking about me in hushed voices. Not just talking about me but accusing me too. Men, women, children, old people... I can't see them but I can feel them all pointing at me. I feel not like the accursed but the accused. And they are afraid of me. I can feel that too; their voices are hushed, and they sound cowed and browbeaten. All that can be heard is a hum, a constant, sinister hum of whispers and accusations. 'Who are these people?' I ask my guide but he doesn't answer, as though he is afraid of breaking the spell that has been created by that ominous drone of voices. 'Who are they?' I ask again, this time raising my voice. The whispering suddenly stops, like a wretched mob of peasants that has been terrified into silence by the sudden anger of their tyrannical overlord. The guide finally speaks up.

'You're asking me? You don't remember what you did?'

'What did I do?' I say, stopping in my tracks. 'What are you talking about?'

He takes me by the arm and pushes me forward.

'Don't pretend you don't know. You're going to pay for everything you did. Everything.'

I am about to fall but manage to keep my balance. My right hand reaches up and removes the blindfolds around my eyes but it's so dark that I can't work out where I am.

'Switch the lights on!' the guide barks. 'Switch them on. Let him see everything.'

The lamps come on one by one, temporarily blinding me. I was right; there are people everywhere. But this is not a hall in a house but a theatre. A large, high theatre with a stage in the centre surrounded by seats and three rows of boxes at the top of the tier stretching up to the ceiling. The theatre is packed to the rafters and all of the burgundy–pink seats and boxes are occupied but not a sound is being made. The whispers of a few moments ago have died down and all that can be heard is the sound of my guide's voice reverberating off the gleaming crystal chandelier that swings overhead.

'Lights! Let him see everything!'

I can hardly see a thing. I know there are people there but I cannot make out their faces. It is almost as though they do not even have faces. There are mouths and eyes and eyes and noses but – I don't know how to describe it – they seem blurred and indistinct. Maybe I know them all, maybe I have never seen any of them before in my life, but they all seem to be looking at me in condemnation. They don't have eyes but I can feel their denunciations and accusations. Who are these people? What am I doing here? I look for my guide to ask him. When I turn around, I see them. And that table… Was that there a few moments ago? The three hooded men that had initiated me into the movement and the table at which they had been seated appear before me.

'How are you going to defend yourself?' the hooded man in the middle says. There is not a trace of warmth or friendship in his voice, but there is no hostility. His voice is clear, crisp and emotionless, like an order from a military officer.

'What? Why should I defend myself? What have I done that needs defending?' I ask in bewilderment. 'I'm sorry but I don't know what you're talking about.'

'Pain', he answers, pointing to the people around us. 'You've caused pain and suffering to all these poor people.'

I look at the people seated around me and for some reason feel a pang of shame and embarrassment.

'I don't even know them. How could I have wronged them when I don't even know them?'

'Well, in that case, let one that knows you tell us'. He turns to the hooded figure next to him. 'Go on. Tell us what he did to you'.

For a moment I hope it is Basri Bey. He was one of the three people that took me into the party and into the movement. It was Basri Bey that told me himself on that ghastly day in the middle of the desert. Just as my hopes that it is Basri Bey begin to rise, the hooded figure stands up. He is thin and frail and he is swaying, as though he can fall at any time. It can't be Basri Bey, as he was not this slim. He had a strong, stocky, powerful frame and he always stood firm and upright. So who is this person? I wait expectantly for him to speak, thinking I may perhaps recognise him by his voice. But instead of speaking, he silently takes off his hood.

The shock almost makes me swallow my own tongue. It's you standing there in front of me. You were the one hidden under that black cape and hood and now you're standing here in front of me, with your red curls and your serene, unruffled face, and your large black eyes staring like two wistful flowers.

'Ester… Ester…' I mumble your name as that is all I can manage to do but you don't say anything in response. Your lips do not move, not to make a sound, nor to smile. All you do is stare blankly at me.

'Tell him then!' the hooded figure next to you hollers. 'Tell him and tell us what he did to you. Tell us how he ruined your life!'

Still you do not talk. Your eyes, lowered the whole time, now wander over to an object on the table. I follow your gaze and see it too – an old Gasser revolver on a flag. Without any flicker of change in your expression, you reach for the gun. The whispering resumes among the audience and is amplified to an excited, throbbing hum as you lift the gun and aim at me. It may not be being uttered explicitly but the audience's wish is palpably clear: they want you to pull the trigger and end my life. I'm not afraid. No, I am not afraid. But I am disturbed, and dejected too. Do you really despise me this much? Have I really hurt you this much? I stand there and berate and curse myself, hoping you'll pull the trigger quickly and put an end to this torment.

'Don't!' one of the hooded figures roars. 'Don't, Ester! This is not your task.'

You turn to face the man with neither hurt nor anger in your eyes. You simply stare at him with the empty expression of somebody with nothing to lose. You then turn back around and look at me. For a second, you seem to come to life and I think – I hope – you're about to say something but all that happens is a wry, bitter smile forms on your lips and you lift the gun to your temple…

'Stop!' I shout. 'Stop! Don't!'

The smile remains. You blink once and then you calmly pull the trigger.

That is when I wake up. I am horrified, and tortured by my own conscience. No matter how hard I try to forget them, no matter how much I try to hide from them, I cannot rid myself of these horrible feelings that leave me in peace when I am awake but morph into nightmares that haunt me as soon as my willpower and my energy levels wane. I do not know how many people I have upset in this world, how many people I have infuriated or disappointed. For all I know, they were even more innocent than you and I may have inflicted even greater evils upon some of them but you are the one that has scarred me and you are the one that is causing this pain. Love is the greatest selfishness in this world.

See? I am still trying to explain and justify myself to you, and yet I am desperate to know about you. I know you are in Paris. That is why I am sending these letters to your father's address there, the one I have. But I know nothing else about you. Tell me, Ester, what have you been doing? How have you been? Are you happy? Are you still writing poetry or have you given up on that? Like me, have you given up on life too? Maybe you've found love. If you have, I am sure he is a better man than me, and smart enough not to leave a woman like you. How devastating that would be for me – to know you are in love again. Although I have no right to do so, I have always hoped you would remain faithful to me. I still do. Yes, it is impossible and pointless, but still, hope I do. Hope, even though eighteen years have passed… I spend days wondering what you are doing. Wondering like crazy, desperate to know. I *need* to know. One way or another, I need to find out, need to get hold of any tiny scrap of information about you and how and what you have been doing, anything, just so I know.

A small note, a small message, saying, 'Ester is fine, she's happy and living in Paris, in a rooftop apartment overlooking *le Jardin du Luxembourg.*' But nothing. No note, no letter, not even a sound... And that is probably how it will remain forever.

How I want a cigarette right now. The craving is real but it will soon pass. That is how it always goes. Like an opium addict going cold turkey, it won't last long. It will soon fade away...

Well, seeing as I've woken up now and have a pen in my hand, I may as well continue with my story. Don't laugh. I may come across as some kind of pompous wordsmith but this is the only way I can express myself, and seeing as I am not a novelist, my shortcomings can be overlooked. And if we're talking about novels, like any decent novelist, we may as well not upset the flow of events. Let us return to the past and let me tell you how I joined the movement's armed wing.

Yanık Halit and Kısır Ismail, they were our targets. And why? Because their intended victim was none other than Talat Bey, the core and the brain of our party and our movement, our guide and leader. If the 'Great Master' was killed; if, that is, we allowed such a thing to transpire, then our movement's brain would be killed along with him.

So those were the political reasons behind our plan but I had my own reasons for wanting to face off with the Albanians. I wanted to prove that I had the gumption, and not just to Basri Bey and this cocksure Mehmed Esad fellow, but to myself too.

We set off the next day, not to shoot them but to carry out a trial run. Our meeting point was the entrance of the Şeyh Hortacı Mosque. Yanık Halit and Kısır Ismail were staying in one of the detached houses on the street that ran past the mosque and down to the sea. Every evening, they had dinner in the Albanian restaurant in the little square just behind the mosque.

When I reached the mosque, neither Basri Bey nor Mehmed Esad were anywhere to be seen. Thinking I was perhaps a little early, I slipped into the grounds of the mosque and headed for the fountain. I had brought my father's revolver with me, just in case, despite Basri Bey's warning not to. I sat on a wooden stool by the fountain and began washing my hands and face, as though in preparation for prayers. There were two other worshippers performing their ablutions by the fountain too. I was watching them while at the same time keeping guard and washing as slowly and as deliberately as possible so I could at least stay positioned there and not be forced to get up before my comrades arrived. But despite my efforts to be as slow as possible, I eventually completed my own pretend ablutions and so I got up and began wandering the grounds of the ancient structure. It had initially been built as a tomb for the Roman emperor Galerius, after which it had served as a church, the *Agios Georgios*, for over a millennium, before being converted into a mosque. I made sure I did not stray too far from the entrance as I stood and gazed at the plump summer roses in the courtyard.

'You got a cigarette?' a voice suddenly asked, startling me. 'A cigarette for a humble believer, if you will'.

It was Tiresias, the local madman, completely bonkers but quite harmless.

'Sorry Tiresias, I don't have any smokes. I'll tell you what, you gave me a real fright there.'

He gave a merry chuckle.

'Why you frightened? How can a man be frightened in a House of God?' His large, blue eyes wandered over the garden. 'Don't be afraid'. His voice suddenly fell to a whisper. 'Even if you're a Muslim, don't be afraid. Satan cannot enter this place. Saint George protects us.'

'Saint George? What are you on about? This place is a mosque now.'

He stood upright in front of me like a petulant child.

'For the moment, but it won't be for much longer'.

I was about to give him an appropriate response when I saw Basri Bey approaching the gate. Like I had, he was heading for the fountain, and Mehmed Esad was right behind him. Both were in plain clothes.

'Alright, alright, on your way now', I said to Tiresias, and headed for the fountain, where I sat down beside my friends, who had rolled up their sleeves and were washing their arms, as though preparing for prayer. Basri Bey got straight to the point, without messing around.

'The Albanians are in the restaurant. They placed their order some time ago so they're now probably taking their first bites while we're yakking away here. We don't have much time. We'll walk behind them, but separately. I'll be on the right hand side of the road, Mehmed, you'll be on the left and you, Şehsuvar, will bring up the rear. We'll stay in this formation, understood? And we'll also try and stay as far away from them and from each other as possible. If they notice us, the whole plan will go up in smoke. Once they've got home and gone inside, we'll get together again. We need to watch them closely, note down every detail so we know who is going to be where, who is going to shoot first and who is going to be shot first during the actual operation. These details have to be crystal clear in our minds before we start, so keep them in mind when we're following them. We need to be ready for any and every possibility that may spring up tomorrow. Got it?'

I silently nodded my affirmation.

'Good. Then let's move'.

Basri Bey left the mosque first, then Mehmed and then me. The sun had long since set but it was one of those bright Salonika evenings when, as my old man used to say, the light from the bay seems to engulf the entire town. It was not a good time to be following those men at all. It would have been easier to hide had it been darker. Still, although I knew they were there somewhere, I could not see Basri Bey or Mehmed Esad anywhere as I approached the small square. For all I knew, they were in some nook or cranny laughing themselves silly as they watched me, the hopeless rookie, wander aimlessly around.

The Albanian Restaurant was situated between a Jewish-owned maritime trading house and the bakery owned and operated by Dimitri the Bulgarian. The maritime trading house had long since closed for the night and there they were, sitting on one of the four tables the restaurant owners had arranged in front of the trading house's shuttered premises. I had clocked the Albanians but far too late. I had been expecting them to have their dinner in a modest, unassuming little place in a nondescript corner of the town to maintain their anonymity, seeing as they had been sent to kill a man as well known as Talat Bey but there they were, right in front of me. I thought about turning around but that would have been highly suspicions so I carried on walking without breaking my stride, cursing myself under my breath for my incompetence and for the abuse Basri Bey was no doubt silently hurling at me from wherever it was he was hiding. And as for that Mehmed Esad; if he'd seen me, which he no doubt had, there was no way he was going to let me hear the end of it. Luckily for me though, the Albanians had not seemed to notice me. One had his back to me, whilst the one with the burn scar on his face had finished his meal and was enjoying a cigarette. As I approached, he lifted his head and our eyes met. There was a disturbing glint in his eye and I began to panic. What if he remembered me and recognised me? It wasn't impossible. I had recognised them from mere photos, after all. What if they remembered me as the man who had been in front of the telegraph office when Şemso was shot? I quickly looked away and slipped into Dimitri's bakery.

'We're shut'.

Dimitri was there and he gruffly waved me away, as though he were waving away a fly. You know Dimitri; he's always been a grumpy old man. 'No more bread'.

Of course, I hadn't come in for bread but I was worried that if I went back outside empty-handed, the Albanians would begin to suspect something was up so I put on an innocent smile and asked, in a sweet, pleading, persuasive voice, 'I wasn't going to buy any bread'. I looked at the cookies on display along the wooden counter. 'Erm, I wanted some of these'.

He looked at them out of the corner of his eye.

'They're stale. Come back tomorrow morning, I'll have a fresh batch for you, straight out of the oven.'

Why did he have to be so honest?

'Actually, it was stale ones we wanted', I said, making it up as I went along. 'My Mum is going to make a cake and she said she wanted some stale cookies to add to the mix.'

He stared at me long and hard and frowned, his eyebrows standing up like a hedgehog's quills.

'What kind of cake?'

'I don't know, Dimitri Usta. One of the neighbours gave her the recipe.'

He shook his head and walked over to the counter, muttering angrily as he went.

'What the hell would your neighbours know about baking anyway? It's going to be a real crummy cake. Still, what do I care? How much do you want?'

I shrugged my shoulders.

'I don't know. Give me a half an *okka*, I suppose'.

A few minutes later, I was walking out of Dimitri's bakery with a packet of stale cookies in my hand. I quickly peeked at the Albanians' table. They were getting ready to leave. Acting as though I was on my way home to deliver the packet in my hand, I walked straight ahead and turned right, into the street the Albanians – according to Basri Bey – were supposed to take. However, we now had a problem; according to our plan, I was supposed to be at the rear but I was now in front of them. according to our plan, but now I was in front of them. I needed a place in which I could wait and hide so I could slip in behind them and follow them.

'Şehsuvar... Şehsuvar...' A voice was calling my name and made me jump. When I turned around, I see Recep the Kurd standing there in front of his greengrocer's store, waving at me. Recep was a good man and my father had helped his family a lot, and Recep's family, decent people, the lot of them, had never forgotten and had helped my mother and I a lot after my father had been sent into exile. Just as I was quietly cursing myself for letting myself get tangled up in this situation, I realised it was actually a stroke of good luck. Recep's shop was beckoning me in; if I could just get inside, then the two Albanians – as well as my two comrades – would walk past without seeing me.

True, Recep was getting ready to bring the shutters down but I didn't need much time anyway.

'What's up, Recep?' I said, heading for his store.

He came out and shook me by the hand.

'All good, thanks to the Almighty. But what about you? What are you doing here? You looking for someone? A house?'

That's what people are going to assume if you stand around like an idiot staring at nothing. Even your average Kurdish shopkeeper will eventually start to get suspicious.

'There's some office space up for rent around here', I said, uttering the first lie I could think of. 'For the law firm. A lot of work is coming our way and our current office is getting a bit cramped.'

'Hmmm, I wonder where it could be?' he said, looking around innocently and earnestly, eager to help.

'Or am I on the wrong street? Maybe it's the next street up. Oh well. So tell me, what's new with you? Everything okay?'

'Can't complain', he said, a smile in his eyes. 'We've only just opened this shop but thankfully it's letting us fill our stomachs.' He gestured to a stool in front of the store. 'Here, take a seat. I'll tell my son to bring out some coffee for us.'

'No, I'm fine, thanks'. I peered into the shop as though seeing it for the first time. 'Wow, you've got a pretty big place here'.

'It is indeed', he said, beaming with pride. 'Here, come inside, I'll show you around'.

I had a quick long down the street before walking in. There was nobody around. I trudged in behind Recep.

'Here, look at this! There's a little grotto in here! They stumbled across it during the renovations. Some Roman ruins apparently, or so they say. They said it was a grave but I didn't see any skeletons or corpses. But it's come in dead useful. I put the empty crates there. It's nice and cool too.'

I was listening to him speak but I was keeping an eye on the street outside at the same time to see when the two Albanians would be passing. Just as Recep began filling a paper bag with apricots, I saw them walk past. To tell the truth, I was quite surprised at how blasé they appeared. There they were on a mission to assassinate one of the most important men in the Committee for Union and Progress, and they were casually strolling through the streets without a care in the world… I was soon brought back to earth by Recep's voice.

'This is the last batch of apricots for this year. Here, these are for Aunt Mukaddes. She'll love them. Say, how is she?'

'Oh, she's just fine', I answered, not taking my eyes off the street. 'But really, Recep, you shouldn't have'.

'Why shouldn't I? Anything for my Aunt Mukaddes. Say, what are you looking at?'

I immediately spun back around.

'That building opposite. Maybe that's where the offices are.'

'Forget it', he said, shaking his head. 'That's Lefter the cobbler's house. He'd never give that place up for rent. Eight kids, he has. Eight. They're crammed up to the rafters in there. He's turned his ground floor into a shop. You think he's going to give it all up?'

The Albanians had now passed us and were walking up the street. Just as I was beginning to wonder where they were, I saw Basri Bey a little further back on the right and Mehmed on the pavement to the left, as agreed, his body leaning forward slightly, his eyes like a hawk's fixed nervously on his prey. Basri Bey, on the other hand, looked like a respectable family man on his way back home from work: calm, confident and content. It was time for me to bid Recep goodbye and take my place in the drill.

'I've got to go, Recep', I said, once Basri Bey and Mehmed had walked past the store, accepting the bag of apricots. 'I'll take a quick look at the next street up and then I'll head on home.'

Of course, leaving such a generous and kind-hearted soul was not going to be that simple. I only managed to leave after he'd filled another bag with some small but scrumptious-looking peaches. Only a rank amateur like me could go on his first drill for a real-life assassination holding a bag of apricots and another bag of peaches. Still, at least my comrades didn't see me step out of the store like that. Even if they had been in a position to see me, my plan was to throw the bags away at the first opportunity. I made my way out of the store, eager to reclaim my position in the drill.

That is when I saw him. A street vendor walking right in front of me, one of those men that wandered the streets selling those multicoloured mastic sweets I used to love when I was a child. He had his stand up on his shoulders and was walking along the street but there was something odd about him. At first, I couldn't quite place it but then it hit me: this man should have been exhausted, seeing as he'd been tramping up and down the streets of Salonika all day in the scorching heat trying to sell his wares, but he looked oddly alert. Shouldering a stand like that all day, setting it down for customers and then hauling it back onto your shoulders countless times throughout the day should have taken its toll on his posture but his back was completely straight and he looked strong and revived and was strolling up the street, a tiger ready to pounce. At first, I paid little attention to him as I did not want to look like an idiot in front of Mehmed Esad but another voice inside told me to keep my eyes on the vendor.

When we turned the corner into another street, everybody was within my field of vision – the two Albanians on the pavement to the right of the street, which led down to the coast, Basri Bey and Mehmed Esad around twenty or thirty metres to their rear, and right behind them, the wandering sweet vendor. The various elements of this motley crew were making their way down towards the sea separately but as a single unit too. When they neared the main road that cut across the street, the two Albanians suddenly stopped. Not because they suspected anything; rather, I think one of them wanted a cigarette. Seeing them stop, Basri Bey slowed down but Mehmed Esad did not break his stride – perhaps he couldn't – and kept on walking. It's not easy, after all. The nerves can get to you. Maybe he assumed the Albanians would not be stopping for long and that they would soon set off again. But the two marksmen were not in any seeming rush. They just stood there, smoking their cigarettes, lost in conversation in the middle of the street. What was even odder was the vendor in front of me… He had also begun to slow down. What the hell was going on? Had we walked straight into a trap? It was not out of the question. After all, we were members of an underground organisation, and just as they are targets for us, we could quite feasibly be targets for them. I immediately put my packages down in the nearest doorway and quickened my pace, but making sure I was discreet so as to not attract any attention. And of course, I kept my eyes firmly fixed on everything that was happening in front of me.

Mehmed Esad was – unavoidably – beginning to near the two marksmen. They noticed him but ignored him, which was perfectly natural. Why should they have been interested in someone they didn't even know? But for some reason, it happened while Mehmed Esad was walking past them. With no reason or warning whatsoever, our young lieutenant suddenly drew his gun and aimed it at them. The two men seemed confused but Mehmed Esad barked at them to raise their hands and they quickly complied. I glanced over at Basri Bey. He was as stunned as I was. What the hell was Mehmed Esad doing? The whole operation was about to be ruined but he seemed so certain of what he was doing and was now addressing the two Albanians in a threatening manner. And that is when I saw the vendor spring into action… In the blink of an eye, his stand had fallen to the ground and he had taken out his gun and pointed it at Mehmed Esad. Then, without even issuing a warning, he pulled the trigger. By now, I was also reaching for my gun but it was too late and before I could even draw it, I saw Mehmed Esad lying in a pool of blood. Quicker and calmer than me, Basri Bey had drawn his weapon and two quick shots later, the vendor was on the ground. I think that is what emboldened me. I drew my gun and began running towards the scene. The Albanians also reached for their weapons but they froze when they saw me sprinting towards them. I pulled the trigger. The one with the scar on his face was the first to fall. I turned my gun on his companion but there was no need as bullets from Basri Bey's gun had already torn into his chest. Their guns fell out of their hands and they both fell backwards onto the ground faces up.

The narrow street was filled with the overpowering smell of gunpowder. Basri Bey walked steadily over to the two prostrate figures and shot them both in the head to make sure the job was done before turning to look at me. He didn't say a word but I understood. I walked over to the vendor, who was lying on the ground in his own steadily congealing pool of blood and already on the verge of death, and without hesitation shot him twice. His body jerked up off the ground twice before coming to rest on the pavement. It was now completely still.

You may find all this horrifying and yes, I suppose it is, but had we not killed them, they would have killed us. Once you enter a fight, you have to adapt to the rules and the conditions of that fight, even if that means getting your hands bloody. Of course, not getting involved in the first place would be ideal but that is an irrelevant detail as I had already made up my mind to enter the fight.

But before I finish this section, let me at least close with a paragraph about Mehmed Esad. A paragraph from the past…

As I'm sure you can guess, Mehmed Esad did not die. He was seriously wounded and had he lost any more blood, he would not have made it to the morning. It's thanks to Basri Bey, who, with my help, lifted him onto his back and carried him to a carriage. We took him to your distant relative, Monsieur David the doctor, that tiny bad-tempered gentleman who liked to wear those gold-rimmed glasses. When he saw us, he thought we had wounded Mehmed. 'What the hell is this?' he exclaimed. 'You may as well have brought me his corpse'. I was worried he would refuse to treat Mehmed Esad but he took him into the hospital straight away, and without any paperwork either. The operation lasted hours and went on until well past midnight. Both Basri Bey and I stayed there at the hospital throughout, although we did not hold out much hope for him as his injuries seemed so severe but he managed to pull through. He was a man of good blood and good stock, I suppose. He was back on his feet in less than two weeks, after which we moved him to a safe house, where I made sure I visited him every day to keep him company and keep his spirits up. I was pretty much his carer in all but name. I did it not because I liked him but because it was a duty. He was still a comrade, despite his faults, and a fellow fighter too and so I stayed by his side and helped him until he had made a full recovery. On the evening before he was due to return to his barracks, Basri Bey took me to one side and said, 'You don't need to come tomorrow, Şehsuvar. We've done what we can do for him. This is where Mehmed Esad's path and ours must diverge. He no longer has a place in our squad.'

I saw Mehmed Esad many times after that evening. We would greet each other and were often seated at the same table and we were even sent on missions together at times but for some reason we never talked about what happened that summer evening. Still, whenever I saw him, whatever the situation or context, he always seemed to have a somewhat sheepish expression on his face. Until yesterday, that is, when he suddenly turned up at the Pera Palace.

The World's Greatest Mystery

Good Morning, Ester (Morning, Day 4)

I may say good morning but it's already late in the day. I was only able to pick up my pen and start writing after midday. When I finished writing last night, I was so tired I almost fell asleep at my desk and only just managed to crawl into bed. When I woke up, it was already noon. I was still so groggy that it was only after I had taken a cold shower that I managed to come round. I got dressed and went downstairs to eat. On the way down, I saw two maids cleaning in the corridor but now that I was free of any suspicions, I don't think they were watching me. The elevator was full so I walked down the marble staircase to the hotel restaurant. The lunch service had not yet started but the head waiter, bless him, had the cooks rustle up a cheese omelette for me, along with a large glass of *ayran*, which I tucked into whilst leafing through the papers.

There was an interesting piece in *İkdam*. Two armed men have been arrested in Ankara, it seems. They have refused to confess to their charges or give a statement but they are believed to be associates of Çerkez Ethem, or Ethem the Circassian, who has fled to Greece. There is talk afoot of a plot to assassinate Mustafa Kemal, with the help of the Greek secret services. Our security services, in response, have made it clear that such plots will always be thwarted and that the ring of steel around the young republic will always be there to defend the life and the honour of the president. I read the piece carefully but there was no mention of any ex-CUP members or any attempt to link this new plot with the assassination attempt in Izmir, which I suppose is something. At least now they are no longer shackled by a fantasy that every and any assassination attempt is somehow connected to ex-members of the CUP.

'Hi Şehsuvar *ağabey*'.

I looked up and saw Reşit standing in front of me.

'Hello there, Reşit, Sorry, I was so lost in the papers, I didn't see you there.'

'Don't worry about it', he said and pulled up a nearby stool. 'How are you?'

He seemed tense and his attempt at a friendly smile did not conceal his unease. Even his simple 'how are you' seemed fearful, as though he was expecting bad news.

'I'm fine, Reşit. So tell me, what's the latest?'

He quickly glanced around.

'I was told somebody came to see you…'

Why had Mehmed Esad's arrival made him so uncomfortable? And what did he care anyway about who came to visit me?

'Oh yes. An old friend from Salonika I haven't seen for years. He went to look for me in my old house in Beşiktaş and then found out I was staying here from the local shopkeeper over there. He just popped round for a chat.'

He stared at me intently, wanting to understand.

'Well, I hope nothing untoward happened as a consequence.'

What was this? Why was he so disturbed by Mehmed Esad's visit?

'I doubt it', I replied, placing the newspaper on the table. 'A visit from an old friend from my hometown is hardly going to hurt me now, is it? In fact, I'm glad he came. It was nice to see him. He's an old friend. We talked about Salonika and the old days.' I paused. 'Why? Do you know Mehmed Esad from somewhere?'

'Oh no. Not at all. How would I…'

But even as he spoke, he looked away. He obviously knew him from somewhere but for some reason did not want to tell me.

'Don't get me wrong, Şehsuvar *ağabey*, I'm just looking out for you. I don't want anything nasty to happen to you. You know as well as I do that these are tumultuous times we've been living in recently. Things are only just now starting to settle down, if at all, and it's hard to work out who is who and who is working for whom. During times of uncertainty like this, decent, innocent people can also get caught up in all kinds of unpleasantness. Basically, what I'm trying to say is that it is perhaps wise to be cautious.' He looked around nervously again. 'If I may be so bold, I would even go so far as to ask you to avoid those whose integrity you may doubt.'

I gave him a reproachful and doubtful look.

'Tell me one thing and be honest – do you know Mehmed Esad?'

He looked away again but then firmly shook his head.

'Not at all. I don't know a thing about him. And that's just it. If I knew the man, I would at least be able to speak with a little more certainty.'

I tried to look unruffled.

'Let's not get carried away now, Reşit. One can't go through life suspecting everybody, otherwise we'd end up having nobody left to talk to. As it is, I've been holed up here for ages. What harm can come from a visit by an old friend?'

But still he would not be reassured.

'I don't want to look as though I'm interfering in your affairs but there are more reliable friends one can find for pleasant conversation. Something has to be afoot for a friend you have not seen for years to suddenly emerge like this out of the woodwork.'

I was now pretty sure he knew Mehmed Esad. For all I knew, he also knew the reason for his visit, but that he did not want to share with me. No, that was something he would not reveal that easily so I chose to just remain as as calm and as casual as possible. I reached out and put my hand on his shoulder.

'You're just overworked, that's all. Don't worry. Nothing is going to happen to me. If everyone ran and hid, how would I possibly find such old and loyal friends?'

His eye lit up.

'There is one person you may be interested in finding, actually. Major Cezmi… You fought alongside him in Tripoli.'

'Cezmi Kenan?' I cried, startled. 'Are you trying to tell me Cezmi Bey is still alive?'

My delight must have been contagious as even Reşit looked pleased.

'Alive and well, apparently. His wife Aunt Munise died of typhus during the Balkan War and, as you may recall, they had no children so Uncle Cezmi is on his own. I pop in to see him once a week. He would be delighted to see you. We can go together this week if you like.' He paused for a moment, lost in thought. 'Who knows, maybe he'll have some information about this old friend of yours. Remember, Uncle Cezmi was one of the security services' top brass during the occupation so he may well know something about this Mehmed Esad friend of yours.'

Cezmi Kenan! He was the man who led after us Basri Bey's death but I had known him long before the war in Libya as we had been together during the suppression of the 31st March Rebellion. Many people found him a little odd but for me, he was one of the bravest men to walk the earth. If the Italians, despite their technical and military superiority and despite their brutality, had not been able to advance from their position on the beachhead in Tripoli during those hellish days when the bombs were raining down on our trenches and the shrapnel fell like hail and the scorching wind raged like an inferno around us, it was because of men like Cezmi Kenan. There were times back then when I would stop and ask what the hell I was doing there and why I didn't just flee but Cezmi Bey was in the thick of it all, running from trench to trench and from ditch to ditch keeping our morale up. Not once, not even for a split second, did I see anything resembling fear in his innocent, almost childlike, green eyes. So yes, it would be wonderful to see him again. Not only that, I was certain he would help me solve the riddle of this Mehmed Esad. The knot Reşit refused to tackle Cezmi Bey would help me unravel.

'I would like that very much', I said to Reşit. 'I haven't seen Major Cezmi for years. I would be delighted to visit him. In fact, why don't we invite him here for dinner? What do you say? Wouldn't that be better?'

His face darkened.

'He won't come. He thinks the hotel is being watched.' He then lowered his voice and, in a whisper, continued. 'He thinks this hotel is a hive of treason and that most of its residents spies and informers.'

It was thinking straight out of the CUP book: doubt everybody, under all conditions. But what if he was right? How were we to know who the people staying in the hotel really were? For all I knew, even Reşit, standing there right in front of me, was on the government's payroll. If he were, he could keep a much better eye on who was coming and going. So if there was a snoop in the hotel, then the prime suspect was Reşit, because he was the one with access to the intelligence. He was the one in the know.

Good heavens, what next? First I was suspecting Mehmed Esad, and now Reşit! Madness. But then again, I am an ex-CUP guy, and suspicion has always been central to our remit. So what about Major Cezmi — what was his part in this charade that was being played out?

No. It couldn't be. Not Major Cezmi. His sense of honour is beyond reproach. He would never get caught up in such cloak and dagger schemes. But at the same time, I have to be vigilant. These are dark times, when it is difficult to know who to trust. I have seen fine men, men of seeming valour and integrity, betray their comrades in the blink of an eye and cross over to join the other side.

I don't know if you'll remember but one day we were discussing literature and asking ourselves why duels feature so prominently in Russian and French literature but not in ours. Neither of us could come up with a satisfactory answer. I remember your Uncle Leon, who was at the table with us, saying, somewhat dramatically, 'Unless you count Ahmed

Mithad's *Hassan Mellah* or Recaizade Ekrem's *Araba Sevdası*, we don't have actually have any novels for them to feature duels.'

I've thought about it many times over the years. Seriously, why don't our novels feature duels? Is it because we are not as brave as the French or the Russians? I doubt it. Courage has nothing to do with one's race or nation. As a nation, we are as brave as any other but as individuals we have not progressed. This is not particular to the Abdülhamit era or to the Ottomans in general; the lack of any true sense of individualism has always been a notable absence here, in these lands, in our part of the world. What we have had instead are despotic leadership cults and a tradition of crushing, overwhelming state power that have created such an intense strain on the common man that the concept of the individual has not been allowed to emerge and to flourish. Nobody has ever managed to be his or herself; instead, they have always felt a need for a leader and a guide, and that is why, I guess, the notion of the duel, a decision by just two people to conduct affairs one to one, has never taken root amongst us. Instead of a mutual arrangement between two individuals, we have always chosen to use force, to simply obliterate that person we view as the enemy. That is why our informed methods over the years have made use of the informer, the ambush and the lynch mob...

To tell you the truth, when I sat down at my desk to resume writing, the opening sentence in my mind was completely different and anyway, I don't think you will have given much thought to what I have just written above. I'm sure you are still thinking about my last letter and about that callous Şehsuvar staring down at the bloodied corpse of the man he had just gunned down on a warm summer night in Salonika. I'm sure you are wondering how the man you once fell in love with, an innocent young adventurer that used to read you poetry and write you stories, turned into a cold-blooded murderer and I'm sure you are cursing his name as you do so. I too have thought about it. Not because of a troubled conscience on my part but simply because I am shocked at the equanimity with which I carried out those acts. Man is the greatest of the world's mysteries. I don't mean that as praise or as damnation; what I mean includes all those binary oppositions. The human soul is a pitch-black terrain that has yet to be truly charted. Imprisoned within the same mind you will find compassion and savagery, courage and terror, reason and insanity and, nestled alongside the wildest of hatreds, the purest of loves. We may, at times, see ourselves as good, decent people but that is not always the case; when we think we are overflowing with love, we are just as predisposed to murder. And the same can be said for the inverse. Some are born and raised in worlds that are so harsh and loveless, we think they would be full of hate and resentment but in reality they are incapable of doing any harm. Most of us do not know who we are; we have not even thought about it. Thinking about it leads to shocking revelations, to events that force us to confront our own souls... Just like the awful events of that warm summer evening that completed my transformation into a murderer.

Yes, it's true. When I got home at midnight that night, I realised I no longer recognised myself. I had just killed a man, and only a few hours earlier too boot, and yet I did not feel any discomfort. I was upset, of course, at Mehmed Esad being shot by the sweet seller, but only a little. Not because of the way he treated me, nor was it because of the way he disobeyed orders and consequently put the mission and all our lives in danger... I was so intoxicated by my own personal triumph, if that is what you want to call it, that I couldn't care less about the dead or the wounded. So yes, it was that evening when I realised what I was. It was that night that I was to make the acquaintance of a completely different Şehsuvar Sami, one that lurks in the darker depths of my soul.

It looked like the caveman lurking inside me had now come out, now that I was free of the weight and the expectations of a certain Emrullah Bey, the man and the teacher that had dedicated his life to bettering the Ottoman education system, that man of peace who also happened to be my father. The strange thing is, I didn't feel any fear, or, indeed, shame. I felt neither... On the contrary, I felt strong; strong and brave enough to take on the whole world. And more importantly, I had been able to use and display this strength and this courage for a sacred cause, to help my nation in the fight against annihilation, to free my people, to help rewrite history. Grand revolutionary words, yes, but I was the one that had changed. Not when I pulled the trigger but much earlier. The transformation had begun when I first joined the movement. I had felt it too, in fact, which is perhaps why I kept it from you when I first joined. Perhaps my pulling of the trigger that evening was the completion of the transformation. The moment when the other Şehsuvar opened his eyes and told me and the world that he had arrived...

Had I told you all this that day, you would have hated me. In fact, you probably already do. Sometimes even I hate myself when I think about what I have done. Sometimes I hate myself and sometimes I pity myself. Yes, I pity myself, because, despite a life of allegedly heroic acts, the truth is I am a wretch that has been tossed around by the winds of fate. And not just a wretch but a fool who was too reckless to see what was about to happen... And not just a wretch and a fool either, but an incurable and foolish romantic too, one who could not see what was unfolding in front of his own eyes, even when he had someone like you by his side trying over and over again to warn him of the dangers.

You may mock me for saying romantic but that is what I am. I have never been a realist and the greatest proof of this is my falling in love with you. As my dear departed mother used to say, instead of finding a nice, decent Muslim girl to marry once I had learnt to stand on my own two feet, I had gone and found a Jewish girl, and not just any Jewish girl but the feistiest and most hot-headed of them all.

Don't get me wrong. These are not barbs or criticisms, but words of praise and admiration. Because experience has taught me that the real issue in this country is our constant submission to authority, our inability to stand up and resist, our misguided belief that silence is somehow a virtue. These habits and practices are the results of an accursed heritage, customs that go back a thousand years and more, and because they are so old, they have crept into our skin and into our bodies. We cannot escape them or discard them as they have lodged themselves into our flesh and our bones.

The more I ponder these truths, the more my respect for you grows, which, when I think about it, is not something I should encourage, as the more you turn into a distant, unreachable jewel, the more I shrink into nothing more than a tiny particle of dust… What's worse is that I was the one at fault, and no explanation, no justification – or attempt at justification – will ever change that. Not now, nor in the future. Nevertheless, I shall continue with my story.

Yes, there is somebody after me… I don't know who they are exactly, nor do I know what their intentions are but the years of experience I have accrued now lets me sense when they are near and lets me feel their breath on the back of my neck. I don't have much time. I don't know who will strike the first blow or who will pull the trigger first… Nor do I have the luxury of being able to choose whom to attack when the time to strike comes. I may not be as defenceless as a gazelle but there is little else I can do but wait and write these letters to you while I wait. I should finish these letters to you before they arrive because I know that when they do arrive, they will not be content with simply destroying my body – they will obliterate all traces of my life, short though it has been. This is why I do not want to waste any more time. This is why I am returning to the past.

The courage and acumen I showed in the mission against the Albanians garnered much praise and appreciation in the *fedai* group and throughout the movement as a whole.

'Your demeanour was that of a true hero, Şehsuvar', Basri Bey said, kissing me on the forehead

'You are too kind, sir', I replied. 'But really, I was just doing my duty'.

'Not in the least', he said. 'I have seen good, brave, upstanding men, men of honour and courage, tremble and freeze in terror in far less dangerous situations. No, this is in your blood, young man. You have my admiration, Şehsuvar. Not only have we eliminated three dangerous traitors, we have also gained a true hero and a servant of the nation in you.'

Gratifying though these compliments were, even greater was the praise lauded upon me by Talat Bey, the leader of our movement. The next day I was sitting in the law office writing a petition for a case that was to be heard in Serres when the door opened and in walked none other than Talat Bey himself, accompanied by Uncle Leon and, interestingly, four plainclothes bodyguards. After the affair with the Albanians, the movement, it seemed, had decided to be more vigilant. The four bodyguards stayed in the hall whilst the movement's chief walked into the office I was in. I had not seen Talat Bey for quite some time and rose to my feet to greet him. When he saw me, he gave me a great bear hug.

'You saved my life, young man', he said, in his usual chirpy manner. 'I am indebted to you. I owe you my life.'

I was so nervous, I didn't know what to say and just stood there shuffling my feet whilst mumbling incoherently.

'May your father rest in peace and light', he went on. 'You've shown the world you truly are the son of Muallim Emrullah.' He turned and looked proudly at Uncle Leon. 'Just as I described, isn't he?'

'Şehsuvar is a good lad', Uncle Leon replied his smile not quite as broad as Talat Bey's. 'I am sure he will go on to accomplish even greater things for the cause.'

But there was no reining in Talat Bey's delight and he sat at the desk without waiting to be asked.

'That he will. The period of autocracy has come to an end. The time for liberty has arrived. Our time… However, it has only just started. We are still far from victory. The state is still run by Abdülhamit's men, and that wily old fox from Kayseri will not give up power without a fight. Every trick and ruse he has learnt in all his years in power he will employ in his bid to hold on to power. At times, he will appear loving and kind like a father, at other times he will say he agrees with us, but be sure that he will be ready to kick the stool from under our feet, just as he did with Mithat Paşa. We need to be vigilant, more than ever…'

'Absolutely', Uncle Leon said, taking a seat opposite him. 'All revolutions begin with a challenge to the regime. We may have ushered in the declaration of a constitutional regime but the requisite institutions have yet to be formed. We have the sultan on one side and parliament on the other. The real struggle starts now.'

I didn't really understand. As far as I was aware, we had won. The *Kanun-i Esasi*, the Law of Fundamental Principles, was about to be passed and a new parliament was to be inaugurated – what more could we want?

'That is why we need to go to the capital', Talat Bey said. 'The palace awaits us. Dersaadet awaits us'. He turned his chestnut eyes towards me. 'You will come with us too. Salonika has done what it needed to do. Now, if we are to influence the world's events, we need to be in the city the entire world is watching.'

It was a great honour for me to be summoned to the capital by the leader of the movement himself but what about you and my aged mother? What would happen to you two?

'Uh, the workload here is, erm, really beginning to pile up', I stammered unconvincingly. 'I wouldn't want to leave Monsieur Leon in a difficult situation…'

Your uncle shot me a reproachful glance, whilst Talat Bey, who obviously did not know about my relationship with you, let out a roar of laughter.

'Don't you worry, Monsieur Leon can look after the work here.' Then, once his laughter had subsided, he went on. 'If it's your mother you're thinking of, don't worry about that either. We'll sort that out too. If she stays here, we'll have someone look after her. If she decides to come with you, then that we can also arrange. But no matter what, you are going to be in the capital with me. New duties await you there. Important, complex and highly confidential duties…'

It was obvious what he meant by important and highly sensitive – it meant settling accounts with our opponents, and not via legal routes either but via the routes we knew best. Back then, that method did not strike me as wrong. I can't remember

whom I heard it from but I agreed wholeheartedly with whoever it was that said revolution starts in the barrel of a gun. If
we did not have the necessary conviction and determination,
we would be endangering the entire nation, not just our cause.
What's more, I liked that way of settling accounts. So yes, seeing
as we're on the subject, I suppose I should confess that I am not
only an incurable romantic but also an irrepressible adventurer.
A love of romance and adventure can be a boon to a novelist,
yes, but no novel can match the pleasure of real-life adventure.
Who knows what adventures and escapades lay in store for me
in the capital? Moreover, Uncle Leon would also be coming
to Istanbul as a member of parliament, which meant we would
also find a way of persuading you to join us there. After all,
you wouldn't have said no to the two most important people
in your life, would you? However, I would soon discover that
I had been gravely mistaken. After the assassination of the
Albanians, I started to realise that I did not know myself, and
after our argument that day in the garden, under the wooden
arbour crisscrossed by vines and garlanded by plump violet
grapes, I realised that I did not know you either. ...

The Love That Will Never Fade

Hello Ester (Evening, Day 4)

It's strange but when I left the hotel this evening to get some dinner, there was nobody watching me. None of the crew assigned to follow me were anywhere to be seen. There were few places for them to hide and with risk of sounding boastful, I would have known were they trying to follow me. So yes, I was sure they had given up following me, probably, I guess, because of Mehmed Esad.

What had he told his superiors? That he would sort it all out and personally hand me, Şehsuvar Sami, over to them? Or did he tell them that there was no reason to suspect me and that I was not a threat to the republic? That they could, in fact, make use of me and hire me to work for them?

Whichever one it was, Reşit's concerns were unfounded. As far as I could tell, it was Cezmi Kenan that suspected Mehmed Esad. He and Reşit must have spoken last night or this morning. But how had Reşit identified and recognised Mehmed Esad? He obviously knew him and had seen him entering or leaving the hotel, and this must have stoked his suspicions. He must have then asked the lads at reception what he had been doing at the hotel, with Ömer reporting back to his boss as per what he had seen. When Reşit found out Mehmed Esad had used a fake name, his suspicions must have been exacerbated even further, making him believe he had a duty to inform me that he was nearby. And what if Reşit is right? What if Mehmed Esad really is a shady character? It is possible, after all. I haven't seen the man for years and now suddenly he turns up out of nowhere, after all this time. Nevertheless, Mehmed Esad's offer is intriguing, and moreover, it is hardly the offer of a traitor. And what about Reşit – how much can he be trusted? He is clearly being influenced by Cezmi Kenan, a man whose honesty cannot be faulted but whose thinking is also linear and predictable. For him, if somebody is not on our side, he is either an enemy or a spy. Perhaps Cezmi has given in to some profound misgiving, a mistake often made by those who have spent years in the secret service and the underground, who always end up suspecting others of treachery and deceit. His paranoia was even more intense during the occupation of Istanbul, when there were so many clandestine organisations and so many secret societies that nobody knew whom to trust.

But meeting Cezmi Kenan may at least help me get a better grasp of the situation. I should be cautious, I suppose, but cautious about what? Not to fall into the hands of extra-national forces, for a start. Not that that is actually a possibility countenanced by the new government. The authorities most probably assume I am one of Kara Kemal's men, one of those fierce ex-CUP members that have not been eliminated in the aftermath of that debacle in Izmir. They probably think I am operating under the leadership of the *Küçük Efendi*, the 'Little Master', now that Talat Bey has left the country, which may actually be partially true, as that is a contact I need if our resistance to foreign occupation is to be revived. What other options do I have anyway? We were members of the same organisation, we knew each other well and we trusted each other. Moreover, we were never against the national resistance movement that began when the occupation of the homeland began. On the contrary, we all, whether it was as a movement as a whole or as individuals, sent aid, munitions and equipment to Anatolia, and at great personal peril too as we risked being tortured, left to rot in Bekir Ağa's prison, sent into exile to Malta or executed. I don't want to bore you with the details but I do want you to know that I have experienced all of the above, except for being killed, of course. I know that nobody wants to listen to the bleating and whining of the defeated, that nobody wants to listen to their complaints and their excuses, and hear about the agonies they may have suffered, and their disappointments, their disillusions and their attempts at apologies... The fact is, in this world, Ester, one must avoid defeat at all costs... One must never become weak, nor succumb to weakness or complacency... If you stumble, you must make sure you don't fall, because if you do, no one will help you back up. If you fall, there you will remain, on the ground, ready to be crushed.

But perhaps we should leave this issue to the side for the moment. We'll come back to it another time...

Where was I? That's right. I'd left the hotel to get some dinner. I walked out of the Pera Palace and headed for Asmalımescit and to a restaurant at the end of the street run by a Viennese couple. Actually, I wasn't that hungry and only managed to finish half of the huge schnitzel I ordered, and that with the help of a large jug of blond German beer. After dinner, I did not want to return to the hotel so I headed for the *Cadde-i Kebir*, which is still trying to adapt to the country's new economy. Although this street opened its arms to the outside forces three years ago when the city was under occupation, I still cannot lose my affection for it and Pera in particular is one of the very few places in Istanbul where I truly feel at home, not that I can go around saying so as if I do, I would immediately be labelled a collaborator or a traitor. But the fact remains, in all of this huge, teeming Istanbul, Pera is the one place that reminds me of Salonika. I don't mean its shops and stores, or the elegance and the beauty of its patrons and clientele, but the way it has embraced and absorbed so many different cultures.

As I walked along the street, I could hear so many languages: French, Greek, Turkish, Armenian, Russian... It was just like our beautiful old hometown. Perhaps this is the only place in the country where the culture of the old empire can still be clearly felt. I walked over to Tünel and sat down in one of the coffee shops lining the arcade there, hoping to enjoy the warmth of the autumn evening. But it was not to be as I was soon overcome by a strange and inexplicable melancholy, a feeling so overwhelming that I quickly paid up and rushed back to the hotel and back to my desk, where I am now recalling the hot, heady days of that summer of 1908.

That summer was to prove pivotal not just to the fate of our vast but impoverished nation but was to also be a turning point in our relationship. At the time, I was aware only of the changes taking place in the country, changes that delighted me because I believed the turmoil would only eventually lead to peace and prosperity for us all. Trying to speculate as to what lay in store for you and I, on the other hand, was a far more arduous task. We had walked together for some time but we had come to a fork in the road and, unfortunately, we had taken different paths. The worst thing is, we were both resolute in our decisions; neither of us wanted to deviate from our chosen path. I suppose the best thing was to not to think about it at all, which is what I tried to do. After all, what importance did our lives have when the nation and the homeland were in danger?

At this point, I suppose I should confess. There were times when I truly resented you for thinking only about yourself when our country was in such a perilous state and when so many of our compatriots were experiencing terrible hardship. Dreaming of sunny days swanning around in Paris, with its posh literary journals, its pretentious discussions about art, its swaggering dandies and oh so feeble and fragile mademoiselles and crusty old madams... I used to really resent the fact that you were cluttering up your mind with airy notions of love and literature, when there were so many things to worry about in the world...

And although I was right in most of my resentments and accusations, I now realise reality has other dimensions too. The decision to dedicate your life to the well-being of the nation can also be seen as selfish, as an act of the ego. But isn't dedicating your life to the service and salvation of the nation and the homeland more virtuous and more meaningful than dedicating your life to the woman you love? It is more praiseworthy and more heroic, with greater sacrifices being demanded and greater dangers confronted, and yet, at the same time, it is somehow belittling and merciless too. More is the pity I did not know better back then. More is the pity, indeed... And so unfair too! This is not my attempt at a confession. I'm just writing down what I feel. The words are just coming out. But wait. Let's not get carried away. It is the summer of 1908 and we are still together...

I don't know if you'll remember or not but we met three days after you presented me with a gift of one of Voltaire's books. You had little idea of what was going on behind the scenes with me but you could clearly sense what your Uncle Leon called 'the approaching catastrophe'. You tried to hide it but you were nervous and uneasy. It was late afternoon and a tired-looking sun was slowly retreating from the skies. The sea was still, like a faded carpet that had been laid out at our feet and was stretched out across the entire bay.

'I think it's the sea I'll miss the most', you suddenly said. 'I mean, when I go to Paris. The only thing missing in that wonderful city is the sea.'

That had always been your style – jumping straight in, without any hint or warning. I remained silent but that didn't stop you.

'We'll go to the south', you went on. 'Especially in the summers. The sea in the south of France is as beautiful as ours, if not more. They have wonderful bathhouses by the sea there. At the end of the day, it is still the Mediterranean...' You stopped and stared at me. 'Are you listening?'

'Of course I am', I hurriedly said, pulling myself together. 'Yes, the Mediterranean is beautiful but it can be very choppy'. I smiled, trying to appear comfortable. 'And we still have our bay. But you're right, life in a city far from the sea is hard'. I opened out my arms and breathed in the sea breeze. 'Tell me, where else will we find such a magical scent?'

You playfully barged your shoulder into mine, oblivious to what any onlookers might have thought or said.

'Don't make fun of me!'

At least the uncomfortable silence between us had been broken.

'I'm not making fun', I smiled. 'You asked and I answered, that's all'. I paused and then asked, 'Seriously, how will we live without the sea? We were born and raised in this city. We grew up on these streets and by this sea. How will we survive so far water nearby?'

You didn't answer, probably because you could guess as to where the conversation was heading, so I carried on.

'But if we went to Istanbul…' I said, glancing over at you, curious as to what your reaction would be. 'Dersaadet… Dersaadet has a sea. It may not be Paris but it is still a capital and it is open to innovation, so much so that it may well be the Paris of the future. All that's happened is that her opportunities have been snatched away from her. She may not have industry, she may be wanting in recent cultural development and many of her people may be simple and uneducated but she has hope.' The expression on your face did not change in the least, so it was impossible to tell what you were thinking but a part of me began to believe you were slowly warming to the idea of moving East rather than West. 'Maybe it is our fate to turn Dersaadet into a new Paris…'

Those black eyes turned towards me and for the first time, I saw those sparks of fury flickering in their dark depths.

'A hundred years, Şehsuvar. A hundred years and more separate us from Paris, and that is taking two revolutions into account. You guys had your revolution yesterday, whilst theirs was one hundred and nineteen years ago. I'm not talking about industry, societal conditions, art or life standards. These are not what form the groundwork for revolutions…. Turning Istanbul into a new Paris is a beautiful dream but it's not possible. Going to Paris itself and starting a new life there is the more feasible option. It is a far more realistic move.'

Your response was just as I had expected but still I persisted.

'But Paris was not always like this'.

'True, a hundred years ago, it wasn't, but now it is. It's a pity but I'm afraid we only have the one life. We do not come back to this world once every hundred years. We have just the one life, and with each passing day, that life becomes less and less. The clock is ticking, the hourglass is there for all to see, and with each grain of sand that comes down, life slips away from us. Those grains of sand are precious, Şehsuvar. Let's not waste them for a freedom the attainability of which is doubtful.'

This time I was silent and began edging away from you. I was dragging my feet but you wouldn't let me get away and you came and stood in front of me.

'No Şehsuvar, I won't do it. I will not waste this precious time we have. I don't want you to either but I cannot force you. That is too great a responsibility.'

I tried to wriggle out of it with an offhand smile and mumbled some empty clichés like, 'Why would you? You are under no such obligation', but they were far from convincing. If anything, I came across as cowardly. You just looked at me silently. Not a single word was uttered. And then you began walking, again without a word being uttered, while I tagged along.

Of course, I was as upset as you were. Yes, I had made my decision but I was also distraught at having let you down. I did not want to lose you, nor did I want our love to end, but an invisible gulf was now opening up between us and with each passing day, it was becoming wider, moving us further apart from each other. A mere five days later, an order came through informing me that I was to go to the capital. Non-compliance would have been out of the question, not that I would have let such an opportunity pass me by anyway. I was not going to the capital for good, no, but that was not something I could not disclose to anybody, which meant I was forced to lie to both you and my mother. I told both of you that I had to go to the capital to sort out some legal affairs for the office but the truth is, I was part of a *fedai* team that was being sent to the capital to guard a delegation of Committee members that was due to hold meetings with the government. You didn't believe the lie, anyway. You listened with an indifferent look on your face, as though to say, *Do whatever you have to do but don't bother me with all these fabrications.*

Yes, I was ashamed at lying to you, deeply ashamed, but I was also furious. You had become so proud and so conceited, so selfish and callous, and yet I could not say so to your face because I had made a promise I now could not keep, whereas for you, nothing could take precedence over love, no event or emergency could be more important than love. I, naturally, did not share that view, and the next day I was the first to board the train to Dersaadet.

Basri Bey was the head of our *fedai* group and before anybody else had boarded the train, he was on board checking every carriage and under every seat, making sure there were no threats to our squad. Luckily, no bombs, guns, weapons or other suspicious objects were found. When Talat Bey and the other members of the delegation took their places on the train, we formed a tight ring of security around them.

Only once during the journey did I enter the carriage in which the members of the delegation were seated, and I happened to overhear Talat Bey angrily mutter, 'Said Paşa is going to discover where the true power lies. We are not like Abdülhamit. Either Said Paşa bows to the will of the people or he resigns from the post of *sadrazam*. It is us or them. There cannot be two authorities in the land.'

It was after hearing this that I realised how critical our visit to the capital actually was. Once more, I was furious with you. We were on this mission of crucial national importance and all you could do was defy me, argue with me and throw my mind into confusion and turmoil. So I decided at that moment not to think about you anymore. I would ignore our little misunderstanding, at least for the duration of our journey and our mission, because the safety of our delegation was of utmost importance. Thankfully, nothing unpleasant or dangerous occurred during our journey to the capital, but one interesting conversation did take place between Talat Bey and myself.

It was late at night and I was on duty in the corridor outside the delegation's compartments. All I could do was stare out at the homeland as it went past, the blurred scenes accompanied by the rhythm of our speeding, jolting train. The crops had been harvested and the chaff burnt by the villagers. The flames that rose up from the steppes into the darkness of the night seemed to hint at an early sunrise. The smell of scorched soil seeping through the windows into the carriage can prompt strange feelings in a man.

'What are you thinking about?' a voice asked, jolting me out of my reverie. I spun around and saw Talat Bey's tired but cheery face looking at me. 'Must be some important business you have left unattended, I'd wager'. Just like Resneli Niyaz, he'd caught me dreaming on the job. I was so raw and so inept, I cannot even begin to tell you how embarrassing it was. I still had a long way to go if I was to rid myself of these weaknesses. But it was the look of a concerned and caring elder brother on Talat Bey's face, rather than that of a commander.

'Thinking of the homeland', I said, mustering up a smile and gesturing to the lands speeding by outside. 'A homeland that is in flames, just like the land out there'.

He peered outside.

'It's worse than that', he sighed. 'Much, much worse, brother Şehsuvar. The country is being torn apart. Yes, we may have started a revolution but we have yet to accomplish anything. Standing before us in all his glory and with all the power of the sultanate and the state in his hands is Abdülhamit. He may appear humbled and subjugated but believe me, he is biding his time, waiting for the opportunity to put his hands around our necks and strangle us. Our mission is a tough one, my friend. A very, very tough mission...' He stared silently out of the window for some time before turning around to look at me again. 'But you seem to have some other business on your mind'. With a sparkle in the eye, he went on. 'Matters of the heart, perchance?'

Whether he knew about you and I or was merely testing the waters, I couldn't tell so I played it safe.

'Not at all. Not when the country is in such a state'.

He took a cigarette case out of his pocket and held it out to me.

'Here, take one'.

As you know, I didn't smoke back then but I took one anyway. He took one out too, placed it between his lips and then, after lighting mine, lit his. We took a drag each and then, as we blew the smoke out, he gently nudged his fez back with the back of his hand.

'In such a state', he sighed, repeating what I had just said. 'That's right, Şehsuvar. For men like us, there is only one true love, and that is love of the motherland.'

'Absolutely, sir', I said, nodding in agreement. 'This land means everything to us'.

He carried on, as though he had not heard me.

'But at the same time, we are still human. You, for example. You're still young, still full of fire. Of course you'll be interested in women. Of course you'll fall in love and get married, but never forget this: women come and go, and there will be a lot of women in your life. One day you'll find them irresistible and vitally important to your life, the next you'll have forgotten all about them. Only one love remains true for us and that is our love for the homeland. Our love for the nation. That is the only love that will never fade. That is the only noble feeling that will remain in our hearts. I'm not saying you should ignore women altogether but never choose a woman, no matter how much of a hold she has over your heart, over the motherland. Believe me, the motherland is more precious than any of them.'

At that moment, I realised he knew about us. Uncle Leon must have told him. Just as you were afraid that I would obey the party's orders and so not come to Paris, so they must have suspected I would follow my heart and abandon the cause and the country.

'You're right, Talat Bey', I said resolutely. 'No love can possibly replace one's love of the motherland.'

I don't know if he believed me or not but he carried on smoking and did not mention the subject again. When he reached the end, he threw the butt out of the window, turned to me and, striking me affectionately on the shoulder, said,

'Well, I should get some sleep, and you should get back to your post. Tomorrow is going to be a tough day.'

After he'd gone, I went back to the window and back to staring at the crimson horizon. I was caught between two worlds and I needed to free myself of the doubt and the hesitation. A decision had to be made. That much was clear. I could no longer lie, either to you or the party. Years later, when I learnt of Talat Bey's marriage to Yanyalı Hulusi Bey's daughter Hayriye Hanım, I remembered what he'd said to me that night on the train and the rage swelled up inside me. I had left the woman of my dreams, the woman I loved, for the cause whereas he had not bothered to renounce his own personal happiness. I felt the same rage when I heard about Enver Paşa's wedding to Naciye Sultan, a member of the royal household. I don't know, perhaps I was being unfair to them. Later on, when I saw the sacrifices they made, my anger subsided. And now? Now I don't even care about these inconsistencies. As Talat Paşa himself said, aren't we all human at the end of the day?

The next day, as we pulled into the station at Sirkeci, a small but vocal crowd was there to welcome us for what was in fact a crucial moment – the core of the revolution had come all the way from the Balkans to the heart of the country itself, to the imperial capital. In the CUP's march to power, we had lived through a historic moment and the crowd that met us at the station welcomed us with joy and affection. They were all sympathisers or members of the movement, people that had proven their worth, and yet we still knew we could trust no one and we did not leave Talat Bey's side for one moment as we made our way to the Bab-ı Âli, the seat of Ottoman government. When we arrived, the delegation was nervous and I heard Talat Bey whisper to our commander Basri Bey to 'be prepared for any eventuality'. Whether he was worried about being arrested or had some other concern in mind, I do not know, but when the delegation went through the palace gates, Basri Bey summoned us and, ignoring the policemen and security officials standing nearby, said, 'Keep your fingers on your triggers, gentlemen. Do not wander. Stay where you can see me, and if I give the signal, do not hesitate.'

As we all looked for suitable places in which to position ourselves and stand guard, Basri Bey signalled for me to stay with him and we walked towards the right-hand side of the Bab-ı Âli's historic main gate.

'Is there going to be trouble?' I asked. 'Do you think the *sadrazam* is really willing to risk a shootout? Because if he does, he knows we can easily take to the mountains any time…'

Basri Bey looked at me approvingly.

'You're going to rise up the ranks quickly, Şehsuvar my boy. None of the other *fedai* here know what's going on. If need be, they'll stand and fight the police, and if need be, they'll stand and die. But none of them actually know why we are here. The fact is, the fate of our revolution is being discussed inside. So bravo, Şehsuvar, my lad. Bravo. You, for one, can see what's going on. And yes, to answer your question, anything may happen. The *sadrazam*, Mehmed Said Paşa, is as wily a statesman as you'll ever meet. He's been appointed *sadrazam* no less than seven times. He is not afraid of taking on Abdülhamit and despite being removed from office so many times, he is still there and still a force to be reckoned with. If he wants, he can have Talat Bey arrested or even resort to force himself. The man is capable of anything, which is why we also need to be prepared for anything. *Inshallah* it won't be necessary but if we have to, we'll draw our weapons and storm the palace.'

Draw our weapons and storm the seat of Ottoman government! It was incredibly daring, not to mention audacious. I remember thinking to myself that the government could have had us all killed right there, even though I then quickly did my best to dispel such dark and foreboding thoughts from my mind. We had successfully brought about a revolution so there was no way they would hurt us now. Now was the time for us to be firm and decisive. We would not become pawns in Abdülhamit's palace intrigues or in Said Paşa's plots and schemes. Yes, if need be, we would kill and die if necessary but what we would not do was betray our principles. Thankfully, none of us wavered and the ageing *sadrazam*, seeing our resolve, realised he could no longer rule alone and buckled. As it is, he was soon forced to resign and hand over the post of *sadrazam* to his bitter rival, Kamil Paşa.

And so the first round with the government had ended, it seemed, in victory for us, and I returned to Salonika jubilant at having played my part in this triumph. But these were petty triumphs. The true tests, the real issues that needed to tackled, were still out there. And, although we were, down to the last man, resolute, determined and brave, we were also – horribly and painfully – raw and inexperienced...

What Does a Single Individual Matter?

Good Morning, Ester (Morning, Day 5)

I was awoken at midnight by someone knocking on my door. While I tried to shake off my drowsiness and work out what was going on, it suddenly hit me. They were here. They had come. For days I had been struggling, trying to tell myself they would not come but now they were here. The funny thing is, I didn't feel any fear. I had felt much greater fear when Kara Kemal was killed, something akin to panic, whereas now I was as serene as a condemned man who has come to accept the finality of his grisly fate. I got up out of bed, slowly and unhurriedly, told them to wait a second, and then went over to the silver-framed mirror on the wall where I smoothed down my hair and tidied myself up as I did not want to look scruffy before my executioners. I walked casually over to the door and opened it. And who did I see peering at me? Who else but Reşit! Of course, seeing a friend standing there instead of the police was a relief but when I saw how flustered he was, I realised all was not well.

'Well, well, what a surprise', I said, welcoming in my unexpected guest. 'How are you doing, Reşit?'

He took a step forward but still glanced nervously up and down the corridor before entering my room.

''Not too good, Şehsuvar *ağabey*', he said anxiously. 'The police are about to raid the hotel. They're looking for someone, apparently. They didn't give us much in the way of details.'

So my gut instincts had not betrayed me – they were going to capture me, and tonight too. I still felt the need to ask.

'Is it me they're looking for?'

He ran his fingers over his hand helplessly.

'I don't know but who else can it be? If that lowlife Mehmed Esad has ratted you out, then I'm afraid it might mean... Oh, Şehsuvar, I told you he couldn't be trusted...'

The poor man was so terrified, I forgot my own woes and tried to calm him down.

'Just take it easy, Reşit. No need to panic just yet. It may have nothing to do with me. Could be just an ordinary criminal.'

He shook his head forlornly.

'I don't think so. The police commissioner sounded like he was dealing with a deadly serious case. When he said an arrest was going to be made at the hotel, my legs almost gave way. If they found out I've come to see you here in your room, I'll be in for it too but I just couldn't stand by and let them catch you unprepared.'

I should admit that I had lost my serenity but I was in a much better state than Reşit, who was shaking like a leaf in the wind, the poor fellow.

'Here, take a seat', I said, pointing to the beige *bergère* by the window. 'I'll get you a glass of water'.

He stared at me incredulously.

'Water? A seat? Şehsuvar *ağabey*, don't you realise what's happening? We're finished. Ruined. They might arrest you thinking you're the killer that has been sent from Greece. It's all over the papers... Çerkez Ethem has sent an assassin over to kill the President! What if they arrest you for that? How will we survive such a scandal? Nobody will dare stand up to refute the charges.'

He sounded deranged, so, hoping it might have an effect, I raised my voice.

'Enough, Reşit! Enough! Just calm down! What is this madness?'

It had no effect.

'What else can I do, Şehsuvar *ağabey*? I'm so scared. Terrified. I have a family, you know. Children.'

'That's wonderful, but remember, I haven't done anything wrong. I'm no fugitive. I'm just another ordinary citizen. And you in particular have no cause for alarm. Had you not been in charge here, I would still have stayed in this hotel.'

I saw the dread in his face start to disappear and so I went on. 'They know me well anyway, those guys, and they know all too well I am not the type to get caught up in such a nasty assassination plot.'

As soon as he heard the word *assassination*, the fear came back.

'I'm sorry my friend, but they have no way of knowing, and even if they knew you weren't involved, they'd pretend you were. They almost had a man like Kazım Karabekir strung up so why should they have any pity for you?' He smashed a fist onto his knee. 'No, no, no, there's something sinister going on here, some game is being played out. That Mehmed Esad did not come here for nothing.'

He was a grown man and here he was almost weeping. I remembered his father, Yusuf Bey, a fearless soldier. Could this really be his son? I grabbed him by the shoulders and shook him.

'Nothing is going to happen to you, Reşit, okay? Try and get that into your head. I'm just another ordinary guest in this hotel, that's all.'

He looked as though he was on the brink of being persuaded when he suddenly began trembling again.

'But they've seen me come up here to your room now. How am I going to explain being here?'

Well, there was no denying that it had been a stupid move on his part.

'Why didn't you just use the phone? Why did you come here in person, and all the way from Şişli too?'

He shot a sideways glance at the telephone.

'I thought they might be listening'.

Which would certainly have been a possibility but whatever the case, I needed to calm this wreck of a man down first.

'Now Reşit, listen to me very carefully', I said looking him straight in the eye. 'You came to the hotel because you wanted to be of assistance to the police if any arrest is to be made. You have had no contact with me whatsoever. You have not been up to this floor, nor have you seen me.'

But he would not calm down. Instead, he sat there, weaving ever more complex and ominous scenarios in his mind.

'What about the other members of staff?' he stammered. 'They've all seen how close we are. What if they tell the police?'

'Let them. We'll tell the police that I fought in Libya alongside your father during the war. You can also tell them we went to the same school. That's hardly a secret now, is it?' I put on my warmest and most trustworthy smile. 'So you can put your mind at rest now, Reşit. Please. Just calm down. Nothing is going to happen. I want you to pull yourself together, go back downstairs and assist the police. Do whatever they want, help them in any way.'

He looked embarrassed and his eyes, wide with fright, blinked.

'What about you? What are you going to do, Şehsuvar *ağabey*?'

I shrugged my shoulders indifferently.

'Nothing. I won't put up any resistance. I'll do whatever they want and go along with whatever they ask. Like a little lamb. Let's see what they're up to.' I gave him a friendly slap on the back. 'Off you go now. On your way'.

After sending Reşit away, I went to the bathroom, washed my hands and face and came back into the room. I was about to start getting changed when I realised I was making a mistake – they needed to catch me in bed unawares. So I sat on the bed instead and began my long wait. Once more, I felt that same serenity. *What does a single individual matter in the face of the will of history?* Maybe you'll remember that line by Ahmed Rıza, a line you used to agree with. For the individual to be happy, society as a whole needs to be happy; that is the whole point, and when examined from that perspective, a single individual is of no value whatsoever.

That is how I consoled myself as I sat on my bed waiting for the inevitable end. There was little else I could do to bide the time. The minutes and then the hours passed and yet there was still no movement or noise in the hallway outside. What were they waiting for?

I remember having experienced similar feelings before, six years ago, again on an autumn night like this, during the start of the occupation. I was on the English forces' wanted list and the house I was staying in Sütlüce had just been raided. The English had not been able to find me for two years as I kept on the move. Whenever things got too hot in my location, I'd leave immediately and move to a new house, which meant capturing me became almost impossible for the English. That is why when I saw some English soldiers standing in front of me one day accompanied by a handful of Sultan Vahdeddin's plain clothes officers, I was shocked. I was even more shocked when the policemen addressed me by name. 'So, Şehsuvar Sami', they said. 'We finally get our hands on you. If at first you don't succeed, as they say, eh?' At the time, I was carrying a fake ID so there was nothing on me to prove I actually was Şehsuvar Sami but they knew all too well it was me. I denied it of course, but they just smirked in response and said, 'We'll see what you have to say at headquarters'. Back then, the police general headquarters were located in the Şahin Paşa Hotel in Sirkeci. (That's right, the security services had hired out a hotel from which to run their operations). I was taken straight up to Kalkandelenli Hasan. We knew each other well but I still looked him in the eye and lied.

'I am not this Şehsuvar Sami person. My name is Kerim Şakir, as you can see from my documents.'

He let out a raucous laugh.

'Wow! Such audacity, Şehsuvar!' he said sardonically. 'It is to be admired. Nevertheless, we have sound intelligence straight from the English high command as to who and what you are. They know who you are and if you don't start telling us the truth while you're here, they'll have you transferred to the Kroker Hotel.' He looked at me with pity. 'I'm sure you are aware of its infamy. Here, we rely on beatings and the odd *falaka*. All crude, unsavoury stuff, to be sure, but not really effective. Over at the Kroker, they have more subtle techniques. They go to work on you for hours so I strongly suggest you start talking. We don't want that much, anyway. Just tell us what your duties are in the movement and what your current mission is and give us a few names and that will be enough. Look, I'm not even asking for all the names. Just three, for instance. Three names and we'll call it a day.'

'You've made a mistake', I said, shaking my head and sticking to my story. 'My name is Kerim Şakir'.

And so they hauled me off to the Kroker Hotel. I stayed there for seven days. Seven days of interrogation and torture. I was questioned by a member of the British intelligence services himself, a Captain Bennett. I won't go into too much detail, but I will say I didn't speak. They didn't get a single name from me, and on the seventh day, I was transferred to the Bekir Ağa Prison. It was there that I learnt something very interesting from Doctor Fehmi Ekrem, the man that tended to my wounds. The man who had given us away was an informer known as Silent John. That's right, an Ottoman agent working for the English. He had infiltrated the security services' high command and had gathered intelligence about me there. And not just me, but others too. That same night, no less than twenty houses were raided and twenty-nine honourable and upstanding patriots were arrested and carted off.

Thinking about those dark days six years ago… Was the same thing going to happen to me now? Were the same pains and the same agonies going to be inflicted upon me again? I began gasping for breath. I stood up and went out on to the balcony. Outside, there was no sign that this quiet autumn night's tranquillity was about to be destroyed. I went back to my bed and back to my silent vigil.

Eventually, as dawn was about to break, there were two knocks on the door, but they did not sound like the prelude to a bust. They sounded more like the gentle, almost diffident, taps of a finger. Of course, I would be lying if I said I was not nervous. I got up, walked over to the door and opened it. It was Reşit again, except this time, instead of terror, there was a look of sheepish jubilation in his eyes. He waltzed in, even though he clearly hadn't slept a wink the whole night.

'You were right, Şehsuvar *ağabey*. All that panic was for nothing. Seems they were looking for some farmer guy called Nazıf who killed his wife and her lover in Bursa. He was upstairs, in Room 505. They found him and took him away quietly and without any fuss. Perhaps I shouldn't say it but he looked pretty innocent, not the type to have killed two people. Quite a fright he gave us, eh?'

'Well, it's all over now', I said, eager to put the affair to bed.

'I'm really sorry, Şehsuvar *ağabey*, for my behaviour earlier. I think I may have overdone it a little. It's just that I'm not used to that kind of situation. Not like your generation. I hope I haven't let you down.'

He seemed so embarrassed and so genuine in his remorse that I felt sorry for him.

'Not at all, Reşit. No problem whatsoever. You've been nothing but kind to me ever since I arrived at the hotel. And you've put yourself in danger for me too.' I took a step towards him. 'But I do have a question for you, and I'd like you to answer honestly. Don't hold back, please. Be honest. If my staying here at the Pera Palace is a problem for you, tell me. I can move to another hotel straight away. As you know, your father has always had a special place in my heart and I do not want to cause you any trouble or harm.'

The pinkish hue spreading across his cheeks was so deep, even the stubble on his face could not hide it.

'Perish the thought!' he said. 'It is no trouble for us at all. Please, stay as long as you like. I admit, I may have lost control a little last night, and I beg your forgiveness. But I would be deeply offended were you to move to another hotel, and I am sure my father, God bless his soul, wherever he may be, would also be mortified. He loved you just as much as you loved him. Please, I beseech you, do not leave the Palace. And please, no more talk of leaving.'

Actually, leaving the hotel would not have been a good move as I needed to stay put until I had solved the Mehmed Esad riddle but my offer to leave the Pera Palace was genuine as another raid on the hotel – whether it be the next day or the day after – was unthinkable and I did not want to disrupt the life of a man who had been nothing but kind to me.

'Now Reşit, look. You have a family to think of.'

He scowled and lifted a hand.

'Please, *ağabey*. No more. We shall speak of this no further. I'm embarrassed enough already as it is.'

He seemed to have made up his mind and was clearly still smarting from his earlier behaviour so I did not pursue the matter further. However, Reşit was still not satisfied and, by way of apology, he treated me to a magnificent breakfast. When I got back to my room, despite a sweet drowsiness that was beckoning for me to lie down, I sat at my desk. My mind's urge to write is overcoming my body's need to sleep.

So yes, years later, this is what I have become. Şehsuvar Sami, the man who used to raid hotels, who used to track down and apprehend dangerous people, who used to question them and interrogate them and then, if necessary, gun them down, is now high up on the list of men that are to be tracked down, arrested, interrogated and perhaps even executed. Quite the turnaround… Still, I suppose there is little point in dwelling on it now so let us return to the past and to our story.

When I got back from the capital, I felt weighed down. I felt I could no longer lie either to you or to myself. I did not have the time for such deceptions anyway. The order had come down from up high that our duties in Salonika had taken on a new urgency and that I was to return to Istanbul as soon possible and without delay. I asked Commander Basri if I could stay another fifteen days in the city, citing my aging mother as the reason, and he consented. The first week I pretty much spent sleeping. Later on I told my mother I had to leave for the capital as I had been offered a job in the civil service, to which she reacted with surprise and delight. But you? I did not say a word to you, although I knew I could not avoid the subject forever. Eventually, we would have to talk. At least talk. That much I owed you.

It was the nearing the end of August and there was a damp breeze blowing through your garden and over the purple grapes hanging down from the vines. We had just eaten some of Grandma Paloma's sumptuous *çörek* and now the two of us were strolling through the garden together. We stopped at the stone pond, the one whose fish had died the previous winter.

'I'm going to join the Committee for Union and Progress.'

That's how it came out. Just like that.

'I've made my decision. I'm going to join the movement.'

You had been looking down but you now lifted your head slightly. I could see your beautiful slender face though your gleaming red tresses as you stared at me in amazement. Actually, I was pretty sure you already knew and that you'd heard about it from someone somewhere through the grapevine. I was waiting for you to throw all my lies back in my face but you didn't. Your response was completely unexpected.

'So are you going to be a killer?'

That was the first time you asked me that question. You really did seem oblivious to what was going on. Maybe you actually were aware of what was happening; you were so certain that I was unable to hide anything from you that you did not even want to entertain the possibility that it was true. Your response threw me completely. All I could do was look away, unable to answer.

'Well, Şehsuvar. Tell me. Are you going to be a killer?'

I should have told you that I had already become one. That I had already killed and that it was for our homeland, and for liberty and fraternity, just as it had been during the French Revolution. *Liberté, egalité, fraternité.* I should have told you that I had killed in the name of those exalted ideals... That it had been a killing that would transform our country and the world... But I couldn't. Instead, cravenly, I spluttered, 'What do you mean? Just because someone believes in a revolutionary ideal, doesn't mean he has to be a killer.'

You shook your head, despondent at my failure to understand.

'Yes, that is generally true… But what about Danton, Robespierre, Saint-Just and Babeuf? What happened to them? First they went on the rampage, and then they in turn were thrown to the wolves. And that was France, remember. This is not France, Şehsuvar. Forget what the maps might say about this also being a part of Europe or what have you. This is the East, Şehsuvar. Life here is hard. It is tough. Without mercy. Everyone here bears a grudge. Everyone in this part of the world has a cause of their own, some account they wish to settle. Even the Jews — yes, we too — are looking to establish a state of our own, and right here too, in Salonika. And do you think the Greeks, Bulgarians, Serbs and Armenians are any different? They all want their freedom, their national independence. They all want a homeland and a state of their own. And that is their right. Nations have the right to establish states and to rule over their own lands. But right now, there is only one state and one land here, and that is the Ottoman state and the Ottoman Empire and nobody here is willing to give up what they already have or hold back on their cause. Those peoples with whom we marched hand in hand for freedom just a few weeks ago and those people with whom we sang songs of unity and brotherhood will soon turn on each other. Mark my words. They will turn on one other and they will slaughter one other. There is only one choice, Şehsuvar: either you become the tyrant or you become the tyrannised. You become the killer or the killed, the oppressor or the oppressed. Yes, I'm afraid it is that simple, and yes, from what I can surmise, you have already decided and are now itching to become an oppressor. That is terrifying enough, but what is worse is that in the end, ultimately, you will lose, and you will then become one of the oppressed. The ones you have hurt will turn around and hurt you. That is how it has always been and that is how it will always be.' You looked at me imploringly. 'Don't do this, Şehsuvar. You're a writer. That is a rare talent. Anyone can join a rebellion but not everybody can write. Instead of hitting the streets with all the others, you should write down what you have seen and what you have experienced. That is much more useful than defending a revolution that simply uses your body as a shield.'

The words were there, on the tip of my tongue, and I couldn't hold back any longer.

'More useful and much safer, too. And if I go to Paris, I will be even safer. There, from a nice, safe distance, we can watch our country tear itself apart.'

I admit I must have sounded proud and brittle but you overlooked it and looked deep into my eyes, desperate to see and understand what was happening in the dim, dark recesses of my mind and my heart.

'You are not a coward, Şehsuvar. Neither of us is. We are not running away. On the contrary, we are trying to create the optimum conditions that will allow us to write about what is happening to us and to our country and our people. How many Şinasi's do we have? How many Namık Kemal's or Abdülhak Hamit's has this vast country of ours produced? How rare such men are and yet you wish to join up with those so-called revolutionaries and *fedaeen*, of which there are hundreds. Don't you see, Şehsuvar? You are different. Overturning a government is one thing, yes. It is hard, but overturning and transforming an entire culture, that is even harder. But you can help accomplish this by writing. By writing your novels.'

You were so sure and so staunch in your conviction that for a moment I was swayed, but only a moment. It was too late. I felt cornered and I was also bristling with a growing anger.

'What makes you think I'm a writer? Having a few stories published in a few minor journals in Salonika makes one a writer, does it?'

'Don't be so harsh on yourself. I know my literature. I have been love with it ever since I learnt how to read and write.' You smiled that sweet, seductive smile. 'And let's not forget that my father is a professor of literature in Paris. But that aside, you do have a gift, Şehsuvar. If you didn't have the gift, I would say so. And it's not just me. Uncle Leon has mentioned it a few times too. He knows it, I know it, and you know it, so why are you pretending otherwise?' You suddenly stopped. The smile on your face vanished and there was a look of shock in your eyes, followed by a look of realisation and massive disappointment. 'You've lied to me, haven't you? You've already joined that movement! Haven't you?' Your eyes bore into me like lead as the words came pouring out. 'You've already taken the oath and joined the CUP! Who knows how long you've been a member now. That time you went to Bitola… When Şemsi Paşa was shot…' You stopped, your hands went up to your head, and you cried, 'Oh my God. I'm such a fool!' You stared at me in disbelief. 'I thought we'd promised to be honest with each other, Şehsuvar? That we would never lie to each other?' You struck your hand against your head. 'Oh my God, I've been such a fool…'

'I didn't want to put you in danger…' I said, spouting the first excuse that came to mind. 'You know as well as I do that the CUP is a secret organization. It has yet to acquire full legal recognition. I did not want you to be dragged in if anything went wrong and I was caught or arrested.'

'Don't, Şehsuvar. Don't take me for a fool. Not now. You may not give a damn about me but at least, out of respect for yourself, enough with these lies. You lied to me and that's the plain and simple truth. If you'd told me that the rebellion was more important and appealing to you, fine, I would have understood. If you'd told me that the motherland is more important than our love, again, I would have accepted it. Even then I would have understood. But don't stand there and give me all this drivel about wanting to protect me.' The lines on your forehead deepened and there were sparks of pure, unadulterated fury in your eyes. 'Who are you anyway to have to protect me? I've been involved in all this since I was a kid. You think my father went to Paris for a laugh? To have some fun? He had to leave this wretched city because his views were seen as too liberal, and not just by the Ottoman authorities but by his own people too, his own community. And Uncle Leon? He has been active in the freedom movement since before you were born. In Salonika, in Paris and in Istanbul.' I could see you holding back the tears. You shook your head in despair. 'I can see I was wrong about you, Şehsuvar. I was horribly, horribly wrong.'

You were right, of course, and I knew it too. I just stood there, a wretched sight, not knowing what to say, desperate to pluck myself out of this mess.

'Fine', I said angrily. 'If you've seen the truth, then there's nothing more to say. I'm going.'

You didn't tell me to leave or to stay. You just looked at me, your eyes, drenched in pain, locked onto mine. But alongside the pain and the dejection was a look of strength and condemnation that was so overwhelming that had I stayed a second longer, I would have fallen to my knees and begged for your forgiveness. Believe me, I am not exaggerating, such was that look in your eyes, and I was so frightened of being exposed and humiliated that I quickly got to my feet.

'See you around then, Ester', I said, trying to sound indifferent. 'I hope you'll be happy'.

You didn't reply. You probably didn't even watch me go. You just stood there by the pool, motionless. By the pool whose fish had long since died in that wild, unkempt garden… An eerie, fading portrait that has been carved into the walls of my memory…

A Game of Revenge

Hello Ester (Noon, Day 5)

Again, I woke up just before noon. The maid has grown accustomed to this and now cleans the room whenever I'm out. Sometimes she has to wait two days before she gets a chance to come in and clean. Like the crew outside, she keeps tabs on my movement as part of her job. Although having said that, the snoops are still nowhere to be seen. The more I think about it, the more I am starting to believe what Mehmed Esad had said but I still need to meet Cezmi Bey before making up my mind. But I have my doubts about that meeting – expecting a man as timid as Reşit to take a marked man such as myself to an old CUP stalwart like Cezmi may well be a pointless exercise. I say stalwart because Cezmi has never acknowledged or accepted our defeat. The last I heard, according to what Kara Kemal told me anyhow, he was working at the Progressive Republican Party's Istanbul headquarters. That must have been around two years ago.

'He's a funny old man, our Cezmi. Just like Enver Paşa, he cannot distinguish between his ideals and reality. He behaves more like a guardian of the republic than a member of the Progressive Republican Party. You should see the way he addresses the police and members of the gendarmerie; like he's still a major in the army and the police and gendarmerie are privates under his command. As soon as I get the chance, I'm going to have to tell him that the CUP are not in power. Otherwise if he keeps on acting up the way he is, he'll not only get himself into hot water but those around him too.'

Kara Kemal was most probably killed before he had the chance to tell the old major to quieten down, which means, in a way, that that particular duty has fallen to me. But for all I know, the Cezmi I meet may be a changed man, especially after the assassination attempt in Izmir. I mean, even a fearless old CUP gunman like Mehmed Esad is now telling me he wants to get on with the government. The world is changing, the times are changing and circumstances are changing, so it is only normal that people should change too, isn't it? Well, we'll soon see. Let's see if I can get Reşit to take me to Cezmi. It may have been his idea in the first place to get us together but the way I see it, the events of last night may have scared him off the idea.

And he wouldn't be wrong, either. Meeting Cezmi could be dangerous. Like me, he is probably also under surveillance. But if I am to solve the riddles that surround me, I need to risk it.

But I have a little time before I leave so let's get back to 1908, to that amazing year of massive hopes and equally massive disappointments. You and I had split up, even though our love for one another had not died and we still loved each other dearly. Although I now realised it was impossible for us to be together, the problem was telling the heart what the mind had already grasped. That was my new nightmare. We had split up and yet you were always with me, wherever I was and wherever I went. The only time I was free of your presence was when I was on duty with my comrades, when my mind was fully focused on our mission. They say that the only cure for heartache is to fill each moment of each day, to keep yourself occupied and to busy yourself with matters so important that the memories of the love you have lost cannot bother you, but that did not work for me because whenever the mission ended and I was left on my own again, that same pain would resurface, that same hidden torment that others who saw my smiling face and assumed all was well with me and my life could not see. Even my mother, bless her, was oblivious to the pain I was in. Before I kissed her hand and asked for her blessings as I prepared to leave for the station to board the train that would take me to Istanbul, she lovingly stroked my hair and, hiding her sadness, said, 'So you're going to work in the government's Translation Bureau, are you, my son? My blessings are with you. It is a great honour. It looks as though the government is trying to make up for sending your father into exile by bringing you to Dersaadet. Well, you've done the right thing in accepting the post, son. It is fitting position for the son of *Başmuallim* Emrullah Bey.' She wiped her eyes with the edge of her muslin headscarf and went on. 'One must not bear a grudge against the state. It's in your stars, to work and earn your living in the capital. What more can I say, son? You have to go. Let us hope death does not come between us.'

But it did. My leaving was one departure too far for her tired, wounded, aching heart and one night, suddenly and without warning, it stopped beating. But we still have some way to go before we reach that point. Back then, if it is death we are talking about, it is those three corpses lying in pools of blood on that narrow street leading down to the Salonika coast that spring to mind. But they were not to be the only deaths. More were to come. To die in old age meant one was one of the lucky few. It was a dreadful age, one in which death at the hands of other men was about to begin. The gunshots on that street that day were the portents of worse to come, of tanks and cannons that would thunder and roar into destructive life only six years later. By that time, we had already lost many of our friends and comrades… But I digress. Let us return to our story and to the capital.

When I arrived in Dersaadet, Basri Bey put me up in a house in Beşiktaş, three hundred metres as the crow flies from Yıldız Palace. So close that I could not help but rib him about it.

'What's all this then, Basri Bey? Are we this close to the palace so it's easier for us to get there and back once it's ours, eh? Is that it?'

Joking aside, I loved that little two-storey house. It had a broad, wooden staircase and a delightful little garden too, much smaller than yours but still adorable. The house used to belong to a barber called Spiros but he'd passed away three years earlier so now his widow, a plump lady called Madame Melina, rented the rooms out. She was a lovely person and was an amazing cook but she hated it when people called the place a house.

'This is a *mansion*', she would say. 'A palace. Bless his soul, Spiros worked night and day to build this place'.

I warmed to Madame Melina immediately. She wore her heart on her sleeve and spoke her mind without holding back, and there was nearly always a cheery sparkle in her huge, heavily made-up blue eyes. It was only when she was thinking about her late husband or his name was mentioned that her expression changed and became sombre. She never had children, which is perhaps why she loved me almost like her own son. And I won't lie, I was also very fond of her. She was like a second mother to me and when I moved to Istanbul for good, I always stayed in that house. Before she died, bless her, Madame Melina performed an act of kindness to me that I shall never be able to repay and bequeathed that house and all her belongings to this simple man from Salonika who first came to her house as a lodger in the autumn of 1908.

Whilst studying at the Imperial High School, Istanbul for me was the *Cadde-i Kebir*, the Grand Street, whereas during the period of constitutional government, my life was centred around Beşiktaş and the *Bab-i Ali*. Not the Bab-ı Âli as in the seat of government but *Bab-i Ali* Street, which is where the offices of Müsâvât Publishing, for whom I supposedly worked, was located. Of course, it was all a cover. Müsâvât were involved in pretty much everything except publishing. I didn't mind the ruse, though, as I quite enjoyed pretending to be a member of a profession I have always admired.

One day in the office, I turned to Kâzım Bey, the man pretending to be in charge of publishing, and asked him if he had any novels that needed translating. 'I may as well do something while I'm here', I said. 'Who knows, we may even have a book to publish in the end.'

He looked at me and frowned.

'Don't bother, Şehsuvar. I'm a retired soldier, not a publisher. What the hell would I know about printing and publishing?'

But I persisted and started paying more frequent visits to a bookseller with whom I would later become quite friendly. I can't remember his real name but I do remember that the local shopkeepers would jokingly call him the 'Vizier of the Sultanate of Books'. He was one of the smartest guys I ever knew and I asked him if he could get me some French novels.

'Come back in three days, young man. There will be a book here for you then.'

And three days later when I returned, just as he'd promised, there was a book there waiting for me. It was Anatole France's *Le Lys Rouge*.

'How about this one?' he asked, handing it over. 'I can also get you the works of Victor Hugo, if you like. Or Stendhal'.

I thanked him and took the book home, which I immediately began translating under the title of *Kırmızı Zambak*. Madame Melina noticed I was retiring to my room early in the evenings now and when saw me reading and writing in the light of the oil lamp on my desk, her respect for me grew.

'Well done, Şehsuvar my boy. I'm so glad I rented this room out to you. Always reading, always writing and making notes, you are. Bravo! Such a lovely sight to see.'

It was only later, much, much later, that poor Madame Melina was to find out that I was actually an assassin for the CUP. Even when I went to Tripoli, she thought I had gone on a business trip for Müsâvât.

I can almost hear you berating me now. *So you lied not just to me but to that poor old woman who was nothing but kind to you?* Well, had I told her the truth, not only would the fear and the anxiety have been too much for her but her respect and affection for me would have received a blow from which there would have perhaps been no recovery. For years, she had thought of me as a gifted writer and she used to scold me all the time, saying, 'All the time translation, translation, translation! It's time you wrote your own novel, my boy! You have a writer's name as it is. *Şehsuvar Sami*. That would look wonderful on the cover of a novel.'

Later on, although her hope had probably began to fade, she never stopped expressing her belief in me. So, as you can see, everyone except me thought I would become a writer but instead of following that path, I spent the most productive years of my life following orders and carrying out political missions. Müsâvât Publications' real purpose was to identify enemies of our party – and who were therefore enemies of the constitutional movement – and to either browbeat them into silence or, if they would not be cowed, have them neutralised. As a result, we had begun our own surveillance, networking and intelligence-gathering operations. Our movement's secret divisions, wherever and whenever they were active, would tell us who was whom, who was working with whom, who could be trusted and who was suspect. And the reason such divisions existed was because we believed we had many enemies, and everywhere too, whether it be in the palace, in government or amongst the people. They could be politicians, civil servants, clerics, journalists, soldiers, tradesmen or merchants… But the worst of all our enemies were Abdülhamit's spies. Admittedly, Serhafiye Ziya Paşa had long since fled to London once the spectre of constitutionalism began to rise over the Ottoman Empire but there were still others sowing seeds of discord all over the country hoping to end the constitutional movement.

Fehim Paşa, a member of a gang of informers, extortionists and traitors that had tarnished the honour of our nation, was lynched by a mob in Bursa. As for the others, who had infested every city in the homeland, we hunted them down, these evil sowers of discord and misery, one by one, name by name, address by address, and we made them pay in the manner they deserved for their treason.

In December of that year, we targeted Ismail Mahir Paşa. He was one of Abdülhamit's most trusted men, and possibly the nastiest of his gang of thugs. When he learnt about his murderous friends' fates, he knew what was coming and so he locked himself up in his mansion, not even daring to stick his nose out of the window. We needed to lure him out so we had sent to him a coded telegraph claiming to be from Yıldız

Palace and stating that the sultan was personally summoning him to his presence. He may have been suspicious at first but in the end, he fell for it and he left his house, which was located near the tomb of Sultan Mahmud. We finally had the chance to give the man with the blood of hundreds on his hands the reward he richly deserved. And no, before you ask, I did not pull the trigger. I was there as backup.

I'm sure that, while you read these letters, you're shocked at how casually I can write about people being killed but let's not forget that it was people like Ismail Mahir Paşa and others like him that only six months earlier had denounced many of the best, brightest and bravest men in the land and had them sent into exile, destroying them and ruining their families' lives, just as they had to my father and my family. And remember, many of those that had been arrested, punished and exiled by the Sultan's men, were innocent and had no connection to our movement or any other.

Don't misunderstand, we were not looking for revenge but had we not acted quickly and decisively, those men we were chasing would have regained power and been back in business. We had to be as smart, as determined and as ruthless as them. And the assassinations were hardly a stroll in the park either. The men we were up against were highly trained professionals, just like us, but they were also more experienced and more ruthless than us. Such was the threat they posed that, once we had taken care of Ismail Mahir Paşa, we shifted our attention to Solak Kani. He was a cunning man, one of the most vicious of the palace spies and the sworn enemy of our movement, and the operation against him almost cost me my life.

It was around the middle of December and the first snows had begun to fall in Dersaadet. For months, we had been trying to keep tabs on Solak Kani but he was a shrewd, slippery character, like a ghost or a flea. He would easily give us the slip and it would take everything we had for us to track him down again. He had lost us a full nine times! Nine times he just vanished into thin air. But we eventually found out where he was staying. It was a two-storey ochre-coloured wooden house just behind the cemetery in Eyüp, right next to the ghouls and the ghosts. The house belonged to a *tellak* called Leb-i Şeker Seyfi, who had worked as an informer for Solak Kani during Abdülhamit's autocratic rule. However, he was not just a masseur, scrubber and informer; the disgraceful wretch also shared a bed with Solak Kani.

Solak Kani had a soft spot for this Leb-i Şeker, whose depravities had gained him notoriety throughout the entire city. Kani did not just have a nasty addiction to opium but he was also so entranced by this pervert Leb-i Şeker that he had to see him at least once a week or he could not be gratified. Thanks to our men out in the field, who had been trailing him for weeks, we now knew that Solak Kani entered that house on Wednesday evenings and left early the next morning during the first call to prayer and so we were also ready, fingers on our triggers, waiting for the order to finally sort him out. Finally, one weekend, the news we had been waiting for arrived. Our intelligence reports had been verified: he was there, in that dark, grubby den of vice and wickedness tucked away by the graveyard. Although it was not a Wednesday but a Friday, Basri Bey, myself and new member of our crew, a youngster from Salonika by the name of Fuad, set off immediately. This Fuad was a decent-looking fellow, nothing like Mehmed Esad. Whether he had the gumption or not, it was still too early to tell, but I did find out early on that he had a love for literature and that his French was at least as good as mine. Actually, oddly enough, his true passion was theatre. He told me he never missed a play back in Salonika, whether it was a local effort or a foreign production. After having somebody like Mehmed Esad, a rude and churlish man with no interest in the arts, it was a relief to have a cultivated man like Fuad on the team.

Well before the morning call to prayers, we took up our positions behind a hill around a hundred metres away from Leb-i Şeker's house, huddled into a small wooden hut that was reserved for the cemetery guards but which was no longer in use. The winding, snow-topped path that snaked through the cemetery to Leb-i Şeker's house passed right in front of us, which meant Solak Kani, if and when he exited the house, would eventually walk straight past us. We knew our calculations were spot on but it was still only on paper. What's more, it was a damp and bitterly cold morning and there was no stove or other form of heating in the hut. Basri Bey had come prepared though, having gained invaluable experience from hunting bandits in the Macedonian mountains, and he took a bottle of cognac out of his pocket.

'Here you are lads. Drink some of this. Should warm the cockles'.

We all had a few sips and it did help but only so much, and we were soon jumping up and down and stamping our feet in a desperate attempt to keep warm. All we could think about was sticking it to that pervert out there and then finding some warm, cosy spot in which to hole ourselves up and let the warmth come back to our bodies. However, the minutes kept ticking by and there was still no sign of Solak Kani. The door to his house remained firmly shut.

'Let's just break in and sort him out inside', Fuad eventually said, growing more and more impatient. 'Otherwise I swear we're going to freeze to death in here'.

Basri Bey, serene as ever, handed him the cognac.

'Don't worry. Nobody is going to freeze. Just wait. That little devil will soon emerge. He has to appear at morning prayers.'

'And what if he doesn't?' Fuad said, holding the bottle but not drinking. 'What if he's still fast asleep? Or doesn't feel like getting out of bed?'

'He will', Basri Bey replied, shaking his head calmly and confidently. 'Abdülhamit sets great store in his men's training and discipline. He has them trained to the highest international standards, which is why the palace guards and his other staff have to show that they are compliant with the Sultan's commands and possess the necessary self-discipline.'

This did not satisfy our young Fuad as he was still shivering with cold and it was making him even more irritable and impatient. He took a generous swig of cognac and passed the bottle over to me.

'Remember Javert?' I asked, taking the cognac. 'You know, the detective in *Les Miserables*?'

'Yeah, why? What's Javert got to do with anything?'

'He was also a policeman with principles. Stayed devoted to his principles to the very end.'

'Javert is an angel compared to the guy we're after', he said as I helped myself to the cognac. 'I don't want to come across as cocky or anything but if you ask me, Victor Hugo overdid it a little. He was always so melodramatic, and so sentimental. Don't you think?'

Job done. I'd got Fuad busy talking about something he loved, making him forget the cold.

'I wouldn't go so far as to say it was sentimental', I said. 'If you ask me, he was quite the realist. He takes a look at good and evil and then analyses them via their causes.'

He sat down on the bare wooden bench.

'But he always depicts people as essentially good, and as decent. Take his hero Jean Valjean, for instance. The man is a veritable monument to goodness. Any more and – God forgive me for even daring to mention it – the man would have been a prophet. Do such people exist in the real world? I'm sorry my friend, in the arts the greatest exposition of the human condition is the comedy. Take the character of Harpagon in Moliere's play *The Miser*. Moliere depicts the man's love of money in such a way, the comic incidents eventually take on a drama all of their own.'

Poor Basri Bey, who wasn't so keen on literature, couldn't hold back much longer.

'Dear me, what is all this? Victor Hugo on the one side, Moliere on the other. If anybody saw us now, they'd think we're here for an author's convention rather than to track down a government spy.'

Just then, the muezzin in Eyüp Mosque began the morning call to prayer. Bless him, he had such a beautiful voice, I almost forgot why we were there. I quickly gathered my wits and was about to tell Basri Bey to get ready when I noticed the wooden door to Leb-i Şeker's house creak open.

'Hold on, hold on', I said, pointing through the broken window. 'Looks like Solak is coming out'.

My two companions both crept up to the window and stared at the house amongst the graves. Fuad was the first to react.

'But that's a woman. Look, she's wearing an *abaya*.'

I squinted and had another look. He was right. It was a woman. There we were, waiting for a tough, moustachioed government agent built like a Janissary but all we could see was this slim woman slipping away.

'That fiend!' Fuad exclaimed. 'Now he's hiring women for the night'.

Basri Bey was frowning but the frown soon vanished and gave way to a wolfish grin.

'That's not a woman, Fuad. That's him. That woman in the abaya is none other than Solak Kani himself!'

I recalled our own lieutenant Atıf escaping to Reseñ in a similar disguise after shooting Şemsi Paşa. If we could do it, why shouldn't the palace spies do it too? We grabbed our guns but we stayed put in the hut, waiting for him to approach. A few minutes later, with an alluring swagger that would have put real women to shame, he passed in front of the hut. When he was five metres past, Fuad and I, at Basri Bey's command, jumped out.

'Don't move!' Fuad shouted. 'I'm afraid this is as far as you go, Solak Kani'.

We both had our guns pointed at him and were ready to pull the trigger but then I heard a shot go off and felt an excruciating pain in my back. The shot had not come from any of us, that much I could tell. Almost immediately after, I heard Basri Bey's revolver go off from the window of the hut. As I fell to the ground, the man in front of me took off his *abaya*, shouted out something about people being shot and began running away. However, it was not Solak Kani that stepped out of the black gown but Leb-i Şeker Seyfi. I remember thinking before passing out in that snowy graveyard in Eyüp that Solak Kani, the sly old dog, had done a real number on us.

When I regained consciousness, I was in an unfamiliar house with Basri Bey and a man I'd never seen before at my bedside.

'He's coming round', the stranger said. 'Like I said, give him a few days and he'll be as good as new'.

While I tried to make sense of what was going on, Basri Bey leaned over and held me by the hand.

'How you doing there, Şehsuvar my boy?' he asked.

I was dazed and a little dizzy but at least I wasn't feeling any pain.

'Thank you, sir, I'm fine'. I scanned the room looking for Fuad but he wasn't there. I began fearing the worst but Basri Bey put my mind at rest.

'Don't worry, Fuad is fine. It's you and your wound that were our real concern and they say you're going to heal in no time.'

So, my beloved Ester, that's how it went. We were not brutes. It was just the world we were living in, the era we were in, the people we had to deal with, life itself. All we were trying to do was bring a semblance of order back to a world that had lost its conscience and its sense of compassion. Of course, the novels make it look so easy but it is never so simple. We had no choice but to take up arms and resort to violence – even if it meant risking our own lives.

The Motherland Is Lost

Good Evening, Ester (Evening, Day 5)

Lady Luck has finally decided to smile upon me – tomorrow we are going to see Cezmi Kenan! Reşit and I spoke over dinner. I hadn't been planning on dinner with him. I had been getting ready to go to the Taksim Gardens, where, according to Ihsan, a new orchestra is scheduled to perform.

'You'll like it, Şehsuvar Bey. They have a German tenor singing songs from *Faust* and *La Traviata*.'

Yes, I'm afraid it's true. I do like a bit of opera, an art form to which I was introduced in your house. I know you've never really taken a liking to it but your Uncle Leon loved it, so much so that he once went all the way to Venice to watch a performance of Verdi's *Rigoletto*. I remember him once jokingly saying, 'It's is the only thing I have in common with Abdülhamit. We both love opera.' Actually, my adventures with opera did not begin in Uncle Leon's law office but with a gramophone and a recording of *Faust* that were amongst the items we seized from the Italians during the war in North Africa. They may have objected at first but even the soldiers I was sharing a tent with soon got used to this most European of art forms and when I arrived at the Pera Palace Hotel, Reşit, upon hearing about my fondness for music, had a gramophone placed in my room.

So yes, just as I was about to leave for the Taksim Gardens to eat while listening to songs about Faust's deal with the devil, Reşit caught up with me in the lobby.

'I'm afraid I cannot let you go, Şehsuvar Bey', he said sternly. 'This evening, you shall be my guest'.

I protested, telling him I had already been his guest that morning but he would not listen and quickly gestured for Ihsan to set our table. And yes, I know you're curious as to what we ate — we started with *düğün çorbası*, followed by *paçanga böreği*, beef fillets in a thick tomato sauce, roasted jellied pheasant and a chestnut dessert. And of course, to top things off, sweet Turkish coffee. While dining on this sumptuous feast, we discussed our forthcoming rendezvous.

'This Major Cezmi', I asked, trying to sound as nonchalant as possible as I ate. 'How did he behave with you? When you went to see him, that is'.

'Oh, he was very pleasant', he answered, without any sign of anxiety or nervousness. 'He seemed very pleased to see me'.

Strange. Very strange... On the one hand, Reşit was scared to death of the police but he didn't bat an eyelid when visiting an old CUP man...

'As you probably know, he and my father were old friends', he went on. 'They fought side by side in the war. His friendship with him stretched even further back than yours.' He paused and then asked, 'We are going, aren't we?' He then glanced around, especially at the next table where an English couple were tucking into their food. Once he was certain they were not listening, he carried on. 'I think he has things to tell you. About this Mehmed Esad character. When I told him Mehmed Esad had paid you a visit, he looked very concerned and told me to bring you to see him as soon as possible. He said he did not want 'that lout Mehmed Esad' causing you any problems. He must know something about all this, Şehsuvar *ağabey*. I think we should go and see him.'

I was desperate to know what he had to say about Mehmed Esad but I needed to stay calm and at least appear unconcerned. I reached out with my fork for the fillet steak.

'Well, yes, that would be good. I'd like to see Major Cezmi too'. I carved off a chunk of meat and then, before putting it in my mouth, asked, 'So when are we going?'

He was reaching out for his wine glass and paused.

'Well, we can go tomorrow. Why wait? Does tomorrow suit you?'

Did it suit me? It was perfect. Best to go soon and sort the issue out before Reşit succumbed to the fear again.

'Tomorrow is fine. What time?'

'How about three or four?' he said, taking another sip of wine. 'Three or four in the afternoon, that is. That's when I usually see him.'

'Deal', I said, reaching for my own glass. 'Let's meet at three in the lobby tomorrow then'.

Our dinner did not last that long as we were both still exhausted from the events of the previous night so we drank our coffees and finished up. I thought about going for a stroll outside but I was suddenly very weary, either because of the food or the wine – or both – so I went up to my room and lay down. I drifted in and out of sleep but then suddenly woke up. I got out of bed and went out onto the balcony, where I looked out onto the city, onto what was once a magnificent capital. There were lights shimmering and flickering everywhere but little of Istanbul's former glory remained; little remained of what was once the queen of all cities. For some unknown reason, I felt a sense of unease and bitterness in my heart. It was the cities, more than any, that had lost during the Great War and Dersaadet was no exception. Now, whatever faults she may have had, she was no longer the capital.

Speaking of faults, to whom are we to point the finger amidst all the carnage and turmoil of the last few years? Who was responsible for all the death and destruction? When did the tide of history undergo this dramatic change? Where and how were such terrible mistakes made? Did we lose because the sultanate had become corrupt and rotten? People now are talking about being unable to adapt to the new regime and to the new way of life. When did this happen, this inability to adapt? Was it with the sudden death of Sultan Mehmed the Conqueror? Or was it with the enmity between the two princes, the two heirs to his throne, and the eventual victory of Prince Bayezid over his brother and rival claimant, Cem Sultan? Or was it the coronation of Selim as Sultan that dragged us into ruination? Was it Sultan Süleyman that made the critical error, when he had Prince Mustafa killed? Perhaps this curse over our soil and our fate began with the Janissaries' brutal and senseless slaying of the young Prince Osman. Did we become this impoverished with the draining of the treasury during the *Lale Devri*, 'the Tulip Era'? Or have we always been ruled by such lopsided and irregular economic forces? When did we hand over ascendency to the Western states? Or should we not look to them in awe or jealousy at all? Was it Mahmud II that set us off on this flawed and doomed path? And the Imperial Edict of Gülhane that reorganised the running of the empire and the government – is that to be seen as a treasonous document? Was Abdülaziz right? Is it true that constitutional government is not our way and not our custom? But isn't that the path all today's pioneers, innovators and civilized nations have chosen and adopted? Aren't all the nations and countries that have rejected the constitutional system sinking and floundering like us into poverty and ignorance? Or have we, as Abdülhamit has stated, simply acted in haste? Is the nation not ready for both a sultan and a parliament? Wouldn't it be prudent to bide our time and wait?

All these questions and conjectures regarding our accursed misfortunes, no matter how logical or illogical, reasonable or unreasonable, went through my mind but then I realised there was little to be gained in dwelling on such myriad speculations. It was too late, and we too were too late. Much too late, in fact. Still, a revolution that has come late is still better than no revolution at all. At least we had had one. Although the republican nationalists posit the 19th of May 1923 as the starting date of the revolution, it began much earlier than that, in the July of 1908, with the uprising that brought the entire country together. Maybe it began even earlier, with Sultan Mahmud II, and is simply being continued now with the emergence and rise of the republic.

I don't know if you remember but Uncle Leon once said, 'The revolution is like a ship on a stormy sea battling giant waves as it tries to reach the shore. The hull of the ship is the people, its masts the organisations and civil society and its sails popular revolt'. When he told me, I appreciated it greatly but I now I see that he was not exactly right. The ship is not trying to reach the shore but is tussling with the waves so it can learn how to stay afloat. The events that make up history are never stable and never the same, nor do they obey specific laws; they do not stay still but are forever in a state of flux, and forever evolving. And most important of all, they are eternal. Especially during the years of the uprising, those huge events erupted one after the other, each carrying a meaning and impact of their own. And then the moment came when the nation, the parties and the individual all lost their hold and their grip on history…

But that was a truth of which we were not aware at the time. On the contrary, we were satisfied, both with ourselves and with the course political life was taking. Despite the events that were unleashed on us after the revolution that began in Macedonia in the summer of 1908, and despite the raw inexperience of its captain, the ship managed to stay afloat, and this was a cause for delight that served only to increase our thirst for freedom. But it was not to last long, and the hurricane that broke loose in the capital soon after plunged the nation, the country and our party into a state of panic and disorientation.

The first blow would come from the Austro-Hungarian Empire, which had been circling around the Ottoman Empire for years like a greedy vulture waiting for its prey's demise. Thanks to their agitations and incitements, the Bulgarians would assume control over the southern part of Bulgaria, and the following day the Austro-Hungarians themselves would annex Bosnia-Herzegovina while Crete would opt to unite with Greece. Although the decision could not be enforced, it was still a crushing blow to us. And of course, none of these events were coincidental. The western nations, Britain above all, were terrified that the citizens of the newly liberated Ottoman state would rise up and when, in the December of 1876, the first Chamber of Deputies was established, the western powers, although congratulatory in appearance and in speech, did everything they could to bring down the Committee for Union and Progress, the organisation that was the leader, pioneer and upholder of the new constitutional era.

What was most astonishing was the role played by the religious fanatics in this nefarious chain of events. Ever eager to drag us all backwards, from the time of Mahmud II to today, they have vehemently opposed every move and attempt to propel the country forward, oblivious to the fact that they are the very reason we have been lagging behind the rest of the world for centuries. At the forefront of this reactionary movement was a sinister man known as Derviş Vahdetî, who was supported by a ragtag mob of madrasah students and semi-literate civil servants and army officers. Together, they formed a reactionary movement known as the *İttihad-i Muhammedî*, or Party of Islamic Unity, and a founded newspaper called *Volkan*, which would spew bile, anger and hatred at the CUP leadership every day.

Had it been just them, then our uprising perhaps would not have slid into the ignominy the way it did, but there was also Prince Sabahattin's Ottoman Liberty Party, the *Ahrar Fırkası*, which exploited the situation in every manner it could. At one point, until only very recently indeed, Prince Sabahattin had been a member of the Young Turk movement but had not hesitated in forming an alliance with the religious reactionaries in order to strengthen his hand. And why? Because Prince Sabahattin hated the movement from which he had been ousted, and he despised Ahmed Rıza, whom he considered his greatest political rival.

Prince Sabahattin and Ahmed Rıza... Both were highly educated and both had brilliant minds but for some reason, they had never seen eye to eye. Their differences of opinion went back to the first Young Turk Congress in Paris, where Prince Sabahattin rested his hopes for national liberation on foreign intervention, an idea to which Ahmed Rıza was ferociously opposed. As it is, the movement was split in two after the Congress, and when the Ottoman Freedom Society, founded by Talat Bey in Salonika, merged with Ahmed Rıza's *İttihat ve Terakki*, Prince Sabahattin found himself side-lined at one of the most important junctures in the nation's history. Eager for revenge, he saw no harm in allying with some of the most conservative forces in the country and exploited every opportunity that came his way in order to regain power.

And so it was this unannounced and sinister alliance, along with Abdülhamit's cunning tactical manoeuvres, that led to the shameful palace mutiny of the 31st March.

I was sleeping when I heard the gunshots. Thinking a raid was taking place, I quickly reached for the revolver in my chest of drawers but nobody was attacking the house. I got out of bed and looked out of the bay window and saw some madrasah students waving the distinctive green, white and red flags that were the banner of the *İttihad-i Muhammedî* movement. Behind them were massed ranks of soldiers and policemen. I had no idea what was going on so I quickly got dressed and rushed downstairs. Madam Melina was by the window, peering anxiously through a narrow gap in the curtains.

'Şehsuvar, my lad', she murmured fearfully when she saw me there. 'The army has mutinied! The soldiers have turned on the government. They are out there right now, in front of the house, with banners demanding Sharia law.' She made the sign of the cross and said, 'We're done for, my boy! Done for. Christ protect us! We're ruined. The country is finished.'

I walked up to her, took her ice-cold hand in mine and tried to calm her.

'Don't worry, Madam Melina. I don't think it's anything important. I'm sure it's just a demand for higher wages. Just sit tight. It will have blown over by noon.'

I had barely finished my sentence, though, when there was an urgent rapping on the door. Poor Madam Melina went as white as a feather. I gently ushered her into one of the side rooms and then took out my revolver.

'Who is it?' I asked. 'What do you want?'

'It's me, Şehsuvar. Basri'.

I can't tell you how relieved I was at hearing my old commanding officer's voice. I hurriedly opened the door and let him in.

'So you heard it all, eh?' he said, noticing the gun in my hand, visibly excited. 'The religious goons have mobilised and are gathering in Sultanahmet. Come on. Let's move.'

'Okay, I'm coming'.

I opened the door to the room Madam Melina was hiding in and smiled at her to try and ease her nerves.

'Don't worry, Madam Melina, it's just an old friend who has come to see me. There's nothing to worry about out there, believe me. Just a few rash, impudent soldiers acting out on the streets.'

The poor woman was so beside herself with worry, she would have given anything to believe me.

'Is that all? So it's not a mutiny? Thank God for that! I was so scared. And God bless your friend too. I was terrified they were going to kill us all.' She looked at me imploringly. 'Don't get me wrong, Şehsuvar Bey, but so much has been happening recently that even a gentle breeze is enough to send shivers down my spine nowadays.'

'Well, there is nothing to fear now. But it would still be best if you stay indoors and keep the door shut. Don't open it to anybody.' I saw the fear return to her face and so I added, 'Just as a precaution, that is. Better to be safe than sorry, as they say.'

When I finally got to walk out of the front door, I saw Basri Bey and Fuad waiting for me under the plum tree outside, which was now beginning to blossom. Together, we set off and dived into the mob of chanting soldiers and students. It was swelling by the minute, and one bearded fanatic, displaying the numerous daggers in his belt to the baying crowd, bellowed, 'Those of you that love your religion and want Sharia – to the Hagia Sophia! Hey, people of Muhammed – to the Hagia Sophia!'

The cry had a particular resonance of course as many important gatherings (and uprisings) had taken place in that historic area. Basri Bey filled us in on the details as we made our way to Sultanahmet with the heaving crowd. 'The mutiny began at midnight in Taşkışla. Soldiers of the Fourth Gunner Battalion turned on their officers, took them hostage and then, with the weapons they had seized, surrounded the parliament building. Soldiers from units stationed at the palace as well as other divisions have also joined the mutiny and are now gathering in Sultanahmet. The mob in front of the Hagia Sophia is growing by the minute, indeed by the second. It doesn't look too good. Who would have ever thought something like this could take place?'

'I told you', Fuad said, breathing heavily. 'The officers in the military have grown arrogant and they look down upon the common soldiery. A number of non-commissioned officers have been dismissed from the army. I said on several occasions that a general feeling of mistrust and disgruntlement has infested the army but nobody seemed to care.' He glanced at the people marching past us and, without even bothering to lower his voice, went on. 'If you don't talk to your soldiers or listen to them, if you don't know what's going on in the barracks, then how can you command your men and your army?'

He was right, absolutely right, and I felt a need to join in.

'The killing of Hasan Fehmi added insult to injury. Why did they have to go and kill a journalist? What else did the murder do except unite the opposition?'

'Let's not rush to judge now', Basri Bey said. His voice carried the necessary authority but no condemnation. 'It's a lot more complex. We don't know for sure if it was our people that killed Hasan Fehmi. Or at least, I have yet to receive any intelligence on the matter. You talk about the non-commissioned officers, Fuad, but look around – madrasah students are out here, too. Seems military service is too burdensome for this shameful lot.' He stared in disgust at the madrasah students milling around us and shook his head. 'Well, whatever it is, it's happening now and we need to think of a way to stop this treachery.'

I was not of the same opinion. This uprising had arrived kicking and screaming. It was enough simply to have seen the mass of people thronging the Hagia Sophia during a prayer and memorial service held by the *İttihad-i Muhammedî* to sense that something big was stirring and that a major revolt was on the cards. The tens of thousands of people that flocked to the funeral of *Serbesti*'s chief writer Hasan Fehmi should have also set the alarm bells ringing. All one had to do was look at the madrasah students, army officers and religious zealots gathered there and see the fury in their eyes to see that the events of today had been threatening to take place. After the killing of Hasan Fehmi, all one had to do was see the way the main opposition newspapers – *İkdam*, *Volkan*, *Yeni Gazete*, *Mizan*, *Osmanlı* and *Serbesti* above all – united against us to know that this day was coming.

But we weren't smart enough to sense this day was coming or figure out something of this nature was in the air because after Said Paşa (and then Kamil Paşa) were dismissed as *sadrazam* and replaced by Hüseyin Hilmi Paşa, we fell victim to a misplaced sense of pride and comfort. Fuad was right. There was an air of arrogance amongst the educated officers, an ugly and incon-gruous feeling of superiority. We felt that our movement was secure and all-powerful and that we had a presence and wide-spread support at all levels of society but that was not the case. We still had many weakness and we had yet to gain power by ourselves.

Of course, I did not share these thoughts with Basri Bey then, not out of a sense of reticence or propriety but rather because I felt there was little to be gained from discussing it when we were experiencing such a setback.

'So where are we going?' I asked. 'Why are we here with these people?'

He winked playfully to hide his nervousness.

'Where else but to Sultanahmet? We may as well make hay while the sun shines, as they say.'

It was not the response I had been expecting and frankly, I was afraid. In fact, I was terrified. If the mob identified us, we would be torn to pieces in the square. Basri Bey could sense my fear. 'There's no need to panic, gentlemen. Nobody there knows who we are. Hardly anybody in Salonika knows we are members of the movement, so nobody is going to know us all the way out here. We're just here to get a handle on this situation and to see what's going on. We won't use force unless we absolutely have to.'

He was right. It wasn't as though we were going to the movement's clubhouse or its newspaper offices. We were on an undercover mission, and we were acting as though our own revolution had never even taken place, as though the opening of parliament and the declaration of the constitution had never happened.

'But we should still remain vigilant', he went on. 'The palace spies are still out there and we don't know who they are or where they may be operating. So whatever happens, we have to stick together in the crowd. Let's stay in sight of one other.'

When we reached the main thoroughfare in Beşiktaş, we only just managed to find places on a horse-drawn tram amongst the throngs of mutinying soldiers. As the tram wound its way to Karaköy, the leaders of the mutiny continued with their chants and their propaganda on the trams and on the streets. In our car, one burly sergeant kept up a rant all the way to Galata Bridge:

'Brothers, we live for the nation, for the homeland and for our faith, whereas the Committee for Union and Progress wishes to destroy our nation, our homeland and our religion! If we let them succeed, neither Allah nor His Prophet will ever forgive us! We renounce all of them: Talat the mason, who wishes to lord over us, Ahmed Rıza, Chairman of the Parliament, who is trying to force hats upon our heads, Hüseyein Cahit, who sows the seeds of discord amongst us with his writing, and Hüseyin Hilmi Paşa, the *sadrazam* and the puppet of the CUP. These treacherous and ignominious men must be dismissed from their positions at once and be subject to the sternest of punishments…'

'*Execute, execute, execute!*' roared the mob in response. Such was their bloodlust, the horses drawing the tram almost overturned the car in fright, not that any of the men on board cared. The sergeant continued with his diatribe. I should hand it to him, he had a powerful voice and he spoke eloquently and earnestly, inspiring all those present (apart from us). We also shouted and applauded to blend in, as we knew we would be lynched in a flash if the speaker or the mob found out who we really were. Actually, we played our parts so well and with such gusto that a nearby madrasah student thrust some green, white and red banners into our hands, which handily completed our disguise. We now looked like just like the other protestors.

While all this was happening, another situation was unfolding that gave us a glimmer of hope. Despite all the passionate and provocative cries and declarations, there was a palpable reticence and restraint amongst the soldiers. And no, this was not some blind optimism on our part but a very real and clear anxiety that could be seen and felt in their expressions. A huge protest was taking place, a real mutiny, yet where it would lead was still unknown. After all, the mutineers were standing up to none other than the government itself. Yes, they were claiming that the palace was on their side but how right were they? It was well known that Sultan Abdülhamit could not abide potentially volatile demonstrations such as this one and that he preferred business to be conducted amicably and concluded in a mutually agreeable manner. Moreover, the government did not need the sultan's permission to order the army to disperse those gathered, whether they were madrasah students or revolting soldiers. Eighty years may have passed but the *Vaka-i Hayriye*, the incident in which the Janissary Corps, seen as a hotbed of dissent against the crown, was eliminated on the orders of the sultan and thousands of Janissaries were killed in one night, was still fresh in the memory and discussed all over the land. True, the soldiers that were present in the square with us that day were not Janissaries but they were still soldiers in open rebellion against the state and the government.

We could see the same unease in the expressions of those gathered in front of the Hagia Sophia mosque during those first few hours. Yes, they were waving their flags, shouting out their slogans and listening to the speeches being made but at the same time they were still nervously keeping an eye out on the square's entry and exit points and whenever there was a hint of confusion or raised voices, they would become even more anxious. By the time the noon call to prayer was being performed, the situation had changed. Another crowd had begun to stream into the square from the *Divan Yolu*, the road that connected the palace and the buildings of state to the district of Sultanahmet. Led by members of the *ulema*, and composed of more soldiers and madrasah students, the arrival of this new group boosted the morale of those already present in the square and soon the roar of the *tekbir* could be heard resonating around the ancient forum. Derviş Vahdetî led the cries that galvanised the crowd, many of whom probably felt like holy warriors in an army about to wage battle against the hated western Crusaders.

Watching this mob intoxicated by its own voice and its own presence, I could not help but think about the people that had gathered not even nine months earlier in Salonika chanting for liberty, equality, fraternity and justice. Witnessing first hand these two critical turning points in our history was an amazing experience, not that I realised at the time. What I felt instead was disappointment and disillusionment. Strangely enough, neither Basri Bey nor Fuad shared my pessimism. They were both focusing on our mission and were busy observing the crowd and registering the situation as it unfolded.

'Let's go and see what's happening over at the *Bab-ı Âli*', Basri Bey finally said after he had gathered as much information as he could from our position in front of the Hagia Sophia. 'We need to see with our own eyes what's happening in the seat of government itself.'

As we were getting ready to slip out of the square, a hand reached out and grabbed Basri Bey by the shoulder.

'Hold on just a minute there, brother. Aren't you from Salonika?'

It was a burly-looking sergeant who stood at least a head higher than all three of us that had grabbed him after seemingly recognising our commandant. All he had to do was shout out to the others and the lynch mob would be upon us.

'No', said Basri Bey, shuffling free of the man's grasp. 'I'm an Albanian from Prizren. Why, what happened?'

The man looked him up and down suspiciously.

'Your name's Basri, isn't it?'

'Who the hell is Basri?' our commandant said angrily. 'My name is Ferruh. Ferruh of Prizren'.

He seemed to hesitate but then he made up his mind.

'Why don't you come this way a second', he said and began pulling Basri Bey away. Fuad stepped in.

'What the hell do you think you're doing, eh?' he bellowed. 'What's with all this pushing and shoving? We're already crammed in. You want us all to get crushed here?'

'Who do you think you are?' I said, joining in. 'Are you trying to get involved or what?'

But he was not the type to be cowed by idle threats and he pushed Fuad and I away with his huge oar-like hands.

'If you ask me, you're the ones getting involved. Get the hell out of my way. I know this guy. He's an *ittihatçı*. An officer from Salonika. A damn *ittihatçı* officer to boot, one of their top guys.' He grabbed Basri Bey by the collar again. When some mullahs nearby heard the commotion and surrounded us, I thought the game was up. *This is where it ends, Şehsuvar,* I thought to myself. *We're going to die here.* I remember what you once said to me:

'This is not France, Şehsuvar. Forget what the maps might say about this being Europe or what have you. This is the East. Life here is hard. It is tough. Without mercy. Either you become the tyrant or the tyrannised. The killer or the killed, the oppressor or the oppressed. In the end, ultimately, you will lose, and then you will become the tyrannised. The ones you hurt will turn around and hurt you'.

So was this the moment? Had it finally arrived? And so soon too? I felt all my plans, and all my ideas, hopes and dreams crumbling into dust. *Just draw your weapon, shoot the sergeant, unload the chamber into this mob of idiots surrounding us and then blow your brains out with the last bullet and end this nightmare,* I remember thinking. In fact, my hand went to my holster and grabbed the hilt when suddenly all hell broke loose.

'We've got him! We've got him! Hüseyin Cahit…! We've caught Hüseyin Cahit!'

The CUP's loyal publicist Hüseyin Cahit was such a loathed individual that the sergeant and the men surrounding us immediately forgot about us and, thinking they had caught an even bigger fish, headed in the direction from which they thought the shout had come.

'They've seriously caught Hüseyin Cahit?' Basri Bey murmured, expressing little joy at having escaped from a possibly nasty and fatal encounter. 'Let's go lads, we might be able to save him'.

So, just when Azrail had decided to release us, we were now heading straight back into the jaws of death. As I've said before, Basri Bey was a brave, brave man, and he strode straight into that teeming mass of people, some of whom just a few seconds earlier had been getting ready to tear us limb from limb. We tried to get nearer the commotion but we could barely move, it was so crowded. All we could make out were the pieces of a Landon car amongst the mob because the person said to be Hüseyin Cahit had managed to start the car and was trying to get away by driving through the baying mob. The cry came up. 'Get him! Get him! Kill him! We want Sharia!' They eventually caught up with the car and tore the poor man to pieces. We later managed to get near the scene and to the battered and broken body of Hüseyin Cahit. It was a ghastly sight. The body was a bloodied pulp lying a few metres away from the wrecked car. The mouth was wide open, displaying rows of broken teeth, and the skin was hanging off his face, his skull almost poking through in places. As the mob dispersed, we approached the body of the dead journalist, but then Basri Bey, who was staring at the body, gestured for us to stop and stay where we were.

'Get back', he whispered. 'Don't come any further. We're getting out of here'. When he saw us staring at him in amazement, he said, again in a whisper, 'This is not him. It's not Hüseyin Cahit'.

That evening we learnt the truth. The man that had been murdered by the frenzied mob was not our eminent publicist but the parliamentary representative for Lazakia, Arslan Bey, who just happened to bear a striking resemblance to Hüseyin Cahit. I should tell you now that it was during this particular incident that I grasped the importance of keeping calm when in such situations. Had I reached for my gun when that sergeant had tried to drag Basri Bey away, then the three of us would have been killed there and then.

That day, the fact that the protest had a religious dimension was a boon for the soldiers present as it helped turn it into a holy campaign, one that had been blessed and sanctioned by the madrasah students and members of the clergy. Around noon, a further one thousand or so members of the navy also arrived, and as the day wore on, the mullahs, madrasah students, officers and supporters of the Ottoman Liberal Party grew even bolder. When rumours came through that the parliament building had been surrounded, that offices of the journals *Tanin* and *Şura-yı Ümmet* had been occupied and that the CUP clubhouse had been looted, the mob let out triumphant roars. What encouraged them more than anything, though, was the government's procrastination. The prime minister's office dithered and it seemed nobody was able or willing to give the order for the rebellion to be crushed.

When the mob realised an official intervention was unlikely, they were even more emboldened. One group attempted to break into the offices of the Ministry of War. Soldiers still loyal to the government fired warning shots into the air and kept them away but even then, when the Ministry itself was under attack, the army could not shoot the attackers, and once this was the case, the protestors' objectives had been realised. Within twenty-four hours, the government had been toppled, and Hüseyin Hilmi Paşa, whom we supported, had been dismissed and replaced by Ahmed Tevfik Paşa. Even then, the mob would not disperse, not until the Minister for War, Ethem Paşa, personally appeared before them in front of the Hagia Sophia. When they were sure they had succeeded and that the sultan had forgiven them, they were content. That is when the mayhem began. In a show of victorious celebration, the

soldiers in the mob, along with a few others, began to fire cele-
bratory shots into the air. People began running away in terror
and the doors and windows to nearby houses were slammed
shut as the local residents did what they could defend their
homes and protect their families and loved ones. The smell of
gunpowder lingered in the air until sunrise...

A number of murders took place too. One of them was
another case of mistaken identity, when Nazım Paşa, the
Minister for Justice, was mistaken for Ahmed Rıza, Chairman
of the Chamber of Deputies, and killed, whilst four military
cadets were also killed on the streets. As three undercover *fedai*
for the CUP mingling with the deranged mobs, there was little
we could do except store everything we had seen, heard and
experienced to memory. We had been up since dawn and
watching all the madness without being able to intervene had
begun to take its toll on our spirits and our bodies. I had a
pounding headache, Basri Bey had an injury to his right foot
and Fuad, who had very pale skin, was burnt from standing
under the sun for so long.

'Maybe we should stay together', he offered as we trudged
home. 'They'll be able to hunt us down much more easily if
we're alone.'

'*Hunt?*' Basri Bey said, glowering at him. 'What the hell is
that supposed to mean? Who's hunting whom? Do you honestly think this pack of jackals is going to get away with this?
Yes, the government may have been overthrown and a new
sadrazam may have been appointed, but that doesn't mean
a thing. It's just a diversion. All bluffs. Can't you see it's the
English behind all this? There are outside forces behind all
of this, behind all of them – Vahdetî, Prince Sabahattin, that
group of officers demanding their 'rights', and behind that sly
old man in the palace. But it won't last long. They'll soon
be defeated. Our lot have started to get together. See? They
couldn't get their hands on Talat or Hüseyin Cahit or Ahmed
Rıza. Preparations have been well under way in Bitola and in
Salonika. The Third Army may strike at the palace gates at any
time, and that is when the enemies of this nation, these traitors,

this motley little alliance, no, this gang of thieves and evildoers, will be crushed like the ants they are and forced to flee. No, my friends, this is not the time to weep, or to lose faith. We shall continue with our mission. We shall remember every detail of what we saw today at the Hagia Sophia and remember the faces of those madrasah students led by that hound Vahdetî and when freedom once more dances through the streets of Dersaadet, we shall hunt down these traitors, find them wherever they are hiding and hand them over to the proper authorities. We shall see justice meted out to them, one by one, and we shall make sure they receive the gravest and heaviest punishment for their crimes.'

Once more, I felt awe and profound respect for Basri Bey. Once again, with his unflinching will, rock steady nerves and his cool, searing sense of judgement in times of crisis, he was an example to both of us, a man and an ideal to be emulated. Still, although our hearts were stirred by his rousing words and his sense of selflessness, it was hard to actually believe that events would develop so readily in our favour. The government had been overthrown in the space of a single day, and both the *sadrazam* and the Minister of War had been deposed and the palace was no doubt, either overtly or in secret, delighted at this turn of events. A mere nine months had passed since the Constitution had been declared and already its promised reforms had been dealt a major blow. Kamil Paşa, who had been dismissed as *sadrazam* two months earlier, must also have been delighted. But, as Basri Bey told us later on that evening, their joy was to be short-lived. The CUP had already dispatched the Army of Action to deal with the reactionary forces that had gathered in the capital and although it would not arrive for another ten days, those that believed they could halt or even reverse the tide of history were about to be dealt a devastating blow.

The Only Thing Keeping Me Alive

Hello Ester (Morning, Day 6)

I woke up early this morning, before sunrise. I had a terrible headache, possibly because of last night's wine, although I doubt it as it was a fine wine and I hadn't really drunk that much anyway. Perhaps it was because I stayed up late writing to you because I could also feel my eyes stinging when I woke up. But more important was the fact that as I wrote, I remembered and relived those days. In one's youth, one can withstand the most trying and terrible events – war, revolution, assassinations and death – but now simply thinking about them is an ordeal for me. It seems I am still reeling from my writing, which perhaps explains the patchy, disjointed dreams I kept having last night. The past is not just a collection of memories but our very lives, nourished by the present and staying with us till we breathe our last. Yes, I know that those without a past have neither a present nor freedom but I often wish I did not have the past that I have. I often, to myself, quietly wish I had not experienced the pain and the torments that I have, that I had not lived the life I have, and last night, I felt those same pangs of regret again. But one must not surrender. One must not give up. No matter how hard it is, or how distressing, I will keep on writing to you, and I won't stop, not until they finally kill me or lock me up to rot in a cell. I shall keep on writing down my memories, even though I know you may never read any of these letters and that you may simply rip them up without even bothering to open them.

The only thing keeping me alive is the need to write to you. And that is why, like an athlete readying himself for competition, I do not have the luxury of relaxing. I cannot and must not be discouraged by headaches, stomachaches or weariness. That is the attitude with which I woke up this morning. I had a glass of water, which helped refresh me, but I still did not feel like going downstairs so I had breakfast sent up to my room. I could not finish it all but the coffee went down a treat, jolting me out of my lethargy and firing up my mind. Afterwards, I was dying to have a cigarette and I even thought about asking room service to bring up a packet but then I gave up on the idea. I have never done anything outside my own volition, which is perhaps the best thing the movement taught me. I have given up smoking and I will never start again. Before sitting down at my desk to write, I went out onto the balcony, not to look at the city but to look up to the sky and take a deep breath.

The skies were overcast, promising rain, and the sea was coated in a grey mist. I could not look at that gloomy view for much longer and so went back in and began writing about spring. It is supposedly the season to inspire joy and hope but the spring of 1909 in Istanbul was far from stirring any such emotions in us...

Just as the revolution had made Salonika all the more enchanting, so it had made the capital all the more ugly. In Salonika, everybody came out onto the streets to embrace the revolution, whereas in Istanbul most people did not want to be seen in public and instead stayed far away from the trouble brewing on the streets. And no, I am not exaggerating; almost all the residents in the city had holed themselves up at home, and the stores remained closed and shuttered for days on end. Although the protestors had got what they wanted, they could not be placated and stormed into the city's many coffee shops and tea rooms and tore down any pictures or slogans on the walls that celebrated our constitutional freedoms, whilst also forcibly cutting the hair of any women they deemed too immodestly dressed and looting the inns and taverns. In such a grand and ancient city, nobody felt safe, least of all the minorities.

The three of us met the next morning in a coffee shop in Tophane. Basri Bey looked distressed, too upset even to enjoy his usual morning coffee.

'The bastards', he muttered furiously. 'They're killing military cadets out on the streets. They have already killed dozens of officers. Somebody needs to tell them to stop.'

'So we kill them', Fuad erupted, like a barrel of gunpowder that had been set off by the spark it had been impatiently waiting for. 'There's nothing else we can do and we're already wearing civilian clothing. Let's hit the streets and shoot whoever tries to get in our way. Might as well. All or nothing.'

Basri Bey looked at him in despair.

'This is not a play about the French Revolution, Fuad, and we are not actors in a play. This is reality. We can't just do the first thing that pops into our heads.'

Fuad was clearly offended at having his love for the theatre thrown back in his face and about to say something when Basri Bey held up a hand to silence him.

'You don't think I want the same, Fuad? You don't think I want revenge for our fallen friends? That I don't want to drown these bastards in the blood they have shed? I do, but we have been given a mission so until the Third Army arrives, we stay put.' He turned and looked out of the window to the sea beyond, hoping almost that a vast ship hosting a huge army would suddenly arrive at the docks and let the men on board save the city. He muttered, more to himself than to us. 'Not long now. We shall soon bring this scum to heel'.

He reached out for his now cold coffee and took a sip. It must have tasted horrible as he grimaced and put the cup down, picking up the glass of water on the table and downing that instead. He wiped his mouth and moustache dry with the back of his hand and beckoned for us to come closer.

'The movement's most important men are in safe houses', he whispered. He saw us hanging on his every word and went on. 'Talat Bey, I mean, and Ahmed Rıza and Doctor Nazım. Our mission is to guard them.'

The pride was palpable in his voice, and I am hardly going to chastise him for it as I felt the same pride myself. I was actually being charged with protecting two men who were, for me, the most important people in the world! Ahmed Rıza... I hadn't seen him since Paris. I began to wonder if he would remember me but then I realised how immature – and pointless – such thoughts were. My own personal feelings? They were irrelevant! I had been charged with a mission, a mission far more important than any personal feelings or desires, a mission that was a matter of life and death. A matter of vital importance, not in terms of individuals but in terms of the revolution and its survival. And there I was, wondering whether Ahmed Rıza would actually remember a young nobody like me!

When we finally got up, the sun was already well up and the sea was shimmering with light. The smell of gunpowder was still on the breeze but there was hardly anybody out on the streets. The only people outside were some students and a few irregular soldiers milling about in groups, chanting slogans, taunting the few people that had come out, telling them that they were now the law and the government, and shooting randomly into the air as though it was a rare skill. We had only just left the coffee shop when a young madrasah student who had probably never held a gun before in his life accidentally shot his friend right there in front of our very eyes in the small square in front of the coffee shop. Can you imagine how many more innocent people were injured, maimed or killed by stray bullets fired by those buffoons?

Basri Bey had not told us where the safe house in which our leaders were hiding was, and we did not ask either, so as to not compromise their security. There were no trams or carriages so we had no choice but to walk. We set off over the Galata Bridge towards Eminönü. There were no bridge officials collecting tolls and nobody seemed to care. About halfway across the bridge, we saw a group of about twenty students marching towards us, waving green flags and demanding sharia law. I saw Fuad reach for his gun. Basri Bey noticed it too and hissed at him to stop. Fuad did as he was ordered. The students didn't actually suspect us anyway; they didn't even know who we were and probably couldn't have cared less. All they were doing was giving a show of strength, so when they neared us, we joined in with their chant.

'*We demand sharia! We demand sharia! We demand sharia!*'

With their fists raised, they marched past and vanished. That was the only action we saw on the bridge. When we reached the New Mosque, we turned right, walked past the Egyptian Bazaar, whose gates were firmly locked, and took the road to Süleymaniye. Once we were on the backstreets, the wandering mobs seemed to thin out and we finally saw local residents leaning out of their windows chatting to neighbours, sharing information and trying to get an update on the situation. The more courageous residents had opened their front doors and peppered us with questions when they saw us walking past, eager for updates. When we told them that the stores, markets and bazaars were still closed and that they should stay indoors, their worries only resurfaced.

'Why doesn't the sultan find a solution?'

'May Allah protect us from the wrath of Satan!'

'The army should put a stop to this disgrace.'

We walked all the way up to Süleymaniye Mosque. The courtyard of that architectural marvel was teeming with madrasah students listening to speeches and waving green banners bearing inscriptions from the *Quran*. Every now and then, a cry of *Allahu akbar* would go up, animating them yet further and amplifying their confidence in their little rebellion, which they saw as a sacred calling, sacred enough that beatings, burning, looting, abuse, insults and murder were all suddenly justified. To avoid getting too close to the crowd, we walked along the thick outer walls of the mosque and then turned into one of the narrow, rickety paths that led to Şehzadebaşı. The path led us out onto a broad thoroughfare, where we saw three looted shops – a tailor, a second-hand bookshop and a bakery. Why they were looted was unclear; perhaps the owners were rumoured to be CUP sympathisers, or were minorities. We walked through the piles of clothes, fabrics, books and bags of flour that had been strewn across the street and then turned right into another long road that thankfully took us further away from the mob and their hullabaloo. We stopped at the end of the street, at a fountain bearing the *tuğra* of Sultan Abdülaziz, next to a shuttered store. Basri Bey leaned over to drink but what he was really doing was looking around and scoping the area. After he'd washed his hands and wet his lips and taken out his handkerchief to dry his hands and mouth, he looked at the direction from which we'd just come to make sure nobody had followed us. Then it was my turn to lean over and wash my hands and face, with Basri Bey watching the street the whole time. Apart from the three of us, no living thing, apart for a yellow cat with sparkling green eyes, could be seen in the area. Once he was certain we were safe, our commandant walked with calm but rapid steps to the brown house behind the fountain and knocked on the door.

'Who is it?' a female voice called out. 'Who are you looking for?'

'It's me, Nusret the dentist', Basri Bey answered. 'Is Ali Cemal home?'

They were all codes, of course, and after the sound of a lock clicking open, the door was opened slightly, allowing the three of us, without rushing but as quickly as possible, to slip inside. The woman in the black yashmak that had opened the door to us retreated back down the hallway and a large, well-built man holding a Lüger in his right hand appeared.

'Hello there, Basri. Good to see you.'

Our commandant responded with a broad smile.

'Well, well, well, Cezmi, my dear fellow, if it isn't you! What a surprise! So you're here too, are you?'

So that, dear Ester, is when I first saw Major Cezmi, the man I am going to meet this afternoon. Back then he was still a captain, not a major, and he had also been charged with guarding the leaders of the CUP, just like us.

'Of course I'm here. Who else are they going to find to guard these important fellows?'

Cezmi Bey and Basri Bey embraced warmly and slapped one another on the shoulders. We would later discover that they had been classmates in the military academy.

'What's the latest then, eh?' Basri asked. 'Tell me, what's going on?'

Cezmi Bey jerked his head towards a closed door.

'Don't even ask. We only just managed to save Ahmed Rıza Bey from that gang of zealots. The man has the heart of a lion, I tell you. The way he behaved out there, it may as well have been a picnic in a rose garden as far as he was concerned. Got into a car and calmly made his way over to the Bab-ı Âli, didn't he? If that mob had seen him, he would have been a goner. When he arrived at the government offices, even the ministers were too scared to speak him. Wouldn't even come out to see him. So what does he do but stay holed up the whole day in the Ministry of Foreign Affairs. When it got dark, Suudi Bey and I went over, straightened things out, covered his face with a handkerchief to hide him and brought him here.'

Basri Bey looked around, expecting to see Ahmed Rıza Bey step out.

'I hear Talat Bey and Doctor Nazım are also here'.

Cezmi gestured with a motion of his head towards the front door.

'They were, but they left. This morning. Ahmed Rıza was not pleased about it but I reckon they made the right move. If those bearded loons find out about this place and force their way in, then both the movement's mastermind and its principle architect will be toast. God knows how we would survive if that were to happen.' He turned and looked at Fuad and I. 'Our friends here are from Salonika, are they?'

Before Basri Bey could answer, the door to the room Major Cezmi had gestured to a little earlier creaked open and a man with a thin, pointy face and regal beard stepped out. It was the man we were all in awe of, the 'Father of Our Freedom': Ahmed Rıza. Seeing him stare at Fuad and I in confusion, Basri Bey immediately stepped in to explain.

'Sir, our friends here have been sent by the party. For your protection.'

A smile of appreciation appeared on Ahmed Rıza's tired face.

'In that case, a warm welcome to you, dear friends. How lovely to see you here, and how decent of you to come.' His wandering eyes came to rest on me. 'Correct me if I'm wrong but... But aren't you that young man I met in Paris? Şahsuvar, wasn't it?'

'Şehsuvar, sir', I answered excitedly. 'Şehsuvar Sami. I'm amazed that you remember'.

There was a warm gleam in his eyes.

'That's right. Şehsuvar Sami. You came to our club in Bonaparte Street in Paris. There was a young lady with you. A beautiful lady with red hair. Stella, I believe her name was.'

He may have mispronounced both our names but I was still delighted that he remembered us.

'Ester, sir. Her name was Ester. Her father Monsieur Naum was a friend of yours.'

He nodded his head gently.

'Monsieur Naum. That's right. A most valuable and cherished man of letters he was indeed. A professor of literature.' His mood suddenly changed and became serious. 'But tell me, what exactly are you doing here? If I remember correctly, you nurtured dreams of becoming a writer. I read the stories you gave me. Not bad at all. I even remember telling you not to give up and to keep on writing. In fact, Monsieur Naum and I once talked about you. He also thought highly of you. So tell me, how is the writing coming along?'

I could the blood rushing to my face.

'Well, the thing is, sir. Well, you know better than I do. It's just that when the country is in the state it is in now... When things are the way they are, well, I don't think it would be right to lock myself away in a room full of books and just write.'

There was neither appreciation nor recognition in his face.

'I see. Well, you've probably made the right decision. Although having said that, finding a writer that could record all that is happening nowadays wouldn't be such a bad thing now, would it?' He looked at the others. 'Wouldn't you say so, gentlemen? The present will soon be the past. Just look at today. We're already talking about the day's events as though they are rooted in history, when in truth, it has only been twenty-four hours. So yes, somebody needs to write all this down, and in the truest, rawest, most honest and genuine form.'

'But one cannot write about it without first experiencing it!' Cezmi said. 'How can somebody who has not felt the fear of our people, who has not felt their worries, woes and concerns, who has not smelled the gunpowder looming over the city like a black cloud convey all that has happened?' He then turned and looked at me with pride. 'Our comrade here has gained invaluable experience which will provide ample material for his future writing.'

Ahmed Rıza listened carefully but couldn't help respond with a slightly stinging note of caution.

'So long as he does not grow disillusioned'. He gave me a hearty punch on the shoulder. 'Such are the difficult times we live in. Politics has become so dirty and corrupt that it can kill off the poets inside us at any time'. He then smiled broadly at us all. 'But let's put that aside for now. Let's go inside. Please, gentlemen, this way. Cezmi, please ask the lady if she would be so kind as to prepare some refreshments for our friends here.'

Cezmi went off to the kitchen while the rest of us went to the room Ahmed Rıza was staying in, a modest affair with few furnishings – four brown velvet chairs, a broad sofa covered by a beige throw and a wooden desk. He seated us all personally, as though it was our home, and then spoke to Fuad and Basri Bey, asking after their health and thanking them again for coming to guard him. After we had finished our coffee, his expression grew more serious.

'So tell me, what is the atmosphere like out there on the streets? Are the riots still going on?'

After a few moments of silence, with all of us hesitant as to who should answer, I spoke up.

'The same as yesterday, Ahmed Bey. Officers are being killed, and women and ethnic and religious minorities are being harried and harassed. Shops with known connections to or sympathies with the CUP are being looted and trashed.'

'But they will lose in the end', Basri Bey interjected. 'They can get as violent and as reckless as they like. They can trash a few more stores and yes, they can hurt and kill even more people, but in the end, they will lose.'

Ahmed Rıza stroked his beard with his right hand.

'I agree. I said the same thing to Talat Bey yesterday. Whatever may have transpired so far, the constitutional movement has pulled through. Had we fallen into the hands of the zealots yesterday, things would have been much worse. But those jackals' days are now numbered.' He stopped, took a deep breath and shook his disconsolately. 'Nevertheless, there are a number of problems that need to be resolved. Very serious problems. We have a hugely inexperienced group. Inexperienced and naïve, and our organisation is still shoddy. And if that were not enough, we seem to have the same propensity for violence and intimidation as… Well, let's just say we are not entirely free of blame for all that has happened recently.' He turned and looked at me. 'The tyrant's greatest achievement is to make those he tyrannises more like him, and I'm afraid Abdülhamit has been an outstanding success in this regard. If we carry on like this, then even if we do gain power, we will have already lost our future. There is a famous saying; one cannot prosper via tyranny, and even if one does, it is eventually ruined. Look at what happened to poor Hasan Fehmi. That was the last straw. The assassination that united the entire opposition against us. Tell me, what was the point of that murder? What was achieved? Why did we have him killed? Only nine months ago, we were extolling the importance of the right to freedom of expression, yet now we are the ones terrified of that same freedom. Tell me, what difference is there between us and Abdülhamit?'

As I listened, it was not so much his words that affected me but the despair in his eyes. Ahmed Rıza was an important man, not just for me but for anyone that cherished liberty. When he returned from Paris, the party welcomed him with open arms and made him a member of parliament and then the speaker of the house. But now, seeing the despair in the eyes of this

Young Turk, I was seeing the despair and the disenchantment of our movement's leadership. When at one point, even under the most trying of circumstances, Ahmed Rıza had flown the banner of freedom for the Ottomans almost single-handedly in Paris, now his innovative, audacious ideas and radical theories in matters pertaining to religion were drawing the ire of the party and the movement. Just as the Macedonian reformists and revolutionaries were viewed with disdain by the capital and by people in the countryside, so within the ranks of the reformists, this brilliant and unorthodox thinker was viewed with suspicion and unease. The number of people that saw his theories merely as eloquent and beautifully articulated remedies that could solve nothing had grown to such an extent that the series of events that were set in motion by the uprising on the 31st March and which would soon escalate in violence would also spell the end of this otherwise brilliant man. What the movement needed was stern, determined and disciplined men of conviction who would obey orders without question, not men like Ahmed Rıza that viewed events with an analytic eye and who did not pull any punches when it came to expressing his opinions. As it is, a few months later, he would come out and admit that the killings were terrible mistakes and that in us and our government, a new despotism had come to rule the land. In doing so, he effectively severed his ties with the party and the movement forever. However, that day, when I saw him in the safe house, such a severance of ties was unthinkable. That day, we faced an urgent and pressing matter – the protection and the promulgation of the constitutional reforms.

We guarded Ahmed Rıza for five days. Some days, we sat in smoky coffeehouses that stank of stale tobacco and listened, gathering as much information as we could, whilst on other days we mingled with the local traders and shop owners who were slowly reopening their stores. Some nights we stood guard on dark street corners staking out the neighbourhood, whilst on other nights we stood by the window, guns at the ready, on the lookout. It was tense, nervous, tiring and often frightening work but I can't complain as over those five days, I also had the chance to listen to Ahmed Rıza and his deeply powerful and moving ideas. Most of them I had already heard before but hearing them from him first hand was an altogether more riveting and educational experience.

When we were alone, he would speak French with me, and Fuad would often join in. On one occasion, they had a heated debate as to the respective merits of Shakespeare and Moliere, with Ahmed Rıza defending the Bard while Fuad fought on behalf of the Frenchman. Ahmed Rıza said that the success with which Shakespeare explored the depths and complexities of life and the human soul made him one of the greatest writers ever; Fuad, on the other hand, championed Moliere with a passion that bordered on fanaticism. He was unable to convince Ahmed Rıza and was so upset, he did not speak to either of us for the rest of the day, which wasn't so bad as it meant I was able to spend more time with the great man myself.

He told me about his time in Paris, and what he had been through there. He even shared with me some of his childhood memories and his memories of the Imperial High School. He also used to write poetry in his youth, and when he was around fifteen, one of his poems was put to music. Although not as much as the sciences, he still attached great importance to literature and the arts, and although he never said it openly, I don't think he really approved of my giving up on my dreams of becoming a writer. I can't say I wasn't surprised but events were unfolding so rapidly, life simply did not allow us to take a step back and reflect.

Eventually, five days later, Ahmed Rıza was moved to another, safer location in Yeşilköy. I still received updates about him but it would be years before I saw him in person again. I shall write about that too when the time is right, but not now. Six days after we moved Ahmed Rıza to his new location, the 'Army of Action', led by Hüseyin Hüsnü Paşa, arrived from Salonika and was at the walls of the capital. The time had come to bring to account the rebels that had held not just the city but liberty itself hostage for ten whole days.

I think I should stop now as the throbbing in my head is becoming unbearable. Or is it my eyes that are playing up? It must be my head as it seems to be exacerbated when I write… I think I'll take a break. I may even take a pill.

No Intention of Surrendering

Hello Ester (Noon, Day 6)

I fell asleep, right there on the *bergère*. I was knocked out, probably because of the pill I took, and was only eventually awoken by the ringing of the phone. I had no idea what time it was when I woke up. Was it past three? I hurriedly picked up the receiver. It was Ömer from reception.

'Hello sir. Reşit Bey wanted me to remind you that you were going to meet him at three in the lobby.'

'What time is it now?' I asked anxiously.

'It's still eleven, sir'.

It was a relief to hear it. I let out a deep breath, thanked him and put the receiver back down. I'd only slept for half an hour but after the fitful sleep I'd had last night, which was probably the cause of my earlier headache, I finally felt a little refreshed and revived. I went to the bathroom and washed my face, and then took out the clothes I'd be wearing for the meeting and lay them out on the bed. I was dying for a cup of coffee but did not want to trudge all the way downstairs to get one so I called to have one sent up. I then went out onto the balcony.

The rain hadn't started but there was a stiff breeze in the air whisking away the black clouds that had been hovering overhead earlier this morning. The morning sun, late to rise, was now shimmering pleasantly over the city's rooftops. Whether it was this glorious sunlight or my excitement at the prospect of seeing Cezmi again or the fact that my headache had disappeared I can't say but there was no trace of the morning's gloom and despair. I looked out in the direction of some noises in the distance; renovations were being carried out on the Tepebaşı Theatre. Seeing the theatre like that took me back… To 1906, the year I graduated from the Imperial High School and the year you came to Istanbul. I picked you up from Sirkeci Station that day, or rather, that evening and we went to the theatre, to a visiting French theatre company's production of *Cyrano de Bergerac*. It was a pretty standard performance but I couldn't have cared less as I was with you. I was so happy, I may as well have been watching the world's greatest actors and actresses giving the finest ever performance of that play. You, of course, did not feel the same.

'The actor in the role of Cyrano is terrible', you said with your usual bluntness. 'But then again, the play is so magnificent, his shortcomings are insignificant. Even this actor can be saved by the writer's poetic brilliance.'

They were the best four days I ever had in Istanbul. Not just in Istanbul, but the best four I've ever had anywhere. We were like a husband and wife blind to the world and the world was blind to us. In the mornings, I'd pick you up from your Aunt Lillia's and we'd spend the day wandering the streets of the city. Remember the ferry tour we took along the Bosphorus and then that boat trip up to Kağıthane? I never did tell you how blissful that day was for me. I was never able to tell you, just like all the countless other thoughts and feelings I have never been able to convey to you.

Anyway, as I stood there lost in my thoughts and memories, a knock on the door shook me out of my reverie. I went back inside. It was room service with my coffee. I gladly accepted the beverage, sat back in the armchair and drank, savouring each sip. I was actually dying to have a cigarette too but I ignored the cravings. I looked up at the clock. It was past eleven. I went back to my desk, picked up my pen and returned to my writing.

The rebellion in Istanbul broke out during the first days of spring. Redbuds were blooming into life all over the city – in the gardens of the old palaces, on the banks of the Golden Horn, on the doors of seaside mansions, in forgotten little

213

neighbourhood squares, in the cool courtyards of the mosques, in the forlorn cemeteries, on the hills leading down to the sea, and in the nooks and alcoves in the old city walls. They all seemed to be adorned with a sweet pinkish hue.

'The imperial flower', you used to say. 'That colour is the symbol of the Roman Empire. It is the colour of those that drank to victory with golden cups and who ruled with fabulous wealth gained through tyranny. It is the colour of treachery and murder...'

Yes, in the space of a single morning, when the city was undergoing yet another rebellion, to go along with the countless others that had broken out before, the imperial flower still bloomed, stubbornly and insistently, seemingly eager to reveal itself, even though fear gripped the blood-stained streets and the stench of gunpowder filled the air like a filthy, grimy cloud.

'It is a symbol of hope', Madam Melina said when she saw the flowers blossom in our garden. 'Whenever this tree is decked out in this way like a beautiful blushing bride, it always brings good news. All these troubles will soon be over, Şehsuvar Bey. Mark my words. They will soon be over. Very soon.'

She must have heard the news that the Army of Action had arrived. In the coffeehouses, the neighbourhood squares, on the streets and in the markets, everybody was talking feverishly about this new development, with equal measures of hope and trepidation, delight and worry. The people were scared; scared of new clashes breaking out, of shops and houses being looted, of being assaulted, attacked and killed. But at the same time, the news that the uprising, which had lasted days, may now be coming to an end was a source of hope for many, who wished for a return to normal life. While the people were caught up in this maelstrom of emotions, Mahmud Şevket Paşa was moving into new lodgings in Yeşilköy and personally taking over command from Hüseyin Hüsnü Paşa of the Army of Action.

As for the government and the parliament, they had been rendered redundant. All parliament could do now was busy itself reading out the telegraphs that were being sent in from all across the empire. Real power now lay with Mahmud Şevki Paşa, and those that grasped this new reality were quick to beat a path to his door. Everyday, a new delegation arrived seeking an audience: representatives from the palace and from parliament, journalists and representatives from the various minorities groups expressing concern over their safety and their properties... Two days before the operation began, parliament was moved to the building which housed the yacht club in Yeşilköy. Ahmed Rıza, who had resigned from his post ten days earlier, was now reinstated as speaker of parliament, along with Said Paşa, and during the very first session, there were demands for Abdülhamit to either abdicate or be deposed.

As for Abdülhamit himself, naturally he monitored the situation very closely and frequently sent communications to the relevant authorities insisting that he had had absolutely nothing to do with the uprising and that he remained true to his word regarding the constitutional reforms. One proposal by parliament was that the Army of Action not enter the city and that a committee be formed to negotiate with the rebels and persuade them to stand down but the proposal was rejected out of hand by Mahmud Şevki Paşa, who was stringent in his desire to see those that had brought fire, blood and death to the city pay the penalty. At the same time, knowing full well that the sultan still commanded a loyal battalion, he was careful to send a communiqué to the palace, stating that no harm would come to the sultan's person as he had had nothing to do with the uprising.

The *Hareket Ordusu*... The Army of Action... It was the force that upset the precarious balance that had been reached and a force in which the current President of the Republic, Mustafa Kemal, was a commander. When news filtered through that the Army of Action was on its way, the effects immediately began to be felt. The rebels sensed that the tide had turned and now it was simply a matter of time before this meaningless uprising would be crushed. 'Rebellions like this are like a litmus paper: these are the times when a society's true character comes through,' your Uncle Leon once said. And he was right. It was just as he said. In the face of overwhelming force, that sordid clutch of hypocrites vied with each other to see who could change their tune the quickest. The first was the press. The same papers that a mere eleven days earlier had been praising the rebels and their acolytes to the skies now turned on Derviş Vahdetî. *Volkan* newspaper described the approaching army as a liberating force, whilst the renegade deputies in parliament now sniffed around for a way to escape the country and find refuge abroad. As for the people of the city, they had begun to find their voice and now spoke out against the reactionaries that had held them captive.

And of course, our own group of *fedai* began making its own preparations for when the Army of Action would finally enter the city and crush the rebels. Once we had finalised Ahmed Rıza's transfer from his house in Şehzadebaşı to a safer location, Cezmi Kenan joined our team. At first, I found his brusque and gruff manner a little disconcerting and off-putting but once I got to know him, I realised he was a good, decent man who meant no harm and I began to warm to him. Nevertheless, when Basri Bey took me to one side one day and said, 'For the love of all things good, Şehsuvar, keep an eye on Cezmi. He's a good man, yes, and he's solid as a rock but he's also rigid and needlessly stubborn. He doesn't bend for anyone or anything, and we don't want that to compromise our mission,' I realised I needed to remain vigilant because our new task was to gather intelligence regarding the barracks.

First of all, we went to the army barracks in Davutpaşa to reconnoitre and to ascertain the soldiers' mood. We changed our outfits, discarding our fezzes and redingotes and replacing them with turbans so we would look more religious and conservative, like the insurgents. When I looked at myself in the mirror, I remember thinking how much you would have laughed had you seen me, but now, looking back, your reaction may have been much, much colder and sterner. Either way…

That morning, when we arrived at the barracks' gates, nobody suspected anything. The soldiers on duty were casually chatting away. They must have heard that the *Hareket Ordusu* was on its way but they did not seem too perturbed. Either they had not grasped the gravity of the situation or their fears had been allayed by their commanding officers, but whichever it was, they seemed calm enough and quite determined to defend their barracks. After staking out Davutpaşa, we went over to Taksim and sat in a park facing the barracks gathering as much information as we could. We saw a sergeant from the city of Konya in the park who was saying, 'If we defeat the army of infidels coming in from Rumelia, then victory shall truly be ours. If we are defeated, then we shall enter paradise waving the holy banner of our faith. There, at the gates of heaven, we shall be greeted by our Prophet, *sallallahu aleyhi ve sellem.*'

There was no fear in his eyes. He saw the approaching army as an army of infidels, with himself and his comrades as soldiers of the Prophet. For them, this was a religious struggle no less, a true holy war...

In the afternoon, we went to the barracks at Taşkışla. The soldiers there seemed at ease too and a corporal addressing the rank and file there also seemed hopeful like everybody else we had encountered that day.

'The Army of Action is nothing more than an ill-disciplined, ragtag band of cowards,' he roared. 'A marauding gang of Christians full of Bulgarians, Greeks and Armenians with not a single Muslim in their ranks. Just as our exalted forefathers put the Crusaders to the sword, so too shall we, with the grace of Allah, grind these infidels into dust.' Nobody spoke of the possibility of defeat or of surrender.

The next day, we went over to Beyazit, all the way down to the Ministry of War. Discipline there was still high as when we reached the gates, the soldier on guard pointed his rifle at us and said, 'Stop. Do not come any closer. This area is prohibited.'

'I'm here about my cousin, Seyfullah', Cezmi Bey began. 'We've been so worried. I just want to know he's okay.'

The frown on the soldier's face deepened and his response was even fiercer.

'What don't you understand about the word *prohibited*, eh? No closer. That's it.'

Other soldiers heard him and rushed to see what the commotion was. I saw little point in attracting attention or, worse, suspicion but Cezmi continued with his little act.

'But he's my cousin. We just want to know how he is', he went on. Basri Bey grabbed him by the arm and pulled him away.

'For God's sake Cezmi, stop it. Let's get out of here before things get nasty.'

After that, we walked along the Divan Yolu down to the Bab-ı Âli. Strict security precautions had been installed all around the government buildings, as well as around the Hagia Sophia. In the gardens of the Hagia Sophia, we spoke to a young madrasah student, still wet behind the ears.

'If I die, I'll die as a martyr. If we win, I shall see the Sharia implemented in our beautiful homeland with these worldly eyes. What else can a human being desire other than Allah?' Everybody else we met spoke in similar terms. 'If we win, we shall have liberated ourselves from those dirty lowlife servants of the Jewish masons and the Christian infidels. If we win, we shall pass through the gates of heaven.'

Leaving the Hagia Sophia, we went down to Dikimevi and from there onto Ahır Kapı station. We didn't see many soldiers down there, so that must have been the rebels' weak point. But apart from that, our conclusion was that the soldiers, the madrasah students and the others that had joined the mutiny were all willing to kill and be killed. Yes, they were anxious and worried but for one, the sultan had forgiven them, and on top of that, they also nurtured wild hopes that the sultan's First Army would come to their aid. If that were to happen, then the entire situation would be dramatically altered and the Army of Action would most definitely be routed. But of course, such a development was not on the cards. Whether it was because he was loath to have any more of his believers' blood spilled or because Mahmud Şevket Paşa had convinced him that no harm would come to him personally it was unclear, but either way, the sultan did not mobilise the divisions stationed at the palace.

The next day, we took the train to Halkalı, where the army headquarters had been set up in the Veterinary College building and where Major Muhtar Bey welcomed us. Standing over a large map of the city, we relayed all the information we had while he made detailed notes in a large, yellowing notebook. Basri Bey explained the situation and the mood in the various barracks and drew him a diagram showing the points through which the army could enter the city.

'The army should attack all the barracks simultaneously', Basri Bey said. 'Rami, Davutpaşa, the Ministry of War, the area around the Hagia Sophia, and the barracks in Taksim, Taşkışla and Selimiye – all must be attacked and neutralised simultaneously, otherwise resistance will grow and they will run to one another's assistance.'

Cezmi agreed.

'Absolutely. The attack must be swift, overwhelming and decisive. They shouldn't be given a chance to get their breaths back. We should take over the barracks before they even know what has hit them.'

And they were right. Absolutely right. However, the victory would not be as easy as they assumed. Yes, the rebels had been stunned by the impending arrival of the Army of Action but they had been quick to overcome their fears, and their leaders had not been idle – their spokespeople, imams and preachers had infiltrated the army and had been trying to twist the minds of the soldiers that were on our side, telling them that they were being deceived and that the approaching army was not a Muslim army but one of infidels, and that if they won, they would kill the sultan. 'They are trying to destroy our religion', they would say. 'If they win, there will be no Sharia and no caliph'. And so, before a shot had even been fired, the psychological battle had begun.

We visited the army command centre at Halkalı to pass on the intelligence we had gathered to Muhtar Bey no less than three times before the Army of Action finally entered the city. He expressed his gratitude each time, but he also seemed to grow more and more despondent on each visit. He had been on the front line ever since the rebellion had broken out and seeing how intense and serious the threat was, he had come to realise that quashing the uprising would not be an easy task. Unfortunately, the outbreak of hostilities was now simply a matter of time. The shedding of blood had become an inevitability but it was the price we had to pay if we were going to secure victory.

Finally, the moment arrived. The army sprang into action late on a Saturday night, eleven days after the mutiny had started. The city awoke before the morning call to prayer to the sound of guns. Bakırköy was the first to fall: after a short skirmish with the soldiers on duty at the ammunitions depot there, our people were in control of the area. The Davutpaşa Barracks were a different story. The engagement there was a long and protracted affair. The mounted cavalry corps that day had been to the palace and on the way back had run into the Army of Action. They immediately opened fire but when our side responded with cannons, they could not sustain their offensive and retreated to beyond the city walls, thus surrendering Davutpaşa to our forces.

However, the rebels had no intention of surrendering. Eventually their retaliation came, with shots fired at the division that had entered via Edirnekapı in front of the Fatih Police Headquarters. When the fire was returned, the madrasah students and soldiers that had taken up positions at the windows of the mosque immediately entered the fray but they were reckless and unprepared and when, after a sustained exchange of gunfire, they realised they would not be able to hold out much longer, they fled, leaving their dead behind.

What was most surprising was the situation at the Ministry of War, where the hero and champion of our freedom, Niyazi Bey of Resen, was alongside Major Fethi Bey of the Chief of Staff. Fethi Bey was commanding our forces there and he called out to the mutinying soldiers:

'You are not to blame here and you shall not be punished. The soldiers facing you are your comrades and your brothers. How can you possibly raise arms against your own brothers?'

And so, with these words, the ministry was subdued and retaken without a single shot having to be fired. Nevertheless, when some volunteers from Resen singled out one officer whom they suspected of incitement to revolt and shot him in front of the others, the soldiers who had already surrendered grew extremely nervous. When Niyazi Bey heard of what had happened, he gave strict orders to his men that if such actions were to be taken, they were to be taken far away and out of sight so as maintain order and prevent hostilities from resuming.

The forces stationed in and around the Hagia Sophia, consisting primarily of volunteers, had arrived that morning at Ahıkapı Station on a darkened train and had reached the square without meeting any resistance, thanks to the intelligence we had provided. Some shots were fired from the courthouse but when fire was returned with even greater intensity from our side, the rebels chose to surrender. The more serious fighting would occur in and around the Bab-ı Âli buildings, and there was a commensurate loss of life on both sides.

As for the little reconnaissance outfit that consisted of Basri Bey, Captain Cezmi, Lieutenant Fuad and myself, we were to join Major Muhtar Bey's forces. Well before sunrise, we took up our positions in the gardens of a mansion in Şişli and huddled down for the long wait. Eventually, when dawn approached and the blackness of night began to turn grey, we heard it. First was the barking of dogs, then a clatter and the neighing of horses, some barked commands, a few snatches of conversation, words exchanged here and there, and then, finally, emerging from a vast cloud of smoke, was the legendary fighting unit we had been expecting for days: the *Hareket Ordusu*. The division we saw was under Enver Bey's command but we also saw Muhtar Bey amongst the troops, cutting a magnificent figure atop his steed. Their mission was to retake Taşkışla whilst ours was to engage with the Topçu Barracks in Taksim. We were buoyed and ready, optimistic and full of hope, with absolute faith and trust in ourselves and in our friends and comrades. None of us entertained the possibility of defeat. The first news to come through bolstered ours and the troops' spirits even further, with Muhtar Bey even going so far as to tease our crew by saying, 'Your intelligence was way off the mark, Basri Bey. One or two shots of a rifle and one shot from the cannon and this band of ragamuffins that call themselves soldiers would have run for the hills.'

But he spoke too early. When we were marching past the Military Academy, all hell broke loose. Bullets began raining down from the windows of the academy and many men were killed with many others wounded but the division did not panic. Enver Bey's unit was the first to respond and a vicious exchange of fire soon began. It lasted minutes and wounded many more. When the rebel soldiers realised they were up against some serious firepower and that they were not up to the fight, they downed guns and fled in the direction of the Armenian Cemetery. A few others sought refuge in the barracks at Taşkışla, which is where the real fighting was to occur.

Their inability to defeat us spurred us on and we marched to Taksim, bristling with confidence in ourselves, our weapons and our men. The people of the city had long since woken up and were waiting with their hearts in their mouths to see who would come out on top in this terrible factional infighting, this struggle between brothers. When the guns stopped, they came out onto the streets to welcome us, waving their banners, and we marched on to the sound of cheers and shouts of praise. Everybody was intoxicated by our victory, as though all the barracks had been retaken, as though the last rebel had surrendered, and a sense of comfort and accompanying negligence began to seep into our troops. It was an ominous sign and something that should have been countered, but at the same time, we did not want to destroy the troops' morale. The men we lost in Taksim Gardens was the price we paid for that negligence and that overconfidence.

Yes, the attack began as our march was nearing the Topçu Barracks. As we prepared to surround the barracks, machine guns nestling amongst the historic flowerbeds of the Taksim Gardens exploded into action, spewing deathly fire in our direction. Two officers and around twenty privates on the front line fell at once and Muhtar Bey's commands rang out across the battlefield.

'Take cover! At the foot of the walls, behind the mounds, behind the gates… Take cover! Do not stay in the open! Everyone, find a safe place!"

It was not just Muhtar Bey; Senior Captain Servet was out there rallying the troops in preparation for an offensive. The soldiers and the officers now knew that this was not a drill but a real and bloody battle. We secured the area around the training grounds and then surrounded the barracks. We were itching to plunge into the foray, especially Cezmi Bey, but Muhtar Bey held him back, sternly rebuking him and saying, 'We have all been given different tasks so I would kindly request that you do not place yourselves in danger unless absolutely necessary.'

It's easy to say but not so easy to follow when machine guns are mowing your friends down. The four of us were crouching behind a carriage whose horses had been killed in the exchange, guns at the ready. We were trying to find a way to respond to the gunfire coming down at us from the heavy artillery in the Taksim Gardens but our pistols were nowhere near enough. Captain Cezmi disappeared at one point but soon returned with four rifles and some extra ammunition.

'These pistols won't do anything but tickle them from this distance', he said and handed out the rifles. 'But these beauties will definitely wake them up!'

He was quite right too but there was a small problem – I had never held a rifle before in my life. Luckily, Fuad came to my rescue and quickly told me what and where the key parts were and how to load and fire it. When I looked at him in despair, he laughed and said, 'Just pull the trigger and to hell with it. Even if you don't hit anybody, at least you'll make some noise. Better than nothing, eh?'

And so I did. I pulled the trigger, not knowing or caring where or what I hit. The same can't be said of Basri Bey, Fuad and – especially – Captain Cezmi. Wherever they aimed their rifles, they caused mayhem and panic. Three turbaned men fell down dead in front of my eyes as a result of their steady eyes. By now, the rest of the troops had rallied and had started to return fire. It looked as though things were going our way. Our forces – ordered, disciplined and trained in tactics and battle – were routing the enemy and the number of dead bodies on the ground around the Taksim Gardens' iron railings was mounting with each passing minute. Realising they were about to be defeated and their lives snuffed out, the remaining rebels – from where they found it, I don't know – waved a white piece of cloth in the air.

'Don't shoot…. Don't shoot… We surrender…'

At that moment, another mistake was made. When our lads stood up without any precautionary measures to accept the surrender and move in to apprehend the rebels, the shooting from within the barracks resumed and more men were lost. We returned fire. A number of rebels, sensing an opportunity, headed for the gates hoping to escape, and many fell lifeless to the ground before they could reach safety. The shedding of blood and the loss of life turned the anger and the enmity on both sides into open hatred. Muhtar Bey gave the order to fire at will and soon the air was filled with the howl, the roar and the shriek of machine gun and rifle fire. Still our weapons were not enough; the Topçu Barracks were sound and the men stationed within had taken up such strong positions that it was all but impossible to hurt them.

'The cannons!' Cezmi Bey bellowed from his position on the ground. 'Why aren't we using the cannons?'

Just then, as though it had been waiting for his command, there was an almighty clap of thunder and the ground trembled. The sound really was incredible. Even though the cannons were not aimed at us, we curled up in the foetal position and stuck our fingers in our ears. I had never felt so scared in my life. This truly was a battle; war in its raw form. The cannonballs ripped through the walls of the barracks, causing massive casualties. And then, suddenly, they stopped. Silence fell over the area. Basri Bey and I exchanged glances.

'Why aren't they returning with cannon fire of their own?' I asked anxiously. 'These are the barracks, after all. They must have cannons inside.'

He gave a wolfish grin.

'Our lads took care of that', he chuckled.

None of the cannons inside had been used as the officers stationed there that were sympathetic to our cause had defused them all.

The silence did not last long though as our cannons soon resumed their grisly symphony, raining fire and death onto the barracks without pause or mercy for what seemed like an age until Muhtar Bey gave the command.

'Cease fire! Cease fire!'

Silence again… Smoke and dust rising from the walls of the barracks and the acrid stench of gunpowder on the spring breeze… Shattered, mangled corpses on the ground, young men's lives snuffed out by their brothers' bullets. Perhaps it was this ghastly and bloody scene and his reluctance for more blood to be shed that made Muhtar Bey intervene, even though he shouldn't have as in battle, there is only one objective and that is to win. If, in war, you are not ready to incur losses, then this can only lead to defeat. Nevertheless, Muhtar Bey, like most of us, faced a dilemma – even if they had been firing at us, the men inside that garrison were still soldiers in his army, and it was this thought that led him to err. Without speaking to anybody, without first consulting anybody, he suddenly rose to his feet. Perhaps he thought he could put an end to the fighting and persuade those men to lay down their arms, like Fethi Bey had during the skirmish at the Ministry of War. Perhaps he thought could put an end to the bloodshed and stop even more soldiers, even more sons of the soil, from being needlessly chopped down.

'What the hell is he doing?' Cezmi Bey seethed. 'They'll shoot him! For God's sake man, get down! Get down!'

Muhtar Bey did not even hear him and he began walking towards the barracks. The four of us watched on with our hearts in our mouths. At first, he seemed to falter but he soon found his belief and after a few metres he strode on more assuredly. Strangely enough, those inside the barracks were also bewildered by this move. Not a sound came out from within, not a word, not even a single shot. As he neared the main gate, we also began to grow in confidence.

'Well, I'll be damned, he's going to do it', Basri Bey whispered next to me, but Fuad and I were so on edge that we couldn't say anything in response. As for Cezmi, his chin was resting on the muzzle of his rifle, his mouth working away nervously as he furiously chewed his lower lip. To tell the truth, the four of us were becoming increasingly hopeful. Even Cezmi Bey seemed to sense a shift in fortune. And then it happened. A bang. The sound of a rifle shot, then another, and then another, and then a hail of bullets. Muhtar Bey staggered back and then collapsed onto his right side. There was another silence, this one far deeper, far heavier than the previous one, and then Basri Bey's roar filled the air.

'Bastards! Attack! Attack! Show these fiends no mercy!"

We leapt out from our positions behind the carriage and ran at the barracks. We no longer cared about death or about being hit; we were just soldiers trying to reach our target. The rest of the company opened fire, and not just with cannons but with pistols, rifles and anything else that could be classed as a weapon. They were all now aimed at the barracks and the inferno that was unleashed was so heavy and so intense that those inside the garrison did not even have time to surrender. As we stormed through the gate, they tried to raise the white flag over their shattered flagpole but it was too late – only more death can appease soldiers who have just seen their comrades mown down.

That day, for the first time, I saw how wild, how savage and how thirsty for blood man can be. And no, I won't go into details about what happened. Not because I have anything to hide either, although there is much I have that should remain hidden. Nor shall I try to distance myself from all those other fallen sinners, as I too was amongst them. I won't lie – I was a part of a deranged pack that tore into its prey with rifles, pistols and bayonets, attacking, hacking and killing in a mad lust for revenge. Whatever they did, I did too.

But this much I will say: whether it was because of exhaustion or someone pushing me I don't know but at one point, I stumbled and fell to the ground. Military boots trampled over me and bloody, lifeless bodies toppled onto me until eventually, all that was left was the sky. A beautiful blue sky: clear, cloudless and pristine. It was less like the sky and more like a mirror, showing us not our faces but our souls. And that is when I felt the remorse. Remorse, regret and a deep, abiding shame that made my face turn red, a red deeper than the one that stained my hands. I felt ashamed of my life and my existence, and ashamed to be human.

It didn't last long as Captain Cezmi's face soon appeared, blocking out the sky.

'What's happened here then, Şehsuvar? You hit?'

All that I had seen and experienced I wiped from my mind. The sounds, colours and smells that had been tormenting me and my conscience, the faces of the youngsters whose blood were staining my hands; all were smothered and silenced. With invisible hands, I strangled the sense of shame enveloping my soul, the unbearable remorse threatening to engulf me and the newfound sense of mercy that was beginning to awake within, me and I leapt to my feet.

'Nothing, Captain. I just fell. That's all.'

A Man's Word Is His Honour

Hello Ester (Afternoon, Day 6)

The Captain Cezmi I met up with today was the same Captain Cezmi I had once fought alongside in the attack on the Taksim Barracks and against the Italians in Libya. It was strange, as though the intervening years had barely touched that stubborn old man. His hairs had barely started greying; there were just a few strands of silver here and there and one or two wrinkles, that's all. And yet this was the same man that had been there with us during our victories and defeats and had experienced even more tragedy in Libya, the Balkans and Gallipoli. He had seen the full horror of war with his own eyes and felt all its ignominy and its shame in his bones and yet there was no sadness or despair in his eyes, nor was there a sense of defeat or remorse about him. The way he spoke, it was as though we were the victors. And this was not an attempt to deceive us, or himself; he spoke with conviction and with a firm belief in every word he uttered. True, for some time, the country had lost its mind and lost its way but that would soon be brought to an end. Not by him, of course, but by patriots such as our-selves assuming the reins of power once more. Listening to him was unbelievable: he really did live in the past, and, to be pre-cise, in those first uncertain but heady days when war had just been declared and we were swept away by the delusion that we would end up victorious…

Wait, I'm sorry, I'm digressing. Cezmi Bey actually did have some important information for me, especially about you…

It may not have been the truth but it was still exciting… The hope that I may still see you again… See, I'm doing it again, getting things all mixed up… I told you I did not have what it takes to be a writer. What I should say first I say last… Anyway, back to where we were. I was telling you how we captured the Topçu Barracks in Taksim but then I had to stop because of my scheduled meeting with Reşit and our planned visit to Cezmi Bey. I took the elevator downstairs to the lobby. Reşit was down there waiting for me. He rose to his feet when he saw me and took his watch out of his waistcoat pocket.

'Exactly three o'clock', he remarked. 'That's what I like about you old CUP guys. You're always so punctual. My father was the same. He would always be there on time. The stated time and place were the time and place he would be there.'

I extended a hand.

'And so it should be, my friend, because a man's word is his honour.'

He put the watch back in his pocket and shook my hand warmly.

'The car is waiting for us outside. We can leave whenever you like.'

The poor guy was so naïve, he had no idea as to how dangerous our little expedition could be. He was, after all, an accomplice to a meeting between two ex-CUP members and I needed him to know this and warn him of the dangers but I couldn't do it without meeting Cezmi first. I needed to gather as much information as I could about Mehmed Esad; only then could I take Reşit to one side and let him know about the potential dangers he was putting himself in. As such, I did not ask him have the car pick us up from the service entrance as this would have caused him unnecessary alarm. If we were going to be followed, then so be it. Not that I cared. After all, Cezmi and I went back a long way – what could be more natural than two old friends getting together? Of course, I was fooling myself. In an age when even the most innocent of get-togethers could be seen as an underground gathering with evil designs, Şehsuvar Sami being seen speaking to Cezmi

Kenan could be seen as a meeting to discuss nothing less than an assassination attempt. If throughout all this, Cezmi had yet to be apprehended and taken inside, then it must have been because he was no longer seen as a threat and was considered a harmless eccentric. That, at any rate, was my hope. If that was not the case, then there was little I could do anyway, and the risk had to be taken.

Nevertheless, as we were leaving the hotel, I still had a quick look around to see if there was anything or anyone suspicious in the vicinity. Everything looked in order; there was no sign of the team that had been following me before, nor was there a sign of any other suspicious activity. I kept my eye out during the journey too, without letting Reşit realise, to see if we were being followed but I saw nothing unusual.

The wooden house Cezmi was staying in in Langa was almost a twin to the house in Beşiktaş Madam Melina had bequeathed to me, although the garden, replete with an impressive array of walnut, mulberry and plum trees, was larger than mine. In front of the house was a well with a tin covering, behind which was a huge woodshed. Captain Cezmi was standing in front of the house waiting for us and as soon as he saw us, he leapt up and opened up his arms.

'Şehsuvar, my brother, finally! Together at last! God bless the man that brought you to me! Tell me, how long has it been?'

'It's been a long time, Captain', I said, embracing him in return. 'A long time indeed. I have not seen you since our last congress. I have been keeping abreast of developments and your heroic escapades during the occupation of Istanbul have been on everybody's lips.'

He blushed, almost like a child.

'Most of it embellished, my friend, I'm sure. You know how our people love to make up stories.' He gestured to the divan on the veranda. 'Please, do sit down. This place is just wonderful in the afternoons. Can't get enough of it, one really can't.' He saw the parcels Reşit was holding. 'Again, Reşit? What have you brought me this time? Didn't I tell you not to go to all this trouble? Thankfully, I have everything I need.' As we prepared to take our seats on the divan, he turned to me and said, 'This Reşit is a fine man. A real good lad, he is. Treats me almost like a father. Such generosity and devotion he shows. Not at all necessary but there you go.'

'Don't say that, Uncle Cezmi', Reşit replied gallantly. 'I made a promise to my father. 'If anything happens to me, Cezmi will be your father and you will respect and honour him the way you honour and respect me. Otherwise I shall disown you from the beyond, you hear me?' Those were his exact words. To the letter. All I am doing is honouring the wishes of my late father.''

Our retired captain waved him lovingly away.

'He's stubborn, just like his father. His old man was a man of his word, no matter what, right to the bitter end. A good, decent man and a man of principle. Tell me, did you know him, old Yusuf the rifleman? Did you ever get to meet him?'

I nodded my head as though the very question was an affront.

'How could I not know him? Captain Yusuf was our neighbour. He was a good friend to my late father…'

'Of course, yes. Now I remember. Your houses were on the same street.' He grabbed a wooden stool and sat opposite me. 'We talked about it in Libya, if I remember correctly. Before you were wounded…' His face darkened. 'I really thought you were done for that day. You were bleeding heavily from your left side. I thought you'd been hit in the heart.'

I crossed my legs.

'It wasn't that bad. It just looked bad, that's all.'

He took out a silver cigarette case bearing an engraving of Salonika's White Tower, flicked open the lid and offered me a smoke.

'Here, light one up. These are from Kavala. You know, those scented cigarettes.'

For a moment, I thought about taking one and lighting up but I stopped.

'Thanks, but I think I'll decline. But that's a lovely cigarette box, by the way. Did you get it in Salonika?'

There was a faint flicker of sadness in his green eyes.

'It's from Salonika, yes, but I didn't buy it. It was a gift from our Basri.'

He took out a cigarette and then showed me the inside of the lid. 'Do you see what's written here?'

I took it and read the engraving.

To my friend and brother Cezmi Kenan... Long live liberty, equality and fraternity! 23 July 1908.

'A memento from the constitutional years?' I said, handing it back.

'That's right', he answered, taking a deep drag on his cigarette. 'He gave it to me the day the constitutional era was declared. God bless his soul, he was a great man, Basri. A truly great man.'

The melancholy was broken by Reşit asking us if we would like some coffee.

'For crying out loud, Reşit', Cezmi growled. 'Sit yourself down, will you? I'll make the coffee.' He stopped and turned to me. 'Coffee or would you like something cold? I've just made some fresh compote with Damson plums from my own garden. Nice and refreshing. It goes down well.'

'Thank you sir, coffee will be fine', I said.

'Great!' Reşit said. 'I'll make the coffees. One plain, and one with sugar.'

Cezmi was growing irate at Reşit's eagerness to please.

'Reşit', he grumbled. 'I thought I told you to...'

'It's no trouble at all, Captain', I said, gesturing for him to sit. 'Don't mind Reşit. He's one of us. Let him make the coffee. He doesn't mind. It will give us a chance to talk.'

'Very well, let's talk', he said, seeing I was keen for us to be alone. He took another drag on his cigarette. 'So, I hear that rat Mehmed Esad has paid you a visit, eh?'

We were finally getting down to business, which, frankly, was a relief.

'Why do you call him a rat?'

'Because he is one', he answered, flicking the ash from his cigarette away. 'He's a traitor. That rat, that *cockroach*, was working for the English.'

I pretended to be amazed.

'But sir, that is a serious allegation. Do we have anything to back up such a serious accusation?'

His face went red with anger.

'Back up? I saw it with my own eyes. My own eyes! The man sold us out, pure and simple. This was when we were in the *Karakol Cemiyeti* during the occupation of Istanbul sending arms to the National Resistance Movement in Anatolia. Back then, there was this English officer we knew called Barney. Barney Stevenson. A colonel, he was. Red hair, red moustache, grey eyes. The man worshipped money. We had a deal with him whereby he would supply us with guns from the armoury at Maçka and have them delivered on a French vessel called the *Ararat* to the Kuruçeşme Coal Yard. You know, the standard procedure with the ammo hidden under the coal to avoid detection. Only three people in the world knew about the deal: myself, Colonel Stevenson and Mehmed Esad. But during the first call to prayer on the morning of the Thursday the ship was scheduled to set off from Kuruçeşme with the weapons on board, the English turned up and stormed the ship. The ship's crew were caught with their pants down and after a skirmish on board, five of our boys were killed and the rest of the crew, the captain included, were captured. You'd think it was Barney Stevenson behind it all but it wasn't because the English had already arrested him the previous day, which means somebody else must have betrayed us, and seeing as it wasn't me, it could only have been Mehmed Esad.'

It seems he had forgotten about the crew members themselves or the workers at the coal yard. Once the English high command got wind of how our arms were to be delivered to the Anatolian interior, they were quick to hire informers in the shipping companies, the coal mines and other such commercial enterprises and when they couldn't hire informers, they had their own agents infiltrate those organisations, which is probably how they found out about the munitions delivery that was to take place. Not that I said any of this aloud to my old commanding officer as I did not want to upset him.

'Did you tell the Committee?'

He took another deep drag and then smiled impishly.

'No, I went one better. I took my trusty old Luger and went over to that rat's house in Tavuk Uçmaz Street to sort him out. Unfortunately, I didn't kill him. He managed to get away with a bullet to his left leg.'

It was Cezmi Kenan to a tee. No questions, no inquiries and no investigation: just shoot the man, no questions asked.

'And what did the Committee have to say about that?'

His face fell.

'What do you think? They said there was not enough evidence, for one, and on top of that, they said firing at another of our officers without their permission was wholly unacceptable. In short, in their eyes, I was the one at fault. Again. Can you believe it? The man was responsible for the loss of all that ammunition, the capture of dozens of our men and the death of five more and I was the one that got the book thrown at him!'

It was just as I had guessed. All the rumours about Mehmed Esad were baseless and unfounded. There had been many such rumours flying around during the occupation, the most famous of which was the rumour that an Ottoman officer going under the name of 'Silent John' was working as a spy and informer for the British forces. We even blamed him for my arrest and incarceration. Whenever we were raided, whenever one of our meetings was located and attacked, whenever a ship carrying weapons for us was seized, the name on everyone's lips was Silent John, the man whose real identity we never learnt. He was slowly turning into a myth, so much so that we soon began to think that there really was no such character and that he had been conjured up out of thin air by the British secret service to demoralise the resistance and break our spirits. The story Cezmi was telling us was of the same type, a story without any rhyme or reason. Had our movement had real misgivings about Mehmed Esad, they would not have given up their investigations into him so quickly. Being accused of working as a spy for the English was not an accusation that one shook off lightly.

'The biggest disappointment was the top dogs abandoning the country,' Captain Cezmi went on, who was now getting in the mood and opening up. 'How can people abandon their country and their people just like that? They should not have gone. Remember the last congress? We were both there. Talat should not have resigned, not from the Committee, or from the government. But he did, and others followed suit, and now look at the state we're in. The country has been left in the hands of third-rate people with third-rate minds. People who we once deemed unsuitable and laughed off as incompetent are now hunting *us* down. They are standing over us and judging *us*. If things carry on like this, they'll kill us all, one by one.'

He was now speaking so loudly that for a minute I felt I had gone back in time to the days when the implementation of the constitution had just been announced and when our speakers were on the street corners extolling the need and the necessity for liberty, equality, brotherhood and justice. To tell the truth, I was a little frightened that somebody passing by would hear us and go to the authorities. If that were to happen...

'Don't worry, Captain. It will all come good in the end. Just give it time. The truth will find its way out, eventually.'

'Like hell it will', he said angrily, stubbing his cigarette out in the ashtray. 'So we should all just sit down, should we, and let truth find its own way, eh? Is that it? That's not how it works, brother Şehsuvar. We need to fight for it. It's the only way. We shall dig up our weapons from where we have buried them and we shall fight, to the death if need be. Yes, to the death. If we have to, we shall die. As it is, one way or another, these bastards will make sure we go down. Look at Karabekir Paşa. They may have released him, yes, but they are constantly on his case, breathing down his neck, waiting for the chance to put the noose around his neck, waiting for him to stumble so they can string him up. And there's no need to smirk like that because they'll do the same to you too, and to me. They'll hang us both. They might even think hanging too good for the likes of us. See what they did to Kara Kemal? Killed him and stuffed him in a chicken coop. No, no, no, it's clear what has to be done. We need to be ruthless, just like we were in the good old days. Bring down the man at the very top. That's what you have to do.' I could see the hatred blazing in his narrowed green eyes. 'Those idiots in Izmir messed the whole thing up. But don't you worry, we'll sort it out in Istanbul! Why do you look so shocked? You know what I'm talking about. Yes, Mustafa Kemal. The president. None of us will ever be at ease in this country while he is still around. That's why he doesn't come to Istanbul, see? Because he's frightened of us.'

He had never really had the strongest grasp of reality but I think now he had lost the plot entirely.

'No more deaths, Uncle Cezmi, please!' Reşit said, bringing a tray bearing three cups of hot, foamy coffee. 'Enough lives were sacrificed during the Great War. No more.'

But Cezmi's mind was set.

'I'm afraid this is how things are done, son', he said. 'The war may be over but the struggle goes on.'

'Just look at the froth on these coffees', I offered, wanting to change the subject. 'You really are a dab hand, aren't you, Reşit?'

He beamed with pride.

'Actually, I'm not that bad when it comes to the kitchen, Şehsuvar ağabey. My mother was often ill, as you may recall, and there was no daughter in the house so the cooking fell to me. I had no choice but to learn. I even did an apprenticeship back in Salonika during the school holidays, in Mikhailidis' restaurant. You remember his place. It was on the same street as that law firm you used to work in.'

Cezmi took a slurp of his coffee, reached once more for his cigarette case with the engraving of the White Tower and lit one up. As the smoke swirled around us, he peered at me.

'That's it. I've been racking my brains all this time trying to remember what it was I wanted to tell you, Şehsuvar. That Jewish guy, the owner of that law office Reşit just mentioned. He was one of us, a member of the Committee…'

'You mean Uncle Leon?' I said, sitting bolt upright.

'That's the one. The very same. They said he was a mason or what have you but he turned out to be a communist. Anyway, whatever he was, this Monsieur Leon had a niece, I believe. A red-haired girl. A bit mental. A wild one. You were always hanging out with her.'

'You mean Ester?' I asked. My heart was in my mouth.

'Ester, Ester! That's it. That was her name, wasn't it? Ester?' My newly awakened curiosity could have killed me.

'What about her? What's happened to her?'

He shrugged and said, 'Oh, nothing's happened to her. Nothing like that. Seems she's in Istanbul, that's all.'

I could not have hoped for more wonderful news.

'She's here? In Istanbul? Are you sure?'

He was rather taken aback at my sudden interest.

'Well, I haven't seen her myself. Cafer told me. You remember Çolak Cafer, don't you? The guy with one arm? He lost an arm after being tortured by the British during the occupation. Went gangrenous, it did. Had it to have it cut off. He wasn't an officer but you knew him. He was from Salonika too, like us. Told me the other day that he'd seen Monsieur Leon's niece in Beyazit wandering around the bookshops.'

Once he said bookshops, I knew it had to be you. They may have mistaken somebody else for Monsieur Leon and the 'niece' they mentioned could have been any other young woman but when they said a Jewish girl from Salonika browsing the bookshops, then it couldn't have been anybody but you. I started peppering him with questions, not even bothering to hide my sudden interest.

'So where is she now? Does Cafer know her address? Is he going to see her again?'

He put his coffee down and held a hand up in the air.

'Hold on, hold on. Calm down a second. That much I don't know. Yes, he spoke to Monsieur Leon too. He told me he went to some place in Galata or something, somewhere like that, but I've forgotten now. But Cafer has the address. 'At the end of the day, he's a Salonika man', he said. 'Jewish or Muslim, makes no difference, he's still one of us and we have to extend a helping hand however we can.' I know you and her had a thing going back in the day so I thought I'd mention it to you but I forgot all about it. Thanks to Reşit here, I remembered.'

Just a few seconds ago, I saw Cezmi Kenan as a lunatic spewing out a non-stop stream of gibberish but now I was hanging on to his every word.

'So tell me, where can I find Cafer?'

His eyes lit up in surprise.

'So she really is that important to you, eh? Well then, it's lucky I mentioned her. If I had known, I'd have mentioned her earlier.'

'Please, Captain Cezmi, sir, where can I find Çolak Cafer?'

He stubbed out his cigarette and shook his head.

'Well, you can't go and find him just like that. Like the rest of us, he's keeping a very low profile nowadays. But don't you worry. He'll turn up eventually. Tomorrow, the day after, soon. Pop round a couple of days from now and I'll have her address for you.'

Actually, I had not been thinking of visiting him again as in his state of mind, he would have just gotten us both into a whole heap of trouble but now you were in the picture, things had changed.

'Very well', I said jubilantly. 'I'll be here in two days'.

An Inappropriate Sense of Compassion

Good Night, Ester (Night, Day 6)

If what I learnt from Captain Cezmi this afternoon turns out to be true, soon I won't need to write to you and what's more, I may also get to leave this hotel. If what he said was true and you have decided to come to Istanbul, then that means you are looking for me. It means you have not been able to find happiness over there and that you have decided to move to my city and with your family too... Well, with what remains of your family. Only your Uncle Leon and your father, Monsieur Naum, remain and I do not think your father would readily leave Paris or the university in which he lectures to come to Istanbul. Perhaps it is just you and Uncle Leon, him leaving Salonika and you leaving Paris. Whatever the case, I shall soon know. I don't remember having felt joy like this in a long, long time.

So yes, perhaps I no longer need to write to you but for some reason I can't help myself. It's as though I come to this room solely to write. No other habit or activity has any importance. So no, I won't stop writing. Even if we get together again and live together, this pen shall not fall from my hand.

Live together? Dear me, will you look at that! My imagination has already started running wild...

This evening I ate alone. Reşit had to go home, as he wanted to spend the evening with his family, the poor guy, so I had some mushroom soup, a salad and a *keşkül* before coming back to the room.

I would like to return to the past, if I may, to the accursed and shameful days of the uprising when the streets of this beautiful city were awash with blood – blood that had been shed by brothers no less – and to the period immediately after that uprising, when death had left such a profound and ghastly impression on me. Yes, I'm talking about the assassination of Şemsi Paşa. The hesitation I felt after we shot those three Albanian bodyguards, the pangs of conscience, the sudden and overwhelming sense of mercy; I never thought I would experience those feelings again. It was not one of those moments in which when I realised it, it was too late, no, it was simply a case of short-lived moral and mental confusion. I was raw and inexperienced and nowhere near hardened enough, and I had suddenly been thrown into the middle of a vicious and terribly real battle. Not a one-on-one bar fight but a real battle, not one suited to a rookie like me. Of course, even more terrible encounters awaited me in the future, encounters in which any hesitation on my part could have proved fatal. I needed to learn so that when the nation needed me, my hand would be steady.

That is what I willed, and that is what all the others said – Basri Bey, Fuad, my comrades in arms, all of them. We had beaten the mutineers, decisively and speedily. The nightmare scenarios of which were all afraid had not come true: Abdülhamit had not ordered his army to turn on us and the palace's Second Division had not fought back. The palace had fallen and without a shot being fired from within. The following day, the mutineers' last bastion, the Selimiye Barracks, raised the white flag and our victory was complete. The constitution would be reinstated and this time for good. Of course, there would be a price to pay; blood would flow and people would pay with their lives. That is what happened during the French Revolution and it would happen again with us. If only that same nightmare had not kept haunting me every time I lay my head down on my pillow.

It was around that time that I first began to have that reoccurring nightmare that for years would wake me up in the middle of the night. When I lay down to sleep exhausted after those two days of bloody fighting... I've written to you before about this nightmare. I am being dragged blindfolded down a corridor in Salonika to an initiation ceremony for the party... Voices whisper around me, but I cannot tell if they are the voices of the living or the dead... The whispers that make my hairs stand on end and send shivers down my spine. And then there is the council that initiates me into the organisation. It's almost like a play, the audience seated around me in concentric circles watching, accusing and condemning me. They may not say it but they hate me. I can feel it. Perhaps it is all the more explicit because they don't verbalise it. And then, out of the blue, you appear and you stare at me, emptily. No smile, no words, nothing. Just that empty stare. And then your gaze slides down to an object on the table in front of me. I follow your gaze. Next to the flag and a copy of the *Quran*, a shiny object. A Gasser M1870 revolver. Without a flicker of recognition or emotion in your eyes, you reach out for the gun. You pick it up and point it at me. The whispers increase. Again, they don't say it but the expectation is there. The anticipation. It is obvious what they want. They want you to pull the trigger and take my life. And I can sense its inherent justice, which is why I do not feel any fear. I feel just a profound sadness, a stabbing at my heart, and shock at how much you seem to despise me. I want you to pull that trigger and end this pain immediately. Then there is the wait, the hesitation appearing in your dark eyes, a bitter smile forming on your lips... And then your unexpected move, that dreadful moment... You turning the gun onto your temple... Me reaching out in horror and shouting 'Don't!' The lack of emotion on your face as you pull the trigger... And then I wake up.

It was back then that I first began to have this nightmare, and it still hasn't left me. For years, I have been having the same terrifying dream with the same terrifying details. Little has changed over the years. The number of seats has increased and the audience has increased – with the seats – over time, with new banks of spectators now rising up to the ceiling, but other than that, little else has changed. The people in the audience, whose faces remain obscured and difficult to make out, still sit in those faded pink seats and condemn me. I don't know if I shall ever be free of this nightmare. Perhaps it will follow me to the grave, who knows. Apart from you, the only other person to know about this dream of mine is Fuad. I never told Basri Bey or Cezmi as they would not have understood. The only thing I revealed to Basri Bey was the hesitation I felt that day when we were about to enter the Topçu Barracks.

'It will soon pass', he said, averting his gaze. 'It's just a fleeting thing. You'll soon get used to all this. We've all been through it. We are fighters, Şehsuvar. We are *mujahidin*, as are those we fight against. It matters not whether they are our soldiers or foreigners – the enemy is still the enemy. If you had not killed them, they would have killed you, and what's more, they would have revelled in their killing of an infidel. Because that is what we are to them. In killing us, they would have secured their place in heaven, or so they believe. I'm sorry son, but yours is the sensitivity of the intellectual, a quite inappropriate and unnecessary sense of compassion. But as I said, it's a fleeting thing and will soon pass.'

But it didn't. Most of the time, I forgot about it, but it never went away. Thankfully, there have been no shortages of events in my life that have helped me forget. Yes, the chief opponents to our movement had been purged. Although not arrested, Prince Sabahattin was forced into exile, while Derviş Vahdetî was captured a few days later and executed, along with seventy or so other men charged with inciting the rebellion. Another development had also taken place, one that had been delayed by the mutiny, and that was the toppling of Sultan Abdülhamit. Actually, the issue had been on the agenda before the recapture of Dersaadet but the *sadrazam,* Mahmet Şevket Paşa, had shelved this particular proposal by parliament for fear of the army's reaction as there were still many in the armed forces that remained loyal and bound to the person of the sultan. But now the time had come to resolve the problem once and for all. As Talat Bey had said, 'There cannot be two centres of power – it is either us or them!'

It was clear whom the 'us' were; as for the 'them', that was a little less clear. In broad terms, anybody that stood against us, including – and chiefly – Abdülhamit, was one of 'them'. But to remove them from the centres of power, we had to start with the sultan, and that is what we did; a mere two days after the attempted counter-revolution had been quashed, the Chamber of Deputies roared its endorsement of the proposal to have Abdülhamit removed from the sultanate and the caliphate.

This incredible news I learnt that afternoon from Basri Bey. After that fortnight of blood and horror, I was at my desk at Müsâvât Publishing, flicking through my translation of Anatole France's novel *Le Lys Rouge*, which I had not opened for quite some time. To put it in a way that would please your sense of style and artistry, I was now trying to cleanse my soul, which had been fouled by the blood of politics, in the pure waters of literature. As I sat there leafing through the pages, Basri Bey walked in. Instead of being delighted, he seemed tense.

'Abdülhamit has been ousted'. Instead of joyously shouting it out, it came out as a mutter, almost a whisper. 'The Chamber of Deputies convened early this morning and forced his removal. He has been replaced as sultan by his brother, Reşad.'

For a man who was ready to sacrifice his life for his ideas, one of which was a monarchy restrained by the constitution, and who was now seeing his dream become a reality, he seemed lost, like a man that had fallen into a pit. He had the bewildered look of a naughty boy who had always argued with his father but now, having lost his father, did not know where to turn or what to do. I did not feel the same. For me, the right decision had been taken. Indeed, it should have been taken the previous July. But seeing Basri Bey like that, I was reminded of something Uncle Leon had once said to me:

'This is not France, Şehsuvar. The people of this country do not actually want a revolution. The revolution is what people like us want, learned people who can see that the state is failing and has fallen into disrepair. This is the age of autocracy, forced exiles, tyranny and despotism but do you think anybody cares? In France, the people poured out onto the streets and stormed the Bastille. Ordinary people – workers, shopkeepers, villagers. But here, people celebrate the constitution by shouting 'Long live our beloved Sultan'. It's going to be hard, Şehsuvar. Very hard. Perhaps it's just a dream. I hope one day we will succeed, of course, but the dream is still a long way away. A long way away. Nevertheless, it is a precious dream and a precious ideal, one we should never abandon.'

How right he was. Despite all our progressiveness, all our revolutionary fervour and all our ideals, when it came to the sultan and to a reckoning with the state, our hands were tied, so much so that we were almost rendered immobile. A thousand-year culture of servitude and submission to power and to royal authority had seeped into our blood and our bones and had turned us into obedient little children. That is why I could empathise with Basri Bey and understand his predicament. No matter how old we were, how wise or advanced in age we were, at death's door even, none of us could escape the influence of the sultan. On the plus side, we had stood up to this influence and had maintained our belief in ourselves and our cause. Ultimately, despite any qualms or misgivings he may have had, Basri Bey was not the type to show any hesitation or vacillation when it came to carrying out his duty.

'Abdülhamit is going into exile', he went on, trying to lift himself out of his stupor. 'Strange, isn't it? For years, he sent our friends and comrades into exile, and now we are the ones exiling him. And guess where he is going? That's right, to our one and only Salonika. He wanted to stay in the Çırağan Palace but his request has been refused and he has been told to pack immediately. You would not believe the panic in Yıldız Palace right now. The family are packing up their belongings as we speak, ready to leave tonight. That means we have to pack too, Şehsuvar. We don't have much time. You'd better go home and get ready.'

I had no idea what he was talking about.

'We're going too, Şehsuvar. Our new mission is to escort Abdülhamit on his journey into exile in Salonika. Let's go, young man. No delays. Off you go. Pack, get ready and then get to the station at Sirkeci. A private train has been commissioned for the journey.' He shook his head, still unable to comprehend the magnitude of the occasion. 'Can you believe it? Abdülhamit is going into exile to Salonika and we are going to take him there!'

For me, this was even more extraordinary than the news that he had been deposed. At first, I felt a childlike delight: I was going back to Salonika and so I would get to see my loved ones, but that delight was soon swamped by gloom. And why? Because you would not be there. You had moved to Paris the previous September and had been there ever since. I found out from your Uncle Leon when he came to Istanbul on the 17th of December, the day the Chamber of Deputies reopened. He seemed pleased to see me, and, encouraged by his affection, I asked after you.

'She's fine', he answered, looking away. 'She's in Paris, as you probably know, with her father at the university. She writes every now and then. She says she is happy there.'

However, he did not seem comfortable telling me this, as though he was struggling with a sense of guilt.

Of course, I did not ask him if you had asked after me because I was sure you hadn't. The Ester I know would never ask, even if the curiosity were killing her. And even if you had asked, what would have come off it? You would not be coming back from Paris and I was not going to leave Istanbul. One of us had chosen the West and the other one had chosen the East. Salonika, perhaps, would have brought us back together but neither you nor I were willing to make that crucial first move, to take that crucial first step... And so, with these gloomy thoughts for company, I began packing my wooden suitcase. Not even the prospect of seeing my mother, whom I had not seen for months, could cheer me up. Thankfully, there was a mission to be completed, and a vitally important one at that – guarding the deposed sultan as we escorted him into exile. Guarding the life and the honour of none other than Abdülhamit, the thirty-fourth Ottoman padishah, the sultan who, after Sultan Süleyman the Magnificent and Mehmed IV, had reigned the longest and who was the man and monarch behind my father's death. By reflecting upon these truisms, I was able to grasp the significance of our mission and was thus better able to chase the images and the memories of you out of my mind and devote myself entirely to our new mission.

The truth of the matter is that, until that night, I had never seen the sultan. It was in Sirkeci that I would come face to face with him for the first time. We had arrived at the station early, before dusk fell. The director of the railway network had commissioned a special train for his unusual passengers. It had three wagons – two ordinary carriages and one bedecked with the requisite comforts and luxury. When I arrived at Sirkeci, Basri Bey and Fuad had already had their suitcases placed on board on the third wagon, the one in which we would be travelling. Our actual commandant for the journey was Staff Major Ali Fethi Bey of Macedonia, the man who had spoken out to the soldiers at the Ministry of War during the rebellion and had persuaded them to surrender. He had been asked by the *sadrazam* himself, Mahmud Şevket Paşa, to escort the ousted sultan to Salonika and had been assigned a squad of thirty handpicked men, including the three of us, for backup. Once all the preliminary checks and inspections had been made to ensure there was nothing untoward on or around the train, we sat down to wait.

We waited a long time. After the evening call to prayer, as the light was rapidly fading, the palace delegation arrived in four cars, greeted in person at the station by Hüseyin Hüsnü Paşa. It felt odd seeing the delegation like that, their shoulders slumped, heads bowed and eyes drawn, people with the look of defeat about them. The group was made up of women, children, servants and, leading from the front, a gentleman in a grey, ashen overcoat. To be frank, it was a sad, desperate sight. The great Abdülhamit, the man who had ruled an empire that stretched from the Adriatic to the Gulf and from the Caucasus Mountains to the Sahara with an iron fist for years and who had made its citizens tremble with fear now cut a tragic and pitiful figure with his hunched back, his thin, drained face and his slow hesitant steps. Years ago, the term 'the Sick Man' had been used in a French newspaper to describe the Ottoman Empire; well, Abdülhamit now seemed the very personification of that sick man. As their belongings were being loaded onto the train, he looked around, as though searching for something, as though there was something he needed and had forgotten. I happened to be closest to him at that moment and we came face to face. Clutching his stomach with his right hand, he gave me a weak, distant smile. I had no choice but to smile in return.

'My dear boy', he asked pleadingly. 'Would you be so kind as to bring me a glass of water? A nice glass of cool mineral water. The pain in my stomach has flared up once again...'

He was not ordering me. Quite the opposite; his tone was gentle and courteous, whilst also completely self-assured at the same time. I sprinted off and hurriedly returned with two bottles of Taşdelen water, as requested. He smiled graciously.

'Many thanks, my lad. May you prosper in life and may you be as grand and as noble as water itself.'

That was the first and last time we spoke at the station. At midnight, the train set off. Nobody came to see them off, to wave handkerchiefs after them as they departed. Abdülhamit and his sons were in the luxury carriage that had been commissioned for them while the ladies of the entourage were seated in the other. We kept our distance as much as possible, but as per our remit, we patrolled the sultan's corridor on a regular basis, not only in case of threats from outside but also because we were afraid the sultan would do something to harm himself. Luckily, nothing of either kind occurred. Just before dawn, it was my turn to keep guard. I approached the first wagon, the royal carriage, and looked around. All seemed calm and well and I was about to turn return to my post at the rear of the train when I heard a voice.

'Excuse me, young man'. I turned around and saw Abdülhamit smoking a cigarette by the door of the carriage. He looked tired. 'Are you not the young gentleman that brought me water yesterday?'

I took a few steps towards him, but made sure I kept a healthy and respectful distance between us.

'Yes sir, it was. May I be of any assistance? Is there anything I can bring you?'

With the hand holding the cigarette, he gestured to my jacket pocket.

'What are you reading there?'

I was so nervous, I could barely grasp what he was saying. I looked down at my jacket pocket and saw the book I had brought along to read on the journey.

'*The Mysteries of Paris*, sir. Written by an author by the name of Eugene Sue.'

He put the cigarette between his lips and held out a hand for the book. I reached down to take it out of my pocket but as luck would have it, it got stuck and the sultan's hand was left hovering in mid-air. Luckily, it didn't last long. I managed to claw it out and handed it to the waiting ex-monarch, who received it almost reverentially.

'I know it well', he said, examining the cover. 'He was a contemporary of Victor Hugo. I had seventeen of his works translated.' He looked up at me. 'Tell me, what do you think of it? Are you enjoying it? Would you say he is as great an author as Hugo?'

I shook my head.

'I am not an expert on literary affairs by any means but I can safely say that he is not a writer of Victor Hugo's stature. What he wrote were essentially suspense stories; murder mysteries. Detective novels of a sort, one can say.'

He gently raised his head.

'One must not be quick to dismiss detective stories, son. Some of my greatest literary delights have come from reading detective stories. Seeing as you are interested in literature, I'm sure you have heard of a certain Arthur Conan Doyle. He is the man that wrote the Sherlock Holmes stories. Wonderful stories they are too. But the saddest part of his tale is that he himself was not even aware of the impact his stories had made and how important they actually were. You see, I once met him in person. He came to the palace, where I awarded him the *Mecidiye Nişanı* medal. I also awarded his wife the Order of Charity medal.' The conversation was beginning to interest him and he closed the door to his quarters and came closer. The overpowering smell of tobacco filled the corridor. 'Tell me, have you read any detective stories?'

Of course I had. In fact, one such book, *The Mystery of the Yellow Room*, had caused a huge row between you and I but I was so nervous I couldn't remember the book at that particular moment. It was quite understandable. After all, it was midnight and I was on a train to Salonika discussing literature with Abdülhamit, the man we had spent years trying to topple.

'I have, sir, most definitely. I am familiar with the Sherlock Holmes stories, for instance.'

He took a deep drag on his cigarette.

'Well, as far as I can see, young man, you are not the most passionate reader of this particular genre.'

'I suppose you could say that', I answered, feeling a little tense. 'I prefer works by the great writers'.

He gazed at me in approval.

'Ah, youth… Indubitably, the most beautiful of life's seasons. Ahead of you lies a long and beautiful life full of mysteries. The mere anticipation of this life is, in its own right, a beautiful thing. But then, later on, further down the road, when one has grown old, shall we say, when one has decoded life's great mysteries, the days are composed of more mundane moments.' He must have thought I was about to interrupt as he was eager to continue. 'Even if, like me, you rule a country which is beset by new problems and new shocks every day, every hour, every moment, life, ultimately, can become tedious. The best remedies for this tedium are detective novels. They set the mind working and keep one's emotions on edge. They keep the mind sharp and take you on unique and extraordinary journeys.' He smiled a bittersweet smile. 'In contrast to journeys such as this one'. He stopped, realising his mistake, and leaned his head to one side. 'Unfortunately, yes, one can be rendered anxious and foreboding but there are so many reasons for one to be apprehensive in our current times, are there not, my lad?'

I felt like telling him to keep his opinions to himself but I couldn't.

'I'm afraid I see things somewhat differently, sir. In contrast to what you have just said, I would say that literature is a precious art form, one that reveals the intricacies of the human soul to its readers. Take Victor Hugo, for instance. It is not so much Jean Valjean's sacrifices that matter but rather the imprint they leave in our minds and in our souls. If that novel encourages me to be a better person, to confront the evil that resides within me and engage and struggle with it, then that means the novel has served its purpose. On the other hand, detective novels, as you say, speak to the mind and the intellect. They are like mathematical problems; brilliantly formulated mathematical problems. They appeal to our mind but alas, we also have hearts and souls…'

I fell silent, thinking perhaps I had overstepped the mark and grown a little too confident.

'If you don't mind me asking, do you perchance write yourself?' he asked. 'Because only a writer could speak about literature with such assurance and mastery of detail.'

I didn't say yes. It would have been a lie anyway, as I had long since given up writing, and even if I hadn't, I would not have told Abdülhamit.

'No sir, I do not write. Mine is just a reader's interest'.

He seemed to believe me.

'And a fine interest it is, too. Keep it up, son. But I would say that you should try writing, too. You seem to have the aptitude.' He pointed to the window. 'Would you be so kind as to open this window so I may dispose of this cigarette?'

I did as requested and opened the window and he threw the butt out into the darkness. Fresh spring air rushed into the corridor. I was about to close the window when he stopped me.

'Leave it open a little while'.

He breathed in the damp air. It reminded me of the conversation I'd had with Talat Bey around nine months earlier, also in the corridor of a train, although that one had been taking us in the other direction, from Salonika to the capital. That day, Talat Bey had been telling me how dangerous Abdülhamit was and how delicate the situation was… And now here I was, talking about literature to that same supposedly dangerous Abdülhamit. Like Talat Bey that night, Abdülhamit was staring out at the fields and the vast steppes racing past us.

I also turned to look out of the window. The moon was fading fast, and a faint sliver of light promising a new day shimmered on the horizon. The fields, groves, meadows and mountains of the prairies and the wilds began to flicker into view.

'Breath-taking, isn't it?' he murmured. 'Such a wonderful feeling. To watch this vast land slowly come to life on a spring morning… This is a beautiful country. A beautiful land….' He turned and looked at me, this time openly and earnestly. 'I had nothing to do with the mutiny. Nor am I against the idea of a constitutional monarchy. It is the timing that is crucial. The people need to be ready for such a change. Thirty-one years ago, the people were not ready for such a transformation or for such an upheaval. But they are now. Believe me son, like you I have no other wish than the welfare and prosperity of our people and for the thirty-one years Allah granted me on the throne, I strived for nothing else. And now look. Look at what they deem to be befitting to me and my family. Predecessors of mine that were deposed were allowed to remain in the capital. Even those that were killed were buried in the capital. But exile? Salonika? From where were these ideas conjured up?'

The scant and temporary consolation that our discussion of literature had provided had vanished. The immensity of the defeat he had experienced was there to see.

'I wouldn't know, sir', I said coldly and sternly. 'They say parliament made that decision'.

He looked up at me wearily and despondently, as though I was the one that had betrayed him, and in a broken voice, asked, 'And you agree with the decision, do you not? You think I need to be punished?'

My silence was damning consent, but I think it had begun to aggravate him.

'Are you an officer, son?' he asked, a newfound steel in his voice. 'A lieutenant perhaps, seeing as how young you are'.

It would have been wrong not to answer.

'I am not a soldier, sir. I have no rank.'

He did not look surprised.

'You must be a member of the movement, in that case. One of the *fedai*, perhaps.' He nodded his head. 'That must be it. Well, you must be an outstanding *fedai*, otherwise they would not have assigned you to such an important mission.' He looked away and turned as if to go, but then turned back around. 'Tell me, lad, who recruited you? I am just curious. How did someone so young and with such an abiding interest in literature become involved in such a murky and dangerous world? Who dragged you into this particular game?'

A voice inside pleaded with me not to answer but I couldn't stop myself.

'You did, sir'.

'What?' he replied, astonished. 'Me?'

'Yes, sir. You'. Each syllable was slow and measured. 'When you sent my father, Emrullah Bey, the Director of Educational Affairs in Salonika, into exile. When you sent him to his death in the desert wastelands of Fezzan. So yes, I'm sorry sir, but I'm afraid you were the one that dragged me into the movement.'

He stood there in stunned silence, not knowing what to say.

'Good night, sir', I said and walked away. As I moved into the next carriage, I turned around to have another look at him. The hunch in his back seemed a little more pronounced, and his face seemed paler… He was not staring wistfully at the beauty of the country as it sped past. He was just standing there, alone in the corridor, not knowing what to do.

A Token of a Conversation

Hello Ester (Morning, Day 7)

I awoke to the sound of rain. And what rain it was. It was as though the sky had been split asunder, as though autumn was taking its revenge after a long, hot summer. The balcony door was swinging wildly in the wind as I had forgotten to close it so I had to get up to close it properly and while I was doing so, I took a look out of the window. The rain was coming down so hard, I could barely see beyond a few metres but I did notice inside the room a small puddle where I had left the balcony door open. I rushed into the bathroom to get some towels, knowing the damp could play hell with the wooden floorboards, when I suddenly sensed a pair of eyes following me. I looked up and saw my own face in the mirror. I looked funny, with my long nightgown, my hair all over the place, a stubborn little beard beginning to form and my uneven moustache, with one end pointing down, the other pointing up. A clown. That's what I looked like. A doddering old clown like the one we saw at the circus in Paris. You know I have always been careful about my appearance, even if I am on my own, and normally it would have been disconcerting to see myself in this state but I was so happy this morning that neither the torrential rain nor my scruffy appearance could bring me down. Indeed, my spirits were so high, I burst out into laughter. And why? Because it is possible that you are here in this city. For all I knew, you were sleeping just a few metres away from me at that moment, and that was enough to fill me with an unexpected and unbridled joy. I shaved, had a lovely bath, got changed and, with a spring in my step, strode down to breakfast.

Even Ihsan, the head waiter, noticed my good mood.

'Good morning, Şehsuvar Bey. So nice to see you looking so happy. And in such horrible weather, too.'

'Morning, morning, morning, Ihsan Bey', I beamed. 'It's not the weather that matters but our state of mind. And anyway, this is just a summer storm. It won't last long. It will have dried up by noon. But enough about the weather. How about a nice omelette this morning? Three eggs should do the trick.'

'Right away, sir'. He turned and took a step forward but then paused, remembering something important. 'Should I bring you the morning papers first?'

I stopped and thought about it.

'Don't bother', I replied. 'I don't want any depressing news to ruin my mood this fine morning.'

The chance that I might see you again had not made me forget about the possible danger I was in, no, but those dangers also seemed to be diminishing. Neither Mehmed Esad's mysterious riddles nor Cezmi's deranged ramblings could have bothered me. Since yesterday afternoon, I have had just one aim: to find out whether you have come to Istanbul or not. Perhaps I could find somebody else that knows this Çolak Cafer. Track them down, knock on their front door perhaps and ask them a few questions... I could pay a visit to Kara Kemal's men. Wait, no. That would be going too far. If Cafer is still laying low, that means it is still not safe. I cannot risk getting arrested, not now, when I am so close to seeing you again. Can't risk getting arrested or having my brains blown out. I need to be patient and keep things simple. I won't have to wait that long anyway, as Captain Cezmi told me to pop round in two days later... Just two days... Less than forty-eight hours before I see him.... Perhaps it would be best if I don't leave the hotel. Not that anybody is following me but there is still little point in aggravating matters. Best to stay in my room and carry on with my writing. At least that way, the time will pass quickly.

'Şehsuvar Bey.... Şehsuvar Bey...'

I turned around and saw Ömer from reception standing to my right.

'Good morning, Ömer'.

'Good morning, sir'. He held out a little envelope for me. 'This was left for you by the gentleman that was here three days ago. The gentleman whose name surprised you at first but whom you then sat and and chatted with in the Domed Tea Lounge.'

He was describing Mehmed Esad.

'Did he bring the letter himself?' I asked, taking the envelope.

'No. Another gentleman brought it. A dark gentleman. Very dark, indeed. He may have been an Arab or an African. He didn't say a single word when he delivered the letter but your name is right there on the front.'

I was about to ask him how he knew Mehmed Esad had sent it but then I saw my shady old friend's name in the top corner of the envelope. I thanked Ömer and watched him walk away before opening the envelope. There was a brief note inside:

I'll be in the Avrupa Pasajı shopping arcade. No. 19. It's a carpet shop. If you come by around noon, we can get something to eat and have a chat. I have very important news for you.

Warmest regards,

Your brother, Mehmed Esad.

No, I won't go. What business do I have with this guy? As I said before, I have nothing to do with politics anymore. Not this side, not that, and nor indeed any other. If I don't go, he may give up. But what if he doesn't? What if he comes here again? What will I tell him? I can hardly say I don't trust him. The best thing will be to tell him I received the note too late. Of course he'll know I'm lying but at least then he'll know I don't want to see him. So no, I decided not to go. I wasn't going to let anyone or anything ruin my mood today so when I finished my delicious breakfast, I came straight back up to my room and sat down to write. It's such a wonderful feeling, this sparkling bright hope. I only hope it doesn't disappear. And it is such a stark contrast to seventeen years ago, to the spring of 1909, when we escorted Abdülhamit into exile in Salonika. What I felt then was an emptiness, a dark and brooding anxiety, a deep and, frankly, absurd sense of worthlessness... That is how Salonika greeted me. Not when we got off the train, not when we accompanied Abdülhamit and his delegation to the Alatini Mansion, no. It was a full two days after I had arrived in the city of my birth, the morning we handed over our watch to the squad that had just arrived at the mansion.

I should tell you about a little incident that occurred to me first. While the ex-sultan was busy settling into the house in which he would reside for three years, the three of us, our little group which had accompanied him from the capital to Salonika that is, were leaving the premises and were about to walk through the gates at the end of the huge garden when a soldier called out to us.

'Wait! Wait! Stop!'

We stopped. Not just me, but Fuad and Basri Bey too. A soldier came running straight towards us.

'The sultan is calling you'.

'Me?' I managed to mutter.

'Yes, you', he replied, standing to attention. 'You need to go and see him'.

Basri Bey chuckled.

'Don't worry, son. His reign is over. He can't do anything to you. He can't send you into exile. Go on. Go and see what he wants.'

My curiosity almost unbearable, I began walking through the garden towards the beautiful marble staircase in front of the large red brick mansion when the ex-sultan appeared at the top of the steps. Clearly, he was expecting me and I naturally straightened up and adjusted my stride to give it more decorum. As I began climbing the steps, I saw that same distant smile on his lips.

'Caught you just in time', he said sheepishly. 'Son, I feel I must tell you something. Please understand, I am truly sorry about what happened to your father. You must have suffered terribly as a result. But believe me when I say I did not wish for anybody to die. I know that is not much of a consolation for you now but it is the truth.' He held out his right hand, which had been resting behind his long robe. He was holding a book. 'However, I would be honoured and delighted should you accept this book. Not on account of what happened to your father. Rather, it is a gift from one lover of literature to another.' Seeing me hesitate, he insisted. 'Please. As a memento of our conversation the other night. A memento of a conversation that, brief though it may have been, for a moment made me forget my own woes.'

Standing in front of me was not a tyrant that had crushed a country and a nation under his heel for nigh on thirty years but a simple lover of literature. I don't know whether he was trying to ease his conscience or hoping to gain the goodwill of as many people as possible that could help protect his family from future threats but he looked so forlorn and helpless that I could not bring myself to say or do anything to hurt him, a frail old man, no matter how much anger I may have had in my heart for him. I accepted the gift.

'Thank you, sir'. I looked at the cover. It was *The Adventure of the Bruce-Partington Plans – A Sherlock Holmes Story*. 'I haven't read this one', I muttered.

His pale face lit up.

'Well, it's a valuable copy. Signed by the author.'

I opened the book and there it was, on the third page – Arthur Conan Doyle's signature. '*To the Great Sultan of the Sublime Porte, With my warmest and sincerest regards.*' I cannot lie. I was moved by the gesture. It mattered not who the man in front of me was or may have been. He was an incurable literature buff and for me at that moment, that was all that mattered. I smiled in appreciation.

'I don't know how to thank you, sir'. I turned and was about to go but felt something was amiss. I turned back around and said, 'I hope you are happy here in your new residence.'

He didn't answer. He just looked at me, a broken, defeated expression in his countenance. I left him there and walked down the steps.

When Fuad and Basri Bey saw me and the gift I had received, they eagerly flicked through it and were stunned when they saw Arthur Conan Doyle's signature there. 'Well, if he ever comes back to power, you'll be set for life,' they laughed. We then said our goodbyes and each went our own way.

I should have been happy. I had returned to Salonika and had completed a mission that was central to our revolution but for reasons I could not fathom, I was not content. I was beset by a vague uneasiness. Walking past the White Tower and down to the coast, the memories of the city still fresh in my mind, as though they had only been yesterday, I realised what it was – you were no longer there. I already knew it but when I grasped it in its entirety, it seemed as though my whole world had come crashing down around me. In the vastness of all Salonika, I was alone and it was the first time I had ever felt something akin to hatred for the city. It was your absence, Ester... You not being near me as I walked around the streets we used to wander together. My yearning for you that silently pulsated like another heart in my body. The image of you, the sound of your voice and the memory of your scent... Your absence only made me think of you even more and it was unbearable.

Now I knew for sure. There were two Şehsuvars: the young wannabe writer that was devoted to you, and the one that had dedicated his life to the tides and the ebb and flow of history; the rebel and revolutionary who was ready to kill and be killed for his cause. They had never understood each other and now they never would. Yes, I suppose you could say it was a form of madness, a form of self-inflicted suffering.

That spring evening, when all the trees of the city seemed to be in wondrous full bloom, I, Şehsuvar Sami, dragged my feet through the front door of my parents' house as though I was carrying the woes of the entire world on my shoulders. Even seeing my mother after so many months could not lift the gloom that had cloaked itself around my heart.

'You've changed, son', she said when she saw me. 'Like you've aged'.

'How can I have aged, mother?' I said, not wanting her to worry. 'It hasn't even been a year since I left Salonika. How can someone age in less than a year?'

She shook her head.

'But you have. The lines on your face have hardened and your eyes have changed. The softness that used to be there has disappeared. You used to have such tenderness in your eyes.' She stroked my hair and asked, 'Are they working you too hard, son?' I mumbled something incoherent in response but she saw through me. 'No, this is not work doing this to you. This is something else. I hope it's nothing serious, my boy. Tell me, Şehsuvar, what's bothering you?'

I wanted to be free of this affliction that had infected my soul and taken over my body… I wanted the energy to shake off this despondency and go back to the past. To better, happier days… I wanted to go back to the old Şehsuvar Sami, the happy, hopeful, carefree, Şehsuvar…

'Nothing, Mum. Nothing's bothering me. I'm just a little tired from the train journey, that's all.' I put on a smile for her and hugged her, an amazing woman that cared for me more than I cared for myself. 'I've missed you, Mum. So much.'

The way she hugged me, breathing in her beloved only son's scent, seemed to lift her worries. Perhaps. I don't know. Maybe her anxieties were still there and she was simply pretending.

'Your being away kills me', she said, still hugging me. 'You should come more often, Şehsuvar. You are not that far away. You get on a train in the evening and you're here in the morning. You should visit your poor old mother more often. I already have one foot in the grave.'

She was right but I didn't take it seriously. I thought it was just a loving mother showing her son how much she loved and missed him.

'I have so much work, Mum, that I barely have any free time', I said, hoping to change the subject. 'But I promise, the next chance I get, I'll visit you.'

Isn't that what we always do? When it comes to our parents, we barely notice them, thinking their love, their selflessness and their sacrifices will always be there for us. It is only when we lose them that we realise how precious they were. And I was no different. Two years later, when we were laying her to rest for the last time, I realised how much she meant to me. But I'm not completely without heart. I begged and pleaded with Basri Bey and convinced him to let me stay on another day, even though I had been granted only two days' leave and seeing and wandering the streets of the city were such a torment for me. I didn't go to your house either. I couldn't. My legs seemed to ache to go to the Jewish quarter but I did not listen, even though your Grandma Paloma was as dear to me as my own mother. I didn't go to your house as I was frightened I would break down if I walked through that front door… And the prospect of walking around that garden without you…. It would have been too much to bear. Even seeing your Uncle Leon would have been a trial for me, so much so that I decided not to visit him either. But as fate would have it, he found me. The morning of my departure from Salonika, he popped round. I greeted him in the guest room.

'So you come to Salonika and you don't even pay me a visit?' he said angrily while we sipped our coffees. 'Don't you have any respect for custom, Şehsuvar?'

He was right too, absolutely right, but I could hardly tell him that I had not visited him as I wanted to keep away from anything that would remind me of you. I did not want him to see me as someone akin to Goethe's desperate young Werther.

'I'm so sorry, Monsieur Leon', I blurted out through my shame. 'I just couldn't find the time. I'm sure you know about our mission here. I was caught up in that. I was going to come round to see you as soon as I had the chance.'

He looked me up and down disbelievingly.

'Şehsuvar, please, I knew you were not going to come. You're a terrible liar, you know that? I'm sorry but you were not going to come and see me. I know the party has all but deleted me from its records forever. That I no longer have a place in the movement. I know what they told you. *Don't you dare visit that socialist Jew.* That's what they said.'

I was stunned.

'Monsieur Leon, please. Nobody has said anything like that. And even if they had, I would not have complied. You have done so much for me… How can I possibly forget your efforts on my behalf? I would never be so disrespectful to you. And as for this exclusion from the movement, I doubt anyone would dare do such a thing to you.'

Now it was his turn to be stunned.

'You really don't know?'

'I don't. How can I? I've been in Istanbul for months.'

The reproach in his eyes was replaced by suspicion.

'So why didn't you come to see me?' He held up a hand to stop me from answering. 'And don't even try telling me you were busy. For two days, you've been wandering aimlessly around the streets and the seaside. You didn't even visit my old mother, and you know how much she adores you.'

I had to deny it.

'Not aimlessly, no. Nothing like that. We were told to bring Abdülhamit to Salonika and we did. We were his security detail. How could I have wandered the streets when I was on such an important mission? If I was walking the streets, there must have been a reason. How is Grandma Paloma, by the way?'

'She's in a terrible state. When Ester left, she seemed to age overnight. I'm scared something may happen to her. To tell you the truth, I'm not doing too well myself. First you left, then Ester. Now I'm pretty much alone in this city.' And then, out of the blue, he asked, 'Have you been keeping in touch with Ester? Do you write to her? Or are you both still…?'

He probably knew the real reasons why I hadn't visited him. Not that I minded as it no longer bothered me but I kept up the lie.

'That's all in the past now, Monsieur Leon. As you yourself said, it was not meant to be. It was all over before I left for Istanbul. Actually, I owe you my gratitude. For your advice back then…'

'Maybe I should not have said what I said that day', he said, sighing regretfully. 'I'm no longer sure that the advice I gave you was correct. Strange things are happening, Şehsuvar. This revolution has been a disappointment, to be frank. A huge disappointment…'

I could feel my anger mounting. A mere nine months earlier he had been telling me that a revolution is more important than love and now he was standing in front of me saying he'd made a mistake.

'I don't understand. What do you mean by "disappointment?"'

He took some time before answering, the eyes wandering over the blues and the greens of the hand-woven carpet on the floor.

'I'd always had misgivings, some of which I'd shared with you. For a revolution to succeed, certain objective preconditions are necessary. Economic turmoil, for one. On top of that, the authorities should no longer be governing with their former efficiency, and should be resorting to tyranny and oppression, with the public no longer wanting to be ruled in the traditional manner. Demonstrations, protests and strikes are also needed… Essentially, what is needed is for the people to express their frustrations, as was the case in France and Prussia. Moreover, certain subjective conditions are also required, such as a class, or classes, that want revolution, a political party that can lead the masses, and experienced, informed leaders. We have classes that want reform but only in a handful of cities, such as Istanbul, Izmir and Salonika. Beyond these cities, there is hardly any industry, hardly any bourgeoisie, petty bourgeoisie or working class worthy of the name. And the few people in the hinterland that are aware of their conditions and want a revolution are few in number and not organised anyway. In addition to all this, and crucially, there is no political movement that can lead and direct the revolution. It's been twenty years since the CUP was established, and look now – the revolutionary impetus has been seized by the soldiery. This is not a promising sign at all. Furthermore, this movement, whether it be soldiers or civilians, is woefully inexperienced. They are learning and improvising as they go along, and this is proving immensely costly to us.

'Just think of the conditions that paved the way for the uprising of the 31st March. Look back to the mistakes we made. We unwittingly brought our enemies together when we began employing the very same oppressive measures we had initially claimed to be against. Tell me, was Hasan Fehmi really a conservative? Was he one of Abdülhamit's supporters? If not, why did we have him killed? To borrow from Saint-Just, are we creating a tyranny out of liberty? If we are, then God help us. Because we both know what happened in the end to Saint-Just and to Robespierre. I'm afraid, Şehsuvar. Afraid that something akin to the Reign of Terror will happen here too. Afraid that the revolution will devour its own children. There are still so many huge issues that need to be resolved. The Ottoman Union is breaking up. All the ethnic minorities – the Greeks, the Bulgarians, the Romanians; all of them – are talking about independence, about setting up their own states. The same with us Jews, too. Some are asking why Salonika shouldn't be an independent Jewish state. These questions have been festering unanswered for so long now that they have become gangrenous, and instead of dealing with the problem, we resort to violence and repression. And that can only mean that we have run out of ideas. That we are helpless. It is still early, yes, it has only been nine months since the founding of the constitutional system, and yes, we can safely say that the party has not yet truly gained power. But with all these other developments around us, one cannot help but be concerned.'

Of course I was not as hopeless as he was but I had heard rumours from the intellectuals of the party, especially from Ahmed Rıza, about these alarming developments.

'I know what you're trying to say', I said calmly. 'And you're not alone in your concerns. Many in the movement are deep in discussion over these issues. But what I don't understand is what happened between you and the party.'

'Deep in discussion, you say?' he said, a look of despair in his eyes. 'Are you sure? Because the points I raised with the Committee were not greeted at all positively here. Tell me, is it different in Istanbul? Are they prepared to welcome – or at least tolerate – different points of view?'

I was going to tell him they did but then I remembered what our very own Basri Bey had once said about Ahmed Rıza in his house in Şehzadebaşı. After a long discussion with that great thinker, Basri Bey discreetly took me to one side and said, 'Be careful, Şehsuvar. These guys' heads are in the clouds. They've been living in Paris for so long, they're blind to the realities of our country. All they do is write and pontificate but when it comes to applying theory to life and reality, they are clueless. The things they write and say can often confuse patriots and *fedai* such as ourselves and cloud our judgement, when what people like us actually need to do is march with belief, conviction and self-sacrifice towards our goal. We do not need empty words or silly theories. For us, they are pointless. Futile. All they do is weigh us down and weaken our spirits.'

Back then, I don't think I knew exactly what Basri Bey meant. I thought he was perhaps jealous that Ahmed Rıza was taking an interest in mé when he, Basri Bey, was the one in charge of our little group but now Uncle Leon's words had opened up new pathways in my mind. That was because his observations and analyses were remarkably similar to Ahmed Rıza's; they examined and evaluated situations from similar points of view, whereas Basri Bey did not share that perspective. Neither did the central committee of the movement. So what was going to happen now? Was there going to be a rift within the movement between the soldiers and the intellectuals?

I thought of Talat Bey. He was not a soldier but a decent and honourable man of letters, a thinker, yet he did not seem to mind working alongside the soldiery and he continued to fight the good fight shoulder to shoulder with men like Enver Bey and Cemal Bey. What's more, he was one of the most prominent and respected men in the movement's upper echelons. So if you ask me, Uncle Leon was falling victim to groundless fears. Perhaps Ahmed Rıza could not quite see the situation from all the necessary angles. Yes, on paper, all seemed easy but installing a new regime in a vast empire was hardly easy; it was one of the most complex tasks imaginable. Of course there would be violence and repression… But it would only be temporarly. Once the structures safeguarding and guaranteeing liberty for all had been effectively and permanently installed, there would be no need to resort to the darker and more sinister methods. And this is exactly what I told Uncle Leon. This and everything else that had been on my mind, and I told him openly, frankly and bluntly.

He listened with an acerbic smile on his lips.

'It seems Talat has really got to you', he finally said, not wanting to argue. 'All I can say is that I hope you do not come one day come to regret what you are doing today. Because I, for one, am already feeling remorse. Perhaps I should not have recommended you to the movement as a member. And as for trying to dissuade you from going to Paris with Ester – I should never have done that.' He paused, truly dejected and overcome by regret. 'I don't suppose you would go to Paris now, would you?'

I had done it. I had actually succeeded in making Uncle Leon think I had forgotten about you. Succeeded in making him believe that the love between us had died. And I was furious at myself for my success and for acting out my role so flawlessly. And yet, at the same time, a spark of hope seemed to flicker into life inside me. There was still time. I could still do it. Tell him the truth, find you and change my destiny forever. But I didn't. I couldn't. It was out of the question. I kept up the act.

'I'm afraid Paris would be out of the question, Monsieur Leon. I have to return to Istanbul this evening. I have vital work to attend to. If you'll remember, you yourself once told me that one can hardly attend to the affairs of the heart when the country is in flames. And you were right. When the country is on a knife-edge as it is now, one does not have time for the flowery oratory of sheltered intellectuals or for the demands of a broken heart. There is only one life for me now, and that is the unity of the nation and the prosperity of our homeland. To even consider any other life would be an insult.'

Hold on. What's that? I think there is somebody at my door. Is it the cleaner? No, it feels as though they have their ear to the door, listening. I can feel them breathing. Who can it be? They are knocking even more loudly now.

It is becoming even more brazen and persistent. They won't stop, whoever they are.

I'm sorry, Ester. I have to go.

I Am Not the One to Decide

Hello Ester (Afternoon, Day 7)

It seems there is no avoiding Mehmed Esad. I didn't go to the address he gave me for lunch so he came to see me instead. Yep, the knock on the door was from none other than my old comrade-in-arms. You may say he was showing some temerity in coming but he said he had his reasons. He said he had important news for me and asked to come in but I did not want to let him in.

'The room is a mess', I said, trying to dissuade him. 'Wait in the restaurant, I'll be down in a tick.'

When I went down to the restaurant, he had already made himself comfortable and was helping himself to a hearty meal. He was so at ease and so self-assured that I may as well have invited him over for lunch. His audacity was quite unbelievable. And on top of that, he actually had the nerve to rebuke me for not showing up!

'Why didn't you come round, Şehsuvar? I almost died of hunger waiting for you.'

I sat down on a stool in front of him and gave him a piece of mind.

'I don't actually remember telling you I'd come, Mehmed.'

He didn't seem angry or offended.

'You angry with me? Is that it?' He smirked and said, 'And there I was thinking we were old friends'.

I placed my hands on the table.

'It's not a matter of friendship but of time. You sent me a letter but you didn't give me enough time.'

He shrugged his shoulders.

'Fair enough, old friend. No need to get tetchy'.

He wasn't angry or anything, just a little taken aback.

'Nobody's getting tetchy. I'm simply trying to explain the whys and wherefores.'

'Understood. Fair enough. My mistake. No need to rub it in. Tell me, what are you eating?' He held the menu out to me. 'I'll say one thing; the food here is outstanding.'

'I'm full', I said tersely, in stark contrast to his convivial demeanour. 'I had lunch with someone else.'

He narrowed his eyes and stared at me.

'A lady friend, eh? Oh well. Actually, that reminds me – what happened to that Jewish girl you used to hang out with? The one from Salonika? Ester, wasn't it? I saw you two together a few times. I'll be honest, I was mad with jealousy when I saw you with her. She was a real stunner. She had a real air about her, eh? So tell me, what happened to her?'

Did he know something about you? Did he also know you'd come to Istanbul? Or was he just fishing around?

'I don't know', I replied, playing it safe. 'I haven't seen her for years. Neither her, nor her Uncle Leon.'

He nodded his head and frowned, as though he'd just remembered something important.

'Ah yes, Monsieur Leon. I bumped into him the other day, as chance would have it. Well, around two months ago. At the Tokatlıyan Hotel. He was sitting with somebody in the lobby.' He cast a quick glance at me. 'But his niece wasn't there. Or at least, I didn't see her. Maybe she was upstairs in one of the guest rooms.'

Those words…. The anger I had been feeling towards him immediately vanished because what he was saying meant the chances of you being in the city had just gone up again.

'Have you seen him since?' I asked. 'Monsieur Leon, that is. You know I used to work as a clerk in his law office.'

He shook his head.

'Nope. Only the once. That evening. We didn't speak or anything. I hardly know the man. Why, have they settled in Istanbul now?'

And then the worm of suspicion began to awake. Did he also know about my meeting with Cezmi? Had he been watching us yesterday? But if he had, how could he have listened to our conversation? What if somebody else had eavesdropped on our conversation and reported back to him? Somebody else… Who? Obviously not Cezmi. Reşit perhaps? Of course not. My suspicions were beginning to grow. Maybe it was Çolak Cafer himself who told Mehmed. But if Mehmed was now working for the government, why would Cezmi's man Cafer even go near him?

'Şehsuvar! Hello? Are you there?' Mehmed said, seeing me drift off. 'Monsieur Leon – has he settled in Istanbul or what? The Jews of Salonika have been leaving in droves ever since the city fell.'

'No idea', I said, pulling myself together. 'I'm hearing about him from you'.

'So you haven't seen that Ester then?'

He didn't seem convinced. What's more, I did not like his brusque and invasive manner.

'No. There's no reason why I should see her.'

The conversation was momentarily cut off by a waiter bringing bread and water. Mehmed must have been ravenous as he tore off a piece of bread and began chewing hungrily on it.

'So tell me', I went on after the waiter had left. 'What's this important news you have for me?'

He leisurely reached for the pitcher of water and poured a glass for himself and then for me before answering.

'I spoke to some of our guys. About you. They want you to work for us. An invitation to return to duty.'

It was my turn to play it cool. I took a long, slow sip of water.

'Well, I must say I'm honoured and I'm also very relieved because at least now they realise I am not a threat or an enemy to the government. But as I said before, I want to retire now. I want to put all that behind me and live the quiet life. Peace is what I need now, Mehmed. I just want to live a quiet life and die peacefully in my sleep in my own bed. If I can.'

For the first time, he looked anxious, even critical.

'So you're evading your duty then'.

I was in no state to argue with him.

'I'm afraid I won't be much use to the nation with this exhausted mind and body. I'll only end up doing more harm than good.' I looked at him earnestly, almost pleading with him. 'I'm in a bad way, Mehmed. Really. The old Şehsuvar is gone. Gone for good. No good can come from me now.'

He leaned back and crossed his arms.

'So how are you going to survive? Where are you going to find money? You don't have a job and no job means no income.' He looked around. 'Although having said that, you must have a little bit tucked away seeing as you're staying in a place like this. But that money won't last forever, will it?'

'Remember Madam Melina?' I said, without any remorse or resentment, a man sharing his woes with an old friend. 'I used to lodge in one of her rooms. Well, she was like a mother to me and when she died, she left everything she had to me. A house in Beşiktaş, a little shop in Karaköy and some cash. I'm living off that at the moment. Yes, you're right, I can't stay here forever. I suppose I'll go and live in the house in Beşiktaş eventually. I don't need much anyway. The odd translation here and there will do. I'll get by.'

The look on his face had changed. He seemed thoughtful and concerned.

'I see. Well, I'm not sure they're the sort to just let you turn around and stroll off into the sunset. No one is going to actually believe that you've left all this behind. And even if the government leaves you alone, the others won't. Of course, I'll speak to them on your behalf but they won't believe any of it, of that I am absolutely certain. If I were you, I'd mull it over a little more…'

I was about to object but he held up a hand.

'Not now. Not this very moment. But just think about it. With a clear and calm mind. Nobody will know you're working for the state. You'll report only to me. What I'm saying is, nobody will be able to accuse you of working for the CUP hunters.'

Was it bait he was dangling in front of me…?

'That's not the issue', I replied. 'I'm not the one to decide who is a killer or a monster. All I'm saying is that I'm not ready for such a position.'

He gave a fake laugh to try and ease the tension between us.

'We can send you off on a holiday, if you like. You can relax, take it easy, sort yourself out.' But then his expression suddenly changed. 'The country is in danger, Şehsuvar, and the government needs experienced men. Men like us. Think about it, properly. You have one day. We'll talk again tomorrow. I'll be waiting in the shop. Pop round in the evening and we can have a few drinks, get a bite to eat and all that.'

So yes, that is what Mehmed and I chatted about. But while this old friend of mine, one that I cannot say I wholly trust, was urging me to think again, I remembered the day years earlier when I met Basri Bey in Salonika in order to join our *fedai* group, because on that day he said the same thing. 'You go home now and think it over.' Back then, the situation was the other way around – I was desperate to join the group and Basri Bey wanted me to be sure of my decision, whereas now Mehmed was trying to force me into something I did not want and moreover did not have the requisite experience for. Perhaps the right response would have been to tell him there and then without even getting up from the table that there was no way I would get involved. But I couldn't, not while living under the constant threat of arrest and especially not when my hope of seeing you again had just been rekindled.

'Fine, I'll pop over to see you tomorrow evening', I said to delay the issue. 'We'll at least sink a few glasses of *rakı* together'.

When I got back to my room, I noticed that the morning rain had stopped. I stepped out onto the balcony and breathed in the damp air. A glorious sun had come out from behind the specks of clouds and had dried the balcony within half an hour but there was also a stiff wind that reminded me in its own way that the warmth would not last and that autumn was on its way. How would I ever find peace? Just when I have thought I have found a sliver of happiness, something comes along and snatches it away. For one, they don't even let me enjoy the newfound possibility of seeing you again. I fobbed Mehmed off today but tomorrow I'll let him know for sure that I'm not interested. I don't want any more missions. No more duties or liabilities, secret or out in the open, and that's all there is to it. Otherwise I'll never be able to rid myself of these people. So I have made my decision and that is that. I now feel something close to relief.

I was telling you about my conversation with Uncle Leon in Salonika, about my, ahem, 'heroics' with him, all the while hiding my longing for you. Yes, in stark contrast to the optimism I feel today, that day I was furious, and that unwarranted rage lasted all the way back to the capital....

Unwarranted? Of course it was not unwarranted. The misery I felt at having lost you coupled with what Uncle Leon had told me had left me despondent. I needed something to cling on to but whatever I tried just slipped out of my grasp, whichever street I tried I just ended up facing a huge wall. It was as though some accursed hand was closing all the doors in my face one by one. Not long ago, a mere nine months earlier, not only had I had you by my side but I had also been filled with grand hopes for the nation's future and its independence. But now you were in Paris, the revolution for which I had sacrificed our love was beset by problems and men like Uncle Leon and Ahmed Rıza, men that had believed fervently in the cause, were now openly expressing their disillusionment. Had I made the wrong decision? Had I thrown my entire life away for nothing? The rage that was engulfing me was a product of my mental and emotional torment.

I was angry as I had not found a way to express my feelings and because I had not found a way out of my situation... Yes, it was a case of helplessness. Helplessness at myself, at you, at the group but especially at my enemies. Yes, enemies. Whoever betrayed the nation, whether they were one of us or not, was now a personal enemy. As though bringing the country to its pitiful state were not enough, they had also ruined my life, which is why I was in such a raging mood that day and why I believed we had to be pitiless and brutal. Basri Bey had warned me before that my intellectual sensitivities gave me an unnecessary sense of clemency that was weakening my resolve and corrupting my soul. 'Yes, Saint-Just was right: we have been forced to exercise the tyranny of freedom, otherwise they would have recreated the despotism of bondage and made our lives hell.' That is what I said at a large general meeting held at a clubhouse in Nurosmaniye, one which Kara Kemal Bey also attended. At the meeting, we discussed ways to counter any activities targeting our revolution, as well as how we should identify any persons and groups that had the potential to stage a counter-revolution and ways they could be neutralised. We all agreed on the need for stern and swift responses. The mistakes that had led to the uprising of the 31st of March had been forgotten and we were now discussing – in a strangely sombre mood – how to deal with our political rivals and eliminate them if and when necessary. We had yet to gain full control and there were still people out there roaming around eagerly waiting for us to slip up whilst their cohorts busily dug our graves.

After the 31st March uprising, the post of prime minister had once again been granted to Hüseyin Hilmi Paşa, while Talat Bey, along with other members of our organisation, had been made ministers. More importantly, the new sultan, Mehmed Reşad, had agreed to work in collaboration with our organisation, which meant we had no more worries when it came to the palace. However, the martial law that had been declared in Dersaadet by Mahmud Şevket Paşa in the wake of the mutiny was still in force. In other words, although the sultan's authority had been seriously curtailed, there were still two powers ruling the country. Mahmud Şevket Paşa, the man who had crushed the mutiny, was more than content to defy the other authorities in the land. He felt compelled by no one, he kept us at bay and he was against any army interference in political affairs. Actually, we were also against the army meddling in politics, despite the fact it was the army that had saved us and the forces of constitutionalism during the uprising. During the group congress convened in Salonika, we had welcomed this caveat with applause but we also knew deep down that without the support of the army, real political stability could not be achieved. More importantly, the Committee of Union and Progress's backbone was drawn from the army.

That is why the Union's most reliable and trustworthy men were sent to the army, to identify troublemakers and traitors and other enemies of the homeland and of constitutionalism. And it was not just the army either; using Kara Kemal Bey's network of relationships, which spread like a spider's web throughout the city, mosques, madrasahs, schools, teahouses, drinking dens, taverns, inns and any other places where people congregated were placed under close surveillance. What people were talking about, their woes and complaints, the people behind them edging them on, who was behind any anti-party and anti-government propaganda; it would all be found out and traitors would be rooted out, one by one.

At the same time, the military courts had decided to embark upon a campaign of tolerance towards opposition youths who had lost much of their previous fervour and who were now proclaiming themselves advocates of liberty. This laxness only emboldened the enemies of the party and created an atmosphere similar to the one before the 31st March uprising, strengthening the opposition. Attacks on the party in the press in particular had begun to proliferate, chief amongst which by the young writer Ahmed Samim in the *Sada-i Millet* newspaper, which was owned by Kozmidi Pandelaki Efendi, a member of parliament in Istanbul. Actually, who the real powers behind the *Sada-i Millet* newspaper actually were was a mystery. Some said the Greek Patriarchate was behind it. How much Ahmed Samim himself knew about this matter was unknown but one thing was certain and that was that he was not shy when it came to writing against us. Maybe it was just the fire of youth but his attacks and his censures continued unabated, despite Talat Bey's personal warnings.

'We have no other choice', Basri Bey said. 'It's not ink that flows from that pen of his but blood. The man is fanning the flames and deepening the animosity and the hatred that exists against us. He is giving succour to the traitors that surround us. We need to sort this business out and soon.'

When he said *sort this business out*, what he meant was the young writer needed to be silenced, and permanently. In other words, he needed to be killed, and the 'soon' Basri Bey wished for came five days later, on a warm summer evening. It was the type of evening that usually inspires people to live, not to kill, one of those sweet evenings when one visits a good friend's house for dinner. Ironically enough, in this case, Ahmed Samim was going to dinner. A few days earlier we had received intelligence that he – Ahmed Samim – would be accepting an invitation to dinner from Muhtar Bey, son of Cemaleddin Efendi, the Şeyhülislam, and we had been following him since morning, from the moment he stepped out of his house. Had we wanted, we could have snuffed him out any time during the day but the order was to wait until darkness so there would be less chance of the killer being seen. Everybody needed to sense that we were the ones behind the killing but nobody was to be sure enough to actually point the finger, otherwise the opposition groups would have a field day.

'It's tonight or never', Basri Bey was told. 'Shut this arrogant know-it-all up for good'.

We don't know who gave the order. Was it from the Central Committee or was it another trigger-happy foot soldier like us who thought the answer to any problem was to reach for your gun? Whoever it was, it didn't matter. Ahmed Samim's card was marked, the verdict had been given, and the poison flowing from his pen would be stemmed for good. There was no other way about it. He was to be killed, and that very evening.

That morning in the house on Cağaloğlu Hill, before we began trailing him, Basri Bey had taken Fuad and I aside and informed briefed us.

'If all goes to plan, we won't be involved. However, if the designated hit man is hindered or for whatever reason does not complete the mission, then we take over and complete the job. We won't all shoot; you, Şehsuvar, will pull the trigger.

If the hit man, for whatever reason, can't do it, then you'll shoot the journalist. But wait for my signal, because I'll be in contact with the other *fedai* group. For everyone's security, it's better they don't know you and you don't know who they are. But we need to be close to the target, especially you Şehsuvar. And you need to be on your toes, because this Ahmed Samim has received numerous threatening letters and if he senses something is up, he'll be up and away. So for the love of God, whatever you do, do not give yourselves away and freak the guy out in any way. Got it?'

Of course we got it. We were like wolves that had their prey cornered and we were waiting for the moment when the guns would go off and the blood would start to flow. After we had trailed Ahmed Samim to the *Sada-i Millet* offices in Ebussuud Street, we took up positions around the building, each of us in a different corner, in different nooks and crannies.

I was sitting in Selami the Arab's coffee shop overlooking the entrance to the *Sada-i Millet* premises. I ordered a nargile for myself, not that I'm a serious smoker, and staked the place out, one eye on the entrance to the newspaper offices and the other looking for the guy that would pull the trigger. He had to be nearby but I didn't see anything suspicious in the vicinity. *Well done*, I whispered to myself. It meant he was doing his job properly. I was hoping he was a good shot too as I did not want to have to kill him. Yes, I nurtured a real resentment towards the opposition but deep down, I believed it was wrong to shoot this journalist. Well, perhaps it was not belief I felt but something more akin to fear. Why were we going to kill him? What harm could he do us? He was just a zealous fool desperate to show off and make a name for himself, a youngster that had been played by that upstart Kozmidi and was drunk on his own ramblings. Another lover of literature, just like me. Of course, if the party had decided, then it was not our place to question whether the decision was right or wrong. But hunting down Abdülhamit's spies, snoops and generals, men with blood on their hands, was one thing; killing someone who fights only with a pen and with ideas was something else, even more so when the assassination of Hasan Fehmi had still not been forgotten.

Of course, I did not convey these misgivings of mine to anyone. As a civilian and volunteer amongst more seasoned professionals, I was hardly one to be noticed and if I was to start criticising this move of ours then who knows what the others would start thinking about me. That is why I desperately wanted the first hit man to succeed, otherwise there was a strong possibility that I would be the perpetrator behind a murder I and my conscience would regret for the rest of my life.

The hours passed and still Ahmed Samim had not emerged from the newspaper offices. I was suddenly overcome by a naïve hope that he had slipped out through another door and disappeared. Perhaps somebody had told him about the plot on his life. Perhaps while we were camped out there waiting for him, he had already boarded the evening ship to Marseille... If only. But that is not what happened. The poor man was simply passing the time waiting for his dinner engagement. Eventually, as the light was beginning to fade, he emerged. He was with somebody, probably another journalist like him. As he walked over to the pavement on the other side of the road, I managed to get a good look at him. He was only a few years older than me, which is odd as for some reason, I had assumed he would be younger. I don't know if it was due to the gravity of what we were about to do to him or because of the compassion I felt for this unsuspecting victim but when I looked at him, a young man, walking straight into his own death, unaware of the danger all around him, I felt I was looking at a junior student from a class at the *Mekteb-i Sultan*.

You may ask why I didn't warn him, why I didn't tell him to run. I couldn't, Ester. I just couldn't, my love. That would have been treason to the party. I was a foot soldier in a cause, and I had been charged with certain duties. I admit it's a strange mindset, a mental oddity, but even if I felt a world of pity and compassion for Ahmed Samim, my only actual wish was that I not be the one that had to pull the trigger. It is a cruel state of affairs, yes, and, more to the point, it is a dishonourable one.... Let him die, just so long as my hands stay clean. That is what it boiled down to. And lurking behind that shame was the fact that I was not even sure I would have had it in me to shoot him, that I would have been able to pull the trigger had the need arisen.

Last night, when I lay down to sleep, I felt the same. The light from the huge full moon was striking my face, and it was giving me the creeps. While my eyes were transfixed on the moon, which looked like a huge limestone disc hanging in the night sky, everything suddenly struck me as meaningless. Everything. Homeland, the party, myself, even you. I just lay there like a lizard flitting from here to there, not knowing what to do under that gleaming full moon. It was terrifying. I switched on the lamp and, thinking it may help, began reading the novel by Anatole France, which I haven't opened for some time. Not to translate but simply to free myself from that cold, eerie silver that had reached down into my veins. But it was no good. My eyes wandered the lines of the text but my mind was miles away, so I put the book down and lay down again. I didn't know what was happening to me. Was I losing my faith? My belief in myself? Maybe it was both. Perhaps Uncle Leon was right. I could still quickly gather up my things and go first to Salonika and from there on to Paris. To you... Who knows how delighted you would be at my arrival. Or would you? I'm not sure you would be. Maybe you've already forgotten about me. Perhaps you've already expunged me completely from your heart and mind. Not that I can blame you. I am the one that made you do it.

I suddenly felt terribly lonely. Utterly alone on a dark night in a vast world. I welled up, a lump formed in my throat and yes, I wept, shamelessly, like a child. Do not see it as a weakness. Rather, it is something quite human, and it did me good. I perked up a little, although the doubts remained. I had played the role of the steely hit man well but I could feel my belief in the cause wavering. For the same reasons, I did not want to be the one that pulled the trigger that day on Ahmed Samim, although if the order did come through, I would have followed him and done what had been asked – no, *demanded* – of me.

So the two journalists set off on Ebüssuud Street and I began following them at a distance of around fifteen or twenty metres. Oddly enough, Ahmed Samim did not appear nervous. He wasn't looking around or behind him to see if anybody was watching or following. Either he was lost in conversation with his friend or he was getting into the spirit of the evening's dinner invitation.

The crowds grew larger as we approached the end of the street and Ahmed Samim and his friend headed towards Sirkeci with the rest of that mass of people. That is when I saw the hit man. He was wearing black, and a fez tilted lightly to one side. As he stepped out from next to the tobacconists on the corner of the street, his right hand was in his jacket pocket, probably clutching the weapon he was going to use for the murder. He was calm and was walking casually. Had I not seen him at the party clubhouse, I would never have spotted him or suspected him either. I don't remember his name but I think he was a Circassian, either from Serres or Drama. I'd heard that he was one of the party's most fearless men but this street filled with people making their way home from work was hardly the best spot to pick for an assassination. How was he going to do it in front of all these people? Before I could even formulate the thought in my mind, Ahmed Samim and his friend had crossed the road. Our Circassian assassin didn't rush though and just carried on walking in front of me before he too crossed over to the other pavement. The two journalists then turned into the street that led to the Central Post Office. I stayed behind the shooter, who had increased his pace. As we turned into the street, I turned around and sure enough, Major Basri and Lieutenant Fuad were ten to fifteen metres behind us. I took a deep breath and turned into the street.

The crowds seemed to have dispersed a little and our young *fedai* had sped up so he was now only a few metres away from Ahmed Samim. My eyes were fixed on his right hand, still thrust in his pocket. Was he taking it out? Was this it? Yes, he was taking the gun out…. My throat went dry. Was he going to do it here? No, he was in no rush. He wanted to keep the distance between himself and his victim until the time and place were appropriate. His target and his companion turned into the street that led down the hill, with the rest of us in pursuit. I suddenly had a strange thought. What if I were to intervene? What if I were to stop our hit man and let Ahmed Samim escape? Of course, I would never have done such a thing, but had I tried, then the others – my friends, no less – would have shot me without hesitation on the spot.

'The punishment for treason must be severe', our beloved major used to say. 'Traitors we can never forgive. If we do, they will only multiply and flourish.'

So no, I had no such intention but if by some miracle Ahmed Samim were to have escaped, then I for one would have been relieved. However, there was little chance of that happening and I carried on playing my part. The street was calm and quiet but my heart was in my mouth. The journalists took another left, towards Bahçekapı, with the man in black hot on their heels. I had to increase my pace to keep up with them. When we reached the main road, I looked up and saw that the Circassian was all but breathing down Ahmed Samim's neck. He seemed tense, which meant we must have been nearing the denouement. I sped up, as though I were about to intervene. That is when the gun went off. Three times in quick succession. The hit man stood there, holding his Smith & Wesson. He must have shot Ahmed Samim in the back of the neck as the poor man fell forward face first, while his friend fled for his life and ran into a nearby bakery to hide.

For a moment, the gunman looked at the body of his victim lying on the ground and then began to walk calmly but rapidly away. As for me, I was rooted to the spot. It was weird but I couldn't take my eyes off the body and the shattered head on the ground in front of me. From one side, he looked a lot like me. Almost as though I had a twin I had never known about. Or had they actually shot me dead and I just didn't know? Was my soul stopping to have one last look at my body before finally departing, the way they say it does? There were people rushing about all around me, a crowd was beginning to gather and there were voices and cries everywhere but none of it seemed to be affecting me. I simply stood there on the side of the road like a statue. Had Basri Bey not turned up, I may have stayed there forever.

'Let's go, Şehsuvar', he said, taking me by the arm. 'We're done here, son. Let's go'. As we moved away, he didn't neglect to give me a ticking off. 'What the hell were you doing back there, stopping like that? Luckily I know you, or I would have thought you were about to pass out at the sight of blood.'

He was absolutely right. The sight of blood had affected me. Not at that precise moment though but long before. Maybe it was when Şemsi Paşa was killed, or when the Albanian marksmen were gunned down, or when the mutineers were being mown down in front of me at the Topçu Barracks.... Yes, the sight of blood sickens me but until that moment, I had never realised. The cause and the revolution had been so hypnotic to me and subsequent events had unfolded so rapidly around me that I had not had the chance to realise that I was repelled by the sight of blood. But now... I couldn't take much more. My body had reached its limit and my spirit could no longer accept what was happening... My mind could perhaps be persuaded but my soul was appalled by all this killing... Yes, blood sickened me. It sickened me when that first gun went off in Bitola when Şemsi Paşa was shot. But it was only now that I was beginning to realise it.

Miracles

Hello Ester (Evening, Day 7)

When I went down to dinner, it was still early and the sun had yet to set. I hadn't had anything to eat since noon and my stomach was rumbling. I had planned to walk along the *Cadde-i Kebir* and get some fresh air but as I approached the Tepebaşı Gardens, I saw a young girl. She was thin, with your build and with red hair like yours. For a second I thought it was you and prayed to the Almighty that it was. I started to walk towards her although I was so excited I could not keep up with her and she quickly slipped into the gardens, seemingly in a rush. I went in after her and although I lost her at first amidst that sea of tables, it did not take me long to find her. She was sitting by herself, her back to me, at one of the tables in front of the pavilion in which the orchestra usually played. I walked up to her, nervously and hesitantly, and the closer I got to her, the more hopeful I became. The way she leaned her head ever so slightly to one side and curled her hairs over her fingers made me think of you. But when I was just a few metres away, before I even saw her face, the painful truth hit me: the last time I had seen you was a good four years ago, and even then you had already become a young woman so how could you have remained the same over such a long stretch of time? Still, I was not discouraged by that fact. And why should I have been? You have always been one for miracles. I did not give up until I saw her face and when I did, she was exactly what I had anticipated; a complete stranger. She was young, very young, no more than eighteen, if at all. When she saw me staring intently at her, she smiled back at me, and quite alluringly too, and I realised she was one of the many ladies of leisure that are to be found plying their trade around the Tepebaşı Gardens. I smiled back but did not go any closer, finding instead another table far from the stage with a wonderful view of the Golden Horn.

I ordered chicken with thyme, a Salonika special, and a Bomonti beer. I knew the dish would be nothing like the way my mother cooked it but I was hoping that the meal would at least have a passing resemblance to what I was used to. However, my hope was in vain. What arrived was a bland, tasteless affair but I was so hungry I covered it with pepper and all the other spices at hand and polished the whole plate off and then ordered another beer. I stared out at the evening sea. It was turning a glistening red in some places, just like the red sheen of your hair, and I gave in to my inner wanderings.

If you have come to Istanbul and I do manage to find you, then I need to think of a new life for us together. Would you like the house in Beşiktaş, for example? Colak Cafer said that you were looking for a house. That means you must be with Uncle Leon. I wonder, have you sold your house and offices in Salonika? Perhaps your Uncle Leon will set up an office here. Not that working for him at this stage of my life is actually a prospect...

Such were my thoughts when I suddenly realised I had lost the plot and I burst into laughter. What on earth was I doing? I still don't know for sure whether you are in Istanbul or not, and even if you are, there is no way of knowing how you will greet me. But if I am to believe Mehmed Esad, you have already been here two months. Had your Uncle Leon wanted, he could easily have tracked me down by now. After all, wasn't Mehmed able to find me? Suddenly, my high spirits fell. What if you really have forgotten about me completely and have come to Istanbul from Salonika simply to start a new life for yourselves, a new life in which there is no place for me? I can almost hear your answer. *Why should there be? After so much pain and so many setbacks and after all the wasted years, why would I want to be with you again?* I had no answer. All I had was a tiny glimmer of hope that perhaps you have not forgotten, and that you still love me.

I could think it, yes, and try to console myself with the thought but the mood was ruined. Walking along the *Cadde-i Kebir* suddenly seemed too much of a trek. As I pondered over whether to order another beer or not, I realised what I needed was not alcohol but a pen. I needed to write so I paid up and headed back to the Pera Palas.

I was hesitant when I first picked up the pen as I didn't know how to start. I kept thinking about how humans can destroy their own happiness with their own hands. Why would a man leave behind a life he loves and wants and dive headfirst into a venture fraught with danger? Why would a man do that to himself? Because of youth and inexperience, and because he did not know himself. Very well. Then let me ask: do we get to know ourselves when we get older? When we are older, do we know what we want? Can our minds solve that riddle? Can a man explain himself to himself? Perhaps yes... Perhaps yes, but only for a moment, a short while, until a new event, a new incident, comes along and rocks him and his mental stability once again. Then the picture changes completely and we once again forget who we are.

That is what happened to me in the wake of the assassination of Ahmed Samim. Not only was I unsure as to what I was doing, I was unable to even clearly analyse the situation. Amidst all my mental turmoil and confusion, it was difficult for me to even say I regretted what I did. Do not misconstrue this as a fear of confessing on my part. If that were the case, I could have easily come up with a solution and split from the party. That I would have been prepared to do. The oath I took would not have stopped me. You know as well as I do that an oath taken over a cause we no longer believe in has no binding power. Don't misunderstand; freedom, equality and fraternity were still sacred values to me but I was no longer sure that the path the party had chosen would take us where we wanted to be. That is why I was confused, and why death at the hands of humans was now unthinkable to me.

The evening after the death of Ahmed Samim, I began thinking more frequently about Şehsuvar Sami the writer. Or rather, with the death of that young journalist, the writer Şehsuvar Sami had begun to take more of a hold over me. In the battle that was taking place between my conscience and my will, it seemed, for the moment, that my conscience was winning. The murders we were committing and the blood we were shedding I could no longer justify by saying it was all for the revolution and for the cause, and when I did try to justify it so, I was no longer convinced. Somewhere along the line, a mistake had been made, one that could be grasped, perhaps even corrected, using logic but something else inside me was now broken beyond repair. It was not a simple case of realising we had made a political blunder but one of actual disillusionment. Like the disillusionment I had seen in the eyes of Ahmed Rıza and Uncle Leon... After what I had been through, I remembered what you had once said and now realised how right you were:

'Life is brutal, Şehsuvar, and that is why man invented art. And we are lucky because we are at least able to write. When life becomes too much, when the days become unbearable, we have a wonderful port to which we can retreat, one called literature. What's more, our writings are not just a shelter for us but can be a shelter for others too and may give them a renewed joy in life. Don't you see? Life would otherwise be unendurable.'

As the writer in me began to grow, I began to remember your words more frequently. Indeed, I was not just remembering you but actually began to find myself talking to you. Once, I was caught doing so at home by Madam Melina. She knocked on the door and asked, 'Şehsuvar my lad, did you say something?' And of course, this new development did not go unnoticed by Basri Bey. I was expecting a stern reprimand, or at least a warning of some kind, but instead I received a polite invitation to dinner.

Remember the Tepebaşı Gardens, where I saw that red-haired girl I thought was you? It was at the entrance to those gardens that Basri Bey and I met sixteen years ago. The commotion from the jazz orchestra playing inside was too much for us so we decided to walk along the *Cadde-i Kebir* up to the Cité de Péra arcade. Along the way we talked about this and that; at one point, even though it was not the done thing with us, we even touched on the topic of literature. Basri Bey told me had not read any other poets besides Namık Kemal and he admitted this was a failing on his part and went on to say how important he knew reading was. I could feel that this was not what he really wanted to talk about and I was waiting nervously for him to get to the point, nodding and agreeing half-heartedly with whatever he said, careful not to disagree or initiate any argument. We carried on talking in this manner until we got to Yorgo's tavern in the arcade. While we're on the subject, yes, the first time I went to Yorgo's was with Basri Bey; after that first visit, I became a regular. It was also that night that I first met the waiter Hristo, who was still a young man back then. Even then he was as jovial and as vivacious as ever.

'Welcome, Basri Bey sir. What would you like to drink tonight?'

'I'll have some *sakız rakısı*, old boy, thanks', he said and looked at me. 'How about we get you an aniseed *rakı*, eh? It's all the rage at the moment. Everyone seems to be drinking it.'

Back then, I wasn't really much of a drinker but I hardly wanted to publicize it so I said, 'I'll have the same as you. I'm not a big fan of the aniseed variety'.

Basri Bey turned back to Hristo and said, 'In that case, open up a bottle of *Deniz Kızı* for us. You still have that brand in stock, haven't you?'

'Sir', Hristo began with a glint in his eye. 'If I did not have *Deniz Kızı* to serve my customers, I would shut this place down. I shall return with your drinks right away.'

The table was set with an array of mezzes, the *rakı* was poured into the carafe and first sips were taken. We felt that sweet burning sensation in our throats and had moved on to the second glass but we had still to broach the topic that was supposed to be the whole point of the evening. I was beginning to think I'd made a mistake and that this was just another normal dinner when Basri Bey began.

'Women, eh? They're sometimes the most important things in our lives'. He had raised his voice and shifted his gaze from his glass to my face. 'The same can be said about love. We sometimes think life is all about love. But that is a big mistake because love, just like a woman's charms, is a fleeting thing. We, however, think it isn't because it gives us such joy, such pleasure. A pleasure tinged with an abiding pain too. But they all come to an end eventually. No matter how deep, how grand or how moving it may be, all loves end. If there is one abiding law in all this, it is that it is fleeting. Those that live their lives according to love eventually end up broken and ruined. It doesn't matter whether it is happy or not, in love the result is always the same.' He let out a deep breath. 'I'm sure you know why I'm saying all this. I'll be straight. I don't like what's happened to you recently. The way you're heading. As though you're no longer with us in heart.'

'Not at all, sir, it's just that...' I began but he raised a hand to silence me.

'Don't bother objecting, Şehsuvar. I know about the Jewish girl that went to Paris. I know how much you love her. I've been through it too. The same heady love. Had I gone about the way you are now, I would have long since married that Romanian girl I fell in love with in Bucharest fifteen years ago. But would I have found happiness and contentment? I doubt it. Men like us; no matter how much we may love a woman, we cannot live our entire lives at her beck and call. We are like the wind, Şehsuvar. We have storms raging inside us. That, indeed, is why we attach so much importance to our women. We see love as this serious, spectacular entrance that will turn our lives into some kind of epic, and for a time, that is what it may be. But it always ends in pain and disappointment. For men with grand ideals, love alone cannot provide the contentment we seek, and it never will. The profound love we feel for our motherland, the unflinching sacrifices we are ready to make for our countries and for the cause; this is what moves us. It is the cause that inspires and satisfies us.'

To be honest, I was stunned. I would never have expected Major Basri to speak so eloquently. He was also aware of the effects his words were having on me.

'Don't make a mistake, son. Do not neglect your duty to your country for a momentary affair. We are living through a historical epoch. Yet greater opportunities and greater duties await us. Yes, any man can fall in love with a woman and any man can feel the pain of love, that I do not deny or denigrate, and yes, these feelings too are important, but how many men can history remember as heroes? How many men can stand and up say without hesitation that they killed and that they risked death for their motherland?'

'It is not dying that matters', I replied. The words seemed to tumble from my lips without any effort on my part. 'But killing, especially the innocent, and killing people simply for their ideas…'

It seemed he hadn't considered that and believed that the matter was simply your leaving. He sighed a deep sigh and lifted his glass of *rakı*.

'In that case, let us drink to conscience…'

I didn't for sure know what he meant but I lifted my glass anyway.

'To conscience'.

We downed our glasses and then banged them down on the table.

'What does conscience mean, eh, Şehsuvar? Does it mean trying to stop the catastrophe as the country rushes head-long into oblivion or does it mean retreating to a corner and watching events from afar in safety, without getting your hands, your mind or your conscience dirty? The country is heading into the abyss, that much is certain, a bloody abyss, and there is only one organisation that can stop it and that is the Committee for Union and Progress. I'm not saying it's going to be easy. In fact, it's going to be very hard, maybe even impossible. And this battle will not be won with guns, rifles, cannons and artillery but with something far more powerful. Ideas. That's right, with ideas. With the mind. But just as the mind can bring about freedom, equality and fraternity, so it can also cause unrest and destruction. Remember the 31st March uprising. I dread to think what would have happened had the insurgents succeeded. I don't mean the savageries they would have inflicted on us personally and our bodies but what they would have done to the country. Just try and picture that.

'So yes, Şehsuvar my brother, this thing we call conscience is not just a case of keeping your hands cleans but also a case of not hesitating in pulling the trigger even when you know it is a cardinal sin to do so. Because what you are killing is a traitor and killing him means thousands of people get to live. Conscience also means being prepared to kill if you have to and if the circumstances demand it…. If you have to then yes, it means killing a journalist or a man who sees himself merely as a 'thinker'. Yes, they may accuse and reproach and condemn you, and call you a cold-hearted, cold-blooded killer. But all that matters in this cause is the unity and the integrity of the country. The rest is just hot air.' He leaned over to me. 'I'll be open with you. If you tell me now that you can't go on, that you've had enough and that you can't take any more, then you can leave the party and the organization as of this minute. And you don't need to be afraid either. You can leave freely and without any fears. If you need money, then I can help you out in that respect too. But if you tell me that you're not going anywhere, that you're in, that you're a part of all this, then you need to sort yourself out. Because we do not have time for *fedaeen* that hesitate at critical moments.'

At that moment, I wanted the earth to swallow me whole. He had summed up my predicament so simply and yet so brutally that I could not summon up the strength to object from any source. And he was right. Nobody had forced me to join the Committee. It had always been my decision. I had wanted it, and at the cost of losing you too. It was not a children's game. A revolution was taking place and history was being written in front of our eyes, and in blood too, and I was not so ignorant or inexperienced as to be unaware of that. I had been involved in politics since my childhood. Or rather, politics had found me in childhood and involved me ever since: it had taken my precious father away from me and sent him into exile. The motherland is people's destiny, no matter how much we try to deny it. Even if I had gone to Paris, I would not have been able to escape or ignore destiny. Had I gone to Paris, my heart and my mind would have still been here, in these lands, and I would have made not just myself unhappy but you too. Yes, my commandant was right. It was time to stop faltering. The time for pondering and reflecting was over and the time for action had arrived. I had chosen my path and it was not a path strewn with flowers weaving its way through a scented garden but a garden reeking of blood and gunpowder that led up the slopes of a fiery volcano.

'I have already decided, Basri Bey', I said breathlessly. 'I had already decided before our meeting in Salonika. My belief in the cause is total.'

'I doubt it', he said, putting me in my place. 'Let's be honest here, Şehsuvar. You have doubts, either about us or about yourself. My dear friend, there is little to be gained from deception. When you and I first met, I told you to go home and think it over until the morning, and now I'm saying the same. Tonight go home and think it through.... But this time, be sure, because there won't be a third time. You know what I mean, don't you? There won't be any going back.'

'I understand clearly and I don't need time to think it over. I've made my decision.' It was obvious from the way he was looking at me that he was not convinced. 'It's true, Basri Bey, sir, that I at one point I may have had some reservations. That I may have lost my way a little. But now I have found it again. Nothing can sway me now. I'll do whatever you ask of me. I swear, I won't cause any more problems for you from now on.'

He sighed, reached for his *rakı* and raised his glass.

'Very well then'. I believe you. To believe in somebody means to vouch for them. In other words, I vouch for you. And to whom, you may ask? To the party. The Committee.

What that means is I accept the responsibility that comes with vouching for you and that is because I know you and I trust you. All I ask is you do not tarnish my name or my reputation.

'Now that that's done, let's drink. To your health'.

I raised my glass.

'To your health, sir'.

He drank but he kept his eyes on me.

'Be in front of the French Post Office in Galata tomorrow at 11.00', he said. 'We have important work to do. And make sure you bring your gun.'

Once he said that, he did not raise the issue again, nor did he allow me to mention it again. We talked about this and that, life and the weather. However, as we were saying our goodbyes to each other in front of the Cité de Péra, he wagged a finger in warning and said, 'We're not playing games here, my friend. No more hesitations. No more doubts from now on.'

It was not a threat. There was no enmity in his voice. All he was doing was trying to underscore to me how important the matter was. Since then, I have looked back many times on our conversation and pondered it. Was he, an experienced committee member and soldier, playing a game that he thought would influence me and change my mind or was he actually revealing his true feelings? Not that I'll ever be sure but I think it may have been the latter. Basri Bey was a honourable man and soldier, and a man of integrity and to the very last, when he died in front of my very eyes, that opinion I had of him never changed.

The conversation chat we had evening that evening banished all my doubts, like a brisk spring breeze. The way I saw it, the writer Şehsuvar in me had been removed from my being, and full control had been given back to Şehsuvar the revolutionary. If you ask if it really did happen that quickly, then my answer is, yes, it did. Don't forget, back then, I was still a young man, and like a fire in a stormy field, I went which-ever way the wind blew. That conversation also had another unexpected effect: the party no longer sent me on missions to clean up writers, thinkers and intellectuals that were considered enemies. I don't who made this decision and I'll probably never know. Maybe the party had enough evidence to suggest that I was not a safe bet on such missions; perhaps Talat Bey had had a say in the matter, or perhaps Basri Bey himself had been involved in the decision. After that conversation, had such a mission been entrusted to me, I would of course have carried it out but at the same time, now that the decision had been made, I was not complaining about it. Fuad and Basri Bey had also been relieved of the rather ugly and unpleasant task of silencing journalists writing for the opposition. From now on, we would be sent to deal directly with illegal opposition groups that were manoeuvring against us, whose activities were on the increase. And one of those planned activities is what Basri Bey was referring to when he told me to be at the French Post Office in Galata at 11.00 the next morning.

The Ability to Forgive Ourselves

Good Morning, Ester (Morning, Day 8)

The rain has started again. Serene, calm, without fuss or commotion, like a woman silently crying to herself. I'm not one of those people that likes to predict what the day will be like by looking at the weather. I don't believe in such absurdities. Storms, winds, rain and clouds may be portents in Shakespeare's plays but in reality, they are just blind forces of nature. And yet despite knowing this, I have a sinking feeling in my heart today. I'm going to see Cezmi, to get news about you. To find out whether there is any truth in the rumour that has brought hope to my world. I'm not going right now but later on this afternoon. I may even hold till the evening as there is no point in meeting the old major if he hasn't spoken to Çolak Cafer. I might even go tomorrow; that way, at least there will be more of a guarantee. Hang on. I can't wait that long. I need to find about you today. I need to find out where you're staying and knock on your door, even if it is in the middle of the night. I know it may not be right or appropriate but I can't take much more.

I went down to breakfast thinking I was hungry but actually all I had was half a slice of bread, a small piece of cheese and some coffee. And no, I shan't read the newspaper today. I'm not in the mood for politics. I should perhaps find Reşit. He may want to come with me. Going to Cezmi's house by myself may not be a good idea. But Reşit was nowhere to be seen so I went over to reception to ask after him.

'Morning Ömer. Is Reşit Bey around?'

'Morning sir', Ömer replied brightly. 'I'm afraid he hasn't arrived yet. Actually, he is normally here at this time so he has either been delayed or is busy with some other work.'

Why was he late? Hopefully nothing had happened to him. I could already feel the doubts and the misgivings gather, those sinister whisperings… I quietly told myself to pull myself together.

'Very well, Ömer. I'll be in my room. Please let me know when he arrives.'

I began walking towards the elevator when I suddenly remembered something else.

'Oh, and another thing Ömer. That friend of mine yesterday…' He had no idea whom I was talking about. 'The one who was here before'.

'You mean the well-dressed gentleman?'

'Yes, that's the one. Did you tell him my room number?'

'Not me, sir', he said taken aback. 'Never. I would never commit such a gross dereliction of trust.'

So how did Mehmed Esad know which room I was staying in?

'May I ask if it is your friend who is suggesting I revealed such delicate and confidential information?'

'No, no, not at all', I said, not wanting to land him in hot water. 'It must be an innocent slipup, that's all. It doesn't matter anyway. I'll be off now. You have a good day. Again, please let me know once Reşit Bey gets here.'

A relatively minor and insignificant issue that was nagging at me yesterday had suddenly turned into something quite alarming. How did Mehmed Esad get my room number? How else but from his own men in the hotel. The big hotels were teeming with moles. The young Belgian waiting in front of the elevator with me this morning, for instance, a tall, well-built athletic-looking man in his thirties – when I saw him, I thought, even he could be a spy but then I laughed to myself. As if Mehmed Esad would bring men over from Belgium to watch over me! It is the hotel staff I need to keep an eye on.

Maybe even Ömer, despite his innocent features. He, more than anybody, knows who is coming and going in the hotel. The Belgian and I got into the elevator and we got out on the same floor. I began walking to my room and he was right behind me. I began walking to my room. He was right behind me when I sensed he had stopped. When I reached my door, I turned to look and saw him enter one of the rooms on the left.

This constant suspicion and mistrust are starting to get me, starting to eat away at me. Telling myself I needed to calm down, I walked into my room but instead of sitting at my desk to write, I stood by the balcony for some time looking outside. The light outside had turned silver and the rain was beginning to pick up. It would last all day, well into the evening. I turned around, stifled by that gloomy weather, and sat at my desk.

I'm sure you were taken aback when you read about the conversation I had with Basri Bey at Yorgo's tavern. I'm sure you were annoyed at my complacency and my indecision. I won't say you're wrong; just don't rush to judge me. Try to put yourself in my shoes before passing judgement. Then perhaps you may understand me, and not just me but yourself and perhaps even mankind too…. That's right, mankind too, because we are not distinct from that great mass. For good or bad, whether cowardly or brave, hesitant or decisive, we are what the rest of mankind is. We may believe we are important but we are not, not in the least. We are all weak, vulnerable beings consisting of mere flesh and bone. And if we did not have the ability to forgive ourselves, then we would not have survived. Will, consistency, determination; these all sound good but if our forebears had stuck rigidly to these ideas then that species known as man would have long since been wiped off the face of the earth.

I'm not saying all this in an attempt to defend myself but simply to remind myself of the weakness lurking in man's disposition. If you're angry at me, furious even, and are censuring me, I fully understand but please do not belittle me. I may have made the wrong decisions, I may have wasted a life coming up to forty years and I may have harmed not just myself but my country, my homeland and even my people... Yes, I confess to all of that but know this: when the world was awash with blood and the country was staring into the abyss, how could I be expected to always do the right thing? Naturally, I wanted to do the right thing, and I was prepared to pay a hefty price in order to do so. But it didn't work out. Yes, I failed, and that is the simple truth. However, I am not the only one to bear responsibility for this. You know as well as I that I am very harsh with myself. I am always first to blame myself whenever a problem arises. And yet in most cases, humans do not want to accept that they are to blame, no matter how much they may have messed up. They are rarely honest with themselves and even when they are, they are quick to whitewash their mistakes and forget about them. Not me. I become uneasy when there is a problem, life comes to a standstill for me, and I see myself as the cause.

But the strange thing is, after that conversation at Yorgo's, I did not blame myself. What Basri Bey's stern words did that evening was to actually stop me staying up all night with a constantly shifting and unsettled state of mental turmoil. That night, after that conversation, I slept like a baby. No nightmares or dark thoughts interrupted me. My mind and heart were totally relaxed and I enjoyed a deep, peaceful, comfortable sleep. The Şehsuvar that had previously been lost in a maelstrom of doubts, hesitation and confusion was waiting in front of the French Post Office the next morning ready for the mission to which he had been assigned. Surprising, yes, but when it comes to the human soul, one needs to prepare for all manner of surprises.

I joined Basri Bey and Fuad, who were seated at a table outside a café on the other side of the road facing the Post Office. Basri Bey greeted me warmly and naturally, with no hint of the previous evening's conversation. As for Fuad, it was clear he had no idea about that conversation. We ordered three coffees and then lowered our voices to discuss the matter at hand.

'They've set up a new squad, the *Cemiyet-i Hafiye*. The name gives it away. The Surveillance Agency. A reference, in their minds, to Abdülhamit's reign. Seems their goals is to wipe out the CUP leadership and deal a serious blow to this country. They are based in Paris and are being led by Şerif Paşa, the former ambassador to Stockholm. Actually, he's an old CUP guy but when things didn't turn out the way he wanted, he turned his back on us and now he has us in his sights. He was sure the 31st March uprising would see us wiped out for good and so on the eve of the insurgency, he slipped off to Paris. Things went south and he realised he was no longer welcome in the CUP but he couldn't stomach it and so he has been sending money and publications from France to support this new *Cemiyet-i Harfiye*. It's clear he has connections in some countries' secret services. This network is a highly devious one and operates behind a wall of protection provided by the *Islahat-ı Esasiye Cemiyeti,* the Ottoman Society for Fundamental Reform, which has been set up completely above board as a legitimate party. The party has a lot of members and divisions and it is only a matter of time before they pick up their guns...' With a nod of the head, he gestured towards the entrance to the Post Office. 'This Hafız Sami fellow we're looking out for is on his way here to pick up instructions from Paris sent by Şerif Paşa. He's here every Tuesday and Thursday, like clockwork. He collects the coded instructions and illegally published material and hands it on to the leaders and members of the group. Our mission is to find out who his contacts are, who these traitors are, and identify their homes, their shops and their places of business. Whatever happens, we cannot give ourselves away. There is to be no intervention of any kind until the order comes through, is that understood? No intervening, no interfering and no detaining. Got it?'

'Got it', Fuad said, scratching the back of his neck. 'So who is going to bring him in? What are we – petty bureaucrats filling in report forms?'

Like me, but for different reasons, Fuad was upset at not being given more responsibilities. He was right, though. Why weren't we out there fighting on the front lines?

'Patience, Fuad brother', Basri Bey said. 'Regardless of our personal inclinations, we must remember we are part of a large group and that group is the source of our strength. We are like musicians in a grand orchestra. By ourselves, there is little we can do, but together we create exquisite music that can move the heavens and the earth. For the moment, all we can do is what is asked of us. That is more than enough. Capturing him and bringing him in for questioning we can save for a later stage and for some other guys.' He glanced at the doorway to the Post Office. 'There he is. Our man. Here to collect the Paris mail'.

We only caught a quick glimpse of Hafiz Sami the courier from behind as he had rushed into the Post Office.

'As always, we'll split up and follow him. If he suspects one of us, the other two can stay on his trail. Although it will be much better if he doesn't suspect any of us, naturally.'

We finished our coffees. Fuad and I stood up, whilst Basri Bey stayed behind smoking his cigarette and bathing in the sunshine. I headed for Karaköy, whilst Fuad made for the hill. Now it was up to chance and to fate as to which direction he would take. As luck would have it, he took mine, strolling casually past on the pavement opposite the German bookshop I was loitering in. I spent a little more time pretending to browse the books there and then fell in after him. Fuad and Basri Bey had most probably also sprung into action. As for Hafiz Sami, the way he was walking, in such a casual and relaxed manner and seemingly without a care in the world, he looked like a man carrying a newspaper rather than material that could bring down the government. He did not seem to have any suspicion that he was being followed or any fear as to what the consequences of his capture could be. Indeed, he was so relaxed, when he reached the seafront, he stopped and hummed a little tune to himself.

There was still time before the ferry arrived. He put his delicate package down on the ground between his legs and lit a cigarette. I couldn't help but think that we may have received dubious intelligence otherwise how could somebody caught up in illegal activities like this appear so calm and carefree? My comrades must have got the same impression because when Fuad and I made eye contact, he looked at me quizzically, subtly turning his hands up and raising his eyebrows in astonishment. It was the same when we boarded the ferry. Our reckless target chose a seat on the top deck and began snoozing in the noon sunshine.

The three of us were amazed but we stuck to our mission. When we disembarked at Kadıköy, our man began making his way to Kuşdili, again with that same languid, carefree stride. He was so calm, that there was a risk that his lethargy would start to get to us too but when Basri Bey caught Fuad and I communicating to each other with our eyes and eyebrows, he gestured for us to pack it in. Hafız entered a two-storey wooden house in a garden on the left of the hill leading up to Kuşdili. When he came out half an hour later, the package he had been holding was gone. Fuad was sent off to track the indolent courier whilst Basri Bey and I took up position in front of the house.

After a twelve-hour stakeout, we realised we'd hit the jackpot. People began streaming in and out of the house, some of whom we had personally identified as enemies of the CUP. The next morning, we submitted our report to headquarters, and events began to develop at lightning pace. A delegation from headquarters met with Mahmud Şevket Paşa, the officer in charge of martial law, to explain the gravity of the situation. The corridors of government power soon began to ripple with activity. We stayed on Hafız Sami's trail as the poor fool went on with his business, happily completing his mission street by street, unaware that he had given himself away to the entire secret service. Our stakeout of the house in Kuşdili continued too, with our squads working in shifts checking out everybody that went in and out of the house and writing up reports on all of them. It was painstaking, detailed, disciplined work but there was one thing that was bugging me. This *Cemiyet-i Hafiye*, this spy network that had been set up, was not capable of starting an insurgency more powerful than that of the uprising of the 31st March and overthrowing the government. Those may have been their goals and their aims but the organisation we had under surveillance was just a bunch of half-hearted and inept fools and it wasn't long before we had found their ten locations in the city and identified their chief, a man by the name of Kemal Bey. On one of those nights when we were lying low amongst rows of tomatoes and aubergine in the little garden facing the house in Kuşdili watching the people walking in and out, I couldn't stand it anymore and asked, 'Should we really be taking these guys this seriously?'

Basri Bey shook his head reproachfully.

'Look here, son. We are no longer young, firebrand irregulars trying to start a revolt. We are now protecting a state and a constitutional government. We are the guardians of that government and we have to protect it not just with guns, swords and rifles but with our minds too. Yes, I'm talking about intelligence gathering. Abdülhamit ruled over this country for thirty years with a network of spies, informers and police. Of course, we are not going to set up a dictatorship the way he did but we do need an intelligence network every bit as strong as the one he had. If we don't, then with the world the way it is now, there is no way we can survive, not as a country or as a people. But intelligence work is never just surveillance, pursuit and detention. Most of the time, we won't be able to carry out arrests anyway. What matters is detaining people when it is politically expedient.' He turned to look at the house. The lights had not been switched off the whole evening. 'You're right, we can't expect a respectable insurgency or counter-revolution from these guys. But what they can do is provide us with a gilt-edged opportunity to prove the value of our organisation to the government.' Seeing the blank expression in my eyes, he went on. 'Let me put it this way. Who gained the most from the 31st March uprising? We did, of course. We are now much stronger than before, both with the government and with the people. If we sort this *Cemiyet-i Hafiye* out at the right time and in the right way and, more importantly, if we can get public opinion on our side, then we can become even stronger. That is why you should not underestimate this lot, especially when you are writing up your report. Otherwise you'll be making a huge mistake – in political terms, anyway.'

It was a completely different Basri Bey I was seeing. Gone was the solemn and dignified soldier obeying every command to the letter; in his place was a smart, cunning intelligence officer. I was at a loss. My trust in him was shaken but my admiration for him was now even stronger. He was not the superficial, one-dimensional person I had made him out to be, and I realised how wrong I had been to underestimate him. On top of all that, I now – finally – understood how critical our mission was. It was no joke: the country's political future and its fate, and therefore life itself, were in our hands. The men in power would act upon the details of the reports we submitted to them. I felt an unbelievable surge of power, but at the same time, I was also hesitant. How right it could it be for us to distort the truth for our own political expedience? But that immediately gave rise to another question: what exactly was 'the truth'? Of what use was a 'truth' that did not allow us to alter the course of history or to bring people happiness? Truth for us was a new country that would be built on the basis of liberty, equality, justice and fraternity. Everything we did and every step we took was for that. That is what I told myself to put an end to the doubts. We needed to focus on whichever aspect of the truth aided us politically and ignore those aspects of the truth that weakened us. We had no other choice if we were to succeed.

And that is exactly what we did. To scare the masses, we used the possibility of a new revolt and portrayed the *Cemiyet-i Hafiye* as a terrifying organisation with nefarious plans. The pro-government newspapers were only too glad to help us. The public were told what we wanted them to be told and thanks to this influence of ours, the arrests, when they came, caused a sensation. The police and security forces tracked the plotters for days and when they did move in, pretty much all of the *Cemiyet-i Hafiye*'s members had been arrested, their homes raided and their bases exposed, all within a matter of days. Only by pure coincidence did their leader Kemal Bey manage to get away, but his wife Şahande Hanım was arrested and charged with being a member of the organisation. Although she maintained her innocence, the evidence suggested that she too was involved. Thus, not only were we able to browbeat the opposition but we were also able to arrest parliamentary representatives like Rıza Nur, who had been stirring up hostility against the CUP. Having said that, Rıza Nur was later released on the personal orders of Talat Bey, but the message got through to the opposition that we were serious.

Abdülhamit used to fill the Bekirağa Bölüğü Prison with freedom fighters and good men, men of the soil, but the prison's new guests were these incompetent would-be rebels trying to bring down the constitutional government. And yes, I will admit now that the treatment they received was horrific. Our men were just as brutal towards them as Abdülhamit's wardens had once been to us. Of course, I am not condoning the treatment meted out to the prisoners as cruelty is a sign of weakness but we simply could not stop certain urges and impulses that had by now seeped into the very depths of the state. Thankfully, I was not involved in any of the interrogations or torture sessions but the day would soon come when our hands would get very dirty indeed. That is because a homeland cannot be defended with rhetoric and flowery language alone. To defend and uphold the state, one must be ready to commit acts of evil.

Losing One's Humanity

Hello Ester (Afternoon, Day 8)

The rain stopped at noon but the sky was filled with leaden clouds, ready to open up again at any moment. I took a break from my writing and went down for lunch. Reşit was waiting for me by the marble column at the bottom of the staircase. He looked excited, rather than nervous or worried, a kind of sweet anxiety writ across his countenance. When he saw me, he rushed up to me.

'Şehsuvar *ağabey*, your English is pretty good, isn't it? A writer has just arrived from England, a young lady. She writes detective novels, or something on those lines. I am going to accompany her to lunch and was thinking you could perhaps join us.'

I thought about Abdülhamid. Had he still been sultan, he would no doubt have been eager to meet the young English woman but I was not in the mood.

'I'm sorry Reşit, I have things to attend to.'

His face fell.

'That's a shame. Do you think my English will be enough?'

'I'm sure it will', I said, slapping him on the shoulder. 'You'll be fine. Who knows, maybe she speaks French... Actually, that reminds me. What are you doing this afternoon? Shall we pay Cezmi a visit?'

He paused to think.

'I can't. I have a meeting with the owner of the hotel. It will probably go on for some time. Competition between the Istanbul hotels is heating up, as I'm sure you are aware. We're going toe-to-toe with the Grand Hotel de Londres and the Tokatlıyan. Quality is key, and we're all trying to outdo one another. Please forgive me this once. Let's do it another day.'

He had just finished talking when a young lady appeared next to us.

'Hello Mister Reşit…'

She had a long, thin face, a very fair complexion and greenish-blue eyes that sparkled with intelligence. Our hotel man immediately straightened up.

'Hello, Mrs. Christie'.

He'd started well, despite his fears, and spoke quite well. Why didn't he have more belief in himself? But that's unmistakably us as a people. Always finding fault in ourselves, always wanting… To be honest, I was a little confused. He was so focused on her that he seemed to have forgotten that I was standing there right next to him. But I was wrong. As he made his way to the dining hall with the English lady, he turned and asked me again, 'Are you sure you won't join us, Şehsuvar *ağabey*? You can talk about novels and stuff.'

'Thanks but no thanks, Reşit. I'm not in the mood for any literary discussions. *Bon appétit* to you both.'

The young lady turned to me too. I bowed my head slightly in greeting and she gave me a gentle but bittersweet smile. I say bittersweet but it was actually almost mournful. I looked down at her hands and yes, she was wearing a wedding ring. Who knows, maybe she was having marriage difficulties or was missing her husband, but I had so many problems of my own to deal with that I did not have the time nor the inclination to ponder the problems some writer I did not even know may have been experiencing. In the dining room, I sat as far away as I could from them. I looked up every now and then to check on Reşit but he seemed to be doing just fine and was talking to the lady without any noticeable difficulty. She, on the other hand, seemed less than interested in what he was saying and appeared to be listening purely out of courtesy. As I said, she seemed troubled, as though she was carrying a sadness she could not conceal no matter how hard she tried. A sadness

I saw and recognised all too well in my own eyes whenever I looked in the mirror.

Anyway, once I had eaten my fill, I went back to my room and decided to write a few more lines before heading out.

The summer of 1910…

After you left me, that grief remained. Like a masochist in love with his own wounds, I carried that longing with me wherever I went. During the Great War and during the subsequent political upheavals that ravaged our country, you were not just a little postcard in the corner of my mirror which my eyes would every now and then wander over but an ache that had seeped into the very core of my heart and which would live with me not just during those heady days we were together but for the rest of my life. I am not exaggerating when I say you were like a second mind residing within my skull and a second heart pounding within my rib cage. And no, these are not memories either; back then, just as it is now, all I could think about was what you were doing in Paris and whom you were with. The anxiety, the chronic jealousy… The books you had read without me, the plays you had seen without me, the streets you had wandered without me; each one, the thought of each one, was a new source of pain for me.

I can almost hear you in response saying, *Well, what about you? Didn't you have other women, other girlfriends?* I won't lie. Yes, there have been other women. I should confess that during those first years in Istanbul, I led quite the charmed life. When we were not out there tracking down and identifying spies and members of the opposition, we spent most of our time on the *Cadde-i Kebir*. I suppose you could say this life of debauchery, if that is the right word, began after I bumped into Arşak Boğosyan.

Arşak Boğosyan was my old classmate from the *Mekteb-i Sultani*. He was a bit of a weakling in school and I used to protect him from the other boys. He was also lazy; most of the time, I ended up doing his homework. But he was a good lad, affable and with a good heart. His family owned vast swathes of land back in Sivas. When the school terms began, he would bring back outrageously delicious sweets, *lokums* and chocolates for the rest of us. Anyway, I bumped into him one day on one of the city ferries and we immediately embraced. He had opened a jewellery shop in the Grand Bazaar with his older brother Bedros and had bought a three-storey building in the Cadde-i Kebir, with two floors reserved for themselves. I knew Bedros well. Unlike his brother, he was a giant of a lad, a real Hercules. Both boys were their father's pride and joy. Arşak was delighted to see me. We hadn't seen each other since graduating from high school and that very same night we went to Galata. The rest just followed. We were soon regulars at Galata's most exclusive haunts and at the *Cadde-i Kebir's* most popular taverns. There was no romantic element to any of this, it was just pure carnal desire we were after, two guys trying to quench the raging fire of lust in their bodies. I'm afraid more than half my wages went to those poor women who were forced to sell their bodies. Most of the time, Arşak wouldn't let me pay. When I objected, he would always say the same thing. 'It's thanks to you that I managed to finish high school. Otherwise they would have kicked me out on my ear after my first year there. So you just sit down and shut up because there is no way I am going to let you pay.'

I soon became a bit of an expert, perfecting my art with those sassy, rich foreign women staying in the Pera Palace or the Tokatlıyan Hotel looking for adventure. A Hungarian orchestra was in town playing waltzes in the Taksim Gardens? Off we went. Jazz at the Maksim? Then that's where we were headed. The best part of it all was that I no longer needed Arşak's money; the women I was with were more than happy to stump up. In fact, the wife of one ambassador grew somewhat enamoured with me, so much so, that we only just managed to avert a major scandal. Thankfully, a mission came up and I was stationed in Egypt for a month and so managed to rid myself of her. But none of them actually made an impression. Not the hookers of the *Cadde-i Kebir* that could perform wonders with their hands and their tongues or any of those rich women ready to give up their lives of affluence and security for some love and romance… All that remained was a sense of depravity in my soul and a feeling of shame in my body. It did not go unnoticed by Basri Bey. However, he didn't object or raise a fuss. One day, he just smiled and said, 'The time has come, Şehsuvar. We need to get you married.'

Was that all? No. Madam Melina would not stop pestering me either, harping on all the time about finding me a bride. Had I not lost her at an early age, I'm sure my mother would have found me a nice Muslim girl from Salonika. Like all parents, her greatest wish was to see me settle down and to hold her grandchildren in her arms. Unfortunately, it was not to be. Her layabout of a son and her early death did not grant her that joy. Yes, I'm afraid I unexpectedly lost my mother that autumn. She didn't even tell me about her illness. 'No point in needlessly upsetting him', she'd said to her sister, my aunt. 'He has important work in the capital'.

I don't know if I would have been able to help had I known but the fact that I was not able to see my mother one last time before she died affected me greatly. While running around in pursuit of my grand ideals, dedicated to the cause, I had neglected the most important person in my life. In fighting for my people and my compatriots to live a more humane life, I had perhaps lost my own humanity… I felt a searing pain, as well as a shame that I knew would never go away. It was not my poor mother I had disappointed but myself. When my father died, of course I had been upset, but I was still a young lad, only just beginning to leave childhood behind and starting on ado- lescence, and the pride I felt in my father having been a patriot helped me get over the loss; at the end of the day, my father died a hero in exile. He was a martyr to the cause of freedom, and to mourn him would have been to taint the honour and glory of his memory. But my mother's death…. The loss of a great woman whose existence I had barely cared about when she was alive was like a slap to the face. My heart ached not just with grief but with remorse too…

My mother's body was in the garden, washed and ready, in a coffin under an embroidered veil, the prayers having already been performed. There were people everywhere. Most, if not all, I probably knew but I couldn't recognise or remember any of them, not then, not now. I just stared at their faces, as though they were creatures from another world. They were all passing on their condolences and urging me to be strong. I do remember thinking, *Who the hell are these people? What are they doing here? When did they become a part of our lives?* All I wanted to do was think about my mother. Think about her, feel her presence, remember her… The woman who had always been by my side, who had never left me, a woman with a vast and generous heart, who had suffered and been through so much. Why wouldn't these people leave me alone? Why wouldn't they let me be alone with my memories of my wonderful mother? Of course, nobody could hear my silent screams. They were busy raising their palms skywards in prayer, the women in one room, the men in another. Some were crying but not for my mother but for their own deceased loved ones or out of fear of their own eventual deaths… That profound and accursed grief inside me was growing by the second. I felt guilt like you cannot imagine yet there was nothing I could do to stem its flow.

We finally set off, a not inconsiderable crowd finally laying my mother to rest. The people present had not come for me, of course, but out of respect for my father Emrullah Bey, the one-time Director of Educational Affairs in the city of Salonika. But they stayed with me until the end, when my mother's old, tired and broken body was finally returned to the damp earth, and not for show either or for me but out of a genuine love and respect for my mother. Finally it was all over and the last handfuls of earth were thrown over the coffin but I was still not alone. It was kind of the people there to stay behind but I needed to be alone for a few minutes with my mother and so, a little brusquely, asked them to leave.

'Please, I would like to spend a little more time here. Just let me be for a moment.'

Some were going to speak up but the imam was an understanding man and said, 'Please, let us do as Mister Şehsuvar requests. It is better for the son to be here during the final moments. Come, let us leave.'

They did not leave straight away. It took a few minutes for them all to eventually trudge off in twos and threes, until I was finally alone with my mother. Why had I never sat down and just talked to her, talked to her for hours on end to tell her everything and let it all out? And why had she never revealed her thoughts to me or shared her woes with me? She had kept her illness a secret from me. And why? So as to not upset me. So as to not busy me with her illness when I had so much else on my plate. If only she had. If only she had made me think of her a little. Something had remained unresolved between us, between my mother and I, and now she was lying inert and lifeless under that mound in front of me. My mother, my dearest precious mother… The woman that had given me life and raised me into a man, and whose every waking moment from the moment I was born was spent thinking about me and caring for me…

The air was damp. A warm breeze caressed my face and dried my tears, as though trying to console me. There were so many images in my head but I tried to pick out my mother's face from the flood of memories… I remembered our last meeting, the day she told me I seemed to have aged. 'The lines on your face have hardened, your eyes have changed. Are they working you too hard, son…?' I remember feeling a lump in my throat that day and how hard it was not to let myself fall apart. Yes, she was right, I had aged, but not then. I had aged now, now that I had lost her and had watched her frail, spent and broken body returned to the earth. Yes, now I had aged. Because until their mothers die, children cannot grow up. I don't know how long I stayed there at her graveside but I eventually got up and walked to the city, to Salonika, to the city of my childhood, to the Salonika where I had lost all my loved ones one by one, to the city which now only had bitter memories for me rather than happy ones.

I did not hate the city now, no. Rather, I looked at it with a mixture of love and pity. At the masses of buildings squeezed in between the sea and the hills, at the collection of ethnicities and faiths always on edge, at the people living with constant fears and anxieties and with the constant prospect of having to flee… A small city in which the people tried to stay alive, in which they struggled simply to exist, to be. For the first time, I felt the city's grief in my heart. I know you'll tell me it sounds absurd; that a city cannot have grief and that it was my own personal pain and grief I was feeling. And you may be right, but what I used to feel in this city were joy and happiness.

My legs seemed to be leading of their own accord to your house. Not because I thought I might find you there but because there was no other place left for me in Salonika. But when I got there, the scene in the garden was one of mourning. The trees were bare, the ground was covered in dry leaves and the little pond was a mess. The only thing that hadn't changed was Grandma Paloma. She was sitting in her usual spot, under the late afternoon sun in the corner of the divan, sifting through some rice on a copper tray. The only thing missing was an old Sephardic folk song on her lips. When she saw me approaching, she looked up, squinted to get a better view and let out a little gasp.

'Oh my! It's Şehusvar! My little lamb, my precious Şehsuvar. My condolences, child. I'm so sorry to hear about Mukaddes Hanım.' She stood up, opened her arms wide and beckoned me over. I hugged her, and I admit, my eyes welled up.

'I'm sure God has taken her into heaven', she said when we let go of each other. 'I know a better life is waiting for her, one of peace and contentment. And now she is back with your father… You know, perhaps we should be happy for her that she did not live to see these dark times.' The grief in her eyes was replaced by worry. 'Ah Şehsuvar my lad, what's happening to us, to our country? Everybody has gone mad. I don't know if the people in the capital know but dark days are coming. The city has never been like this. People are turning their backs on others. All the backbiting, the whispering, the rumour-mongering. Everyone is doing it. And I mean everyone. Greeks, Bulgarians, Romanians, Muslims…. They are turning away from one other and the hatred has begun to seep in. They say the people have begun arming themselves. I'm scared, Şehsuvar, my boy. So scared. A terrible calamity is approaching and we are just watching it get nearer. Fools, all of them! They'll destroy themselves and the world too. Your mother was beloved by the Lord and she was lucky enough to get away from this world before the catastrophe strikes. God willing, I will be next.' She raised her hands skywards. 'Dear Lord, you are my only hope. They are soon going to take over this city but before they take my beautiful hometown away from me, I entrust myself to the hands of your Azrail… That is my only wish.'

Her voice, as well as her body, slightly bent with age, began to tremble.

'You're worrying needlessly, Nona Paloma', I said, taking her by the arm back to the divan. 'Here, let's sit down'.

She just sat there with her hands in her lap, looking helplessly at me. I put aside my own grief and pain and tried to console her.

'You're worrying needlessly, really. Rest assured, the government knows what is going on and it has taken all the necessary measures. Nobody will dare upset you or take anything from you. All this confusion will soon be sorted out. We shall forge a new Ottoman unity and all the nations and faiths of the Balkans will once again live side by side as brothers. All shall be free to speak whichever language they choose and worship at whichever house of God they choose, free from any interference. All shall respect all. And why? Because that is what the Constitution commands, and nobody is above the Constitution.'

To tell the truth, even I did not believe what I was saying, but I dearly wanted to because if what I was saying did not come true, then Grandma Paloma's much darker prophecy would come true instead.

'Inşallah', she said, listening carefully to what I had to say. 'I have little hope but my dearest wish is that what you say happens.'

She looked anxiously up at me, her black eyes circled by grey rings. It was probably the first time she had really looked at my face.

'You've aged, Şehsuvar', she sighed. 'You were such a handsome lad. What happened to you?'

First my mother and now Grandma Paloma. What were these women seeing in my face? I was overcome by a strange feeling, a wistfulness of sorts, but I could not tell whether it was for myself or for these women. I tried to laugh it off but even in that I failed.

'Mum's death has been hard to take...'

I don't think she heard me.

'Ester is the same', she went on. 'The last time I saw her, she looked terrible. You can't imagine how much it hurt me to see her like that. It was as though the poor girl had just given up, and so suddenly too. Like a flower withering away before its time. Ah, Ester! My little darling, my little girl, my wild flower! How I miss her, so very much. She misses us too, of course. All this absence, all these distances, all this longing for our loved ones to return! A curse on it all! All this pain, because of people being wrenched away from one another. It's the same for you, isn't it? You didn't even get to see your mother one last time. But what is old age to a man of your youth? I mean, how old are you? And I said the same to Ester.' Her face suddenly lit up. 'Actually, she was here two months ago, although she didn't stay long. She used to love Salonika but last time she was here, she barely left the house. Stayed by my side almost the whole time. Of course, I didn't mind, but it's not right for a young girl to be cooped up in a house all day like that. All the joy vanished.' She looked at me. 'All the joy went from her, just as it has from you.' And then, with childish innocence, she asked, 'Do the two of you write to each other?' And then, before I could answer, the next question. 'You two used to be so close. What happened? Did Paris come between you? Or was it Istanbul?' Again, she did not give me time to answer. 'I know and I'm not afraid to say it. Other cities are dangerous, and the big cities are even more dangerous. The crowds, the lights, the pomp, the glitz. They stop people from thinking properly. About loyalty, wisdom, attachments… All those things vanish in the big cities.'

She was needling me, maybe both of us at once. But I should confess that when she told me you were unhappy, I was secretly pleased as it meant you still loved me and that Salonika meant nothing to you without me. It also meant that I still had a chance if I came to Paris.

'Did she ask after me?' I asked. Well, I didn't ask so much as listen to the words trip off my tongue by themselves. She stared at me vacantly. 'Ester, I meant', I repeated, a little louder. 'Did she ask after me?'

Instead of answering, she pulled her copper tray in towards her, narrowed her eyes and stared at the white grains.

'You know, my eyes don't see as well as they used to. I think I can sort this rice but actually I can barely see a thing. Poor Leon almost broke a tooth yesterday on a stone in his rice.'

She was dodging the subject but I pressed on.

'Did she ask after me, Grandma Paloma? Did Ester ask about me?'

She glanced up at me with a look of disappointment and despair.

'No', she said and went back to staring at her rice. 'She didn't. You know what she's like. She's stubborn, just like her mother, bless her soul.' She paused and then turned to me. 'But she responds to acts of goodness. She is helpless against affection. When somebody apologises to her, she yields and forgives immediately.' She then shook her head forlornly. 'But she never takes a step back. Like I said, she is as stubborn as a mule, that girl.'

In her own way, she was telling me to write to you and apologise. Seeing you sad had upset her and now she was dabbling in some matchmaking in an effort to make her one and only granddaughter happy. For all I know, she had spoken to Uncle Leon about the matter too. But the poor woman did not know that my own hands were tied, that my mind was a mess and that I could not apologise to you or go to Paris even if I wanted to, and nor could I tell her as it would have upset her terribly so I changed the subject and asked after Uncle Leon.

'He drinks, day and night', she said lifting her arms up in a show of helplessness. 'He used to console me, and tell me everything would turn out right. But now he barely talks. Yes, even he has given up and lost his joy. He took a particular turn for the worse when Ester left for Paris. That's when he really hit the bottle. He numbs the pain with wine. Thankfully, he loves his job and has not let that go. This morning he went to Drama. He'll be back soon. Why don't you stay for dinner? He'll be delighted to see you.'

'Thanks, I'd love to but I have to get the evening train back to Istanbul. You know how it is. Matters of state can't wait. I need to be back at my desk first thing in the morning.'

She reached out and held my hand.

'Don't go anywhere. I'll make you a coffee. I also have some *samsa* dessert for you.'

I couldn't say no and so I stayed and watched her get up, with aged, faltering steps, and bring the sweets and refreshments. The coffee, as usual, was perfect and the dessert simply delicious. As I was leaving, she held me in a warm embrace.

'If I never see you again', she said, her eyes misting up. 'Don't forget me. I'm not just Ester's Nona Paloma but yours too.'

I bent and kissed her hands.

'Always', I said. 'You are the only grandmother I've ever known. And now you are not just my grandmother but my mother too. And you always will be.'

She couldn't hold back the tears any longer.

'Ah Şehsuvar my lad…. Sweetheart. Life could have been so much better. But people. Foolish, blind people, will drag the whole world down with them into mayhem.'

I left her in her usual place on the divan but as I was leaving I turned around to look at her. Her frail body and her black clothing seemed to bestow upon that garden, and its faded flowers and yellowing leaves, an inexplicably delicate but overwhelming grandeur.

No Choice But to Fight

Hello Ester (Evening, Day 8)

All my fears have come true, one by one. I wasn't wrong. There is somebody out there trying to drag me into a bloody plot. And somebody close to me, too. Someone who smiled at me and shook my hand and looked ready to help but who in actual fact was digging my grave. It was this afternoon that I finally grasped this terrible truth, when I walked into Cezmi's house and saw his lifeless body lying in a pool of blood. That's right, this afternoon…

I left the hotel late in the afternoon. Of course, before setting off, I looked around for anything usual and I kept my eyes open for any strange activity after I'd got into the carriage but there was nobody following me. That did not, of course, mean I could relax. When we arrived at his street in Langa Bostanları, I did not get out in front of his house. I paid the driver at the end of the street and then began walking back to the house once he had disappeared. If anybody had been following me, it would have been impossible for me not to notice on that dim, sunless one-way street. But there was still nobody there.

The garden gate was not closed but I didn't attach too much significance to it. Maybe Cezmi Bey had left it open. I walked beneath the fruit trees up to the front of his house. Silence reigned in the garden. Save for the faint chirping of some sparrows, there was not a sound to be heard. When I neared the house, I noticed that the divan we had sat on out front two days ago was unoccupied. Knowing he would not be one to sit inside on such a stiflingly hot day, I looked around but the old warhorse was nowhere to be seen. I called out to him but there was no answer so I walked over to the veranda and called out to him again. 'Major Cezmi… Mister Cezmi, sir… Are you there?' Not a sound. Seeing as the garden gate had been left open, perhaps he'd gone out and was signalling to me that he would be back soon? I decided the best thing would be for me to wait. As I headed for the divan, I noticed the house's front door was open… Or was it? I wasn't sure so I gave it a little nudge. It swung open.

'Major Cezmi… Sir… Are you here?'

Again, that heavy, foreboding silence. I just stood there by the door, not knowing what to do. Something wasn't right. An old CUP hand like Cezmi would not be this lax, especially when he was gearing up for a showdown with the government.

A voice inside told me to leave, to get the hell out, but I didn't. I couldn't. I poked my head through the open door and looked around but it was so dark, I couldn't even see the furniture clearly. I walked in, knowing I shouldn't have. As I waited for my eyes to grow accustomed to the darkness, I walked over to the window to the left and pulled open the thick, tightly drawn curtains. Light reluctantly swept into the wide hallway. I drew open the curtains in front of the other two windows and then walked up the stairs to the first floor. The door to the room right in front of me was wide open. Inside, I walked over the hand-woven carpet that was spread out across the wooden floor near the door and when I was a few metres away, a familiar smell hit my nostrils: the smell of dried blood. I wasn't scared but I wanted to make sure and so walked gingerly towards the room. When I reached the door, the full horror revealed itself to me. Major Cezmi had fallen to the floor right by the door. He had a wound on his chest, clearly from a knife or dagger of some sort. There was anger in his eyes. I looked down at his hands and saw dried red stains on his fingernails. Clearly, he had fought back against his assassins and put up a fight, which was hardly surprising. I couldn't imagine him doing anything else. Submitting to his assailant was not in his nature. The hatred and anger etched into his now frozen eyes were evidence enough of what had happened. When I reached over to close his eyes, I saw the Lüger by the bedside. He may not have had time to pull the trigger but he had drawn his gun, which meant he must have been expecting an attack like this, which was hardly surprising as anybody planning an attack on the government must surely know he has put himself in danger. So he had pulled out his gun but had not fired it. I looked around for some clues and then heard a sound. Was it him? Was it the killer? The sound wasn't coming from the house but from the garden.

I looked out of the window. Three policemen – two in uniform, one in civilian clothing – were walking under the plum tree and towards the house. Now what was I to do? If they saw me there, they would naturally have me down for the murder of Cezmi Bey and if I was hauled in, there would be no way out. I started to fret but the panic didn't last long as an exit had presented itself: the window I was standing next to did not have any bars on it. That would be my way out. But I had to bide my time and wait until the men were on the veranda before I jumped. I opened the curtains and opened both windows. When I heard footsteps on the veranda, I jumped but, as luck would have it, one policeman had stayed behind and when I landed, we were almost eye-to-eye. He was unprepared though, and before he could work out what was going on, I began sprinting towards the back garden. Actually, it was a foolish thing to do as I didn't know what was waiting for me there. But what else could I have done?

'Stop! Stop or I'll shoot!' the policeman shouted.

Instead of stopping, I ran even faster. Of course, he fell in after me and it wasn't long before his two colleagues had joined him. It seemed like a mile away when in actual fact, it was only around fifty or sixty metres but eventually, as I ran to the rear of the house, I saw a wooden fence and without a moment's hesitation, I leapt over the fence and into the neighbour's garden, where there was a huge shepherd dog stretched out on the lawn. He saw me and lifted his head. I was in serious trouble now and was getting ready for him to attack but all he did was look at me, give a little growl and then go back to his evening snooze. I carried on running and didn't look back as I did not want to slow down but I was sure the policemen were after me. As I was making my way through the garden gate and out onto the street, I heard voices cry out, 'Watch out for the dog! Careful now, he looks like he's going to attack.'

The policemen were cut off by an ominous growling and then the dog began to bare its teeth. He may have gone even further and attacked his intruders, for all I know. Whatever happened, had that dog not been there, I would have been a goner. I ran through the gardens and the allotments and out onto the street lined with wooden houses. There were no policemen there thankfully, not uniformed or plan clothes. Nevertheless, I had been seen and identified and they now knew my face, which meant I could not spend any more time than necessary in that neighbourhood. I hurried away to the main road, where I was hoping to find a carriage that could take me back to the hotel. As luck would have it, as soon as I hit the main road, I saw a carriage on the corner and got straight in.

When Ömer saw me arrive, naturally he was bewildered at the state I was in but I ignored him and walked straight over to the elevator, which took me up to my room. I took off my clothes, which were drenched in sweat, and had a bath, which did me good, helping to calm my nerves a little. I then sat down on my bed with my back against the wall and started thinking.

Who could have killed Major Cezmi? Who else but the government's secret agents. So in other words, Mehmed Esad. And why not? For him, it would have been killing two birds with one stone – he will have rid himself of a fierce *ittihatçı* whilst also getting rid of a suspected English spy. But didn't Mehmed Esad know what Cezmi Bey had been saying about him? Well, why wouldn't he? I'm sure Cezmi had been under surveillance, just like me. Spies and snoops must have been all over him, right under his very nose, watching his every move. And if they had mentioned the rumours in their reports to Mehmed Esad… But still, it was difficult to be absolutely sure.

And then it suddenly hit me. How was I going to find you now? Çolak Cafer had your address and now it would be impossible for me to reach him. If I were to go back to Cezmi's house, whether it be to pay my last respects or for the funeral or for whatever other reason, Çolak Cafer may also turn up, yes, but it was not a risk I could take as Cezmi's killers would have me arrested for the murder on the spot. So yes, it was most probably the government's intelligence services that had killed him and they would have no qualms about framing *me* for the murder. Don't get me wrong, it's not like I am not upset about what happened to him. It has hit me, and hard, and it has scared me too. But I had nothing to do with it and the more I sit back and reflect on the incident, the more I start to see reason. I had nothing to do with it and, more importantly, I did not leave any clues behind. They won't find me. But still, the same question keeps hammering away at me: how am I going to find you now? Uncle Leon… Isn't he staying at the Tokatlıyan Hotel? That means he must have provided the hotel management with a home address and Reşit knows people at the Tokatlıyan so he can easily get that address. But how am I to tell Reşit that Cezmi has been killed? The man is already a nervous wreck, making an issue out of everything, no matter how trivial. What if he suspects me of the murder? But will he? No, surely he wouldn't go that far. He knows me too well. So yes, I'll tell Reşit. When? Now? No, he is still in his meeting with the hotel owner. Tomorrow. Tomorrow morning. That will also give me time to sort my head out.

Even if I hadn't actually sorted out any of these issues, just reliving them and putting them in order in my mind gave me some semblance of relief. And you know what they say: if there's no solution, then that means there's no problem.

Evening had arrived but I was still not hungry. Even if I had gone down to the restaurant, I doubt I would have been able to eat.

I got out of bed, went out on to the balcony and just stared at the city. It was getting dark outside, and Dersaadet was getting ready for another normal autumn evening. I switched on the lights and sat down at my desk. I thought writing tonight would be hard but on the contrary, the words just flowed. I was back from Salonika, after returning the woman that had given me life back to the soil.

Fuad was waiting for me at Sirkeci Station. At first, I thought Basri Bey had sent him but when he started talking, I realised he had come of his own accord. To be honest, I was surprised as I had always sensed an unspoken rivalry and animosity between us. Seeing as I was just a civilian and he was a full member of the Committee, I had always assumed he looked down upon me but it appears I had misjudged him. He was impatient, yes, and impulsive, but he had a good heart and he was also one of the smartest, most intelligent soldiers I had ever met. I looked him up and down out of the corner of my eye. He was carrying my wooden case, walking alongside me, unaware of what was going through my mind. When he saw me looking at him, he smiled under his sandy moustache.

'So what are you up to this evening? I have a couple of tickets for the Ferah Theatre. They're showing Mınakyan's *An Untimely Wedding*. How about we go?'

I could see he was trying to make things up with me and I appreciated it but I was just too tired. On the train, my memories had not let me rest. Nearing morning, I was close to something akin to restful sleep when I was snatched away by a terrible nightmare. In the dream, Salonika was in flames. Everything was on fire – people, birds, trees, houses, everything. I was running towards the sea with a wooden bucket to get some water to put out the fire. Ridiculous, yes, I know, but it was a dream after all. Anyway, the more I ran, the more the sea retreated. Poseidon, the old Greek god of the sea, was dragging the water away from me, as though it were a vast blue fishing net. All of a sudden, the Gulf of Salonika had been transformed into a literal gulf, a huge hole, full of sunken, seaweed-ridden ships, dead fish, empty bottles of wine, empty jars of olive oil and even some human skeletons, but not a single drop of water. I just stood there, caught between a waterless sea and a burning city. I then felt something hot and turned around. The burning city had grown feet and was now walking towards me. Burning houses, cars, trees, birds and even half-burnt people were all there, all approaching me, from all directions and rapidly too... Soon the flames began licking at my body. I woke up screaming. Everybody in my compartment on the train was looking at me in fright. After that, I couldn't get back to sleep and just stared out of the window until morning. That is why I had to turn down Fuad's offer, even though I would have very much liked to see the play.

'I'm really tired, Fuad', I said awkwardly. 'Another time. Seriously, I'm so tired, I'll probably fall asleep as soon as the curtain rises.'

He nodded amiably.

'Not to worry. Another time then. It's not like the days are going to run out!'

But it was not to be as events abroad were beginning to develop rapidly. As though we did not already have enough enemies, another foe had emerged on the Mediterranean coast. Yes, I'm talking about Italy. Seeing the uprising in Yemen, the turmoil in the Balkans and the political crises in the capital, the Italians were now ready to tear off a piece of what they saw as the crumbling Ottoman pie for themselves. All the other great powers were getting ready for a piece so why not the Italians too? That is why they had dispatched troops to Tripoli. I had already read about it in *Tanin* but Basri Bey filled me in on the details.

'You know, the country is being rocked by political earthquakes. Ibrahim Hakkı Paşa has resigned, and that wily old fox Sait Paşa has become *sadrazam* once again. However, his entourage consists of nothing but weaklings and cowards. They do not have the stomach to stand up to either the British, the French or the Russians, so don't expect them to declare war on the Italians either. And that means we are the ones that have to step up and take action. We shall go to Tripoli under cover. Some of our comrades have already set off and are on their way there now. In a way, yes, we are stationing ourselves there. This is not being carried out with the knowledge or the approval of the state. As the steadfast *fedai* of the party and as loyal servants of the nation, we shall not cede an inch of land to the enemy. We shall show those pasta-eaters what it means to attack Ottoman lands! And let it be a lesson to any others that harbour any nefarious intentions. So get ready lads, get packing and as soon as we have obtained the necessary documentation, we are heading off to Tripoli. I don't need to say it but we are going to kill or be killed so if there are any people you need to say goodbye to, go and say your goodbyes. If there are blessings you need to receive, go and get them.'

Fuad went straight to Salonika to receive blessings from his mother and father and his fiancée of three months. I, however, had no one. No one except Madam Melina. She was my landlady, but she was also a woman with a generous and loving heart.

I thought about writing to you, to tell you that I was off to war and that I would perhaps not return, to ask you for forgiveness and to tell you that I still loved you dearly but I was afraid you would mistake it for weakness on my part. If anything were to happen to me, you were bound to find out sooner or later anyway. Perhaps it was best this way; to be shot and killed whilst defending one's homeland, for a rather unspectacular life to at least be snuffed out in a glorious fashion. For me, that was the ideal way to go because with each day, I was becoming increasingly alienated from myself. Even though I stood firm against those that were attacking the party, out of habit perhaps, I could sense that something was not right. My greatest fear was that we could and would turn into tyrants ourselves, and I knew all too well that dying as one of the oppressed was far more honourable than living as an oppressor. That is why I was actually quite relieved when Basri Bey told us we were going to Libya. That brutal and unforgiving war would perhaps put an end to the torments of my mind and my soul. I was not in the least afraid or worried. Rather, I was excited and impatient.

Impatient to sail to Africa, reach land and do battle with the invading Italian forces.

But I needed to wait first. For one, we did not leave for another ten days. When we finally did set sail, on a sunny autumn morning, it was on a ferry called the *Ismailiye*, which was owned by the Hidivye Company. It was heading for Cairo, after which it was scheduled to go on to Tripoli. I was travelling as a reporter by the name of Faruk Ziya for the newspaper *Tercüman-i Hakikat*, while Fuad chose to be a theatre director named Ismet Naci travelling to Egypt to stage a play at the famous Library of Alexandria. As for Basri Bey, he was travelling as a preacher named Nizam Sabri. Basri Bey was the son of a mufti and spoke Arabic fluently and so he was already well-versed in the ways and words of religion, more than any of the rest of us anyhow, enough to wiggle his way out of a predicament were one to arise. It was only much later that I found out that it was Kara Kemal that was able to procure so many official documents so efficiently and so quickly. I also learnt later on that the decision to go to war in Libya had been taken in Enver Bey's house in Beşiktaş and that the soldiers and officers present there on that day would later go on to play decisive roles in our country's struggle for independence. Not that it would have made much difference to me had I known any of this at the time as I was too busy mulling over a strange coincidence – less than a month after my mother's burial and I was setting off to the lands in which my father had died. You know I'm not exactly the superstitious type but I couldn't help but wonder whether this coincidence had any deeper significance. The prospect of seeing the place in which my father lived and breathed his last and knowing there was a chance I could fall and die in defence of my country and motherland in the same place arose strange feelings in me.

Basri Bey, on the other hand, was pensive. I assumed he was upset as he would be far from his wife and child but it wasn't just that; the silence in which he had entombed himself was a result of his knowing just how grave our mission in Libya was. In stark contrast, Fuad and I argued about Stendhal's *The*

Red and The Black for most of the journey. As two young men, the protagonist Julien Sorel's tumultuous state of mind and his mistaking personal ambition for love had struck both of us. Whereas Fuad looked at the issue from a moral and spiritual angle, seeing Sorel as somebody of weak character, I tried to convince him that Sorel was a victim of the system. We eventually arrived at the same conclusion though, and that was that Julien Sorel would make an outstanding character for a play. Perhaps our pointless rows and squabbles on such an insignificant topic were an attempt to momentarily forget the reality of our voyage into what would be a hellish inferno. That is probably why we were still engaged in our vain little literary discussion when we sailed into the port at Alexandria.

Yes, we reached Alexandria safe and sound but Egypt was now under British control. While we were fretting about any potential problems at customs and the probability of a police inspection, we ran into another, unexpected problem: quarantine. Because of an outbreak of cholera in Istanbul, our ship was taken into quarantine and we stayed in port for four days before the British finally let us go. We made contact with our people in Alexandria and after a few days rest in the party's safe houses, we managed, after a great deal of trouble, to get seats on a train that would take us to the Libyan border. The train journey lasted hours and was hellishly hot but we eventually reached the border. However, our problems were far from over. Indeed, they were just starting, because we now faced a journey of hundreds of kilometres and it was a journey that could only be taken by camel. In this regard, we were lucky as the caravan we were joining had set aside a Hecin camel for each for us. The Hecin camel is not a creature to be underestimated; it is the swiftest camel in the desert and even after the most arduous journeys, it barely registers any discomfort. All it does is look dolefully at you with huge, fearful eyes.

We rode the camels for days over shifting sands that were sometimes as white as milk, sometimes the colour of honey and at other times the colour of wheat. After every fifty kilometres or so, we would stop at a well and try to cool down with water that was as warm as blood, but no matter how much we tried and how much we drank, the sand got everywhere, and into our noses and mouths, making the very act of breathing a war of attrition. We reached Derna first, where Mustafa Kemal greeted us. He was from the same town as us, and he and Basri Bey went back a long way. He was delighted to see us and did everything he could to make us feel at home and help us relax, despite the rudimentary facilities.

'Winning this war is going to be very hard. Our men are fighting heroically and we've managed to stop the Italian advance. They're hemmed in on the coastline, and can't get out of range of our cannons. But we cannot let them leave, either. The government should realise we have this advantage and press for a favourable peace treaty but unfortunately, nobody in Dersaadet is aware of the situation...'

'What about Enver Bey?' our commandant asked. 'He's always sending good news back to group headquarters'.

Mustafa Kemal's face fell.

'I'm sorry to say this Basri, but if you ask me, Enver is dreaming. He mistakes what his wishes for reality. As far as he's concerned, we've already crushed and routed the Italians and all the Arab clans are on our side. Now he's talking of founding an Islamic state loyal to himself personally that would cover Tripoli, Tobruk, Benghazi, Derna and even Fezzan. However, the reality on the ground, as you'll soon see, is completely different. We have very few men facing down an Italian force consisting of something approaching one hundred thousand men, and they are better armed and better equipped than we are. The people here hate the Italians, yes, especially the Senussi, and that is our only advantage. In other words, the situation is dire. But there is nothing else we can do but fight.' He took a drag from his cigarette and then went on. 'I don't know, perhaps everybody here is simply fighting for his own honour, for his own conscience.'

That night, I did not agree with Mustafa Kemal. He was overly-despondent in my opinion, and neither Basri Bey nor I could find sufficient reason for such gloom.

'Chin up lads', he said to us as we went to our tents. 'It's just a misunderstanding between Mustafa Kemal and the party. And we all know about his animosity towards Enver Bey. But he's a fine soldier and you can trust him with your lives. He's a true patriot, a man who will fight down to his last drop of blood. So, let's not dwell on all this, eh? Sometimes even the finest soldiers have their moments.'

The next day, during the morning call to prayer, we went to Enver Bey's base, located on a rocky outpost one hundred metres above sea level, high enough that one could make out the invading Italian ships on a good day. Enver Bey's some-what ostentatious tent was set up in a hilly area and one could immediately feel and see its difference. He sent for us when he'd been told we had arrived. On our way to his tent, we bumped into a bedraggled-looking guy wearing Arab clothing, who stopped and hugged Basri Bey when he saw him and spent a few moments in discussion with him. After he'd left, Basri Bey turned to us and whispered, 'That's Kuşcubaşı Eşref. A Circassian. He's a good man, Eşref, a brave and talented *fedai*.'

It was a name we would come to hear many more times while in Libya and over the subsequent years. He would go on to become one of the key figures in the state's intelligence agency, the Special Organisation, which would be founded two years later.

Enver Bey stood to greet us when we entered his tent. Like Mustafa Kemal and Kuşcubaşı Eşref, he had also grown a beard, which made his teeth look even whiter when he smiled. But he also looked tired, and not just because of the beard. Like the rest of us, he had been caught out by the trying circumstances and they had taken it out of him. The young officer that had addressed the crowds from a balcony in Salonika when the con-stitution had been declared was gone and had been replaced by a grizzly middle-aged man. But he was still fit and strong, still steely in his determination, still burning with fire. He shook each of us by the hand.

'It's good to see you here, Basri…. You have no idea how much I need you guys here. We are trying to create an army here from people who do not know how to fight a war.' He gestured to the cushions on the floor. 'Please, gentlemen, take a seat'. We sat down in the traditional manner, our right legs curled up beneath us. 'Things are in our favour, though. Morale is high. The Italians are penned in and they are scared. They dare not move out of their garrisons. As for the locals, they are swarming to join us, but they need to be organised and trained to fight. That is why we need experienced men like you here. In short, you've come just in time, Basri. It really is a relief to see you here.'

In contrast to Mustafa Kemal, Enver Bey was optimistic and his words lifted the spirits, but within the year, Mustafa Kemal would be proven right. Of course, at the time, I did not know and did not care. For a young man who had come to fight for his country, it was emotions that mattered, not logic. Inspiring rhetoric is a thousand times more effective than simple, basic truths. However, there was one thing Enver Bey had said that made me pause and think. The experienced men he needed to train the locals were Basri and Fuad. I, on the other hand, was not a soldier and knew pretty much nothing about the art of war. So how could I help train the locals? I was worrying for nothing because I soon realised that when Enver Bey said military training, what he meant was the act of war itself. I would see that with my own eyes eight days later when we engaged with an Italian division.

The Italians really were hemmed in on a long strip of the coast, trapped between the sea and their ships to the rear and barren wasteland and our forces in front. To win the war, they needed to advance over the wasteland and overrun us, whereas we needed to keep them penned in on that coast and hope to strangle them into submission in that sweltering Mediterranean heat.

Of course, intelligence was vital. The Italians usually attacked at night, wanting to advance as far as they could inland without being noticed. It was the same this time; the division we were facing waited until it was dark before they began their offensive, their objective being to attack us from behind. But before they could even begin to move, intelligence had reached us. A unit under Basri Bey's command consisting of twenty or so Ottoman *fedaeen* and one hundred hardened warriors from the Senussi clan had taken countermeasures. The Italians were spotted towards midnight, marching slowly and carefully forward with great discipline. We had taken up position between the rocks on the hills on either side of the road the Italians were marching upon. The Italian commanding officer obviously did not want to leave anything to chance and had dispatched three men as scouts to check the route the battalion was going to take. We watched carefully, barely breathing, not making a sound. The three Italians advanced about a hundred metres into the area in which we were hiding. They stopped every now and then to listen to the sounds of the night, to listen out for any activity or a trap but not a sound could be heard except for the crickets resuming their chirping after being nervously silenced by our arrival. The Italian scouts must have decided the route was safe as they had turned around and were walking back to their friends. Just then, however, one of the Arabs in our company had to sneeze, and not just one, the poor lad, but three sneezes in quick succession. The three Italians cried out in shock and panic and began running back to their comrades. And then, in the darkness of the night, came Basri Bey's roar.

'Attack, men! Attack! For God and the nation!'

This was followed by a deep, rumbling chant from the young Senussi fighters: 'Allahu akbar…. Allahu akbar… Allahu akbar…'

The guns went off at the same time and the three Italians crumpled to the ground. After a few moments, uncertainty during which their comrades tried to work out what was happening, they took up their positions and waited. We had lost a crucial advantage. Had they walked into our ambush, it would have been easy to overcome them but now we were facing an entire Italian battalion over open ground and even if we did manage to repel them, one did not to be a soldier to realise that most of us would not see out the night. Still, Basri Bey had given the order to attack and there was no going back so we took up our rifles, revolvers and swords and plunged forward. That is when it happened. I thought it was a miracle but what it actually was was proof of Basri Bey's tactical brilliance. There was a glimmer like the glow of fireflies in the darkness to the right of the Italians, followed by the sound of gunshots. The Italians did not know where to turn or to whom to respond – the Ottoman soldiers charging at them as though charging at death itself or this sudden, surprise attack on their flanks. It is difficult to say who was the first but the soldiers in the company around fifty metres away from us abandoned their artillery and began running for their lives back in the direction from which they had come. Of course, we did not give up the chase and as the sun began to rise, we had taken around twenty Italians prisoner. They had lost fifty-seven men, with only ten or fifteen managing to save their skins. On our side, we had eleven wounded and six martyred...

When we got back to base, Basri Bey summoned everybody that had fought in the battle and gave us a stern scolding regarding the many mistakes that had been made. Muhammed bin Tarık, the sheikh of the Sennusi clan, suggested finding the man that had sneezed and punishing him but Basri Bey did not agree.

'It was not a case of treachery or even cowardice. It was just inexperience, and a bit of bad luck, so there's no need for punishment. But we do need more discipline. More discipline and more training.'

I have a feeling he sensed something would go wrong, otherwise why would he have positioned that second company to outflank and surprise the Italians like that? I now realised why Enver Bey had been so pleased to see us. He knew Basri Bey well and having a soldier like him by his side had revitalised him and boosted his morale. As for me, Basri Bey was fast turning into something beyond a hero and nearer a legend in my eyes. As far as I was concerned, he was near flawless and should have been recognised as such, to the extent that, in my opinion, he should have been in charge of our forces out there. I liked Enver Bey, sure, but Basri Bey was on another level for me. Had he been in charge of the forces there, the Italians would have long since been routed and pushed into the sea. I didn't say so out loud, naturally, but I believed it wholeheartedly. The successive victories he commandeered over the course of the following six months and the way he turned a group of young and brave but raw and inexperienced men from the Sennusi clan into an effective and conscientious fighting force elevated Basri Bey in my eyes into something approaching a deity. So long as he was on our side, no battle could be lost. He was, for me, invincible and immortal.

Wait. The phone is ringing again. Who can it be? Mehmed Esad? Yes, it must be him. I'd totally forgotten about him and our meeting this evening. Seeing as I hadn't turned up, he must have come to the hotel to see me. I'm sorry Ester, I have to answer the call or he'll start knocking on the door.

Give Me an Honourable Death

Hello Ester (Evening, Day 8)

It wasn't Mehmed Esad but Reşit. His meeting had just finished and he was calling to ask me if I was hungry and would like to eat with him. Of course, what he really wanted was to find out what I had talked about with Cezmi. I was in no position to refuse so I made my way down to the restaurant. In the lift, I bumped into that English woman, the one that writes detective novels. We didn't speak, as you can guess, but she smiled when she saw me, although that sadness was still there in her eyes. I found Reşit downstairs talking to Ihsan. I thought he would be telling him which food to bring but it turned out a customer had lodged a complaint and Reşit was giving Ihsan a stern talking to about cleanliness. However, he straightened up when he saw me and adopted a politer tone.

'Please, Ihsan, if you wouldn't mind. The complaint went all the way up to the owner. Let's be extra careful when it comes to hygiene.'

Poor Ihsan turned crimson red.

'Of course, Reşit Bey', he replied courteously. 'It must have slipped past us. I can assure you, something like that won't happen again.'

Reşit was eager to put the issue to bed.

'Excellent. That's that sorted then. Back to work, eh? Oh look, here's Şehsuvar Bey. Would you be so kind as to bring us something to eat?' Ihsan bowed and headed off. Reşit turned to me and said, 'It's a treacherous game, this hotel business, my friend. Here I am breaking my back trying to make sure every-thing goes smoothly but all it takes is a little carelessness by one person and the whole thing goes south.' He would have carried on with his diatribe except he saw the look on my face. 'What is it, Şehsuvar *ağabey*? Has something happened?'

Before giving him the terrible news, I sat down.

'It's Major Cezmi', I said in a steady voice. 'He's been killed'.

He froze. His eyes bored into mine. He was so shocked, he couldn't even ask me how but I went ahead and gave him all the grisly details. When I told him he'd been stabbed, he started to sob, a grown man weeping like a child right in front of me. I didn't reach out to console him but just let him cry. Once he had calmed down, he began to think a little more clearly.

'So who was it? Which fiend do you think did this?'

I raised my arms in a gesture of helplessness.

'I don't know. I only saw Cezmi two days ago, but you were seeing him quite regularly. Did he mention anyone? Anyone that had threatened him or posed some kind of danger? Any arguments or fights he'd had…?'

'None I can remember. I don't think he had any grudges with anyone. As I'm sure you know, he did have a short temper and was quick to lose his cool with anyone and everyone when it came to politics but he never even mentioned any outstanding arguments or disagreements with anyone, let alone any actual physical confrontation. There may have been some quarrels but he never told me so I wouldn't know. But who would want to kill Uncle Cezmi? He was the sweetest man in the world.'

Reşit really was a simpleton. The man he was calling 'the sweetest in the world' was a vicious brute who would not hesi-tate in pulling the trigger on anyone that dared cross his path or annoy him, something he had amply demonstrated numerous times. We sat in silence for a few seconds, just staring into the distance, until eventually he said, 'So you weren't able to get Mademoiselle Ester's address then…?'

The opportunity I had been looking for had come knocking.

'Unfortunately, no. But apparently her uncle Leon stayed in the Tokatlıyan two months ago. He may have left an address with them.'

'Well, if he did, then we can easily get it. The manager of the Tokatlıyan, Ali Çetin, is a good friend. I'll give him a ring tomorrow and find out.' The worry returned to his face. 'What if the police turn up here at the hotel and ask me about my connection to Cezmi? What do I tell them then?'

'Tell them the truth, Reşit. Tell them Cezmi was a friend of your father's and that is why you used to visit him. But whatever you do, don't mention me. And for god's sake, don't tell them I saw the body, otherwise there will be all kinds of trouble. And you'll be dropped right in it too.'

He wasn't afraid but there was a sliver of suspicion in his eyes.

'Seriously, Şehsuvar *ağabey*, why did you run from the police? If you tell them the truth the way you say I should, wouldn't it be better all round?'

'No. The Izmir assassination attempt is still fresh in people's minds, and in cases like that, the first names on the list of suspects are ex-CUP men, men such as myself. I'll never be able to get rid of them or their attentions. Actually, that's their aim in the first place. To put guys like us either inside or six feet under. Just like they've done with Cezmi.'

'Well, you know best'. The questions in his mind had not been answered but he at least appeared convinced. 'But please, Şesuvar *ağabey*, I'm begging you, be careful. Especially with this Mehmed Esad fellow.' He was suddenly hit by a thought. 'Or was it him? Was he the one that had Uncle Cezmi killed?'

'I doubt it', I said, not wanting to explore that particular avenue too deeply. 'Even if Cezmi's worries were real and justified, Mehmed Esad would never get involved in a murder like this. Him and people like him are after much bigger fish. They wouldn't waste time killing retired ex-CUP guys.'

He didn't ask anything else. The food arrived but the atmosphere had soured and we got up after only a few cursory bites.

Despite what I had said to Reşit, I couldn't stop thinking about Mehmed Esad. He was the prime suspect in the killing of Cezmi. If not him, then his friends and his people were. It was Mehmed Esad that revealed to me that he was working for the state secret police and it was he that asked me to join him. Who knows, maybe, despite all my efforts and all my vigilance, they had followed me to Cezmi's house. Two days ago and today… But if Mehmed really did have Cezmi killed, then shouldn't he have done it before? Cezmi and I had already met and he had told me everything he knew. Something wasn't right. The picture just didn't add up.

I went back upstairs and wandered aimlessly around my room, pacing up and down on the Persian rug that covered the floor from wall to wall. I came to a stop in front of the large beige Chinese vase and stared at the storks by a lake of water lilies painted on its exterior. My eyes then wandered over to the wooden clock on the wall. It was 22.13. Too early to go to sleep, and I wasn't tired anyway. If only there were somebody with whom I could talk, somebody to whom I could let it all out… But alas, there is nobody. Even Reşit suspects me. True, he looked convinced earlier this evening but even I can't be sure that he won't go straight to the police and grass me up once his shift has finished. So once I again I realise that there is nobody in this world with whom I can share with my woes. That is why, once again, I turn to you…

Maybe you're angry at me for writing to you in such detail about the war and sharing with you my memories of the battles. 'Haven't we seen enough blood?' you may ask. 'Haven't we suffered enough and experienced enough pain and heartache? What point is there in describing, in all its gory detail, the killing of other human beings, as though it is some kind of accomplishment?' If that is how you think, then I'm afraid you're mistaken. Yes, at the end of the day, war is murder, a form of ritualised mass killing, but it is not only that. War has a far deeper meaning. I'm not talking about defending one's country or that kind of thing. I'm talking about people and what it means to be human. I'm talking about all of man's feelings, fears, acumen, savagery and courage coming together and exploding into the world. I'm talking about war as part of the human condition. About the kind of creature we are... The tragic fact is, man is one of the few species that enjoys killing, whether it be just a single victim or whole groups. This is why I am writing to you about the war, to let you know how deeply that bloody encounter affected me and how much it changed me.

Seeing as I am being this candid, I suppose there is another confession I should make while I'm at it. As Basri Bey said, I was a man with an innate aptitude for the art of war. Maybe it was because one of my forefathers was a fine warrior, I don't know but I do know that war was in my blood. The war in Libya made me realise this. I adapted easily to the conditions out there, to the infernal heat of the day and the icy cold of the night. Fuad was the same; apart from a shivering fit he had in the second week, which lasted a full three days, he didn't have any major problems in North Africa. As for Basri Bey, on day one he was already demonstrating why he commanded such respect as a soldier. Indeed, he was one of the main reasons why the local Bedouin fighters wanted to join our company. The locals were strong and brave, brave enough to stare death in the face without flinching, but training was another matter and instilling in them the discipline necessary for war was more difficult than getting one of their camels to jump over a ditch. The fault, I suppose, ultimately lay with us. The Arabs were our people and were part of our country and they had lived under our suzerainty for hundreds of years – indeed, at the time, they still did – so if they were not up to scratch, then the fault, if anything, lay with us, with that six-hundred year old jugger-naut that had once been the bane of empires worldwide and which had ushered in new historical epochs but which was now at the mercy of others. I'm talking, of course, about the Ottoman Empire...

Anyway, back to our story. Without the support of the Arab clans, we would not have been able to hold off the Italians. But to talk of a uniform sense of fealty and loyalty amongst the Arabs would be a mistake. Some nurtured dreams of a inde-pendent state of their own, although most of the clans with a national awareness and national aspirations were based in Egypt. The clans in Libya, in contrast, were ready to turn on us at the drop of a hat, not because they sensed that the Ottoman state under which they had lived for so many centuries was about to implode but for far cruder reasons – such as a chest of gold. Not most of them, mind, but there were many like that, and we lost a lot of fine men because of them. The worst part of it was that we often confused the decent, upstanding patriotic clans with the more treacherous ones, which meant making the right decisions was not always easy or indeed possible.

The news that would turn our lives upside down came that Monday. An Arab fighter by the name of Beşir El Hamid, one we trusted and who had proven himself in battle, came to us with news that another clan in the interior wished to join our ranks. The chief of that clan, a certain Mahmud Faiz, had at his disposal five hundred armed men, eight hundred camels and three hundred horses, all ready to fight alongside his 'Muslim brothers' against the 'infidel Italians'. However, it was on the condition that he be greeted with full honours in a high-ranking Ottoman official's tent and that the deal be signed only after he and the Ottomans had sat down together to dine. It was not actually that an unusual a request as honour, for the Bedouins, was paramount: they liked to be respected and, conversely, hated being mocked. Enver Bey was delighted when he heard the news.

'Didn't I tell you the Arab clans of the interior wanted to join us? When I first arrived here, we had nine hundred desert warriors. Now we have thousands of trained soldiers on our side, and we are going to get more.' In fact, he was so delighted at this development that he began to throw caution to the wind, at one point even going so far as to suggest going in person to speak with the clan chiefs. He was like an impatient young officer trying to prove his worth rather than a seasoned veteran capable of analysing the finest details. Luckily, Basri Bey was on hand to provide a dose of reality.

'Absolutely not, Enver Bey. The desert is not safe and anyway, you are needed here. We shall go and speak with this Sheikh Mahmud and finalise the deal.'

That afternoon, we formed a twenty-five man company, including myself, Fuad, our medic Mevlüt and Kasım Çavuş, Beşir El Hamid (the man that had brought us the news) and nineteen dependable men. The following morning, before sunrise, we set off for the entrance to the Gazâl Valley, located around a hundred kilometres in the interior, which is where Mahmud Faiz's clan were camped as there were countless oases located in the valley. We all had Hejin camels, which meant under normal conditions we would have reached the valley before dawn the next day, although we had to slow down as the day wore on and the noon sun began to beat down on us.

Our first designated stop was at an oasis known as the Ayn-el Kabûl, fifty kilometres into our journey. We had been there before, around two months earlier, chasing up intelligence that claimed the Italians had spread out into the desert, but we found nothing. But I should tell you that the best water in the desert was to be found at that well. And not only that, it offered an amazing view, with the oasis located at the foot of a small amber-coloured mountain with three jutting peaks cut from a single giant slab of stone that seemed to suddenly emerge from the sands. The well was surrounded by reeds, palm trees and large lilac-coloured flowers which I could not identify but which seemed to be staring at us in an ominous manner as if trying to tell us we did not belong there. Don't think for a second that just because some of us were born and grew up by the sea that we dismissed that seemingly paltry trickle of water as insignificant. After the vastness of the desert, that tiny little trickle was like the ocean itself.

Things started going wrong for us at Ayn-el Kabûl. First, our very own Bekir Çavuş, from Üsküdar no less, fell from his camel. At first we thought we had just fallen asleep but then when we saw his body going into convulsions on the sand, we realised he was having an epileptic fit. Mevlüt, our medic, cut an onion in half and pressed it into Bekir Çavuş's mouth to bring him round. It worked. Bekir opened his eyes and stared at us, but he barely knew who or where he was. It was when we tried to get him on his feet that the actual scale of the calamity hit us – poor Bekir had broken his leg in his fall. Mevlüt gave him a strong painkiller but he looked worried.

'He needs help and now', he muttered. He was staring at Bekir's leg, which was beginning to swell up. 'Otherwise it may get a lot worse'.

'It's not far to the oasis', Basri Bey said impatiently. 'Can't it wait until then?'

'Well yes, it can if he has to', Mevlüt replied, wiping the sweat from his forehead. 'But it would better if the leg was treated sooner rather than later'.

'You guys go on ahead', I said. 'We'll stay behind and catch up with you at the oasis later on'.

Basri Bey was not sure but Fuad offered to stay behind with me.

'I'll stay here too. We can catch up with you later'.

Basri Bey looked down at Bekir, who was writhing in pain, and then towards the Ayn-el Kabûl. He stared into the steamy, sweltering distance for some time and then turned to Fuad.

'There's no need for you to stay. Şehsuvar can handle it'. He then turned to me. 'Five of the Senussi men will stay here with you. We'll go on and you can catch up with us once you're ready. Take it easy and gather your strength but don't waste any time. Yes Mevlüt, I'm talking to you. You have a tendency to take things slow. You need to sharpen up, my lad.'

'Understood, sir', Mevlüt replied and gave a nervous embarrassed smile.

Basri Bey gathered his men and they set off, whilst we hurriedly put up a tent and carried poor Bekir inside. First, Mevlüt located the break and then bandaged and stabilised it using a sheath. He was good, yes, but he really was slow. Maybe it was because he liked to be thorough in his duties, although I should admit that he was faster than usual this time. Nevertheless, the treatment still lasted more than an hour. Once we had prepared a stretcher for Bekir, we hit the road but we were at least a good two hours behind the main party and Bekir's stretcher was not helping us make up for lost time either. Still, our spirits were high. Bekir's moaning had stopped and he was now in a deep sleep. We advanced under scorching desert sun, dreaming of the Ayn-el Kabûl's cool and refreshing waters ahead.

When riding a camel, one cannot help but feel heavy and lethargic. Riding over that vast monotony, you soon realise you are helpless and vulnerable and so you try to adapt to the surroundings. You end up, in an almost semi-conscious state, surrendering to the surroundings. If you do not, that huge unchanging sea of sand and that heavy foggy sky become unbearable. As our little band led by the slow but steady pace of the camels trudged across the desert, we were suddenly awakened from our stupor by what sounded like champagne bottles being popped open in the distance. The Senussi were the first to realise what was going on.

'Gunshots', Fahad Kerim said. He was sitting up straight on his camel and listening to the wind. 'A gun fight must be taking place in Ayn-el Kabûl'. He fixed his light brown eyes on me. 'They've ambushed the others'.

Holding firmly onto the camel's reins, I turned to Mevlüt.

'You stay behind and keep an eye on Bekir. We're going. Let's go lads. On the offensive!'

We struck our camels and rode fast for the oasis. As we approached the small three-peaked rock, the gunshots became louder and clearer but when we were about a thousand metres away, the sounds suddenly stopped. All that could be heard was the soft thud of our camels' feet padding on the sand and the keffiyehs we had wrapped around our heads whistling in the wind. I was near panic. What if our friends really had been jumped and killed? No, there was no way Basri Bey would let something like that happen. He must have faced a hundred ambushes before and he had survived all of them. He also had Fuad with him to warn him if they were walking into a trap. Not only that, but the Arab mujahedeen they had with them were not to be underestimated, especially that Beşir el-Hamid, who was the bravest and smartest *mujahid* I had met so far, a man who could sense a trap a mile away, a man who could talk to the earth and the wind and who could pick up the enemy's scent no matter where he might be hiding. There was no way anything could have happened to them. So why had the noises stopped? Why hadn't our friends, seeing us coming, not raised their rifles and greeted us with cries of victory?

As we approached the mountain, glowing amber under the fiery sun, I felt the cool of the oasis but I could also smell gunpowder, a smell I had come to know well. I was so worried and so angry with myself at being late that while Fahad Kerim and the other mujahidin got down off their camels and took up their positions, I hurtled straight into the oasis. Had any of the ambushers been there, I would have long since been toast but there was nobody there. There were no shouts, no shots and no cries. There was just a maddening silence. And that is when I saw the blood… A dark red liquid, oozing into the lagoon. I saw three Senussi warriors lying lifeless amongst those large-petalled lilac-coloured flowers, the name of which evades me now. All three were stark naked too. The desert bandits must have stripped them of everything they had. I came down off my camel and had a look around. The area around the water was filled with the naked and looted bodies of the Arab fighters. They must have been shot while they were drinking… However, Basri Bey and Fuad were nowhere to be seen. I must admit, I was relieved as it meant they may have escaped. While the other Arabs, seeing their slain friends, began howling in grief, I had already slipped away from the lagoon to look for Basri Bey and Fuad but there was no sign of them anywhere. I was beginning to think they may have been kidnapped and were being held for ransom when I heard gunshots. I fell to the ground and took up position but there were no follow up shots. One of the Arabs pointed to the area at the foot of the rock.

'There. Over there'.

I turned to look at where he was pointing and saw what looked like Fuad's blood-soaked head. He had taken up position behind the rock and was probably too exhausted to even call out so he had fired his gun to get out attention. We ran straight over to him. Yep, it was Fuad. He was covered in blood, and right behind him was Basri Bey, lying motionless on his left side. I was distraught as I thought he was dead. Normally, death would not have fazed me as I had become so used to seeing dead bodies but when you see the body of someone you love and admire, it's hard to stay composed, no matter how experienced you are. I realised that when I saw Basri Bey lying there like that in a pool of blood. In my eyes, he was more than a man. As I said before, he was something approaching a myth, an invincible hero, the only man I would have trusted to the absolute and very end. When I saw him like that, I actually thought the war was over and we had lost. At that moment, my belief – in myself, our men, the motherland and the party – disappeared. Now that Basri Bey was dead, it was all over.

Fuad's croak of pain brought me back to my senses.

'Help... Help.... Why are you just standing there? Help, for god's sake.'

I shook myself out of my reverie and ran to him.

'Fuad! Fuad, are you okay?'

'I'm fine', he said, his blue eyes boring like hot coals into mine. 'I've been hit in the leg but I'm okay. Basri Bey is seriously wounded though. He needs your help.'

Fuad's selflessness hit me hard and shamed me. He was caked in blood but still he did not panic or give in to fear and thought only of his commandant.

'You're not in good shape... Your head... Your head is bleeding.'

'It's nothing. I wasn't hit there', he said, controlling his breathing. 'A piece of rock came flying up during the gunfire and got lodged in there. It's nothing. It hasn't gone in too deep.'

I looked over at the rock and sure enough, it was covered in pockmarks, a sign of how intense the skirmish must have been.

'I'm fine, just a bit shaken, that's all', Fuad went on. 'I don't think the wound to my leg is that bad either. Go check up on Basri Bey.'

I signalled for one of the Arab mujahidin to look after Fuad while I went to check up on Basri Bey. He hadn't moved the whole time and was still lying there on his left shoulder. I tried to turn him over onto his back without hurting him and heard a little groan. Thankfully, he was alive.

'Basri Bey… Basri Bey…. Sir, are you okay?'

His eyelashes trembled and there was a flicker in his eye. He recognised me. He said something but I couldn't make it out so I leaned forward with my ear to his mouth.

'Lift me up', he wheezed. 'Lift me up or I'll choke on my own blood'.

With the help of one of the mujahidin, I got him into a seated position with his back against the rock. There was a dark red blotch on his khaki shirt over his stomach. He licked his dry lips.

'Water… For the love of God, some water… I'm burning up.'

I wet my handkerchief and dabbed it onto his lips.

'More… More…'

I wet his lips again.

'Hold on, Basri Bey. Hold on, Mevlüt is on his way.'

'No point, Şehsuvar', he sighed, a look of pained resignation in his eyes. 'There's nothing Mevlüt can do here'.

He was so resigned to his fate and so ready for death that I couldn't hold back my tears.

'Don't say that. You're going to make it. Nothing's going to happen to you.'

He reached out with his right hand and grasped my arm.

'Don't cry. Why are you crying?' He seemed to be coming round a little. 'Here, come closer…'

I dried my eyes with the back of my hands and did as I was told.

'Beşir el Hamid…' he said with great effort. 'Beşir is not a traitor. It was just bad luck. That's all. Bad luck. We ran into bandits. It's not Beşir's fault. Don't blame him.'

'I know. They shot him too. The poor guy bought it.'

'I saw him get shot. So he bought it, eh…' He tried lifting his head and gazed out at the lagoon. 'And they've taken the camels too, haven't they?'

He was right. There wasn't a single camel left.

'I'm afraid so. They took all of them. But don't worry, we'll find a way out. We'll get you back to base.'

He tried to smile but failed, his body wracked by a violent coughing fit. When it subsided, he took a deep breath.

'It's not dying I'm afraid of but not dying', he managed to say. 'How long before sunset?'

The bloodstain on the front of his shirt swelled the more he spoke.

'Still some way to go. A good three or four hours'.

'They'll be back when it gets dark…. The bandits. Maybe even earlier. I'm sure they're watching us from afar. The other wells are controlled by more powerful tribes so this is the only watering hole they have. You need to get away from here immediately.'

I wasn't sure what he meant.

'What do you mean *you*? We're all leaving together.'

Once again, I saw that pained look of acceptance.

'Don't, Şehsuvar. There's no need to pretend. If I try and leave this place in this heat, I'll be dead within half an hour, and I'll only be slowing you down anyway.' I was about to object but he silenced me. 'Now listen well. They may be the hardest tasks you ever have to complete but there are two things I want you to do for me.' He gestured to the revolver by his right knee. 'Take that'. I picked it up and held it out to him. 'You keep it', he said, nodding his head. 'You're the one that is going to use it'.

It dawned on me what he wanted.

'No way, sir. I can't'.

'You will', he said gently but firmly. 'You owe it to me. That autumn night in Salonika, I was one of the men that accepted you into the movement. I have always believed in you, even when you stumbled and slipped up. But more than that, I have always loved you like a brother… So yes, Şehsuvar, I have the right to ask this of you.' He looked at the gun in my hand. 'You have to do it, Şehsuvar. You need to give me an honourable death. You cannot leave me alive for those savages.'

'We won't leave you here…'

'Don't waste your words. It's the end of the road for me. That much is clear. My story ends here. In this valley. Nobody can help me now.' He looked out of the corner of his eye to one side. 'But you can still save Fuad'.

When I turned and looked, Fuad and I were, from a distance, eye to eye. He didn't say anything but I realised he was thinking the same as Basri Bey. I could even see that he was ready to pull the trigger on our commandant if I couldn't do it myself. I turned back to face Basri Bey.

'That's not all', he went on with a pained smile. 'I want you to tell my wife about my death.' When he saw my reaction, he held on to my wrist. 'You can do it. You have to. I know you better than you know yourself, Şehsuvar. You're strong. Think of it as a test. Like that afternoon I took you out to see what you were like with a gun. Like that evening we took out the Albanian hitmen.' He was struck by another coughing fit and blood trickled out of his mouth. 'Come on, Şehsuvar', he said, spitting the blood out. 'Don't make me beg to die. Do it, I'm in agony here. Do it. Finish off the job.'

My right hand seemed to lift up the gun and point it of its own accord.

'Good lad', he said, encouraging me. 'Good man, Şehsuvar. That's the way'.

I tried but my index finger just would not pull the trigger.

'Come on! Don't make me wait! Do it, Şehsuvar! Do it, man! Pull that trigger! Do it! What are you waiting for?'

My finger pulled the trigger. The shot echoed around the entire oasis. Basri Bey's body heaved and jerked. Not a sound came from his lips. No gasp, no groan, no spluttered last words. There was just a look of gratitude in his eyes…. And then, like that amber rock that had stood silent in the middle of the desert for centuries, he was still.

The Walking Dead

Good Night, Ester (Midnight, Day 8)

A storm whips up the desert and flings the sands over us. It is incredible to behold; in front of our very eyes, one sand dune is swept away, only for another to be almost instantly created in its place. The wind is so strong that we have to lie face down on the ground and hold on to each other in order not to be lifted up and swept away. There are three of us – Fuad, Basri Bey and I. Yes, I know Basri Bey is dead but I still do not find it odd having him there next to us, and neither does Fuad, who is clinging on to my arm with his right hand. We are lying still on the ground, the wind howling in our ears, the grains of sand thrashing around us, striking our hair and our heads like hot sparks.

'Memories!' I shout above the din. 'Think of happy moments from your lives, happy memories, and hold on to them! Hold on to your most precious memories!'

Fuad does not respond but Basri Bey begins to say something.

'I remember an oasis', he mumbles. 'Like a piece of paradise that has fallen to earth…'

He is only mumbling, yes, but I can hear him clearly, as though the storm is not there, as though its winds are not trying to turn us inside out and fling us into oblivion.

'I'm exhausted', he goes on, losing himself in his story. 'As though I have been on the road for days and have not closed my eyes for days. My whole body rattles with every step the camel takes, and is swinging like a pendulum. It's hot. So hot, if

I reach out, I'll be able to touch the sun. That is when the oasis appears in front of us...'

I listen to Basri Bey and feel his words come to life. Not even that, I become Basri Bey myself. There is no more Şehsuvar Sami; I am just the sum of what my beloved commandant sees, hears and feels. I am the one swinging like a pendulum on a camel, I am the one losing my mind in the suffocating heat.

A piece of heaven hidden away in a little valley... The lagoon is surrounded by lush green trees and the cool of the oasis hits us from hundreds of metres away. The camels pick up the scent of the water and speed up, now almost racing each other to get their first. When we get there, I lose myself in the water. We all do; commandant, common soldier, volunteer, young old, it makes no difference. We are all overwhelmed, all reduced to an almost childlike state, as we drink in this sudden splendour. The bottom of the lake is stunning, almost like a coral sea, the stone at the bottom sparkling like a rainbow. I can't help it and dive in. The silverfish, blue crabs and seaweed-green turtles are my new companions. The water is incredible. I don't want to get out. I want to stay there in the water, with the little fish swimming amongst the rocks and stones of myriad colours. But then someone catches me. I try to pull my legs away but in vain. He is so strong, I cannot get away. I turn around to see whom it is but I cannot make out a face. All I can see is a figure in black, swiftly pulling me away. I am helpless, like a harpooned dolphin. I finally manage to get out of the water. The man throws me onto the rocks. It is surrounded by dead soldiers, the dead bodies of my friends, comrades and brothers-in-arms. They have been ruthlessly mown down and their blood forms multiple red rivulets flowing down from all directions into the blue of the lagoon. I pull myself together and stand up but the figure in black has pulled out a gun and is pointing it at me. A sandy *keffiyeh* covers his head and a black veil covers his face. His eyes gleam with hatred, with an undeclared loathing, and that is what makes him so threatening and so ominous. But I don't flinch. I don't feel the slightest twinge of fear.

'Who the hell are you?' I holler. 'What do you want?'

'You', he says from under his mask. 'I want your life. Now. Right now.'

And then before giving me the chance to speak, he pulls the trigger. Three times. I fall to the ground but I don't feel any pain, as though it's not me that has been hit but somebody else. In fact, I want to get up and fight back, kill him with my bare hands, but I can't. I can't move. My back seems stuck to the hot sand. The man calmly approaches me, gets on his knees and leans over me, the gun he used to shoot me still in his hands.

'I've never liked you, Basri Bey', he murmurs. 'I've always hated you but I've never been able to tell you, which only made me hate you more. You stole my life. You ruined me.'

I shout out in a rage.

'Who the hell are you? What do you want from me…?'

He wordlessly removes the veil from his face and I let out a scream.

I see myself behind the mask. Myself, Şehsuvar Sami, and I have shot Basri Bey three times…

Three knocks on the door wake me up. I sit up breathlessly in bed. Someone is knocking on the door. But who… What is going…

Wait. Has the knocking stopped? No, it's started again. I stagger out of bed, still reeling from my nightmare, and walk to the door. Who can it be? The police? Mehmed Esad? Still in a daze, I hear someone call out to me.

'Şehsuvar Bey? Şehsuvar Bey, are you okay?'

Whoever it is, he sounds worried. Has he heard my nightmare or what? I open the door anxiously. Halim Bey, the hotel's night watchman, is standing in front of me.

'Are you okay?' he asks again.

What on earth is going on?

'I'm… I'm fine. Why?'

'You screamed', he says, looking over my shoulder and scanning the room behind me. 'And not just once but a few times. The guest in the next room told us. Agatha Hanım, the English writer. She was worried. Thought something had happened to you.'

'I'm fine, really. I just had a bad dream, that's all. Please apologise to the kind lady on my behalf.'

But Halim was not convinced. He just stood there, waiting, it seemed, for some further explanation.

'That's all, Halim Bey. Thank you. Good night'.

He eventually left, leaving me on my own to stare at my unkempt bed and look back on the nightmare. What was it all about? Was my subconscious blaming Basri Bey for everything? That would be unfair. Basri Bey had never forced me into anything; everything I had ever done with him I had done of my own volition. Of course, he had wanted me to join the armed wing of the movement but he had questioned me every step of the way to make sure I was certain of my decision. No, if there was anybody to blame for what I had gone through, then it was not Basri Bey, God bless his soul, but Şehsuvar Sami. Yes, I often like to refer to myself in the third person, especially when I am criticising myself. It makes things easier. It makes me feel as though he is standing there in front of me.

I was a damp, sweaty mess thanks to that nightmare so I got changed and went back to bed where I tossed and turned this way and that but it seemed I had killed sleep as well as Basri Bey so I got up and went to my desk. Seeing as my old commandant had woken me up, I may as well continue with him.

I was back in Salonika. Back in my hometown for the death of someone close, for Basri Bey. I was back in town to pass on the news of his death.

Refiye Hanım just stared at me. Like Basri Bey during his last moments, her eyes just stared straight ahead, boring into mine. It was hard but I repeated what I had just said to her.

'Refiye Hanım... Basri Bey has been martyred... Unfortunately, we were not able to save him... My deepest condolences.'

A tiny cry escaped her lips.

'Ah...'

Her frail body shook, as though she had been hit by lightning, but she managed to maintain her decorum. It was clear she had been expecting this news for years and was thus duly prepared.

'When did it happen?' she asked, trying to hide her surprise amidst her grief.

'On the 13th of August', I replied.

'Three months ago!' she cried. 'Why didn't you tell me before?'

'Basri Bey did not want the news to be passed on to his family via letter or telegraph', I said gently. 'He asked me to pass on the news to you personally. He was totally against the idea of you being informed another way.'

She wiped away her tears with her hand.

'That's true. He hated things like that. He used to say that handing over a piece of paper to the family of a fallen man saying he has been martyred is the height of insensitivity. He always used to go in person to the family of the fallen to give them the sad news.'

Encouraged by her stoic resilience, I went on.

'That's true, Refiye Hanım. He did not want either of you to suffer such an indignity, which is why he told me and reminded me many times that I would come in person to tell you should it happen. Please accept my sincerest apologies for being so late. Actually, I would have been even later but I was sent home early because I was shot. As soon as I was discharged from the hospital, I set off for Salonika, as per the promise I made Basri Bey. I wanted to fulfil my promise to him.'

'You were with him when he died?' she asked, seeming to have calmed down.

'I was', I said. I could not look into her hazel eyes as I answered and looked away. 'I was with him when he was shot'.

The way she stared into the emptiness, as though trying to relive those fateful, final moments, was eerie.

'How... How did it happen?' she asked, ignoring the grief that was growing heavier with each passing second.

For a moment, I thought I should tell the truth. That I shot her husband on his request. Not even on his request but on his order. That I had to shoot him as I had been ordered to do so.

But I couldn't. It would have been a second blow for the poor woman, a blow too much.

'I'm sorry', I said, playing for time. 'I'm afraid I don't understand…'

'Her lower lip was trembling and her voice was cracking'.

'How did it happen? Basri, I mean. How did he die?'

She could not hold back any longer and began sobbing before I could answer. She covered her face with her aged hands, streaked with varicose veins, and wept. All I could do was sit and wait in silence. In the midst of her crying, she looked up at a photograph on the wall of Basri Bey in his army uniform gazing down at me with what seemed to me to be gratitude, as though he was sending a message of thanks down to me from the heavens. You may think it absurd but at that moment, I needed all the support I could get, even if it was imaginary. Thankfully, Refiye Hanım was a strong woman.

'My apologies', she said, collecting herself. 'Do forgive me. Such a sight I must be. In front of you like this… I really do…'

'Please, do not feel the need to hide your feelings from me. Please see me as a brother. God rest his soul, Basri Bey was a hero to us all.'

She began sobbing again.

'God rest his soul… A blessing for the deceased… And he is deceased now, isn't he? Lord, I can barely believe it.'

She held on this time and wiped away the tears.

'How did it happen? Did he suffer? Please, tell me the truth.'

'He did not suffer', I said, shaking my head firmly. 'It was all over in a second. His last words were, "I lived with my honour intact and I die with my honour intact. Tell my wife and son not to grieve for me, and that they should both walk with their heads held high, without fear. There is nothing to mourn. It is the highest rank any soldier can attain: the rank of a martyr. What more could a man and a soldier wish for? Please tell Refiye not to be sad. Blood shed for the sake of the motherland is never shed in vain."' Yes, I was lying but my heart ached just as much as hers. As it is, I couldn't keep it up much longer. 'And then… And then…' I started before breaking down. Şehsuvar

Sami, who only a month earlier had seen his friends killed in the heat of war, broke down and wept like a baby. Refiye Hanım put aside her own grief to comfort me.

'Please, Şehsuvar Bey, do not cry. Let us fulfil Basri's final wishes together. You're right, the rank of martyr is the most exalted and sacred of them all. No matter how painful it is for us, we must be stoic and dignified in the face of our loss.' I looked up through my tears and saw a look of resignation and compassion in her face. 'I don't know if he ever told you but he loved you very much. Like a son. Like a brother. Maybe it is because of your age. Because you reminded him in some way of our son Nail…' She paused. Her eyes welled up again. 'Ah, Nail! My boy. How am I going to tell the poor lad his father has died?'

'I can tell him. Seeing as I'm something of an older brother to him…'

She reached out and held my hand, in the same way her husband reached out and held my hand in the middle of the desert on that tragic day.

'Basri Bey was not wrong. You're a good man, Şehsuvar Bey. But breaking this tragic news to our son is my duty. You have already done your duty, and for that I shall be forever grateful. You shall always have a home here in Salonika. A home, a mother and an older sister. Whenever you are in trouble or in need of the comforts of home, my door shall always be open to you.'

Those were the last things I ever heard from that brave and upstanding woman. I got up and left, leaving Refiye Hanım alone to battle with that grief for which she had been preparing for years and which would never dim.

It felt good to be outside. The spray from a stiff breeze that had blown in from Mount Olympus had left a light coating of moisture everywhere. I breathed in the air, clean and fresh after the rain, and began aimlessly wandering the cobblestoned streets. I had left my suitcase at the station so I suppose I should have gone back to pick it up or just got on the first train back to Istanbul but for some reason, my legs seemed to be taking me to the coast. Not to the White Tower or the gardens but towards my youth… Back to my memories, which had seeped into every street and every corner of the city. Back to the day I received the news of my father's death… To the year I began at the Imperial High School. How proud I felt that day. And then the moment I first laid eyes on you… The way you appeared before me when I knocked on the door of Monsieur Leon's office. That nonchalant smile on your lips, your red hair falling over your shoulders like a fluttering banner, your huge black eyes, throwing down a challenge to the whole world… Then our lovemaking in that dark room stacked high with grim case files… Not just our bodies but the writers, poets, feelings, ideas and ideals that brought us together… And then, a full five years ago, again on an autumn day like this, my joining the CUP without your knowledge… Maybe it had been on this street, in that building over there behind me, in that mouldy hall… How full of hope I had been back then. Full of hope and faith, so sure of myself. I wasn't just going to save my country, I was going to save the world, and with you by my side too. And yet now, all that I once believed in had been shattered. What we had once believed to be grand victories were now, one by one, turning into defeats. I now see that all that heroism, all those sacrifices and all those deaths were pointless. It's as though we were destined to lose, no matter how hard we tried and how ardently we believed. As though it was pre-ordained… No matter how hard we tried, it was all in vain. We were never going to climb out of that deep, bloody pit. Destruction, betrayals, rebellions… Tyranny, corruption and poverty… All the accusations we used to fling during the Abdülhamit era were now being flung again, and the people were being ground up in the millstones of history like little grains of wheat… Such was my state of mind as I wandered the streets of our ancient city, the thoughts besieging me, when the miracle occurred. That's right. Out of nowhere, a few steps away from the sea of our childhood, the sea that was now turning green after the rains, there you were.

Standing there in a long sandy dress, with your huge eyes and flowing red hair. At first, I couldn't believe it. I thought it was a mirage brought on by the increased sensitivity of my emotional meanderings. I closed and then opened my eyes again, and almost pinched myself to see if I was actually awake, but ultimately there was no need as you had seen me too. There was a flicker of that old smile of yours on your lips, the one I had seen the first time I saw you: bold, alluring, defiant. But it was not to last long as your expression changed almost immediately into an ice-cold look I had never seen on you before. An icy demeanour behind which you were hiding your body as well as your mind. Perhaps I should have turned around and left then, or perhaps I should have spoken out and asked you why you had done that. If nothing, I could at least have adopted an equally defiant and estranged expression myself but I didn't. I wouldn't have been able to anyway, had I tried. Instead, I walked up to you and smiled.

'Hi Ester. It's nice to see you again.'

You indulged me with a smile but one bereft of any warmth.

'Hello Şehsuvar. How have you been?'

I felt emboldened hearing you at least take an interest in me.

'Pretty good… How do I look?'

The disappointment was all too evident in your olive black eyes.

'You've changed. You've… I don't know, and I'm sorry, but you've aged. Your features have changed.'

I was stunned. What you had just said… Just like my mother and just like Grandma Paloma. I tried to shrug it off.

'Well, you know how it is. Things are tough at the moment. A person can change overnight.'

You looked at me with understanding, almost with sympathy.

'Yes, I heard you'd been in the war. Libya, wasn't it?'

So you'd been keeping track of me. I was pleased. But I did not tell you I had been injured because I did not want to upset you or make you think I was looking for pity.

'I was', I said. 'I arrived in Salonika this morning. An errand to run, if you will. Not a very happy one, but there you go.'

There was a genuine expression of sadness and sympathy for me on your face.

'What was it like, over in Libya?'

I couldn't help but smile a bitter smile.

'Horrible. Just horrible. As you would expect from a war'.

'But you won', you replied, with what looked like a mocking glint in your eye. 'That Enver Bey of yours performed wonders out there. You stopped the Italians from advancing inland and now you're going to establish a grand Muslim union and revive the Ottoman Empire under the banner of Islam. Or so it said in your CUP newspaper.'

I know you were needling me but I ignored it.

'I wouldn't know about that but we did stop the Italians. They couldn't beat us in the battlefield so they decided to incite the Balkan states against us. We had to leave Libya but the locals are continuing the resistance. The Italians are going to have their work cut out for them out there.'

'And what about our work?' you said angrily, shaking your head. 'You think it's going to be easy for us in Macedonia? I don't know if you've had a chance to wander around Salonika and talk to people but the atmosphere here has changed. I've never seen anything like it here before. I used to sense the hostility but now they're not even afraid to come out and say it. The Greeks, the Bulgarians, the Serbs, the Montenegrins… They're all saying the same things. That our time is going to come. It's not just the Muslims they're threatening but us Jews too, saying we've collaborated with the Turks all these years and that we are responsible for the suffering inflicted upon them. They're telling us that centuries of tyranny are coming to an end and that Christ will return.'

There was real worry in your voice. Not just the anger you felt towards me but real fear, even I thought you were hamming it up a little. Yes, the Serbians, Bulgarians, Greeks and Montenegrins had declared war on us but their armies were weak and their weapons and equipment were wholly inadequate.

'You're worrying needlessly', I replied. 'Nothing will come of it, especially not here. There is no way they can get their way here. Not here. Come on, Ester. This is Salonika we're talking about.'

'Well, that's not how it looks from Paris. They're not calling the Ottoman Empire 'the Sick Man of Europe' any more. They're calling her 'the Walking Dead', and everybody wants a piece of the corpse. I'm afraid this country does not have any friends. Even those that look like friends are just after the largest piece of the pie. Everyone agrees that the Ottoman Empire is finished. Everyone except you, that is. Oh, I'm sorry, you and your people. Your organisation. Your 'party'. The party that began as a struggle for freedom and ended up creating a despotism worse than Abdülhamit's.'

To be fair, I had been thinking the same before I bumped into you but you said it with such force and venom that I felt the need to defend myself.

'You may think so', I said, my voice rising. 'But an empire that ruled the world for six hundred years does not collapse that easily. Those Western governments looking to colonise us are all dreaming. They'll never win. No way. We'll soon show them who the walking dead are.'

Even while I was speaking, I realised how idiotic I sounded, and it infuriated me. The whole thing was like a bad dream. There we were, face to face for the first time in four years, and I was arguing about politics with you. True, you started it and you were being provocative, but I could have let it pass. Even better, I could have opened up to you and told you what I was really thinking and how I really felt; in other words, I could have told you that day the things I am writing to you now. They haven't changed, so I could have told you then. But I didn't. Even though I loved – and still love – you dearly, and even though you were and are irreplaceable for me, I carried on with that pointless argument. Whether it was pride, stupidity or stubbornness, I simply do not know.

'Yes, we have our problems, and yes, we have not been able to deliver complete freedom or political stability. And that is because we have not acquired full control of the government and do not have the power we need to deliver. We have always had to share power with others. The pashas had our hands tied, and now the opposition parties do nothing but play into our enemies' hands. Under these conditions, we can only...'

'Stop, Şehsuvar. Please. Just stop, for the love of God'.

There was no anger in your eyes. Just pity. I remember it all too well, the way you were looking at me, the look in your eyes. An unbearable, embarrassed and embarrassing pity.

'You've lost your grip on reality. Don't you see? You've lost power in this country. Don't you know what's been going on?'

You were right. While we were fighting out in Libya, a new government had been formed. Our party, the CUP, had become the opposition again, whilst our rivals, the Hürriyet ve İtilaf Fırkası, the Freedom and Accord Party, had risen to power, with our leaders, Talat Bey in particular, having played quite the role in the outcome. While stubbornly stressing that they would not share power with Mahmud Şevket Paşa, the Minister of War, they ended up losing all power. However, as luck would have it, the new government was as inept and short-sighted as we had been. Instead of improving the country's lot, they had made it even worse. Poverty was rampant and the disintegration of the empire was gaining momentum. The news coming in from the Balkan front was no less dismal. We were losing everywhere and death and destruction followed in our wake. I was privy to all this information and knew that the country was headed for the abyss but there was nothing I could do but hope. Despite the relentless defeats and disappointments, I had yet to lose faith in ultimate victory.

'I am', I said. 'It's not easy you know, saving an entire country. It took years for the French Revolution to bear its fruits, and our country faces even sterner, graver tests. Under these conditions...'

'Enough, Şehsuvar, enough!' You didn't just say it; you screamed it, right in the middle of the street. 'How can you be so blind? Even Uncle Leon has woken up to what is going on. What have these men done to you? What's happened to you? Who has twisted your mind like this? I don't get it. Really, I don't.'

'Nobody can twist my mind', I said coldly, incensed at the way you were looking at me and talking to me. 'They couldn't if they tried. I make my own decisions and I act on those decisions myself. I am fighting for my faith, for my country and for my people. Those bastard Westerners are all liars. All they're doing is spewing out propaganda, nothing more. Yes, we will win. We will triumph. I believe that wholeheartedly. What is there not to understand?'

I saw your eyes mist up. That is when I realised you still loved me. That is when I should have gone down on my knees, apologised to you and begged forgiveness. But I didn't

'I don't understand', you said, shaking your head with that same look of pity. 'I'm sorry, but really, I don't understand. But I guess it doesn't matter now'. You held out your hand. 'There's no point in carrying on with this conversation. So long, Şehsuvar. It was nice to see you. All the best.'

And do you know what? That broke me.

I was gone. My soul and my body were broken, but still I stood there, someone absolutely convinced of themselves and of the righteousness of their cause. I shook your hand, which was even colder than the look on your face. And then, without any reaction, you walked away.

Save Yourself, Soldier

Hello Ester (Morning, Day 9)

I wrote all night, until dawn, until my fingers began to ache and my eyes began to sting. When I finished, I did not go to sleep. I felt strangely awake and alert. They say the best form of thinking is writing, and they must have been right. Writing is the best method of clarifying not just the past but the events of today too. My mind, free from the chaos of likelihoods and possibilities, was now beginning to see things much more clearly. When I went out on to the balcony, I was greeted by a spectacular autumn morning. Yesterday's rain had left behind a little coolness before vanishing from the city and I felt an unbearable urge to go out and wander the streets... To wander the deserted streets and walk by the closed shops while everyone was still asleep or only just waking up... I got changed and walked out of the hotel.

There was nobody around. On the corner of Asmalı Mescit Street, two night watchmen, approaching the end of their shift, yawned languidly. As I made my way around the narrow streets, I greeted some shopkeepers opening up their premises eager to catch the early bird. I stopped in front of a restaurant run by a Viennese couple to say a few words to a stray dog with beautiful eyes as it stretched out lazily and waited for a bone to be thrown its way. He didn't mind my stopping to talk and wagged his tail listlessly in reply. It reminded me of the Kangal dog I saw yesterday; he hadn't minded me much either. I must have some kind of effect on dogs as they clearly don't see me as someone to take seriously.

When I turned left at the *Cadde-i Kebir*, my nose picked up a lovely aroma. A few steps later, I realised where it was coming from: the Lebon Patisserie. Were they actually open this early? No. The shop was not open to customers but the bakers must have long since started work, baking the world's most sumptuous cakes and pastries, many of which I remember well from my days as a student at the Imperial High School. As I walked through the Aynalı Pasaj arcade of shops, the path opened out and people emerged. I walked past the frozen gaze of the mannequins in the window of Madam Cecile's famous seamstress' shop, the one you had always liked but had never mustered up the courage to enter. It had yet to open. The Karlmann Arcade, which used to be known as the Bon Marché, had opened its gates but was not yet open for business. We went there together when you came to Istanbul but of course we didn't buy anything, not even a single scarf, as we couldn't afford anything there. Now, though, if I could track you down, I'd buy you anything you want from there, even though I'm still not a rich man… There I go again, getting carried away with my dreams. As though I've already found you, as though you would actually accept a gift from me. But if you have come to Istanbul, then there is still hope, a hope that perhaps should not be dismissed so readily.

I carried on walking along the *Cadde-i Kebir*. The outer gates of the Saint Antoine Church were locked but a few metres on from there, Monsieur Leduc the florist had already opened for business, the scent from his array of red, pink and yellow summer flowers infusing the entire street. When the street reached Imperial High School, it broadened out and led straight on to Taksim Square but I did not feel like walking all that way. I was feeling a bit peckish so I took a left on to the street that led to Pera House, the building that housed the British Consulate. I couldn't help but take a quick glance to my right and to the *Avrupa Pasajı* arcade. That is where Mehmed Esad's carpet shop, which I had forgotten to visit last night, is located. The arcade was still shut but it would soon be opening. Seriously, what was I going to do with his guy? I needed to know what Mehmed Esad was going to do with me. I had a few possibilities in mind but I still wasn't sure. I left the mystery behind by the entrance to the *Avrupa Pasajı* arcade and walked over to the restaurant on the corner.

The restaurant was called *Nefaset* and was owned by old Uncle Kemalettin, a stout gentleman from İnebolu. He had always been kind to us as students and never turned us away, even when we were broke; he made sure we left with full stomachs. Uncle Kemalettin has long since passed away and the restaurant was passed on to his son but he turned out to be good for nothing so the restaurant ended up with Rasih, the head cook. Although the food isn't as good as it used to be, the lentil soup they make in the mornings is still out of this world so I ate my fill there. After a coffee made by Rasih himself, whom I remembered from my student days, I decided to come back to the hotel. It was enough wandering for one day. When I got back, even Ömer had yet to turn up. Without delay, I came up to my room, hoping to catch some sleep but to no avail. The fresh sparkle of the new day had got to me and I couldn't get to sleep. Not that I minded. I need to write. To write non-stop, to let it all out, everything in my heart and mind, and get it all down. If circumstances will allow, that is; who knows what may happen in the wake of Cezmi's murder. That is why I have to be quick and write a lot more so here I am at my desk, casting my mind back to that miserable day in Salonika when we broke each other's hearts.

I just stood there in the middle of Salonika, frozen, not knowing what to do without you. I had no home to go to and no friend that would open his doors to me. I couldn't go to Uncle Leon's or Grandma Paloma's as they would assume I was coming after you and my self-esteem would not allow me to be lowered in such a manner. If only... If only I hadn't let pride get in the way and had gone instead to your home to see her one last time. Yes, I was furious with you because you had neglected to tell me that Grandma Paloma had had a stroke and she was at death's door. You did not have the right to keep that from me. Grandma Paloma was just as much my grandmother as she was yours and the love and respect I had for her was genuine. And my respect for her was not without reason, either; she had a far better grasp of the situation than most of our party's leaders and her reading of our country's independence was a lot more accurate and incisive too.

I should have boarded the train and gone back to Istanbul, back to our old and tired capital where all kinds of plots, schemes and intrigues were being played out. But I couldn't go. Invisible ties bound me to Salonika and I couldn't tear myself free of those binds. I felt there was something I needed to do, a task I had to complete, but I didn't know what it was and the more I neglected it, the larger it loomed. I walked down to the White Tower and to the garden where Basri Bey and I had met four years earlier. I sat at the same table, ordered a sweet coffee and looked around with love at the city, a city of so many languages and so many faiths, a city in which an ideal could be found in every heart. Apart from my memories, I had no more ties to Salonika but I still had nothing but love for her, and it was a love that would never die as it is that city that has made me the person I am. I was born there, it was there that I became acquainted with life, in all its glory and with all its afflictions, it was there that I learnt to live and it was there that I had the best days of my life. To deny any of that would be a betrayal. The fact that on that day I felt so utterly alone and helpless had nothing to do with the city. I would say it was because of the choices I had made but that still would not have been enough. I could say it was the role history had carved out for us but that would also be wrong. I could say it was just bad luck but even that would not be right. Perhaps it was all of them together that had brought me down so low. And not just me, but the whole of humanity too… And to make matters worse, those were not even the darkest days; worse was to come. A ghastly future lay in wait for us and for the rest of the world. Of course, I didn't know that at the time. Four years earlier, when I had sat down at that same table with Basri Bey, I may not have been the eternal optimist but I had hope. Indeed, it was pretty much all I had. Without that hope, there would have been no reason for me to live.

It felt good sitting in that shaded garden overlooking the sea and feeling the autumn air on my skin as I let my mind wander. The grief was still there but at least the despair and the gloom had gone. After taking the last sips of my coffee, I decided to board the first train to the capital but there was one more visit I had to make before leaving. The city had still one sacred piece of land that belonged to me: my mother's grave.

I'm glad I went as the grave was in a sorry state. The stone was crumbling, and the earth over the grave was covered in wild grass. I took off my fez and my military jacket and set to work cleaning it up but before long, the wound in my back began to play up and I remembered what Doctor Şakir had told me: 'I'm discharging you but your wound has not fully healed so no heavy work or lifting or you'll tear the stitches apart and if you do that, you'll be in a world of trouble...' Still, I cleaned up my mother's final resting place as best as I could and then sat down on a nearby slab. I told my mother about Libya and what I had been through there and asked her to forgive me for not being able to visit my father's grave while I was out there. I had wanted to pay my respects to my father but I hadn't had the chance because of the war.

'But don't worry', I said. 'Father is no longer alone out there. I left a friend out there with him. My commanding officer, Basri Bey, a brave and honourable man. I'm sure they've already met, as like father, Basri Bey had no concern other than the welfare of his people and his country. And like father, he sacrificed his life without a moment's thought, leaving behind a wife and child. It looks like it's going to be my turn next. I shall follow in their footsteps. It's not as sad with me as I won't leave behind a grieving wife and child. But I promise you now, and this is a pledge, that while I am still alive, I shall keep on visiting you. This grave will never be left unattended or unkempt.'

While I was there having this one-sided conversation with my dear departed mother, I felt somebody coming towards me.

I looked up. It was Tiresias, the local lunatic from Freedom Square.

'You got a smoke?' he asked, sitting next to me. 'Come on. Give one of God's poor wretches a smoke, eh?'

I'd always liked Tiresias, but he'd also grown old. His hair and his beard were greying and he must have been losing his eyesight too as he was squinting. I reached into my pocket and took out my cigarettes.

'Here, take the packet.'

He took one and handed the packet back to me.

'Just one. I only have the right to one. Any more would be a sin.'

There was little point in arguing so I put the packet back in my pocket and lit his cigarette. He half-closed his eyes, took a deep drag and then released a cloud of grey smoke out into the wind. He was murmuring something as he did so but I couldn't decipher what he was saying.

'Speak up Tiresias, I don't know what you're on about.'

He straightened up, with a swiftness that was surprising for his age, leaned over and whispered in my ear.

'Get away from here. Now. Right away.'

'And why should I do that?' I asked mockingly. He cast a furtive glance around.

'Saint Demitrios has awoken', he whispered. 'And he is coming to save the city. He is going to take the church back from the Muslims. And not just the Muslims. He is going to crush the Jews, the Bulgarians and the Vlachs. All of them. Salonika will be ours and ours alone. So go, while you still have time. Go. Save yourself, soldier. Take whomever you have, dead or alive, and whatever you have, and go. I'm telling you, Saint Demetrios is coming and he is holding the banner of the Christ.'

I laughed at poor Tiresias but a month after I got back to Dersaadet, Salonika fell. That's right, my beautiful city, which had been conquered by none other than Sultan Murad Han, father of Sultan Mehmed the Conqueror, and had been under Ottoman rule for nearly five hundred years, was overrun, and without a single bullet being fired either.

Of course, the fall of Salonika had nothing to do with Tiresias. The real reason was obvious: it was Hasan Tahsin Paşa, enemy of the CUP, whose inept and incompetent government's politics of fear and cowardice ceded the city to the Greek army without even bothering to defend it. If our losses had been restricted to Salonika, then we could have perhaps acknowledged the defeat and consoled ourselves by saying we would regroup and take the city back but we had also suffered heavy defeats in the Balkans and the new Minister for War, Nazım Paşa, did not have the experience or the knowledge necessary to direct a military campaign. When fighting broke out in the Balkans, for example, he saw nothing wrong with discharging around one hundred thousand men from our army. Morale in the army was shot and there were now serious rifts between the CUP-supporting officers and another group of military officers that called themselves the *Halaskâr*. Yes, I'm afraid there were now mutinies against us amongst the common soldiery. Like us once upon a time, these officers that called themselves the *Halaskâr Zabitan* were organising within the ranks of the army but their only targets were us: the CUP guys. I don't deny that our party's mistakes were a critical factor in creating these rifts. Despite the decision taken at our congress not to involve the army in politics, at the first opportunity that is what we did and we plunged straight into the government's affairs.

Not that any of that mattered by then. The grand collapse had already started. I should confess, I never expected the collapse to be as horrific as it was and I used to be furious at you for once again being right, only then to realise how stupid I was being, after which I would try to refocus my fury on to myself. That was the insanity I struggled with for days. What's even more surprising is that it wasn't just me but the rest of the party members too; they were all perplexed, and none of them knew what to do. The Balkan states' armies were at the gates of Istanbul, and the Bulgarians, for example, were only just stopped at Çatalca. But the fall of Salonika was a huge setback for us and was a shock not just for me but for nearly everyone else in the party as well; a real catastrophe. For those of us that had been born there, we would never be able to return and walk its streets, or, and this was the most agonising, pay our respects at the graves of our dead. The pledge I had made to my mother just a month earlier would now be unfulfilled. It wasn't just Salonika we had lost but our childhood, our youth, our dead and many of our memories; whole parts of our lives had gone, along with the city. Talat Bey was particularly dismayed by the loss of Salonika, even though he was from Edirne. When we bumped into each other at the party's branch offices in Nuruosmaniye, he was almost apologetic and asked, 'Tell me, Şehsuvar, have you managed to bring your mother, Mukaddes Hanım, to Istanbul?' When I told him my mother had passed away a year earlier, he was embarrassed but also defiant and did his best to console me. 'Don't grieve for her', he said, 'Her grave shall not be neglected. Salonika will be ours again soon...'

Even he knew he was lying. Just as my father's grave in Fezzan has been lost to time, so too will my mother's grave in Salonika eventually be lost. But I was not angry at Talat Bey. What else could he have said? He was the leader of our movement and our organisation and as such, he could hardly go around saying it was all over and that we had lost and that it was best to just give up. Like the rest of us, he had aged before his time; the lines on his brow had deepened and his black hair was turning grey. Moreover, as we chatted, he revealed some surprising secrets to me.

Actually, Fuad and I had gone there to speak to Kara Kemal. Fuad had returned to the capital a month after me, and many of the other soldiers, rather than wasting time in Libya, were coming back in small groups to the capital to get ready for redeployment in the Balkans. However, like the rest of us, Fuad's mind was a mess and after Basri Bey's death, he was at even more of a loss, which is why we had come to talk to Kara Kemal in Nuruosmaniye, where, luckily enough for us, sitting next to 'the Little Master' Kara Kemal smoking his *nargile* was none other than 'the Grand Master' himself, Talat Bey, puffing away on a cigarette.

We talked in the committee room, which was so full of smoke from our cigarettes we could barely see each other. Talat Bey was pleased to see me. We had bumped into each other numerous times over the years but had never had the time to talk and had not actually spoken since our interesting little chat on the train from Salonika to Istanbul years ago. He was very affectionate towards Fuad too, asking after him and his family, and congratulating him on his heroics in Libya. As for Basri Bey, he already knew, and had known for some time. 'An exceptional man of the cause, a soldier of honour, and a true patriot', he said, his eyes clouding over. Kara Kemal also knew Basri Bey very well and he turned to me and said, 'What you did was not easy, Şehsuvar brother. Yours is just as heroic an act as Basri's. I don't know if I would have been able to do it had I been there...'

Talat Bey, however, was not keen on the line the conversation was taking.

'Of course you would have. We all would have! You are putting a friend and comrade out of misery. You are putting an end to his agonies while also preventing the enemy from capturing him alive.'

I actually did not want to discuss it. As far as I was concerned, a man's courage should be used productively and not end up in his friend's death.

'So what are dealing with, Talat Bey?' I asked, changing the subject. 'What's going to happen to our country? While we were out there defending Libya, the Balkans slipped from our grasp, the Bulgarians are now almost in our face and Kamil Paşa's government is hunting down the CUP.'

He lit a new cigarette with the glowing stub of the last one and took a deep breath.

'We need to be patient, Şehsuvar', amidst a cloud of smoke. 'Sometimes the greatest virtue is knowing how to wait. Sometimes one has to leave life to chance, which is something, unfortunately, our party does not seem capable of doing. So yes, now is the time to pause and reflect. To evaluate and assess and, more importantly, to assess ourselves. We have made a terrible mistake.' He shook his head sternly. 'It's not easy to admit but it's the truth. I'm talking about Mahmud Şevket Paşa. Forcing him to resign from the Ministry of War was a fatal error. He was a balancing element. He may not have known it but he was preparing the groundwork for our entry into politics but we were unaware of this and we took Damat Ferit's Freedom and Accord Party far too seriously.'

Judging by his frown and his twitching right eye, it seemed Kara Kemal did not agree. He put aside the pipe from his nargile and spoke up.

'That may be so, Talat Bey, but it's not just the Freedom and Accord Party we're up against. What are we going to do about Colonel Sadık's Halaskâr officers? The situation amongst the soldiery is dire…'

'That is the very fear that led us to err', our movement's leader said. 'When the Albanian officers took to the mountains and lent their support to the Halaskâr officers, it made us panic and believe that what happened to Abdülhamit in 1908 would also happen to us. But the fact is, circumstances on the ground had changed. Most importantly, we are the ones that inaugurated the parliament and we are the ones that had the constitutional system implemented, whereas the opposition were trying to turn back the wheels of history. I mean, some of those fools actually even considered bringing Abdülhamit back from Salonika and reinstating him on the throne! But these are all minor details. Because at the end of the day, the reason for our defeat is our overconfidence. We became intoxicated by power and we failed to properly gauge reality. That is why we were unable to grasp the importance of the role Mahmud Şevket Paşa has had to play in all this. We forgot that Said Paşa, who abandoned us, is an ancient foe. We became so sure of ourselves and our position that we assumed things would come to a standstill if we took a back seat. But politics hates a vacuum, and when we retreated, the opposition groups suddenly emerged and they obtained their seals of approval and their seats. And now, they have not only dragged the country into chaos but they have started their offensive against us too.'

'So why are we still ignoring them then?' Fuad asked excitedly. The desert sun and the desert winds had bronzed his complexion, as it had mine, and the strain of war had hardened the lines on his face. 'Seeing as they wish to break the law and dissolve parliament, we should get together and give them a show of strength to let them know who we are. We can sort them out in one night and finish them off for good. Most of the army is on our side. Enver Bey and our other officers are legends in the eyes of the military. I don't know what we are waiting for. Let's mobilise and save our country.'

'I'm of the same opinion, brother', Kara Kemal said, his eyes gleaming. 'Actually, this same matter was discussed at the Congress in September. We asked ourselves why these guys were allowed to operate so freely and why we should not just step in and take power back from them...' He looked over at Talat Bey. 'But for some reason, our suggestions were not accepted.'

'Don't even think about it, Kemal!' Talat growled. 'It is military operations like that that would drag the country further into ruin. When there are rumours still flying around that we won the elections by force, entertaining such thoughts and adopting such an attitude will only harm us and the movement. In politics, a certain level of violence is acceptable but if a political party casts aside all other means and methods and reaches straight for the gun, it is doomed to failure, even more so in a country like ours, where the problems just keep piling up and growing ever thornier. If we resort to force and force alone, then defeat will only be a few steps away.'

Kara Kemal, however, was not so quick to give in.

'But that is not what most of the delegates voted for during the first round at the Congress...'

'That's because the armed wing wants us to carry out a coup'. He turned to face Fuad and I. 'I don't mean you two but there are some in that faction that are...' He was struggling to find the right words. 'A little hot-headed, shall we say. A little too zealous. They shoot first and think later, whereas what we need is to think things through over and over again. Courage, valour and sacrifice are important, of course, but they are not enough. One needs the right political approach first. A sound strategy, the proper tactics.' He must have mistaken our silence for disavowal as he then asked, 'Isn't that so, gentlemen?'

'I agree with you on that, Talat Bey', Fuad said, not even feeling a need to hide his anger. 'In Tripoli, one of our *fedaeen* killed one of our aides for no reason. Shot him dead, and in one of the paşa's tents no less. All the poor aide did was criticise the CUP men and he ends up paying for it with his life, whereas the *fedai* was not punished at all.'

He was talking about Yakup Cemil, who shot Lieutenant Şükrü in the tent belonging to Ethem Paşa, commander of the Tobruk Zone in Libya.

'That is what I meant, yes', said Talat Bey, who clearly knew about the murder. 'Such unpleasant incidents do not help our movement in the least. Rather, they serve to harm it. Which is why for us, the optimum route is the one lain out by the law. It may be a long and tiring one but it is the only route that will bring us lasting victory.'

No one could touch Yakup Cemil or his accomplices as they were protected by Enver Bey. As for Talat Bey, it didn't matter how much he claimed to be against these acts of terror and aggression, he knew all too well that at the end of the day he had to work with those fedaeen. In other words, he needed the strongmen. That is until they turned their guns on him, although we had yet to reach that stage.

'Our focus at the moment is on the war in the Balkans', Talat Bey went on. 'We need to put aside all our divisions and join in the defence of the motherland. The Bulgarians have to be stopped. This is the number one national priority and we need to help the government in any way we can. If we play our political cards properly, history will be on our side. We need to exercise patience and wait for that moment to arrive.'

That is what he said, in that cloudy, smoke-filled room. And believe me, Talat Bey meant it but just three months later, whether it was down to helplessness or the whims of politics, he was forced to embrace everything he had just condemned in that room. The Committee for Union and Progress would soon carry out a coup and take over power.

Wishing for Help from the Dead

Hello Ester (Noon, Day 9)

Mehmed Esad has not given up, and nor will he. Of course, I am not surprised, as no CUP man, regardless of whether he is an old hand or a rookie, gives up easily. When I went down for lunch, Ömer came running up to me to give me the news that Mehmed Esad had come while I had been ensconced in my room. He had made his way to the elevator without even bothering to ask anybody but was stopped by Ömer, who spotted him and told him I was not in my room and that I would not be back until the evening. Actually, I had not instructed him to say anything of the sort but it was hard not to admire his initiative.

'I don't think you would have liked it, sir', Ömer said when he saw me at lunch. 'I can't say I've taken much of a shine to that gentleman myself. He strikes me as, how should I say it, a little arrogant. A rather conceited fellow, if you ask me. When he realised he would not be allowed upstairs, he left you a note. But he also said, 'I've left him this note but I'm telling you too. Make sure he knows. I shall be waiting for Şehsuvar Bey this evening.' Yes, sir, those were his exact words. It's not my place to say but it would perhaps be wise if one were to keep one's distance from this gentleman.'

Indeed it wasn't his place to say so but I did not want to hurt his feelings so I thanked him, took the envelope he was holding out for me and sent him on his way. This is what the note inside said:

'Şehsuvar, where have you been? I'm not joking, we really need to meet, and urgently. There is some serious business going on and you are involved. The meeting we were supposed to have yesterday I've moved forward to today. I shall be expecting you this evening. Regards, Mehmed Esad.'

So we had now moved on from insistence to veiled threats. What could these incidents and events involving me possibly be? Cezmi's murder? Of course not. How would he know I went to Cezmi's house? What if he did know? I doubt it. It must be something else. But what? I have not done anything wrong. Not that it means much as even if I haven't, they would still invent a misdemeanour for me, the way we used to do back in the old days of the Ottoman Secret Service, the *Teşkilat-i Mahsusa*. After all, eliminating individuals and groups that posed a threat was all that mattered, wasn't it? Having said that, I am not so sure now. If their intention is to eliminate me, then why send a man like Mehmed Esad? All they have to do is kill me, just like Major Cezmi, and be done with it. Why prolong the matter? On the other hand, when so many ex-CUP guys are swinging from the gallows or are being sent to the dungeons to rot, why would they want to work with me? How can they trust someone like me, a man who was once close to Talat Bey and who had carried out highly sensitive assignments for the *Teşkilat-i Mahsusa*? No, Mehmed Esad is definitely up to no good and I will not be keeping my appointment with him. Let them come and arrest me if they want. At least that way, I will be able to stand trial. Even if the trial is not a fair one, at least the defence I put forward will be on record. So no, I will not comply with his request. I made my decision and sat down to eat but I still felt uneasy. I ordered a glass of wine, hoping it would help ease my nerves, but the first glass had no effect so I ordered another, after which I began to feel a little better. I got up without even ordering a coffee and was walking towards the elevator when I heard Ömer calling out to me.

I turned around. He was walking towards me flanked by two men in trilby hats. What, so now Mehmed Esad was sending plain clothes police officers to speak to me for not keeping our appointment? But there was still time before our scheduled meeting. In that case, who were these guys?

'These gentlemen are from the police', Ömer said. 'They would like to speak to you'.

The distress in his voice was quite palpable. I, on the other hand, smiled, prepared as I had been for some time now for any eventuality.

'Is that so?' I said, turning to the two men. 'And what seems to be the matter?'

'Perhaps we could find a quiet corner first?' The one with the upturned moustache reminiscent of an old CUP member said.

I shrugged my shoulders.

'How about the restaurant? Lunch is over, so nobody will disturb us.' We walked back to the table I had just vacated. 'I would ask you if you'd like anything to eat but I'm afraid you may misunderstand.'

'Thank you, we're full', the one *sans* moustache replied.

There was no hostility or animosity in their manner and I wanted to make a good impression before we began talking so I asked them if they would like some coffee. Actually, before they could even reply, I called Ihsan, who hurried over.

'How would you like your coffee?' I asked.

'No sugar', they both replied. I gave the order and turned back around to face the two men.

'Yes gentlemen', I said. 'I'm listening'.

They got straight to the point.

'Do you know a Mister Cezmi Kenan?'

So, it was all out in the open. But how was I to answer? If I said I didn't and they knew I had gone to his house, then I would be shooting myself in the foot, but if I said yes, then there was a chance I would be playing into their hands when they had nothing to go on. But seeing as they had come to see me about Cezmi, they must have had some information that indicated we were at least acquaintances. At that moment, another possibility hit me. What if these men were the two policemen that had chased me yesterday? Thank God neither of them had seen my face and the clothes I was wearing now were not the ones I had been wearing yesterday.

'I do', I replied casually. 'We are both from Salonika and we fought together in Libya.'

The clean-shaven one's face lit up.

'You were in Libya? My father also fought there.'

No, these gentlemen were not from the political division. I reckon they were from homicide.

'Really?' I said, genuinely interested. 'Under whom? Enver Paşa?'

His face fell.

'Actually no, under Mustafa Kemal'.

It was a serious *faux pas* on my part and I immediately tried to set it right.

'We were with Mustafa Kemal at first but then we had to split. Had we remained with him, I am sure I would have met your father. Tell me, how is he? I hope he is in good health.'

He bowed his head.

'My father joined the ranks of the martyred', he said. 'But not in Libya. In the Balkans'.

'May Allah have mercy on his soul', I said, offering my condolences.

'And on all our fallen'.

'Why are you asking after Major Cezmi?' I then asked, as though it were but a minor afterthought. This time the one with the beard answered.

'Why don't you let us ask the questions? When did you last see Cezmi Kenan?'

Straight to the point… If they knew I had gone to that house, then replying in the negative would immediately make me a suspect. But what if they didn't know? But if they didn't know, why had they come to see me? And so soon, too – not even twenty-four hours had passed since the murder had taken place.

'I saw him three days ago. He invited me over. He has a lovely house with a garden in Langa, which is where I went. We had a nice chat.'

I kept my eyes on their faces the whole time I was talking, curious as to how they might react, but they remained straight-faced, giving away neither doubt nor excitement. I don't think they saw me as a killer, which would imply that they did not have any evidence or witnesses that could proclaim me a suspect.

'Why do you ask?' I asked, as though giving in to my own curiosity. 'Has anything happened to Major Cezmi?'

'He's dead', the one whose father had died in the war replied. 'Stabbed to death in his own home'.

'What?'

'I'm afraid so. Somebody entered his premises and stabbed him in the heart'.

'But how? Who? Was it thieves? Burglars?'

'Possibly. We're looking into it. Mister Cezmi kept a diary and we saw your name in it. He mentioned your visit three days back, the one you just mentioned. A certain Reşit Bey was also mentioned.' He looked over to reception. 'It appears Reşit is the manager here. We asked for him but he has yet to arrive at the hotel.'

'Cezmi Bey was friends with Reşit's father, Yusuf Bey. They were in the military academy together. Reşit Bey had been helping Cezmi.' I shook my head in astonishment. 'How can such a thing a happen? A man who was as strong as an ox just three days ago killed…'

The clean-shaven one looked on indifferently.

'Did he have any enemies? Any people that bore him ill will?'

This one with the moustache seemed more alert and focused on his remit but actually they were both as amateurish as each other.

'I don't know', I said, feigning bewilderment. 'I hadn't seen Major Cezmi for years so I have no information as to the people with whom he had been fraternising or what kind of relationships he formed with them. He didn't mention anybody in particular when we met, nor did he seem to be under any kind of threat. Or at least he didn't say anything of the sort to me. He was a brave man, Major Cezmi. And a strong man too. I'm shocked, I tell you. Really. How could the killer have possibly overpowered him and… And with a knife too…'

'Maybe the killer was not alone', the one with the moustache said. 'Maybe it was more than one person'.

'That must be it', I said looking at him as he stared back waiting for confirmation. 'If it was just one person, Major Cezmi would not have let him off…'

He was an astute fellow, this officer, and he looked down at my arms.

'Would you be so kind as to take off your jacket and roll up your sleeves?'

Good for them. So they had noticed the blood under Cezmi's fingernails.

'Of course'. I did as requested and showed them my arms, which they proceeded to carefully examine. I carried on feigning innocence and asked, 'What are you looking for?'

'If you leave the hotel, please leave an address at which you may be found', is all they said in reply. 'If necessary, you may be asked to come to the station to submit a written statement.'

And then, suddenly, they upped and left. I stared at them in genuine bewilderment as they made their way out. Was that it? Is that how a serious murder inquiry is conducted?

I began ambling back up to my room, mulling over what had just happened. And then, while I was opening the door to my room, it hit me. Mehmed Esad was communicating with me in his own personal way. He was sending me a message: *Look, I know what you've been up to but I don't want to arrest you so I'm sending these two oafs after you instead. But if you do not turn up tonight, I won't be so accommodating.* There could be no other meaning behind his sending two bungling police officers to question me. As I said, a good CUP man, no matter how old, does not give in that easily. Perhaps it would be best to change tack; not keeping my appointment with him may not be the best idea. But first I needed to warn Reşit. He should never have told them that I had gone to see Cezmi last night. I called Ömer on the telephone and, calmly but firmly, said, 'I would like to speak to Reşit Bey the moment he arrives. It's very important so please inform me as soon as he gets here.'

'As you wish, Şehsuvar Bey'.

I put the phone down. I was now convinced that there were people out there conspiring against me. But instead of fear, what I felt was excitement, a strange thrill at having upended their little game, at revealing their plot, at being in the middle of this political riddle…. And what about the risk of being arrested or killed, you may ask? None of it matters. The only fear I have is the prospect of never seeing you again and of not being able to write to you again. Which is why I have to continue, while I still have time and while I am still free. And so…

The winter of 1912 hit the capital like a nightmare. And I am not just referring to the military defeat we had recently suffered but a real catastrophe. The devastation wreaked in the Balkans had hit us hard. Aside from the violent, vicious deaths of thousands of soldiers and civilians, thousands of others that had been forced to abandon their homes and their villages were now streaming into Istanbul. A city that was already struggling to feed its own people had turned into a teeming nest of hunger and cholera. The squares, mosque courtyards and street corners were filled with men, women and children groaning in pain as a result of disease, hunger and cold, and they were begging for help. My late father had once told me that the collapse of a large state gives rise to scenes of horror and I could now see how right he was. But I also felt a strange satisfaction. You know I am not a heartless man and I'm sure you can guess how upset I was at seeing those women and children and those refugees writhing and moaning in pain but as well as distress, I also felt a strange relief. Relief that our party was not in power and that the police were not commencing proceedings against us. It was the relief of not being under pressure… Over the previous four years, we had been subjected to so many denunciations and had been so widely vilified and maligned that I now, in a way, saw the absence of accusers as a blessing. And yes, I know that you will say this a shunning of responsibility, but it felt good nonetheless.

Yes, the government of Kamil Paşa, which had been responsible for the defeat in the Balkan War, was also a fierce opponent of the CUP. Using the war as a pretext, they could have
declared every last member of our organisation a traitor, but
the truth is, the mistakes made by a government that had
dragged the country to ruin, and the mistakes made by Kamil
Paşa, an admittedly brilliant man, had had nothing to do with
us. Nevertheless, in spite of this, our men did not hesitate in
fighting to their last breath during the conflict once it broke
out, not just as a point of national principle but as an ethical
position too. Talat Bey must have been having similar thoughts
to mine for him to offer power to the İtilaf Fırkası on a golden
platter from the summer onwards and be willing to leave the
post of *sadrazam,* first to Ahmed Muhtar Paşa and then to
Kamil Paşa. This ostensibly 'passive' stance had, in my eyes, an
ethical quality to it, as it is my belief that Talat Bey did want to
risk becoming a tyrant himself.

I should also confess this outlook was in part thanks to you.
Perhaps it was also a virtue given to me by art. It was not winning
that counted for me now but being right; standing not by the
strong but alongside the vanquished and the oppressed, and this
new outlook gave me a strange contentment, one I had not felt
for a long time. For some time now, I had been questioning
my beliefs. The constitutional system was faltering and it felt
as though our revolution was incomplete. More importantly,
the movement of which I was a part had been compromised
and seemed to have turned into the kind of power it had once
so sternly and vehemently condemned. But now we were the
opposition again, which let me see myself as a revolutionary
once more, as a defender of the downtrodden and a soldier for
the nation, and that is how it was supposed to be. Seeing as we
were willing to sacrifice our lives, it was not riches or power for
which we were to be striving. As dedicated men, we needed to
live unblemished lives and die untainted deaths. Unfortunately,
this quaint contentment I felt was not to last very long. As Talat
Bey was to later explain, we could not sit idly by and watch the
country get swallowed up and disappear. Ultimately, we would

have to assume power. The decision would eventually have to be taken and implemented, even if it meant turning into the very tyrants and coup plotters we so abhorred.

It was January, and a relatively warm night for that time of year... We had taken up our posts around Beşezade Emin Bey's house in Vefa Square, inside which a meeting was being held. Neither I nor Fuad nor any of the four men on duty with us outside knew the details or content of the meeting. We were merely keeping watch, as per orders, but we could grasp the gravity of the meeting inside by the people we saw emerging from the darkness of the street and hurrying into the house: Talat Bey, Ziya Gökalp, Miralay İsmail Hakkı, Fethi Bey, Mithat Şükrü, Doctor Nazım and the man from whom we were now taking our orders, Kara Kemal... Yes, we were now part of that outstanding network set up by the Little Master in the capital consisting of hundreds of people from various diverse backgrounds and professions. We were not complaining. If anything, we counted ourselves as happy to be able to take up the struggle against the new despots. We had been charged with protecting the leaders of a movement that was standing up to the arrests and the prosecutions being carried out by Kamil Paşa's government. A number of our leaders had managed to evade the police raids on our movement, with many deciding to flee overseas. Indeed, we had already engaged in gunfights on a few occasions with government agents but luckily nobody was hurt on either side. However, if the situation were to continue like this, the shedding of blood would soon be unavoidable as the government would not rest until it had completely eliminated the Committee for Union and Progress and we were convinced that the meeting that was taking place that night was going to tackle all these issues head-on and come up with viable solutions.

What was striking, however, was that Enver Bey was not attending the meeting, which made me wonder whether a rift had appeared in the movement. I mean, how else to explain the absence of a man like Enver from such an important meeting, a man who was seen by the people as a true hero?

I did not express any of these thoughts to Fuad of course but oddly enough, he must have been thinking the same thing as he turned to me and asked, 'Why isn't Enver Bey here? Has something happened between him and the party?'

'I doubt it, Fuad', I said, masking my own misgivings. 'I'm sure there are valid reasons for his not being here. He would never turn his back on the party, nor the party on him.'

I was trying to calm Fuad but the truth was soon revealed. Enver Bey had not come to the meeting so as to not threaten its security. He knew he was the subject of intense surveillance and scrutiny. As champion of the nation's liberty, the soldiery held him in high esteem, and this terrified the government into monitoring his every move and tracking his every step.

The meeting in the house in Vefa Square went on late into the night. We spent hours patrolling the streets, taking up positions in our respective corners and checking to make sure nobody was around, smoking the whole time until our mouths reeked. At one point, Fuad narrated Euripides' play *Medea*, which he had seen a week earlier and which he was still raving about, reciting some choice lines for us. The heroine's power, fuelled by that intense jealousy, must have left a huge impression on him but for some reason, he could not understand how she could kill her own children as a form of revenge against her husband. It made me think about you, Ester. Don't get me wrong, I'm not implying you would kill anybody of course, especially not children… But whenever I hear talk about women and that secret, overwhelming power they possess, it always makes me think of you.

So anyway, as we stood there prattling on, the front door opened and the people at the meeting began filing out in ones and twos. The Little Master was the last to leave, and he did not look happy; clearly, the gathering had not gone as intended. We escorted him home but he did not say a word about the meeting and we made sure not to ask, although we were dying to know. We didn't have to wait for long though as a week later another meeting was held in the same house, this time with Enver Bey in attendance and Fethi Bey absent. It wasn't a huge loss, as although Fethi Bey was a brave soldier and a loyal CUP man, he did not have Enver Bey's standing in the movement. In other words, a decision could be taken without Fethi Bey present, so I saw no reason to fret over his absence.

We kept our weapons at hand and again began pacing the dark streets. This time, however, the weather was not so mild; a stiff icy breeze was coming in from the sea and kept us on our toes the whole night. Just when we thought we were going to freeze to death, the meeting ended and the committee members began exiting the premises. This time, the meeting had gone on until dawn and the fatigue and sleeplessness were getting the better of us but we were buoyed when we saw Kara Kemal coming out of the house looking delighted. The meeting had clearly gone well.

'All done', he said, blowing into his hands to warm them up. 'We'll sort those traitors out once and for all. Get ready for a massive operation. We shall soon be in action.'

The operation to which he was referring was a planned attack on the government. The movement that had taken to the hills before the 1908 revolution to usher in constitutional reforms was returning to its roots. When Talat Bey discovered that Kamil Paşa's government was preparing to cede the city of Edirne as part of a proposed peace plan with the Balkan states, he was no longer willing to just 'wait and see'. Now he was planning on taking over by force, using the fury and indignation that would be roused amongst the masses by this territorial loss. Nevertheless, the decision had not been taken that day at the meeting in Beşezade Emin Bey's house. Fethi Bey was against a coup, saying, 'The age of secret societies and clandestine resistance movements is over. Let Kamil Paşa and his government sign the peace treaty. The people will be enraged and then we will duly prepare for elections. That way, we will simply be voted into power.'

That is why Kara Kemal had been so frustrated when he left the first meeting. But at the second meeting, the one which Enver Bey attended and from which Fethi Bey was absent, Talat

Bey got what he wanted and the decision was made to carry out a coup. Indeed, at this meeting, Enver Bey did not hold back and scolded the members there for having not decided to do so at the previous meeting, telling them it was a crucial moment, not just for the movement, but for the whole country, and that they either liberate themselves from Kamil Paşa and his government, who were about to give the country away to outsiders, or they all sink. Nobody opposed him.

The date set for the coup also seemed deliberate: the 23rd of January, a Thursday. The declaration of the constitutional era took place on the 23rd of July, so we couldn't help but wonder if that particular day was chosen intentionally. We didn't know for sure and it was Kara Kemal that told us that Talat Bey himself had chosen the Thursday as he believed Thursdays were auspicious days. However, there were other, more significant, reasons behind the coup falling on a Thursday. It was on a Thursday, Thursday the 23rd of January 1913 to be precise, that the answer to a statement issued by the foreign powers was to be issued by the office of the *sadrazam*. In other words, Kamil Paşa's resignation and a new government made up of hand-picked men would be demanded. The second meeting at the house in Vefa must have proceeded smoothly as not only the date but the time of the planned coup was also agreed upon: 15:00 on the 23rd of January.

Days before the coup, Fuad and I began preparing. We spoke to the people on a list given us by Kara Kemal, all of whom had become members of the party even before Resneli Niyazi had taken to the hills. None of them asked what it was all about or how, when or where the decision had been taken. Indeed, they all said that if that was the decision and the plan, then of course they would be there but the excitement and the zeal of old had gone. We were all suffering from a crisis of conviction. The subtle unravelling that had taken place in the country and the rotting decay that had enveloped the nation had infected the movement and its members too. It felt as though we were slowly but inexorably losing our belief in the cause. For all

I know, we had already lost it but nobody was actually openly saying so.

Lieutenant Fuad was all too aware of this dark turn events were taking but neither of us spoke of it. Even if we had, what would it have accomplished? We had no choice but to give in to the chain of events and let fate decide. As always, we rolled up our sleeves and performed our duties to the best of our abilities. The day before the coup, we walked up and down the hill that led from Sirkeci to the government buildings a dozen times and then some, noting down the coffee shops, the clubs and the hotel bars in which our men would be positioned. We then informed them of their positions and also reminded them not to attract any unwanted attention that could endanger the operation.

Despite our preparations and the warnings we had issued to our men, I must have been a nervous wreck the next morning as Madam Melina, before I had even left the house, asked, 'Şehsuvar my boy, what's wrong? You seem so nervous this morning. Is everything okay?'

'I'm fine', I replied. 'I'm just applying for a new job. One with better pay and conditions.'

Luckily, she swallowed the lie but I still ate a few more bites so she would not worry before hurriedly getting up from the breakfast table to leave. It was cold and wet outside, the rain a dirty, fickle drizzle. When we gathered at the spice merchant Üsküplü Necip's storerooms in the Egyptian Bazaar for a final meeting, it was approaching noon. As we were entering the storerooms, we bumped into Yakup Cemil and another army officer who was as large and as imposing as him. They had just met Kara Kemal and were on their way out. When he saw us, Yakup Cemil sneered. He wasn't what you would call my biggest admirer and he made it clear he did not like Fuad, either. Still, we brought our hands up to our chests in greeting to which they gave faint nods of their heads in response.

We found Kara Kemal in the dark depths of the storehouse, sitting on a wooden stool in the flickering light of a gas lamp gathering up some notes that were spread out on a huge wine cask. When he saw us, his face lit up. He didn't seem worried; things must have been going as planned. Enver Bey and his men were waiting at the Ranges Inspectorate and Talat Bey and Sapancalı Hakkı were sitting in a modest little coffee house on one of the side streets, whilst the men that would cut off the government's communication with the outside world once the coup began were stationed around the Post Office. The division known as the *Uşak Taburu*, charged with guarding the government buildings, had pledged not to put up any resistance.

We informed Kara Kemal that our reconnaissance mission had led us to conclude that we did not have enough men out there, whether it was in the clubs and coffee houses in Sirkeci or in the lounge of the Meserret Hotel, but he seemed unperturbed.

'No need to panic, gentlemen', he said with his customary coolness. 'We still have time. They'll turn up. But that doesn't mean you two let up in your surveillance. I have placed my trust in you two more than any others in this operation.' He glanced at the door. 'You two are smart and alert, and I know you won't get carried away in the heat of the moment, unlike some people I could mention. I would like you two to stay with Talat Bey. Enver Bey will be guarded by his men, but we need to make sure Talat Bey is safe. During this operation, any one of us may be shot or killed but the movement's leaders cannot come to any harm. Our freedom as a nation depends upon them. What we are trying to accomplish here is tough but we need to stay strong and stay focused. Just as we dethroned Abdülhamit, so shall we depose Kamil Paşa. Of that, I have not the slightest doubt and neither should you. You have to believe.'

And what if we didn't believe? What then? What difference would it make? Still, the men he said were going to turn up didn't. Whether it was because they got the fear or because they thought the coup was a mistake or because their faith in the movement had been shaken, it's hard to say, but at one o'clock, there were very few familiar faces in the local clubs and coffee houses and on the streets and street corners. Of course, the men that had turned up were all loyal, steadfast and committed *fedai* that had proven themselves in battle but our numbers were still small. With such few men, carrying out a raid on the Bab-ı Âli and bringing down the government of the Ottoman Empire, no less, was simply not possible. To even undertake such a venture was to walk straight into the arms of death. I was mulling over the possibility of the operation being called off when the order came through from Kara Kemal, stern as ever.

'No turning back, gentlemen. Death if needs be, but no retreat. Let's move.'

We were all supposed to meet in front of the General Offices of the Military Inspectorate of Ranges at 14:30. The wheels had been set in motion, the arrow had left the bow: the Bab-ı Âli was to be stormed and the ruling government was to be brought down, whatever the cost. We were sitting in the tea-room of the Meserret Hotel when the order came through. We had half an hour to reach the assembly point but first we needed to get to Sirkeci to inform the others. We went into all the premises in which our men were stationed and pushed our fezzes back on our heads with our hands, this being the agreed signal for us to mobilise, and then made our way back up the hill towards the Bab-ı Âli. By this time, there were only about sixty of us in total. It did not bode well and I could see Fuad wistfully stroking his moustache.

'Perhaps we should say our goodbyes now, Şehsuvar old boy', he said with a resigned smile. 'Because I don't know if we're going to come out of this in one piece or not.'

'Of course we will, Fuad my brother' I said, not wanting to appear doubtful and also wanting to boost his morale. 'We've been through much worse. This is child's play.'

He looked me up and down sceptically.

'*Inshallah*. Still, best to say our goodbyes anyway. Just in case. I don't want to leave this world with any loose ends dangling about.'

I stopped and gazed affectionately at him.

'Then I guess this is farewell, old boy. And you should say it too as I may not see the day through either.'

We embraced warmly, and it was at that moment that I realised that it was not Talat Bey or Kara Kemal or anybody else that I was closest to in this world but this man, this honourable soldier and loyal son of the soil. Since I had known him, and it may not have been that long a time, we had been through so much and had faced and overcome so many challenges and hardships together. Most importantly, throughout it all, we had never wavered in our dedication to our country. We had not stolen a single penny nor eaten a mouthful of food that could be considered haram, and it was this integrity that had brought us closer together, closer than brothers. And of course, underlying this bond between us was the great Basri Bey himself. We were bound to each other through him and because of him.

'If only Commander Basri were here with us', Fuad said, seemingly reading my mind as we climbed the hill at Cağoğlu. 'I'd have felt better with him here'.

'Me too, brother', I said, surprised and heartened by his forthrightness. 'If Basri Bey were here, we'd feel so much safer and have all that more belief.'

He turned around and looked at the little group following us. He then sighed and said, 'What can we do? We can hardly ask for help from the dead. We just have to place our trust in ourselves and our guns. God willing, we shall succeed.'

Resign, Your Excellency!

Hello Ester (Early Evening, Day 9)

The sun was still up when I entered the shop in the *Avrupa Pasajı* arcade. The light reflecting off the glass ceiling of this arcade, an equal in beauty of which one could find only in a European city, had lost its lustre but was still strong enough to keep the darkness away and the gas lamps unlit. Finding the only carpet shop in the arcade was not hard. Inside was seated a dark – very dark – gentleman with a pockmarked face, probably the man that had come to the hotel the other day to bring that message. When I greeted him and walked in, his dark, bloodshot eyes bored into me.

'I'm looking for Mehmed Bey', I said casually. 'Mehmed Esad. Is he around?'

He just stared at me and then raised a finger. I didn't know what he was trying to say so I asked him again.

'Mehmed Esad… Is he around?'

Again, there was no reaction or response, except for the waving of the finger. I was beginning to think I had come to the wrong place when my friend's voice came through from the upper floors.

'Şehsuvar… Is that you? Come upstairs.'

There was a wooden staircase behind the handmade curtains. As I walked up, I was hit by the heavy, musty smell of rugs and carpets. When I reached the upper floor, Mehmed Esad was standing there waiting for me.

'Finally! You've finally made it to our little store, my brother. We were about to close the file on you for good.'

I wasn't really paying much attention but I shook his outstretched hand and asked, 'Who's the surly fellow downstairs? Doesn't he speak Turkish? He didn't even have the decency to answer me when I asked after you.'

He glanced at the stairs and then back at me.

'You mean Ruşeym? Sorry about that, old chap, but the poor fellow can't speak. He was a member of a pro-Ottoman tribe out in Egypt. The English cut his tongue out. We came back together from the Suez. He worked as a courier for me during the war. He's such a good man and so loyal and what have you that I couldn't let him go so I brought him here with me.' He pointed to a stool by a little table atop of which were a silver cigarette case, a crusty old ashtray and a large box of matches. 'Here, take a seat'. I did as requested and he took a seat facing me. 'What will you drink? Our guy here makes a fine coffee, over a real coal fire too. What would you say to a couple of strong, hearty coffees?'

I wanted to give the impression that I was in a foul mood, even though I wasn't, to get Mehmed Esad to stop beating around the bush and get to the point.

'No coffees for me', I said tetchily. 'I've already told you, I've left this business behind. Why all this insistence, Mehmed?' He was taken aback by the sternness in my voice, which only emboldened me further. 'Why? Tell me, what do you want?'

He seemed embarrassed, to the point that I even think I saw his beardless, clean-shaven face blush.

'No insistence at all, old boy… It's just that you said you'd think about it and…'

'That's what you think but I've already made up my mind, Mehmed. I'd already made up my mind when I got back from exile in Malta. No more politics, no more secret underground stuff. It's not for me. If you really are a friend and you want to do me a favour, then get me a job in the Translation Bureau. You know my French is pretty good so at least let me be of some use to the country in that respect.'

He sniggered.

'Don't laugh, Mehmed. My decision is final. I'm not getting involved in any more dirty work, not for the state, nor for anybody else. I'm deadly serious. Like I said the other day, I want a peaceful life. I want to live in peace and die in peace. So please, stop running after me. Stop with the badgering. I implore you, let's put this one to sleep, for the sake of our friendship. I don't want that ruined.'

He wasn't laughing anymore. Where there had been that notorious sneer of his was now a look of deep disappointment.

'You're the one that is going to be ruined'. He was calm but he articulated each word clearly and carefully. 'Stop playing the innocent, Şehsuvar. They know what you're up to.'

My tactic had worked – his tongue had been loosened. I needed to keep on winding him up.

'Everyone knows what I've been up to. I've never hidden it. I joined the CUP in 1907 and remained a member until the movement broke up. We were defeated and the case was closed. Now I am not a member of any party. Not the Committee for Union and Progress, not the Progressive Republican Party and not the People's Republican party either.'

'Don't bother, Şehsuvar', he said, staring at me. 'You've said all this before but the reports that have come through to us say something quite different. You're still in touch with the CUP guys.'

Was he talking about Cezmi? Was he threatening to set me up as the fall guy for Cezmi's death?

'They know you've met Ziya Hürşit and that Sarı Edip Efe and Abdülkadir Bey, the ex-governor of Ankara, were there with you.'

What on earth was he on about?

'How could I have met those guys? They're all dead. They were all hanged for the attempted assassination of Mustafa Kemal.'

He stared at me with a mixture of despair and pity.

'Before that, Şehsuvar. A month before the assassination attempt in Izmir. You met them last May. There's no point in trying to deny it. You were present at Ahmet Şükrü Bey's house in Şişli and you spoke there. Your name is mentioned in Ziya Hürşit's personal statement.'

I had forgotten all about it. Yes, it had been during first week of May the previous year. Ahmet Bey had invited us to his home but it had not been political in nature or in intent.

'So?" I said angrily'. 'Ahmet Şükrü Bey was a friend of my father's. I've known him since his time as a teacher in Salonika. He invited me to his house for dinner but I didn't know who else had been invited. If I'd known Ziya Hürşit and Sarı Edip Efe were also going to be there, I would not have gone. And anyway, there were others there, four or five others, who had nothing to do with the Izmir assassination. Are you telling me old friends getting together for dinner automatically leads to an assassination attempt on the Gazi himself? As it is, Ziya Hürşit and I had had a major row at the table that day, and yes, it was about the republican government of today. Everyone knows how much they disliked Mustafa Kemal Paşa and his government. I was about to object, as the words they were using were bordering on the abusive. In fact, that is why I left.'

He was barely listening and what he did hear, he hardly believed.

'That's not what Ziya Hürşit's statement says. Worse still, some people in the secret service believe that you were the real brains behind the Izmir plot. That Kara Kemal sent you to that meeting personally as he was being tracked by the police and could not attend so he sent you to speak on his behalf. You gave the assassins the intelligence they needed.'

I was absolutely stunned.

'Have they lost their minds? Why the hell would I get involved in an operation that is bound to end in disaster with a bunch of people I despise? That is absurd! Absolutely absurd! How can they fall for such a lie? For such a blatantly false accusation?'

I realised then that we had started to switch roles and that he was trying to get under my skin. I needed to calm down and apply reason. My old friend looked rather pleased with himself. He reached out for a cigarette, lit it unhurriedly and took a long, leisurely drag.

'I wouldn't know about that, Şehsuvar old boy', he said, blowing smoke out of his mouth. 'But that's the situation, it seems. Of course I believe you. I know damn well you would not get involved in such an amateurish plot.'

'So why didn't you stand up for me and defend me? Why didn't you tell them you know me, that you know what kind of guy I am and that you know I wouldn't get involved in such madness?'

'How do you know I didn't stand up for you? If it hadn't been for me...' His voice trailed off. He knew he'd gone too far. 'I did stand up for you, Şehsuvar. And at the risk of causing them to start suspecting me. Don't forget, I'm an old CUP guy too, which means they have their doubts about me too. Not that I care. Let them. And you want to know why? Because you saved my life. But if you don't start cooperating with us, I can't make any guarantees about what will happen next. I'll be frank – I won't be able to protect you.' I was about to ask him if he was blackmailing me when he raised the hand holding his cigarette. 'No, I'm not forcing your hand. If you don't want to, you don't have to work with us, and it might be that nobody will interfere. But if someone does start getting involved with you, then I won't be able to help.'

I smiled sardonically.

'And you say you're not forcing my hand?'

'Not at all'. For some reason, he had lost his cool and his voice had come out needlessly high. 'Can't you see I'm trying to do you a favour? You're just brushing it off. I'm doing what I can but you don't care. Don't you see what's happened to you, Şehsuvar? Don't you trust me at all? Or are you really still in league with those CUP guys?' His eyes were flashing with anger and he took two long puffs of his cigarette in quick succession. 'I'm sorry old boy but you're being so tight-lipped that even I'm starting to have my doubts about you.'

I pretended to be moved and even a little embarrassed.

'I know you mean well, Mehmed, and I know you're out there putting yourself on the line for me. But I'm not being tight-lipped or anything. I've answered all your questions so far, if you haven't noticed, and if there is anything else you'd like to ask then I'll be happy to help you there too, to the best of my knowledge, of course. But how can I tell you something I know nothing about? I keep telling you, I no longer have anything to do with the Committee.'

He stubbed his cigarette out angrily in the ashtray.

'Very well old boy. If that's the way you want it. Here I am putting my neck on the line for you and what do I get out of it? Nothing. Well, seeing as you don't care, there there's no point in risking myself any further.' He pouted miserably, as though filled with remorse. 'You know best, Şehsuvar. That's it from me. I won't call you or bother you anymore. God help you, my friend…'

He was laying it on too thick, talking not like an old comrade but a member of my family, a close friend or relative whom I had betrayed and caused huge distress. Maybe he'd told his boss not to worry and that I would immediately fall in line and now that I hadn't, he was in a spot of bother. Indeed, that was possible but so what? The situation was clear. I could just let it go and tell myself that Mehmed's predicament was of no concern to me and get on with my life but it was a little bit more complicated. The meeting that took place before the assassination attempt in Izmir really could spell trouble for me. Even then, when I'd heard about the attempt on the President's life, I had been worried and when the details began leaking out and Ahmet Şükrü Bey, Ziya Hürşit and Sarı Edep Efe's names were mentioned, I actually starting to panic. The straw that broke the camel's back was the death of Kara Kemal. It was after that that I decided to move to the Pera Palas, so they wouldn't find me alone at home and kill me there the way they had Major Cezmi… Speaking of which, why hadn't Mehmed mentioned that incident? If he wanted to convince me, then that murder, which was still fresh in the memory, would have been highly effective. I looked at him as he sat there frowning.

'Come on Mehmed', I said, slapping his knees amicably. 'Aren't we friends? What's with the long face? We've been through so much together. Far worse than this. We can work our way out of this.'

'I don't know', he said, not giving in. 'Can we? It's up to you, Şehsuvar. I've said what I had to say. The decision is yours now. Do whatever you want.'

He was trying to come across as nonchalant but he wasn't sure what I would do. He knew that I could still reject him, even though I was cornered. I have long since given up on the pursuit of wealth and worldly possessions; even my own life has ceased to have any real value for me, and Mehmed Esad knew this. But there are of course some things in the world more painful than dying.

'Fair enough', I said, straightening up. 'You were right, Mehmed. Chatting like this on the fly doesn't do the trick.' Seeing me stand up, he began to panic. Was I walking away? 'Let's meet again tomorrow evening. But somewhere else this time. And with a couple of glasses of wine and a bite to eat too. The Taksim Gardens, for instance. There's a new orchestra playing there apparently, so we can listen to some music while we sort all this out.' I tried to look more understanding. 'I'm sorry, I know this issue has started to become a headache for you but hopefully tomorrow we can reach a decision.' He was delighted and stood up, as though I had already accepted his offer.

'Excellent. At the end of the day, you stand to gain a lot. Good. Now that you'll be working with us, it's taken a huge weight off my shoulders. But I swear, on my honour, you stand to gain a lot more from this collaboration.'

There wasn't a trace of his earlier sullenness. Forget intelligence work; Mehmed Esad couldn't even make a decent poker player. However, I must confess, I still couldn't work out what his game was, and until I accept his offer, I don't think I will. We said goodbye, promising to meet tomorrow evening at the Taksim Gardens.

So, my dearest Ester, that's how it is. Once you're a marked man, you can never get away. Either you get back in the game or you hand over your life. But surely there is a third option?

There must be. A chance for me to start a new life, a new life with you, perhaps. But that can only happen if you are in Istanbul, otherwise there is no point to any of this. And in order to make the right decision, I have to find your Uncle Leon first as he is the only person who can give me reliable information about you and your whereabouts. I am not without hope. I know I will find him. And I am not scared either, not of the government, nor of other people. On the contrary, trying to solve the riddle of all these successive events is sweetly enticing. On the other hand, there is in the background the constant worry that at any moment an intervention may occur, which is why as soon as I got back to the hotel, I sat down at my desk, picked up my pen and went back to those wonderful heady days of the past.

Where was I? Oh yes, I was describing that historic event that would determine the fate of the country and one whose imprint on the nation would perhaps be felt for years. The storming of the government on the 23rd of January, 1913… Fuad and I walked up the hill together in the drizzling rain. When we turned right at the Iranian Embassy on the corner, we saw a small group assembled amidst a sea of red and black fezzes. Suddenly, in front of the *Pembe Köşk* mansion, which we had been using as our General Headquarters for some time, Enver Bey suddenly emerged sitting astride a white horse. He had about him the air of a general commanding an army of thousands, convinced of his imminent triumph, but the crowd that had gathered there was pitiful in size and of the few that had turned up, it was enough just to look at their faces in the rain to know that most of them did not believe any good was going to come from the operation in which they were about to take part. I would not be exaggerating if I were to tell you that of all the people gathered there in that little crowd, only Enver Bey seemed unworried. He was utterly convinced that the planned coup would liberate the motherland, vindicate the party and guarantee him glory. Call it what you will; self-confidence that came from having overseen so many victories in life or madness created by a daring-do that has broken free of the prison of the rational mind, but he was convinced he was destined to make history.

But let me not take anything away from Filibeli Hilmi and İzmitli Mümtaz, who stood on Enver Bey's right and left respectively; neither of those honourable and reputable men of the movement were showing any fear either. Like us, they may also have had their doubts about the efficacy of our attempted coup but they grasped their guns anyway and rode bravely on into the jaws of fate, finding comfort in the thought that if they were going to die, they would at least be sacrificing their lives for the cause and would be dying honourably. As we approached the street corner, Yakup Cemil and Mustafa Necip also arrived and hurriedly took their places alongside Enver Bey. The movement's bravest and most fearless men had assembled. The scene was complete.

As for Fuad and myself, we, along with Mithat Şükrü, were charged with protecting the real mastermind behind the coup, Talat Bey, who simply smiled when he saw us at the meeting point. He also looked tense. He was probably disappointed, like the rest of us were, at the paltry turnout. Although he was trying – without success – to hide his frustration, he had not given up hope and was desperate to see this operation concluded successfully, no matter the cost.

And so our motley crew advanced up the street that turned on to a hill that led to the seat of government. We were calm but resolute to the last, but when we reached the Ministry of Public Works and saw the soldiers guarding the entrance, a ripple of anxiety passed through the crowd. Facing us was a well-equipped battalion and if they decided to open fire, the chances of us getting out in one piece were minimal indeed. The tension began to mount when a voice rang out across the street.

'Beloved citizens, people of this glorious land, brave sons of a country that has been exploited for years…. The time has come to say no to this treachery and to speak out against those that have given away our country! The time has come to give them the answer they deserve!'

Ömer Naci, the movement's propagandist, had climbed the steps of the Ministry of Public Works and was addressing the nation crowd and the nation as a whole.

'My brothers, the true inheritors of this red and green banner. At this very moment, a grave crime is being committed in the Bab-ı Âli. As we speak, the government of Kamil Paşa is about to hand over our beautiful beloved city of Edirne to the Bulgarians.' He pointed to the government offices. 'Yes, there, in that building over there, at this very moment, a vile and heinous document is being prepared. A document of treachery and perfidy. A text of surrender. And with this text, another cherished and beautiful piece of our country, drenched, nurtured and protected by the blood of countless martyrs, is being surrendered by our own government. If we turn a blind eye to this, then it is simply a matter of time before the capital itself, bequeathed to us by our glorious ancestors, is also overrun. If we remain silent, then the Ottoman state shall cease to exist in this world.'

At first, Ömer Naci's roared words seemed to increase the tension amongst the assembled crowd, with some of the people there even beginning to drift towards the edges but the more he spoke, and with bristling confidence and conviction too, any traces of trepidation were soon banished and the crowd regrouped. Of course, it would be a lie to say all our fears had dissipated; our ears were listening but our eyes were on the soldiers of the *Uşak Taburu* battalion guarding the Ministry and their rifles. Indeed, Yakup Cemil and Mustafa Nacip had come to the front of the crowd and had reached for their own guns but thankfully the officers commanding the battalion were members of our party and carried out their duties to the letter. The soldiers charged with guarding the *Bab-ı Âli* merely stood on and watched.

Although this served to lift our spirits, something even more important then happened: people passing by began to join us. Yes, strangely enough, some of the people walking by on the hill began streaming towards us, ignoring the rain that was now pelting down, and when they saw Enver Bey, their excitement grew. Ömer Naci's words were now really working the crowd up.

'He's right, you know', one porter said. 'As though losing the war wasn't enough, now they're going to give Edirne away to the Bulgarians.'

A nearby medical student voiced his agreement.

'What else would you expect from a dotard like Kamil Paşa? That traitor is going to give this country away to the English piece by piece!'

One gentleman, a typographer, had become quite emboldened and was now clinging on to one of Enver's horses' stirrups.

'Save us, Enver Bey! Save us, hero of the revolution!' Filibeli Hilmi struggled to get the man off but he held on, shouting, 'The motherland expects! The country expects! If it's not going to happen now, then when?'

Enver did not respond, acting as though it had nothing to do with him, and maintained his position and his posture. The real change took place in Talat Bey, whose face lit up and in whose eyes disillusionment was now giving way to hope. Not wanting to lose the crowd's newfound support, Ömer Naci said, 'Forward, dear friends! Let us march to save our country and to punish its traitors!'

The crowd answered as one.

'Forward, brothers! To lift our fallen banner from the ground and to save the fatherland!'

Fuad and I looked at each other.

'Looks like it's kicking off', I muttered happily. 'And this time it looks like we might actually pull it off'.

Fuad, however, was not so sure.

'Well let's not let our guard down just yet, Şehsuvar old friend. All we have here is a mob. One gunshot and they'll be off like a flock of frightened birds. It's the *Bab-ı Âli* where we're going to be really tested. We still don't know what to expect there.'

Talat Bey was listening in on us and nodded in agreement.

402

'Absolutely. So stay sharp, boys, for the love of God. No sudden movements. And don't let your nerves get the better of you. What we need now is clarity of the mind and clarity of vision. We need minds free of passion, excitement and zeal. And more importantly, stay close. We mustn't lose sight of each other. Right, let's move. We don't want to be lagging behind.'

The crowd was growing by the second and we were now walking towards the *Bab-ı Âli*. Indeed, we forced our way through the crowd and were trying to get to the front so as to not fall behind Enver Bey. As we neared the government headquarters, the tension began to mount again. The *Uşak Taburu* battalion guarding the building had been warned but seeing such a large and angry crowd marching towards them, the soldiers, especially the younger ones, grew fearful and pointed their weapons at us. In response, many in the crowd reached for their own weapons. All it needed was one finger on either side to pull a trigger and we would have a bloodbath on our hands. Ömer Naci's deep growl came to the rescue once again.

'Gentlemen!' he said, addressing the soldiers. 'Gentlemen, pray, what are you doing? Those guns are the people's guns. They are to be used against the enemies of this country, not us. The enemy is not here. He is in Çatalca. Those guns should be pointed not at us, the people, but at the Bulgarians in Çatalca.' He gestured with both hands to his chest. 'But if you don't agree with me, then go ahead and shoot. If you too are involved in the destruction wrought by those currently inside this building, then go ahead. Shoot. Shoot me now.'

One by one, the soldiers downed their rifles. Up went the roar from the crowd, 'Long live the nation! Long live the army! Long live the soldiery!'

While all this was going on, Enver Bey's horse had already entered the *Bab-ı Âli's* gardens. He deftly got down from his horse onto a stepping stone and was soon joined by others, including Yakup Cemil, İzmitli Mümtaz, Filibeli Hilmi, Mustafa Necip and Sapancalı Hakkı. We were keeping an eye on Talat Bey and Mithat Şükrü, who was standing next to Talat. They were watching proceedings closely. Talat Bey pointed to the crowd gathered in front of the building.

'How are we going to keep all these people under control? If they find a way inside, all hell will break loose. If that happens, we'll have neither a government nor a coup!'

'The doors', Doctor Ağabeydin Bey said. 'Close the doors. Don't let any unauthorised persons enter.'

Once our team was inside, the doors were slammed shut and we were making our way through a corridor towards the office of the Prime Minister when two soldiers suddenly emerged and blocked our path. They did not know what was going on, however, and they paused when they saw uniformed officers standing before them. Sensing an opportunity, Sapancalı Hakkı gave the command.

'Attention! Present arms! Make way!'

The two men immediately stood aside and waited at attention. Our group moved on to the main reception area whilst Sapancalı stayed behind to instruct the soldiers.

'Well done, men. Now, these doors are under your watch. Nobody is to enter under any circumstances.'

'Yes, sir!' the two men cried in response and stood to attention, still not clear as to who was doing what.

Luck had been on our side so far but when we entered the reception area, an officer emerged from out of nowhere and began firing at us, the first shots of the day. It was not an auspicious start for him as our lads responded with a hail of bullets and he fell to the floor. Gunshots, shouts and screams filled the air. The wheels had been set in motion and the people inside must have caught on so we needed to be vigilant. Nafiz Bey, the aide-de-camp, finally realised the government was under attack. He reached for his gun and stood before us but luckily for us he was a terrible marksman and none of the shots he fired hit any targets. Mustafa Necip, on the other hand, hit him with his first shot. Nafiz Bey did not die, though, and managed to escape to his office, despite his wound, with Mustafa Necip hot on his trail. Inside, we heard two gunshots fired off in quick succession. The first came from Necip's Gasser, whilst the second sound came from Nafiz Bey's gun. When we entered the room, we found both of them writhing on the floor covered in blood. Mustafa Necip was badly wounded, and there was little we could do for him. His fate was in the Maker's hands now. Unfortunately we had to leave him there, in clear discomfort, as we had a mission to complete. We needed to get to the *sadrazam's* office and force Kamil Paşa to resign while he was still in a state of shock and confusion and so more open to our demands.

We had only taken a few steps when another aide-de-camp, Tevfik Bey of Cyprus, appeared. There was no desire to talk or negotiate, nor was there any trace of mercy or hesitation. Instead, the shots rang out instantly and the poor man fell to the floor. Talat Bey was clearly unsettled but events were unfolding so rapidly now that any vacillation or confusion on our part could have spelt our ruin. Talat Bey bent down and whispered to me, 'Steady, Şehsuvar. Steady. Careful now.'

Yet we were way past being careful. This was a raid on the government we were carrying out, a coup, and although we were few, not expecting any blood to be shed would have been rank naiveté. We did not have time to sit and debate; we needed to get to Kamil Paşa's office as quickly as possible and so we kept on. Or at least, we tried to keep on when suddenly the huge figure of Çerkez Nazım Paşa, the Minister of War, appeared in front of us. As soon as he saw Enver Bey and Talat Paşa, he knew what was going on. He was neither surprised nor frightened. He simply looked Enver Bey up and down in fury.

'What the hell do you think you're doing?' he growled. 'Is this what we agreed upon? This is an outrage!'

Enver Bey stood to attention, the years of training and practice making the act almost involuntary.

'Sir, the situation is critical. The people demand the resignation of the *sadrazam*. Kamil Paşa must immediately relinquish his office.'

He was calm in the extreme but he was not holding back or mincing his words either.

'The people?' Çerkez Paşa exclaimed. 'Which people? Who the hell do you think you are? Enough of this! Clinging on to some fancy notion of 'the people'. What you are doing here is scandal and you shall pay for…'

He was cut short by a gun resting on his temple. Yakup Cemil could not take the invective any further. He had taken out his revolver and was now pointing it at the side of the Minister's head. None of us actually believed he would pull the trigger. We just assumed he had done it to silence the Minister or that he was perhaps considering taking him hostage. His victim must have the thought the same as he glared at him and snarled, 'What do you think you're doing, you little cuckolded…' Those were to be his last words. Yakup Cemil pulled the trigger. The Paşa fell to the floor. He began frothing at the lips and the pink foam soon gave way to a much darker, thicker liquid, and his body began trembling on the silk carpet like a leaf in the wind.

'What the hell have you done?' Enver Bey shouted. 'Yakup, what the hell have you done?'

'Nothing', he replied, staring at the writhing body on the ground the way Nazım Paşa had been looking at us, a mixture of disgust and contempt. 'He was never going to listen anyway.'

Before anybody could even respond, he pointed his gun at the body and fired another shot. Talat Bey was enraged.

'Enough! No more shooting!' He turned to his comrade-in-arms in a fury. 'This is not what was agreed upon, Enver. We can't go around shooting everyone in our path. That is not how it's done. If one more person gets killed, I am out of here, understand? Understand?'

Yakup Cemil and his friends were beginning to look at him disdainfully. With my hand close to my gun, I approached Talat Bey, whilst Fuad was eyeing up Enver Bey's *fedaeen* nervously. Enver eventually broke the silence.

'Fine. Everyone, calm down. Yakup, put the gun away.' He turned to face the Big Man. 'What to do, Talat? It's done now. We can't bring back the dead but if we don't move fast, this operation is going to fail. So let's look sharp and get that resignation from that old goat.'

He was right. Five people had been killed but the operation had yet to achieve its aim. Talat Bey lifted his arms upwards in exasperation and muttered something on the lines of, 'God give me patience', before falling in line behind his comrades.

Kamil Paşa was sitting by himself at his wooden desk in his office. His guards had fled upon hearing the gunshots and had left the old man to fend for himself. He was as white as a sheet and was biting his lower lip nervously, while his long beard seemed to be quivering. He looked less a mighty vizier and more a weak and helpless old man who had been betrayed by his good-for-nothing sons. He knew all too well that it was no use trying to escape and so he sat there, resigned to whatever fate had in store for him. He had seen and experienced so much during his long years as a statesman, with four terms as the *sadrazam*, the highest office in the land, that nothing, it seemed, could shock him anymore. As our little group approached, he tried to smile and failed, but he eventually managed to break the silence.

'Yes, gentlemen, what can I do for you?'

His voice was high but it did not waver. He was nervous but he had not allowed fear to get the better of him.

'Resign, Your Excellency', Talat Bey said, getting straight to the point. 'We have come here to request your resignation, sir.'

The old man looked at each of us one by one before gesturing to the window.

'I would first ask you to bring the hostilities outside to an end. I will not have our countrymen slaughtering one other. That is unacceptable.'

What he was actually doing was requesting his own safety. Talat Bey nodded in acquiescence.

'Fear not, sir, we do not wish for any more blood to be spilled either. However, and unfortunately, events spun out of our control at one point. But do not be alarmed. As of now, no further shots shall be fired. No more sons of the Ottoman state shall have their blood shed.'

His doomed face lit up for a second before he reached for a sheet of paper emblazoned with the official seal of the office of the *sadrazam* and began writing. When he'd finished writing the letter, he handed it to Enver.

Talat and Enver put their heads together and read the letter.

'I'm afraid this will not suffice, Your Excellency', Enver said, handing the note back. 'It is not enough to say you are resigning at the request of the army but out of respect for the will of the people, too. It is not just the army but the people that want you out too.'

The experienced man of state was stalling.

'Your resignation, Your Excellency', Talat Bey intoned menacingly. 'Please do not prolong the matter'.

The *sadrazam* realised he was playing with fire. He wordlessly took back the letter and began writing a new one. This time, when it was ready, Talat Bey took it and read it.

'That's better'. He then turned and raised his voice so we could all hear.

'To His Most Exalted Majesty;

At the request of the people and the army, I do hereby comply with their demands and tender my resignation. All authority and command reside in the most exalted and sublime office and person of His Majesty, the Sultan.'

A False Sense of Security

Hello Ester (Evening, Day 9)

I almost didn't open the door. After dinner, I came back upstairs, put my stool out on the balcony and sat down to contemplate the city in the coolness of autumn and to reflect on what Mehmed Esad had said to me. He wanted me to work with him but he hadn't told me what kind of work it was going to be. But seeing as I had rejected his offer and there was little he could do about my decision, there was actually no reason for me to worry. What was troubling me was the matter of Major Cezmi. For instance, why hadn't Mehmed mentioned his murder? Surely the fact that our old commandant had been killed was a more urgent issue than the meeting and dinner I had attended at Ahmet Şükrü Bey's house just before the assassination attempt in Izmir. Had they wished, they could have easily pinned the blame for the murder on me. Who knows, perhaps Mehmed Esad wants to keep the murder for a rainy day, another ace up his sleeve to be used when he sees fit...

Anyway, those were some of the issues I was pondering when there was a knock on the door. It was late in the evening but again, I wasn't that worried as I had met with Mehmed Esad in person, as per his request, so there was little point in the police bothering me now. And indeed, when I opened the door, it was Reşit. Assuming he would be beside himself with worry because of the police visit earlier this afternoon, I began thinking about how to calm him down when he blurted out,

'I've just come back from the police station.' He walked in and slumped into the grandfather chair. 'A full one hour I spent talking to them'.

There was no panic or fear in his expression. On the contrary, he looked calm and relaxed, and in his eyes were the relief and happiness of a student who has passed a particularly difficult exam. I sat on the edge of the bed and listened.

'When I got back to the hotel, I called you but you had already left. Ömer filled me in on the situation so I went over to the police station. They directed me to the officers that wished to speak to you. I told them everything I knew. How I knew Uncle Cezmi and why I went to his house; I gave them all the details. The only thing I hid from them was your second visit to his house, but if you ask me, even that didn't have to be a secret as the police reckon the killer, or killers, were burglars and broke into his house with the intention to steal. As a result, they have no reason to suspect either of us.'

Poor Reşit. Clueless as to what was actually going on. An invisible hand was protecting us both, a hand most probably belonging to Mehmed Esad, who had also had the Cezmi case assigned to those two rookie officers. Not that I said any of this aloud to Reşit.

'Oh God, no, don't', I warned him 'Don't tell them I went to the scene of the crime otherwise some meddlesome police officer will get involved and get us both into trouble. If the police think Major Cezmi was killed by a burglar, then so be it. No point in us denying it.'

'So you don't believe them?' he asked, eyeing me up and down suspiciously. 'You think someone else murdered Uncle Cezmi?'

I knew I had to be careful with what I said.

'No, not at all. I also think it was thieves that killed him. How could I possibly know more than the police?'

But he wasn't convinced.

'Do you think he may have been killed because he was ex-CUP? I overheard your conversation. He wasn't holding back in his criticisms of the government, that much I can tell you.'

I had to cut him off before he reached what for him could have been a highly disturbing conclusion.

'I doubt it. Why would they take Major Cezmi seriously? God bless him, most of the time he was away with the fairies.'

'That's true but they're saying the police went on the hunt for CUP guys after the attempt on the President's life in Izmir. And Uncle Cezmi was also...'

He was a smart guy, our Reşit, but there was little he stood to gain from solving the riddle.

'Oh, come on. If the government really went after anyone and everyone that claimed to be CUP, then there would be nobody left in the country. And that includes our President, our Prime Minister, our Ministers and most of the members of parliament. Nearly everyone at every level of government is an ex-CUP man, isn't he? No, this is nothing more than a nasty, everyday burglary. You know the house. You know it had no protection. Anyone could just waltz straight in. The man's economic situation was obvious too, and there are so many impoverished people in the country, all it takes is for just one of them to sneak into that house, draw a knife and...'

'That may be so but Uncle Cezmi was hardly the type of guy that could be overpowered so easily. I mean he was old, sure, but he was still tough, still strong. He still had it in him. And he was no stranger to a fight, either.'

I opened my arms outwards in a gesture of helplessness.

'We don't know how many people broke into his house. It may have been more than one, and they may have been experienced guys. They may have got him while was asleep. After all, he was found lying on the ground.'

'It's possible, yes', he sighed. 'You're right Şehsuvar *ağabey*. The police will do what they have to do.' He got up from the chair. 'Well, I guess should be off', he said and began heading for the door when, after a few steps, he stopped, in front of the Chinese vase. 'That's right, I almost forgot. I spoke to Ali Yunus, the manager of the Tokatlıyan. He's expecting you tomorrow afternoon. Said he'll be happy to help you any way he can. He said you should pop in and the two of you can go over the list of guests over a nice cup of coffee. 'If the person he is looking for has stayed with us, we'll find him, no problem,' he said. He also said if the person you're looking for left an address, he can have it sent to you. He's a good lad, that Ali. Honest and reliable. Doesn't make promises just for the sake of it. If he says he'll do something, he does it.'

'Thank, Reşit. Really, I don't know how I'll ever be able to repay you for all your kindness.'

'Not at all, Şehsuvar *ağabey*', he replied graciously. 'It was nothing. All I did was send a simple telegram. I hope you find it, this address. Well now, if that will be all, I shall wish you a pleasant night.'

It was a simple wish but the news he had given was already making it a very pleasant night indeed. I am going to find you, one way or another. A new life, perhaps, is waiting for us. Fate, perhaps, is going to present us the opportunity we missed eighteen years ago. It may sound stupid, yes, but why not? I was ecstatic. Thrilled and overjoyed, like a teenager all over again. Tomorrow afternoon I will be heading straight for the Tokatlıyan Hotel. I need to get in touch with Uncle Leon straightaway. Who knows, perhaps you'll be there when I find him? But I should get back to my writing, back to where I had left off.

That rainy day when we carried out the first coup d'état in these lands and forced Kamil Paşa from office would be the beginning of a five-year period during which our party would be the sole source of power. But according to Talat Bey, who would take on the position of Minister for Internal Affairs in the newly formed government, we had still not fully taken over the reins of power, an observation that was not completely incorrect, as a few hours after the attack on the *Bab-ı Âli*, Mahmud Şevket Paşa was appointed the new *sadrazam*. While we were still holed up in the government buildings, Enver Bey, with Yakup Cemil by his side to make sure there were no more fatalities, was heading for the palace, while Mahmud Şevket Paşa had already left his home in Üsküdar to accept the new position that was about to be offered him. His Majesty

Sultan Reşid, who, since his first day on the throne, had always taken great pains to cooperate with us, was not surprised by these developments as he had accepted the resignation of his *sadrazam* without question or protest. He listened contentedly when Enver Bey announced, 'Your Most Benevolent Majesty, the government of Kamil Paşa has proven itself incompetent in matters of state and has left the people and the nation destitute. As a result, Kamil Paşa has acquiesced to the demands of the people and resigned. I do hereby present to Your Majesty his resignation.' When Enver had finished, the sultan replied with one simple sentence, 'God bless you son, for saving me from those men.' As for the recommendation that Mahmud Şevket Paşa be appointed *sadrazam* and Talat Bey the temporary Minister for Internal Affairs, he found both terms agreeable and gave his seal to the documents detailing the appointments.

Of course, these changes to the government were not being decided upon as the coup was taking place but had been settled earlier, most probably during that final meeting that had gone on until the early hours of the morning in Beşezade Emin Bey's house in Vefa Square, with the decision and the offer probably being delivered to Mahmed Şevket Paşa himself soon after. As for our great sultan, he had chosen to turn a blind eye to these latest developments, despite his legendary arrogance, and, in order to preserve the authority of the throne, he agreed to the new *sadrazam* and new government that were being offered to him on a silver tray. Yes, a new phase was beginning, but the issues that needed to be dealt with were the same. Perhaps that is why when Mahmud Şevket Paşa climbed the steps of the *Bab-ı Âli* carrying a document signed and sealed by the sultan ratifying his appointment, his usually stiff and upright posture had gone and he seemed to be hunched over, like Sultan Abdülhamit had been years earlier, as though the duties he had agreed to take on were already beginning to weigh him down.

'Don't you think is weird?' Fuad's question brought me back from the windows of the *Bab-ı Âli* to the interior of the room. 'Why are we making the man we forced to resign as Minister of War only seven months ago the *sadrazam*?'

'Politics and all that I suppose', I mumbled, not knowing what to say. 'We're living through such topsy-turvy times, white has become black and black is now white.'

'That's all well and good but how is Mahmud Şevket Paşa going to work with us? Doesn't he know that it was Talat Bey himself who had him removed from the Ministry?'

It was a germane question and I was having similar doubts myself but I did not want to discuss it at that particular moment.

'Well, they must have come to an agreement. Such are the current circumstances, I suppose everyone has to compromise somewhere down the line. There is little point in asking such questions, not when the enemy has advanced all the way up to Çatalca. The time has come for us all to assume our responsibilities and do our duty.'

'And what's that supposed to mean, Şehsuvar?' he snarled. His voice had come out unusually harsh and he didn't realise how jarring it was. 'Are you saying I'm not doing my bit? That I'm not doing my duty? That I'm frightened? Do you think I am shirking my responsibilities? Or that I'm hiding or running away? So we become bad people when we speak our mind now, do we? You think we shouldn't speak up when mistakes are made. When there are shortcomings? That we should just shut up?'

Actually, I felt the same but for some reason I felt an idiotic urge to defend our leaders.

'Come on Fuad, it's nothing like that. I'm not saying we should shut up but there is a time and an occasion for everything. First Ahmet Muhtar Paşa and his government were a bane to us and then for another six months it was Kamil Paşa and his government. If we hadn't intervened, they would have sent us either into exile or to the dungeons. Thankfully we're free of them now. I mean, look. For the first time we are actually forming a powerful government. All I'm saying is we need to brace ourselves a little more, exercise just a little more patience and then…'

He cast me a moody glance.

'I'm all for exercising patience but if we don't succeed this time, then I don't know how much more the people of this country will put up with us.'

I laughed a fake laugh and pointed to the crowds demonstrating outside the *Bab-ı Âli*.

'Is that what you are worried about? Come off it, Fuad! The people are on our side. Look! Don't you see it? That crowd is getting bigger by the minute. We've won, Fuad, my brother. We've won.'

'I don't know, Şehsuvar', he said dejectedly, not bothering to try even a fake smile. 'I hope we've won but I'm not sure we have.'

I held him by his shoulders.

'Of course we have. You're fretting for nothing. You were like this this morning too. Remember? You said we wouldn't make it through to the evening. Well, we have made it, and we've come through in style, thank you very much.'

'Hopefully you'll be proven right', he said and bowed his head. '*Inshallah*, this time I'm the one who'll be mistaken.'

But he knew he wasn't wrong and worse still, so did I. Forming a government under those circumstances was madness. We were surrounded on all sides by enemies and our lands were whetting the appetite of the Great Powers. As for us, we were like an old wolf with rotting teeth and dulled claws trapped amongst a horde of wild beasts, each more savage and bloodthirsty than the other. Forget great powers like England, Russia and Germany, we could not even stand up to our one-time vassals the Bulgarians. We had deposed Kamil Paşa as *sadrazam* because he had been ready to surrender Edirne to the Bulgarians but we ourselves could barely defend the historic second capital of the Ottoman Empire. The situation on the front was grave. Eventually, straight after the formation of a new government by Mahmud Şevket Paşa, Enver Bey's plan to liberate Edirne ended in total disaster. Hinting at problems in coordination, Enver Bey accused Fethi Bey and Mustafa Kemal Bey of the Bolayır Division of dereliction of duty. In turn, Fethi

Bey and Mustafa Kemal Bey claimed that they had acted alone and could not wait for the other battalions and companies to join them and as a result, the blame lay with Enver Bey.

As our Chiefs of Staff bickered and squabbled and pointed fingers of blame at one another, the situation on the front was turning into a catastrophe. The defeat that was threatening to drag us down into a quagmire of shame and recrimination was becoming a reality. On the 26th of March, we were forced to surrender Edirne to the enemy. Yes, it's true. The Ottoman banner would no longer flutter from the elegant minarets of the Selimiye Mosque and the sound of the *ezan*, the call to prayer, would no longer be heard on our jewel of a border town. It was not just a case of an ancient city that had once been the Ottoman capital; even more calamitous was the fact that the peace treaty signed in London had brought the Thracian border back all the way to the Enez–Midye Line. Now only the Çatalca defensive line stood between Istanbul and our enemies.

We had done everything, perhaps even more, we had said we would to bring down Kamil Paşa's government. Of course, it would have profound political ramifications. The Freedom and Accord Party, which supported the former *sadrazam*, was not standing idly by but was instead inciting the people at every opportunity against Mahmud Şevket Paşa and his government. In the wake of the coup, the opposition press was also growing louder and more fiercely outspoken in its criticisms, all of which were designed to stoke people's fears.

We had managed to do something very difficult indeed and that was to unite the entire opposition against us, so much so that we would eventually have to deal with a plot that included a vast array of enemies of the CUP, from Şerif Paşa in Paris to the liberal Prince Sabahattin and from the former *sadrazam* Kamil Paşa to Damat Salih Paşa. At the head of the plot was Çerkez Kâzım, or Kâzım the Circassian, whom I knew personally, a miserable and contemptible man. He used to be a member of the CUP but he had crossed over to the Freedom and Accord Party. However, he was not to be underestimated;

he was one of the leading lights of the *Halaskâran Zabıtler*, the 'Saviour Officers', and he was brave – and violent – to the point of lunacy. After the shooting of Nazım Paşa, a Circassian like him, he began nurturing a profound and almost insatiable loathing of the CUP.

'If they are going to be this ruthless in their use of force, then why can't we?' he would say to the servile wretches that gathered around him. 'A bullet each to the head and we will be rid of them. Seeing as they seized power by force, then we can do the same. We can overthrow them by force and seize power for ourselves.'

We knew he was speaking like this because of the informers we had planted in his ranks, and those same informers also let us know the details of their planned insurrection and the people that would be involved. That particular plot was being dealt with by Admiral Cemal Bey, the Warden of Istanbul. He had been appointed to this position by Mahmud Şevket Paşa himself and would later go on to become one of the party's three leading pashas. Of all the CUP guys, it was Cemal Bey whom the new *sadrazam* trusted the most. Yes, it's true. The new premier still had doubts about us and did not fully trust our party or our movement, which was odd as there were no reasons for him to have such misgivings: our enemies were one and the same.

The financial source of all this plotting and scheming was Şerif Paşa. He was based in Paris but he still had powerful supporters in the palace. Damat Salih Paşa, for one, never hesitated in lending his support to the coup plotters. We had also spotted him meeting Prince Sabahattin, although the prince had played it smart and had kept his distance from them as he was against the idea of a violent insurrection. Most probably it was the British behind it all. The names of Major Tyirel and Fitzmaurice, the interpreter from the British Embassy, were mentioned in the reports. Most painful of all was the fact that our hands were tied and we could not ask the British Embassy to account for those two gentlemen or to provide details about them due to the terms and conditions of the capitulations.

This pack of delinquents was planning a series of assassinations of leading figures such as Talat Bey, Cemal Bey, Azmi Bey, Emanuel Karasu and, most important of all, the *sadrazam* Mahmud Şevket Paşa, hoping to create a climate of instability and chaos in which they would offer their own candidates for leadership of the government, just as we once had. They had two candidates for the premiership: the first was Kamil Paşa, whom we had deposed during the coup on the 23rd of January, and the second was Prince Sabahattin. Whether it was pure coincidence or a deliberately planned trip is hard to tell but it was around this same time that Kamil Paşa was returning from a trip to Egypt. Upon learning of his return, Cemal Bey, the Warden of Istanbul, had dispatched his assistant to Kamil Paşa's estate to inform him that some sinister figures were planning on carrying out a number of assassinations in the capital and that the best thing for him would be to return to Egypt. Of course, Kamil Paşa, ever the astute one, made it clear that he was under no obligation to return to Egypt and that he would, in fact, be staying in the capital, which served only to confirm our suspicions that the assassinations would soon be starting and that there really was a clandestine network in play that was now mobilising and preparing to overthrow the government. In response, we increased our surveillance and intelligence-gathering activities and went to even greater lengths to get a better grasp of the situation and make sure we were up to date on the latest developments.

Fuad and I had taken up our posts outside Kamil Paşa's residence, where we had been instructed not to let anybody in or out. We did as instructed, even when Fitzmaurice, who was supposedly an official interpreter for the British Embassy but whom we all knew was a spy for the British government, turned up one morning at the gates of the estate. Of course, his arrival there was not a coincidence. Kamil Paşa had contacted the British embassy and explained the situation to them, and had openly – and quite brazenly – requested help from them. When Fitzmaurice saw us, he feigned surprise.

'Morning, gentlemen. In what capacity, may I ask, are you here?'

'Official business', Fuad replied calmly. 'We are protecting the mansion'.

He smiled courteously.

'I see. Well, if you wouldn't mind, I would like to enter the premises to speak to Kamil Paşa on behalf of the Ambassador, Sir Gerard Lowther.'

'Unfortunately, that will not be possible, Mister Fitzmaurice', Fuad said, replicating the envoy's polite smile. 'Much as we are delighted to see you, I'm afraid you cannot see Kamil Paşa as he is under house arrest, if you will, as per Ottoman law. We have been instructed by our superiors not to allow anybody to enter these premises. And I'm afraid that extends to loyal and honourable friends such as your good self.'

Fuad made sure he emphasised the words *loyal and honourable friends*. Fitzmaurice's face darkened but only for a split second. He was soon his jovial, smiling self.

'I see. Oh well. It seems I have come all this way for nothing then.' He paused before continuing. 'Well, I trust Kamil Paşa is in good health?'

'Very much so', Fuad replied. 'His Excellency is in fine health, by the grace of God.'

'That is indeed good to hear. Very well gentlemen, seeing as I have been barred from entering, I shall be on my way. A good day to you both.'

And so he departed, ever courteous and ever the gentleman. But as soon as he was back at the embassy, he wasted no time in raising hell and sending the ambassador to visit Mahmud Şevket Paşa to lodge a complaint. In response, Mahmud Şevket Paşa, who was unaware of the gravity of the situation, summoned Cemal Bey and sternly reprimanded him.

'All these problems we need to deal with and you want to go and rile the English up too?' It was only the next day that Cemal Bey, who loved Mahmud Paşa like a father and who was thus stunned to be so harshly rebuked by him, was able to reply.

'There is a grand conspiracy afoot, Your Excellency, and if we do not act, we face calamity. There is a plan to have the entire government killed, your good self-included, after which the coup plotters intend to assume power and reinstate Kamil Paşa as *sadrazam*.'

After he had been convinced and realised how serious the situation was, Mahmud Şevket ignored the pressure being applied by the British and agreed to have Kamil Paşa kept under surveillance and so Fuad and I returned with our crew to our positions in the cherry tree grove in front of the ex-*sadrazam*'s beautiful mansion. Having woken up to the threat, the government was now playing it shrewd and it was paying off. Kamil Paşa now knew there would be no help from the British and so returned to Egypt. Indeed, he went down to the docks in Sir Gerard Lowther's private car, with Fuad and I following close behind. At the docks, Fuad pointed to Kamil Paşa and said, 'He's not going because the English aren't going to help him but because Çerkez Kâzım's network turned out to be so utterly incompetent.'

He was right too. Decades spent in affairs of state meant Kamil Paşa had learnt through experience whom he could trust and whom he couldn't. The few days spent in Dersaadet had allowed him to work out Çerkez Kâzım and what kind of man he was and he was now convinced that the best course of action for him would be to quietly return to Egypt. And yet, even though he was nearly eighty years old, he could not curb his lust for power. Like his ancient and bitter rival Said Paşa, he would never give up his quest for power so long as he was alive. Moreover, Said Paşa had been *sadrazam* a full nine times, whereas this ill-starred old man had only been appointed to that post four times.

Kamil Paşa slipping back to Egypt in despair was followed by Prince Sabahattin fearing for his life and seeking asylum in a ship registered with the French Embassy. Both incidents helped us considerably. Moreover, we had identified all the members of this sordid gang as we had their primary meeting place, a building in Glavani Street in Beyoğlu, under strict surveillance.

The premises were being rented by the traitor Şerif Paşa's man Pertev Tevfik, who lived on the upper floor, whilst on the lower floors were the offices of the *Müdafa-i Milli* newspaper. However, in renting out these premises, their real aims (at first) had been to organise activities against our party and to have a place in which they could organise opposition to the government. However, they were now well past the stage of peaceful opposition and mere debate. Under the leadership of Çerkez Kâzım, they had become a movement of dissent and discord, itching to engage in violence. But they were too late. Who was meeting with whom and where and how; we knew it all now. The intelligence we had gathered was priceless and had given us some control over the situation, but this had also gone some way to dispelling our worries and thus giving us – and Cemal Bey most of all – an unnecessary and quite unwelcome sense of confidence. There was another reason why we had not started making arrests: we wanted to catch these guys red-handed and thus hit them with the heaviest penalties possible.

However, Captain Kâzım was as experienced as us. Like us, he had survived the political storms of the last five years and had survived numerous plots, schemes and scandals. Like us, he had faced all manner of trials and tribulations and had not buckled. He had managed to expertly evade our spies and escape to Romania, where he recouped and gathered his strength. Indeed, it was this last move, his escape, that had lulled Cemal Bey and the rest of us into a false sense of security, leading us to believe that the opposition had been so soundly routed that they would not be able to regroup.

The model for their offensive was our very own attack on the *Bab-ı Âli*. However, not only were they not as well organised as us, the men in their ranks who were fighting for their cause did not have the necessary discipline. All they had in common was a loathing for the CUP, but when it came to political operations, those motivated solely by hate are doomed to fail. That is why we were not taking the group set up by these renegades seriously enough. Seeing as many of the men they were relying on had either been dissuaded or deterred and their ringleaders had fled, we assumed the group had broken up and was therefore not worthy of our time and our attention. It was a critical mistake. As the old saying goes, never underestimate your opponent. That, alas, is what we had done and we were going to pay the price for doing so. A very heavy price, indeed.

The True Power in the Land

Good Morning, Ester (Morning, Day 10)

I froze when I read the newspapers this morning. The plot is much deeper than I suspected. I don't know exactly what is going on but I do know that there are people out there plotting against me in a big way. I'm talking about the murder of Cezmi Kenan. The newspapers have finally got round to writing about it, and what a piece they turned out. This is what the third page of *İkdam* newspaper wrote:

> *A mysterious murder in Langa! Retired Army Captain Cezmi Kenan, who it transpires had been living alone, has been found dead in his home, the victim of a stabbing... After searching the premises, the police found an extensive haul of ammunition in the dry well in his garden. It is still unknown why there was such a cache of rifles, pistols and hand grenades stored on the premises. Noting that the victim was formerly a member of the İttihat ve Terraki movement, the Committee for Union and Progress, the authorities suspect that the arms may have been intended for use in an operation with a political aspect. The investigating authorities have also announced that they have identified photographs of the victim with Kara Kemal, one of the former leaders of the CUP, and that the murder may be linked to the attempted assassination of the President in the city of Izmir. As one of the suspects in the Izmir case, Kara Kemal*

*committed suicide in the house in which he was hiding in July
of last year when he realised he was about to be captured and
detained.*

Cumhuriyet and *Vakit* gave similar accounts of Captain
Cezmi's death. Clearly the reports had been written by the
same person and then passed on to the press. There was
nothing surprising or untoward about that. We used to do the
same when we were in the *Teşkilat-i Mahsusa*. What was astonishing was a marked man like me not being noticed in such an
important murder investigation. If one was to go along with
the newspapers' reports, I had long since been arrested and
questioned. And yet the two policemen that turned up yesterday barely even saw me as a suspect! So what were they up
to? Well, what else could it be but Mehmed Esad trying to gain
some time? And it was obvious that they were the ones behind
Captain Cezmi's murder. Of that I had no doubts once I had
read about the ammunitions cache. They must have seen the
old man as some kind of threat.

But a man like that would have been under surveillance
twenty-four hours a day, which also meant it was impossible
for them not to know that I had gone to see him. And yet here
they are letting me roam around as free, relatively speaking,
as a bird. Why? Again, it's probably thanks to Mehmed Esad.
Seeing as they were the ones that killed Cezmi, there are no
perpetrators out there they need to track down. Seeing as they
are hoping I am going to join them, there is no point in them
arresting me. That is why I am still a free man.

It all sounds very reasonable but why didn't Mehmed Esad
mention Cezmi? It was bugging me last night but now it has
taken on even greater urgency. Why was Mehmed keeping
quiet, if he knew that I had seen Cezmi's corpse, and indeed
that I ran away to avoid being captured? To test me…? That
must be it. It's the only reasonable explanation. They do not
trust me enough. He said so himself, that there were people
within the secret service that believed I was still in touch with
the old CUP guys and was still involved in their activities, and

they are using the death of Major Cezmi to test me, to see how far I can be trusted. That is why I should have told Mehmed about what happened when I met him. I mean, what if my predictions are wrong? What if Mehmed really doesn't know anything about the murder and it was actually another squad within the state apparatus that carried out the killing? In fact, what indeed if the incident really is just a case of an ordinary attempted burglary going horribly wrong and the police, in the course of their investigations, have by pure chance stumbled on to the armaments cache? In that case, would I not have just needlessly given myself away? And isn't that when the actual crisis of trust and confidence will begin?

It's all so convoluted. Basri Bey used to always tell us to be frank. 'Sometimes being tight-lipped can lead innocent people to their deaths.' And that is exactly my predicament now. I have not committed any crime, nor have I behaved inappropriately. All I did was visit an old friend in his home and yet now I find myself a suspect in a murder case. No, I need to disentangle myself from this mess and tell Mehmed what happened and convince him that I have had nothing to do with the murder. Maybe that way I will also be closer to knowing the truth as even if Mehmed does not know about this incident, he can look into it, investigate and find out its true causes. Yes, that is what must be done. This mystery should not be busying my mind any more. I have to get back to my writing so, before I head off to the Tokatlıyan Hotel, I should tell you about the assassination of Şevket Paşa.

Yesterday evening I ended by telling you about the price we would pay for underestimating our adversaries. It would be very costly indeed, but none of us knew at the time. When the news of the attack came through, we were sitting in the small lounge of the *Pembe Konak*, the 'Pink Villa', which served as the CUP's headquarters. Talat Bey was talking to us about the need to establish an intelligence-gathering organisation in the wake of our attack on the *Bab-ı Âli*. Not an organisation that would replace ours but one that would be present and active all over the country, and indeed overseas. A body that would act as both the sword and the shield of the homeland, an organisation with no name but of the type that soldiers and civilians such as ourselves had been able to bring to the theatre of war over the last five years in places like Libya and the Balkans.

'Even within this brief period of time, our movement has proven its courage and it needs to be recognised and legitimised', Talat Bey was saying. 'It is time for you all to take on more serious responsibilities and face perhaps even greater dangers.'

And then, while he was speaking, the news of the assassination came through.

'Mehmed Şevket Paşa… He's been shot'.

It was Cevdet Hulusi, speaking out of turn from the doorway, with a look of shock on his face.

'They've shot Mehmed Şevket Paşa. In Beyazit. In front of everyone.'

It was not so much shock I felt when I heard the news but a deep sense of remorse and guilt. How could we not have predicted it? Fuad and I exchanged glances. He was thinking the same, shaking his head dejectedly. Çerkez Kâzım, the head of that little band of malignity that we had so horribly underestimated, had played us all. Kara Kemal was the first to speak out.

'Is he dead? Is Şevket Paşa dead?'

'I don't know', Cevdet Hulsui gulped. 'But his car is a mess. Peppered with holes. The Paşa fell forward and just lay there, immobile. Blood all over the place. The inside of the car was dripping with it. His aide, Ibrahim Bey…. He was shot too. They both fell.'

'Was there anybody else with them?' Talat Bey asked furiously. 'Don't tell me the sadrazam himself was out there on the street with just a single aide by his side?'

Cevdet Hulusi's head dropped, as though he were to blame for the incident.

'Eşref, the Chief Aide de Camp, was also there and there were bodyguards and other chauffeurs too. Forgive me, I'm having trouble thinking straight at the moment…. But no, he was not alone. There were others there too, although I don't know the exact number. I only saw it by chance. I was at the Grand Bazaar and when I heard gunshots, I ran out on to the main road. You wouldn't believe how many shots were fired. Anyway, by the time I got to the car, the perpetrators had already fled. Poor Eşref Bey was wandering aimlessly around with his gun in his hand, not knowing what to do. When he realised there was nothing he could do, he had the car taken to the Ministry of War. That is where the news is coming from.'

We hurried off to Beyazit so we could be at the Paşa's side. Grim news awaited us at the historic building that housed the Ministry. Mahmud Şevket Paşa, one of the most powerful men to emerge in the country over the last five years, had died. It was Cemal Bey that informed us, with deep sorrow.

'We have lost the Paşa'.

The proud soldier that only four months earlier had climbed the steps of the *Bab-ı Âli* was no more. The body, the hair now white and the beard stiff, was in the office at the Ministry and the wounds on his tall, lean body were still open and still bleeding. The doctor, Doctor Lambeki, was talking about the five bullets lodged in his body, the worst being the one that had entered through the right ear and come out of the left.

'That was the first one', said Captain Eşref, who had been in the car at the time, and who was now standing in tears by the Paşa's side. 'The men that did this were professionals. Calm and composed. Luck was on their side too. Had it not been for that funeral, our car would not have slowed down.'

Kara Kemal could not help but ask.

'So you're saying they staged a fake funeral procession so they could kill him?'

'No, Kemal Bey', Eşref answered. 'The funeral was a real one but it worked in the killers' favour. When the mourners passed by in front of us, we had to stop. Little did we know they were waiting to ambush us. It seems they had been watching the Paşa for some time and had rehearsed their operation a number of times. They knew that the Paşa left for his office at eleven every day. They'd worked out the route his car took.

Memorised it. For all we know, they may have tried to kill him yesterday or the day before but hadn't succeeded. They approached us on our blind side. There was no one on that side. We didn't see them.'

We couldn't quite work out what he was saying as he was speaking in fits and starts. Talat Bey stepped forward and took him by the arm.

'Here, come this way'.

We followed them to a nearby study, where Talat Bey pointed to one of the stools in front of the desk.

'Take a seat please, Eşref Bey'. He turned and looked at us. 'You too, gentlemen'. While we all sat down on the nearest available chair or stool, he sat on the chair behind the desk that once belonged to Mahmud Şevket Paşa. Only Cemal Bey remained standing, as though it seemed superfluous and pointless to seek comfort when the nation's capital was under siege. The Great Master looked at him quizzically, his expression asking why he was not seated, but the Warden of Istanbul raised his hand and gestured that he was fine on his feet. Talat Bey did not persist and went back to the captain.

'Now, Eşref Bey, I know you have just been through something shocking and I also know you loved Mahmud Şevket Paşa dearly. But you are also a soldier, so I implore you, please, be strong. Leave your feelings to one side for the moment and tell us what happened in that car.'

Talat Bey sounded serene but also confident and assured. The captain straightened up and began.

'Very well, sir. Well, um, it happened like this, sir. Well, what happened was…. It was like this… We were in the car, the usual six-man squad with the Paşa. We had just left Beyazit Square when the funeral procession appeared and was passing by in front of us. We stopped and waited. Nothing seemed out of the ordinary, nor were there any suspicious characters in the vicinity. As the procession went past, two shots went off. Before any of us could even respond or ask what was going on, the Paşa had fallen onto my lap. When I turned around to look to the rear of the car, I saw a nasty-looking fellow holding a gun.

He had the look of a horse thief to him. I drew my weapon and jumped out of the vehicle to give chase. If only I hadn't. If only I had stayed with the Paşa.' His eyes welled up and he looked as though he was about to start sobbing.

'Captain, please', Talat Bey said sternly. 'We shall have plenty of time to mourn later but right now we need clarity of mind. Tell me, why do you think you should have stayed with the Paşa?'

'Because, sir, while I gave chase to that person, the other members of his team were gifted their opportunity. The person that fired the first shots was not alone. As soon as the others saw me give chase, another one of their team approached the car. He shot Ibrahim Bey, Personal Secretary to the Paşa, and then emptied his gun into the body of the Paşa. The nightmare didn't end there, either. The others drew their guns and opened fire on the car. All in all, twenty bullets hit the car. When I got back, having been unable to catch the first guy, the others had all, unfortunately, vanished. I rushed into the car. Mahmud Şevket Paşa was still breathing and I immediately had the car brought here hoping he could still be saved, but alas, as you can see…'

The tears began flowing.

'Çerkez Kâzım', Cemal Bey muttered. 'We should have arrested that bastard when we had the chance. Maybe we should have just put a bullet through his head instead, without even bothering to arrest him.'

Something had been bugging me ever since the news of the assassination had come through and I finally came out with it.

'That's all very well and good, Cemal Bey, but isn't he in Romania?'

He held his arms outwards in a gesture of despair.

'That's what we thought but he must have returned. But I swear to God, here and now, by the memory of this great man he has murdered, I will find him and make him regret coming back.'

'The state does not feel fury, Cemal Bey', the Great Master said, rising from his seat. 'It simply does what needs to be done, that is all. That is a given. Right now, what we need to do is find a new *sadrazam*. The government cannot be without a leader. Not now, during these fragile times.'

He walked towards the door, his speech seemingly over, but after a few steps, he stopped and turned to look at Cemal Bey.

'As the Warden of Istanbul, you'll know better than I but if the assassination of the Paşa is the signal of the beginning of a plot, then that means there will be more murders. It is therefore just as important to find the perpetrators as it is to protect the leaders of this country. It would therefore be wise to increase security around the government and the party's principal figures.'

'It shall be done immediately', Cemal Bey replied, unfazed at being addressed in such a manner. 'Be assured, the killers shall not succeed in whatever nefarious plot it is they have cooked up.'

Like everyone else dealing with Çerkez Kâzım and his cronies, Cemal Bey felt personally responsible for what had just happened. Finding Mahmud Şevket Paşa's killers and punishing them was not just an urgent official duty but a way for us to redeem ourselves and our consciences.

As of that moment, the hunt for the killers began in the capital. Leave for all soldiers, police and security personnel was annulled and the search began in the capital, street by street, house by house. It was not just people linked to Çerkez Kâzım that we rounded up and interrogated but everybody and anybody we suspected of misconduct as we strived to reach into every cell and every node of the network we were up against. The first piece of good news came in the afternoon. A well-known marksman by the name of Topal Tevfik, or 'Tevfik the Lame' – the second man to fire at the already wounded body of the Paşa and the monster that mowed down his aide Ibrahim Bey – was arrested in a trading inn in the area around Beyazit.

At the interrogation, at which I was also present, Tevfik, a lout with no political consciousness or awareness whatsoever, began singing like a canary at the first slap Fuad planted on his face. The information he gave us was sound and we soon began rounding up the other gang members one by one. They were all strong and imposing men but as soon as they saw the stick with which they were to be beaten, they began whining and whimpering like stray dogs.

As we reined the members of this bloody plot in, the party had prepared a final farewell for Mahmud Şevket Paşa, one befitting his status, rank and memory. At the funeral the next day, the crowds were huge. I saw then, for the first time, how a nation could adore a single soldier. In the case of Mahmud Şevket Paşa, the adoration may have stemmed from the fact that he had always maintained a distance between himself and the CUP, despite having himself been a supporter of the constitutional reforms.

Seeing that incredible mass of people uniting the whole country and witnessing and experiencing first-hand the emotions of the people that had gathered there to pay their last respects inspired us even further in our efforts to find the killers. Day and night we were out there, following up every lead, looking up every possible piece of evidence, right through to the end, and ultimately our determination and our efforts began to pay dividends.

One of the suspects we brought in, a man by the name of Hakkı, took us all the way to Beyoğlu and a house on Pire Mehmed Street, where the network was based. We immediately had the house placed under surveillance but we could not raid the premises as the tenant was a British subject. Official contact was made with the British and the seriousness of the situation was explained but the embassy made heavy weather of the issue and was unwilling to grant us permission to enter and search the house. Here we were in our country, on our own land, looking for the people that had shot and killed our own *sadrazam* and we were still dependent upon the beneficence of foreigners! It was a wretched and disheartening feeling, one that an increasingly irate Cemal Bey could no longer bear and he eventually told us all that enough was enough and gave the order for us to break in.

We took up our positions on Pire Mehmed Street, broke the door down and stormed in. We were a highly experienced crew made up of soldiers, police and civilians but once we were inside, we were met by a hail of bullets coming at us from all angles. Fuad and I managed to save ourselves by hiding behind a large cupboard but Captain Hilmi Bey, who was a couple of paces in front of us, took a shot to the stomach. Of course, we fought back but they had taken up much better positions than us. The exchange lasted hours and Samuel Bey and Levi Bey, two police chiefs that were with us, ended up wounded.

Çerkez Kâzım and his gang were resolute, and were intent on dying if they had to rather than surrendering. As for us, we were stuck in our positions behind various pieces of heavy furniture or up against the walls. We could not move forward nor could we retreat and pull ourselves out of that mess. Every now and then we would shoot but we could not even see what we were shooting at.

They were surrounded and had no way out but they were all brave men and skilled marksmen and it was not easy capturing them. Cemal Bey, watching on intently, decided upon another approach and that was to bring Çerkez Kâzım's old comrades-in-arms Kuşçubaşı Eşref, Mümtaz, Yakup Cemil and Hacı Sami to the house. When those old hands arrived, we handed over our spots to Yakup Cemil and Hacı Sami. But when Yakup Cemil introduced himself to those camped inside and shouted, 'Put your weapons down so we can end this amicably', Çerkez Kâzım and his men began firing once again. Yakup Cemil was enraged. He shouted, 'What are you shooting for you, sons of whores?' and he and his crew returned fire. But it was in vain. Nothing was accomplished except for some needlessly spent cartridges lying around and the sharp acrid smell of gunpowder wafting through the neighbourhood. While Çerkez Kâzım and his gang exchanged verbal blows with Yakup Cemil, Kuşçubaşı Eşref and Mümtaz saw their opportunity and climbed up on to the roof. We went up with them to help. Mümtaz leant over a hole that had been made by the firemen and announced his presence to the men inside.

'Mümtaz, is that you?' Çerkez Kâzım replied. 'What the hell are you doing here? What do you want?'

'I mean you no harm', Mümtaz replied amicably. 'We don't want any blood spilled. Eşref is here with me. Why don't you give yourself up? There is no way out.'

After a few moments' silence, Çerkez Kâzım spoke up.

'If we lay down our guns and surrender, they'll be all over us like rats. The insults and the mockery will never end. The whole world will laugh at us.'

Kuşçubaşı Eşref now joined in the tense exchange.

'Nothing like that will happen, Kâzım. Nobody is going to insult you. I give you my word. If you lay down your arms, nobody will touch a hair on your head. I swear on my honour. You will be tried fairly and justly.'

The silence this time was longer.

'Very well', Kâzım eventually growled. 'Very well. I shall take your word for it. I trust you. We're coming out. We're surrendering.'

And so, one by one, they came out of that godforsaken house in Pire Mehmed Street.

That is how we captured their men. And we made sure we honoured Kuşçubaşı Eşref's promise and delivered them to the authorities without insult or abuse. However, we did not hesitate in questioning them thoroughly to get the names of the people involved in the plot. Of the names unearthed, there were two that would require real courage on our part if we were to haul them in. One was Prince Sabahattin, the son of Abdülmecid's grandson Damat Mahmud Celalettin Paşa. Actually, in this particular incident, he had kept his distance from Çerkez Kâzım but there was no doubt that he would have happily finished us all off given even the tiniest of opportunities. The other person was Damat Salih Paşa, who was married to Münire Sultan, the granddaughter of Sultan Abdülmecid, and whom we all knew was the conspirators' financier. Interrogating two members that had the support of the palace was of course not easy but the CUP now wanted to prove it had come of age and send out the message that we were now the power in the land and that anyone that disobeyed us or conspired against us, or tried to take up arms against us, would face the severest consequences and penalties.

That is why the actions that were taken were so decisive and, to some, so seemingly harsh. The Ministry of War sentenced twelve people to death, including Damat Salih Paşa and Çerkez Kâzım, whilst elven others, including Prince Sabahattin, were tried and condemned to death in absentia. As a warning and a message to others, the twelve, despite protests by the French government, the palace and indeed by Sultan Reşad himself, were hanged in Beyazit Square, where Mahmud Şevket Paşa had been gunned down.

Betrothed to Life, Married to Death

Hello Ester (Afternoon, Day 10)

The Tokatlıyan Hotel is on the *Cadde-ı Kebir*. It opened a few years after the Pera Palace but it is just as famous. As students at the Imperial High School, we had walked past it many times, watching elegant gentlemen and beautiful, chic ladies waltz in and out of its front doors, a reminder to us of the presence of an entirely different world out there. All of us, without exception, dreamt of one day staying in that hotel. I don't know about my classmates, but the dream had at least come true for me as I used to frequent the hotel during my years with the *Teşkilat-ı Mahsusa*. Not for pleasure, of course, but to track down spies. The Tokatlıyan, the Pera Palace, the Grand London Hotel… Those were the kinds of places where the foreign heads of the treacherous underground networks that were causing mischief and mayhem all over the country could be found. But now it had been some time since I had come to the Tokatlıyan. I entered the grand lobby, walked across the huge Afghan carpet towards reception and asked for Ali Yunus Bey. Reşit, bless him, had seen to everything and a few minutes later I was seated on a velvet chair in the hotel manager's office waiting for the customer records to be brought to me.

'We've had a lot of guests from Salonika', Ali Yunus told me. 'Especially Jews. The richer ones, of course. We've had guests stay a few days and others that didn't leave for months. Some went to Izmir, others stayed and settled in Istanbul. So in that respect, it is quite possible that Monsieur Leon has spent time with us. However, as to whether he left a forwarding address or not, I cannot tell.'

The customer records arrived before the coffees. Ali Yunus opened the large ledger on his desk and peered at me over his glasses.

'What was Monsieur Leon's surname?'

'Azuz', I replied, getting to my feet and bending over the records. 'Leon Azuz... He was seen here around two months ago.' I stopped and hesitated and then added, 'We can also check his niece's name. There is a very strong possibility that they came together. A lady by the name of Ester. Ester Romano. You may remember her. A very attractive lady, with large black eyes and red hair.'

When Ali looked at me tellingly, the look on his face suggesting he knew what the heart of the issue actually was, I realised I had gone too far.

'They lived together in Salonika, you see, so they may well have come to Istanbul together.'

He looked away and smiled.

'Don't you worry, Mister Şehsuvar. We'll soon track down this Miss Ester too.'

However, despite his words and our efforts, we found neither your nor Uncle Leon's name in the registry. There were people from all over the world in the hotel records; journalists, businessmen, scientists, scholars, soldiers and artists, people from different continents and different backgrounds, but neither of your names were there in the ledger. We went over it a few times too, just in case we had missed something but again, we could not see your names. Had Mehmed Esad lied to me? If he had, why? Why would he lie to me? What did he stand to gain by deceiving me? Ali Yunus seemed to sense what was going through my mind.

'Perhaps Monsieur Leon only came to the hotel for dinner. Or he came for a ball or a meeting. What I mean is, his being seen here does not necessarily mean he stayed.'

He was right. Who knows why and in what capacity Uncle Leon had been there? He was right... So now how was

I supposed to find you? How and where was I supposed to find Uncle Leon? I thanked Ali Yunus Bey and left the Tokatlıyan. It was hot outside. The early afternoon sun was beating down on the *Cadde-i Kebir*. It was one of those hot, damp, muggy Istanbul days that make it so hard to breathe. I had barely noticed it on the way to hotel as I had been so buoyed by the prospect of tracking you down but now, as I headed back to the Pera Palace with all my hopes shattered, the heat and the damp suddenly felt insufferable and cloying. What was going to happen now? Had my dream, the hope I had been nurturing for so long, been snuffed out? Çolak Cafer, the old CUP guy from Salonika… He was the key. Indeed, it wasn't Uncle Leon he'd told Cezmi he'd seen but you. So yes, he was the person I needed to find. But Cezmi was dead so how was I to find him? As I was walking past the *Avrupa Pasajı* trading arcade, it hit me – Mehmed Esad. I could just ask him! But first I would have to tell him that I had accepted his offer. I had no other choice. If I was to remain free outside, I had to collaborate with him. Obviously there was no other way he would indulge me in my right to life. And Çolak Cafer…? I had to find him, no matter what. Otherwise how else was I going to find you?

The sweat was pouring off me when I got back to my room. I headed straight for the bathroom and spent an age under the water. When I got out of the bath, I ordered an ice-cold lemonade and sipped it leisurely in the shade of the balcony. I still had a few hours to kill before my meeting with Mehmed Esad. I went back inside, sat at my desk and went back thirteen years, to an Istanbul plagued by political upheavals.

The assassination of Mahmud Şevket Paşa had been a great experience for us. It's true, yes, sometimes a disaster can be more useful than a seemingly favourable incident, and over the last four years, the assassination had been the standout example of this principle. Whenever there had been a violent uprising, an assassination or a secret plot, the party had always emerged stronger. So it had been on 31st March and so it would be after the assassination of Mahmud Şevket Paşa. Cemal Bey's witch hunt would soon bear its fruit – anybody that stood against the party, not just those involved in the plot against us, would scuttle away in fear, whilst those that could not flee would make sure they remained unseen and unheard. Moreover, Mahmud Şevket Paşa's killer had offered us an even greater gift than just letting us crush the opposition: since 1908, we had been dreaming of and longing for power to ourselves and that dream was now about to be realised. It had been five years since the declaration of the constitutional era but now, finally, we could talk of a CUP government in the true sense of the word. Sait Halim Paşa had been made *sadrazam*, but crucially, Talat Bey had been appointed Minister of Internal Affairs.

We were all overcome by an almost festive wave of optimism. Except for Fuad. No, he did not shun his responsibilities; that was something he never did. He was there, even during the most dangerous assignments, steadfast and tenacious no matter what the mission, but for some reason he could not free himself of his misgivings. He was listless, and very often seemed outright dejected, as though he had given in to some despair. Had I not known him and his courage, I could easily have mistaken the mood he was in, coupled with what he and I had been through over the last few days, as him succumbing to a mortal dread. But whatever it was, the fact remained he was one of the bravest and most upstanding men in our unit, which meant his gloom could be a result of a private matter, an affair of the heart. I put it down to him being upset at not being able to bring his fiancée Mahinur and her family to Istanbul, despite his considerable efforts.

His childhood sweetheart – and distant relative – Mahinur was the only woman Fuad had ever wanted to marry. Usually, he never talked about her and kept his private life secret, the same way he kept the party's affairs close to his chest. However, in the wake of Basri Bey's death in Libya and the grief we felt as a result, alongside the strange effect war can have on people in that it often brings them closer together, he could no longer keep it in and he opened up to me about his love life. It was after dinner one evening. We were lying on the ground on a hill smoking our cigarettes and looking up at the stars.

Caught in a storm we are, carried out to sea
Our union, my love, will have to wait for the next world…

Fuad sighed deeply and said, 'Ah Şehsuvar, my old friend. I'm telling you now, if God wills it and we get out of here alive and in one piece, the first thing I'm going to do when we get back home is get married. I swear I'm going to do it. I should have done it by now. My mistake. The minute I get back, I'm going to bring Mahinur to Istanbul. She's always been curious about the capital. Bless her, she always looks at me with those beautiful blue-grey eyes of hers and asks, 'Tell me, Fuad, which is more beautiful – Salonika or Istanbul? Is the sea around Istanbul bluer than ours? Are the streets brighter? Does it have bigger theatres? Will I ever get the chance to watch a play in Istanbul?' And I always reply, 'Yes, it is more beautiful than Salonika, its sea is bluer and its streets brighter. And yes, its theatres are larger. And yes, one day we shall watch Moliere's *Tartuffe* in the famous Ferah Theatre together'. And then she puts on her jealous face and asks, 'What about the girls there? Are they beautiful? They say the girls there are so beautiful and so alluring'. To which I reply, 'Yes, they are indeed beautiful and alluring, and they dress impeccably well. But none of them are as beautiful as you. None of them can hold a candle to you, Mahicim, my dear…' And then her freckled cheeks blush with shame and she says, 'Liar. You say this to me because I'm here with you but the moment you set foot in Pera, you forget all about me.' Bless her, how is the poor thing to know I've never done it with a woman? Whenever the name Dersaadet is mentioned, she conjures up scenes from Sodom and Gomorrah. But one day I'll bring her to Istanbul so she can see it with her own eyes… Yes, I know we are living through difficult times and yes, I know what they say; that we are betrothed to life but married to death. I know. But who isn't in danger? Who isn't suffering? I'm going to marry Mahinur.'

He was not able to bring her to the capital, though. He was too late. Before he could bring Mahinur to Dersaadet, Salonika was lost. Wrenched away from us. And Fuad, like the rest of us, could only watch on helplessly, his eyes ablaze in fury. For the first few weeks, we harboured dreams of reclaiming Salonika and reuniting with our loved ones, but our hopes were crushed by our numerous defeats in the Balkan War and the Bulgarians advancing almost to the gates of the capital. Any hope of being reunited with our loved ones rested on a mutual population exchange negotiated by the respective states. The only solution was for an immediate end to the continuing conflict in the Balkans and for a long-term peace agreement to be signed. It was not just Fuad that nurtured these expectations. Mine were the same. I had not heard from you since leaving Salonika. You may have come back from Paris, for all I knew. Maybe you were still there, in our hometown… And that last encounter of ours – how awful that had been! Perhaps if we were to meet again, we could make amends… Perhaps we could rekindle… Yes, I know. I know it is all futile, all in vain… I know there is no more hope for us.

Anyway, I was talking about Fuad's dejection. Hoping it might help, I invited him one evening to the *Cadde-i Kebir*, and to one of my preferred haunts, Yorgo's famous tavern in Cité de Péra. As always, when we arrived, the waiter Hristo, the man with eyes and ears everywhere, was running the show. Mezzes, hot dishes, entertainment… After knocking back a couple of glasses, I started the conversation in earnest.

'Any news from Salonika? Any news from travellers? Any letters, messages or personal greetings?'

He stared at me vacantly, as though I was talking about something completely irrelevant.

'What? What was that?' he stuttered, but soon pulled himself together. 'Oh, yeah… Salonika. Nothing there I'm afraid, Şehsuvar. The last I heard from there was two months ago. I bumped into Müfit, Mahinur's cousin on her mother's side, her maternal aunt's son, in Üsküdar. He'd arrived six months earlier. He told me they were all doing well and were biding their time, waiting for the right moment to leave the city. But what with the war and all that, they daren't leave. Their Uncle Naki is getting on too, so he can hardly be expected to hit the road with two daughters in tow. There are soldiers all over the place, Greek and Bulgarian. And even if you did find a way past them, there's the bandits and the deserters up in the mountains to deal with…'

I knew it all anyway. He'd already told me about bumping into Müfit but he was so lost in his own thoughts, he'd forgotten he'd told me. If it wasn't love or matters of the heart, it had to be something else bothering our Fuad but before I could probe him, he came out with it.

'Actually, it all comes down to the same thing: the war in the Balkans. We cannot be with our loved ones, nor can our country be safe from harm if we do not win this war. And we're not winning it, Şehsuvar. It looks grim, old boy.' He reached for his *rakı* and raised his glass. 'We are now in power. We can now take any decision we like and pass any ruling we desire and yet nothing is happening. We toppled the government and assumed power ourselves, promising to liberate Edirne. And yet that beautiful and sacred city is still in enemy hands. I cannot see friends of mine that know I'm with the CUP. They may not criticise me openly but I cannot bear to see their accusatory looks, the condemnation writ large all over their faces. If things carry on the way they are, it won't be long before we cannot even show our faces in public.' He looked at me pleadingly. 'What do you think, Şehsuvar? How are we going to sort this mess out?'

Instead of answering, I clinked glasses with him.

'Let's drink first. Here. *Şerefine*'.

'And to you, my brother. *Şerefine*', he said and returned the gesture.

'It's not the best situation, no', I said, putting my glass back down on the table. 'My landlady Madam Melina is also worried. 'The Greeks have already taken Salonika,' she says to me, 'Which means the Bulgarians will soon take Istanbul. They're going to rename it Tsargrad. That's what they're saying down in the shops and the markets. Is that right, Şehsuvar my boy? Are we going to lose this beautiful city?' The people are frightened and worried, yes, but the situation is not so hopeless. For one, we have staved off a very dangerous plot. That alone is cause for hope, and we have to start somewhere. Getting a crumbling empire back on its feet is hardly an easy task. You know that.'

'Please, Şehsuvar', he said in a dejected and hurt tone. 'Don't. Not you, of all people'.

I wasn't sure what he was saying but he carried on.

'Five years, Şesuvar. It's been five years since we ushered in the constitutional era. It's hardly the blink of an eye now, is it? And what progress have we made? What victories can we talk of? And don't talk to me about Libya. Yes, we went there, we fought, but in the end we surrendered that land, land consecrated with Basri Bey's blood. We handed it over to the Italians and came scuttling home. And then there's Salonika, which we have not been able to hold on to either. How much worse can it get? We handed our relatives and our loved ones in the city of our birth over to the Greeks.' He lowered his voice and continued morosely. 'You can forget any talk about the empire getting back on its feet. That is not going to happen. If only we could defend the territories we already have. That alone would be enough for me but I'm afraid that won't happen either. I'm afraid our lives will become hell once our dreams have turned to dust.'

Fuad's relentless pessimism over the last few days had begun to get to me.

'That won't happen', I said sternly. 'We may lose our lives but it won't be in vain. This great country of ours, this great nation of ours, will rise once more. We've been through dark times before. Think of Beyazit the Thunderbolt's crushing rout at Ankara. The Ottoman Empire was in pieces after that but it rose again and became stronger than ever. What are a mere five years in the vast expanse of history? Was the Ottoman Empire formed in five years? Something like a hundred years passed between Osman Bey and Sultan Mehmed the Conqueror, and even that is considered a relatively short period of time. So don't despair, Fuad my brother. We are not just fighting the Bulgarians; we are at war with the Great Powers too. You think Mahmud Şevket Paşa was killed by that ragtag bunch of crooks? We both read the report, didn't we? Wasn't that Fitzmaurice from the British Embassy involved in bringing that lowlife Çerkez Kâzım back to Istanbul from Romania? And it's not like we don't know that the British secret service, which considered Mahmud Şevket Paşa the Germans' man, was behind the assassination? You think this plot is not payback for our attack on the government? And I haven't even mentioned Russia yet...'

He shook his head, as though none of what I had said had registered.

'I know all this, Şehsuvar. I know all too well about the discord the foreign powers are creating here. True, we are not in the position we were in six hundred years ago, but we do have six hundred years of experience. And that makes the losses we are incurring and the horrendous mistakes we are making unacceptable. Can things be any more shameful? You say it was a few crooks that shot Mahmud Şevket Paşa. That it was that bum, Çerkez Kâzım, who was behind it. Well, who the hell are they? Who the hell are these people that dare open fire on their own *sadrazam*? They were also patriots like us at one point. You know full well that Çerkez Kâzım was once part of our setup, a member of the CUP, and yet now we call him a traitor and a lowlife. Tell me, how is our cause helped by capturing these so-called lowlifes and traitors, by beating them up at the Bekiraǧa Barracks, by torturing them and, indeed, hanging them from the gallows as a message to the world? I'll tell you what. It doesn't help our cause at all. It doesn't solve anything. On the contrary, all it does is make our problems worse. So now, let me ask you this: let's say tomorrow or the day after, one of us, you or I, begins to disagree with the party's policies and speaks out and tells them that what they are doing is wrong; how do we know we won't also be branded traitors and lowlifes?'

His voice was actually trembling.

'Come off it, Fuad! Apart from us, there is no party. We are the party, we are the state, we are the government and we are the country too.'

He shook his head in despair.

'I'm not so sure. True, no one in the party has drawn their weapon yet. Nobody has been shot. But that is because we had never been in power before. But we are now. And now we may be forced to stand against our own comrades and fight them as well as the Great Powers. Believe me, if such a schism occurs in our ranks, then we will be the first to be declared traitors.' He paused, unsure as to the veracity of what he was saying. 'I don't know. Maybe you'll save us. After all, you're closer to the people at the top. Isn't that so? Talat Bey was friends with your father, and Kara Kemal has nothing but respect for you.'

He was laying it all on the table and I don't know if I deserved it. I was trying to help him and in return I was being hit by a barrage of accusations and denunciations. For a second, I was taken aback and didn't know what to say. As for Fuad, he simply knocked back his *rakı* in one go, as though it would offer some kind of consolation, and didn't even bother to wait for my response. This time, there was no offer of *şerefe* from his lips, nor a clinking of his glass against mine. Was he in the throes of making a crucial decision? Was this some kind of parting of ways for us? And if so, what had I done to deserve it? Like him, I was just another simple *fedai* following orders. But when I stopped to ponder it a little, I came to realise that Fuad was actually right. I too had my doubts, but I had never actually come out and verbalised them. Only once had I expressed my misgivings, to Basri Bey, and in that very same tavern to boot. I had taken his conciliatory words on board and, resigning myself to my fate, had continued with the movement, carrying out their orders to the letter. However, that did not mean I should just stand there and let myself be vilified.

'You're wrong, Fuad', I said smiling affably and trying to hide my anger. 'So wrong. I don't mean what you said about the movement. I may not be as bleak about it but a lot of what you said makes sense. But there is one issue on which you are definitely mistaken. Forget the party. There is no one on this earth closer to me than you. Yes, I admit it. If I have a true companion in this scorched, troubled land, a true brother in the cause, then it is you. Yes, I adore Talat Bey, I respect him, and the same goes for Kara Kemal. But I never went to the front with them and never fought the enemy with them at my side. When I was shot, they were not there by my side. Only you were there. You. My brother. And when you were shot, I was there next to you. So I'm afraid you're mistaken, Fuad. Mistaken and misguided. Ours is a friendship that has been tried by fire. Yes, if you do wrong, I'll warn you and reproach you, and yes, I may even fight you, but I would never betray you. I would never betray you or sell you out or abandon you. I need you to know this, so please get it into that thick Salonika head of yours.' I calmly reached for my glass and clinked it against his. 'Now, let us drink. Şerefe. To honour and glory. To the glory of our friendship, which will never be broken, even if we lose our entire country, every square inch.'

Fuad, however, could not reach for his glass. He had never been adept at expressing his emotions and now his whole body trembled as he began to slowly weep. It was then that I realised he was a true friend and I began to love him even more as a result.

Nevertheless, when I woke up the next morning, I felt a terrible emptiness inside. And no, it was not a hangover, but an emotional emptiness. I got up, did my best to shave and freshen up and then had breakfast at the table Madam Melina had prepared for us. We chatted about the state of the nation but the emptiness that had gotten hold of me, that doleful despondency, would not go away. I left the house and walked down to the sea. I didn't feel like taking the tram so I walked along the coast instead and reflected on my conversation with Fuad the previous evening. On the way he had opened up to me so – for him – frankly, and the way I had tried to counter his despondency. On the transparent walls I had put up around my mind whilst trying to convince my old friend. And it wasn't just a case of thinking but feeling too, so much so that the barriers I had placed in front of my mind began to collapse one by one. There under the summer sun with the breeze coming in from the sea, I could feel long-forgotten memories stirring back to life in my mind. The words you said to me in your garden in the wake of the 1908 rebellion.

I'm not talking about politics, or democracy or rebellion here. I am talking about the essence and the meaning of existence. Why are we alive? Do we have a purpose? That is the issue and the question of existence. It is the ancient wound in our souls…

The ancient wound in our souls… What is that? Believe me, I had started to forget. The ruthlessness of everyday political life, the succession of plots, murders, intrigues and deaths. Anatole's France's novel *Le Lys Rouge*, which I had bought with such excitement and anticipation when I first came to Istanbul, a book I had planned on translating. In fact, where is my copy of that book? I wonder where it is? And it wasn't just your words that sprang to life in my memories but your Uncle Leon's protests, Ahmed Rıza's analyses and, indeed, Abdülhamit's concerns – they were all in line with what Fuad had said to me the previous night.

You can forget any talk about the empire getting back on its feet. That is not going to happen. If only we could defend the territories we already have. That alone would be enough for me but I'm afraid that won't happen either. I'm afraid our lives will become hell once our dreams have turned to dust.

It wasn't his own life my old friend was worried about; what he was questioning, and so late in the day too, were the ideals for which we had always been ready to lay down our lives. Whereas you had already done it, five years earlier, during the first days of the rebellion, when we were all full of hope and drunk on the dream of victories we thought were just around the corner. Yes, we had dreams of victories back then, whereas now it was the winds of defeat that were blowing over the land. The defeat of the territories lost in the five years between the declaration of the constitution and now, the countless casualties, the lost innocence and the loss of our moral high ground as the champion of the underdogs, the downtrodden and the wronged. Even our foiling of a murderous plot just a few days earlier would not be enough to save us. All it had done was condemn us to imprisonment in the same vicious circle. For five years we had been trying to capture the bridge and eventually we did but when we began commandeering the ship, we realised the whole thing was rotting and falling apart, from the engine room to the deck, from the hull to the cabins, even the crew manning the ship. The situation was hopeless and we were finished, truly finished, and we could not see a way out. We could not abandon the ship, nor could we just stand by and watch it sink. It was then that I realised that the previous night, I wasn't the one that had opened Fuad's eyes. He was the one that had opened mine.

When the Wolf Dies in the Forest

Good Evening, Ester (Evening, Day 10)

Although darkness had descended over the city, it was still scorching hot, with no wind to provide some relief. It was more like summer, rather than blessed autumn. I thought the Taksim Gardens would perhaps have a few breezes but even there not a single leaf fluttered. I sat at a table in the terrace bar overlooking the sea. At least that way I would be facing some open space and could perhaps get some air. Mehmed Esad had yet to arrive but he would soon be there. The other tables were only now beginning to fill up. Although the smartly-dressed gentlemen and their respectable lady companions had yet to arrive, the young and extravagant playboys and the heavily made-up girls out for a bit of fun and who could smell the money in the young lads' pockets were already out in force and had taken their places at the tables. The flirtatious glances, the coquettish covering of the mouths with expensive handkerchiefs to hide their giggles, the seductive swinging of the head, the flicking of the hair and the eventual merging of the tables were all precludes to a night that would end in the fire of love. The orchestra, from Hungary apparently, had already begun playing Hungarian and Romanian folk songs. When the burly waiter came trundling along, I ordered some Üzüm Kızı *rakı*, which has just come out this year, salad, a plate of white cheese and a plate of cranberry beans. Mehmed arrived and planted himself down on the table before my order arrived.

'Sorry, old chap', he said breathlessly. 'Had a customer at the shop. Real talkative fellow. Wouldn't shut up'.

'Not to worry. I've only just got here myself'. With a jerk of my head, I gestured to the kitchen. 'I ordered a *rakı*. Is that okay or would you like something else?'

'*Rakı's* fine'. He took off his fez and placed it on the table. 'Actually, a nice, cold beer would go down a treat in weather like this but beer makes you feel bloated.' He wiped the back of his neck with his handkerchief. 'This is really crummy weather, eh? I walked here from the shop and now I'm caked in sweat.'

I looked out towards the sea with some faint hope and muttered, 'Who knows? We might get a breeze from the sea later on. It can't stay like this forever…'

He smiled, folded his handkerchief and put it back in his pocket.

'Still, it's not that bad. Remember Libya? The heat and the humidity there were another level altogether, weren't they?'

Opportunity had come knocking.

'Did you know Cezmi?' I said, getting straight to the point. 'Cezmi Kenan. He fought in the war in Libya too.'

He narrowed his eyes and tried to remember.

'You mean old Hawfinch Cezmi? How could I not know him? He was our commandant. He was a bit eccentric but he was a good man. A brave, pious man, the likes of which I have yet to see anywhere else. He was always out there right at the front leading the line. Fearless he was, as though he thought he could not die. We used to warn him and tell him not to but he would just laugh in our faces and say, 'Don't worry lads, nothing will happen to me. I'm protected by magic charms. No bullet can hurt me.' Actually, you know something – he's never been shot. A light wound to the hip during a trench battle once, that's all. Say, how is Major Cezmi? Have you seen him recently?'

Was he testing me? Or did he really not know? I opted for honesty.

'Major Cezmi is dead', I said calmly. 'Strange you don't know, because chances are it's your lot that killed him.'

His expression changed instantly.

'That's harsh, Şehsuvar. Very harsh, indeed. Were you there?'

That is when I knew he knew about Cezmi's death and that he was testing me.

'I was not there when he was murdered, no, but I saw him twice', I said and went on tell him about my first meeting with him at his house and then the day I came across his dead body. I did not spare any details and he listened intently without interrupting once.

'If only you'd told me all this before', he said despondently. 'Had you done so, we could have stopped his murder. And yes, you're right, it does look like one of our jobs. We have squads like that in the organisation but they work independently of us. Yes, I read about the murder in the newspapers. If I'd known, I could have stopped them. It's a shame. A real shame. Actually, this was one of the things what I wanted to talk to you about. What we want is to stop important people such as yourself and Cezmi being hunted down and killed like this. We are asking you to come back to work for us. For the service and for the common good, that is. There is no more CUP or *Teşkilat-ı Mahsusa* or *Karakol Cemiyeti*. What we have now is a republic that needs protecting. We have a parliament that has been established as a result of the grand march that began with the revolution of 1908. Those are your words. True, we do not have an opposition party but rest assured, one will eventually emerge. Yes, our democratic foundations may be a little shaky but that too will eventually be settled. At the moment, our duty is to defend this republic.' He put his fez back on and looked at me, his brown eyes searching my face intently. 'So what say you, Şehsuvar? Have you made up your mind?'

I gently pulled back and his face fell. He must have thought I was declining the offer.

'I'll work for you but on one condition. Just one. I don't want a large salary or some fancy title. I don't care about any of that. But I need to find Monsieur Leon. Yes, I'm talking about Ester. She is still very important for me.'

He could hardly believe what he was hearing.

'You mean that Jewish girl? That old flame of yours? You're not serious, are you?'

Had I been in his shoes, I would have reacted in the same way. An old CUP hand who had dedicated his life to a cause and who had been through so much and faced so many dangers was still chasing after his childhood sweetheart, like a pathetic love-struck high school student.

'I am serious, Mehmed. Right now, there is nothing more important to me than finding Ester. I don't care how it's done but I have to find her. Otherwise I don't think I'll ever be able to sort myself out mentally. If I don't find her, I doubt I'll be able to apply myself to any work. So yes, that is the situation. I don't expect you to understand. Just know that it is the truth.'

He was finding it difficult to understand and trying to work out whether I was deceiving him in some way or just making up a tired old love story in order to get rid of him.

'After all these years, and after going through so much upheaval…' He looked at me suspiciously. 'You're not having a laugh at my expense now are you, Şehsuvar?'

I was beginning to lose my temper.

'What is that supposed to mean?' I said, my voice coming out harsher than I wanted. 'Do you think this is all a joke?'

'No, no, nothing like that. I just thought…'

He suddenly started laughing. That's right. He sat there right in front of me and laughed in my face. I wanted to get up and leave. Why should I stay and talk to him while he mocked my most intimate feelings? He saw the hurt look on my face and immediately pulled himself together and tried to make amends.

'I'm sorry, old boy. Really, I'm sorry. I was just a little taken aback, that's all. Wasn't expecting anything like that, you see. We've all been there, my friend. We've all experienced that nightmare and been through that pain.' He looked at me with a mixture of envy and admiration. 'But after all these years… I take my hat off to you, Şehsuvar. Really, I do.' The laughter had gone and he was now talking to me like an understanding old friend. 'This must be what they call true love. Don't worry, old boy, I'll do everything I can to help you. But perhaps you should have checked out the Tokatlıyan Hotel first.'

I shook my head.

'I did. Monsieur Leon has not stayed there. When you saw him there, he must have been there for something else, a dinner or a meeting. We may not find Monsieur Leon but there is somebody else that can help. Cafer. Çolak Cafer from Salonika. He said he saw Ester at the second-hand booksellers' market in Beyazıt. If we find Cafer, we'll find Ester.'

He narrowed his eyes in thought.

'Fair enough. We can ask around for this Cafer. We'll find him in the end, sooner or later, that much is for sure. But if you say we need to find him quick…'

'We do. As soon as we can'.

The *rakıs* arrived and we started drinking. After that, we did not talk about my future work. He didn't mention anything and I didn't ask. We talked about Salonika and about our childhood and youth. After a few *rakıs* had been downed, he was a little worse for wear and was getting carried away. 'Don't you worry, Şehsuvar old boy, if this Cafer fellow doesn't show up, we'll just go straight to Salonika. I swear, we'll go. Either officially or on personal business but we'll go. We're going to find Ester, no matter what.'

The more he spoke like this, the more embarrassed I began to feel. Perhaps I'd been wrong about Mehmed Esad. Perhaps my aging old friend really only wanted the best for me. It was only when we were parting ways that he said something that stuck in my mind. The bill had been settled and we were at the Taksim Gardens' exit. A pleasant breeze was blowing in from the sea and we were both sporting huge drunken grins.

'Thanks for the meal, Mehmed', I said, shaking his hand. 'But next time, I'm paying'.

He shrugged his shoulders.

'You pay, I pay, what difference does it make? After all, we both have the same employer now. That reminds me. Pop around tomorrow afternoon and I'll give you an advance.

We'll also have a chance to talk about the job.' I thought he was going to say goodbye but he stopped and did not let go of my hand. 'It really is love, isn't it, Şehsuvar? This whole Ester thing. I mean, there's not some other little story going on, is there?'

What, so now he didn't believe me? If that were the case, then the entire evening's conversation had been a sham. I pulled my hand away.

'What else can it be, Mehmed? You think I'm playing spy games or what?'

He wasn't offended. Rather, he looked at me with a strange dolefulness.

'Well, that is the name of our game, at the end of the day. Spy games are what we will be playing. That's a task handed on down to us from above. But I hope this Ester business is not like that. It's not, is it?' He looked as though he was afraid he would live to regret what he had done. 'You still love her, right?'

He actually appeared to be less upset at the possibility that I was lying to him and more worried that my love for you was not real. And it wasn't just the *rakı* talking, either; who knows what love stories he had concealed in his own past.

'It's all real, Mehmed. Everything I've told you. I don't know about Ester, of course. It's been so long. So many years have passed but my feelings for her are the same.'

He smiled and thumped me on the shoulder.

'Good. I'm glad. There should be things of beauty in this otherwise wretched world, don't you think? Anyway, have a good night, my brother. Don't forget, tomorrow afternoon. I'll be expecting you.'

It was around midnight when I got back to the hotel. My head was spinning a little and I thought about ordering a coffee but in the end decided on some fresh air instead. Outside on the balcony, I was greeted by a glittering darkness. There were so many stars in the sky, all so luminous, and seemingly so close to us too. I sat on a stool and stared up at the stars. For a moment, I imagined what it would be like to be up there, to be one of them. To be alone but content up there in that vast, endless space… If only I had wings. If only I had the strength. If only I was not bound by the laws of physics so I could fly up there and lose myself in that twinkling darkness… With these thoughts and wishes in my mind, I dozed off. It's embarrassing, I know, but yes, like an old wino, I fell asleep right there on my stool on the balcony and was awoken by the sound of seagulls squawking angrily on the roof of the hotel. The din they were making was incredible; cats in March are nothing compared to the noise of the fighting that was going on up there on the roof. I looked back up at the sky. It seemed to have lost some of its magic and now didn't seem so enchanting to my eyes. I walked back inside, brushed my teeth and thought about going to bed but then, as I passed my desk, I noticed the blank pages and so, after a moment's pause, I sat down to write. That little nap and the fresh air have recharged my mind and now I find myself drifting back to the past, back to the summer of 1913.

It was a stifling hot day in Istanbul, just like today…

'We need a victory', Kara Kemal was saying. 'It may just be a little one but we need one nonetheless.'

We were sitting in the office of the Ministry of Internal Affairs in the *Bab-ı Âli*. Talat Bey had personally summoned us: Mithat Şükrü, Kara Kemal, Kuşçubaşı Eşref and Fuad. Of course Fuad had to be there… I had asked him to come myself so that he would understand that he and I would always be together, no matter what the circumstances, and that our fates would always be intertwined, whether we won or we lost.

So yes, we had gathered at the *Bab-ı Âli*. We were now the ones sitting in the same building in front of which we had once fought for our cries for liberty, fraternity and equality to be heard. Where the Minister of Internal Affairs used to silence us by destroying our ideas and, if necessary, our bodies, his chair was now occupied by Talat Bey. Whenever the opportunity arose, like today, the Great Master was fond of inviting over for discussion those people in the movement for whom he felt a kinship so he could, while running the government, also keep abreast of developments in the movement and listen to what we had to say on the important topics of the day.

'That is the only way the people can be swayed', the Little Master, Kara Kemal, was saying. 'That is the way their trust in the government is gained. If we are to implement a long-term national economic plan, we need their trust because there is no way we can bring the people prosperity in the short term. As far as we are concerned, we need to create a flourishing local economy. It's possible, yes, but it will not happen immediately. So in order to give the people some hope and to fire them up, we need to record a success, a victory of some kind, even if it is just a minor or temporary one. Otherwise running a government under these conditions may prove very tricky indeed.'

The sweat was pouring off us. The weather was like the state of the nation itself – heavy, oppressive and almost unbearable. The fezzes were off, the starched shirt collars were open and the staff were running back and forth from the kitchens bringing us endless supplies of iced sherbet. For some unknown reason, however, the only person not perspiring in that room was Talat Bey. He turned to Kara Kemal and gave a wolfish grin, as though he had a delightful piece of news waiting for us.

'How about the liberation of Edirne?'

It was like a bolt of lightning running right through us, despite the stifling heat and the clamminess of our clothes. Kara Kemal almost jumped out of his seat.

'I'm all for it! But how?'

Talat Bey looked at each of us with a jubilant glint in his black eyes.

'Our intelligence reports state that the Bulgarians are mobilising for war against the Serbs and Greeks. They have already started pulling back their troops from our front.'

We all turned to look at Kuşçubaşı Eşref, who had fought alongside us against the Italians in Libya, as we all knew that any reports that had come through from the Balkan front had to have come through him.

'The information is correct', he said serenely. 'The Bulgarians are drunk with victory. They have defeated the Sublime Porte itself and now they've turned their rapacious gaze towards the smaller states of the region. They do not want to lose or share with the others the territories they have occupied and they are not chasing their dream of a Greater Macedonia. Their secret intention is to come all the way down to Salonika and so they have recalled a substantial number of troops in preparation for an engagement with the Serbs and the Greeks. If things carry on the way they are now, they will have to recall even more. However, it's not going to be easy for them as they are not just facing the Serbs and the Greeks but the Montenegrins and the Romanians too. Because these are allegedly 'small' states, they are making the critical mistake of not taking them seriously. In war, every soldier and every rifle matter.'

'When a wolf dies in the forest, the jackals tear each other to pieces, as they say', Talat Bey said. 'We kept telling them that an Ottoman union was the best way forward but they wouldn't listen. Well, this is the result.'

'Well, let them tear one another to shreds', Kara Kemal muttered merrily. 'As long as we don't get entangled in their mess, let them get on with it.'

Kuşçubaşı Eşref piped up.

'No sir, that would be a mistake. We cannot do that. We cannot and must not leave them be. Do you not see? This is a huge opportunity for us. The path has been cleared for us to liberate Edirne and Kırklareli and to reclaim the territories we lost in Thrace.'

Fuad could not hide his excitement at what he was hearing.

'My God, yes, Eşref Bey is right. What are we waiting for? Let's get going.'

'If only it was so easy, young man', Talat Bey replied, still smiling assuredly. 'We first need to make an announcement to the Western powers. We need a sound reason before we mobilise.'

'The reason is ready, Talat Bey', Kuşçubaşı Eşref said straight away. 'The Bulgarians are violating both the Çorlu Armistice and the terms of the Treaty of London, which stated they were to retreat to beyond the Midye-Enez Line. Well, have they? They have not moved an inch, which means any action now taken against them is legitimate. As for the Westerners, they're confused. Just think about it. The five states they have been supporting for years against us are now at each other's throats.'

He took a sip from the glass of raspberry juice in front of him.

'Actually, Enver Bey thinks along the same lines as you do. Fethi Bey, too. In fact, the *sadrazam* Sait Halim Paşa also thinks it is time for us to act. But there is a split in the government. On the one side are those that say if we go to war and fail, the fallout will be disastrous, while on the other side are those that say our enemies' going to war with one another is a sign and a blessing from God and that we should immediately march on Edirne. But Ahmet Izzet Paşa, the Minister of War, is playing along with both sides. He is terrified that the blame will fall on his shoulders if things go wrong.'

Seeing as his preferred *nargiles* were not allowed in government offices, Kara Kemal helped himself to a cigarette from Talat Bey's case and reached for a lighter.

'When has he not been terrified? Let them be afraid. Of course the army should march on Edirne. I agree with Eşref Bey. The Bulgarians are offering us victory on a silver platter. It would be the height of stupidity to let this opportunity go begging.'

Talat Bey listened quietly to the discussion. After lighting a cigarette for himself and then letting out a large plume of smoke, he looked at the Little Master and smiled knowingly.

'That's all well and good, Kemal, but just now you were talking about the need for reviving the economy. Forget about going to war with a fully-equipped army, when basic drills cost so much, where are we going to find the money for such a vast operation?'

Kara Kemal's face fell.

'Well, yes, Talat Bey, of course the financial aspect of any war is important too. But we will not get an opportunity like this again. If necessary, we can take on loans, and at higher interest rates if necessary, and we can provide collateral. But we have to send the army to Edirne.'

Talat Bey did not say yes or no but it was obvious from the way he was acting that he had made his decision. Clearly he wanted to see Edirne freed more than any of us there, not just because he was born on that border town but also because victory there would legitimise once and for all the CUP-led government. In other words, he had already made up his mind before he had even invited us in to discuss the matter. In calling us to speak to him, he was just trying to glean the thoughts of the men in the party. Obviously, he had held high-level meetings with others before our arrival. We were to learn after the liberation of Edirne that when asking where the money for the war would be found, he had, earlier that afternoon, already agreed upon a loan of the necessary one and a half million gold pieces from the State Tobacco Company.

And so, on the 21st of July, one of the hottest days of the summer, we liberated Edirne, and we did it without battle or military engagement. The intelligence that had come through to us from the front had been correct – most of the Bulgarian forces had been recalled, and the ones that had remained could not possibly face up to our forces and so they either retreated or surrendered. The Ottoman banner once again fluttered atop the minarets of the Selimiye Mosque.

The liberation of Edirne had the effect Kara Kemal had expected. The nation was buoyed and respect for the CUP grew. Of course, it was like a festival atmosphere for us. Barely two months had passed since the assassination of Mahmud Şevket Paşa but the government had recovered and the city that had been the second capital of the Ottoman Empire was ours again. Undoubtedly, the person to benefit the most from the march on Edirne was Enver Bey. Seeing as any reports from the front went straight to him first and that he was privy to all that was going on there, he had already worked out that the Bulgarians would not have been able to withstand an assault and when the march to Edirne began, he leapt on to his horse to lead the troops, despite suffering from chronic appendicitis pains. He was the first officer to enter the city, and thus gained the sobriquet of 'the Conqueror of Edirne' to go alongside his other title of 'the Hero of the Liberation'.

There was no denying that Enver Bey was a brave and formidable soldier and that he was desperate for Edirne to be delivered from the hands of the enemy, just as we were all were, so much so that we also knew he would lay down his life for the city if necessary. But he was also manoeuvring to raise his own profile and boost his own reputation. That is the real reason he had taken command of one company and had moved to the head of an army that was already on a victory parade. Something similar had happened during the uprising of the 31st March. The commander in charge of the Army of Action then had been Hüseyin Hüsnü Paşa, whilst its staff officer was Mustafa Kemal. The army, which had arrived days earlier, had been ready to enter Istanbul but orders then came through from the General Headquarters of the CUP saying that the army should hold from entering. The Army of Action, under the command of Hüseyin Hüsnü Paşa, was made to wait in the district of Halkalı and the order was given for there to be no attack or movement of any kind until Mahmud Şevket Paşa and Enver Bey had arrived in Dersaadet.

The same thing was happening now and in the struggle to assume command and responsibility for the victory and be seen as the great liberator, Enver had again come out on top. Ultimately, after the recapture of Edirne, the unstoppable rise of the 'Hero of the Liberation' would begin. Having the trust and respect of the army and the support of brave and battle-hardened men like Yakup Cemil in the movement meant that within a short period of time, Enver would soon hold the fate of the government in his hands and neither Talat Bey's politics of appeasement nor Cemal Bey's more hawkish stance would blunt his ambitions. He would have a decisive role in all our fates, a role that, unfortunately, did little in terms of benefit for the country. Of course, at the time, it never occurred to any of us that things would reach such a point. The regaining of Kırklareli and Edirne – in other words, of all of Thrace up to the River Meriç – had lifted the gloom that had fallen over the nation. Even that dark despondency that had overwhelmed Fuad had gone. Our chests now swelled with pride and we could happily tell the people that we had kept our promise to liberate Edirne. Kara Kemal was right – the victory had altered the political mood of the country completely.

Yes, maybe we were mistaken and were acting a little too hastily. We were setting up a new state, one that would be in line with the circumstances and the expectations of the new era, but it would not be completely severed from the centuries-old traditions of the Ottomans. The creaking old institutions needed to be revitalised, outdated laws needed to be reformed and an entirely new bureaucracy needed to be built. Moreover, our positions had to be clarified. So far, we had simply been known as *fedaeen*, as the armed wing of the movement, and during the wars in Libya and the Balkans, we were a 'volunteer' battalion, but now, whether it was via law or decree, we needed to be recognised and instated as officers of an official state institution. With risk of coming across as arrogant, we had completed near-impossible tasks to protect the state and to ensure the continued existence of our people and yet we still did not have official status as government workers. All it needed was a slight change in the winds and for a new party to come to power and form the government and they would waste no time in accusing us of being an unrecognised paramilitary outfit and therefore a threat and subsequently have us incarcerated. Moreover, the state institutions that paid our wages, the Ministry of War above all, would be in serious trouble.

Although I tried a number of times, upon Fuad's insistence, to raise the matter with Talat Bey, for some odd reason, he either skipped over the discussion or just plain dismissed it. However, I managed to catch him alone one day, after the regaining of Edirne when he was looking particularly pleased, and I broached the subject with him.

'Come to the *Bab-ı Âli* tomorrow', he sighed. 'Let's put this issue to sleep once and for all'.

The following morning, I was there as requested at Talat Bey's offices but he was so busy it was only until after the noon prayers that I was granted an audience with him. He did not have his usual paternal warmth about him and after a few perfunctory greetings and a run-of-the-mill inquiry into my health, he rather said, rather brusquely, 'Tell me, Şehsuvar, why are you so persistent on this topic? Is someone forcing you to do this?'

I won't lie; I was deeply upset by the questions.

'No-one, Talat Bey. We just want our status to be clarified, that's all.'

'*We*, you say?' he asked, a deep ridge forming between his eyes. 'Who is this *we*? Who wants it? Is it Enver? Is he a part of this?'

'Heavens, no', I said, taken aback. 'Why would he be? I'm sure you know that we are not that close, either with Enver Bey or with his friends.'

He stared at me long and hard as though he was not sure, as though it was possible that I was lying, before placing a hand on my shoulder.

'I'm sorry, Şehsuvar', he said, his voice and expression softening. 'I had to ask, you see, because Enver has raised the issue a few times too. There's also the matter of...' He could not finish the sentence and instead just shook his forlornly. 'Now look, Şehsuvar. I'll be frank with you. You're right. We should have sorted out your legal and official status by now. But I have some reservations.' He looked into my eyes, expecting understanding on my part. 'Important reservations. You know how much influence Enver Bey wields amongst you *fedaeen*. You may think this is irrelevant but actually, it is of crucial importance. This is between you and I but Enver Bey is constantly criticising and disparaging the Minister of War. Yes, Ahmet Izzet Paşa has made mistakes. Of course he has. He's a soldier from the old school and is not the type to make quick decisions and implement them promptly. But the man is dedicated to his work and does not neglect his duties in any way. I swear, with God above as my witness, whatever we asked of him during the Edirne operation, he delivered. Enver has a different game in mind, however. He wants Ahmet Izzet Paşa removed from office so he can be appointed in his place. Apparently, he has even approached the *sadrazam* in person and said he – the sadrazam – should make him Minister for War 'for the good of the country and its independence'. Poor Sait Halim Paşa, when he came to see me, he was almost purple with fury. 'Talat Bey,' he said. 'For the love of all things good, this cannot happen. Talk to that man, please. If you do not deal with this matter promptly, the integrity and reputation of not just the government but the Ottoman state itself will be compromised.'

I met with Enver and told him that his rank and experience in affairs of state were not enough for the post. He seemed convinced but soon afterwards, I received a visit from Yakup Cemil, of all people. Hardly a coincidence that soon after my little chat with Enver, that thug came knocking on my door and quite openly, indeed quite threateningly, asks, 'Why don't you make Enver the Minister for War? Is there anybody else in the country more qualified for the post than him?' Of course, I gave that hoodlum a piece of my mind but I know that lot won't stop. Enver is stirring up the *fedaeen* and they're egging him on in turn. As though they're the only ones who love this country, as they're the only true patriots. Anyway, that is why at this moment in time, I'm afraid I can't do what you're asking. If I do, then I'll only be baiting a group of men who are already unpredictable enough. I'm sorry but I'm afraid I'm going to have to postpone it, both for the sake of the unity of our party and to make sure the government does not slide into uncertainty and chaos.'

I was happy that Talat Bey had chosen to be open with me but the appearance of fault lines in our movement was making me nervous. I remember what Fuad had said to me: *We are the ones in power now. And we now may be forced to stand against our own comrades and fight them as well as the Great Powers. Believe me, if such a conflict does break out in our ranks, then we will be the first to be declared traitors.*

I didn't think Talat Bey would have us declared traitors but were it to continue the way it was, a clash seemed inevitable. It was not long ago, a mere eight months earlier in fact, in that same building too, that Yakup Cemil, the man who had shot the ex-Minister for War without even batting an eyelid, did not hesitate in pointing his gun at Talat Bey. So yes, at that specific moment in time, our legal status was not the main issue. The key issue was keeping the man who was the brain of our movement alive.

'I see, Talat Bey', I said. 'I understand. Not to worry. It can wait. Tell us, what can we do to help? That is the more pressing question now.'

He looked at me gratefully.

'Thank you, Şehsuvar. Thank you, dear brother. I knew you would understand. And bless you for asking. However, taking too many precautions may prove detrimental. We need to resolve this matter amongst ourselves, calmly and amicably, via discussion. We must not let matters spill over into the public arena. Whatever happens, we cannot allow ourselves to slide into moral decay and political corruption. The chief enemy of morality is neither money nor women but power. Power bereft of morality makes either thieves or degenerates of men. Unfortunately, man has not yet managed to tame that force known as power, and it is doubtful he will in the near future. I'm talking about all of us too, not just Enver Bey. No man can bear the momentous burden of power alone. It is only by uniting that we can pull through. Just as we have survived so far by banding together, in the same way when in power, we must rid ourselves of these corruptive influences by being there for one another, by helping and critiquing one another, amicably and agreeably. Otherwise, God forbid, we shall end up doing to ourselves what our enemies have been unable to do to us.'

This Is Not Ankara

Good Morning Ester (Morning, Day 11)

Strangely enough, I woke up well this morning. It didn't feel as though I had downed so many glasses of *rakı*. Just as I was putting it down to the few moments I had spent sitting on the balcony and sobering up last night, I looked up at the cuckoo clock and realised it was nearly noon. Well, if you sleep till that late, of course you're going to feel good… Breakfast must have already ended in the restaurant downstairs so I called reception and ordered a cheese omelette, toast and coffee and then went into the bathroom to wash. The food arrived while I was shaving. Ihsan brought it up on a tray himself, along with the day's papers and…. What was that? A gift? A phonographic record…?

'A gift from Reşit Bey', he smiled. 'A German guest forgot it in his room so we thought you should have it as you would appreciate it more than anyone.'

I thanked him and picked it up. It was Puccini's *La Boheme*. A love story set in Paris… The story of events in a garret, just like the story we envisaged for ourselves… A sad story, yes, harrowingly sad, but also a real love story, not one that had been cut off halfway like ours.

Ihsan placed the tray and its contents on the table and made his way out while I placed the record on the gramophone. After a few hisses and crackles, the music began. Of course I thought of you, of the grand hopes we had lost, of our younger days, of those youthful exuberances that would never be relived… When the first part of the opera ended, my appetite had vanished. Once more, I was spiralling down into my wretched misery.

I was looking for you, I was collaborating with dark, mysterious characters whom I did not know in order to find you, and yet a voice inside me was telling me that we would never meet again. If you had come to Istanbul, wouldn't you have called me? Otherwise why would someone like you even come to Istanbul? You would need a reason. A visit to Uncle Leon perhaps…. Yes, you would have come for that. But wouldn't you have wondered about me? Not even a little? Would you not have asked after me? Asked around to see what has happened to me? If your Uncle Leon was in Istanbul, he would have found me for sure. We have a shared past, shared acquaintances and shared friends. So why? Why were you not looking for me? I looked over at the record playing on the gramophone. I wanted to pick it up and smash it into pieces but then I realised how stupid that would be. And then I also realised how equally meaningless my despondency was and how I needed to shake it off. As I scanned the room, I noticed the newspapers next to my uneaten meal. I began flicking through them, hoping they would help distract me and perhaps even lift my mood.

Cumhuriyet, *İkdam*, *Akşam*, *Hakimiyet-i Milliye*… I read them all, one after the other, but there was nothing of importance in any of them. Furthermore, they seemed to have forgotten all about the Cezmi case too. The common news, emblazoned in huge lettering on the front pages of them all, was the news that the President himself, Mustafa Kemal, who had not been in Istanbul since the 16th of May 1919, would finally be honouring the city with a visit next year. It was unclear yet whether he would be staying in Dolmabahçe or Beylerbeyi Palace, and another point of uncertainty was when he would be visiting, with some saying it would be around the beginning of spring and others hearing rumours of a visit nearer the end of summer. I remember a conversation I had with Kara Kemal, when I'd asked him why 'the Gazi' had not come to Istanbul and whether he was angry at the city and its inhabitants for whatever reason. With his usual serene demeanour, he replied, 'I don't know, Şehsuvar. Perhaps he's afraid of an assassination attempt. Remember, this is not Ankara. This place is crawling with spies and safeguarding his security would be seriously difficult. So perhaps the guys over at National Security did not agree to a visit. All you have to do is look back and remember that English spy called Mustafa Sagir. He had gone in so deep, he was right under Mustafa Kemal's nose. If they hadn't woken up in time to his presence, he would have killed the Gazi in an instant, just like that.' The late Major Cezmi was the same. He also thought the President did not visit because he was afraid of assassination, only this time Cezmi himself was the one that wanted to assassinate him. Unfortunately for him, he didn't live long enough to see his plan through. Or maybe that's why he'd been killed in the first place...

But if one was to look at the newspapers, such threats to the President no longer existed, which was a relief to know. The country needs to be free of this undeclared and unofficial state of war and return to something resembling a state of normality. A people constantly being told about another Kurdish rebellion or the disbanding of an opposition party or another assassination attempt in Izmir or some other town needs some peace. Maybe this is the context in which I should deal with Mehmed Esad's offer. Maybe the government of this Republic really does want to make peace with everybody now. Just imagine: a multiparty republic instead of a one-party state... A free press that points out and critiques the government's mistakes and shortcomings... A free and open government, not an oppressive one like the one formed by the CUP... How wonderful it would be! Then why did they have Cezmi killed? Actually, I still was not sure about that. Maybe another motive or reason will eventually emerge regarding his murder. Ultimately, the truth will out and we'll know what happened...

I just looked up at the clock. It is past twelve. I need to get a bite to eat and start writing as I'm meeting Mehmed Esad this afternoon. Yes, I shall not give up looking for you. Of course

468

not. No matter what that voice inside me says, nobody will ever stop me from finding you.

Just as 1908 led us to a bright new start filled with hope, so 1914 would be the first step towards calamity. It wasn't as though we were all spellbound by some needless and unfounded optimism but nobody was expecting a disaster of such massive and horrific proportions. I'm talking, of course, about the Great War. About the slaughter of people from all over the world at the hands of their fellow men and about the shedding of blood for more land, colonies and oil. About the Great Powers' and the super rich's relentless and unending lust for more money and greater profits. That calamity, the like of which the world had never seen, was gradually but inexorably closing in on us. We all knew. We could all sense it, and we were all trying desperately hard to avert it. Many of us were doing all we could to avert a war but there were others that were in the pro-war camp and the anti-war camp was too late to respond. They had been unable to stop the people that would decide to join the war from taking up the key positions in the apparatus of government. Incompetence, cowardice and excessive punctiliousness had destroyed all vestiges of common sense. The bullies and the thugs in our movement were in command.

Yes, I was blaming everybody for it, Talat Bey most of all, the same Talat Bey whose drive and belief I had once never doubted. But drive and belief are not enough to govern a country. Doesn't lifting a country that is staring ruin in the face back on to its feet require more? Was it possible to take the right political path and to continue on that route without an organisation made up of people who have sworn to dedicate their lives and their energies to it and who are ready to make the ultimate sacrifice for it? At one point, yes, we did have such a party. But now I was not so sure. We seemed to have lost the trust we once had in each other. That unshakeable sense of brotherhood and selflessness had been sacrificed for the sake of individual gain. Yes, Talat Bey's desire for us to overcome our corrupting urges by relying on one another and by being open to reflection and constructive criticism now just sounded like wishful thinking. Enver Bey would not give up in his attempts to become the minister, nor would the *fedaeen* stop acting like a second government and cease their interfering in ministerial affairs.

Around a year after our coup and the announcement that we had – finally – become the sole power in the land, the state now actually had not two but three heads. Sait Halim Paşa may have been the premier but there were three other men that wielded huge influence over the government: Talat, Enver and the party's rising star Cemal. Yes, we had one parliament, one government and a centuries-old palace but the final word in affairs of state always came down to one of these three men. Even worse was the fact that these three individuals, who were members of the same political party and who shared the same political vision, had now reached the stage where they were in open disagreement when it came to vital matters of national interest. We were falling apart but it was not being done behind closed doors. Rather, the whole country was watching it happen.

Enver Bey was not the only one that wanted to become Minister of War. Cemal Bey, who had become a central figure in our political lives after the assassination of Mahmud Şevket Paşa, was also after that post. It was incredible. Men that had once fought valiantly and honourably against the despotism of the state were now rivals vying with one other to climb the ladder of state officialdom. If it were to continue in this manner, then it would be just a matter of time before the guns began going off within the party.

With an uncanny sense of intuition, Fuad had foreseen it all yet so many other important figures, Talat Bey included, had not stopped to think that the factional divisions within the party would become so vast. As for me, one particularly shameful episode in order helped me grasp the depth and the gravity of this new state of affairs.

I'm talking, of course, about Enver Bey's operation. For some time now, the 'Hero of the Liberation' had been meaning to go to Germany for an operation for his appendicitis. Enver Bey was convinced it was only in Germany, where he had been stationed for two years as the government's Berlin attaché, that the doctors with the requisite skills for the operation could be found but for some reason he suddenly made a U-turn. As for me, it was only by pure coincidence that I found out about the operation.

The January of 1913 was bitterly cold. The waters froze over and the snow on the streets did not melt for days. We saw birds freeze to death and fall to the ground. One morning, when I woke up, I could not see Madam Melina anywhere, which was unheard of as usually she would not leave the house without preparing breakfast for me. I thought she may have gone to visit a neighbour when I suddenly heard moans coming from her bedroom. I knocked on the door but there was no answer. I gently pushed the door open. Madam Melina was in her bed looking very weak indeed. I touched her face. She was burning up. I placed a cold wet towel on her forehead and then went to the cupboard to see what medicines she had but I could not find anything. I ran out on to the street, hailed a carriage and somehow, after strenuous efforts, got her in.

There was a doctor I knew from Salonika at the German Hospital by the name of Salim Ensar and I instructed the driver to take us there as quickly as possible. The whole journey on those icy roads, all the way to Sıraselviler, I was terrified the poor woman would die in my lap. Nevertheless, I managed to get her to the hospital and once I'd hollered at the nurse standing at the entrance to get a move on, he and I managed to get Madam Melina onto a stretcher and carry her inside. The staff appeared in a flash and began tending to her but I told them I urgently needed to see Salim Ensar, the in-house internal medicine specialist.

'He's on the lower floor', a plump nurse said. 'He's operating on another patient down there right now. Someone quite important, apparently. He's been there for some time now. If you wait, he'll soon be up.'

Madam Melina's moans had turned into wheezes and we did not have much time to spare so I ran down to the floor below and into a long corridor lined with doors on both sides.

Which door would Salim Ensar be behind? I tried the first but it didn't open. The second door opened but there was nobody inside. As my hand reached for the knob on a third door, I suddenly felt a gun on the back of my neck.

'Hold it right there. Don't move. Hands up'.

I was stunned. I tried to turn around to see who it was but I received a sharp blow from the gun on my head.

'I said don't move'.

After crying out in pain, I tried talking to the mystery person.

'Look here, my friend. I don't know what you're trying to do but you're making a big mistake'

'I think you're the one that is making the mistake', he said and hit me again, and in the same place too.

'What the…! Why are you hitting me?' I spun around and came to face to face with Yakup Cemil. That's right, our very own Yakup Cemil, glaring at me through narrowed eyes! Standing next to him was Atıf, the same Atıf that had shot Şemsi Paşa five years earlier in Bitola, a man who was not just a hero of our movement but who had also been – at one time – one of my own personal idols.

'What the hell do you think you're doing?' I shouted. 'Don't you recognise me?'

'You'd better put your hands up, Şehsuvar', Atıf warned me. 'We need to frisk you'.

What was all this idiocy about? What were they up to? They knew who I was and yet their hostility remained.

'What's going on here?' I asked. 'Why the hell do you need to frisk me?'

With his free hand, Yakup pushed me up against a wall.

'We're looking for the gun, pal. The gun you are going to use to shoot Enver with.'

'What?' I was too stunned to talk. 'What in God's name are you talking about?'

'You know damn well what I'm talking about'. He turned to Atıf. 'Well? What are you standing there like that for? Search the man!'

'Have you both lost your minds or what?' I cried while Atıf began searching me. 'Why the hell would I shoot Enver?' I looked around the empty corridor. 'And what the hell is Enver doing down here anyway?'

'Don't pretend you don't know', Yakup said, openly belittling me. 'The real question is, what the hell are *you* doing down here? Running around like a mad man flinging all the doors open one by one. What's your game, eh? Who are you looking for?'

Something fishy was going on, that was for sure, so I took a deep breath and tried to explain myself.

'My landlady has a fever. Madam Melina... The poor woman may have pneumonia. She's taken a turn. I heard her moaning in pain this morning. When I found her, she was lying helpless in bed looking a complete state so I brought her here. I was looking for a friend of mine down here. Doctor Salim. Salim Ensar. What the hell are you guys doing here? Why did you attack me like that, like I'm carrying a bloody knife or something?'

'Don't try and play games with us', Yakup Cemil hissed. 'We know full well why you're here. We know the reason.'

'What reason, for crying out loud!' I shouted, finally losing my cool. I pushed away the gun that was resting on the tip of my nose. 'If you don't believe me, go upstairs and see for yourself. The poor woman is up there on a stretcher too weak to even stand.'

'I'll show you weak', he began and raised his gun to hit me in the face when Atıf stopped him.

'Hold on, hold on. He may be telling the truth. I mean, he doesn't have a gun on him for a start.'

Yakup didn't bring the gun down on to my face but he was still not convinced.

'Then he left it upstairs', he said suspiciously. 'Left it up there with his boys while he came down here so he could case the joint, assess the situation, see how many we are down here. Then he was going to go back up and tell the others. I'll bet you anything that brat Fuad is in this hospital somewhere.'

I couldn't take much more and lashed out.

'Enough! Enough of this madness! Why would Fuad come here? Why would we shoot Enver Bey?'

Atıf looked confused, whilst the hatred etched into Yakup's face was beginning to soften.

'And what the hell is Enver Bey doing in this hospital anyway? Or… Hold on. He's not hurt, is he? He hasn't been attacked or anything, he? Don't tell me there's been an attempt on his life?'

The two brutes exchanged glances, unsure as to whether I was being serious or just acting. Eventually, Atıf spoke up.

'You stay here', has he said to his brooding friend. 'I'll go upstairs and take a look around. Let's see if old Şehsuvar here is telling the truth, eh?'

Yakup, however, was not so sure.

'Don't worry', Atıf said. 'I'll be careful'. He then looked at me and gave a sly laugh. 'You're the one that should be careful. You know how cunning this college boy here is.'

As Atıf sped away, Yakup gestured with his gun to the door I had just opened.

'This way please, Mister Şehsuvar, sir. You and I will wait over here.'

I did as I was told. After all, he had the gun. But I made sure I let him know what I was thinking.

'What you're doing here is absolutely disgraceful. You're going to regret this,' I told him but the bully of the barracks was ready with his response.

'Actually what you're planning on doing is the disgrace. Sending Enver off to Germany and making Cemal the Minister for War while he's away, eh?'

I sputtered out my disbelief but in return, I got a rough shove in the back and a snapped order to get moving. 'Pretending you know nothing about it as well, I see. So Enver goes off to Germany for an operation leaving the field free for your Great Master and Cemal Bey to do what they want here. But Enver is nobody's fool. Didn't fall for your little plot, did he? Didn't rise to your bait, did he? That's why he chose to have the operation here, see? And of course, the moment you all found out, you decided to deal with him once and for all. Get rid of Enver Bey and then say he didn't make it through the operation, eh? Is that it? Isn't that why you're here?'

I was going to ask him if he actually believed what he was saying but he pushed me again.

'I didn't tell you to stop. Keep going. That's it. This way. Step inside.'

'Alright, alright. No need to push'.

I entered the room and walked over to the small table.

'Stop', he said. 'Stop. Now turn around and face me'.

I turned around. There was a gap of about a metre between us. He was pointing his gun at my face. The back of my head was stinging horribly and I could feel something warm trickling down my neck. Probably blood but I had to ignore it.

'Do you actually believe what you are saying?' I asked again. 'Talk sense, Yakup. We're all on the same side. Why would I want to kill Enver Bey? He's a hero to all of us.'

'You should ask yourself', he said despondently. He was now actually looking at me like a hurt child. 'Why don't any of you want Enver Bey to be Minister of War? You trying to tell me that that incompetent fool Izzet Paşa is a great soldier, is he? The man's a walking corpse. He can barely stand up and yet he's still the Minister. Why should he run the army when a man like Enver Bey is available?'

'You're right, Yakup', I said, hoping to calm him down by humouring him. 'I agree wholeheartedly but that decision is above both you and I. It's not our call. If there's a problem, then those responsible in the party and the government get together, talk it over and hammer out a solution. But suspecting one another? Pulling guns out on one other? Where is that going to get us? Didn't we all fight side by side for this country? Aren't we all soldiers fighting for the same cause? Haven't we all sat down at the same table and broken bread as brothers?'

'As brothers, eh?' he smirked. 'Exactly! That's what we've been trying to say all along. Tell me, why is it that Talat Bey can sit comfortably at that table as Minister for Internal Affairs but

Enver Bey has to be held back? Why is it that Cemal Bey can be made Minister for Public Works but making Enver Bey the Minister for War is somehow a step too far? Why? I'll tell you why. Because Enver Bey is a soldier. Because he chooses to go to the front and fight, rather than put his feet up in Istanbul and twiddle his thumbs. Who was the first person to take to the mountains in the fight to usher in the new constitution? Who fought hand to hand against the enemy out on the front line?'

It was infuriating listening to him lecture me, as though he was the one that had made all those sacrifices.

'You're preaching to the converted', I said. 'All those incidents you just mentioned – I was there too. Bitola, Salonika, Istanbul on the 31st of March, Libya… I was there. Remember?'

His frown disappeared and he averted his gaze.

'I don't mean you. I saw the way you fought in Libya. And I loved Basri Bey too, God bless his soul. I'm talking about the people that sit in the capital with their feet up and cause harm to the honourable sons of the soil while we are out there on the frontline fighting the enemy.'

'Then why are you still pointing that gun at me?'

The frown reappeared, the eyes narrowed and his arm, which had started to relax, was now pointing the gun at my face again.

'Enough with all these word games. I ain't falling for them.'

I shook my head dejectedly.

'Word games, eh Yakup? You think it's an enemy standing here in front of you?'

'I'm not joking, Şehsuvar. I swear, I'll pull the trigger.'

He would have too. The fact that he hadn't already done it was surprising enough. But he was behaving so foolishly and so recklessly that I lost my cool. I undid the buttons on my coat and tore into him.

'If you're going to do it, then do it! Go on! It's not like you haven't done it before. Only this time it's one of your own. Not that that makes any difference!'

We stood there, glaring at each other. It was all so ridiculous, being cornered in a hospital room like this, while the blood oozed from my throbbing head, but I no longer cared what happened.

'Okay, take it easy', Atıf's voice came through, breaking the tense silence. 'Şehsuvar is telling the truth. He really has brought his landlady here.'

Yakup Cemil turned to look at his friend but he was still not convinced.

'Well, are you sure it's actually her? They could both be lying, you know.'

That was going too far even for Atıf.

'I saw her with my own eyes, Yakup. The poor woman is up there burning up. For God's sake, put the gun away.' He turned and looked sheepishly at me. 'Sorry, Şehsuvar, old friend. It's just that seeing you madly flinging all these doors open one by one like that...' His gaze slid down to my coat. 'There's blood on your coat collar. Oh my god, your head is bleeding...'

He was shameless enough to actually express concern for me.

'No big deal, Atıf', I said, heading for the door. 'It's nothing. Now if you both don't mind, I have to go and find this doctor before poor Madam Melina pops it.'

I had only taken one step when a voice called out to me from behind.

'Hey, Şehsuvar! We've made a terrible mistake here. We're really sorry, but there's no need to make a big thing of it, eh? Talat Bey doesn't need to know. You know, for the sake of harmony in the party and all that.'

I turned and looked at Atıf with daggers in my eyes.

'No need to tell me. I'm not going to do anything that will threaten the unity of the party.'

I was about to walk off when I noticed Yakup Cemil smirking at me. I walked right up to him and said, 'Now look here, "pal." If you ever point that gun at me again, you better not lower it without pulling the trigger. If you do, I swear, you'll live to regret it.'

He grinned a nasty, malicious grin and replied, 'And don't you ever push away a gun I'm pointing at your face. If you do, I promise you, you'll be even more regretful.'

I didn't tell Talat Bey about the incident. Indeed, I didn't even mention it to Fuad either, just to be on the safe side. However, word got round to Talat as Yakup Cemil began bragging to the others that he'd given one of Talat's men a sound whack on the head. When Talat Bey saw me, he asked if me if Yakup Cemil had attacked me. I told him it was nothing serious but he was so incensed he wanted to know the details and so I had to tell him. However, I didn't want to cause a rift between him and Enver and so I also told him it was all Yakup Cemil's idea and that he had been acting on his own initiative. The Great Master nodded thoughtfully.

'I just wish it were that simple, Şehsuvar. But don't you worry, we'll sort all this out, and in a manner that befits our party and the government.'

The matter was resolved but not, as he had wished, in a manner befitting the party and the government. Rather, it was resolved in a manner that suited Enver's needs. He was made Minister of War at the beginning of the year. Cemal Bey was not left unsatisfied either and he was moved from his post at the Ministry of Public Works to the Ministry of the Navy, which meant that control over the Ottoman Empire was now de facto being shared by the three leaders of the Committee of Union and Progress. But of course, for Enver Bey, who was soon after awarded the title of pasha, even though it contravened the rules and the wishes of the army, sharing power was not enough…

Vultures Circling Over an Old Man

Hello Ester (Mid-Afternoon, Day 11)

When I left the hotel, it was around mid-afternoon. On the way out, I saw the English author at reception. She was checking out with a large group that was leaving Istanbul on the Orient Express. She smiled when she saw me. I even think she was going to stop to talk to me and ask me how I was, after having heard my screams the other night, but I was in no state to converse or explain what had happened and so I gave her a simple but courteous greeting and made for the door.

Outside, a restrained sun was gently, almost bashfully, warming up the city. The suffocating heat of yesterday had gone and a cool breeze was waltzing through the streets. The autumn we know so well had arrived. As is my habit, I looked around to see if anyone was watching me but there was no one. I suppose it is only expected that they would stop following me, seeing as I'll soon be working for them.

I picked up speed, despite the heady, lethargy-inducing sweetness of the weather. Mehmed Esad and I had not agreed upon a time but he had said something along the lines of afternoon, which meant I needed to walk a little faster if I was not to be late. As I was hurrying past the entrance of the Karlmann Arcade, which looks out on to the Tepebaşı Gardens, I bumped into someone. He was a small fellow and fell tumbling to the ground when we collided, the poor thing. It was my fault. I was in such a hurry, and so needlessly too, that I had not seen him coming out.

'I do apologise', I said, reaching out to help him up. 'I didn't mean it'.

The man stared at me.

'Şehsuvar…? Is that you?'

I remembered him now: the voice, the face, the look in his eye. It was an old classmate from high school.

'Arşak…? Wow! It is you!'

He grabbed my hand, got up and we embraced. He then looked me up and down.

'You've aged', he said, genuinely sad. 'But then I suppose I've aged even more'.

And he was right. His face was haggard and he looked at least around sixty, not that I said so.

'Oh come on, not that much. A little longer in the tooth than our first day in school perhaps, that's all. And that's only because you've got a few white hairs. So tell me, what have you been up to? How's business?'

'I don't live here anymore', he said, a little sheepishly and a little despondently too. 'I moved to Paris'.

'Why? Why did you leave Istanbul?'

'Well, I… I just did', he said and looked away. Obviously, he didn't want to talk about it so I didn't press him.

'But you're not going back straight away, are you? If you're here, let's meet up. We can have a few drinks, get something to eat and have a good old chat. You know you don't find taverns in Paris like the ones we have here.'

He smiled bitterly and shook his head.

'You know something? You're right. They haven't got inns there like ours. Sure! Let's meet up. Tomorrow evening at Maksim's, okay? I've heard a lot about it and I'm curious what kind of place it might be.'

I was delighted to have the chance to get together with an old friend.

'Excellent. Tomorrow. I'll wait for you at the front door'.

'Done'. He shook my hand firmly. 'Tomorrow at eight'.

As I carried walking along the European Arcade, I began thinking that my generation's time was up. Time has not only been quick with us, it has also been unfair. So many partings, so many deaths and exiles... Everyone I bump into seems to have aged; all the people from my past I happen to encounter seem to have grown old and given up. There is little point in denying it so I might as well accept it and come to terms with it otherwise I will barely be able to look myself in the mirror in the mornings.

When I got to the carpet store, passing by all those wild and colourful shop windows, I found Mehmed Esad on the ground floor. Rüşeym, the dark, mute gentleman, was nowhere to be seen. Mehmed was sitting on a stool drinking soda water from a green bottle and making a face.

'I hope it helps', I said as I walked in. 'You got a stomach ache or what?'

'Don't even ask. Too much of that fried aubergine, my friend. Stomach's been giving me hell me since last night.'

I was walking towards the other stool when he raised a hand.

'Let's not sit here. It's far too open. You go upstairs. I'll lower the shutters from the inside and come up and join you.'

He was right. It was hardly wise discussing supposedly top-secret government business in such a busy and crowded area. I went upstairs, where I saw a table on which were some sheets of paper featuring pencil-drawn pictures of human faces. Arab faces full of pain and suffering... Did Mehmed Esad also have a talent for art that he had kept hidden from us?

'Those are Rüşeym's'. I turned around and saw Mehmed Esad standing at the top of the stairs. 'This creature called man is a mystery, Şehsuvar. Can you believe a man without the ability to speak, and one without any education either, can conjure up such amazing pictures?'

A philosophising secret service agent... Not that I minded. It was nice to hear and I even managed to smile, although Mehmed misunderstood.

'I'm talking nonsense, aren't I?'

'Not at all. On the contrary, you're quite right. There's creativity inside everyone and one day it just erupts and comes to the surface... If only Rüşeyim could get some kind of formal training.'

'If only'. He sat on the chair behind the table. 'Well, what are you still standing for? Take a seat.' I did as told. 'I talked to some friends about this Çolak Cafer business. They're going to start making enquiries today. He must have been scared away by what happened to Cezmi and is now probably laying low somewhere. We'll find him eventually, of that you can be sure, but it may take some time. I just wanted you to know I'm on the case.'

'And Cezmi? Who killed him?'

For some reason, he looked away.

'We don't have any definitive information. My colleagues are making enquires. It could be something quite ordinary, to be honest. No, don't dismiss the possibility so quickly. You know what happened to Niyazi of Resen.'

'How could I not?' I smiled. 'I was the one that took him the coded message ordering him to take Tatar Osman Paşa to the mountains. A day later, the constitutional era was declared.'

'That's what I mean. Niyazi was a giant of a man. Put the fear of God into his enemies. They were so scared of him, they thought bullets couldn't harm him. That they would just bounce off him. And what happened to him in the end? Did he come to his end in front of a British firing squad? Or was he hanged after being tried in a Court of Independence? No. He was shot dead by some useless, no-good bum. The reasons behind the murder are still unknown. What I'm trying to say is that Major Cezmi's case may be similar. We'll soon find out...' He opened one of the desk's drawers, took out a yellow envelope and gave it to me. 'This is your first advance'.

I glanced down at the envelope.

'Looks like the government of the Republic is doing better than the Ottomans', I chuckled. 'Our wages were always paid late'.

'The country should not hold back in its sacrifices for those who in turn are ready to sacrifice all for their country,' he said proudly. He noticed I had not taken the envelope. 'This is yours, Şehsuvar. You've earned it. Please take it.'

It would have been meaningless to refuse the money after having agreed to work with him so I picked up the envelope and put it in my jacket pocket. But I still couldn't hold back a wry smile.

'Why are you smiling?' he asked.

'Oh, it's nothing. It just feels weird getting paid by the government after all these years.'

'You deserve it, Şehsuvar', he said, looking at me admiringly. 'You're a good man. An honest man. That's why we were so intent upon working with you. There are so few honourable men around nowadays.'

'Well', I went on, still mockingly. 'What are this supposedly "honest" man's duties going to entail? What is he going to do for this fine country?'

'We need the old CUP guys', he said, unfazed by my sarcastic manner. 'We need to get in touch with them'.

'What for? What are you going to do with them?'

He shook his head.

'It's not what you think. We're not going to arrest or kill anybody. We're going to hire them, the way we have hired you. We want them to work for the good of the country. Why fight us when they can fight our enemies instead?'

'So they'll be armed? They'll be sent out to kill?'

He brought his hands together on the desk.

'Well, if the people on the other side are armed... If they try to take out one of us... But that won't be your job. We don't want you to shoot anybody. All you have to do is find the old CUP guys for us. But the serious ones, the heavies, the ones that were deep in, the experienced ones... We have no need for the ones who just drew or wrote or talked nonsense. We need guys like that friend of yours. The one who was also from Salonika, like you and I.... Fuad. He was a lieutenant in the organisation at one point, like me. Where is he now, for instance? We need guys like him. Cezmi, for example, would have been no good to us. Yes, he was a standout guy, brave and all, but he was hardly a sensible chap, and he ended up giving himself away anyway. The guys we need are as smart as they are experienced and courageous. Because this is under-cover stuff we're dealing with here.' He fell silent, giving me a few moments to think clearly. Seeing as I did not have any questions, he carried on. 'So what we want from you are guys like this. I'm talking about a group that will begin operations next year so we need to have the group up and running by the end of the year. We need time to prep and organise them. You know how it works.'

That is when I began to realise that the group was being set up to carry out a specific mission. It was the groundwork for a major operation that was going to be carried out the following year.

'Will these guys be official state employees?' I asked, probing him.

'Of course they will, but nobody will know about it. We shan't announce it and they won't tell anybody. That's how it has to be if we want the operations to be run successfully. But don't worry about that. We'll fill them in on that part. You just get us in touch with them. That will be enough for us. If you like, you don't even have to be personally involved. Just give us names and addresses, places where we can find them, and we'll handle the rest.'

'Handle the rest', I muttered. 'How are you going to handle it?'

He knew what I meant.

'If you like, I can swear on the *Qur'an*. We are not trying to arrest them, nor do we have any intention of eliminating them. There are so many of them anyway, which one would we start with? As you said, everyone in this country, all of us, we were all CUP once. We're not involving you in some plot. All we are doing is offering some proud patriots a chance to serve their country again. Ex-members of the Special Organisation, those that worked for the *Karakol Cemiyeti* during the occupation and the war of independence, old CUP hit men... We know these guys are all miserable, that they feel aggrieved and are waiting for the summons to serve again. You know that feeling too. That feeling of anger and unease at why the government of the new republic does not see you, at why Mustafa Kemal does not acknowledge any of you. Isn't that so? That's how you feel, isn't it? That's how the others feel, right?'

He was right. There was nothing in what he had said that could be refuted. If he was telling the truth, that is, and if he didn't have other, darker, intentions, although it was admittedly too late to dwell on such a possibility now. If he was lying and he really was tricking me, then I would no doubt find out in the course of my mission, which is why I didn't raise any objections.

'You're right, Mehmed. That is how they feel. If you ask me, they'll grab the government's offer with both hands. They'll jump at the chance. Right, I'll start looking around. Tell me, is this going to be our meeting place? Will we always meet here? And will I carry on staying at the Pera Palace? Or should I go back home?'

'I don't think you should leave the Pera Palace, at least not for not. Stay there a little longer. And don't worry about money. We'll cover the costs. We can meet either here or at the hotel. Maybe even over a few drinks now and then. That way, we won't be attracting too much attention. I mean, who's going to suspect two old friends getting together for a few drinks?'

Who would suspect us anyway? I thought to myself. Who would bother following and watching us if we both worked for the state? I tried not to dwell on it as I assumed my old friend knew something I didn't. And I was also glad at being able to stay in the Pera Palace a little longer, at least until I tracked you down. When I left Mehmed Esad's, I went straight back to the hotel, even though it was a glorious evening and things now seemed to be working in my favour. The huge, imposing walls of the labyrinth I am stuck in are beginning to come down one by one, and with little effort on my part either. It's as though an invisible hand is helping me... But something isn't quite right. I don't know what it is but it is making me uncomfortable. It isn't something that can be understood rationally but more a feeling, a feeling acquired through experience. It is all too good, too right and too logical, and things never go so smoothly and so flawlessly. Something isn't right. I don't know what it is but I can sense it. I am sure something is wrong. I'll find out soon enough anyway so...

When I got back to the hotel, I sat at my desk and went back to the darkness of 1914. Winter had come to an end and the first traces of spring could be felt in the air. Although it had been two months since Madam Melina had left the hospital, she was still a little gaunt and was often struck by coughing fits. However, the worst was over and she had all but returned to her former health. Of course, my standing in the house was at an all-time high and she was treating me like royalty. We were experiencing major shortages but with the ingredients she did manage to get her hands on, she was cooking up wonders. She kept my room warm all day, as though I was the one that had just recovered from an illness and not her, and my clothes were washed, dried and pressed on an almost daily basis, my every need and whim lovingly catered to. I would not be exaggerating were I to say that I had not seen such affection and such appreciation from my dear late mother. It was on one of those typical mornings when she had prepared a sumptuous breakfast that she handed me a copy of the day's *Tanin* newspaper with a smile and said, 'Your Enver Paşa has finally got what he wanted. He's now a member of the royal family.'

The news was on the front page of the paper. The headline read *'Enver Paşa joins the imperial household'*. Underneath was the news that 'Enver Paşa, the Minister of War, Hero of the Liberation and Conqueror of Edirne, has married Naciye Sultan'. It went on to say that a number of distinguished guests had attended the wedding, which took place at Damat Ferit Paşa's mansion.

'They say she's on the young side. But Enver Bey is a handsome man. He has a certain charm...'

When they were engaged, Naciye Sultan was still just a child, around eleven years old. Actually, it was a political marriage and had taken place at the request of the CUP, the idea being that some of the hostility that existed between us and the Ottoman nobility could be defused were some of us to marry girls with royal blood. That is why, for example, Hafiz Hakkı, one of our men, married into the royal family. However, with Enver, things took on a strange turn. Despite having never seen each other and having only ever communicated via letters, Enver Bey still fell madly in love with Naciye Sultan. Even Talat Bey, who absolutely despised discussing people's private lives, could not help but comment on this odd arrangement.

'That's our Enver. He's a strange man. Head over heels for a woman he's never seen and only knows via his mother's description of her. In love, just as he is in politics, he's chasing after illusions rather than reality.'

I remember Zabit Akif, Enver Bey's aide-de-camp, telling me in Libya that Enver wrote whenever he could and that, 'It is only during two activities that that look of intense passion appears on Enver's face – when he is waging war and when he is writing.'

There were those that saw Enver's marriage as part of his wish to become Minister of War and of his coveting the title of pasha before having attained the requisite seniority. Fuad, for one, said, 'Our patriotism and our devotion to the party, the movement and the revolution aside, there is one other characteristic that we have in common; apart from Prince Sabahattin and a few others like him, we all rose up from the lower or the middle classes. Perhaps that explains our attitude when it comes to the palace. Our distaste at the padishah wielding absolute power is the root of our desire for constitutional reform. But at the same time, we are caught up in a strange contradiction. On the one hand, we have this deep resentment of the palace, while on the other we bemoan the fact that we are not in its place. And this accursed paradox permeates all of us in the party, from the very top all the way down to the guys in the lowest ranks. And if you ask me, Enver Bey is also tormented by this bind. That is why he insists upon the post at the Ministry of War, and it is also why he has waited a full three years to marry into the imperial household. He wants to accrue as much as glory, honour, rank, title and reputation as he can before the wedding because he hopes to narrow the gap in social class between himself and his bride-to-be.'

I couldn't agree or disagree with Fuad's observations in full because I did not know Enver that well. But I did know that he was an incredibly ambitious and driven man.

'So, Şehsuvar my lad', Madam Melina said, bringing me back to the here and now. 'Tell me, when are we going to see *your* happy day?'

I folded the paper and put it away at the edge of the table.

'When I'm Enver Paşa's age. He must be around thirty-three or so now. I still haven't reached thirty.' I gave a little chuckle. 'And anyway, where am I going to find the right girl? The times are hard, Madam Melina. Decent, honourable people are hard to find.'

'Alas my boy', she said, naïve enough to take me seriously. 'You're right. The country is in such a state, it's hard to tell who is who. But surely you must have known a nice girl in that Salonika of yours? A nice decent girl from a good family?'

For a second, I thought about telling her about you. About the first time we met, about the love that bloomed between us, about our unfulfilled dreams, about our tragic story and its unsatisfactory finale. But then I decided not to. She was a decent and sensitive woman and I did not want to upset her.

'I'm afraid I don't, Madam Melina', I said, reaching for my coffee, now starting to get cold. 'There was no one in Salonika and there is no one here'.

At that moment, it struck me: history treats some with love, while with others it is merciless. While it brings some people together, others it wrenches apart. I'm talking about the events that began in 1908. While the constitutional period hindered any chance of happiness I had with you, it brought Enver Bey and Naciye Sultan together in marital bliss. And no, I am not bitter at anyone or resentful towards them in particular. Nor am I saying that this is our fate, because it is my choices and my decisions that have led to this and I therefore have to bear the consequences. But I also realised another truth while at that breakfast table. As a country collapses, some people rise to the top. When a nation is beset by ill fortune, others sense their opportunity and make hay, as the saying goes. Enver Bey was one of those that had come out on top. There was no great victory of any substance at hand of which to speak and the country was spiralling downwards into madness, so what cause did he have to act so triumphantly and so jubilantly? Yes, we may have recaptured Edirne but we had also lost even greater swathes of territory. The masses were struggling to make ends meet, nobody knew what independence would bring, belief in a better future had vanished and few, if any, had any hope left. Resignation and surrender seemed to careering through the land like a hurricane and worse still, the Great War was looming.

It was time to be smart. The general feeling in the party was that we needed a sound and expert plan for peace, not a rash foreign policy adventure. Whether it was Talat Bey, Cemal Bey or Cavit Bey, no one in the party wanted us to take part in the bloody conflict that was knocking on the door, but unfortunately, the country was not being run by common sense and reality but by power. He who had the power had the right to speak and decide, and recently, it was neither Talat nor Cemal that had that kind of power, either in the workings of the party or in the government, or, indeed, in the country as a whole. Since 1908, the man whose star had been rising was Enver Bey, 'the Hero of the Liberation' and 'the Conqueror of Edirne', and now a beloved *damat* of the palace. Had Talat Bey played it shrewd and not made him Minister of War, the end results would have been different but now nobody could stop him in his wild pursuit of his ambitions. Forget about stopping him, nobody could even stand in front of him. And that is exactly what happened, or rather, failed to happen. During that scorching hot summer, just six days after the start of the war, a secret military alliance was signed with the Germans. That's right. Just a few days after the Serbian nationalist Gavrilo Princip killed Archduke

Ferdinand, the heir to the throne of the Austro-Hungarian Empire, we signed an agreement with the Germans.

Actually, the negotiations had begun a lot earlier. Like everyone else, the Germans also knew that war was imminent and they wanted the Ottomans on their side, no matter what. However, things were a little more complicated on our side. For some reason, the Ottoman delegation kept the negotiations secret not just from the British, the French and the Russians but from the government and the party too, Cemal Paşa included. And, whenever there was shady business afoot, our help was needed.

The task of picking Talat Bey up from his location and escorting him to the mansion where the talks were being held without the knowledge of the general public fell once again to Fuad and I. We had no idea about what was going on. We just assumed that Talat Bey was going to be dealing with sensitive and confidential matters, seeing as he had summoned two *fedaeen* to guard him rather than his official state bodyguards. And of course when we saw Enver Bey amongst those attending the meeting, we realised how important our mission was. However, we did not realise the talks were about a possible alliance until we saw Baron Konrad von Wangenheim, the German envoy to Constantinople, turn up, the last of the participants to do so, and stride purposefully into the small garden that made up the grounds of the mansion.

'Well, that's that then', Fuad muttered. 'Looks like we're going to war alongside the Germans.' I was sitting in the driver's seat of the car parked in the shade of a magnolia tree on the corner of the street, where we had a clear view of the house. Fuad was slumped on the seat next to me.

'I doubt it', I said, basing my views on what Talat Bey had been saying. 'We'll remain neutral in this war. It's another issue they're discussing with the Germans.'

He had been staring at the house but now he turned to look at me.

'You're so gullible, Şehsuvar. The stage is being prepared for a play in there. A play more dramatic than anything

Shakespeare ever wrote. A tragedy that will drown the entire world in blood.'

'You see everything in theatrical terms', I said, trying to make light of it.

'You want to bet on it?' He sounded very sure of himself. 'And I mean a real bet. Dinner at the Tokatlıyan, not some titbits at a dive like Yorgo's tavern.'

I was a little confused but I was game.

'If you're up for it, sure. But how will we find out what they're discussing inside?'

'You're going to ask them', he said with a smirk. 'You're Talat Bey's guy after all, aren't you?'

I shook my head.

'Are you mad, Fuad? No way. They're holding top-secret discussions in there and you think I'm just going to swan on in and ask them what it's all about? No way.'

'Very well, then we'll get the Great Master to talk together'.

'And how is that going to happen?'

'Leave that to me', he said, opening a window to let in some fresh air. 'But when it's your turn to talk, don't you go all quiet. You better talk too.'

After three hours of talks, an irate looking Talat Bey emerged and climbed into the car.

'Let's go, gentlemen', he said despondently. 'You can drop me off at the top of the hill in Zeyrek where you picked me up the other day.'

I started the car, which juddered into life, and we set off. As we were leaving, we saw Enver Paşa and Baron Von Wangenheim leave the mansion together and, in contrast to Talat Bey's gloomy countenance, they both looked quite cheery. Baron Von Wangeheim was smoking a cigar, whilst Enver Paşa puffed happily away on a cigarette. Indeed, they looked positively buoyant as they ambled through the garden, and it had not escaped Talat Bey's notice either, as he also watched them carefully until we were out of sight. If a question was going to be asked, then now was the time but Fuad was sitting there as quiet as a mouse. Evidently, I was the one that had to take the bull by the horns.

'Talat Bey', I began courteously. 'If you wouldn't mind, I would like to ask you something.' I was trying to catch a glimpse of his face in the rear-view mirror while I spoke.

'What...? Sorry. Erm, yes, of course Şehsuvar.'

He had caught me looking at him in the mirror and now he was staring at me. I shifted nervously in my seat.

'You don't have to answer, of course. What I mean is...'

He was a smart man and when he saw I couldn't finish what I was saying, he sensed the topic.

'Sure I'll answer', he shrugged. 'Why wouldn't I?'

'What I mean is, if it's something confidential....'

'Ask away, Şehsuvar. Stop blabbering and just get on with it.'

Well, he had given me the all clear. I was free to ask.

'Are we going to be allies with Germany? Because I thought we were going to remain neutral when the war begins? Or has the Central Committee changed its mind?'

The anger on his face when I looked at him was so intense, I instantly regretted asking him. I was also furious at myself for falling for Fuad's silly bet.

'Give me a cigarette', Talat Bey snarled from the back seat. 'I smoked all mine back there. Give me one of yours.'

Fuad was the first to react. He opened his case and held it out for the Great Master, who took one out and lit it unhurriedly. The inside of the car was soon filled with the sweet scent of burning tobacco.

'How can we be neutral if a war has yet to start? Is this the information your sources are providing you?'

He was openly mocking us and I thought he was about to give us both a stern scolding when Fuad stepped in.

'Please, Talat Bey. We're not that naïve. It's just a matter of time before the Austro-Hungarian Empire attacks Serbia. You think they're going to take the assassination of Archduke Ferdinand lying down?'

He laughed. 'Well, at least you're keeping close tabs on international events. Kudos to that.'

'Well, if we don't know what's happening in the wider world, we can never truly know what's happening at home.'

He took a deep drag from his cigarette.

'Very true. Many of the problems we're facing today have their origins in overseas developments. Yes, war is on our doorstep. On that we can all agree. So tell me, what do you two think we should do? What are your recommendations?'

'Remain neutral', I said without hesitation. 'After all, wasn't that the party's original decision? Why do we want to get involved in what may be a very bloody conflict?'

'You're right', he sighed. 'We have no business in it. And you're also right in saying the party's original decision was to stay out of it. Actually, if you look at it, we can still stay neutral. Nothing has been signed yet. But to remain neutral and stay out of the war, we need a lot more power than we currently have. That is why even a peace agreement may still be signed. Because we cannot defend ourselves by sitting at the table with this pack of wolves that can smell blood and simply tell them we're not getting involved so please, kindly don't come interfering in our affairs. And shall I tell you why we can't tell them that? Because we are amongst the causes of the war that is soon going to break out.

'That Serb Gavrilo Princip's assassination of Franz Ferdinand in Sarajevo is just the pretext. The real reason behind this impending war is not the assassination of the Archduke but the insatiable greed of the Great Powers. We tried, my friends. Believe me, we tried. Cavit Bey went to England with an offer, Cemal Bey tried to sway the French, and just this last May, I was in talks with the Russians. None of them want to form alliances with us. They all have their eyes on our lands. They are like vultures circling over an old man, waiting for us to give up the ghost.'

He fell silent and looked away helplessly at the street rushing past.

'They want all of this. All that is out there. These houses, these trees, this sea, this city. Whatever brings them money, whatever we have, everything. If we declare our neutrality, there is no guarantee that the Russians won't invade Istanbul. 'We'll fight to the last man, to the last drop of blood,' we say.

That is all well and good but the country cannot be defended with heroic oratory and bombastic statements.'

He looked at me again in the rear-view mirror.

'So you tell me, gentlemen. What are we to do in such straits? What do you say, Şehsuvar? What's your suggestion?'

Neither of us said anything in response, even though there was so much to say. For instance, we could have told him that had we not stormed the *Bab-ı Âli* and overthrown the government of Kamil Paşa, we would now not be standing off against the British, because the British thought Germany was behind our coup. We could, for instance, have said that perhaps the French would not be against us now had we not been on such cordial and intimate terms with the Germans. We could have also said that instead of approaching the Russians with a sudden offer of friendship when there was nothing substantial on the table, it would have been better to take a long-term view of our relationship with them and build up the friendship over the years incrementally. But we didn't say any of these things because I believed in Talat Bey's honesty and his despondency was proof enough for me. Had I not believed him and had I openly spoken my mind and criticised him, it would not have made much difference anyway. And had he listened to my criticisms and taken them into consideration and even agreed with them, that would not have done any good either because Talat Bey was no longer the power in the country. It was Enver Paşa, and no matter what we or anybody else said, he would do whatever he wanted and whatever he thought was best. He would listen to no one, not in the party, nor in the government. So far gone was he that he would even invent the 'Enveriye Alphabet', his own alphabetic script for the army. Furthermore, the German supply wagons sent to our country would not bear the stamp of 'Ottoman Empire' but a new word: 'Enverland'. I suppose it was only right, as the man of the moment, the ruler in the new era, was the glorious Enver Paşa. So yes, it was too late for us to speak up. We would be allies with Germany because that it what Enver wanted and we would join the Great War because that is what the Germans wanted.

Ignoble Alliances

Good Evening, Ester (Evening, Day 11)

I wasn't wrong, Ester. I had been right to worry. I'd sensed it all along. Nothing ever goes this smoothly. I had a feeling something would go wrong eventually. But I must confess, even I had not been expecting this much. A huge surprise, a thrill, a hope reborn... Yes, someone tonight made my nightmare come true. I'm talking about the nightmare I keep having, the one that takes place in the theatre. There I go again, losing my train of thought. I need to calm down. Calm down and relate everything that happened to me this evening one by one.

I'd eaten dinner in the hotel. I'd come down a little late, I think because I can no longer stand people. By this time, only three tables in the restaurant were occupied. I found a table in a quiet corner of the restaurant and ate my fill. A pleasant breeze was drifting in from the half-open window next to me. After dinner, I decided on taking a stroll, to get some fresh air, stretch my legs and enjoy the rather delightful autumn evening. I did not plan on going too far, just past the American Consulate, up to the 6th Municipality Headquarters and from there on to the square by the tramway tunnel, and perhaps stop to have a nice cup of coffee in one of the cafés there... That was the plan but alas, it was not to be.

Initially, when I stepped outside, I noticed nothing unusual but as I was walking past the Kroker Hotel, I had this awful feeling that I was being watched so I stopped and pretended to examine the displays in the windows of the Kroker

Hotel before turning around to see if I was being followed. There was nobody there. Just a car in front of the Pera Palace with its headlights on, which was quite normal as dozens of cars stopped by the hotel entrance every day. In short, there was nothing on the street that could be considered suspicious. Perhaps it was because of my bad memories of the Kroker Hotel that I felt I was being followed, of the effect of those seven unspeakable days I spent in its bloody, mouldy basement. By way of explanation, I told myself it must have been my sub-conscious remembering Istanbul during the occupation and the long walks I used to take through its eerie streets back then but only fifty metres later, I heard the sound of an approaching vehicle. I didn't pay much attention to it as there are cars driving along that street all day but after I had taken a few more steps, I heard screeching brakes. Before I could make head or tail of the situation, a car had pulled up next to me, the doors were flung open and two masked men jumped me. I managed to punch one of them in the face but I was not quick enough for the other one and he struck me on the head with a heavy object. My head started spinning and I felt I was going to throw up.

Then everything went dark.

When I came round, I found myself sitting on a stool. My hands were free but I had been blindfolded. I wanted to take the blindfold off when I heard a voice.

'You've forgotten. You've forgotten, Şehsuvar. You cannot take that blindfold off until we tell you to.'

The voice was familiar. I'd heard it before, many times, but I couldn't put a name to it.

'If you'd only forgotten your oath, that would still be forgiv-able, but you've forgotten everything about our party.'

What was going on? What the hell was he talking about?

'You can take the blindfold off now'.

I untied the black cloth. The sudden light hit my eyes, making me squint. Sitting on three stools in front of me were three men wearing black gowns with black hoods covering their heads. We were on a stage, a theatre stage, just like the one in my dreams, except this time there was no audience.

The rose pink seats were all empty, and I knew you wouldn't be there either. But the décor was the same as in my dreams and the place looked familiar too… I was pretty sure it was the Ferah Theatre on Şehzadebaşı Street, where I had been so many times to watch the plays.

'You swore an oath', the man with the familiar voice said. A hand came out from under the gown and he pointed at the table. 'You swore on the *Quran*, the flag and the gun. You swore to fight down to the last drop of blood in your body for freedom, brotherhood, equality, justice and the motherland.'

I was having what the French call *déjà vu*. Or was I dreaming again?

'So tell us, Şehsuvar Sami, Member Number 1117 of our fraternity, son of Emrullah Bey of Salonika, Head Teacher and School Inspector. Why have you not remained loyal to your vows?'

No, this was not a dream. This man was deadly serious. That is when I felt the pain. My head was throbbing and I was bringing my hands up to the back of my head to rub it when the same voice bellowed, 'Answer the question! Tell us, why have you not honoured your vows? Why have you betrayed your fraternity, your cause and your comrades?'

'I have not betrayed anybody', I said, lifting my arms and rubbing the back of my head. 'There is no longer a cause for me to betray'.

There was no open wound but there was a walnut-sized swelling on the back of my head. I then realised what was going on. All this was a test. Mehmed Esad still had doubts about me and so he had set up this little theatrical number to test my nerve. The fear that had begun to slowly creep up on me evaporated and I no longer saw the situation as serious. In fact, it was beginning to strike me as ludicrous. The man in the gown, however, was still completely immersed in his role.

'So you've lost faith', he said, in the manner of a judge.

I smiled bitterly and shook my head.

'No, I haven't lost my faith. Our party lost, that's all. At home and in the international arena, we were defeated. And quite soundly too, I should add.' I glanced at the *Quran* and the flag on the table. 'I have not wavered from my vows or my pledge. I fought for years for those ideals and I shed blood for them, others' and my own. But we lost. The Committee for Union and Progress is over. I shall not deny that I had a role to play in this. But there are countless others that must be held to account before I am accused.'

He paused but not for long.

'Very well. What if the movement were to be re-established? What if it were to recommence its activities?'

Either these men were idiots or they did not know me at all. Here they were, trying to ambush me in the most… I started laughing at the absurdity of it all.

'What are you laughing at? What's so funny?'

'I'm sorry but isn't all this just a tad ludicrous? You hit a man on the back of the head and knock him out and then you try to coax him into a joining a secret society!' There were a few moments of silence before I continued. 'I joined the CUP willingly but you brought me here by force. Tell me, how will you be able to trust someone you have coerced into joining the party?' I looked at each hooded figure in turn, as though I could see their faces. 'Gentlemen, don't you realise? It's all over. There is no longer a Committee for Union and Progress. If you want to fight for your country, then lend your support to the republic. Wasn't that our goal in the first place?'

'But they slaughtered our friends', the man in the middle shouted. 'They killed Kara Kemal, the man you once worked with. They killed your closest comrade-in-arms.' All of a sudden, he removed his hood.

My jaw dropped. I could not believe what I was seeing. There in front of me was perhaps the only true friend I had ever had, the man I had loved more than a brother: it was Fuad. The voice I had been trying to identify was his, but still I had to make sure. I looked at his thinning hair and at his slightly greying moustache. 'Fuad, My friend, My brother! Is it really you?' I asked.

Despite my surprise and delight at seeing him, he remained stern and aloof.

'Yes Şehsuvar, it's me. I could not bear to see you being so indifferent and so callous and so I came myself. Don't you realise, Şehsuvar? We have to do something. They're killing us. Don't you see that? They're hunting us down and killing us, one by one, wherever they find us.'

While he spoke, my mind began churning out the possibilities. Was he in cahoots with Mehmed Esad? Had he sent Fuad to test me? Is this why Mehmed Esad had been asking after Fuad earlier?

'And we're just going to be quiet, are we? How much longer can we remain silent in the face of this oppression?'

He was trying to rile me up so he could found out my real opinions and my true motives. I didn't care but I did not want to lose the prospect of finding you so I said what needed to be said.

'These are brutal times we are going through, Fuad', I said calmly. 'History is being written anew and terrible mistakes may be made. We need to wait. Ankara will soon know that things cannot go on like this. Eventually...' I smiled. 'Tell me, old friend, how are you? Where have you been all these years?'

He looked disappointed.

'Forget about all that now. So what you're saying is you're out?'

I held up my arms to stop him.

'Out of what, Fuad? Don't you see? It's over! There is no more party! No party, no movement. What we did have, Mustafa Kemal has finished off. Nobody now will allow you guys to regroup. Mustafa Kemal warned Kara Kemal years ago. Told him in no uncertain terms that he was not prepared to share power with anyone. Told him during the War of Independence, before the Republic was even founded, when they didn't even have power. Aren't you aware of the consequences of the attempted assassination in Izmir? Haven't you been following developments? They almost hanged a man as eminent as Kâzım Karabekir. So I'm sorry, my dear Fuad, but there is no point in getting entangled in an unnecessary adventure. Can't you see there is no more CUP?'

'Then why are you still in touch with them?' he said, his nostrils flaring angrily. 'Why are you still in touch with the old guys?'

Was he talking about Cezmi? Who else could it be? I could see now how meeting our old captain had been a ghastly mistake on my part, the consequences of which I was still having to endure.

'Well, you know Cezmi, bless him. He was an old friend. You and I even met him together. During the 31st of March Uprising, at the house in Şehzadebaşı. You remember, don't you? I went there because I hadn't been to that house in ages.'

'I'm not talking about Cezmi', he said gruffly. 'Cezmi was a wretched old fool. He was soft in the head. I'm talking about your meetings with Mehmed Esad. Why are you meeting up with an old *ittihatçı* if the CUP is now defunct?'

Well, well, well. This was a turn! Had Fuad decided to play his hand? Or were they trying to find out what I was thinking about Mehmed Esad? Or perhaps they were trying to figure out how tight-lipped I could actually be?

'Yes, he's an old *ittihatçı* but he's also an old friend. I don't care if he is ex-CUP or not, I see him because he's an old friend of mine. Before you joined Basri Bey's squad, Mehmed Esad was one of us. You know that. Now, we just have a few glasses of *rakı* and chinwag about the old days. You can come along too and join us one day if you like. We'll have a few drinks and reminisce. But I'll say one thing now and that is that Mehmed does not have any connection with the old boys. I can even say he approves of the current government's policies.'

He looked at me suspiciously.

'So he didn't ask you for anything?'

'Of course not', I said, keeping up the lie. 'What could he want from me? A partnership? A venture? What?'

He didn't believe me. He knew perfectly well what was going on between Mehmed Esad and I; they were in it together and were testing me out. What they were doing was commendable and most certainly worthy of respect; it is how a secret service should operate. But I was in no mood to congratulate them on their professionalism. I just smiled and pointed to the two other hooded men.

'Are these two guys just going to sit there like this the whole time?'

'Well, if you're not going to join us', Fuad answered, staying serious, 'Why should I show you their faces?'

I didn't want to become embroiled in a prolonged debate and so I retreated.

'You're right. You're absolutely right. But I'm still happy to see you, old friend. None of these theatrics were actually needed, by the way. You've known all along that I've been staying at the Pera Palace so you should have just stopped by. In fact, the offer is still there. Pop in and we'll have something to eat together and remember the old days.'

A devilish glimmer flashed in his blue eyes.

'You don't think we're going to let you out of here alive, do you?'

'Well, I can't say you were that hospitable in bringing me here but I'm sure you'll be a lot more courteous when escorting me out.' I looked down at the revolver on the table. 'Somehow I don't think you're going to shoot an old friend who wishes you no harm. You are not that foolish, nor that cruel.'

The last sentence I uttered in a stinging tone.

'My apologies', he said, looking away. 'If you hadn't resisted, we wouldn't have hit you. But you went and broke our man's nose. Took us ages to stop the bleeding.'

My hand went up to the back of my neck again. The swelling was still there, and it was getting bigger.

'Yeah, well, your boys aren't that bad either. Still, not to worry. We're made of sterner stuff. That much is to be expected.' I looked at him affectionately. 'But I am happy to see you again, really, and I'd love to see you again.' I looked around at our surroundings. 'How did you manage to get the Ferah Theatre, by the way? Is this place being run by an old CUP guy or what?'

He smiled proudly.

'You underestimate us but we still have people on the ground.'

I wanted to get up but he signalled for me to sit down and turned to the other two mystery figures.

'If you could leave us alone now'.

Such was the authority in his voice that there was no need for him to raise his voice, repeat the command or provide any kind of explanation. Like two actors damned by only mild applause from the audience, they shuffled off stage.

'So did you find Mahinur?' I asked once they were out of sight. 'Last time I saw you, you told me you were trying to bring her and her family over. Did they manage to get here during the population exchange of 1923?'

His face fell.

'Afraid not, Şehsuvar. I couldn't find them. Neither her nor her family. She upped sticks and left Salonika in 1915 with her family. With her father old Uncle Naki, her mother Aunt Mevlide and her sister Mahperi. That was it. Nobody has seen or heard a thing about them since.' He sighed. 'All I can do is hope that they have survived and that they have settled down in some village somewhere in Macedonia. I hope she's settled down, found a husband and had kids.'

I was quiet. I didn't know what to say.

'So tell me, Şehsuvar old chum, how have you been? You got a job? How have you been getting by?'

This was the real Fuad talking now, the old Fuad, a friend who cared.

'An inheritance. Left to me by a Greek lady who wasn't even a relative… You knew her, actually. Madam Melina, my old landlady, God bless her soul. That wonderful lady left everything she had to me in her will. It lets me live a modest life. I also do some translation work, that kind of thing.'

'And marriage? Kids?'

I shook my head glumly.

'Afraid not, old boy. Never got married.' I noticed the look of concern on his face at my answer and felt the need to clarify. 'But I'm fine. I never really wanted to get married anyway.'

'Something to do with Ester?'

I was not expecting such a question. I was going to say no but I had told so many lies in my life by now that I was fed up.

'Yep. Something to do with her. I never managed to close that particular chapter, Fuad. It may not be love... But a feeling of incompleteness. A feeling of being stuck in the middle. Halfway. Like I have two lives. One, the life I have led and am living now, and the other, the life I could have had with her. The second one froze the day she left me...'

I suddenly blushed. Why was I sharing such personal information with him? Yes, he knew about you, and there was a time when we were close enough to share our secrets but years had passed since and the man standing in front of me now was not the same man I once knew and loved. For all I knew, he could be an enemy out to hurt me.

'I don't know if you've heard but Monsieur Leon is in Istanbul.'

It was like a bolt from the blue. He said it with a hint of sadness but I didn't mind. What mattered was that it was a lead that could – perhaps – take me to you. He saw the gleam in my eyes and went on.

'It's true. One of our men, a reliable one, bumped into him. Even sat and chatted about the old days with him. He lives here apparently...'

I didn't even bother with patience or niceties.

'His address? Can we find his address?'

Clearly he could but for some reason he hesitated. Or was he going to blackmail me too, like Mehmed Esad? Dark thoughts began forming in my mind when he spoke up.

'Sure we can. I'll send someone over to your hotel tomorrow. He'll give you the address.'

All my worries had gone, as had the throbbing pain in my head.

'Thanks, Fuad. Really. Thanks a lot'.

We shook hands warmly but before I left, he went back to being the party man.

'Think things over again. I'm thinking of reforming the party. Bringing it back. Actually, I have a plan. I can tell you about it if you like. If you change your mind, that is.'

I shook my head firmly, as though to say, *don't do this to me, Fuad,* but he didn't care.

'We'll meet again. You think things over. We'll meet again.'

So, darling Ester, that's how it is. An adventure that began this evening with fear and trepidation ended in a fresh surge of hope. Fortune has smiled down upon me. Let us now see what the future will bring.

When I got back to the hotel, I asked for some ice from the restaurant and pressed it down on the swelling on the back of my head. Once I began feeling better, I sat at my desk. I was still unable to make sense of what had happened. There were logical explanations, yes, but the ones I was coming up with were all tenuous, to say the least. I really did not know what was happening. The last time Fuad and I had seen each other was the winter of 1914, a full twelve years ago, before leaving for the Iraqi front with Süleyman Askeri Bey. Süleyman Askeri Bey was one of the first directors of the *Teşkilat-i Mahsusa*, the Ottoman Secret Service, and we were under his command. Fuad and he did not see eye to eye at first but once they got to know each other better, they warmed to each other. And once the Great War started, they could not stand the plots and intrigues raging in Istanbul and asked to be posted to the front. I remember something Fuad said to me as he was leaving. 'There is only way to maintain one's honour in this day and age and that is to die. And that is what I am going for. To make that happen.'

Since then, I had received news about him only in dribs and drabs. Some say he had gone with Enver Paşa to rouse the Central Asian Turks to revolution, whilst others say he had gone to Anatolia to join the National Defence Movement. It was hard to tell which pieces of information were true and which were just rumours, and yet now here he was, right in front of me, and a die-hard CUP man again, in stark contrast to the winter of 1914, when his view of the party had been nearing rock bottom. Had defeat changed his stance? That would have been odd, as defeat should have only increased his mistrust in the party, as it had for most of the rest of us. So anyway, the long and the short of it is that I am being dragged along in a mystery I have yet to unravel. However, one thing I am sure of is this, and that is that it will not last long and that the games and the duplicities will soon be revealed, which is also why I need to finish my story as soon as possible. I need to write it all down for you because if and when this mystery is solved, I do not think it will end well for me.

So let us return to the past, to the summer of 1914. Talks with the Germans were proceeding at full speed and no doubt Talat Paşa, Enver Paşa and Baron von Wangenheim were all present at those top-secret meetings. Sometimes guys from our side and other, trustworthy guys from the German camp would be seen coming and going from the various buildings in which the meetings were being held. The final meeting took place in Sait Halim Paşa's *Aslanlı Yalı* mansion in Yeniköy, on the shores of the Bosphorus. It took place six days after the Austro-Hungarian Empire had invaded and occupied Serbia, signalling the first manoeuvres of what would, tragically, turn into the Great War. The world was on tenterhooks and it was just a matter of time before the conflagration that was enveloping Europe reached us. We were the first to go in and were soon followed by Enver Paşa and Baron Konrad von Wangenheim. The three men that would decide the fate of the country were in the building together.

'You see, Şehsuvar?' Fuad said to me. 'The agreement will be signed today. They finally swayed Sait Halim Paşa. Any other way and it would not have been possible. The disaster that Talat Bey has been trying to warn us about for so long is becoming a reality.'

I tried to keep things light-hearted.

'Okay, okay, I get it. You win. I accept it. Don't worry, you'll get your slap-up meal at the Tokatlıyan.'

He didn't even smile. He just shook his head with the pessimism of a seer that could sense the impending catastrophe.

'Don't bother. There's nothing to celebrate. There are no winners in our bet. We've all lost. The war began a week ago and now we are entering into an alliance with the Germans. This is not going to end well, Şehsuvar. Mark my words.'

I didn't know what to say so I stayed silent. However, when Talat Bey came out of the meeting, he did have some good news for us, although it was about another matter.

'Two weeks from today at eleven o'clock, go to this address', he said and handed us a piece of paper. 'Süleyman Askeri Bey will be expecting you. You too, Fuad my lad. You'll be going too.' He gave a chuckle. 'Looks like your company is about to go public.' He looked surprised as he expected us to be happy at the news, as though it was something we had wanted for a long time. 'What's wrong? You don't seem overly happy?'

'Are we going to war?' It was Fuad that asked. All respect and reserve had been cast aside and his blue eyes were almost insolently fixed on the Great Master, challenging him. 'Have we joined the Central Powers?'

Talat Bey was taken aback and was rather stern in his response.

'No. What gave you that idea? Nobody is going to war. We're just taking necessary measures to ensure we are not harmed by the war, that's all.'

Fuad did not believe him, naturally, while I was still unsure. I truly believed that the Great Master did not want to enter the war but Enver Paşa was another matter and Talat Bey simply could not get Enver to listen. Nevertheless, I didn't think Talat Bey was the type to give in easily and I just assumed, hard task thought it was, that he was out there playing for time and trying to keep the Germans on our side whilst preserving our neutrality. Fuad did not press Talat Bey any further and the matter was closed. However, after we had dropped Talat Bey home, Fuad and I went to a restaurant for dinner, where he suddenly and unexpectedly asked me if I would be going to the meeting with Süleyman Askeri Bey. I stopped stirring my soup and looked at him. He looked pensive, as though he was on the brink of an important decision.

'Of course I will. Why shouldn't I? The work we've been doing honourably for so many years will finally be made legitimate.' I stopped. 'Why? Aren't you going to be there?'

'I don't know, Şehsuvar. Really, I don't know. My head is all messed up. If I could, I would just up sticks and leave but the memory of our fallen comrades just won't let me. And anyway, there's nowhere for me to go. No city, no homeland, no country. I don't know, Şehsuvar. I swear, I don't know, brother. But don't you think it's odd that an organisation that's been top secret for years is now being brought out into the open, right when we are on the brink of war? And by Enver Paşa too?'

'How do you know Enver Paşa is behind it?'

He looked at me incredulously.

'To whom does Süleyman Askeri report? Who is he close to? I bet you it's none other than our very own 'Hero of the Liberation' behind this decision.'

He uttered Enver Paşa's title with such disdain that I felt the need to warn him.

'Please, Fuad, don't talk about Enver Paşa like this in front of others. These are dangerous times we're living in. We don't know who is who and who may be listening in. No point in looking for trouble we don't need.'

His face fell.

'Just look at us. We're all members of the same party, all fighting for the same cause, and yet when it comes to expressing our feelings, we hesitate, as though we don't have the freedom to speak. And don't even get me started on fraternity, equality and justice.'

As always, he was right, but it fell to me to guide him in the right direction and keep a lid on things.

'That may be true but remember, Rome wasn't built in a day. Declaring independence is one thing but getting the support of the people is another matter entirely. It can't be done by laws or decrees. We need to get into their minds and make the concept of freedom a part of their lives, a part of their being. Liberty, fraternity, equality and justice: we have never abandoned these aims but we need to get the country back on its feet first if we are to achieve those goals. What we need is patience, resilience and trust…'

He'd heard such rhetoric so many times before that it no longer affected him and so I didn't persist. But I still felt the need to mention our meeting with Süleyman Askeri.

'But you have to come to this meeting. There is no point in turning your nose up at it when you don't even know what it will be about. And Süleyman Askeri is not a bad guy. I met him in Bitola, during that episode with Şemsi Paşa. He played a big part in getting Atıf out of that place in one piece. He also fought in Libya, and he fought well. Showed us all what he was capable of. And during the Balkan Wars, he went behind enemy lines and organised our guerrilla forces. In fact, he was Chief of General Staff for three months in the Turkish Republic of Thrace. Yes, he may be Enver Paşa's man but he's no Yakup Cemil. We hardly know him. Who knows, he may be a better man than we're making him out to be. This party is full of heroes. Men like Basri Bey.'

'Very well, Şehsuvar. I'll come. But not because I have any hopes or expectations from it but because I have no other options.'

When we parted ways that evening, he cut a dejected figure but he would later thank me for persuading him to come to the meeting. On the other hand, all Fuad's predictions were beginning to come true, and starting the very next day too. Only a day after we were told to meet at the *Aslanlı Yalı* mansion, Germany would declare war on France and two days after that, she would invade Belgium. There was no hiding it now – a bloody war had started in earnest and armies were now being sent off to invade and occupy other countries. But Talat Bey had also been right: the Ottoman state had not joined the war and had not declared war on anyone, which was good news for me at least as it allowed me keep on hoping that our leaders would find a way to keep us politically neutral throughout the conflict. That, however, and tragically, was not to be the case.

Two weeks later, when we met Süleyman Askeri at the Secret Service headquarters, the war was getting ever closer. As we walked through the wooden double doors, I was as nervous as Fuad. Much as I tried to pretend the situation was normal in order to dispel any fears and concerns Fuad may have had, I could not forget that unpleasant little incident with Yakup Cemil in the hospital and knowing Süleyman Askeri was as loyal to Enver Paşa as Yakup Cemil was, I was unsure as to how we would be greeted. However, when he saw us, I realised my fears were in vain. Süleyman Bey greeted both of us with great warmth and affection.

'I am so glad to see you, my dear friends', he said, shaking our hands. 'The last time we were together was in Benghazi. I swear by the Almighty, brother Şehsuvar, that day I thought you were dead. You had lost so much blood, it was a miracle you pulled through. Believe me, I was so relieved when I heard you were back to full health.'

It was tempting to believe he was saying it just for the sake of appearances but I felt he actually meant it.

'Thank you, sir', I said, smiling appreciatively. 'Thanks to you, I was able to evade Azrail himself. Had you not forced those Italians back, I would have been stranded there in the middle of the battlefield, amongst the dead and wounded. Had the enemy gotten their hands on me, I would have been done for.'

'No need to thank me', he smiled. 'We do what has to be done. How could I leave behind a friend and comrade? The shame would have killed me.'

He was wearing a lieutenant colonel's uniform and must have been in his thirties, although he looked older. The hairs sticking out under his fez had already begun to grey, but his full handlebar moustache was still coal black. He called for coffee and the three of us spent a few minutes in casual conversation. Once we had finished our coffees, he pushed his cup away on the table.

'Well, gentleman', he said, his tone now more authoritative. 'By the Grace of Allah, we are together again and once more, we shall fight shoulder to shoulder. It is my sad duty to inform you that I cannot promise you an easy time but we can at least know that we, as an organisation and a unit that has been fighting for this country since the declaration of the constitutional era, will now operate as an official and publicly acknowledged body. We shall no longer have to hide ourselves or the heroism, glory and honour of our admittedly and, so far, brief history. As you well know, in the two years that have passed since Libya, the dark clouds that have been gathering over our country have yet to be dispelled. Instead, they have become greater in number, as well as darker and denser.' He paused and looked at us, eager for us to understand. 'Are you up to speed on the latest incidents to have taken place? Have you heard about the recent hostilities between ourselves and the British?'

'Are you referring to the affair with the two ships, *The Sultan Osman* and *The Reşadiye*?' I asked.

He nodded.

'I'm afraid so. The English have done a number on us. What they have done is nothing less than piracy, brazenly seizing two ships that were agreed upon years ago and which have been paid up in full. They have not handed over our ships.'

'Winston Churchill says they did it because of the war', Fuad said, trying to dig into the matter a little. 'It's not just Ottoman ships but all foreign-registered ships built or being built in English shipyards that have been impounded.'

'He's lying', our new commandant said. 'All lies. What they want to do is weaken us and our forces.'

However, like Fuad, I also had my doubts.

'But why, Süleyman Bey? Aren't we a neutral country? Why would they want to disarm us?'

'What do you think? Why do you think they would do something so blatantly illegal?'

I didn't want Fuad to feel exposed so I decided to answer.

'Because of our friendship with the Germans?'

He looked me up and down, trying to figure out how much we actually knew and how certain we were of the information we had.

'Actually, no. We have enjoyed cordial relations with the Germans since the reign of Abdülhamit. Our people still remember Kaiser Wilhelm's visit in 1898. And as for the late

Mahmud Şevket Paşa and Enver Paşa, they are both in the pro-Prussia camp. That's not a secret. So no, none of this has anything to do with our closeness to the Germans. The English are just trying to stir up trouble, that's all. No matter what we say or do, they are still going to attack us. At the moment, they are just laying the groundwork for their eventual offensive. Why should they hand over warships to a country they are soon to go to war against?'

'There's talk of a secret agreement', Fuad said, testing the waters. 'Rumour has it that our government has signed an agreement with the Germans and the British intelligence service has clocked on to it, which is why...'

I noticed a flicker of fury in Süleyman Askeri's eyes.

'See? The British have already begun their counter-espionage operations. By spreading these lies, they're hoping to win the international community over to their side. When they attack us, they'll turn around and tell the world that we've been collaborating with the Germans. I expect even more agitation to take place on our territories. The Armenians, the Arabs, even the Kurds... They'll try to get the Kurds to revolt. Assassinations, bombings, uprisings, the whole lot. Mark my words, they'll try it all. That is why we are here. That is why our organisation exists. So we remain vigilant and stop any of this happening.'

Because we had already spoken with Talat Bey about the German issue, we were already a step ahead of our commandant, not that we could tell him. One thing we were not sure about was whether this new chief of the *Teşkilat* was aware of the latest developments or not, and if he was, which was highly likely, how willing he was to actually share it with us.

'What about this affair with the German ships?' Fuad said. 'What use would a neutral country like ours have for ships like that?'

'Think of it as a form of retaliation, brother Fuad. Retribution. The Ottoman Empire is a great power. Do you think we'll just sit quietly by and let the British confiscate two warships of ours that have been paid fully paid for?

Just think about it. Not only have they taken our ships, but they have failed to reimburse us too. Thankfully, however, we have been given the chance to take our revenge. Two German ships, the *Goeben* and the *Breslau*, were recently cornered by the British Navy and they sought refuge in our waters, in Çanakkale. To surrender the ships to the British would have meant declaring war on Germany so we did the logical thing and told the British that we had bought the two German ships and hired the services of their crews. This was our response to the British seizing our warships.' He smiled mischievously. 'Of course, the ships' names were changed to the *Yavuz* and the *Midilli*.'

The explanation was enough for me but Fuad, naturally, had to object.

'Excuse me commandant, but you're saying we did not hand over the German ships to the British in order to avoid having to go to war with the Germans and yet, in keeping the ships and changing their names, are we not engaging in a hostile act against the British? Because according to rumours circulating around the corridors of power, Enver Paşa, who gave the order for the German ships to be accepted, also ordered the local forces to open fire should any English ships breach the Çanakkale Straits. Were such a situation to arise, God forbid, would we not then be at war?'

'Nobody is going to war, my good man', he answered, beginning to sound irate. 'You think going to war is that easy? Of course, that doesn't mean that we'll never join the war. The international borders are most probably going to be redrawn after this particular conflict and there are moments in history when being neutral may as well mean being on the losing side. We no longer want to be the side that suffers territorial losses, which is why we need to show our strength. However, we need to do this not when the enemy wants but when it suits us. In other words, we need to exercise patience, whilst at the same time we continue with our preparations. Because in this war, the worst thing that can happen is to be caught unprepared.'

'Or to be the victim of a fait accompli', Fuad intoned. 'To be the plaything of other powers. To send our soldiers to the front to do the bidding of another country.'

There was no restraint in his voice, no hesitation. He was so sure he was in the right that he was openly defying the man that was soon to be our commanding officer and stating his own opinions. I thought we were in for it and that Süleyman Bey would send us packing, or perhaps do something even worse, but nothing of the sort happened. On the contrary, he seemed to agree with Fuad.

'You're right, brother', he said, clearly moved. 'This nation of ours has no other friends besides itself. So whatever we need to do, we shall do by ourselves. You're right. The Great Powers act only in their own interest. Britain or Germany, it makes no difference. We should therefore aim to protect ourselves and safeguard our own independence. But that does not mean we cannot enter into alliances with other nations. And I'll tell you why. It's because the days when the Ottomans could defy the entire world are over. The blunder now would not be to form an alliance but to form a dishonourable and ignoble one. That is what we must avoid. And that is why we need to know exactly what both our friends and our enemies are up to. In other words, we need to know what the Germans the British are planning. We need to be able to foresee any political or military attempts to attack our country and our people and stop such villainy before it happens. Now, when a bloody conflict has started a stone's throw away from our borders, the need for sound intelligence is greater than ever.'

The more he spoke, the more his voice was infused with feeling. No, he was not talking just for the sake of it, to sway us or stall us; he really meant it and he was getting carried away by his own words.

Of course, there were things he was not telling us. He knew all too well that we were about to go to war alongside the Germans but he also thought we had no other way out. Perhaps he believed that if we were to win the war with the Germans, we could revive and restore the ailing Ottoman state. In other words, he was thinking along similar lines to myself and Fuad. The only difference was, he was being a little more reserved, a little more tight-lipped about it all.

'So gentlemen, you have not been chosen for this post simply because you are loyal patriots willing to sacrifice your lives for the good of the nation. Your political acumen and your powers of analysis, as well as the wealth of experience you have amassed over the years, are also of critical importance to us. The state and the nation have never been in such dire need of your services as they are today. What I ask of you is simply this: that you do more than you have done over the last eight years. There is no other way we can save our lands, which are slipping through our hands. There is no other way we can restore the unity of our people and our nation. Yes, these are hard times, dark times, but my faith in a glorious and beautiful future is absolute. And why? Because I shall be fighting alongside honourable men such as yourselves; men that have been tested by fire, steel and blood. I can't tell you how thrilled I am at being under the same roof as you both, at being granted the prospect of fighting alongside you and, if necessary, falling in battle besides you. So once again, my brothers, I welcome you both.'

To be honest, I was swayed by his speech but Fuad still had doubts. However, when Fuad excused himself from the room, Süleyman Askeri saw his opportunity, sidled up to me and whispered, 'I know about the rather unsavoury incident that took place between you and Yakup Cemil. I also spoke with Enver Paşa. He knows about the incident and he told me to tell you that it was Yakup's idea. 'Tell Şehsuvar that he is a gift bequeathed to us by our beloved Basri Bey and that we have no secrets from him. We can trust him with our eyes closed in all matters because we know he trusts us too.' So what I'm trying to say, Şehsuvar, is that you don't need to worry about that particular incident. You are one of the shining stars of the party and its *fedaeen*. I mean it. I'm not exaggerating. And let me also say this. That so far, you have not been assigned to missions worthy of your intelligence, courage and experience.

You are capable of so much more. But don't worry. We intend to rectify that mistake.'

I won't lie. I felt a surge of pride at hearing such compliments but I still could not shake off my unease. Fuad, for instance, was just as important and as valuable a *fedai* as I. He was as smart and brave as I supposedly was and his political judgement was as sharp as mine, if not sharper. Moreover, he was reliable... And yet I was the one receiving all the praise. Still, I did not want to ruin the mood or let my mind take a dark turn. A part of me wanted to believe that Enver Paşa really had heard about – and been upset about – my little altercation with Yakup Cemil and that he really had said all those things to Süleyman Askeri to pass on to me.

A Betrayal of Their Own History

Good Morning, Ester (Morning, Day 12)

The telephone is ringing persistently in the desert tent but nobody is answering it. There are no officers or soldiers on patrol. What is this place — are these the barren hills of Libya? The gleaming shores of Çanakkale? The lush green forests of the Balkans? The vast, endless sands of the Yemeni deserts? The phone keeps on ringing, as though it will never end, as though it is desperate to pass on some news of woe. At my wits' end, I eventually lift the receiver. I am expecting a furious rant from an enraged commandant but what I hear instead is a more restrained and altogether more urbane voice, that of Ömer from reception.

'Good morning, Şehsuvar Bey. I do hope I am not disturbing you. I would just like to inform you that you have a visitor.'

I realise I am in my bed in the hotel.

'I wouldn't have disturbed you like this but he is insistent,' Ömer went on. 'He says you're expecting him'.

Who could it be? I hadn't been expecting anyone. What new nonsense was this? With great difficulty, I opened my tired eyes and squinted up at the clock on the wall. The time was eight thirteen. Who could it be at this ungodly hour?

'He says he's from your hometown. He looks like a war veteran of some kind. He's got an arm missing.'

'Cafer', I muttered happily. 'Çolak Cafer!'

'That's what he says his name is, sir, yes. Cafer. I asked him to wait for you in the Domed Salon but he refuses. He's standing here now in front of me waiting for you.'

That was difference with Fuad. In the evening, he says he'll do something, and by the morning he's got it done. Whatever promises he makes, he keeps. A few minutes later, I was dressed and downstairs. He was a thin man, Cafer, one of those guys that looks so frail, you'd think a gust of wind could blow him over, and the sight of the right sleeve of his jacket swinging in the air beside him made him look even more unimposing. However, when he saw me, he gave a wolfish grin, displaying rows of uneven teeth stained black by tobacco. There was a look of recognition in his eyes, staring out from the deep sockets either side of his long nose. We must have seen each other before, seeing as he was also from Salonika, but I didn't recognise him or recall having met him before.

'Pleased to meet you, Şehsuvar Bey', he said, offering his left hand. 'My apologies for coming early but I have instructions from Fuad Bey.'

I shook his hand warmly.

'Not at all. I'm so glad you're here. Here, let's go to the restaurant and sit down. Let's have some breakfast.'

He looked in the direction to which I had gestured and flinched.

'Erm, thanks Şehsuvar Bey but I've already had breakfast.'

'Please', I insisted, thinking he wasn't used to hotels such as this one. 'At least some coffee'.

The apprehension in his eyes deepened.

'Best I don't right now…'

'Well, as you wish. In that case, we can sit over here', and we settled down in two seats by the marble column to the right of the hotel's entrance. 'However, I won't let you leave without sampling the coffee we have here.'

I ordered two coffees before he had a chance to object. When I turned back around, he was staring nervously ahead.

'So yes, Cafer Bey, tell me. How are you? I trust you're in good health?'

'Thanks to the Almighty, I'm doing well, Şehsuvar Bey.' He raised his head and there was a glimmer in his eye. 'You won't remember me but I used to work with your late father at the

Education Directorate as an assistant clerk. I was young back then, only eighteen or so. God bless your father, he was a good man. A man of wisdom and insight. Just like Fuad Bey, and just like your good self. You know, this country and the people of this country need people like you, Fuad Bey and your late father…'

'That's very kind of you, Cafer', I said wanting to put an end to the praise. 'So tell me, where did you see Monsieur Leon?' He recoiled, as though he'd been caught red-handed. 'That's why you're here, isn't it? To share information with me about Monsieur Leon?'

He smiled, showing his dirty teeth again, and fixed his gaze on me.

'Yes, yes, that's right. Monsieur Leon is also a good man, like you. Yes, he may be Jewish and all but he's a lot more upstanding than a whole load of people who call themselves Muslims.' He could see the irritation growing in my eyes and came to the point. 'That's right, you were asking me where I saw him. I saw him in Beyazit, in the Booksellers' Quarter. He didn't recognise me. I mean, why would he? How would he remember me, after all? So I went up to him and introduced myself. He was happy to see me and invited me to his office.'

It was wonderful news. Uncle Leon had settled in Istanbul! I could barely contain my delight.

'He has an office, you say?'

'Why yes, and not too far away either'. He pointed with his left arm. 'Just up the road, in Galata. You know the street that leads from Şişhane to the tower? Well, it's on that street. On the right. Number 32. A three-storey stone building, it is. His offices are by the entrance. But don't bother going in the mornings. He only opens after one.'

I made a mental note of the address but what I really wanted was to ask about you. Cafer, however, was rattling away.

'I went twice. To his law offices, that is. You know how a lot of us came here as part of the population exchange three years ago? Well, I needed some paperwork done and Monsieur Leon, God bless him, helped me out. Like I said, he's a good man.'

'What about his niece? He had a niece called Ester. Did you happen to see her at his offices?'

At first, he seemed stumped but then his eyes lit up.

'Ah yes, the girl in the photograph? Yep, I saw her photograph on his desk in a silver frame. Didn't see her in the flesh, though. She may have been there but I didn't see her.'

And yet Cezmi said Cafer had spoken to you in person. So what did that mean? Was this frail but sinister man telling lies? I doubted it. Why would he lie to me? Cezmi must have made a mistake, or his memory must have played tricks on him. Still, I needed to dig around a little bit more.

'So you didn't see her at all? Was she there at the time?'

His lower lip drooped.

'I don't know, Şehsuvar Bey. It wouldn't have been right to ask, either.'

A waiter brought us our coffees and placed them on the marble table in front of us. He waited for me to start drinking as he thought it would be impolite to drink before me.

'*Afiyet olsun*', I said and reached for my cup. I glanced down at his hand. His index finger was yellow from years of smoking. 'Go ahead and light one up, Cafer'.

His addiction outweighed any sense of propriety.

'I will, if you don't mind'. He reached into his pocket, took out a silver cigarette case and began fumbling around in an effort to open it. He was having some difficulty and I was about to give him a hand when he finally managed to get it open. He held out the case to offer me a smoke.

'No thanks', I said. My gaze slid down to the case. It looked familiar. Where had I seen it before? After Cafer took one out, placed it between his lips and then closed the case, I remembered. It was Cezmi's cigarette case. The one with the engraving of the White Tower on it. But wait… That didn't necessarily mean it was Cezmi's. More than one of the same case could very well have been manufactured. There was one easy way to find out though.

'Nice cigarette case you've got there. Looks like it's from Salonika. Do you mind if I have a look at it?'

'Not at all', he said, not suspecting anything, and handed it to me. 'My brother brought it over for me from Salonika. It's the only memento I have of the old hometown.'

I opened the case's lid admiringly.

'My father had one of these', I lied. Engraved on the inside of the lid was the following: '*To my brother, Cezmi Kenan... To liberty, equality and fraternity! Long may they reign! 23 July 1908.*' Once I had seen that message, I handed the case back to him and went back to my coffee.

So they had killed Cezmi. Not just Cafer on his own but with Fuad and his acolytes. The same people and the same group that had abducted me last night. One question haunted me as I sipped my coffee. Why? Only yesterday Fuad had told me that he was going to revive the *İttihat ve Terakki*. If that was the case, why kill one of its heroes?

'So you live here, do you?' Cafer asked, interrupting my ruminations. 'You ain't got a house or anything?'

I smiled genially.

'I'm staying here for the moment, yes. But not on a permanent basis. I'll be checking out very soon. A couple of days later.'

He didn't ask any more questions. He finished his coffee and then had another cigarette before leaving, as courteously as he had arrived, happy both to have done his duty and to have seen someone from the old hometown. It was hard to believe that this shy, cautious, almost timid, man had, only a few days earlier, been involved in the bloody murder of a much loved friend.

That was all I could think of as I made my way up to my room. What was going on? Or was Cezmi the spy? As if. Only one thing gave Cezmi's life meaning and that was the party. Despite everything that had happened, he had never lost his faith in the cause. In fact, that is why he was killed. When the ex-members of the CUP were under such strict surveillance, abducting someone on the street in the middle of the city and acting out an oath-taking ceremony, and in one of the city's most well-known theatres too, was hardly the done thing. So what does he want from me, old Fuad? There is only one possible answer: he wants to be sure. To be sure about me. This all a game, one Fuad and Mehmed Esad have concocted together. That's right, together. They are in it together. There is no other explanation. But what if I am wrong? What if they aren't working for the same people? What if one of them is lying? Questions, questions, questions... Questions crowding my mind, questions to which I have no answer. But even in the midst of all this uncertainty I am still happy as I have finally found a way to find you. This afternoon, I shall visit Uncle Leon and find out what I can about you. However, I still have some time so here I am, at my desk.

Yes, the year was 1914... The Great War had begun, although we had yet to enter the conflict. Our first mission as part of a now transparent and legitimate *Teşkilat-i Mahsusa* was to identify the British and French agents in the government and in the parliament. The mission had been entrusted to us by Süleyman Askeri himself, who, when he assigned it to us, told us how important it was by saying, 'The situation is critical, gentlemen. Seven states are at war with each other. We may not be at war but there are spies and agents all over Istanbul running amok. We do not expect any harm to come from the Germans but those that are working for the French and the British can strike at any time with sabotage or assassinations. What's worse is that these agents may not even be foreigners but Ottoman citizens, men despicable and ignoble enough to actually carry out such treachery. I therefore put it to you, gentlemen, that our mission is to expose these traitors and to put to an end their nefarious dealings.'

It was easy to label people said to be working for foreign states as traitors without knowing who they were but when we saw the actual list, Fuad and I were stunned. It was impossible not to be shocked, such were the names on the list. When I saw the names of Cavit Bey, the Minister of Finance no less and Ahmed Rıza, I could not believe my eyes.

'They've lost their minds', Fuad said. 'Suspecting your closest friends and colleagues? What the hell does that mean? Cavit

Bey has been a member of the party since its inception and Ahmed Rıza is its intellectual head. You even count Ahmed Rıza as a friend. Tell me, how can they possibly be agents?'

There was fury in his eyes as he spoke.

'I'm at a loss too, Fuad old friend. If these guys are agents, then the country is done for. Why are we even bothering with all this? No, this can't be right. Someone has made a terrible mistake somewhere. Perhaps it's the Germans taking our lot for a ride.'

'I don't know if it's the Germans taking us for a ride or us them', he said uneasily. 'Not that it actually matters at this point. It's obvious that we've thrown our lot in with the Germans and no political will or military power can change that. All we can do now is hope and pray that the Germans don't lose. Otherwise, it will all be over for us. We'll be ruined.'

It was discomforting seeing Fuad so utterly despondent and so resigned to what he saw was an inevitable and ghastly fate. I felt I had to step in.

'Hold on there, Fuad. It's not all over yet. I mean, if needs be, we can go and tell Süleyman Bey about all this. We don't have to stand aside and let this horror show go on, do we?'

'That sounds lovely, sure, but what makes you think Süleyman Askeri will listen to us? He's a soldier and an officer, and a man of deep conviction too. He carries out orders that have been issued from above. His opinions won't be different because he has no doubts about the cause. And he expects the same from us – to carry out his orders without question, without second thoughts. But Talat Bey is different. He may appear to be giving in to Enver Bey but for all we know, he is still looking for a way for us to remain neutral. *He* may listen to us. He may intervene and put a stop to this madness.'

He had a point. What he should have done was immediately speak to Talat Bey and explain these latest oddities to him but then I remembered Talat Bey did not trust Fuad the way he did me. I did not want to see Fuad to be seen as a trouble-maker and so I said, 'You're absolutely right, brother. I'm going to go and see Talat Bey straight away and talk to him. Yes, we are under orders, but at the same time we should be allowed to voice our criticisms of what we see as a bad decision and, if need be, have the decision revoked.'

He smiled a wry smile.

'You go and talk to him. It will make a change to me being the one making the objections.'

I felt the need to defend him, thinking he was offended.

'Don't get me wrong, we can go together if you like.'

He reached out and tapped me affectionately on the arm.

'Don't worry about it, Şehsuvar. I know you mean well and that you're only trying to protect me, and for that I am grateful. It would be better for you to go and speak to Talat Bey. But I don't think Süleyman Askeri should know about it. It may be very unpleasant if he finds out. He has his doubts about us as it is, and if he finds out about this, he'll trust us even less.'

'Don't worry. Talat Bey knows when and how to be discreet. Whatever you say to him stays with him.'

I was glad he was being so understanding and that afternoon I headed straight for the *Bab-ı Âli*. This time, the Grand Master greeted me cordially and listened to what I had to say, almost like an older brother. I even thought I noticed gratitude in his expression at one point. When I was done, he leaned back in his chair and said, 'My thanks to you, Şehsuvar, for your concern. I have to say I concur with what you have just said. The two people you have just mentioned are honourable men. Cavit Bey, for one, is our Minister of Finance, and as for Ahmed Rıza Bey… Yes, he has been opposed to us for some time now but his integrity and his honour cannot be doubted, not even for a second. Accusing these two upstanding men of working for the benefit of another country, let alone spying for them, is preposterous! Nevertheless, the situation is clear. It is well known that both Cavit Bey and Ahmed Rıza Bey want us to join the anti-German alliance in this war, whereas we are doing our utmost to maintain our neutrality.'

'But Talat Bey, there are those both in the party and in the government that are pro-German. They do not want neutrality. Rather, they wish to enter the war alongside the Germans.

And what with those two German ships being granted sanctuary in our waters, the pro-German camp's hand has been significantly strengthened.'

His expression darkened and he cast a quick glance at the door.

'If you'd be so kind as to close the door' he said'.

I'm afraid it's true. Even in his own ministerial office, he could not relax. None of us could. We all suspected one another, all of us. Who was in whose camp, who was working for whom, who could be trusted, who couldn't; the parameters shifted and changed every day. Not even every day but every hour. I did as I was told and shut the door but even then, Talat Bey could not shake off his concerns.

'You're right when you say there are those amongst us that want to side with the Germans and go to war. But their hand was not strengthened by *The Goeben* and *The Breslau* finding shelter in our waters but by the British not handing over the ships we had bought from them and paid for in full, *The Sultan Osman* and *The Reşadiye*. The number of people stressing that we have been friends with the Germans since the reign of Abdülhamit whereas the English have plain sold us out has begun to multiply. There is a massive espionage and intelligence game being played out right now, Şehsuvar, as we speak. The Germans, the English, the French, the Russians; you name them and they are involved, and in trying to stay out of the war under such trying and delicate circumstances, we are having to perform political acrobatics of the most ludicrous kind. The situation is such, that every word uttered and every promise made carries some kind of significance and whether we like it or not, whether we want it or not, we are thrown off balance. So yes, men of repute such as Cavit Bey and Ahmed Rıza Bey may never knowingly attempt to harm us but they may act in such a manner as to unwillingly serve the interests of one side over the other. As the government, it is our duty to be aware of such misguided actions and thus minimize the harm that may be inflicted upon our country. That is why we are duty-bound, troubling though it may be, to observe these esteemed gentlemen, to be aware of any mistakes they may have made and, if necessary, to confront them and speak with them face to face in order to know their thoughts.'

'I know it appears a deeply unpleasant duty, a despicable one even, but we have no other choice. Let me state now that what you are doing now is the most difficult task of all.'

Seeing no objection or response from me, he seemed to relax, and even smiled an oddly devilish smile.

'And so long as you are discreet and play smart, nobody will know.' He then perked up, as though he had been struck by a great idea. 'You are already acquainted with Ahmed Rıza. I think you should go and see him. He's staying on a farm in Çengelköy, an old family property of his. Just knock on the front door, sit down and talk with him. I'm sure he'll be more than happy to divulge his views to you, and when he does, you'll be able to form a judgement regarding his stance and his opinions. Moreover, I doubt Süleyman Askeri will object. On the contrary, he'll be delighted.'

Every time I met Talat Bey, I left his presence with conflicting emotions. Yes, he had once again, on the surface at least, convinced me but something wasn't right and I felt a deep discontent as I left.

I did not see Fuad that evening. We were going to meet at a coffee house in Tophane where I was to recount the details of my meeting with Talat Bey but I was so disturbed by what had transpired in the meeting that I could not bear the prospect of meeting Fuad and having to go through it all again and so I went straight back home to Beşiktaş. Madam Melina was pleased to see me back early but I was in no mood to sit and chat with her either so after I had eaten, I went up to my room and lay down, early though it was. I tried to get some sleep but it was no use. No matter how much I tossed and turned, I could not get to sleep. I got up. The room was hot and stuffy so I opened a window. A breeze coming in from the sea cooled the room a little and I went back to bed, but again I could not sleep. It was a hard night, dotted by sleep and sleeplessness and by dreams and nightmares weaving in and out of each other.

I woke up to the sound of chirping swallows and to a bright new day. It was a glorious morning, far removed from the torments of the night, and beautiful enough to almost make me forget my nightmares. I know what you're going to say; that my personality is like the wind anyway, blowing this way and that, and that my happiness and my sadness are equally fleeting, like gusts of wind. Perhaps I had been overly affected by the events of the previous day and, thanks to Fuad, things had seemed far more alarming than they perhaps actually were. I felt reborn that morning when I woke up. So strong, in both mind and in body, that I felt I could tackle any problem in the world, no matter how formidable it may appear. With this newfound optimism, I jumped out of bed and decided to go straight to Çengelköy after breakfast, sit with Ahmed Rıza in his farmhouse and have a long, honest and open chat with him. I had not seen him for a long time and I was sure he would be happy to see me. To add the icing to the cake, the party would have its report. Perhaps I would not even have to tell Fuad about it either, which I was sure Süleyman Askeri would understand. At the end of the day, wasn't secrecy the prime currency of our organisation?

I crossed over to the other side of the Bosphorus from Beşiktaş by canoe, flagged down a horse and carriage and headed up to Çengelköy. When I eventually found the farm, after asking around, it was around noon. I walked through the maze of plum, cherry and peach trees towards the two-storey house, an admittedly modest affair. Far away, a dog barked lazily three times and a donkey brayed. I think a rooster may have crowed too but I'm not sure. That was all I heard in terms of sounds. The front door of the stone house was wide open. I rang the bell but I don't think anybody heard and so, with few other options available to me, I stepped inside.

After the heat of the noon sun outside, the anteroom was comparatively cool. I walked into an ample lounge and looked around. There wasn't a soul in sight. I was about to shout out if anybody was there when I heard a click. Somebody had stepped out from the door facing the lounge's narrow window but because the light was coming out from behind whoever it was, I could not make out the face. After I had taken a few steps forward though, I recognised him. It was Ahmed Rıza. He frowned at me through narrowed eyes until he finally recognised me.

'Şehsuvar my lad, what brings you here? Have you come here to arrest me or to kill me?'

I didn't know what to say. I just stood there in the middle of the lounge rooted to the spot.

'Here, come this way', he said, seeing my surprise. 'I was only joking. They wouldn't let a man like you do that.' He paused and looked me up and down. 'You're an educated man. No, they'd get one of their more hard-hearted brutes to do that particular job.' He extended a hand. 'Welcome, welcome. Please. Come this way. Have a seat.'

Instead of sitting down on the divan with the red drape towards which he was gesturing, I stayed where I was and smiled sheepishly.

'My apologies if I have disturbed you. I haven't seen you for some time and I thought I might pop in to see how you were.'

He didn't believe me but he didn't want to gloat at my discomfort either.

'Very kind of you. Please, don't stay standing like that. Have a seat.'

The divan was hard, uncomfortably so, but I didn't let it bother me and sat down, while he sat down on a sandy-yellow chair in front of me. The lines on his face had deepened and his beard and hair were greying but he still looked to be in rude health. One could see in his eyes a pride in not having surrendered and in knowing he was defending what he believed in, no matter what the circumstances may be. Perhaps it was this very stubborn belief that was keeping him going, both mentally and physically. After all, at the end of the day, he was still one of the few men in the country that commanded respect wherever he went, and my view of him would not change, despite the social upheavals, the political earthquakes and the moral degeneration that would soon follow. Yet all I could think of was how I was to approach him, a wily and highly astute politician, who had quite clearly sensed my purpose in visiting him as soon as I had arrived?

'I saw that friend of yours', he said, relieving me of the many thoughts crowding my mind. 'Two years ago, in Paris. Monsieur Naum's daughter. Mademoiselle Ester'.

I could barely believe what I was hearing. I had gone there to get him to talk but instead I had been stunned into silence!

'She seemed in good health. She was about to start her studies in literature. She had even joined a radical women's rights group in Paris. Her books are being published out there.' He paused and looked at me, seemingly preparing the *coup de grace*. 'She did not ask after you but I told her about you. How you had protected me during the events of 31st March and about our conversation in that house in Şehzadebaşı. And I also told her this: that you had wasted a great talent and that it was a terrible pity. If only you had devoted your energies to writing instead of politics. I'm afraid you are one of many hundreds of able and talented young men that this era has lost.'

I squirmed on the already uncomfortable divan.

'That's very kind of you, Ahmed Rıza Bey, but it is doubtful whether I had such a talent in the first place. All I have ever written are a few scribbles and notes here and there. No novel, no grand tales, nothing. I think Ester may have exaggerated when it comes to my writing ability but...'

'Ester did not pay you any compliments. As it is, she barely mentioned you. She merely listened to what I had to say. Yes, she frowned and listened eagerly and nervously to what I had to say about you but she did not ask any questions. When I had finished, this is what she had to say about you. 'There are two types of people in this world, Ahmed Rıza Bey. Those that are thrown into the fire and those that fan the flames. Şehsuvar is one of the former. The political storms that ravage our country have determined his fate and whisked him away to another place. I won't say it's a shame because it was his decision. There is nothing for me to do except hope he is happy.' I don't know if it means anything to you at all but those were her words.'

Of course, it meant a great deal but I did not tell him. What it meant was that you had abandoned all hope when it came to us. That I no longer even roused your ire. *There is nothing for me to do except hope he is happy.* That was the worst, the most painful thing to hear, as it meant you had closed the file on me and on us. *Let him do what he wants, I don't give a damn* is what it meant. The aching sorrow and the intense anger I began to feel were awful and to make it worse, I could not show any of it to Ahmed Rıza Bey. The man had caught me completely unawares. I was a wreck. Like an experienced boxer, he had let loose on my already weakened and crumpled soul with a crushing blow. Noticing the prolonged silence, he stared at me, his eyes boring right into my mind, seeing right through me, and, almost mockingly, he said, 'Mademoiselle Ester may not be concerned but I am. Tell me, Şehsuvar, are you happy? Have you found what you were looking for?'

'Who does?' I couldn't even stop the words from tumbling out of my mouth. Nor was it a lie, or an attempt to cover things up. It was exactly how I felt. 'Especially nowadays, when the country is spiralling into madness. When people are this wretched and are searching desperately for an excuse to slaughter one another, tell me, how can one be happy?'

'Perhaps you're right', he murmured. 'It may not be possible for one to be happy but one can be content, even now, when the world is being consumed by this hellish war. What matters is doing the right thing. What matters is not killing others and not being the cause of another's death. I say this both for ourselves and for our country. So long as we remain neutral and do not become a cog in the German war machine, then even in the midst of this conflict that rages around us, we can still be content. So long as we do not kill and do not die...' His face took on a bitter expression and he shook his head in despair. 'But that will not happen. Your people have already dragged us into this war.'

'Actually, no. Talat Bey is totally against us entering the war. The ministers are opposed to an alliance with Germany.'

He stared at me incredulously.

'How can you be so naïve? You're only saying this to get me to talk, aren't you? Because if you were actually this green, they wouldn't keep you on board.'

I was about to protest but he raised his right hand.

'Please. Do not disgrace yourself any further in my eyes.'

My face turned crimson red but Ahmed Rıza Bey ignored it – if he had even noticed it – and went on.

'I know very well why you came here, Şehsuvar. Don't worry, I shall give you what you want. My opinions are hardly top secret, anyway. I express them openly. In parliament, in the press and in conversation with friends. So yes, first of all, I am against entering the war with the Germans. Such an alliance would spell our ruination. But it is not just an alliance with the Germans I am against. I am also against any agreement with the British. What the fools in your party have failed to grasp is this: we are not a party to this war. We are the target. The Great Powers are licking their lips at the prospect of getting their hands on the Ottoman Empire. What we need is to nurture an independent political stance in order to protect our territories, not ally ourselves with any one or more of these rapacious powers that are intent on changing the map according to their own needs. Yes, it will be hard, very hard indeed, and there is always the chance that by not taking sides we risk being sidelined. But we have no other choice. We should have realised this, accepted the challenge and done everything in our power to succeed.'

'We still can', I managed to blurt out before he continued.

'No, it is too late now. The Trojan Horse has entered the keep. And not just one but two. *The Goeben* and *The Breslau*; they are the Trojan Horses. Just because their names were changed to the *Yavuz* and the *Midilli* does not mean they have suddenly become Ottoman ships. The actual objectives here are something else entirely. Those in charge are waiting to make one last move to finally sever the already strained relations with the pro-England camp. Kaiser Wilhelm himself concocted this entire scheme. You can write it down if you like: it is just a matter of time before those two ships spell doom for us. The Germans have not had the victory they expected on the French front and the Russians have the Austrians cornered, which is why the Kaiser now more than ever needs our cheap and cheerful soldiers, soldiers whose lives are cheaper than a glass of water. And mark my words, they shall get what they want…'

That day, I stayed at Ahmed Rıza's house and we talked until early afternoon. He did not for a moment think I was there on an innocent visit but he still had some faith in the concept of empathy and in my sense of decency. He did not throw me out when he could have and indeed asked me to stay for lunch not out of a sense of courtesy and hospitality towards a guest but because he still harboured a faint hope that I could change. There was also a possibility that he wanted me to pass on a message to his former comrades.

Mürşit Ağa and his wife suddenly appeared out of nowhere and in a flash, they had cooked a meal and set the table. That day on his farm, I had the tastiest meat stew I have ever eaten in my life. After the meal, while we sipped on ice-cold cranberry juice, he said, 'In any political party, there should be a concordance between the thinkers and the organisers. The thinkers and the intellectuals may not mingle with the masses as much as the leaders do, as the burden of knowledge brings its own set of worries, woes and responsibilities. But the leaders of a party have only one duty and that is to establish a strong party with a sound and robust sense of belonging and in order to accomplish this, more than anything they need to win over the masses. This is why, most of the time, they flout both the party's principles and general ethical principles. Moreover, they often clash with us, the intellectuals, claiming we are obstructing them. This is what is happening to the Committee for Union and Progress now. The party leaders, in collaboration with the army, have purged the thinkers from the party but in doing so, they have also purged the party of its principles. They no longer care about liberty, fraternity, equality or justice. Talat Bey and Enver Paşa are no longer the men of liberty and of belief that they were in 1906. They have become the very regime they swore to overturn. Whatever criticisms they had of Abdülhamit and his reign are now just as applicable to them, perhaps even more so.' He smiled a bitter smile and then shook his index finger, almost dictating the words to me. 'In your report, I would like you to say this. That I, Ahmed Rıza, have never lied to the people or to the party. I defend today the same principles I was espousing twenty years ago. However, the party's current leaders have betrayed not only their own ideals but their own history as well, and for this, neither the nation nor history shall forgive them.'

Fighting for a Lost Cause

Ah, My Dearest Ester! (Early Evening, Day 12)

Once again, I went back to the hotel an unhappy man. Unhappy, disappointed and in pain... So you hadn't returned to Istanbul. Not to Istanbul or to me. And how convinced I had been that you had returned and that I would find you! They were all just empty dreams. Empty dreams and foolish optimism... I had needed to feel hope of some kind and so I had come up with a huge lie in order to create that hope. It was nothing but a flagrant case of self-deception...

After leaving Uncle Leon's office, I wandered the streets aimlessly, not knowing what to do. I just let my legs carry me wherever they felt like going. I went down to Kasımpaşa first, down to the shores of the Golden Horn and walked along the seafront, the way I used to do back in Salonika. I was distraught and wracked with pain, grief and remorse, as though we had split up that day and not years earlier. I sat down on a bench. I could hear the voices of children diving into the sea: wild, frivolous, carefree and joyous. I hated them, and I hated their joy. I got up and walked, for kilometres, but no matter how much I walked, there was no escape, no way out. I was trapped, walking around and around in a vicious circle of fire. Not one of the conditions that had made me leave home twelve days ago and move into the Pera Palace Hotel had changed. I was facing the same threats now that had been a cause for concern to me the day I moved. Life had rejected me completely. No new opportunities would be proffered now. Seeing as you had not come back, any prospects of happiness I may have once clung on to had now vanished for good. I was back in the state of mind I had been in twelve days ago, and it was only right because it was at least rooted in reality.

When I tired of walking, I went back to the hotel and back up to my room. My pen and the sheets of paper on my desk were calling out to me but I had lost the urge to write. What difference would it make were I to write? What would change? I went out on to the balcony but I did not stay out there for long. I could no longer even bear to look out at the tired old city. For a fleeting moment, I thought I could perhaps up sticks and move to Paris but what use would that be? It would be just another disappointment, another mental and emotional disillusionment... I went back inside, placed the recording of *La Boheme* on the gramophone player and listened to the scene when poor Mimi dies. My eyes welled up and I wept, silently at first but then loudly, bawling and sobbing. It felt good, and the more I cried, the more relieved I felt. Not that the pain inside me went away or the grief died down but at least I was now free of that accursed indecision. Our story is an incomplete one but that doesn't mean I should also give up on my writing. No matter how hard it is for me, I have to finish what I want to say. And when I realised that, I could almost hear your voice urging me to write. *You need to write, Şehsuvar. Write it down.*

So I sat back down at my desk, which was waiting for me in silent expectation, and transported myself back to the year 1914... The Great War had started, yes, but first I should tell you about today, about what happened in your Uncle Leon's office. Finding the location was easy but when I got there and knocked on the door, nobody answered. I lifted the brass knocker shaped as the head of the Medusa and knocked again but still there was no sound. I was about to turn around and leave when a voice called out.

'Şehsuvar! Şehsuvar, is that you?'

When I turned around, I was face to face with Uncle Leon. He had aged. His hair had fallen out and his face was wrinkled and lined like dried earth. He had become an old man, in every sense of the word.

'Hi', I smiled. 'I was just about to leave'.

'I open in the afternoon', he explained. His dark eyes were peering out at me intently from under those low eyebrows, trying to work out why I was there. 'We deal with courtroom papers and proceedings in the mornings.'

He was hardly happy to see me but he did not let impropriety get the better of him and he shook my hand.

'How are you, Şehsuvar? It's been quite some time.'

I nodded ruefully.

'It has indeed, Monsieur Leon. As long as it takes for a mighty empire to fall into ruin and for a republic to be established...'

For the first time, there was a hint of warmth in his expression.

'Well put. You always did have a way with words.' We were still standing in the doorway so he beckoned me inside, not that he really wanted me in his office. 'Please, do come in. We can sit and talk.'

He had never behaved so formally and so coldly with me before. Had I not been nurturing a hope of finding you, I would not have accepted the invitation.

The office was considerably smaller than the one he used to have in Salonika but it had the same reddish-brown furniture he used to have in his old premises.

'I don't get much work nowadays. Don't have the strength and drive I used to have. Or the patience. I can barely stand people nowadays.'

When he sat down on the brown chair behind the mahogany desk and I sat on the chair facing him, I saw your photograph. You were smiling and wearing that reddish-orange dress that suits you so well. You looked beautiful, so very beautiful, but the photograph was not telling your story. You were posing for the camera but were not yourself. Your rebelliousness, your indifference to the world, your defiance; all the idiosyncrasies and nuances that make you the person you are were missing from that photo. All I saw was one of countless young and carefree girls full of life and joy that can be seen anywhere. It was not you.

'So Şehsuvar', Uncle Leon said, bringing me back to the here and now. 'To what do I owe this pleasure, and after all these years?'

'Actually, it was only this morning that I learnt you were in Istanbul. Had I known, I would have long since have come round. There are one or two things I would like to discuss with you.'

He was unmoved and looked at me in resignation, as though to say it was too late.

'Life, I suppose. People drift apart from each other…' His eyes – bloodshot from too much drinking – suddenly took on an enquiring hue. 'You're not in trouble, are you? This Izmir assassination thing, that is. The government is rounding all your lot up. The old CUP guys. Bringing them all in for questioning.'

I felt like telling him that he was once a CUP guy but I did not want to start an argument with him before finding out about you. There was little to be gained in annoying him.

'That had nothing to do with me. Ever since my return from Malta, I've stayed out of politics.'

Like the others, he did not believe me.

'You mean you haven't joined the Progressive Republican Party? All the old CUP guys are there.'

I shook my head sternly.

'No, I haven't. The last I was in was the secret service during the occupation, as part of the resistance. That's when I was captured. I was held in the Bekirağa Bölüğü Prison for some time before I was exiled to Malta. After the liberation of Istanbul, I did not get involved with any party or movement. And nor will I. Politics, it seems, docs not bring me any joy.'

He smiled bitterly.

'Don't call it politics. Call it the CUP. It hurts me to say it but the CUP's politics ruined this country and ruined our lives. I don't know how it could have been any worse.'

'Tell me', I said, wanting to change the subject. 'When did you leave Salonika and come here? Was it during the last population exchange?'

His face darkened.

'We came before that. When Istanbul was under occupation. It was dangerous, but staying in Salonika was no longer possible.' His voice fell. 'And I don't know how much longer we'll be able to survive in Istanbul. Don't get me wrong, I'm not complaining. Jews all over the world are facing the same predicament. It would seem God created us so we would constantly move from one place to another...'

As he spoke, I couldn't help but dwell on one thing. He had said *we*, not *I*, which means he had not come to Istanbul by himself. Did that mean you? I was desperately trying to think up a way of asking him without letting on when he gave me the bad news.

'Ester did not come. She said Istanbul was not the right place for her. I think she believes that the chain of events that caused her so much pain began in this city.' His voice was plain and without feeling. 'She stayed in Paris. She is in good company there. She has good friends. Her third book of poems was published this year and has been received quite well...'

'She must be happy, doing something she loves.'

'She is indeed happy', he said, stressing the last word. 'And she's married a fine man. A Jewish painter. He loves Ester deeply. The wedding was last June.' He stopped and examined my face. 'Why the long face? Or did you still think there was a chance? That she would forgive you? Please, Şehsuvar. Don't. You know Ester better than that.'

No, he was not being cruel. In fact, there was something close to pity in his eyes.

'Forget about her, Şehsuvar. Forget her. There is no Ester for you now.'

That is exactly what he said. Those were his words. If he had said, 'Get out of here, get lost', it would have hurt less but he remained courteous to the end, to the extent that he shook my hand when I was leaving and told to me to pop in for a cup of coffee whenever I felt like it. I was not angry with him, nor with you; if there was anyone that had incurred my wrath, it was me. Once again, I hit the streets in despair, back to reality, back to facing up to the empty truth of the hopes to which I had been clinging, to the multiple dreams, each more beautiful than the last, which had woven their spell around me. I went back to the hotel and back to my desk, and look, here I am, pouring my heart out to you, telling you everything, knowing you won't even read these lines, knowing they will do me no good... But still, I shall not give up or leave this halfway. I shall keep on writing to you, until I have said what needs to be said, until I have written down the final lines, which, incidentally, I do not think are that far away.

After my meeting with Ahmed Rıza at his farmhouse in 1914, I wrote a rather comprehensive report in which I detailed what I had gleaned from my conversation with him. In the report, I stated that he was sincere in his thoughts, opinions and beliefs and that the evidence at hand did not lead to the impression that he was in contact with any foreign governments. I was, in my own way, trying to defend him but there was no need as soon after, everything Ahmed Rıza had predicted began to come true.

It was on the 29th of October that the fuse that would lead to the all-consuming fire was lit, although I was not to find out until the following day, on the 30th of October 1914... A Friday... I'll never forget it. It was a sunny morning, the first day of the Feast of the Sacrifice. When Madam Melina called out to me, I was still asleep in bed. I had been up till late reading a novel. It was a time in my life when I was rediscovering my love of literature. The previous day I had gone all the way over to Beyazit and popped in to see Vezir, whom I had not seen for some time, and have a coffee with him. He had set aside for me a special edition of Flaubert's *Madame Bovary*, a gorgeous leather-bound version in the original French with illustrations. Although I had read it before, I was hooked on the first page. The pages kept turning and when I finally went to bed, it was nearly dawn.

'Şehsuvar Bey... Şehsuvar Bey, my lad...' I woke up to Madam Melina standing by my door calling anxiously out to me. 'Your friend Fuad Bey is here. He's waiting for you downstairs.'

Fuad? I was instantly awake. Why would Fuad come here? The last time he had been here was with Basri Bey. That was five years earlier, during the 31st of March uprising. Now what had happened? Was it the Russian spy, Korsakov, the one whose trail we had lost in Kumkapı? Had Fuad tracked him down?

'Thank you, Madam Melina. I'm awake now, I'm coming', I said and sent her on her way. I quickly got dressed and went downstairs, where Fuad was sitting in the kitchen, chatting with Madam Melina and sipping on a coffee. When he saw me, he got up and embraced me.

'*Eid Mubarak*', he said, before leaning into me and whispering, 'I have important news. We need to talk'. Then, in his normal voice, he went on, 'Sleeping in on such a beautiful day, Şehsuvar? What gives?'

I sat down on a nearby stool and answered, 'Don't ask, Fuad old boy. Went to sleep late last night. Couldn't get up.'

Madam Melina could sense something was up but she was discreet enough not to let on and played the part of the gracious host immaculately.

'Fuad Bey says he won't have breakfast, Şehsuvar Bey. Perhaps you can speak to him. I cannot let him sit in this house without having something to eat. Perish the thought!'

'Please, Madame. As I said, I'm full. Otherwise I would gladly sit and enjoy breakfast with you.'

'Very well', she said, getting up. 'In that case, I shall prepare Şehsuvar Bey's breakfast.' However, she was still not satisfied and before disappearing into the kitchen, she turned and said, 'I shall prepare a dish for you too. Just in case you change your mind.'

Fuad bowed respectfully. Once she had left, he turned to me, his face like thunder.

'We've gone to war, Şehsuvar. They said they would, by hook or by crook, and by God, they've done it. They've plunged us into the war.'

'So it's official, is it? We've declared war, have we?' I asked.

'Declare? We've already gone on the attack, Şehsuvar! The Russians. Bombed their ports at Odessa, Sevastopol and Novorossiysk.'

He told me that the navy had set sail for the Black Sea on the 27th of October, ostensibly to carry out naval exercises. Admiral Souchon, the German commander of the Ottoman fleet, had used the exercises as an opportunity to open fire on the Russian ports. Ahmed Rıza's predictions were coming true. On the other front, the Germans, who had not achieved the victory they had been expecting, wanted to drag our men, whose blood and whose lives were cheaper than dirt, into the conflict but most people in the government, as well as a critical faction within the party, wanted us to stay neutral so what was needed was a fait accompli, and that is exactly what they had with the two German ships, *The Goeben* and *The Breslau*, now known as *The Yavuz* and *The Midilli*. It was all done with Enver Paşa's consent and encouragement, naturally.

'So now what?' I asked worriedly. 'What does Talat Bey have to say about all his?'

He shook his head in despair.

'What does it matter? We are now at war and that's all there is to it. I just hope we survive now that we're bang in the middle of it. God help us.'

The details we were to learn after the Eid festival. Neither the government, the parliament nor the party knew about the attack on the Russian positions. Said Halim Paşa, the Prime Minister, resigned after news of the attack but then agreed to stay on in the post after Cemal Paşa intervened. As for Süleyman Askeri Bey, his account of the event may as well have been lifted from an official press release.

'The Russians opened fire first and our forces responded.'

It was the government line too, but this blatant lie was not going to be of any good to anybody. We were no longer teetering on the edge of a cliff. We were now tumbling down into an abyss, one with no end in sight. Anyone with an ounce of sense was aware of our predicament and as such, Oskan Efendi, the Minister for Post and Telegrams, Süleymanül Büstani Efendi, the Minister for Trade and Agriculture, Çürüksulu Mahmud Paşa, the Minister for Public Works, and Cavit Bey, the Minister of Finance, all immediately resigned as they did not wish to join the war cabinet.

What disappointed me the most was Talat Bey's silence. He had accepted the situation without protest. Even the *sadrazam* Said Halim Paşa had done more in response. But the question was why? Was it because he was afraid of Enver? Or because he sincerely believed that we had no other option but to join the war too? Perhaps it was both, but what was even more astonishing was the way Cemal Paşa had acquiesced. It was easy to understand Enver Paşa as he had always been one to mistake his fantasies for reality but what had made Talat Paşa and Cemal Paşa submit so silently and so meekly? It meant that the three leaders of the party secretly believed that we would emerge victorious from the war. But that was just speculation, a crazy gamble in which the odds of our winning were very low indeed. Yes, over the previous half-century, Germany had risen spectacularly as a nation and had amassed a formidable army but facing us were the Allied Powers and they were far superior to us in both weaponry and troop numbers.

For Germany, the situation was quite clear. Although the Ottoman state was about to cave in, it still ruled over significant swathes of land and had a huge population. More importantly, as the Caliph, Sultan Mehmed Reşad was the political and religious leader of Muslims worldwide and the Germans hoped that by calling for a jihad, a 'holy war', the sultan would inspire the Arab world and the Muslims of India to rise up in revolt against England and France. And to this end, three days after we entered the war, Sultan Reşad did indeed declare a jihad. It was the 14th of November. Fuad and I were free so we helped bring the 'Fatwa for a Grand Jihad' prepared by the Şeyhülislam Hayri Efendi from Süleymaniye to the Fatih Mosque. After Ali Haydar Efendi had read out the decree in the courtyard of the mosque to rapturous applause and cheers from the crowd, who then went on to roar the *tekbir*, the oneness of God, Fuad whispered in my ear, 'They'll be celebrating in Kaiser Wilhelm's palace tonight.

He's going to open his finest Rhine wine to accompany his succulent roast pheasant. They've finally got what they wanted.'

'And what about us, Fuad? What's going to happen to us?' I asked amidst the deafening din of the gathered soldiers and civilians crying out in jubilation at what they believed was a crucial step in the revival of the glorious Ottoman past.

He shrugged his shoulders.

'What was going to happen has happened. It's done and dusted. I should have chosen acting and you should have stuck to writing. But that was years ago. It's too late now. There's no turning back from this. This is the end of the road, Şehsuvar... The best we can wish for is a quick and painless death. Preferably on the battlefield, fighting side by side, you and I... The bayonet, the bullet, shrapnel; I don't care which. I'm ready. I don't know about you but I want to go to the front. The Caucasus, Iraq, Yemen, I don't mind. So long as there is a battlefield on which I can die with honour.'

I was in complete agreement. I was tired of talking to Talat Bey, of listening to the same political drivel. I did not want to argue with Süleyman Askeri Bey either. Fate had decided our paths. A large and not insubstantial number of the country's men, the ones old enough to wield a gun, were going to die in the war. That much was inescapable, and like Fuad, I also wanted to be one of the lucky ones that would die on the battlefield defending the motherland during the first offensives, and it was with this wish and intention in mind that we approached Süleyman Askeri Bey a few days later.

'We would like to volunteer for the front', Fuad declared, quietly but confidently. 'We believe we will be of far greater service to the motherland and to our country on the front, rather than in the capital.'

He stared at us intently for a few moments before his expression turned into one of almost childlike innocence.

'Don't worry, gentlemen. We shall go to the front together. All I ask of you is a little patience first. Let's let the dust settle and then we shall set off to fight side by side. At the moment, continue with your duties and wait for further instructions.'

We were in no mood to wait as our patience had been exhausted. We wanted to grab our guns as soon as we could, stand in front of the enemy and then drink the sweet nectar of martyrdom... But it was not to be. Life would not even grant me that much, even though I was fully prepared. The little money I had left I had given to Madam Melina and told her to buy supplies as rumours of war about to break out meant that essential items such as flour, sugar and paraffin had become extremely hard to find in the stores and I did not want the poor woman to struggle. I had already used my own influence to stock the house with as many essentials as I could.

The call to the front finally came at the end of November, with the British occupation of Basra.

When Süleyman Askeri Bey summoned us, we were certain this was the moment we had been waiting for and we rushed to the meeting in a state of great excitement. I was even planning on writing you a long letter before setting off for the war as I did not think I would be coming back. Of course, the letter was not going to be as detailed and as wide-ranging as these but at least I would have written down my feelings for you, as well as my thoughts on various other matters. But alas, events did not develop the way I had hoped.

When we arrived at the headquarters of the security services, twelve other people had already arrived. They were all from our *fedai* crews and were all brave, decent, honourable patriots being sent to Muslim-majority areas to organise the local populations into armed resistance against the Allied Powers. As for us, Süleyman Askeri Bey's aide came and told us that our meeting had been delayed by two hours as a summons had arrived from the government urgently requesting the commandant's presence. We didn't mind. We'd been waiting for that moment for days, another couple of hours was not going to faze us. Fuad and I made our way out and settled down in a coffeehouse down the road. Fuad ordered a nargile, while I ordered a sweet Turkish coffee. When our orders arrived, I took a sip and then began.

'What if we're wrong, Fuad? What if we beat the British and the Russians and actually win the war? Victory does not always have to be about guns and soldiers. At the end of the day, there are so many other factors that can prove decisive in a war Weather conditions, the soldiers' morale on the day of a crucial battle, anything.'

He let go of the nargile and sighed in despair.

'What difference does it make, Şehsuvar? Even if we win this time, these guys will still ruin the country, one way or another.'

There was a question that I had been asking myself for some time now but had been too afraid to actually ask out loud. This time, I just came out with it.

'Is it really that bad? Don't you have any faith left in the party?'

He looked up at me tellingly.

'Do you?'

'Well, the people still believe in us', I said, trying to encourage him rather than voice my own opinion. 'Just look at how they greeted the decision to go to war. The excitement and the enthusiasm. The marches in support of the government are still going on.'

'Just because everyone believes the same lie does not make it the truth. They are misguided fools. A herd of simpletons that cannot grasp the immensity of the disaster that is about to hit them.'

He looked and sounded – to me – like a hopeless soldier fighting for a lost cause.

'Don't blame them. What do you expect them to do? The truth is so awful, they feel the need to cling on to a lie.'

He bowed his head.

'Like I said, the only way for us to maintain our honour is to die.'

I didn't answer, and we didn't say another word until we left the coffeehouse. When we got back to the building, Süleyman Askeri's aide greeted us at the door.

'Şehsuvar Bey', he said in a commanding tone. 'The commandant would like to see you in private.'

Now what was that supposed to mean? Fuad and I exchanged glances but he didn't look surprised.

'Everything happens for a reason', he said in that stoic manner of his. 'Go on. Go on in and speak to the man.'

I found Süleyman Askeri Bey at his wooden desk, which I had always thought was unsuited to him, signing a stack of documents.

'Take a seat, Şehsuvar', he said. 'Look at all this. Documents, documents and more documents. Non-stop signatures, that's all they want. It never ends, I tell you.' He signed a few more forms and then put down his pen. 'Now I know you are keen to fight on the front but I'm afraid I have bad news for you. I have just returned from the Bab-ı Âli. Talat Bey wants you to stay in the capital.' I was about to protest but he cut me off. 'And he has a point, too. All the top men in our organisation are heading for the front. Kuşçubaşı Eşref, Atıf Bey, Nuri Bey, Yakup Cemil, Cezmi Kenan, Mehmed Akif... You name them, they're going. We are fighting on ten fronts, Şehsuvar. Hardly an easy task. In some areas, we need to train and organise the local Muslims, the way we did in Libya. In essence, what we need to do is turn peasants into soldiers. But don't worry. You won't be sitting idle in the capital. One cannot win a war without fortifying the rear lines. The duty that has fallen to you is perhaps even more critical than the ones for those at the front.'

He said it so sternly and with such finality that I dare not question or disobey him. When I stepped outside, Fuad saw the miserable look on my face and immediately understood.

'Well, it's all for the best I suppose, old boy. At least I won't have to worry about Istanbul now. Whenever I think of the old city, I'll know she is in safe hands.'

It wasn't long before we said our goodbyes. A month later, Süleyman Askeri Bey and Fuad set off for Basra. It was the last time I saw Fuad.

Until last night, that is...

Evil Stalks This Land

Good Night, Ester (Night, Day 12)

I was so stunned and my heart so filled with grief that I would have postponed my rendezvous with Arşak if I knew I could see him another time. But the fact remained it was highly unlikely that I would ever get the chance to see him again. For years we had been classmates, sitting next to each other in class, wandering the same corridors and sitting and chatting in the same playgrounds. Just as Fuad had been a central figure in my early adulthood, so Arşak had been an irreplaceable part of my adolescence. Whenever I left Salonika and came to Dersaadet, he had been there for me and had never held back in his help, whether it be material or emotional. He is one of the few people in this world to whom I owe a life debt, so I was happy to be seeing him. Talking to him would perhaps help me a little as there was nobody else with whom I could share my woes. I had yet to work out Fuad's true aims and even if he was telling the truth, he was approaching me not out of friendship but for his own personal gain. Mehmed Esad was no different. Only Arşak was seeing me as an old friend, without any secret agenda or political subtext. Or so I told myself as I stood by the gates of the Maksim five minutes before our agreed meeting time. Arşak had yet to turn up but the venue's lights were on and smart, beautifully dressed men and women had already started making their way inside.

'Why don't you step inside?' a voice asked. I turned around and saw a stocky and affable-looking black gentlemen staring kindly at me. 'It must be tiring standing around like this'.

He spoke Turkish with an accent but was otherwise quite fluent and assured. I assumed he was one of the musicians as it would have been odd for him to be picking up customers from the street. I was about to tell him I was waiting for a friend when I heard Arşak.

'Hi Şehsuvar'. We shook hands and Arşak turned to the other guy. 'You must be Frederick Thomas. My heartiest congratulations. Your reputation has spread all the way to Paris.'

'Is that so?' he smiled. 'That's wonderful to hear. We've been telling people that we've opened a modest little place in Istanbul.'

'Well, let me tell you, Mister Frederick, whenever my friends find out I'm going to Istanbul, they tell me to make sure I visit the Maksim.'

His large black eyes gleamed with pride.

'Please pass on my warmest regards to your friends in Paris. And please, the first round of drinks are on me.'

I wasn't quite sure what was going on. While walking in, I turned and asked Arşak.

'He's the owner of the Maksim?'

'Didn't you know?' he asked, baffled.

'How would I know, Arşak? I thought the owner of the Maksim was some Russian guy that had escaped the revolution. You know, a Belarusian or something. And then suddenly this black guy appears out of nowhere…'

He chuckled.

'Well, you're still right, in a way. Frederick Thomas did arrive here from Russia. He came with others who were escaping the revolution there. He's American-born but he left the States to escape slavery and ended up in Russia. Just when things began working out for him, the poor sod goes and finds himself in the middle of a revolution and so he disguised himself as an American citizen of Belarusian descent and escaped to Istanbul. He's a smart guy. See how he's picked himself up and made something of himself here too.'

As Arşak uttered the last sentence, I had already begun scanning the surroundings. The plates and glasses on tables draped in gleaming white cloths, the subtle lighting giving the place a soft glow, the Russian waitresses....

'Say, how come you're so interested in entertainment venues?' I asked.

He looked up at the crystal chandeliers swinging from the ceiling and then back at me.

'Don't ask, Şehsuvar. We're thinking of moving into the entertainment business in Paris. But when I say entertainment, don't think of cabarets like the Moulin Rouge or girls dancing the can-can. Something on a smaller scale. A little more discreet.'

'You and Bedros?' The light in his eye seemed to vanish when I asked but I foolishly charged on. 'Tell me, how is he, your older brother? I haven't seen him for ages.'

'Bedros is dead'. Rather than grief, there was something closer to reproach in his voice. 'Eleven years ago. Along with the rest of my family'.

He was of course talking about the deportations of 1915. That terrible, heinous decision made by the CUP after the military rout at Sarıkamış, on the advice of the German General Staff, to exile the Armenians of Anatolia to forestall any possibility of them collaborating with enemy forces. He was talking about the tens of thousands of Armenian citizens, including women, children and the elderly, that lost their lives during the relocation process. It was one of the biggest tragedies of the war yet there I was still playing the innocent.

'Really? But... But how?'

He looked at me incredulously.

'They were killed during the deportations. When they were being taken from Sivas to Lebanon.'

'If only I'd known'. The words seemed to fall from my lips of their own accord. 'Had I known, I may have been able to...'

The pain in his heart was all too visible in his eyes.

'Which one of them would you have saved, Şehsuvar? There were two hundred people in our family. How would you have selected the ones to be saved? My mother and father? My six siblings? I had twenty-three nieces and nephews. What about them? Would you have saved them? And my aunts and uncles and their children… I'm sorry, Şehsuvar, but you wouldn't have been able to save anybody.'

'Good evening'. We were interrupted by a blue-eyed Russian lady smiling sweetly at us. She was not that young but she was stunning and she was pointing with her slim and elegant fingers to one of the tables near the front of the stage. 'Please, come this way. Mister Thomas asked me to show you to your table.'

She had caught us at such a terrible and inopportune moment that I didn't know what to say but Arşak stepped in.

'Why, thank you. Yes, that is a wonderful spot indeed. Let's go, Şehsuvar.'

We walked silently to the table and sat down without even looking at each other.

'If you'll excuse me for just a moment', the waitress said, still smiling, and hurried off.

'She's beautiful, isn't she?' He had always had a penchant for charming and beautiful women but this time I sensed he was saying it just to break the uncomfortable silence that was weighing us down. 'I tell you what, my friend, these Russian ladies really are something. A different breed altogether, eh?'

I looked at him tenderly. He was a slight man but he had a huge heart.

'How did you find out?' This time I looked him in the eye and asked. 'Who told you about your family?'

Again, his expression changed. His gaze slid down to the white tablecloths and lingered there for some time before he sighed and lifted his head.

'I found out myself'. He had tears in his eyes and he nodded his head softly. 'Yep, I found out myself. But months later, when it was already done and dusted. I was in Çanakkale at the time. On the Seddülbahir Front. You may not know but I volunteered during the war, along with a few others from the *Mekteb-i Sultani*. I was stationed all over the place during that nightmare. I'm sure you've heard about the war in Çanakkale but whatever it is you heard, I can assure you it was a hundred times worse. It was hell. I was one of the lucky ones as I didn't catch typhoid or dysentery. I was shot once but it wasn't a serious wound. But while I was out there, hunched down in that trench, sleeping in the mud and the filth, what concerned me was not my own survival but the fact that after April, I'd stopped receiving letters from my brother Bedros. I was no longer getting any news from back home and I was starting to worry. Of course, you always find reasons and explanations. I told myself it was war and the letters may have been lost in the post. But the worst thing about it all, the most painful thing, was that while I was scared that they might be distraught thinking I had died, they were already dead.' Tears began streaming down his face. 'They've all gone, Şehsuvar. All of them. From my grandfather Abig all the way down to my youngest nephew Vaçe. I haven't found any of them. Neither them nor their graves.

'I learnt about it after I was discharged from the army. When I got back to Sivas, back home. Have you ever seen a village without a single soul? Have you ever experienced a silence so overpowering and deathly that it can make your ears howl in pain? Have you ever witnessed all your sweetest childhood memories turning, one by one, into nightmares? Because I've been through it all, Şehsuvar. I kept asking myself why. Why had they killed my whole family? You can say it was war and that circumstances change in wartime. You can say that Armenian rebels were collaborating with the Russians. And I know that some of our people, like the Greeks and the Bulgarians, wanted to establish their own independent state and that the Ottomans wanted to defend themselves and ensure their own security. Yes, I understand all that, but does any of that justify the deaths of so many people? Was it really necessary to take so many lives and to shed so much blood? Was it really necessary for so much cruelty and brutality to be unleashed?

'It reached the point, Şehsuvar, when I could no longer live in this country and so I went to Paris with the intention of never setting foot in this place again. But you know how it is. It's hard to let go… I may not know which field or ditch they are in or which river's murky waters are their final resting place but at the end of the day, my family's final resting places are all here, in this land. That's why my legs keep bringing me back here. I was in Malatya two weeks ago, in a place called Hasan Çelebi, a valley amongst some steep mountains. Apparently that is where they were killed. They gathered the men together, took them to the top of the mountain and then went to town on them with knives, hatchets, axes and whatever else they had at hand. Then they threw the corpses down the mountainside for the birds and the wolves to feast upon. I have yet to find any trace of them. There is a curse upon this land, Şehsuvar. It's as though the fields in this country have been nourished by blood, not water. As though it is rage that flows through our mothers' breasts, rather than milk. As though it is some wild, vicious light that illuminates our days, rather than the rays of the sun. Something harsh, merciless and cruel… I can't think of any other reason behind the slaughter, behind the sheer lack of conscience, behind the insane brutality of it all. I don't give a damn about this group or that group. We were all Ottomans. None of us were better or worse or superior or inferior. We were all in it together… And yet. I tell you, Şehsuvar, evil stalks this land. An unrelenting evil that grows bigger and stronger with each passing day.'

He fell silent. He did not even bother to wipe away the tears streaming down his face. I didn't know what to say either. The two of us just sat there. Me and my old childhood friend. There was little point in me saying that when the order came for the deportations to begin I had protested. Nothing could ease his pain. No reassuring glance, no consoling word, no gentle touch. Perhaps it was time and only time that would eventually help him forget the pain. But that day was still a long way away.

'Gentlemen, your menus'. The waitress had returned but even she noticed the sudden change in mood at our table and there was a flicker of uncertainty in her blue eyes. 'I'll leave them here. Please call me when you are ready to order.' And with that, she disappeared.

Arşak reached for a serviette and wiped his eyes and his cheeks.

'I'm so sorry, Şehsuvar. I've ruined the evening.' He smiled a bitter smile. 'But we're used to living with pain, aren't we? One part of us cries, while another part laughs. Although how it can laugh is another matter. Because it is the ones left behind that have to deal with the pain.'

I reached out and touched his hand affectionately.

'I'm so sorry for you, Arşak. Really, I'm so sorry. If there was only something I could do to…'

He shook his head.

'Thanks Şehsuvar, old friend, but there's nothing anybody can do for this.'

The all-black musicians of the Abyssinian Orchestra began playing, signalling that dinner was now being served. Arşak looked over at the musicians.

'Right, that's enough', he declared, pulling himself together. 'We didn't come here to cry. Let's order, shall we? What shall we drink? Vodka?'

'You choose', I said, amazed and also relieved at his strength and maturity. 'It doesn't have to be vodka. We can drink *rakı*. Seeing as it's probably hard to find in Paris.'

He looked around with an exaggerated zeal for the waitress.

'Where has she disappeared to?'

'She must be in the kitchen', I said and looked around for her.

And then I saw him.

Standing by the bar, next to Mister Thomas the owner. It was none other than Mehmed Esad. A coincidence or was he following us…? If he was following us, why? So he could…? Surely not? That would be daft. And even if was following us, why was he personally doing it? He could easily have sent a couple of his underlings out to do the job. What struck me was how friendly he seemed to be with the restaurant owner, the two of them raising their glasses in friendship and clinking away. I was a little uneasy seeing him there. If he saw me, he would definitely want to come over and sit with us and he was the last person I wanted sitting with us. Things could easily become very unpleasant between him and Arşak, a prospect that was making me increasingly worried. I got to my feet.

'Sorry Arşak, a friend is over there at the bar. Let me just go over and say hi, otherwise he may be a little offended. You order the food for us. Anything you like.' He was about to object but I stopped him. 'Not a word. Remember how you always used to choose whenever we went out to eat, telling me us Salonika folk didn't have a clue about good food and decent meze? Well, you're going to choose today too.'

A wonderfully innocent smile appeared on his aging face.

'Very well then! But no whining about my choices! None of that, *I don't like this* and *I don't like that* nonsense!'

I brought my right hand up to my chest by way of acceptance and left. Mehmed Esad saw me before I was even near him. The owner of the club had gone.

'Well, well, well, Şehsuvar! You're here too, eh?'

We shook hands.

'I'm here with an old friend'.

He peered at the direction from I had just arrived to see who I was with. I pointed our table out to him.

'An old classmate from high school. We bumped into each other. He wanted to see the Maksim.'

He narrowed his eyes and stared at Arşak.

'An old CUP guy?'

'Oh no, he was never one of us. Just an ordinary guy trying to make his way in the world. Tell me, what are you doing here?'

'I came here to see someone but he's not here.' He lifted his glass of vodka. 'I'm just going to polish this off and then I'll be on my way. Tell me, Şehsuvar, while we're here, have there been any developments? I know it hasn't been long but... Well, time is becoming a factor. Have you managed to establish contact with anyone?'

If my encounter with Fuad had been set up and arranged to test me, then I had to tell Mehmed Esad about it but I still wasn't sure. I played it safe and spoke in vague terms.

'I'll tell you about it when we get together. I'll pop by soon. In the near future.'

He seemed content with the answer and raised his glass.

'In that case, cheers. I have a feeling we shall soon obtain some very pleasing results'.

'Cheers'.

Mehmed Esad made his way to the exit and I went back to Arşak and our table.

'I've ordered some magnificent mezzes for us. And *rakı* too.' He was not over the grief of a few minutes earlier and he couldn't have snapped out of it had he wanted to anyway but he was putting on a brave face. 'They've got caviar too but I don't know if we can trust them. Hard to tell whether their caviar will be the real thing and whether it will be fresh or not.'

'And a good thing too. Whoever heard of drinking *rakı* with caviar?'

I had barely finished my sentence when Thomas turned up at our table. He may well have heard me as he planted a huge bottle of vodka down on our table.

'I know you're going to be drinking *rakı* but you should try some of this first.' He turned to the waitress behind him and said, 'You can put them down over there, Larissa.' From a tray, she took some glasses, a few slices of bread, some butter and a bowl of jet black caviar and placed them on our table. Without asking, Thomas sat down on one of the free stools, gestured to the food and said, 'These are on the house'. He then reached for the vodka and filled the glasses. 'This is one of my special bottles. One of the ones I brought with me when I left Russia.' He put the bottle down and raised his glass. 'Şerefe, gentlemen!' He brought the glass to his lips but then stopped. 'But all in one go, please!'

We downed the shots. The ice-cold liquid stung our throats on the way down but it clearly hadn't done the trick for Thomas, who had already refilled our glasses. Arşak was only too glad but I felt I had to stop him.

558

'Let's wait a little. I'm not used to drinking vodka this quickly.'

Thomas' big black eyes widened in surprise.

'Really? Despite being friends with Mehmed Esad? I saw you with him just now. You seemed to be on very friendly terms. I will say one thing; Mister Mehmed does like a drink. Vodka, gin, whisky, you name it. And he can really hold his drink too. Doesn't matter how much he's had, he's barely affected by it. He'll get up from the table and stand straight as a die. No swaying or lurching about with him!'

'How come you know Mehmed Esad?' I asked, more to keep the conversation going rather than out of genuine curiosity. He placed his hands on the table.

'We've known each for a long time now. He was a great help to me once. When I first arrived here from Russia, I opened a dance club in the Stella Gardens in Şişli. This was during the occupation. The English were in charge of our area and the local officers made our lives hell. We had beautiful girls working at the club. The English soldiers would hit on them but the girls would just ignore their advances and that is when things would get ugly. It was nasty stuff at times. Real disgraceful scenes. The British tried closing us down a number of times but each time Mehmed Esad would step in and sort it out. He had contacts at the British Headquarters. He got on with the Brits like... How do you say it? Like a house in flames? Is that it?'

'Like a house on fire', Arşak corrected him. 'In other words, they got on really well.'

'*Like a house on fire*. Exactly. And they did. They got on really well. They were good friends.' He pointed to our glasses. 'But enough of that, gents. Drink up. This little beauty loses all its charm if you let it get warm.'

As we knocked back the drinks, I still thought Mehmed Esad was innocent. Just because he had been close to the British during the occupation did not necessarily mean he had collaborated with them. He may have established contact with them in order to obtain information and material that could have been valuable to the resistance. Yet, on the other hand, the situation could hardly be deemed completely innocent when one combined what Thomas had unwittingly told us with the incident involving the British raid on the ship that Major Cezmi had described to me. Moreover, it was highly unlikely, indeed all but impossible, for the British intelligence services to be duped wholesale by a CUP guy like Mehmed Esad. So how did he manage to convince them?

Thomas eventually left, and Arşak and I chatted away, mainly about our plans for the future. At one point he told me to come to Paris, telling me I had a home there and that I was free to stay whenever I liked. I was grateful for the offer and told him I would take him up on it one day. But throughout the conversation, I couldn't help but think about Mehmed Esad and the possibility that he had been a double agent.

My mind was still busy with the same question when I got back to my room and my desk at the hotel. If Mehmed was a spy, then what was Fuad's role in all this? Were they both, independently yet simultaneously, conspiring against the government? Or were they rivals scheming against each other? Were they investigating each other? Fuad, for one, had actually articulated his suspicions when he came straight out and asked me why I was still in touch with that an ex-CUP guy if the party was defunct. Indeed, there was a warning and an admonition nestled amongst his remark. My mind was in a whirl. What if, as I actually assumed, they were not in fact testing me and were not in touch with one another? Possibilities, misgivings, doubts, suspicions and illusions… My mind was working overtime but questions and doubts do not obtain results. I remember what Basri Bey used to say. 'Without the right questions you won't get the right answers.' I needed to find the right questions, both to ask myself and to ask Fuad and Mehmed Esad. I did not feel like writing while my mind was in such a tumult so I lay down on my bed. I tried to get some sleep but it was no use. I tossed and turned but still my eyes would not stay shut. Tormented by my restlessness, I got up and opened the balcony door. Cool fresh air streamed in. Outside, the city was like a vast ship that had silenced its engines and dimmed its lights and was now bobbing gently in the autumn breeze. I didn't stay out on the balcony for long. I came back inside and sat at my desk, hoping writing would help dispel the confusion in my mind.

It was the right choice. The best way to put an end to the ever-expanding battle between possibilities in my mind is to write about the war that was the bloodiest conflict the human race had yet to experience. The Caucasus, Iraq, Syria and Palestine, Çanakkale, Galicia, Macedonia, Romania, Yemen and the Hijaz, Iran, Libya… The land battles, the naval engagements, the trench warfare, the war in the desert, the battles for the mountains… Retreats during which thousands of soldiers drowned in the sea, sieges lasting months, bayonet battles in which death reigned supreme… Hunger, cold and disease… Typhus, dysentery, malaria and cholera, and Azrail crushing mankind in his deathly grip… Men, women, children, the elderly… Thousands, hundreds of thousands, millions of fatalities… Poor, innocent people whose graves and final resting places may never be found…

Of course, I am not going to describe every front, every slaughter, every victory or every defeat during that brutal four-year conflict but I will touch upon a few key incidents of the war and how they impacted our lives. The war began in the summer of 1914 and we joined – or rather, we were forced to join – it in the autumn of the same year.

Towards the end of the war, Cemal Paşa, when asked why we had entered the war, gave the following answer: 'So we could pay wages! The Treasury was empty. We did not even have the money to procure bread for the army. The Germans, who were all too savvy of the situation we were in, offered us money in return for an alliance, and we accepted.'

However, if you ask me, this explanation is not only incorrect, it is also shameful. The fact is, all three of them – Cemal Paşa, Enver Paşa and Talat Bey – believed that our troubles as a nation would be dispelled with victory. Enver Paşa, in particular, dreamt of uniting the Islamic world and the Turks of Central Asia under one banner and restoring the heady days of the Ottoman Empire, with himself, naturally, the leader of this new force. But there was a yawning chasm between his fiery, lofty dreams and reality. Ultimately, a series of crushing defeats in the months immediately following our entrance into the war would serve as a wake-up call for us but by then it would be too late.

Whether it was the workings of fate or a lack of the requisite military experience on his part I do not know, but the first defeat came at Sarıkamış, where Enver Paşa himself was commandeering the men. On the 19th of December 1915, when Enver gave the order to the Third Army to attack by famously saying, 'Ahead of us lie honour, glory and fortune! To the rear are infamy, misery and death', he had a perfect plan in which he would have the Russians surrounded. However, he failed to take the weather conditions into account and this naivety alone cost tens of thousands of our men their lives without even a shot being fired as they froze to death on the Allahuekber Mountains. What was even more disgraceful was the fact that once Enver Paşa knew defeat was imminent, he abandoned the battlefield (on the 15th of January) and rushed straight back to the capital. Not only did he not tell a soul about the defeat, he also barred the newspapers from writing the truth about what had happened there. I only heard about the horror because Talat Bey himself told me about it.

'It was a disaster, Şehsuvar. An absolute catastrophe. Thousands of our men, thousands of good, loyal, honest soldiers died up there in the mountains. But Şehsuvar, for the love of all things holy, do not let on. There is no need to lower our people's morale any further. The later they find out about this mess, the better.'

A short time after this disaster, we would have our second big defeat. This time it was the forces led by Cemal Paşa that were crushed. As the night of the 2nd of February sneaked into the morning of the 3rd, the Fourth Army, under Cemal Paşa's command, was routed by intense machine gun fire from the British while attempting to take control of the Suez Canal. In total, we lost around six hundred men, a paltry figure perhaps compared to the nightmare of Sarıkamış, but for Cemal Paşa, who saw himself as 'the Conqueror of Egypt', it was a massive blow. Both men reacted in similar ways. Enver Paşa held the Armenian gangs responsible for his defeat. 'Had it not been for them, we would not have suffered such a catastrophe.' And that is how the seeds that would sprout into the idea that would lead to the Armenian expulsions, and which would wipe out Arşak's entire family, were sown. As for Cemal Paşa, he began conducting a brutal and merciless political campaign in Syria and Palestine, executing Arab nationalists who were calling for independence and sending around two thousand people picked out from the local tribes into exile in Anatolia, Thrace and the Balkans.

So yes, the Great War commenced with these two routs but come spring, we would have a stunning victory, a true epic written by ordinary soldiers. I'm talking of course about Gallipoli and the Çanakkale Front. As a result of the bloody engagements there and the heroism of our men, the French and British navies were unable to pass through the Çanakkale Straits and the countless land operations undertaken by the Allied Forces would all end in failure. Battling hunger and disease as well as incoming fire, a superhuman resistance by our troops thwarted the will and the designs of the enemy and eventually ended in their retreat on the 9th of January 1915. However, there was also an unpleasant incident on this front between Enver Paşa and Mustafa Kemal, who had been promoted to the rank of colonel as a result of his successes in the region of Anafartalar. When Enver Paşa visited the front but did not stop by Anafartalar, Mustafa Kemal handed in his resignation but Liman Von Sanders, the commander of the armed forces on the front, rejected his resignation and personally asked Enver Paşa to smooth things over with Mustafa Kemal.

The news of this unpleasant incident did not take long to reach us. Once again, Talat Bey's reaction was interesting. 'I don't get Enver Paşa at all. Really I don't. He's becoming obsessed by this Mustafa Kemal. Yes, Mustafa Kemal may have been quick to react during the 31st March Uprising and reach Istanbul first, and yes, they may have had their differences during the Balkan War but a seasoned soldier like Enver Paşa should not be envious of or bothered by a subordinate officer. Mustafa Kemal is a talented officer, no doubt about that, but Enver is none other than the 'Hero of the Liberation'. His name has become legend. Enver is making a mistake, as far as I can see. He is lowering himself and his reputation in the eyes of the people around him.'

At the time, I would never have revealed my true thoughts to Talat Bey because I knew all too well how fickle he was and how frequently he changed his mind but now I am free to write what I truly feel. I can't say I knew Colonel Mustafa Kemal – now the President of the Republic, no less – very well back then so I won't comment about him but I'm sure you have worked out by now that I did not hold Enver Paşa in the highest regard. That being that, let us return to our bloody subject matter.

Our second major triumph of the Great War would take place around a year later on the banks of the Tigris River, at Kut ul Amara. An English garrison had taken up position there and the Sixth Army, under the command of Marshall Von der Goltz, had them surrounded and had cut off all their contact with the outside world. Many of the Indian troops in the English divisions were starting to weaken and fall to hunger and disease as they would not eat the horsemeat their comrades were forced to eat as a result of the blockade. The conditions out there were so grim that it was not just the besieged that were in danger but the besiegers too, to the extent that Marshall Von der Goltz himself died of typhus, after which Enver Paşa's paternal uncle Halil Paşa, a year younger than Enver, would assume command of the army and not only bring the English general Charles Townshend to his knees but bring his prisoner of war to the capital.

Apart from these two victories, there were few other successes worth mentioning. However, one event that did move me deeply was the death of Süleyman Askeri Bey, who had been posted to Basra. Fuad told me about it in his last letter.

Until the end of April 1915, Fuad used to write to me regularly from the Iraq front. When he first met Süleyman Askeri Bey, Fuad had had his doubts but now he was in awe of him and praised him to the skies. It's such a shame that in his last letter, he had to give me the sad news about our commanding officer.

The letter was sad, so sad one could almost feel the pain resonating between the lines. It all began when Süleyman Askeri Bey was wounded in the leg on the 20th of January 1915 in a skirmish with a British unit during a reconnaissance mission. He was immediately taken to Baghdad Hospital but Süleyman Bey was so eager to fight that he ignored the doctors' orders to rest and wait until the wound had been treated and headed straight back to the front to fight. That's right, wounded and on a stretcher, he commanded a 9,000-strong division that fought for weeks on end against enemy battalions. The decisive encounter with the British would come on the 12th of April 1915 on the outskirts of the Bercisiyye Forest, during a brutal battle. At first, we seemed to be winning but the British brought in reinforcements and the situation changed. Over half our men fell, in what turned into an unexpected and crushing defeat. Although he knew the battle had been lost, Süleyman Askeri Bey did not turn and flee but instead stood his ground and personally oversaw his men's retreat. As his division retreated, guarding him as they did so, he turned his gun on himself and shot himself in the head with his final bullet.

I read Fuad's last letter with tears in my eyes. And then I thought of Enver Paşa... The same Enver Paşa who, knowing defeat was imminent, handed over command of his forces at Sarıkamış to another officer and returned to the capital.

Enver Paşa – the so-called 'Hero of the Liberation'.

A Malevolent Rain

Good Morning, Ester (Morning, Day 13)

I woke up in a terrible state this morning. I had a strange feeling in my mouth, a painful pressure on my palate, most probably from grinding my teeth while I slept. I'd had so many dreams… So many colours, sounds and silhouettes… So many streets, squares and faces… A random, fragmented sequence of events… I couldn't remember any of them. I was exhausted, both mentally and physically, and so fed up that I could barely drag myself out of bed. If I could have just stayed under that warm blanket, just stayed in the room and let nobody touch me without the need to be protected from anybody, well away from all kinds of trouble… They were all hopeless fantasies, of course. I knew they were not going to leave me in peace and so, resigned to my fate, I dragged myself out of bed.

The breakfast lounge was quieter than usual. For the sake of conversation, I asked the waiter what was going on.

'What's happened, Ihsan? The hotel looks like it has been emptied out.'

'The Orient Express passengers have left, Şehsuvar Bey', he replied gravely. 'But they'll be back soon'. He didn't seem to mind, despite the seeming seriousness of his tone. He had a quick glance around and then said, 'At least this way we'll have a little breathing space.' He then realised his remark could be misconstrued and so hastily added, 'I don't mean you, of course. You're one of us, sir.' He glanced down at the half loaf of bread still on my table and the cheese that was just sitting there. 'You've hardly eaten a thing. How about I get the chef to make you a lovely omelette, sir? And some freshly squeezed orange juice to go with it perhaps?'

Any other day and I would have gladly accepted his generous offer but this morning I really wasn't in the mood.

'Thanks, but I think a coffee will be enough. And a glass of water to go with it. Cold water, though. I think I overdid the *rakı* again last night.'

'As you wish, sir', he smiled and went off, leaving me alone with the day's papers. *İkdam* was on the top of the pile so I began with that. One of the columnists was still discussing the issue of Mosul, claiming that in 1918, the British had acted unlawfully and violated our rights as a nation. He was right too but after the signing of the Treaty of Ankara last June, what could be done? Another columnist was discussing the significance of the rights and freedoms granted to the women of the country by the recently ratified Civil Code, rights which women in many European countries had yet to be granted. He was also right when he said they were important rights, even if most of the women in our country were not even aware that they now had such rights... On the front page of the paper was a photo of Süleyman Bey, the Governor of Istanbul, with the accompanying headline: *Our city is ready to welcome His Excellency, the President.* I pulled the paper towards me to read the article when I heard a familiar voice.

'So after eight years, Mustafa Kemal is coming back to Istanbul.'

I looked up. Standing over me and sporting a cheeky grin was the last person I had been hoping to see at this time of the day. I was speechless. Fuad, on the other hand, looked completely at ease.

'Morning, Şehsuvar. What's with the surprise? Don't you remember – you're the one that called me?' He stopped and pretended to be unsure. 'Or have I made a mistake?'

'No, no, you're right', I said. I stood up. 'It's just that seeing you here all of a sudden is a bit of...' We embraced. 'Welcome, Fuad, welcome'. He struck me affably on the shoulder. I pointed to a nearby stool. 'Please. Take a seat. Are you hungry? How about a bite to eat? They do a particularly outstanding breakfast here.'

He unhurriedly sat down and placed the leather bag he had in his hands on his knees.

'Thanks, I'm full. But I wouldn't mind a cup of tea.'

'Tea?' It was yet another shock.

'Don't ask', he replied sheepishly. 'Got used to tea on the front during the war, didn't I? I haven't given up coffee completely but I do like a nice cup of tea every now and then.' He opened the bag on his lap and took out a vinyl record. I read the label. It was a recording of Puccini's famous opera *Tosca*. He held the record out to me with a playful smile. 'Here. It's for you. You used to drive us insane with your damn operas back in Libya.'

'Thanks', I said, gladly accepting the gift. 'I love this one. Absolutely love it. I have a gramophone up in my room so I'm going to listen to it right away.'

'I won't lie. I haven't listened to it, and I don't really want to either but I did read up about it. They say it's a love story but I don't think it is, to be honest. It's a story about friendship, if you ask me. The story of a man who risks his life to save his friend from the clutches of the government.'

There was a warmth in him today, in his looks and his voice. It was just like the old days. He was open and honest, like the friend I used to have, as though he had not gone off to Basra in the autumn of 1918 to join the Great War and the events of the ensuing years had not actually happened. But it was still hard to tell whether the warmth I saw in him was genuine or not. I asked Ihsan to bring us some tea and then turned to Fuad.

'So tell me, what have you been doing? What's the latest? The last time you wrote to me was May 1915. You wrote to me with the news of Süleyman Askeri Bey's death. After that, I didn't hear another peep from you.'

His face fell.

'Süleyman Bey was one of the bravest soldiers I ever knew. In my whole life, there were only two deaths that shook me; one was Basri Bey's, the other was Süleyman Askeri's. But when I look at what's happening around us now, I am actually glad that they died and did not live to see the shame and the ignominy in which we are mired today. I'm talking about our own friends, Şehsuvar. Our own people. Okay, they may not have been our friends but they were comrades and they fought alongside us for the same cause. I'm sure you know what's happened to a lot of the lads from our old crew. Theirs are stories of true heroism, Şehsuvar. True heroism but also terrible pain. Horrible stories they are. Very painful to hear.'

'You're right, Fuad old boy. No one can accuse of holding back when it came to sacrifice and courage but when I look to the past…'

'Enough of the past', he said, cutting me off. 'What's happened has happened. Let us look to today.'

This was not my old friend sitting in front of me but an ex-CUP guy trying to use me for his own ends. He placed both his hands on the table and looked me sternly in the eye.

'Tell me, what the hell are you doing, Şehsuvar?' Was he genuinely curious or was he trying to warn me about something? He checked our surroundings and then back at me. 'Here. In this hotel. What are you doing here?'

'I told you', I mumbled. 'I'm just taking it easy'.

He reached out and took me gently by the arm.

'No, you didn't tell me. And I don't think you're taking anything 'easy'. Tell me the truth. What are you after, Şehsuvar?'

I tried to smile but failed.

'Noth…. Nothing', I muttered. His eyes bored into mine.

'Please Şehsuvar, be straight with me. We may not have seen each other for years but you're still my best friend, and trust me, I am still your best friend in this world.' He looked at me with something close to pity. 'You know what I'm getting at, don't you? I don't want you to get hurt. So tell me, what are you playing it?' Before I had a chance to reply, he pointed to the copy of *İkdam* newspaper on the table in front of us. 'Is this it?' He reached out, picked it up and showed me the news I had just been reading. 'Or are you after Mustafa Kemal too, like us?'

My jaw almost hit the floor.

'What? What are you talking about, Fuad? What do you mean about Mustafa Kemal?'

Instead of answering, he carried on staring at me, but this time his lips had curled into a sneer. I couldn't help but look over at the paper again and the headline: *Our city is ready to welcome His Excellency, the President.*

And that is when it hit me. Like a bolt of lightning, the mystery was revealed and the picture, in all its naked glory, seemed to take shape right in front of my eyes. How could I have missed something so stunningly simple? How could I have been so caught up in so many insignificant and distracting details when the truth had been obvious all along? Mehmed Esad coming to the hotel, the plain clothes police no longer following me, the murder of Cezmi Kenan, Fuad abducting me... It was all so simple. I now knew what they were planning. Not just Mehmed Esad but Fuad too. Despite the immensity of the shock, I stayed calm and carried on playing the fool.

'What? You're going to kill Gazi Mustafa Kemal? You made a hash of it in Izmir so now you're going to finish it off in Istanbul? Is that it?'

He gave a sly grin.

'Why are you pretending you have nothing to do with it? You're just as much a part of it as we are. Come on Şehsuvar, enough of the acting! There must be a reason why you're staying in this luxury hotel when you have a lovely little place of your own just down the road in Beşiktaş.'

'Of course there's a reason', I snapped. 'As an ex-CUP man, I'm afraid for my life. I don't have your power or your resources. I don't have an organisation guarding me. And I don't want one either! My only concern is that if I am captured or killed, the news gets out and the people of this country know about it. That's why I'm staying in the Pera Palace.'

The clouds of suspicion in his eyes seemed to disperse but Fuad had never been the type to give in easily.

'And Mehmed Esad? What about him? Why are you always meeting up with him?' Before I could answer, he went on. 'And don't you dare try any of that 'he's an old friend' nonsense with me. Both you and I know you can't stand the guy. More importantly, he can't stand you. So there must be another reason behind your meetings with him. An important reason.' He looked at the newspaper again. 'Something like this, eh? Tell me, am I wrong?'

The time had perhaps come to show my cards. I leaned back and began.

'If Mehmed Esad is still working for the party, then shouldn't you, more than anybody, know about it? Seeing as you're one of the heads of the CUP now, you should know what he's up to.'

He just stood there, staring. I thought he was going to come out with an explanation but instead he asked, 'How well do you know Mehmed Esad? Before you began seeing him recently, when was the last time you saw him?'

He looked as though he really wanted to know. Perhaps he wanted to trust me.

'Probably before the occupation... Yes, that's right. It was after you'd left for Basra with Süleyman Askeri. So it must have been around the end of 1914. We ran into each other at the General Headquarters. He told me he would soon be heading for the front too. I didn't see him again after that.'

'So you never saw him during the occupation? Because he was also working for the *Karakol Teşkilatı* at that time.'

'Nope. I didn't see him or hear anything about him. As it is, I was captured during the second year of the occupation and shipped off to Malta by the British.'

'The British', he said, hissing the words between his teeth. 'The British... You know Mehmed Esad was in contact with the British during the occupation, don't you?'

I remembered what Cezmi Kenan had told me and thought about telling Fuad but then thought better of it. I decided to exercise patience instead and let Fuad reveal what he knew first. There was no point in showing all my cards straight away.

'Not back then. Not when I was with the *Karakol Teşkilatı*, nor when I was incarcerated in the Bekir Ağa Bölüğü Prison.

And I didn't know about it during my exile in Malta either. No one saw Mehmed Esad as a traitor.' I was then struck by an outlandish idea. 'Why don't you ask him yourself? I can bring you together if you like. Arrange a meeting so you two can talk face to face. In fact, he told me he wanted to see his old friends from the CUP.'

'Is that so?' he said, twitching uneasily on his stool. 'Why would he want to meet ex-CUP guys?'

Just as I had expected. His reaction was a sign that I was on the right tracks.

'Well, that I don't know but he asked after you by name.'

His face went darkened.

'After me? How?'

'Oh, just off the cuff. Nothing serious. 'What's that friend of yours Fuad doing? He was a brave chap, and a good soldier.' That's all he said.' And then, as though I had only just noticed his curiosity, I went on. 'What's going on, Fuad? Is there something going on between you and Mehmed Esad? Do you have an issue with him or what? Why is he so important? At the end of the day, he's just an ex-soldier doing some business. But if you like, you can meet up with him face to face. He's not far from here, either. Just up the road, in the European Arcade. How about we finish our drinks here and go and pay him a visit?'

He kept his eyes on me the whole time. There was no concern or anxiety in his blue eyes, just the cautiousness of a man trying to solve a riddle. He eventually looked away.

'Not right now. But... But...' His blue eyes came back to me. 'Let's meet at the Ferah Theatre tomorrow. Bring Mehmed Esad. We'll be able to talk in peace there.'

'Fine by me. I don't mind. Problem is, Mehmed Esad has to agree too. I can't consent to the arrangement on his behalf. I'm sure you understand.'

'Don't you worry', he said with a sly, almost malicious smile. 'He'll be delighted by the suggestion'.

So, my dearest Ester, that is the conversation that took place between myself and Fuad. It was strange. There was once a time when I would have trusted him with my life but now I barely recognised him. He left after he finished his tea but not before reminding me about our appointment.

'So tomorrow at eleven? I'll be expecting you both. It could be a nice little get together, eh? Hopefully it will be as interesting as the conversation you had with him.'

I pretended not to notice his little insinuation.

'Done. If Mehmed Esad agrees, we'll be there tomorrow at eleven.'

As soon as Fuad left, I sent a message to Mehmed Esad with one of the hotel staff. *We need to meet. Events have taken an unexpected turn. I'll be at yours this evening at five. Regards.* I then went up to my room and stared at myself in the silver-framed mirror. I looked alert and focused, almost happy. Perhaps old Basri Bey was right when he said it was in my blood, this business… Actually, no, it wasn't the truth. It was nice of him to say so, and nice to hear, but it wasn't true. There was no need for me to lie to myself. I may have looked pleased but I had grown tired of the plots and intrigues and I did not want to be a part of any sinister scheme. Not a part, nor a target. But first I have to extricate myself from this quagmire into which I have been unwillingly dragged. If I can, that is. Either way, I can sense that I am nearing the end of the road. The mystery will be revealed tomorrow and the knot will be unravelled. At the Ferah Theatre at eleven o'clock…. But before that, I need to finish my writing. Seeing as the mystery will be solved tomorrow, I will be leaving the Ferah Theatre either a free man or a dead man. So here I am back at my desk, my mind wandering back to the final years of the Great War.

From 1914 through to 1918, as the Great War raged on, I stayed in the capital. Actually, it was more a case of being unable to leave, rather than choosing to stay. Talat Bey would not grant me permission to leave. He kept me by his side like a shadow, one that kept him up to date with all the latest developments, not just those of our enemies but of our rivals and indeed people on our own side too… So yes, I was working for the *Teşkilat-i Mahsusa*, the Ottoman Secret Service, gathering news from our men on the various front lines, from Istanbul to

Baku and from the Crimea to Baghdad, and providing them assistance whenever and however I could. But that was not my only duty. I was also charged with keeping tabs on Enver Paşa and Cemal Paşa's activities and reporting back to Talat Bey if I noticed anything suspicious or untoward. Yes, the names Talat, Enver and Cemal were inextricably linked to the running of the country and yes, the bond between the three men who had shouldered the burden of the state may have been stronger than that of brothers but the fact remained, none of them trusted the other two. Indeed, as the defeats began to mount up, the cracks and splits between the factions following the three men began to show, to the extent that in 1916, rumours reached us that Cemal, who held Enver responsible for the defeats, was planning a coup. The Minister of Internal Affairs at the time, Talat Bey made it clear that he was utterly against any such plan, even in rumour, and the three men then rallied and regrouped saying they were 'all for one and one for all'.

Actually, looking back, Talat Bey was consistent in at least one aspect of his political life and that was his pragmatism in government. His being a comparatively relaxed fellow able to remain upbeat and hopeful during even the most trying of circumstances played a large part in his success, as was his ability to find a middle path and bring conflicting parties to the negotiating table in order to keep the political ship afloat. Although some of his CUP peers saw this and criticised it as the clumsy politics of desperation, Talat Bey had managed to remain a balancing force within the organisation and my clandestine mission was to protect and support his politics of reconciliation and unity. But my work was hard as I was still seen as Talat's man, whereas the directors of the *Teşkilat-ı Mahsusa*, in contrast, were – in the main – closer to Enver. Its last deputy chairman, for instance, Hüsamettin Bey, had worked alongside Enver for years and was one of his most trusted men. So if by chance I was to give myself away and it got out that I was gathering information for the Minister of the Interior, then it wouldn't just be my position and reputation on the line – the entire government would be thrown into turmoil.

But it was not just the conflicts between the pashas that we had to deal with in the capital. Unfortunately, disheartening news from the front just kept on coming. The Central Powers were reeling from one defeat after another and we as a nation were in terrible straits, suffering from hunger, misery, disease and depravation. To top it all off were the terrible accusations of corruption... The short-sightedness of men like İsmail Hakkı Paşa, who was in charge of overseeing the execution of Kara Kemal's economic programme, which was supposedly devised to revive the national economy, led to many setbacks and the party was hit by a barrage of charges and allegations. Added to these woes were our German allies' demands, which were increasing day by day. The pressure soon began to tell on Sait Halim Paşa, the *sadrazam*, who voiced his discontent at the situation, a discontent that was not necessarily unreasonable. German intelligence officers were running wild in the Ottoman high command and, in the name of the alliance and cooperation, they were listening to our every word and knew our every step. And although Sait Halim Paşa was right to be concerned, he was wrong to openly express his alarm, when he should have approached matters with the decorum befitting a minister of the state rather than a reckless and outspoken member of the public.

'We need to bring an end to this war', he would say.

'Those that committed atrocities during the deportation of the Armenians should be brought before courts and made to stand trial.'

'We must not let war profiteers flourish and fatten themselves whilst the masses live on dry bread.'

'We should not bow to every German demand.'

Of course, these grumbled declarations were all recorded by the Secret Service and sent to Enver Bey. But what must have infuriated him more than anything were the *sadrazam's* calls for peace.

'What the hell kind of premier does he think he is?' he once growled to Talat Bey, whom I was with at the time. 'While our men are out there performing heroics and sacrificing their lives for the country, this man is all but an emissary for our enemies. He's bad for our troops' morale.'

Talat Paşa, as always, tried to placate his friend and comrade, telling him to be patient and that the situation would eventually be dealt with. Well, it had to be, otherwise the Prime Minister and the Minister for War would soon be at each other's throats. Eventually, two weeks later, at a meeting at the party headquarters, Sait Halim Paşa was removed from office on the recommendation of Kara Kemal and Talat Paşa was pronounced the new *sadrazam*. Enver Paşa was delighted at the news but surprisingly, Talat Bey did not share his enthusiasm.

When I congratulated him upon his appointment to the post, he replied, 'Thanks, Şehsuvar, but I'm afraid there is not much to celebrate. It's a heavy burden… A heavy, heavy burden indeed.'

I thought he was talking about the front and said, 'Don't be downcast, sir. The war's final die has yet to be cast. Fortune may yet smile upon us.'

He smiled a bitter smile.

'It looks like you too have been infected by my idiotic optimism.' He then reached out and touched my arm to reassure me he was speaking in jest. 'Yes, our work on the front is hard but that is not what worries me. Let our pashas and our generals worry about that. They are more than equal to the task.' He deliberately emphasised the word *pashas*. 'No, what worries me, Şehsuvar, is how we are going to find food for our people. Food, fuel and medicine. Our people are hungry and sick, and they are freezing. If things go on like this, our civilian casualties will surpass our military losses.'

I had seen Talat Bey worried before but this was the first time I had seen him look so utterly downcast.

As the defeats and the dejection piled up at home, there were two developments in 1917 that would be decisive in the outcome of the war. The first, which was to our detriment, was the Americans entering the war in April with the British. They would not be engaged in battle directly against us but they brought fresh blood to the Allied Forces and it was a major blow to our troops' morale, which was already dangerously low. There was also a fear amongst the *Teşkilat* that morale at home would be hit so hard by the American entry into the war that it could lead to people rising up in revolt. However, that particular fear was quite unfounded as it was clear that a people that had, throughout history, fawningly submitted to the will, whims and dictates of the state and its masters had long since forgotten how to revolt. Back then, I admired that particular characteristic of our people but when I look back at it now, I can't help but wish they had risen up and overthrown us in a bloody rebellion.

However, the revolution that did not take place in our country exploded into life in November that year in Russia. Your Uncle Leon's socialist comrades toppled Czar Nicholas and opened up a path to peace, albeit a partial one. The deposing of the czar was a boon not just for the Russians and for the workers of the world but for us too, coming as it did during our darkest hour. After the Bolshevik revolution, the formidable foe we had been facing for so long in the East was suddenly and unexpectedly no more. The Russians were retreating from Eastern Anatolia, ceding to us the cities of Kars, Ardahan and Batum. Talat Bey was beginning to regain some of his former cheerfulness and after a long, long time, the word 'victory' began to be uttered again in the party's general headquarters. And why not? There was still a chance that we could emerge victorious. Indeed, if you asked Enver Paşa, the possibility had always been there and now we were edging closer to our ultimate triumph. But the truth is, although the year 1918 began in high hopes for us, it would end in despair and defeat. But before I write about that looming disaster, let me tell you about the events that were unfolding in the palace.

1918 was not just a terrible year for the people but also for the Ottoman dynasty. On the tenth day of February, we received news that the former sultan Abdülhamit's health had taken a turn for the worse. Although no one had asked me to do so, that Sunday evening I got up and went to Beylerbeyi Palace In 1912, before the loss of Salonika, he had been brought back to the capital and had taken up residence in Beylerberi Palace, where he had been living a quiet life, keeping to himself and desisting from playing any role in state affairs. When I heard the news that his illness was at an advanced stage, I don't know why I felt the urge to visit him. Perhaps it was because of the conversation we had had a decade earlier when I had escorted him into exile or the memory and the impact of the book he had given to me as a gift. Or perhaps it was just a simple case of respect for one's adversary. But the fact remains, if, years earlier, someone had told me that the day would come when I would attend the funeral of the sultan who was responsible for my father's death, I would have uttered all manner of curses in that man's face. At the palace, I found the sultan's personal physician, Atıf Hüseyin Bey, who told me that his royal patient had passed away. He had taken a turn for the worse ten days earlier but a few days later he had begun to recover and only yesterday, the doctor told me, he had informed him that he was feeling fit and fresh and revived and had sent the doctor away. However, that same evening, he began feeling poorly once again and the next day at noon he passed away as a result of coronary failure. I didn't want to see the body and I know they would not have let me anyway, had I asked.

On Monday, the body was placed on a steamboat and brought to Topkapı Palace, where it was washed, prepared and wrapped in a shroud. Following the noon prayer, in a ceremony befitting the sultans, he was laid to rest in the tomb of his grandfather, Mahmud II. I don't know why but I was greatly moved by the funeral. It wasn't just the final rites of a once powerful sultan I was witnessing but the end of an era. Yes, the war was still raging but one did not have to be psychic to know calamity was not far away and the death of Abdülhamit was one of the omens of the terrible fate that lay in wait for us.

That year, Abdülhamit was not the dynasty's only loss. Not even five months later, the reigning sultan himself, Mehmed Reşad, would pass away. He had already been poorly but the more he heard about our defeats on the front, the more he saw the poverty and hardships heaping up on his people and the more he saw his country slip into ever greater peril, its fragile independence hanging in the balance, the more he retreated into himself. Unable to defy the demands of the party, Sultan Reşad became increasingly despondent and all but severed himself from the affairs of state. He made sure he avoided any matter that would upset him and even refused to attend certain ceremonies at which his presence was mandatory. Indeed, it was just such a ceremony that was the cause of his death – he passed away nine days after suffering a fall while inspecting the religious and sacred artefacts that were housed in Topkapı Palace.

Although the death of the two sultans had a profound effect on the palace and the people, it would be hard to say that those running the country shared in their grief. The death of Sultan Reşad may have been a cause for concern for Enver Paşa and Talat Paşa, but the sultan-to-be, Vahdeddin, could not stomach the Committee for Union and Progress. His powers would be somewhat limited but the prospect of having on the throne a sultan who held the CUP in open disdain, and during such trying times too, had the potential to be very awkward and this fear was further intensified on the day of his coronation. As Vahdeddin was walking past the *Bâbüsaade,* `the Gate of Felicity', on the grounds of Topkapı Palace towards the Bağdad Köşkü mansion, he suddenly stopped and asked one of his aides, 'Where is my walking stick?' Those present were mortified and didn't know what to do but it wasn't long before the truth was revealed – the walking stick in question had been forgotten in his villa in Çengelköy. The sultan, who considered the walking stick auspicious, was horrified and cried out, 'This is a calamity!' Enver Paşa was standing next to him at the time but I doubt he gave the incident much thought as he was too busy with his own preparations for a plot against the government and his comrades in the party. I found out about the plot when Talat Bey invited me to his house. The invitation made it quite clear that the meeting was to be secret: *Please make sure no one notices you arrive.*

'I've called you here on urgent business', he said, not even bothering to wait for our coffees. 'I have a mission for you now that is far more important and far more delicate than anything you have done to date. And it needs to be done promptly.' He waved his index finger for emphasis. 'There are rumours that Enver Paşa is planning a coup. They say he is readying forces both in Istanbul and on the Anatolian side of the city to attack the government and arrest and detain its officials. I need you to find out how much truth there is in these rumours. And it needs to be done soon. Time is of the essence in this particular case, Şehsuvar. I cannot stress that enough. Time is of the essence.'

I did not know the ins and outs of the case and felt compelled to ask.

'Why would Enver Paşa do such a thing? Of all the people that wanted you to be *sadrazam*, he was one of the most vocal.'

'Ah Şehsuvar', he sighed. 'All manner of guile is possible for a man who has lost sense of reality. Enver Paşa believes the government is going to sign a peace treaty with the British, independently of the Germans, and in the event of this happening, it appears he will be ready to strike with his men and assume power. I would like you to find out the truth. Find out what is really going on. But please, be careful. No one should know about it.'

I did as instructed and after some snooping around, I found out that the rumours were true. Enver Paşa and his friends had a military strike force ready that could take over the government within a matter of hours. When Talat Bey read my report, he was livid.

'Friends for all these years and he still does not trust me! He is still running around with all this clandestine secret society madness!'

Of course, Enver Paşa, when challenged, was ready with his answer.

'Yes, I do have forces ready. But they are not there to overthrow the government but to stop adventurers like Yakup Cemil from carrying out a coup.'

He knew the truth but Talat Bey still accepted this answer. Indeed, at one point, when the matter was being discussed, he even said, in order to excuse Enver Paşa, 'He's not doing it to protect the Germans but because he still thinks we can win the war.' But history has a powerful memory, powerful enough to record our mistakes and our ineptitude, and the logic of this memory is based on reality, not on illusions like Enver Paşa's. History favours no one and grants privileges to no one, regardless of how strong they may be or how much power they have, or how despotic they are. The incompetent, the ineffectual, the inept – ultimately, they all pay the price. And not just them but those that turned a blind eye to their maleficence will also be unable to protect themselves from the judgements of history. It wouldn't be long before the reckoning took place and when it did, it would again be the Great Master that rebuked Enver.

The autumn of 1918 was perhaps the darkest of any the Ottoman Empire had experienced. The outcome of the Great War had now been all but settled and our defeat was inevitable. Everything else was irrelevant. All that was missing was the official declaration of what was already known. Talat Bey had gone to Berlin to ensure we formed a united front with the Germans that would allow us to maintain a common stance for the rest of the war and then broker an acceptable peace. We were all desperate to find out what we could salvage from the mess. It was still debatable as to how honourable (or not) our defeat was but at least our dignity had not been dragged through the mud. It was with this scant consolation in mind that we hoped to be able to make something of the end game. But even that hope was dashed. When Talat Paşa arrived in Berlin, the Germans had long since decided to act alone and go on ahead without us.

I remember the Great Master's return from Berlin as I was there amongst the many others waiting for him at Sirkeci Train Station. Despite being tired, he put on a brave face and stopped to chat with some journalists. He even cracked a few jokes with them. But as someone that knew him well, I could tell something was wrong. The smiles, the laughter, the overstated bonhomie; none of it was genuine. As he was leaving the station, he beckoned me over with a jerk of his head.

'You ride with us, Şehsuvar. I need to speak to you.'

I was surprised as he had always tried to keep our closeness a secret, or at least not announce it to the world. But when I got into the car, I understood why he had asked me to join him. Once we were alone, his body seemed to give way and the conviviality he had shown with the journalists at the station gave way to a look of resignation. As the car made its way to the palace, he sighed.

'Do you remember the day we came to the capital from Salonika? Those were hard times. We were on our way to a meeting with Sait Halim Paşa. We didn't even know if we would make it out of the meeting alive. But at least we had hope...' His eyes seemed to mist over. 'Yes, we had hope. And it was a realistic, legitimate hope too, one that could become real. But this time we have failed, my friend.' He let out another deep sigh. 'It's over, Şehsuvar. This time it really is over. We've lost the war and sooner or later we will lose our mandate. I don't care about my own life but I just hope and pray that we don't lose the entire country too.'

He looked so dejected and so broken, I could not bring myself to ask him what had happened in Berlin.

'Of course we won't, Talat Paşa', is all I managed to say, but even I did not believe it. He smiled and took out his cigarette case. He lit a cigarette, blew plumes of smoke into the damp autumn breeze, and gazed pensively out at the murky blue-green sea.

'Let's see. *Inshallah*, you will be proven right.'

Outside, a colourless, scentless rain was falling almost malevolently over the city.

A Fragmented Homeland, a Disintegrating World

Good Night, Ester (Night, Day 14)

I treated myself to a feast in the Pera Palace restaurant this evening. I selected the dishes myself: fillet of sea bass, roast beef with vegetables, spiced *Ali Paşa* rice with turkey, deep-fried spring rolls with cheese and artichokes in olive oil, followed by a dessert of *kadayıf* with clotted cream and then coffee. I also asked Reşit to join me but warned him before he sat down that it was all on me and that our friendship would be over if he objected. He saw how serious I was and decided not to raise a fuss but he was curious as to what it was all for.

'What are we celebrating, Şehsuvar *ağabey*?'

I couldn't tell him it was farewell meal so I was forced to lie to him.

'It's my birthday today, Reşit old boy. Yes, yes, I know celebrating birthdays is not really our thing and is one of those things foreigners do. And I can't say I'm a big fan of birthdays but today I just feel like having a slap-up meal for the occasion…'

'Well, in that case the wine is on me', he said cheerfully, swallowing the lie. 'I have two bottles from my own collection just for occasions like this.'

I accepted the offer and I'm glad I did too as the wines were simply marvellous…. But wait, I'm getting ahead of myself again. Let's get back to where we were.

After I posted my last letters to you from the hotel's post office, I went to the Orient Bar as that is where I was to meet

Mehmed Esad. If you remember, I sent him a note telling him there had been new developments that we needed to discuss and that I would be at his place at seven in the evening. Well, one of the hotel staff brought me back his reply. *My dear brother Şehsuvar, I'm afraid my place is not suitable so I'll be at the Orient Bar at the time you specified. Regards…* I didn't waste too much time worrying about why his shop was good enough for two earlier meetings but not anymore. And anyway, the Orient Bar was easier for me.

As I made my way to the bar, I saw Rüşeyim sitting in the lobby. He was completely still, a black marble statue staring at a single point in front of him, waiting patiently and loyally for his boss. He looked so engrossed in what he was doing that I assumed he wouldn't see me walk past but he did and he got up out of his chair to greet me. I smiled in return and moved on.

When I walked through the door into the dimly lit saloon, Mehmed Esad was sitting at a table by a large window overlooking the street and sipping a cognac. The bar was relatively quiet for that time and, like his man Rüşeyim, he was lost in his own thoughts. He did not notice me until I was standing right next to him. When he saw me, he snapped out of his musings, welcomed me with a broad smile and shook my hand.

'Ah, Şehsuvar! Good to see you, old friend. Here, take a seat.'

'Have you been waiting long? You should have sent someone up to tell me you'd arrived. I was in my room.'

'Oh no, I've just arrived', he answered nonchalantly and then looked down at the honey-coloured liquid in his snifter. 'Not that I mind. Lovely stuff, this cognac. Just wonderful'.

I signalled to the barman to bring me the same. When I turned back around, I noticed Mehmed Esad was watching me, just as Fuad had been, with an intense, burning curiosity, although Mehmed Esad's expression was wilier and more cautious than Fuad's. It was a look that wanted to know and wanted to understand.

'So, tell me. What have you been up to since we last met? Although having said that, we only just met yesterday, eh?'

Actually, what he really wanted to ask was what the hell all these new developments I had mentioned in my note were. I don't know why he was being so cagey.

'I'll tell you one thing, Mehmed. Sometimes things happen in the space of just twenty-four hours that can turn your life upside down. Of course, you'll be the one to decide whether what I am about to tell you is important or not.'

'What's going on, Şehsuvar old boy? Out with it, eh?'

'Well, I've found Fuad', I murmured. 'Remember you were asking after him the other day?'

'Well, that's good news', he said, relaxing a little. 'Did you get to talk to him? What's he up to?'

I could have lied outright but I chose to play safe.

'Actually, I'm not that sure as he spoke in very vague terms. You're involved in all this, Mehmed. I'll tell you what he said and then perhaps you can make something of it.'

He crossed his arms over his chest.

'Of course. I'm listening. What did he say? Does he regret his actions or what?'

I shrugged my shoulders.

'Not really. No regrets. He hasn't changed at all. The same mindset, the same thinking. Basically, he is still doing his CUP thing. But if you ask me, he's a bit confused. A bit unstable, if you will.'

Like Fuad this morning, he stared straight at me and listened attentively, but again, he was calmer and more cautious than Fuad had been.

'What do you mean?'

'Well, he was angry. Furious, to be honest, but he didn't actually seem so self-assured. He looked determined enough to face death but at the same time he was doubtful enough to question what he was doing… He seemed to be caught between two poles of thought. Between two feelings.'

I stopped talking when I saw the barman approach. I waited for him to put my drink on the table and leave before resuming.

'If you ask me, Fuad is desperate. On the one hand, he has his memories and his principles, which make him who he is, while on the other there is this crushing blow he has yet to come to terms with. If he could just see that the new government actually stands for our ideas and ideals, he might relax…'

Mehmed was listening in silence. I reached for my glass.

'Let's drink. To old days'.

'To friendship', he said, clinking his glass against mine. 'To everlasting friendship'.

I took a sip of the burning liquid. It was hard to tell whether he had deliberately emphasised the word *friendship* or if it had just been wishful thinking on my part.

'What does he think about the government?' he asked.

I screwed up my face and shook my head.

'We didn't talk much about the government but he cannot stand Mustafa Kemal. And he is furious at the people behind the assassination attempt in Izmir. Said they were amateurs and had messed the whole thing up. I think he sees the President as the main problem. He had nothing bad to say about Ismet Paşa, for instance.'

It was impossible not to notice the relief in Mehmed Esad's eyes. He reached into his pocket and took out a packet of cigarettes.

'So was he alone or what? Was there anybody with him?'

I gently shook the snifter in my hand but decided to answer him before taking my next sip.

'He may have a tiny crew but I don't know how many they are. As far as I can see, they're operating by themselves… What I mean is, I don't think they are in touch with any other CUP people. But they are on the lookout for new members and more importantly, they are thinking of creating a new organisation, a proper one. He wanted me to join. To take revenge for Kara Kemal and what have you.'

'And what did you say?'

'I told him exactly what I told you. That I'm no longer involved in any of this and that I want to die peacefully in my sleep… He was disappointed, of course. That's when I mentioned you. He remembers you. I didn't tell him that you work for the government now. I told him that you were confused like him and that I can arrange a meeting if he liked. I thought he would refuse but he didn't. His only condition is that I be present at the meeting too. The poor guy sees me as some sort of cover. A safety valve, if you will.'

I reached out for my glass and took another sip of cognac while Mehmed lit another cigarette.

'How did you find him? It can hardly be considered a coincidence, him finding you like that…'

Of course, Mehmed was not the type to simply carry out what was asked of him and he first wanted to be sure he would not be putting himself in danger. My role was to dispel any misgivings he may have had.

'Of course it wasn't a coincidence. He came to see me this morning. That's right, here. The manager of the Pera Palace, Reşit, is from Salonika. He must have found out from him that I've been staying here. It had been some time since we'd last met. A full twelve years, to be precise.' I stopped. 'Hold on, old boy. Are you telling me you don't have any information on Fuad? That the state's intelligence agency isn't keeping an eye on shady characters like him?'

He averted his gaze and, after tapping some ash into his ashtray, began his attempt at an explanation.

'Actually, we were but Fuad is a smart chap and we lost his trail. So it's a good thing you managed to make contact with him.' He took a deep drag from his cigarette. 'So what's your take on the whole thing? Do you think he's serious? You think he means it or is he up to something?'

I looked at him and shrugged.

'That's for you to decide, Mehmed. I've gone rusty. You know I've been out of this game for years. I've told you everything I know. Laid it all on the line. The rest is up to you.'

'Fair enough', he said disconsolately. 'Tell me, back in the day, before the Great War began that is, what was Fuad's relationship like with the party?'

'Terrible', I replied. 'Absolutely terrible, in every sense of the word. In fact, that is why he wanted to go to the front. To put an end to a life of torment with an honourable death.'

'But he survived, didn't he?' Mehmed said, almost jubilantly. 'He came back in one piece'.

'He did indeed. Maybe that's why he's so miserable and so angry'.

'Just like Niyazi of Resen', he muttered. 'Just like Yakup Cemil. A tragic end for those guys'.

'Absolutely. They died for nothing. Especially Yakup Cemil... His death was awful. And a warning to us all.'

His face fell with grief. It was hard to know whether he really was upset or just wanted to appear that way.

'He was executed by firing squad, wasn't he?'

He seemed to have forgotten all about Fuad. We were, after all, talking about our shared past, and to be honest, I was glad at the change of subject as it meant Mehmed's suspicions had begun to disperse.

'Yep. Over by Kağıthane Bridge'.

His eyes narrowed and his moustache quivered slightly.

'Were you with him at the time?'

I downed the last of my cognac before answering.

'I was. I was there throughout it all. Back then, I was one of the directors of the Secret Service. As soon as Yakup Cemil was arrested, I went to see him. I don't know if you remember or not. It was July 1916 when he was brought to the Bekirağa Bölüğü Barracks Prison. He still had his guns on him and no one there dared try to take them away from him. As for Yakup Cemil, he was extremely tense. He wouldn't sleep, nor would he eat out of fear they were trying to poison him. He said to me, "I don't want some cheap, shitty death. If it's going to be done, let it be done properly. Let's die the way we lived." It was only when he finally fell asleep from exhaustion after two nights without sleep that the soldiers managed to jump him and grab his guns. He was charged with attempting to stage a coup d'état and planning to assassinate various government ministers. Apparently, there were people that had personally heard him speak of his intentions. There were even some that claimed he had said, "I'm thinking of staging another attack on the government and of taking out Enver Paşa and replacing him with Mustafa Kemal".'

'He's too late', he said, as though Yakup Cemil had not died. 'He should have done it before Enver Bey assumed power. Before he had been awarded the title of *paşa*.'

'How could he have known what was to happen? How events were going to unfold?' I said, feeling a need to defend the movement's legendary marksman. 'Like everyone else, he thought we would emerge from the Great War triumphant. In fact, he had proved his brilliance during the war. He'd been sent to the Caucasian Front at the head of a ragtag force of two thousand men that had been plucked from the jails and spared the noose. If you ask me, it was Enver Paşa that had Yakup Cemil sent there. Enver knew he could not handle him and so had him sent as far away from the capital as possible. But like I said, Yakup Cemil was no pushover and he still made a name for himself out there. He was pivotal in our victories in Batum and Ardahan, when we pushed the enemy back and reclaimed our territories. But he would not sit still and be content with those victories. He began quarrelling with his commandant and, worse yet, his treatment of the troops took a nasty turn. Very unpleasant rumours began circulating and reached us in the end. The worst of the rumours was that after one particular defeat, he had sixteen soldiers executed by firing squad. There must have been some truth to the rumours because Mahmud Kamil Paşa, Commander of the Third Army, eventually grew tired of Yakup and had him sent to Bitlis. But Yakup Cemil wouldn't calm down there, either. Not content with bullying the soldiers there, he began tyrannising the local Armenians, who refused to hand over their youngsters to the Labour Battalions. Throughout all this, he kept up his stream of letters and advice to Enver Paşa, telling him what needed to be done for the war effort. He was eventually posted to Baghdad, but even there his crude and violent behaviour continued and when it led to the deaths of some soldiers, his commander lied to him and told him Enver Paşa wanted him in the capital and that he would be of greater use to the country there and sent him packing to Istanbul.

'It didn't take long for Yakup Cemil to learn the truth when he reached the capital. Enver Paşa was not as friendly towards him as he used to be but the Ministry of War still rewarded him by promoting him to the rank of major. Whether this was done out of respect for the good old days or done simply to silence a wild and unpredictable man, it is hard to tell. Naturally, Yakup Cemil scoffed at the promotion; he expected more. Why wasn't he being made a pasha or an army commander? Amongst the many reports received by the Secret Service were some that stated that Yakup Cemil had been threatening none other than Enver Paşa. Had it stayed at that, he may still have saved his skin but the rumours that he was planning a coup were beginning to grow louder. Indeed, Yakup did not hide the fact that he held Enver responsible for our defeats during the during the war and began all but shouting out in the streets that he would bring about peace to the nation once he was in power. He may as well have signed his own death warrant and indeed, on the 13th of July 1913, he was duly arrested.

'He and his cohorts were tried after being disarmed at the Bekirağa Bölüğü Prison. Some of his companions were sent into exile while others were acquitted. As for Yakup Cemil himself, he was sentenced to death. I was with Talat Bey when he signed the verdict for execution.

I asked him if it had to be execution and whether exile or a prison sentence may not suffice. He stared straight at me and in a stern and unwavering tone said, 'I no longer want to listen to the screams of innocent people suffering as a result of disasters brought about by misplaced compassion.' He then sealed the document with the ministerial seal. Yakup Cemil was executed on an autumn day. There wasn't even a trace of fear in his eyes. When he saw me, he shot me a defiant look.

'So you're finally getting your revenge, eh?' he said. 'You're finally getting what you wished for.' I shook my head sadly and told him it wasn't personal and that it was just politics. He must have appreciated the remark as he gave a dry smile and said, 'Indeed it is, brother Şehsuvar. Nothing but damned dirty politics.' He then turned to the soldiers that were lined up in front of him rifles at the ready and, as though they were men under his own command, bellowed, 'Well, what are you waiting for? Let's get on with it. Take good aim and keep those hands steady. If the punishment is in accordance with the Sharia, then it cannot hurt. There can be no victory without deference to the government!'

'The head of the firing squad blew his whistle and fourteen rifles went off at the same time. But Yakup, as you know, was one tough nut and he didn't die straight away. He was writhing on the ground for some time…'

I had only started talking about it to distract Mehmed but the more I spoke about those events and remembered them, the more I began to be affected by them. I could almost see the details of the execution, as though it had taken place only yesterday. A bloodied body ripped apart by a hail of bullets, a broad face turning a ghostly white and soldiers barely believing that the man they had just shot had really died.

'He was a brave man', Mehmed said admiringly. 'Whether he was right is open to debate but there is no denying the man's courage. And that's why I keep saying we need to win over men like Fuad. To stop them going the same way as men like Niyazi of Resen and Yakup Cemil.'

'Well, you'll have to convince him first. And like I said before, I can't do that. You're going to have to find a way to explain things to him yourself.'

He took one last drag from his cigarette and then stubbed it out in the ashtray.

'Don't you worry. I'll handle that'. He looked at me with a look of complete self-assurance. 'I mean, look at you. You were hesitant at first too but you came round in the end. You were convinced. Your bringing Fuad to me will be more than enough.'

I raised my eyebrows and opened my arms out in a gesture of helplessness.

'I've been trying to get it through to you. Fuad won't come o you. He doesn't trust anybody, and that includes me. Why do you think he came to my hotel in such a flustered state this morning, as though he was being followed? He's scared, the way I used to be. He's worried something is going to happen to him.'

'Well, how are we going to meet then?' he said irately. 'Are you saying he won't agree to a meeting?'

'He will but he says at a location of his choosing. The Ferah Theatre. Tomorrow, if it suits you. You know the Ferah Theatre don't you? It's undergoing renovations at the moment, and as far as I can tell, Fuad has been in touch with the people carrying out the restorations. He'll be waiting for us there at eleven o'clock. If you can't make it, I'll still go by myself. That's what I told him. I told him I'd come but that I couldn't vouch for you.'

His eyes stayed on me for some time before he replied, quite nonchalantly, 'No problem. We'll go there together. I'll pick you up in the morning from the hotel.'

I turned to the barman to order a drink and to hide my reaction.

'Two more cognacs please'.

'Thanks but I'm going to have to decline', Mehmed said. 'I need to get going, Şehsuvar. I have another meeting lined up.'

And so we said our goodbyes and parted. I don't feel as though I have set a trap for my old friend because even I don't know what is in store for us tomorrow. I am in just as much danger as Mehmed and Fuad. But perhaps I am wrong. Perhaps nothing untoward will happen and an amicable agreement will be signed at the Ferah Theatre. But if my own feelings and predictions are correct, then I also need to be prepared for some serious action, and that is why I wanted to turn this evening's dinner into a banquet. I was also glad that Reşit joined me; if something is to happen to me, then he'll know that dinner was a thank you present of sorts. We sat until late, talking about Salonika, about its streets, squares, houses and thoroughfares, about its sea and how it has a different smell to Istanbul's, about our childhood and our schools, about the foods cooked in Salonika's homes and about our families, whose fina resting places are all in Salonika… When the last of the other diners had left and the restaurant was ours, Reşit finally gave in to temptation and began singing an old folk song. 'Salonika, Salonika, may you be left in ruins / May the waters wash you away, your rocks and your soil / May you be left, like me, without a friend in the world / Death, cruel death, stop for just three days / Take this accursed love of mine and give it to another…'

I'm back in my room. Despite knocking back two large bottles of wine, my head is fine. Even if my head were spinning, it wouldn't matter because I have to write to you. This may be my last letter and my last chance to write and so I think I should complete my story and write down what I have to say. It won't be difficult because I'm going to tell you about the turning point in my life that came in 1916 and how the end of the party dragged me into a whole new world. The wretched end to a twenty-year adventure, the slow extinguishing of a revolutionary fire that had been kept alive with grand hopes… It was perhaps just a small footnote in history but it was an entire lifetime for us. For some, it meant the dungeons, torture, exile or even death. For some, it was spectacular triumph, for others, crushing and shameful defeat. For some, it was heroics worthy of legend, for others it was treachery and infamy of the lowest order. There were sublime loves, unforgettable sacrifices and bitter woes, all, ultimately, ending in broken lives, a fragmented homeland and a disintegrating world…

It was the 2nd of November 1918… A warm night, a remnant of the last days of summer. I was at home. I had just finished dinner and was sitting at the wooden table under the now bare plum tree in the garden waiting for the coffee Madam Melina was preparing. I was exhausted, having been at the party congress all day. I had gone with Cezmi Kenan, to what would be the last congress at the *Pembe Köşk* mansion. It was a bleak affair. Very bleak indeed. That day I came to realise that organisations, like people, also have a spirit, a spirit that gains character and a persona with its rise and collapse. Just as we had felt the same joy, the same sense of freedom and the same shared delight with the nation years earlier in

Salonika, converse feelings had now taken over. We all now felt the same disappointment, the same despondency, the same deep pain. I had attended numerous CUP congresses over the years and had never experienced such a heavy and forlorn atmosphere, even when we were under intense pressure from a government that regarded us as its sworn enemy and was applying all the power it had at its disposal to make our lives hell. All one had to do at this congress to gage the mood was to glance at Talat Paşa, who was in the chair speaking. Yes, he was doing his best to appear calm and confident but when he was describing what the party had been through over the previous few days, his voice began to tremble and he could not hold back his tears. Perhaps that is why he did not prolong the matter and ended his speech by saying, 'I am resigning from the Central Committee of the CUP and am hereby handing over administration to the Grand Council.' He had been removed from the post of *sadrazam* just sixteen days earlier after the formation of a government under the leadership of Ahmet Izzet Paşa and he was now, of his own accord, renouncing leadership of the party. I was heartbroken but Cezmi Kenan, who was sitting next to me, rather than feeling downcast, was furious.

'They are making a terrible mistake. They should not be stepping down, nor should they be resigning from the government. That is exactly what Sultan Vahdeddin wants. Now watch. The occupying forces will make us pay ... This cannot be allowed. If necessary, we shall have to take up arms again.'

If only it were so easy. If only the matter could have been resolved with guns but those days had long since passed. We were now in a far more precarious condition. The question bothering me that day was the same one disturbing most of the other party members at the congress that day and that was: what happens now? Others spoke after Talat Bey, of course, and how beautifully they spoke too! Such flowery rhetoric and such sophisticated and urbane proposals we heard, followed by fiery debates and grand plans and even grander promises. But none of them -- not one – had an answer to the simple question of 'What happens now?' We had lost the Great War, our guns had fallen silent, our banners lay crumpled in the dirt and the people and the nation were at the mercy of enemy forces. Danger was lurking nearby and it was just a matter of time before the occupying armies arrived at the capital.

It was in an utterly demoralised state that I returned to Beşiktaş. However, there was a nice surprise waiting for me when I got home as Niko, Madam Melina's distant cousin and a fisherman, had brought over two bluefish, which, after days of rationed black bread, were nothing short of a banquet for us. Madam Melina, bless her heart, got to work grilling the fish and when I saw the rocket and spring onion from our neighbour Hacı Ilyas' allotment added to the salad and the sudden appearance of a bottle of consecrated wine that had been kept aside for just such an occasion, my woes seemed to momentarily vanish and I felt, as the saying goes, like king for a day. After we had eaten our fill and were enjoying the sweet drowsiness of full stomachs, I could no longer refuse the tempting call of the warm night drifting in through the open window and stepped outside into the garden to drink my artificial coffee (made from chickpeas, no less) under the plum tree. Outside, I noticed a car parked by the front gate. Who could it be at this late hour? When I leaned forward to get a better look, a silhouette slipped into the garden. I jumped back in fear but then, when the silhouette stepped out of the darkness, I saw that it was Ömer Bey, Talat Bey's aide.

'Hello there, Ömer. No bad news, I hope?'

'No, no, nothing like that. Just that Talat Bey would like to see you.'

'I see. When? Tomorrow?'

He shook his head firmly.

'No, Şehsuvar Bey. Now. Right now. We need to go.'

'What, are we going to the Hagia Sophia?' I asked, unnecessarily concerned.

'No, Talat Bey is not at home. We're going to Arnavutköy. To Ihsan Namık Bey's home.'

Ihsan Namık was an honourable man, someone Talat Bey trusted, but why would he be at his house this late? Had the occupation forces already arrived? Were we about to set up a national resistance movement, as Cezmi Kenan had proposed at the congress that morning? Clearly, important things were taking place but either Ömer did not know about them or had been told not to divulge the details.

'In that case, let's go', I said but then I noticed Madam Melina coming down the stairs carrying a tray. I walked over to her, took the cup and took two swift sips.

'I'm so sorry, Madam Melina', I said, putting the cup back on the tray. 'But I have to dash. Hopefully you can make a fresh cup when I get back.'

'Nothing bad is happening, is it?' the poor woman asked anxiously as I made my way to the gate.

'Oh no, there's nothing to worry about. I'll be back soon'.

Once we were in the car, Ömer tapped the driver on the shoulder.

'Right, Şakir, let's be off. But keep an eye out, the way you did on the way here. If you feel something is up, let me know.' He saw me looking at him quizzically and muttered, 'Precautions. Just precautions'.

The journey was short and thankfully we were not followed. We didn't talk in the car but our minds were teeming with increasingly dark and ominous thoughts throughout the journey to Arnavutköy. As soon as I stepped into Ihsan Namık Bey's waterfront mansion, I knew what was going on. They were sitting at a table on the ground floor. Dinner must have finished some time ago, and there was a heavy and desolate atmosphere in the room. At first, I didn't know why. Talat Paşa was sitting and chatting with his young brother-in-law Hayreti, whilst their host, Ihsan Namık Bey, was pacing up and down nearby. In other words, there was nothing unusual or untoward at first glance. But then I saw the suitcases in the corner of the room and I realised why there was such a heavy atmosphere in the house. The Great Master was leaving. A sudden decision, yes, but he was leaving us to fend for ourselves. At first, I was furious. How could he leave like this, without asking us, without consulting us, without hearing what we had to say? But when I saw the embarrassed expression on Talat Paşa's face, my initial impression began to change. He rose to his feet.

'My apologies, Şehsuvar, for dragging you all the way out here at such an inconvenient hour. You know I wouldn't have called you had it not been of some importance. Please, take a seat.'

I nodded a greeting to Hayreti and sat on a nearby stool. The Great Master did not mince his words.

'We're going Şehsuvar. The main leaders of the party, that is. And yes, tonight. We're leaving the capital. We have no choice. We're leaving but we are not running away.'

It would have been more prudent of me not to ask but everything was happening so quickly and I was so shocked that the words just seemed to fall from my lips.

'Are you going to Anatolia?'

He paused. No, they were going abroad. He knew what I was thinking, which served only to increase his embarrassment.

'God willing, we shall eventually', he said, looking askance. 'But we first we need to step back and get a sound grasp of the situation. I'm sure you of all people will know and appreciate that one cannot formulate a new strategy until the dust has settled and we have a sound understanding of our circumstances. Right now, our priority is this issue of the occupation. If our fears are realised and the occupation does happen, we shall be straight back. We are hardly the type to avoid our own country's courts.' I was listening in silence and so Talat Paşa went on. 'There are two reasons why I called you here. First, we have worked and fought side by side for decades so I wanted you to hear from me in person that I have left the country and not from another. Secondly, I have a request. I would kindly ask you to look out for my wife Hayriye Hanım and the other members of my family. Hayriye Hanım is a strong, brave and capable woman but we have dark days ahead of us and if she should perchance need help, then...'

'Do not worry, sir. I shall look after them as my own family.'
He smiled gratefully.

'I know, Şehsuvar. You've always been a good man and a trustworthy friend.' He sighed a deep sigh and stared at the sea quivering in the darkness outside the open window. 'We have seen so much and been through so much and still we have survived so I am sure we shall pull through this too. These dark days will soon just be bad memories.' He turned back around to face me. 'I shall always have the fondest memories of you, Şehsuvar. I shall think good things when I think of you. I hope I may also have a place in your memories.'

I could feel a knot forming in my throat.

'Of course, sir. Anything else would be inconceivable'.

I think his eyes were also filling up and he looked away before suddenly getting to his feet.

'Well, I don't think I should keep you here any longer. The streets are not safe and we don't want you to be too late.'

I also got up.

'I can stay if you need me. For security purposes, I mean.'

'Don't you worry about that', he smiled. 'That's been taken care of'. He opened out his arms. 'Here, let me embrace you. Who knows when we shall see each other again.'

We would not see each other again and I think he also sensed it as he embraced me warmly. I realised at that moment that Talat Paşa, for me, was not just a party leader; he had also been a father figure to me, and I felt the same mixture of reverence, respect and affection for him that I used to feel for my father. And now, ironically, he was being sent into exile, just like my father.

When Talat Paşa told me he was leaving, I was not worried, even though I should have been as I was one of the CUP's marked men. Obviously, Vahdeddin's men and the occupying forces' spies were keeping tabs on my movements and eventually, after two years fighting the occupiers, I was arrested and tortured by the British and sent into exile to Malta for two years.

Obviously, I was crestfallen when saying goodbye to the Great Master but it never occurred to me to think our leaders were abandoning us to save their own lives, because that was not the case. The outcome for all three would be terrible. Within four years of secretly boarding a German submarine and fleeing the country, Enver, Cemal and Talat, the three powerful heads of the İttihat ve Terakki, would be gunned down in their new abodes abroad.

I also grasped another truth that evening on the way back home from Arnavutköy and that was that Talat Bey's departure, like Abdülhamit's death, had huge symbolic power. It signified the end of an era: our era. It was not the General Congress that had taken place that morning but history itself that had pronounced judgement upon us, and it had signed, stamped and sealed its verdict without pity. After that ill-starred night, the *İttihat ve Terraki*, the Committee of Union and Progress, was obsolete.

Turning Us All into Killers

Good Night, Ester (Night, Day 15)

It is late and I am still sitting at my desk.

Before starting this letter, I placed the record Fuad had given me on the gramophone. When Floria began her sad song, I started writing. Whether this is a good thing or not, I don't know but yes, Ester, I am still alive. I am free from danger and have overcome the obstacles that were in my way. It may be something akin to a miracle but yes, I am still alive…

Whereas this morning, when I was getting into Mehmed Esad's car, I didn't know if I would make it back to the hotel alive. Last night, after I had written my goodbyes to you and had put my pen down, I sat back and looked back on the chain of events, starting with my first encounter with Mehmed Esad up to my abduction by Fuad, but unfortunately, all the coincidences, all the words that had been spoken and the details and the possibilities that I managed to recall only led to the same results. Tomorrow the riddle would be solved, I told myself, but the real question was, what would the unravelled riddle result in? At one point I thought about going to my house in Beşiktaş to get my father's beloved old service revolver (which I have held on to almost like a sacred relic), not so I could defend myself from an ambush but so I could take them down with me on the way to the grave when they did jump me, but I then decided against it. What would be gained by more people dying? Who would benefit? The situation was clear. History had passed its verdict. Our party had been routed, and its members were broken and scattered. Personal costs would naturally have to be paid.

Actually, whatever it was that might have been lying in store for me at the Ferah Theatre, I deserved a long time ago. For instance, what difference is there between me and the millions of innocent people that lost their lives during that tumultuous era that began in 1906? Most of them were innocent and had little to do with the terrible human tragedy that was taking place, whereas I had been on the front lines of those bloody games since the very beginning. And as if those rivers of innocent blood were not enough, I had actually stood up and volunteered to kill. If there is such a thing as divine justice in the world, then it is simply unacceptable for me to still be alive when so many innocent people have perished.

So yes, that is how I prepared this morning for the worst but the worst did not happen. I survived that ghastly meeting in the Ferah Theatre and emerged in one piece.

The car came to pick me this morning at exactly nine thirty. There were three people in the car besides me: the driver up front, Rüşeyim sitting next to him Sphinx-like as ever, and Mehmed Esad. As always, Mehmed Esad was smartly dressed and the scent of his cologne filled the car. He was trying to look cheerful but I could see that he wasn't. He was tense, like a trickster preparing to make his killer move but with fear and the prospect of failure clouding his zeal. The more we spoke during our journey, the more his anxieties began to surface. For one, he kept mentioning Cezmi's death and asking me if there had been any new developments.

'If there were, wouldn't you be in a better position to know?' I eventually said irately. 'It's your people that are in charge now. All you need to do to find out is ask them.'

'No need to get angry', he said, tapping me affably on the knee. 'I've asked them too but they haven't heard anything. They're still focusing on the robbery.'

'So you suspect Fuad then, do you?' I asked, testing the waters.

'Fuad? Well, yes, I suppose he may have been involved. He may even confess, who knows? But then again, for all we know, Cezmi may have been killed by burglars breaking into his home.'

It was at that moment I realised why he was so nervous. It wasn't Fuad he was worried about but me. After meeting me, Cezmi had been killed and he was now worried the same might happen to him… He really was a terrible intelligence operative, our Mehmed. But it was far too late to start worrying about that. I looked over at Rüşeym sitting serenely in the front seat. Mehmed had clearly brought him along for protection. I then noticed the long frock coat he was wearing. He had not worn such a garment before when I had seen him and I now realised he was wearing it to hide the gun he was carrying. The bulge on the left side of Mehmed's coat had not escaped my notice either. He too was armed.

We stopped and got out of the car in front of the Ferah Theatre but how we were to get in was a real mystery. The entrance was a mass of planks, beams and metal plates, bundles of rugs and carpets and piles of bags and construction materials. I looked around for an entrance when a voice startled me.

'Hello, Şehsuvar Bey'. I turned around and saw Çolak Cafer staring at me with a strange gleam in his eye. He gestured to a side street. 'This way. We can use the backstage entrance'. We made our way down the side street, Cafer talking to me the whole time, and only acknowledging Mehmed Esad with a stiff nod of the head. 'The renovations are on hold for a week while they wait for the arrival of some curtains from Paris.' He glanced at Mehmed Esad. 'In other words, you won't be disturbed'.

'Good', I muttered. 'It would have been hard to hold a conversation with all that banging and crashing going on around us.'

'Has Mister Fuad arrived?'

The question was asked by Mehmed Esad and it was asked in a curt, commanding and rather rude manner as a way of informing Cafer, who had barely looked at him, that he, Mehmed Esad, was actually the guest of honour and he was therefore the man to be addressed. Cafer was not fazed though and just smiled, showing rows of stained yellow teeth.

'He has, sir. He's waiting for you inside'.

Inside, the place was a complete mess. There were seats and pieces of seating, old fabrics, ropes of various colours, costumes, swords, shields and even a wooden horse lying around but we somehow managed to navigate our way through the mess without tripping up.

And there he was. As in our previous encounter, Fuad was on stage. Had the atmosphere not been so tense, I could have burst out laughing. Here was an ex-Committee man wanting to revive the organisation and carry out a series of assassinations and yet he could not resist his own theatrical urges. He had even found a stage for such a critical meeting! However, this time, he did not have a black cape or two goons flanking him. He was sitting at the head of a wooden table staring at a pile of papers. There were four stools around the table. He must have heard our footsteps on the wooden floor as he looked up. Upon seeing us, he got to his feet.

'Well, well, well, gentlemen...' He turned to Mehmed Esad first and shook his hand. 'Welcome. Welcome. How have we been keeping since we last met?'

The tension in Mehmed's face dissolved and he broke out into a bright smile.

'So you remember me...'

'Why wouldn't I? We bumped into each other so many times at the General Headquarters. We even spoke a few times.' He looked him up and down a few times. 'Although I must say, you've changed. Like the rest of us, you're showing your age.'

'But you haven't changed a bit', Mehmed replied. 'You're still that same young lieutenant I saw years ago.'

'Is that so? How is that even possible? All these years have passed and you're saying we have nothing to show for them? No wrinkles, no lines, no wounds, no scars?'

The reproach in his voice was subtle but still perceptible.

'We're old hands though, aren't we, Fuad old boy? We're not the type to give in so easily. We're sound of body and mind, deep down. Life is not going to conquer us that easily.'

I shook my head in exasperation.

'Speak for yourself, Mehmed! If you ask me, I am exhausted. In body and mind.' His face fell so I quickly moved in to make up for my blunder. 'But seeing old friends like you looking so fit and strong has done me the world of good. Lifts the spirits, don't you know.'

Fuad let out a roar of laughter.

'Ah, one can see now that you were groomed by Talat Bey himself! Neither of you wanted to hurt my feelings and yet you've revealed yourselves quite wonderfully in the process.'

What on earth was he on about? I was not in a position to be offended but I was at that stage in my life when I did not want to take such remarks sitting down.

'He wasn't just my leader, Fuad but, as I'm sure you'll both recall, leader to us all.'

Another bout of uproarious laughter echoed around the empty theatre.

'Of course he was! Nobody is denying that!' He turned to face Mehmed. 'Isn't that so?'

Mehmed shrugged his shoulders.

'Of course not. Why would I? We all have a shared history, a shared past. Talat Paşa was leader and chief to us all. Not excluding Enver Paşa, of course.'

'And let's not forget Cemal', Fuad added. 'And now all three have passed away'. He gestured to the stools. 'Gentlemen, please. Don't just stand there. Be seated.'

I sat facing my old friend, while Mehmed sat on the stool next to mine. I glanced over at the other, vacant stool, something that did not slip Fuad's attention.

'That's Cafer's spot but there is still some time before he makes his entrance.' I looked around but Cafer was nowhere to be seen. 'Isn't that so? Seeing as this is a theatre stage, every prop must have some purpose. If there is a fourth seat at the table, then that must mean it is for somebody.'

Like me, Mehmed did not quite grasp what he was getting at and looked around the hall, expecting somebody to appear from amongst the empty seats.

'Not yet', Fuad said. 'Not yet. In the theatre, just as in life, one has to make one's entrance at a certain time.'

There was a strange timbre to his voice. He was like a seasoned actor, slipping skilfully into his role.

'I am of course referring to that wonderful innovation, the play… Why the surprise? A play is being performed here. And it is called…' Seemingly forgetting, he looked down at a sheet of paper in front of him. 'Ah yes. The play is called "*Who is the Traitor?*"' He saw us squirming uncomfortably and whispered to us both to reassure us. 'But don't worry, this is just a theatrical performance. I mean, how could there possibly be a traitor here amongst us? No, no, this is just a play. A wonderfully exciting play.'

I shifted on my stool. It was all getting very silly. I glanced at Mehmed out of the corner of my eye but he looked calm, calm enough to mumble a response.

'I must say do like the theatre. I once had an opportunity to watch a performance of Abdülhak Hamit's play *Finten*. It was a delight.'

I had always considered myself a lover of the arts but what jewels we had hidden amongst us! I had always known about Fuad's passion for the theatre but suddenly hearing Mehmed Esad, a man I had always considered crude to the point of being a vulgarian, express an abiding interest in the arts was astonishing.

'I think it's time we had a little chat'. Fuad must have been having fun as there was a joyous twinkle in his blue eyes, which had now turned to face me. 'Let's start with you, my dear friend. I feel I must ask: where have you been all this time, Şehsuvar? What have you been doing? Who have you been working for? Come on! Fill us in on the details why don't you?'

He could act out any role he wished as far as I was concerned but I was not going to let him toy with me the way a cat toys with a mouse.

'What the hell are you playing at, Fuad? What do you want? Just spit it out.'

He slowly lifted a finger to his lips.

'Come on, Şehsuvar. Out of the two of us, you know more about the arts then I do. Good art does not 'spit it out'; it expounds via hint and allusion.'

'We did not come here to take part in a play. Why don't we just get to the point?'

He narrowed his eyes and looked me up and down with fake suspicion.

'If you carry on like this, our audience will think you are our traitor'. He leaned over and whispered, 'Or are you?'

'This is getting too much. Any more and I'm out of here.'

Mehmed touched me gently on the arm.

'You're not going anywhere'. He smiled and looked at Fuad. 'You'll have to indulge Şehsuvar, I'm afraid. He hasn't quite warmed to his role yet. Why don't you start with me?'

'Very well', Fuad replied. He stared at me with mock petulance before turning to his newfound volunteer. 'Very well, yes, let's start with you. Tell me, my little cherub, what did you do during the war? Under whose command were you?'

Mehmed all but squared up to him as he answered.

'I was in Suez. During the war, I was under Cemal Paşa. I took part in operations in the Canal. The first and the second offensives. Both ended in failure, unfortunately.'

Fuad looked down at his sheets of paper.

'And then you came back to Istanbul', he murmured pensively. 'In the September of 1916'.

Mehmed was surprised but kept up the performance.

'That's right', he said, coughing to clear his throat. 'I was wounded during the second offensive'.

'But you did not return to the front after your recovery. You stayed in the capital.'

Mehmed was clearly disturbed at Fuad having so much personal and confidential information about him.

'Because I was not in a fit state to fight'. His voice had taken on a stern edge now. 'I assumed duties away from the front. In the *Teşkilat-ı Mahsusa*'.

'Is that so?' Fuad said, with exaggerated surprise. 'So you must have seen Şehsuvar a lot. Perhaps you worked together?'

I shook my head.

'No. I last saw Mehmed in 1914'.

Mehmed let out an angry sigh and answered.

'Ours was a covert group. Not known to everyone in the *Teşkilat*.' Mehmed was becoming more and more irate but Fuad didn't seem to care.

'Hmmm. A covert group', he said, adding a tone of mystery to the words. 'Tell me, Mehmed. Do you speak English?'

'No. I know a little French but I speak it so badly it's not even enough for me to score with foreign ladies.'

'And what about you, my oldest and dearest friend', Fuad said, this time addressing me. 'Can you speak English?'

'Why are you asking these questions? What are you getting at? Just get to the point.'

He suddenly turned serious. I thought he was going to finally end the game when he grinned a manic grin and whispered, 'Silent John'. He assumed an expression of fear and went on. 'Have you heard of Silent John? He's famous spy. Well, more a myth, really. I'm talking about the occupation years. Of course, you'd know more about him as his name appeared on just about every arrest warrant. Every move we made was in his shadow but he was never captured. His true identity was never revealed...' He brought his right hand down gently on to the table. 'But that's enough information for the moment. Let us return to our question. Tell me, Şehsuvar, do you speak English?'

'Yes, I can. Not perfectly but enough to get by. I picked it up during my exile in Malta. Why?'

'Oh please, don't misunderstand. I'm not accusing you of anything but one would assume that knowing their language would be useful for somebody that was spying for the English, wouldn't one?'

'Well of course', Mehmed answered. 'Otherwise, how would they communicate? How would they communicate in their reports, in their coded messages and in face to face meetings?'

My two old friends had now formed a united front and were accusing me. I wouldn't have been surprised had they declared there and then that I was the mysterious agent known as Silent John. Before coming, I knew something was going to happen but I had not expected something this low and contemptible. I got to my feet.

'That's enough. I can't take any more of this ridiculous charade.'

In a flash, Fuad pulled out his gun and pointed it at my face.

'Şehsuvar, please. Have a seat. You're ruining the flow of the play.'

I couldn't even tell if he was being serious or just playing. He eventually lowered the gun and murmured, almost pleadingly, 'Come on Şehsuvar, we're having fun here.'

'God give me strength', I muttered and sat back down.

He put the gun down on the table.

'Why did you have to go and lose your cool like that? Did anybody call you a spy? All we did was ask you a question. Isn't that so, Mehmed? Did we point the finger at anybody here?'

The other one grinned in enjoyment.

'Of course not. It's just a play, after all. A theatrical number'.

'Exactly', Fuad said cheerily. 'And now we shall summon the person that will fill this empty seat. It's time for the fourth actor to take to the stage.' He turned and shouted to the wings. 'Cafer, my little lamb! Cafer! The audience is waiting for you.'

Çolak Cafer appeared, made all the more disturbing by that empty space where his right arm should have been. He seemed nervous and approached us unnecessarily quickly. Were we going to talk about Cezmi now? Was I going to be framed for that too?

'Try and be calm, Cafer', Fuad told him. 'I know you're nervous but try to stay calm. And whatever happens, stay in role, otherwise the play will be ruined.' He pointed to the unoccupied stool. 'Yes, you can take your place now'.

The poor man quietly did as instructed and sat on the stool facing Mehmed Esad.

'Do you remember *Yüzbaşı* Bennett?' Fuad asked drily. 'Captain Godolphin Bennett? A captain in the British intelligence services during the occupation.' Once again, his lips were curled into that disturbing, annoying smile. '"Captain"' is the English word for *yüzbaşı*, isn't it, Şehsuvar?'

'Yes, it is. Captain'. I was fed up with the whole thing by now.

'Alright, no need to get tetchy. I was just asking about one word. So yes, this Captain Bennett was a highly accomplished English officer but, as is always the case with the English, he was stealing the glory of an Eastern man. And that is because it was one of our own who was the real story behind Captain Bennett's achievements. I am referring, of course, to Silent John. Had it not been for the reports written to Captain Bennett by the legend that was Silent John, there was no way that Englishman could have thrived the way he did.'

'And you really believe in the existence of such a man?' I asked. 'No one knows him, no one has ever seen him and no one has ever met him. Our intelligence services always thought he was an imaginary figure concocted by the British.'

'Marvellous!' He roared in delight and pointed at me. 'See? Now that is what we call improvisation, isn't it, Mehmed? Aren't we all glad now that I didn't let him leave?' He looked at Cafer and nodded. 'Yes, this is where you come in. You can now read your lines'.

Cafer was like a bumbling, unskilled actor stepping out on stage for the first time not sure as to what he was supposed to do. Fuad tried to spur him on.

'Come on, then! Get on with it! It's not hard. Just tell them what you told me. What you went through in November 1919 in the basement of the Kroker Hotel. Come on man, don't be shy! They'll love it.'

Cafer gulped and began, all but staring at me.

'Erm, yes. Let me, er, tell you. I was, ahem, captured. In a boathouse near Poyrazköy. Unexpectedly. In the middle of the night. The Ottoman police and the English surrounded us. We were shipping guns to Inebolu. The first three operations had gone smoothly but during the last one…'

'They were raided', Fuad said, unable to hold back. 'During the gunfight, six men were killed and they carted Cafer off to the Kroker Hotel for questioning. Isn't that right?'

'That's right, Fuad Bey. They took me away to the torture chambers.' His eyes shone with anger and there was more courage in his voice now. 'They wanted names and addresses. Wanted to know who ran the *Karakol Teşkilatı* and where it was being run from. They wanted to know it all. I didn't tell them so they beat ten tonnes out of me. Beat me up till I fainted and when I fainted, they poured water over me to bring me back around and then beat me up again. Beaten to a pulp, I was. Forget my friends, my own mother wouldn't have recognised me if she'd climbed out of her grave and seen me. When they realised they were not going to get anywhere by brute force, they hung me up by my right arm. That's right, by just one arm. I stayed there for hours. When they brought me down, I couldn't move it. They interrogated me again and again but I didn't speak so they hung me up again, by the same arm. I don't know how long I was up there. Hours I suppose. I lost count. Eventually, I lost consciousness. Then I heard voices. Voices echoing off the cold walls of the basement. One of them was saying, 'His arm is in a bad state. If we don't get him to a doctor, it will turn gangrenous.' And yeah, they were speaking Turkish. They didn't care because they thought I was out for the count. But then they suddenly stopped talking. Two people stepped inside. I squinted through my closed eyes to get a look. One of them was that English officer, the other was a Turk. I was in serious pain but I carried on pretending to be asleep. What surprised me was the English officer speaking Turkish. But more important than that was the fact that he kept calling the other guy "John."'

'Silent John?' Fuad asked. 'Did you hear him address him by the name Silent John?'

'No. He called him John. Just John'.

The three of us were all hooked on what Cafer was telling us.

'Well, did you get to see the man's face?' Fuad asked. 'What did he look like?'

Cafer was turning to look at Mehmed Esad when a gun went off and the poor fellow clutched his chest and then collapsed onto the table.

'Put the gun down'. My body, of its own accord, turned to face Mehmed Esad, who was pointing his own smoking gun at my old friend and comrade. 'Don't try anything stupid, Fuad'. I could see the disappointment and frustration in my ambushed friend's blue eyes but he held on to his Luger.

'I said put the gun down!' Mehmed Esad bellowed.

Fuad just stood there with the gun in his hand, hesitating. I couldn't wait much longer. Mehmed's entire attention was on the gun and so I took my chance. I jumped on him but he was a wily one. He moved before me and pulled the trigger. Two guns went off at the same time but only one groan was heard. It was not Mehmed that was hit but Fuad and when I saw my old friend fall over backwards, taking the stool with him, I pushed Mehmed over with all my strength. We both fell to the ground. I grabbed both his wrists to stop him firing his gun again and we began grappling on the ground. He was much stronger than I had anticipated. Try as I might, I could not wrestle the gun out of his hands, nor could he overpower me. There we were, writhing on the floor of the theatre's dusty stage, when I felt something hard on the back of my neck. Mehmed smirked.

'Rüşeym. You've finally decided to turn up'.

Rüşeym was standing right behind us holding Fuad's Luger. There was little point in resisting now and I let go of Mehmed's arms. We both stood up. Mehmed looked at me with a look of astonishment. He wanted to know.

'Why? Why did you attack me, Şehsuvar?'

Instead of an answer, I offered a question of my own.

'Why did you shoot Cafer?'

The answer came from Fuad, who was groaning on the floor.

'Don't you get it? Because he is Silent John'.

He had been shot in the right shoulder. It was not a fatal wound but he was bleeding heavily.

'I'm afraid he's right', Mehmed said gently. 'I was Silent John. That nickname was given to me by Captain Bennet. Named me after the Baptist, Yahya. I'm sure you'll know, Şehsuvar, that the English call our Yahya 'John the Baptist'. But I swear to the

Almighty Allah above, I never had any love for the English. Everyone had a side and I chose mine. Yes, it's true, I had lost all faith in the party and in you guys, and I think it's quite obvious to us all that I was not wrong in that regard. I decided back then to work for myself and for my own good. I could have died in Suez. I was one of thousands of soldiers that were shot there and it was only because of pure luck that I was taken to hospital and managed to survive. When I opened my eyes and came round, I vowed there and then never to put my life on the line for anybody again. Not for any party, movement or organisation. And by the by, I had no particular desire to be a spy. I just happened to bump into Captain Bennett. He was an interesting guy, with a great interest in eastern culture and we became friends. However, our initially innocent conversations soon turned into a lucrative partnership… And no, there is no need to look at me like that, with such loathing. You're not better than me. You can stand there and accuse me and condemn me and berate me as much as you like but that won't change the fact that we are all killers. What we have been through has turned all of us into killers.'

He looked at Fuad with derision.

'Fools like you are still trying to keep the party alive when it's all over. The old CUP guys' days are over and they will not be coming back. The new CUP guys are running the show now. Yes, Talat, Enver and Cemal may be dead but their ideas live on in the new republic.' He shrugged his shoulders. 'Not that I give a damn. Let those ideas live on. All I care about is my money.' His expression then became a little embarrassed. 'Yes, I lied to you Şehsuvar, and for that I am sorry. I'm not working for the Republic or anything like that. On the contrary, I'm going about the preparations for an assassination that will bring this government to its knees. Of course, I do not want to kill you as I cannot forget that you saved my life back in Salonika. But I'm sure you'll appreciate that in such circumstances, one has few options. What's more, I am not the one responsible for all this.'

He turned and pointed his gun at Fuad.

'It's this idiot who is trying to stay loyal to that gang of old CUP hands. Yes, dearest brother Fuad. If you hadn't ruined everything, then together we could have erased Mustafa Kemal from the stage of world history. What those old and incompetent ex-CUP buffoons could not do in Izmir we would have done together here, in Istanbul, next year. That is why I wanted to meet you guys in the first place and that's why I was bringing all the old CUP people together. So we could do it as a group. But I guess I'll have to do it without you guys now.'

'How do you know I'm a CUP guy?' Fuad asked, dragging himself forward towards Mehmed by his left arm. He asked again, this time his tone demanding an answer. 'Who told you I was a CUP guy?'

'Aren't you?' The man that had just shot Fuad was beginning to have his doubts. 'Then why did you agree to meet me?'

Fuad grinned slyly, despite his pain.

'To stop your planned assassination of the President next year'.

Mehmed blinked.

'What the hell are you talking about? Your silly little play has ended. It's my play that has started now.'

'I don't think so, Mehmed', Fuad said, still grinning. 'My play is still going on. But neither you nor I have the lead part in this play.' He turned and looked at me. 'Yes, it's this one here. Our dear friend, Şehsuvar. Moreover, your role comes to an end here. What's also funny is that as your role ends, so does your life.' He casually turned around and addressed the Egyptian holding the Luger. 'Shoot him, Rüşeym'.

Before we could work out what was going on, Rüşeym pulled three times on the trigger. Mehmed did not even have time to move or respond and, with a look of astonishment on his face, toppled over in front of Rüşeym. He opened his mouth and tried to utter a few words but what came out was unintelligible. A pool of crimson liquid appeared on the floor. I was as stunned as Mehmed and just stood there, not knowing what to do.

'Don't just stand there like an idiot', Fuad shouted, bringing me out of my shock. 'Get me to a hospital'.

And so Rüşeym and I helped him up and into the car, although I kept an eye Rüşeym throughout. I now realised Fuad had been working for the government all along and although I sensed he had been lying to me, it had never occurred to me that Mehmed was Silent John. Rüşeym, however, had come as a total surprise and I kept my distance from him until a doctor emerged from the operating theatre in Cerrahpaşa Hospital to inform us that Fuad was stable and would pull through. Once we had the good news, Rüşeym came up to me and shook me warmly by the hand. I, however, was not as genial in return. I have never liked turncoats, whoever they may be working for, although I would be lying if I said I did not admire his stealth. All along this man, as still and as quiet as a statue, had been working for the Republic's intelligence agency.

Speaking of which, the hospital was soon filled with members of the agency. Indeed, at one point, one of the men that had been following me – the man with the brown cap and black leather jacket – took me by the arm and held me tight, warning me not to try and escape in an attempt to apprehend me. It was only when Fuad eventually came round and ordered him to release me that they let me go. And so, eventually, I was able to make it back to the hotel and carry on writing to you.

Ah, my dearest Ester! There is so much more I wish to tell you. This will not be last letter to you but I am so tired, I can barely keep my eyes open. I am exhausted, really. I need to get some sleep. This is enough for tonight…

When I Began Losing My Country

Hello Ester (Evening, Day 16)

Yes, I'm beginning with a 'hello', although this will be my last letter to you.

And no, I do not expect an answer, nor do I wish to alter or influence the course of your life. I just hope you understand. After I have written the last line of this letter and the last full stop is in place, I shan't be sending you any more. However, I shall never say goodbye to you. I may write 'goodbye joy' or 'goodbye happiness' or even 'goodbye hope' but my pen shall not write the words 'goodbye Ester'. Not because there is a chance we may be reunited but because I shall take this half-lived love of ours and this endless longing and this profound pain of mine to the grave. I am quite certain that I will never sit at this desk again. I have written enough, recounted enough and narrated enough. Any subsequent word will just cheapen life. It will render what we have been through ordinary and will stain the sanctity of my love for you. Nevertheless, I should get to the point. As one of our famous critics once wrote, the sentimentality of the novelist is an insufferable thing...

I woke up in serious pain this morning, a result of our little tête-à-tête with Mehmed Esad in the Ferah Theatre yesterday. When I looked at my body in the bathroom mirror, it was covered in bruises. Well, I suppose we're not as young as we used to be and our fighting days have long since been over. But there were so many questions racing around in my head that I quickly got dressed and rushed out of the Pera Palas to the hospital in Cerrahpaşa to see my old buddy Fuad, whom I no longer trusted in the slightest.

Although his left shoulder was heavily bandaged, he was in good spirits and he greeted me cheerfully. There was not a trace of guilt or remorse in his demeanour. Not a trace. He even had the nerve to tease me.

'Well, well, Şehsuvar, old boy, you're here early. I knew you'd come but I must say, I wasn't expecting you here so soon.' He then turned to the agent in the black leather jacket sitting next to his bed (and who'd most probably been there the whole night). 'Why don't you wait outside a little, Yasin?'

Yasin hurriedly gathered himself together and left, but not without a brisk nod of acknowledgement in my direction. Fuad pointed to the vacant stool.

'Over here, Şehsuvar. Take a seat'. I did as asked. 'So tell me: when did you work it out? That I'm working for the state intelligence agency, that is. When did you figure it out?'

He was trying to subdue what he thought was my anger but he had it all wrong. I was not angry. Indeed, when I think about it, I have long since forgotten that particular emotion, which is why I was able to respond quite serenely.

'I first suspected it when you abducted me that evening. During that travesty you staged at the Ferah Theatre. No real CUP guy with an ounce of loyalty to the party would even consider turning an oath-taking ceremony we deem sacred into such a farce. But knowing your love of the theatre, it began to dawn to me that you were perhaps capable of such impudence.' He gave a silent, sly grin. 'However, I still wasn't sure but when I saw Çolak Cafer holding Cezmi Kenan's cigarette case, my suspicions grew.'

He grimaced.

'Ah, Cafer! So he went and nicked the cigarette case, did he? The fool.' He looked away, showing signs of shame for the first time. 'We did not mean to kill Cezmi Kenan. We were only going to have a poke around to try and work out what he was up to. Çolak Cafer told us that Cezmi had an arsenal stockpiled at his house and we just wanted to find it. But of course, Cezmi had to be there when we arrived and being Cezmi, instead of cooperating, he went for his gun. You know Major Cezmi. Had we not killed him, he would have killed us all.'

I had told myself the same lie so many times that it was now impossible for me to actually fall for it but I was in no state to argue with Fuad or to stand there and make accusations against him. Even if I was and I did argue with him, what would it have achieved?

'I wouldn't know about that, Fuad. But I was distraught over Major Cezmi's murder, as you can imagine. He did not deserve such a cheap, treacherous end. He deserved better. He deserved to die in battle, for instance. I don't want to say any more about it. His murder is between you and your conscience. As to your question, I realised you were working for the government's security apparatus when you came to the Pera Palace and gave me that record.'

'The opera', he said, his blue eyes lighting up.

'*Tosca*, yes. But more important was what you said after you gave me the record. You said you had been reading about the opera and its story and learnt that it was a love story. But you then said you thought it was really a story about friendship. 'The story of a man who risks his life to save his friend from the clutches of the government.' That is when the penny dropped. When you said those words, I realised you were working for the state and not for the Committee for Union and Progress.' I paused and looked my old friend in the face. 'I know you saved my life. Had you not been working for state intelligence, I would have long since rotted away in a prison cell or perhaps be swinging from the gallows. But if I have to confess, then I should say that I do not feel any gratitude to you for this. And that is because life no longer has any real value for me.'

There was a look of derision on his face.

'Then why are you here? Why are you here talking to me?'

'Because I was worried about you. At the end of the day, you're still a friend...'

He looked at me disbelievingly.

'Yes, I suppose I did want answers to some questions', he said and looked at me, challenging me to open up.

'And what might those questions be?'

'How did you move from the CUP to the National Resistance movement? That's what I need to know first. Because during the war, when we were heading off to Basra to fight, although you were still a little unclear about it in your head, you were still a member of the *Teşkilat-ı Mahsusa*.' He tried to get up but slipped. 'Give me a hand, will you? Just put that pillow behind my back. That's it. Now if you could just help me up. Careful, careful. My shoulder is still killing me.'

I helped him sit up and then sat back down.

'Thanks. Now, let me help you with some questions you may have. After Süleyman Askeri died, I joined Halil Paşa's unit in Baghdad. However, Baghdad fell to the British soon afterwards. We retreated back to Aleppo, with the 7th Army. That is where I first met Mustafa Kemal. He was staying at Salih Fansa's villa. He had handed in his resignation and like the rest of us, he was fuming and at a loss as to what do do. He was not in the best shape physically as he was still recovering from a bout of jaundice but he was kind enough not to disappoint a group of officers and agreed to talk with us. He remembered me from our encounter in Libya. He even asked after you. 'There was a young man with Basri Bey, a friend of yours. A civilian. How is he?' The seeds were sown that day in that villa in Aleppo; they germinated during the War of Independence and eventually bloomed into a full-blown friendship. Yes, I joined the National Resistance Movement, where I fought against the Greeks. I was on the front line during the 'Great Offensive' and was with the first Turkish units to enter the city of Izmir. After the declaration of independence and the founding of the republic, I was entrusted with a number of important and confidential cases. Obviously, my having worked for the *Teşkilat-ı Mahsusa* was a factor in my being chosen for those missions.'

'So you were the one that had me followed?' I asked, pretending to be offended. He bowed his head sheepishly.

'What choice did I have? We hadn't spoken to each in years and I had no way of knowing what you were thinking. Moreover, the party was reforming and organising underground and we knew that most of them could not stomach Gazi Mustafa Paşa. Forget stomach him, if they could, they would have ended his life in the blink of an eye. And in Izmir, during the bungled assassination attempt, they finally nailed their colours to the mast.'

'Please Fuad, don't. There was no such assassination attempt. It was merely in the planning stages. But I should congratulate you. You made the most of that ludicrous plot and you came out smelling sweet. A highly successful espionage operation, if I may say so.'

He tried to object but I cut him off.

'No, I'm not criticising or censuring you. It's the nature of the beast. This is what happens in the struggle for power. But I had nothing to do with the Izmir assassinations. Just like many of the CUP guys you had strung up on the gallows.'

He shook his head like a guilty child.

'We know you were not involved in that particular affair, Şehsuvar.'

Hearing that, I lost my temper.

'Then why did you follow me?'

He suddenly began coughing, one eruption after another, and he signalled to the jug of water on the bedside table. I filled a glass and handed it over to him. He guzzled it down greedily and then, after a succession of deep breaths, said, 'It's the cigarettes, see. Not the wounds. Haven't been able to quit that nasty habit.'

I took the empty glass and placed it on the table.

'We followed you because we wanted to know you and understand you. No, we did not suspect you of being part of a movement plotting against the government. We already had a lot of intelligence on you, whether it was your exile in Malta or your behaviour upon your return to Istanbul. We also know that you were not a member of the Progressive Republican Party, despite a personal invitation from Kâzım Karabekir Paşa.

Neither did you give in to the exhortations and urgings of Doctor Adnan Bey, for whom you had a great deal of affection. You also kept a cordial but keen distance from Kara Kemal…'

I listened in absolute amazement.

'Then why didn't you leave me alone?'

'You still don't know why? Because we wanted to recruit you. We wanted you to join us in the state intelligence network. We would have been working together like in the old days. So we tested you out, gave you a run.'

'What? You mean all this was some kind of examination?'

He smiled contentedly.

'Absolutely. We'd known about that rat Mehmed Esad for ages but we didn't bring him in because we needed to establish his overseas contacts. Mehmed Esad was basically a mercenary, a spy who would snoop for anybody that stumped up enough cash. He was most probably getting his payments from a law office set up in Beirut and funded by the British. Seems he was planning to have Mustafa Kemal assassinated next year during his official visit to Istanbul. That's why he contacted you. So you could track down other CUP guys and bring them to him. But we had Mehmed Esad in the palm of our hands. We were following him and watching his every move…'

I suddenly recalled another figure.

'And Rüşeym? How did you get him to come round?'

'We didn't. He approached us, around two years ago. And no, not because Mehmed Esad had mistreated him or anything like that, but because the British had betrayed the Arabs. You know how the British promised the Arab nationalists their own independent state if they rose up against us? Well, when the Ottomans upped sticks and left the region, the British forgot all about their promise. You know why Rüşeym can't talk? The British cut his tongue out. He's an honourable fellow, our Rüşeym, and he could no longer bear watching Mehmed Esad pass intelligence on to the British.' He stopped and beamed. 'You have to admit it. Rüşeym was a master stroke.'

'It was indeed', I said, nodding appreciatively. 'In fact, the whole thing was put together quite brilliantly. An outstanding plan, if I may. But it has come to nothing.'

I stopped, to let my words sink in.

'What? What do you mean its come to nothing?'

'Because I'm done with this business, Fuad. I'm fed up with it. Tired of the whole thing. I can't take any more. I'm in a bad way, Fuad. I won't be able to do it. Even if I say I will, I won't. I've lost the edge. I'm not talking about getting old or any of that guff but about the drive and the desire. You may have stood up and vouched for me and you may have valued me more than others, more than you perhaps should have, but it was in vain, my old friend. I'm no longer the Şehsuvar Samil you used to know. I'm done. The spirit is not there anymore and the body is wilting. What you see now is a tired, defeated and broken man.

'I cannot accept your offer'.

He just sat there in silence, trying to work out whether I was serious or just playing mind games. He finally realised I was serious but even then, he was not convinced.

'You're always saying things like that. You were the same when we were in the Teşkilat. You'd get down, you'd grow despondent and give in to defeatism, but you'd always bounce back. And the same will happen this time. I'll tell you what. Go on home, sort yourself out and think it over. I know you'll come back. I know you well, Şehsuvar. True, I haven't seen you in years, but I know you well. You know this work. You got a taste of its dangers once. You tasted its thrills and its risks and its delights. And more importantly, you liked being in touch with power. I know all this about you. And why? Because I'm just like you…'

'I'm sorry but that's not me anymore', I said, getting to my feet. 'I'm not like you anymore. All the best, Fuad. I wish you all the success in the world.'

I began making my way out. He called out after me.

'Wait, we haven't finished'.

I ignored him and carried on walking to the door.

'Hold on. At least take these letters then'.

I froze. Of course! How could I have missed it? They had been intercepting my letters! I spun around, absolutely livid. He retreated into the folds of his bed, like a naughty child wanting to be forgiven.

'I was the only one that read them. Really. Trust me, I showed no one. It was just me… And had I not mentioned them just now, you would have never known. But believe me, I was going to send them on to Ester after reading them. I just wanted you to know.'

I was in no mood to listen to his excuses.

'Where are the letters?' I bellowed. 'Where are they?' I was so angry and shouting so loudly, Yasin rushed into the room with his hand on his holster but Fuad waved him away.

'It's okay, Yasin. Don't worry. Everything is under control. Tell me, is Suavi here?'

'Yes sir', Yasin answered, still not knowing what was going on. 'He's gone to the shops. You said you wanted cigarettes.'

'Good. That means he'll be here soon. Now, I'd like you to take Şehsuvar Bey here with you to my office at headquarters and open my cabinet. In there, you'll find a yellow box containing some letters. Give Şehsuvar Bey the box, okay? The entire box, as you find it, with all the letters inside.'

Yasin and I left the hospital. We found the yellow box and I immediately opened it and looked inside. They were all there. The letters I have been writing to you for the last fifteen days.

Eventually, I made my way back to the hotel… I opened the box and spread the letters out on the desk. What was I supposed to do with them now? Post them, of course. But why? You've started a new life for yourself in Paris so what's the point of bringing you fresh anguish and threatening your happiness? But at the same time, you have a right to know all this. Even if it makes you unhappy, you should know my thoughts and feelings and what I have been through…

I did not decide straightaway. I gathered up the letters, stuffed them back into the yellow box and once again sat down at my desk to write to you.

So yes, these are the last lines of my last letter to you... Maybe you are also curious as to whether I will accept my old friend's admittedly tempting offer. Maybe you are of a similar mind to Fuad and you think that, after much hemming and hawing, I will eventually accept his offer. If you do, I don't blame you as I know that I have been inconsistent many times in the past. But this time it is different. This time there will be no turning back. Before, I had reasons for my involvement in that dark, dirty and bloody world. Reasons that legitimised my involvement. But not anymore. Now, I have no ideal, no dream and no country... I may be in rude health but I feel as though I am slowly dying... I remember writing in my first letter to you that death begins with the loss of our cities and ends with the loss of our homeland... And I also asked what this home-land actually consists of. Is it a handful of earth and vast seas? Is it deep lakes, rugged mountains, fertile plains, lush forests, crowded cities and remote villages? I now realise that for me there has only ever been one homeland and that was you... I began losing my country the moment I lost you. Yes, I am dying, gradually but inexorably. The earth that encloses my late mother and my friends now calls out to me. I can feel it. You may tell me that Fuad's offer represents a chance for me to start a new life and that I can renew my love and my lust for life if I accept it. But no. I absolutely and categorically will not accept it and that is because the stormy, tumultuous life I have lived over the last twenty years has taught me this one truth: that the secrets of the state are darker than those of the earth.

Farewell, My Beautiful Homeland

Interest in historical novels has been increasing of late. A new novel detailing the last twenty years of the life and activities of the Committee for Union and Progress now lines the shelves of our bookstores. The novel is entitled 'Farewell, My Beautiful Homeland' and has finally been published by Yeni Asır ('New Century') Publishing. It was written by Şehsuvar Sami, who put a gun to the side of his head on the 2nd of November and ended his own life. In the foreword to the French edition published by Gallimard in 1931, the renowned French poetess Ester Dauphin wrote the following:

We are all going to die. Everybody will, eventually. Sometimes all that is left behind are memories scattered by the wind; sometimes it is unforgettable works of art. The book you are currently holding in your hands was written by a man I once dearly loved. His was a wild and unsettled life dedicated to a grand love, a remarkable ideal and a lost country. I do not know if his was the right way to live but I can say it was a life lived honestly and truthfully. All that is left of that life are these words and these lines… These are the last heartrending and harrowing remains of that life.

(translated by Rakesh Jobanputra)

Glossary

ağabey: older brother; affectionate term for a (slightly) older man
ayran: refreshing drink made with yoghurt, water and salt
Başmuallim: Head Teacher
Çerkez: Circassian
çolak: one-armed
çörek: a sweet or savoury pastry similar to a scone, bun or muffin
damat: groom, or son-in-law
düğün çorbası: a soup made from meat, flour and fat, served traditionally at weddings
fedai: a member of an armed group or armed wing of a political organisation; paramilitary
fedaeen: plural of *fedai*
Gazi: a title given to men that have fought in defence of the faith and/or the country
Gazi Paşa: Mustafa Kemal Atatürk
ittihatçı: member of the Committee for Union and Progress
keşkül: a milk pudding made with almonds and coconut
lokum: popular sweet commonly known as Turkish Delight
muallim: a teacher or learned man
nargile: hookah or shisha
okka, an Ottoman measure of weight, standardised during the latter stages of the empire at 1.28 kilograms
paçanga böreği: a deep-fried pastry filled with pastrami, cheese and tomato
paşa: pasha or general

rakı: an alcoholic beverage made using grapes, figs, plums or other fruits, often infused with aniseed; popular throughout Turkey, the Balkans and the Middle East

sadrazam: Chief vizier or chief minister, a post equivalent to prime minister

sakız rakısı: rakı flavoured with mastic

şerefe: said when drinking, similar to 'cheers' in English; lit., 'to (your, our) honour!'

Şeyhülislam: the highest accepted authority on Islamic affairs in the Ottoman Empire, and, along with the vizier, second in power to the sultan

tekbir: 'Allahu akbar', the declaration that 'Allah is the greatest'

tellak: a male attendant and employee in a hamam (Turkish bath) who washes and massages the clients

Teşkilat-i Mahsusa: 'the Special Organisation', the Ottoman secret service

tuğra: the royal or imperial seal; the seal of the sultan

ulema: the global community of Muslims

usta: expert; a title given to master craftsmen and artisans